New York Times, number one bestseller **P.C. Cast** is an award-winning fantasy, paranormal romance, and young adult author. She was a teacher for many years, but now concentrates on writing and public speaking full-time. Currently she divides her time between Oklahoma, Grand Cayman Island, and Scotland.

Visit her website at www.pccast.net

Goddess of the Rose

P.C. Cast

piatkus

PIATKUS

First published in the US in 2006 by The Berkley Publishing Group,
A division of Penguin Group (USA) Inc., New York
First published in Great Britain as a paperback original in 2011 by Piatkus

A CIP catalogue record for this book
is available from the British Library.

ISBN 978-0-7499-5351-5

Typeset in Jenson by Hewer Text UK Ltd, Edinburgh
Printed and bound in Great Britain by CPI Mackays, Chatham, ME5 8TD

Papers used by Piatkus are natural, renewable and recyclable
products sourced from well-managed forests and certified
in accordance with the rules of the Forest Stewardship Council.

Mixed Sources
Product group from well-managed
forests and other controlled sources
www.fsc.org Cert no. SGS-COC-004081
© 1996 Forest Stewardship Council
FSC

Piatkus
An imprint of
Little, Brown Book Group
100 Victoria Embankment

This book is for everyone who fell in love with the Beast, and then was truly disappointed when he turned into a handsome prince.

Acknowledgments

I would like to thank Mark Stelljes, the rosarian I consulted as I researched this book. Mark, your information was invaluable! Any rose mistakes are mine and mine alone.

A special thank you to my goddess editor, Christine Zika, for understanding that the beast really did need to be a beast. (And thanks for that lovely horn scene, too!)

An adoring thank you to my amazing agent and friend, Meredith Bernstein.

A wink and a thanks to the fabulous 'Lunatics' who helped brainstorm the personification of Dream Stealers.

And thank you to my high school students whose brains I picked for the dream-weaving scenes. See? Teenagers really do have brains!

Dear Reader,

Okay, I'll admit it — authors have favorite books. I know, I know, books are like children and we don't always want to admit to liking one better than another, but it's true. The Goddess Summoning books are my favorite children.

As with my bestselling young adult series, the House of Night, my Goddess Summoning books celebrate the independence, intelligence, and unique beauty of modern women. My heroes all have one thing in common: they appreciate powerful women and are wise enough to value brains as well as beauty. Isn't respect and appreciation an excellent aphrodisiac?

Delving into mythology and reworking ancient myths is fun! In Goddess of the Sea *I retell the story of the mermaid Undine — who switches places with a female U.S. Air Force sergeant who needs to do some escaping of her own. In* Goddess of Spring, *I turn my attention to the Persephone/Hades myth, and send a modern woman to Hell! Who knew Hell and its brooding god could be hot in so many wonderful, seductive ways?*

From there we take a lovely vacation in Las Vegas with the divine twins, Apollo and Artemis, in Goddess of Light. *Finally we come to what is my favorite of all fairy tales, 'Beauty and the Beast.' In* Goddess of the Rose *I created my own version of this beloved tale, building a magical realm from whence dreams originate — good and* bad — and bringing to life a beast who absolutely took my breath away.

I hope you enjoy my worlds, and my wish for you is that you discover a spark of goddess magic of your own!

P. C. Cast

Prelude

Once upon a time, when men still believed gods and goddesses walked the earth, Hecate, Great Goddess of Night, was granted dominion over the crossroads of man. The dark goddess took her charge seriously, for not only did she stand watch over mortal roads and byways, Hecate guarded the crossroads between dreams and reality . . . between the corporeal and the ethereal. Her dominion was the place from which all dreams, and the magick they create, originated. Thus, the Goddess of Night became Goddess of Magick as well as Goddess of Beasts and the Ebony Moon.

Ever vigilant, Hecate called to her service a monstrous beast of olde. Willingly the beast swore to be the goddess's Guardian of the Crossroads and to do her bidding. This creature was the perfect melding of man and beast; son of the Titan Cronos, he was a being like no other. As reward for his fidelity in answering the goddess's summons, Hecate gifted her Guardian with the heart and soul of a man, so although his appearance was monstrous, Hecate felt secure, entrusting him with the protection of the boundaries of the magickal crossroads, which the goddess christened the Realm of the Rose, as well as the Priestesses of the Blood, who served Hecate there. For centuries, the Guardian stood faithful, following the dictates of his sacred trust, for he was as honorable as he was powerful and as wise as he was mighty . . .

... Until one Beltane. The Guardian knew his duty. But alas, even a great Guardian can grow weary. Our beast did not err because of cruelty or greed; his only mistake was in loving unwisely. He broke trust with his goddess, and in a flash of rage, Hecate cast a spell over her Guardian and the Realm of the Rose. The realm would have no High Priestess, and the Guardian would sleep eternally unless the beast was awakened by a woman who carried the magickal blood of Hecate's priestess and was wise enough to see the truth and compassionate enough to act upon it.

And so the Realm of the Rose despaired and the Guardian slept while their goddess waited ...

Part One

Chapter One

'I've been having those dreams again.'

Nelly straightened in her chair and gave her what Mikki liked to think of as her Clinically Interested Look.

'Would you like to tell me about them?' she asked.

Mikki shifted her eyes from her friend. Would she like to tell her? She uncrossed and then crossed her long legs, ran her hand nervously through her hair and tried to settle into the wingback chair.

'Before I answer that question, I want you to answer one of mine first.'

'Fair enough,' Nelly said.

'If I tell you about my dreams, how will you be listening? As my friend or as my shrink?'

The psychiatrist laughed. 'Please, Mikki! We're at a coffee shop, not my office. You're definitely not paying me a hundred and twenty dollars an hour to sit here with you. And let's not forget' – she leaned forward and exaggerated a whisper – 'you've been my friend for years, but you've never been my patient.'

'True, but that hasn't been because of my lack of issues.'

'Oh, definitely,' Nelly said with purposeful sarcasm. 'So you gonna tell me, or do I have to use my secret shrink tricks on you to get you to divulge?'

'Anything but that!' Mikki raised her hands as if to fend off an attack. Then she shrugged her shoulders. 'Well, they're the same as the others.' Noting Nelly's knowing look coupled with her raised eyebrows, Mikki sighed and rolled her eyes. 'Okay, maybe they have changed some lately.'

'Could you see his face this time?' Nelly asked gently.

'Almost.' Mikki squinted and stared at a spot above the cozy brick fireplace in the corner of the coffee shop. 'Actually, I think I could have seen his face this time, but . . .'

'But?' she prompted.

'But I . . .' Mikki hesitated.

Nelly made an encouraging sound.

'But I was so preoccupied I couldn't make myself concentrate on his face,' she finished in a rush.

'Preoccupied with . . . ?'

Mikki stopped staring at the hearth and met her friend's eyes. 'I was preoccupied with having the most incredibly erotic dream of my life. I really didn't give a damn what his face looked like.'

'Well, well, *well* . . .' She drew out the word. 'I don't remember you describing sex in the other dreams. Now I really am interested in the rest of the story.'

'That's because they weren't . . . or maybe I didn't . . . oh, I don't know. For some reason they're changing.' She struggled to describe what was happening to her. 'I'm telling you, Nelly, the dreams are getting more and more real.'

The joking sparkle went out of Nelly's dark eyes, instantly replaced by concern.

'Talk to me, honey. What's going on?' she asked.

'It's like the more realistic the dreams get, the less real my life is.'

'Tell me about your latest dream, Mikki.'

Instead of answering her, Mikki twirled an errant strand of thick, copper-colored hair and bought time by sipping her

6

cappuccino. She and Nelly had been friends for years. They'd met at the hospital where they both worked and had been instant girlfriends. On the outside they had little in common. Nelly was tall and slender – dark with an exotic beauty – a gift from her mother's Haitian blood. She towered over Mikki's five-foot-seven-inch frame. Where Nelly was dark, Mikki was fair, just as where her friend was slender and graceful, Mikki was voluptuous and earthy. But instead of being jealous of or put off by the differences in their exteriors, the two women had, from the moment they'd met, appreciated each other for their uniqueness.

It was a solid friendship, founded in trust and mutual respect. And Mikki had no idea why she was so hesitant to tell Nelly about the dreams, especially the last one . . .

'Mikki?'

'I'm thinking of where to start,' she prevaricated.

Nelly gave her a little half-smile and sipped her own cappuccino before taking a delicate bite from her chocolate biscotti. 'Take your time. All good shrinks have one thing in common.'

'I know, I know . . . you're all annoyingly patient.'

'Exactly.'

Mikki fiddled with her coffee cup. She really did need to get this dream stuff straightened out. It was becoming too weird, in a hypnotic, seductive way.

But she was stalling, and not just because she was hesitant about revealing such intimate details aloud, but also because part of her was afraid her friend – who really was an excellent psychiatrist – would have some kind of magic words that would cure her.

She wasn't sure she wanted to be cured.

'Hey, it's just me,' Nelly said softly.

Mikki gave her a tight, appreciative smile, drew a deep breath and began. 'Okay, this one started the same as the others.' She picked nervously at her fingernail polish.

'You mean in the canopy bed?'

'*Huge* canopy bed in the *enormous* bedroom,' she corrected and then nodded. 'Yeah. It was the same place, only it wasn't as dark as it usually is. This time a little light was coming into the room through a whole wall of windows. I think they're called' – Mikki searched for the word – 'mull-something-or-other . . . panes of vertical stripes of glass. Know what I mean?'

Nelly nodded. 'Mullioned windows.'

'Right, I think. Well, whatever they're called, I noticed them this time because they were letting in some light.' Mikki's gaze was trapped by the cheerily burning fire as she relived her dream. 'It was a soft, pink-tinted light that must have been dawn,' she said dreamily and then caught herself and continued, 'Anyway, it woke me.' She hesitated and a small, half-laugh escaped her throat. 'It even seemed odd in the dream – having my dream self wake up to experience another dream.' Mikki shrugged her shoulders. 'But I woke up. I was lying on my stomach, and I could feel someone brushing my hair. It was wonderful. The "whoever" was using one of those big brushes with soft, wide bristles.' Mikki grinned at her friend. 'You know there are few things better than having your hair brushed.'

'I'm with you on that one, but hair brushing is not sex.'

'Okay, it's been a long time, but I'm fully aware that hair brushing is not sex. I'm not at the sex part yet, I'm just at the why-I-was-so-relaxed-and-happy part,' Mikki said, giving Nelly an impatient look.

'Sorry for interrupting. Just pretend like I'm not here.'

'Is that shrink-talk stuff?'

'Nope. It's I-want-to-hear-about-the-sex-part stuff.'

Mikki grinned at her. 'In that case, I will gladly continue. Let's see . . . I was so relaxed that I could feel myself drifting. It was bizarre – like my soul had become so light that it lifted from my body. It was then that everything got freaky.'

'Explain freaky.'

'Well, there was a rush of wind. It was like the breeze had all of a sudden picked me up and carried me someplace. But not really *me*. Just my spirit me. Then there was a settling feeling. It startled me, and I opened my eyes. I was back in my body, only now I was standing in the middle of the most incredible rose garden I have ever seen, ever even imagined.' Mikki's voice lost any hint of hesitation as she fell into the description of the scene. 'It was breathtaking. I wanted to drink the air like wine. Roses were all around me. All my favorites: Double Delight, Chrysler Imperial, Cary Grant, Sterling Silver . . .' She sighed happily.

'Any Mikado Roses?'

Nelly's question brought her back to reality.

'No, I didn't see any of my namesake roses.' She sat up, giving her friend an irritated look. 'And I really don't think this is happening to me because my mother thought it was clever to name me after her favorite rose.'

Nelly made a conciliatory gesture with her hand. 'Hey, you have to admit, Mikki,' she said, pronouncing the nickname clearly, as if to erase the word *Mikado* from the air around them, 'that it's weird that roses, in some form, appear in every one of your dreams.'

'Why should it be odd? I'm a volunteer at the Tulsa Municipal Rose Gardens. I raise my own roses. Why should something that has been such a big part of my life not figure into my dreams?'

'You're right. Roses are an important part of your life, as they were your mother's—'

'And her mother's before her, and hers before her,' Mikki interrupted.

Nelly smiled and nodded. 'You know I think it's a lovely hobby, and I'm completely jealous of your ability to grow such beautiful roses.'

'I'm sorry. I shouldn't be so touchy. I guess I'm running short on sleep.'

Worry shadowed Nelly's expression. 'You didn't tell me that you're not sleeping.'

'Oh, no, it's nothing,' Mikki said briskly. 'I've just been taking too many papers home from the office and staying up too late.'

Please don't ask me any more questions about that, she thought, glancing at Nelly as she hastily stirred and then sipped her cappuccino. She didn't want her to know that her exhaustion had nothing to do with lack of sleep or too much work. All she wanted to do was to escape to her dream world and sleep, and even though she never felt fully rested after she'd been to that fantasy world of dreams, she felt compelled to return night after night.

'Mikki?'

'Where was I?' she floundered.

'In the beautiful rose garden.'

'That's right.'

'And things were getting freaky.'

'Yeah.' Mikki let her eyes fall back to the fireplace. 'For a while I just walked among the roses, touching each of them and appreciating their beauty. My guess was right, it was early morning and the air was fresh and cool; the roses were still sprinkled with dew. Everything looked like it had just been washed. The garden was circular, and the roses and their terraces formed a kind of labyrinth or maybe a maze. I wandered around and around, just enjoying myself.'

Mikki's smile wavered, and she paused before beginning the next part of her dream. She could feel her cheeks coloring. Her eyes shifted abruptly to meet her friend's curious gaze.

'Do not tell me you're embarrassed!'

Mikki gave her a sheepish grin. 'Kinda.'

'Please recall that you and I have gotten Brazilian waxes. Together. In the same room. Get over it and give me the details. Plus, if all else fails, remember' – she took another big bite of biscotti and continued through a full mouth – 'I'm a professional.'

'Don't remind me,' Mikki mumbled. She took a deep breath. 'Okay, so I'm in the rose garden and then I suddenly felt him. I couldn't see him, but I knew he was behind me.' She licked her lips. Unconsciously, Mikki's hand moved to her throat. Her fingertips slowly stroked the sensitive skin at the base of her neck as she spoke. 'I started walking faster, because at first I felt like I should get away from him, but soon that changed. I could hear him behind me; he was gaining on me. He wasn't being quiet or trying to hide. His noises were feral . . . dangerous . . . it was as if I was being hunted by a fierce, masculine animal.'

Mikki tried to force her breathing back to normal. Her body tingled with a flush of heat. She could feel the drop of sweat that made a hot, wet path between her breasts.

'You were afraid?' Nellie asked.

'No,' Mikki said in a whisper that her friend had to lean forward and strain to hear. 'That's just it. I wasn't afraid at all. It thrilled me. It excited me. I wanted him to catch me. When I ran, it was only because I could tell it provoked him – and I wanted very much for him to be provoked.'

'Wow,' Nelly said on a rush of breath. 'Sexy . . .'

'I told you so, and it gets better.'

'Good.' Nelly bit into another biscotti.

'I ran naked and laughing. It felt like the wind was my lover as it rushed over my body. I reveled in every grunt, every huff, every growl made by the man-thing who pursued me. And I wanted to be caught, but not until he was very, very eager to catch me.'

'Well, for God's sake don't stop there. Did he catch you?'

Mikki's gaze became introspective, and her eyes moved back to the fireplace.

'Yes and no. As I said, I was running and he was chasing me. I came to a sharp corner in the labyrinth and I turned, then stumbled, and fell into a pit. When I hit the bottom it should have hurt, but it didn't because my fall was cushioned.' Mikki's lips twitched and then curved into a seductive smile. 'It was cushioned by petals. I had fallen into a pit that had been filled with a bed of rose petals. There must have been thousands of them. Their scent filled the air and caressed my body. Every inch of my naked skin felt alive against their softness. And then his hands replaced the roses. They weren't soft. Instead, they were rough and strong and demanding. The difference between the two sensations was incredibly exciting. He stroked my naked body, moving from my breasts down my stomach and my thighs. He caressed me exactly as I would have touched myself. It was like he had the ability to tap into my dreams and he knew all my secret desires.'

Mikki paused to brush a strand of hair from her face. Her hand was shaking, but not wanting Nelly to notice, she hurried on with her story.

'It was darker in the pit than it had been in the gardens, and my vision was hazy, almost like the scent of the crushed petals had created a fog of perfume that obscured my vision. I couldn't see him, but wherever he touched me I was on fire. Before then in all of the dreams I had felt his presence, like he was an insubstantial being, a ghost or a shadow. I had known he was there, but he had never pursued me, never touched me. And I had certainly never touched him. But in the pit of roses, everything changed. I could feel his hands on me, and when I reached for him, I could actually touch him, too. I pulled him to me. And he . . . he felt . . .'

Mikki gulped and closed her eyes tightly in remembrance. 'He felt thick and strong and incredibly big. I ran my hands up and down the width of his shoulders and his arms. His muscles were like living stone. And I felt something else . . . he was . . . he had . . .' Mikki swallowed around the sudden dryness in her throat. Could she really tell Nelly? Could she tell anyone? Remembering, it was almost as if she was there again, in that pit of sensation and fragrance. Her hands had moved up to bury themselves in the thick mass of his hair. She had intended to turn his face to hers — to open her eyes and to finally, finally see him. Then she had touched them. Horns. The man creature who was stroking her body into an excitement she had never before experienced had horns.

No! She couldn't tell Nelly; it was just too crazy. And her friend definitely knew crazy. Instead, she said in a rush, 'He had some kind of costume on. It was leather — hard leather, all across his chest. Like . . . like' — she searched for the word — 'like an old-fashioned breastplate. It was unbelievably erotic — those hard muscles being barely covered by that hard leather. I let my hands feel him — caress him. His face was buried in my hair, right here.'

Closing her eyes, Mikki's right hand moved slowly up, pulled forward a mass of her reddish curls and sank her hand into them near her right ear.

'This is where his face was, so it was easy for me to hear every sound he made. When I stroked him, he moaned into my ear, except it wasn't really a moan – at least not a moan a human would have made. It was a low, deep growl that went on and on. I know it should have scared me. I should have screamed and fought, or at the very least been petrified, frozen with fear. But I didn't want to be away from him. That horrible, wonderful, beastlike sound excited me even more. I felt like I would die if I couldn't have him – all of him. Arching up to meet him, I could easily feel his erection. He was grinding it against me.'

Mikki swallowed again. 'And then he spoke. His voice was like nothing I've ever heard – a man's, yet not. An animal's, but not really. The power in it rumbled through me and it was as if I could hear him within my mind, too.'

When she paused, Nelly prompted breathlessly, 'What did he say?'

'He growled into my ear, "We must not . . . I cannot . . . It cannot be allowed to happen!" but his words didn't stop me. I could feel his desire in them as surely as I could feel his hardness between my legs. I begged him not to stop as I clutched at his clothes. I wanted them off him; I wanted him naked against me. But it was too late. I was already climaxing, and all I could do was wrap my legs around him as my body exploded. The orgasm is what woke me.'

Chapter Two

Nelly cleared her throat before she attempted to speak. 'Oh, my dear sweet Lord, I agree with you. That was definitely more realistic than the other dreams – and sexier.' She fanned herself with a napkin.

'I could have seen his face, Nelly. It was there, right beside my own face the whole time, and I knew that even though the pit was foggy, there was enough light for me to be able to see him. I could even feel him staring at me, but I refused to open my eyes. I didn't want to see what he was.' Silently, she acknowledged that she had lost her nerve. After she'd felt the horns, she'd been afraid to see him. She hadn't wanted the fantasy to be shattered by the reality of what he might be.

'Was that because even though you were excited, there was a part of you that was afraid, too?'

Mikki took her time answering Nelly, wondering if she was talking to her friend or the psychiatrist. 'Maybe. But I don't know whether my fear was because of what I might have seen, or because if I saw him the spell might be broken and I would never dream about him again,' she admitted.

'The spell?'

Mikki shrugged her shoulders and smiled sheepishly. 'What would you call it? What's happening feels more like magic than psychosis. Or at least it does to me.'

Nelly returned her smile. 'You know my attitude about that

kind of stuff. I think there are many magical things about the human brain, but they all have causes rooted in science.'

'Now you do sound like a shrink.'

'Stop, you flatterer.' Nelly's eyes shifted to her watch. 'Oh, crap! I have to get going soon.'

'Scary freak coming in to unload his problems on you?'

'Of course. It's my favorite part of my job.' Nelly dunked her biscotti in the remaining cappuccino. 'Wait, didn't you say something earlier about the dreams becoming more realistic and the world around you seeming less real? Did something weird happen?'

'I thought you had to get going.'

'Soon, but not this instant. I still have biscotti to devour. So give up the rest of it.'

Mikki sighed. 'You never forget anything, do you?'

'It's all part of my very expensive training.' She waved the soggy biscotti at Mikki. 'Continue, please.'

'Okay, okay. It happened yesterday. I was crossing Twenty-first Street, going from Woodward Park to my apartment. Thursdays are the evenings I volunteer at the Rose Gardens, remember?'

'Yep.'

'Well, it was a little after dusk. I got finished later than usual – there's just so much to do to get the roses ready for winter, and with the pain-in-the-ass construction in the third tier, well, we're way behind. Anyway, I was crossing the street, and I heard something weird behind me.'

Mikki paused and squinted her eyes in reflection.

'Something weird?'

'I know it sounds crazy.' Mikki gave a nervous laugh. 'But who better to tell crazy stuff to than my shrink girlfriend?' Nelly narrowed her eyes at her. With a little unconscious gesture of defiance, Mikki tossed back her hair before she continued. 'Okay, I heard this . . . this . . . *noise* coming from behind me. At first I thought it had something to do with the play they're rehearsing in the park.'

'Oh, yeah. Performance in the Park runs the first week of November. I'd almost forgotten. What is it they're putting on this year?'

'*Medea*,' Mikki said, slanting a grin at her.

'So a weird sound coming from that play wouldn't have seemed too surprising.'

'Exactly, except I heard a roar, and even though I haven't read the play since high school, I don't think there are any wild animals in *Medea*.'

'You heard a lion?'

'I don't know . . . It sounded a little like a lion . . . only different.'

Mikki paused again. She knew very well how the roar had differed from any normal zoo beast. It had sounded lonely – heart-wrenchingly, totally, horribly, lonely. And somehow human, too. But there was no way she was going to admit that to her friend. She wasn't *that* crazy – at least not yet. Instead, she hurried on with the rest of her explanation.

'Yes, I realize the zoo is way over on the other side of town, and even if the lions or whatever animals were roaring their heads off, there's no way I could hear them at Woodward Park. But I swear to you I heard a roar. As you can imagine, it surprised me, so as soon as I reached the sidewalk I turned around. The park was hard to see because the air was filled with waves or thermals or . . . I don't know what the hell to call them. You know, like currents of air rising from a hot blacktop road in the middle of summer. I thought something was wrong with my eyes, so I blinked and rubbed at them. And when I opened them again, the park was gone.'

Nelly's eyebrows drew together. 'What do you mean, it was gone?'

'Just that.' She shrugged one shoulder. 'Gone. Disappeared. Absent. No longer there. Instead, there was a huge forest of trees.'

'Well . . . Woodward Park has trees,' Nelly said, as if that was explanation enough.

Mikki made a scoffing sound through her nose. 'Oh, please. I don't mean some attractive, well-manicured trees conveniently spaced around man-made waterfalls and azalea hedges. This was a *real* forest. The oaks were huge, and it was dense and dark.' She shivered. 'If I had walked into it, I would have been swallowed.'

'Did you hear the roar again?'

Mikki shook her head. 'No, everything was very silent. Weirdly silent now that I think about it.'

'Did you experience any other sensory impression during the hallucination?'

'You sound like a shrink when you talk like that.'

'Just answer the damn question.'

'I smelled roses.' Mikki's lips curled in a smile.

'At least you're consistent.' She grinned at her friend. Then her look sobered. 'What caused it to end?'

Mikki grimaced. 'Some bubba in a pickup drove by, gunned his motor, and honked while he yelled something incredibly articulate like "*Whoo-hoo! You are one hot mamma, Red.*" That effectively killed the fantasy.'

'As it would any fantasy that took place anywhere except a trailer park,' Nelly said.

'Ugh.' Mikki nodded in agreement. 'So am I bananas?'

'I don't think "bananas" would be the medical term I would use.'

'Nuts?'

Nelly shrugged. 'Clearly, you're some kind of fruit.' Then her expression turned serious. 'All kidding aside, Mikki, I need to know how this is making you feel. Are you afraid?'

Mikki answered slowly, maintaining eye contact with her friend. 'I'll admit it makes me nervous. I wonder what's going on inside my head, but I'm not afraid. It's never made me feel afraid.' She drew a deep breath before she finished her answer. 'Honestly, I don't want to sound like a freak or some kind of a pervert, but the dreams have become incredibly sexy. Hell, even the weird vision made my heart pound and gave me that fluttery feeling like I'd just been kissed by someone who really knows what he's doing. I hate to admit it, but I'm more horny than horrified.' She bit her bottom lip. 'Is that awful?'

'Nope,' Nelly assured her quickly. 'I'm glad you don't feel anxiety or fear. Actually . . .' She gathered up her purse and checked her lipstick. 'My professional opinion – although you didn't technically ask for it – is that your imagination is working overtime because it has been forever since you've been laid.'

'That's what you'd tell one of your patients?'

'You are not one of my patients. And my friend, you are not crazy.'

'I'm just creative and horny?'

'That's my guess. Or I could write you a referral to a good neurologist.'

'A neurologist!' Mikki's panic caused her voice to go shrill. 'Do you think I have a brain tumor or something?'

'Please do not freak. There are a variety of neurological problems that can cause symptoms like you have been experiencing.'

She stood, grabbing her briefcase from beside the chair. 'If it gets worse and is really bothering you, you might want to have some bloodwork run or whatnot.'

'Is "whatnot" another medical term?'

'Just like "bananas" and "nuts." ' Nelly leaned down and gave her a quick, hard hug. 'Don't worry about it. Just go on with your life as you normally would, because you *are* normal. Oh, and don't forget that I'm fixing you up with that professor who is in town to lecture at TU.'

Mikki groaned. 'Now I really do wish you thought I was nuts.'

'Stop it. This date will be good for you. Just don't act like you hate all men. It really doesn't make for a good first impression.'

'I don't hate all men. I even like men. In theory. It's just that the past thirty-five years have trained me to believe that they will eventually disappoint me.'

'Uh, that's not such a positive attitude either.'

'Fine. I'll try to be good.'

'I didn't mean for you to be good – just don't be cynical, and don't worry. You're totally okay.' Nelly hugged her again and then hurried out the door.

Mikki frowned and checked her watch. She'd have to get going soon, too. Drinking the rest of her coffee, she muttered to herself. 'Don't worry? Oh, sure. I saw *Phenomenon*. John Travolta thought aliens had visited him – until he died from *his* brain tumor. Aliens ... a sexy beastlike dream lover ... what's the difference? I think we're both screwed in more ways than one.'

Chapter Three

'Nursing Services, how may I help you?' Mikki answered the ringing phone as she glanced at the clock. It was just a little past noon. Would the day never end?

'May I speak with Mikki Empousai?' the man asked.

'This is she.' Mikki tried to keep the impatience out of her voice. It was probably another drug rep trying to schmooze her so he could get to her boss. As executive assistant for the director of Nursing Services at St. John's Hospital, it fell to her to screen salesmen and other time-wasters from her director. But it certainly was an annoying part of her job. Didn't those guys ever give up?

'Mikki, this is Arnold Asher. I'm calling to confirm our date tonight.'

'Oh! Uh . . . oh,' Mikki stuttered.

'You sound surprised. Did I record the date wrong in my BlackBerry?'

Through the phone Mikki could hear him tapping the little electronic screen.

'No, I haven't forgotten. I've just had a really busy morning,' she lied. The only thing on her mind after her breakfast with Nelly had been her brain tumor and getting through the rest of the day at work without some kind of tragic, foaming-at-the-mouth psychotic episode. Briefly, she tried to recall if her bra and panties matched. God, it'd be embarrassing to be admitted to the psych ward wearing tacky lingerie . . .

Arnold's voice intruded into her musings. She'd almost forgotten she was on the phone with him. Almost.

'Our mutual friend, Nelly Peterson, told me your favorite restaurant is The Wild Fork, so I made a reservation for seven o'clock. Will that work for you?'

Mikki stifled her urge to break the date. She really was being unfair to the guy. He had a nice voice, and Nelly wouldn't fix her up with a guy who was anything less than attractive and interesting. She ignored the thought that attractive and interesting always seemed to hide arrogant and irritating under their onionlike layers of nice clothes and good manners. She could practically hear Nelly yelling at her, *Give the guy a chance!*

'Yes, dinner at The Wild Fork sounds wonderful, and it is one of my favorite restaurants,' Mikki said, forcing her voice to be enthusiastic.

'Great! How about I pick you up at about six thirty?'

'No!' she said a little too quickly, and then to cover her abruptness, she laughed gaily like she'd lost every one of her brain cells. 'There's really no need. I live just down the street from the restaurant. I'll meet you there.'

'I understand completely. Whatever would make you more comfortable.'

Was his tone patronizing?

'That's what I prefer,' Mikki said firmly.

'Then it's a date. I'll see you at seven o'clock at The Wild Fork. How will I recognize you?'

Mikki rubbed her forehead, already feeling the beginning of a tension headache. Or was her brain tumor acting up? She seriously hated blind dates.

'I'll be the redhead with the rose in my hair.'

Warm laughter filled the phone, surprising Mikki with its allure.

'Well, I definitely won't mistake you for another woman,' he said, still chuckling softly.

Hoping he could hear the answering smile in her voice, Mikki said, 'That's the idea. And I hope you're as charming as your laugh. I'll see you at seven.'

'I'm looking forward to it,' he said.

'I am, too.'

She hung up and smiled at the phone, realizing that she really was looking forward to meeting the man behind the voice. She was still smiling when her boss, Jill Carter, rushed out of her office.

'Mikki! Call all the other directors' assistants. There's been a major accident on the BA Expressway. A bus filled with senior citizens on their way to Vegas rolled. They're bringing old people in here in droves. We'll need all the hands we can get to process them.'

'I'm on it,' Mikki said. She was punching phone numbers before Jill finished speaking.

THREE hours later the ER still resembled a geriatric battlefield, but at least Mikki thought it was finally beginning to seem like the hospital staff was on the winning side.

'I think the only ones who haven't been processed yet are those two little old ladies over there.' Patricia, executive assistant to the director of security, nodded her head at the far corner of the ER waiting room.

Mikki sighed. 'I'll take the lady in the red skirt if you take the one in the orange polyester pantsuit.'

'Let's do it,' Patricia said, already heading to her charge.

Mikki nodded. Man, she was tired. She felt as old as the ancient grandma she was approaching. Reminding herself firmly that even though she was tired and stressed, she hadn't just been through a bus accident, Mikki plastered a friendly smile on her face. The old woman's eyes were closed and her head was tilted back against the sterile tile of the ER wall. Her wealth of silver-white hair was caught up in an elegant French twist, and up close Mikki realized that the long, full skirt was made of rich-looking cashmere, as was the matching sweater. A thick, iridescent strand of pearls hung almost to her waist, and elegant pearl drops decorated her ears. A white silk scarf was wrapped around her left hand. The middle of the scarf was stained brown with dried blood.

'Ma'am?' she asked softly, not wanting to startle her.

The woman didn't respond.

'Excuse me, ma'am,' Mikki said a little louder.

Still no response.

A horrible sinking feeling nested in Mikki's stomach. What if the old lady was dead?

'Ma'am!' Mikki tried unsuccessfully to keep the panic from her voice.

'I am not dead, young lady. I am simply old.' The woman's voice was husky and attractive, rich with a soft, rolling accent. She enunciated the syllables of each word carefully.

But she didn't open her eyes.

'I'm sorry, ma'am. I–I, uh, I didn't think you were dead, I just thought you were asleep. It's your turn. I can take your insurance information now.'

She opened her eyes, and Mikki blinked in surprise. The old woman's eyes were startlingly clear and a vibrant, deep blue. If hope had a color, it would be the blue of the old woman's eyes, and Mikki was struck speechless by their beauty.

24

The deep, soft lines at the edges of the woman's eyes crinkled as she smiled.

'You should try to always tell the truth, my dear. You are a dismal liar. But do not fret. I am most certainly alive – for the moment.'

She held out the well-manicured hand that was not wrapped in a scarf, and Mikki automatically took it, helping the woman to her feet.

'Yes, ma'am,' Mikki said stupidly.

'I have always thought that the title of "ma'am" should be reserved for young women who desire to appear older, or old women who have given up on life. I am neither. I prefer *signora*, the title Italians give their women. It sounds so much more interesting, does it not? But you may call me Sevillana.'

Mikki's smile slipped off her face. 'Did you say Sevillana?'

'Yes, that is my given name. Is there something wrong, my dear?'

Mikki helped Sevillana into the chair in front of the registration desk before she answered. 'No, nothing's wrong. It's just that I know the name.'

'Do you?' The old woman raised one delicate silver eyebrow. 'And what is it you know?'

'I know it's the name of a rose, a Meidiland Rose that originated in France. It's a brilliant scarlet in color and very hardy. It makes a great hedge, and it blooms for almost four straight months.'

Sevillana smiled with surprised appreciation. 'I knew there was something special about you.'

Mikki tried to return her smile, but she was still disconcerted by the odd coincidence of their names. Plenty of roses had been named after people – the JFK rose, the Dolly Parton, the Princess Di – but she'd never met anyone else who had been named after a rose. Retreating into the familiar, she tapped her computer and pulled up the new patient profile screen.

'What is your last name, ma'am, I mean, signora?' Mikki asked.

'Kalyca. Spelled k-a-l-y-c-a.' She took an insurance card from her purse and handed it to Mikki. 'And what is your name, my dear?'

Mikki glanced up from the computer screen. Automatically, she opened her mouth to tell Sevillana her nickname, but something in the old woman's knowing gaze made her hesitate.

'Mikado,' she admitted.

The smile that lit Sevillana's face seemed to wash decades from her age. 'Oh, my! Another lady of the roses. What a lovely surprise.'

'It's certainly unusual,' Mikki agreed, with a hint of sarcasm.

Sevillana studied Mikado carefully. 'As you age, you will learn to appreciate the unusual, no matter in what form you discover it. Or it discovers you.'

Mikki closed her lips on the ready quip that came to her mind. There was something so wise in the old woman's eyes that she felt her normal defenses slip.

'Do you really believe that?' Mikki asked suddenly.

'Of course, my dear.' Sevillana's incredible eyes were sharp. 'The unusual is as close as we can get in this world to experiencing real magick, and magick is the breath of life.'

Mikki would have liked to have questioned the old woman further, but just then a nurse stepped officiously up to them.

'I believe you're my last patient.' The RN helped Sevillana to her feet. 'Let's take a look at that hand.'

'It is nothing but a scratch,' the old woman said as she let the nurse lead her from the desk. Then, glancing over her shoulder, she met Mikki's eyes and spoke clearly and distinctly. 'I have received far worse wounds from pruning my roses without gloves.'

Her words caused a shock of surprise to explode across Mikki's skin.

How did the old woman know?

Mikki was still staring thoughtfully at the doorway through which Sevillana had disappeared when her boss squeezed her shoulder, making her jump.

'Didn't mean to scare you, Mikki. I just wanted to thank you. I appreciate your help today. It was above and beyond the normal call of duty.'

'Oh, no problem, Jill. It was a nice change from regular office work.'

Jill looked at her assistant closely. She noticed the dark circles under her expressive eyes and the unusual paleness of her skin. Mikki had been her assistant for five years, and the director had come to depend on the no-nonsense way she kept the Nursing Services office running smoothly, but lately her assistant had begun to worry her. She had become increasingly absent-minded, and just two days earlier Jill was almost positive Mikki had been sleeping at her desk. Perhaps it was time her assistant took a vacation. And maybe she needed a raise, too. Jill would hate to lose her to one of their competitor hospitals, and that new heart hospital had just opened on 91st Street. They were probably recruiting heavily for experienced employees. She made a mental note to look into the raise and bring Mikki one of those cruise line catalogs first thing Monday morning.

'Why don't you knock off early today? It's been a long week.'

Mikki smiled in surprise. 'Thanks! I do have a big date to get ready for.'

Jill grinned at her assistant. 'I'll keep my fingers crossed.' Then she looked around to be sure no one could overhear her before quipping, 'You know, a hard man is good to find.'

Mikki giggled. 'This one's a professor.'

'Well, here's hoping that his' – Jill paused, omitting the word and waggling her eyebrows suggestively – 'is as big as his brain. See you Monday.' Then she departed, swinging her hips jauntily in time with her characteristically saucy stride.

Mikki was still smiling as she turned off the computer. It was as she clicked the mouse that she noticed the laminated insurance card.

'Ah, damnit! I didn't give Sevillana back her card.'

Mikki grabbed the card and rushed through the door to the inner area of the emergency room. The nurses' station was located in the middle of the large center arena. Mikki recognized the unit secretary who sat behind the tall counter. As usual, the petite brunette was busy typing orders into the computer.

'Hey, Brandi, what room is Sevillana Kalyca in?'

'Seven.' The harried secretary didn't even glance up at her. 'That's a name that is hard to forget.'

'Thanks.' Mikki headed to the door marked 7. 'Hope it quiets down for you tonight.'

'Fat chance,' Brandi muttered.

Mikki knocked on the closed door.

'You may enter,' the old woman's distinctive voice called.

Mikki opened the door and peeked hesitantly into the room. Sevillana beckoned her in with her good hand. Her left hand was propped up on an aluminum arm that pulled out of the side of the examination bed. Someone had draped the shiny surface with a blue cloth. Mikki could see the laceration that slashed across the meaty part of her palm. It was slowly seeping blood.

'Come on in, my dear. The nurse has gone to collect some instruments with which to fix this.' She nodded at her hand. 'Apparently, I need stitches.'

'I'm sorry,' Mikki said automatically. 'I hope it doesn't hurt too much.'

'It is a small thing, Mikado.' Sevillana gestured to the chair beside the bed. 'Please, sit. It was kind of you to look in on me.'

'I brought you this.' Mikki handed her the insurance card, feeling chagrined that she hadn't really come to check on her.

'Thank you. I would never have remembered where I left it.' Sevillana took the card and smiled warmly at Mikki.

Mikki sat. She tried to keep from staring at the old woman's wound, but like a horrible accident passed on a highway, her gaze kept being drawn back to it. And there was something else about Sevillana's palm. Mikki squinted, trying to get a better look at it.

'Blood is fascinating. Do you not think it so?' Sevillana's voice was hypnotic.

'The color always reminds me of roses,' Mikki said softly. She forced her eyes from Sevillana's injured hand to her face. 'I don't mean to sound like I'm a blood-crazed ghoul. It's just that freshly blooming roses and new blood share such a unique color. I don't understand why that should have a negative connotation,' she finished defensively.

Sevillana's amazing blue eyes pierced her. 'You are wise for one who is so young. For me, it took many years to understand that there is no negative connotation in what you say. Roses and blood do share many of the same traits, which is, truly, a wondrous thing.'

Mikki took a deep breath.

'How do you know about roses and blood?' she blurted.

The old woman's answering smile was wise.

'Here we are!' The nurse hurried into the room carrying a tray filled with sterile instruments. She was followed by a female doctor Mikki recognized as being one of the new residents. 'Doctor Mason is going to get you fixed right up.'

The doctor glanced at Mikki. 'Are you a relative?'

'No, I'm Jill Carter's assistant.'

'You'll have to leave.'

Mikki nodded and looked apologetically at Sevillana. 'I have to go. It was really nice to meet you, signora.'

'Wait a moment, my dear.' Sevillana reached for her purse, which was lying next to her on the examination bed.

'Ma'am, if she's not a relative, she really must leave,' Dr. Mason said.

'I understand that, young woman. I am not asking that she stay. I simply have something I must give her,' Sevillana said in a tone a mother would use to admonish an errant child.

Without waiting for a response from the doctor, the old woman's uninjured hand disappeared into the bowels of her huge, baglike purse, and when it emerged, it was holding a small glass bottle. The bottle was no longer than Mikki's little finger, and it was shaped like a slender tube. There were knobby protrusions up and down the length of it. Mikki thought the design looked vaguely familiar.

'Here, my dear. I want you to have this.'

Sevillana placed the vial in her hand, and when she touched it, Mikki realized why it looked familiar. It was a perfect glass replica of the stem of a rose, complete with tiny thorns.

'It is a perfume I had made for me when I last visited the island of Crete off the coast of the always lovely Greece. In the past, it has brought me good luck and more than a little magick. My wish is that it may do the same for you.'

30

Mikki's hand closed over the bottle. 'Thank you, Sevillana,' she called as the nurse ushered her toward the door.

'*Remember . . .*' the old woman whispered after Mikado.

The door closed with a soft click.

Chapter Four

Mikki's apartment was a sanctuary. She'd signed the long-term lease five years before and hadn't been sorry once. She lived on the top floor of the small complex. It was a spacious, quiet place, but she hadn't decided on it because of its interior. She'd chosen it because of its location. The view from her wrought iron balcony, which wrapped from her living room past her bedroom, looked directly out on Woodward Park. Woodward Park adjoined her favourite place in the world – the Tulsa Municipal Rose Gardens.

Mikki checked her watch as she stepped onto the balcony. Almost six thirty. She had just enough time. She drank in the wonderful view of Woodward Park and noted that nothing wavered or shifted in the air. The park was simply the park. Briefly, Mikki strained to catch even an echo of a lonely roar, but except for the occasional car that whizzed past on 21st Street and the workers who were putting finishing touches on the stage for the play scheduled to open in a couple nights, everything was silent and ordinary. The October evening was pleasantly cool. The sun had just set, but the sky seemed reluctant to relinquish the remnants of its light. Slate blended with mauve and coral in the fading day. Mikki knew the colors would wane quickly, though. Tonight there would be a new moon, which meant the only light afforded by the night sky would be from its stars.

She mentally shook herself. She'd better stop daydreaming and hurry if she was going to get to the restaurant before her date.

The breeze stirred and Mikki breathed deeply, savoring the sweet scent of roses – her roses. The balcony held five large clay pots in which lived five exquisite examples of expertly tended rosebushes. All five were the same type of rose. Mikki had long ago given up mixing her roses at home; she knew what worked best for her – consistency and meticulous care. Her success surrounded her. All five bushes were in full bloom, and the blooms were more than just the typical last-minute blossoming show before winter called them to dormancy. Her Mikado Roses were miraculous.

The outer petals of the fat blooms were red, but not just any red. The scarlet of Mikki's roses had been compared to rubies, fire, and blood. As the blooms unfurled, the brilliant red merged with gold until the base of the rose appeared to have been dipped in a glass of expensive sherry.

Mikki had been winning the amateur category of the annual All-American Rose Selections Garden Show for the past five years. Her co-volunteers at the Tulsa Rose Gardens liked to joke that no one could beat her because she had some kind of magic potion she poured on her roses. Each year they would make a big production of begging her to share her secret.

Mikki smiled and accepted their praise – but she never joked about having a secret rose potion.

Mikki put down the watering bucket and the little toolbox that held her various pruning shears and other rose gardening implements. She approached the first bush. Frowning, she pinched off a small leaf that to the untrained eye looked healthy, but to Mikki's experienced gaze spelled a potential problem.

'Powdery mildew,' she said with disgust. 'I knew the last couple nights had been unseasonably cool, but I thought the temperatures during the day would offset any negative effects.' She caressed one of the blooms lightly, speaking to the bush as if it were a child. 'It's too early in the season. You won't want me to bring you inside yet. I guess I'll have to start covering you at night.'

Moving from plant to plant, Mikki inspected her charges. She found no more offending leaves, but she made a mental note to check the forecast before she went to bed. If the temperature was going to drop to anywhere around forty degrees, she would cover the roses.

Returning to the toolbox, she selected a medium-size pair of shears. Quickly making her choice, she moved to the rosebush that sat closest to the sliding glass doors leading to her bedroom. With sure, experienced motions, she held the stem of a delicate, just opening bloom, and in one quick motion made a vertical cut in the straight, green stem. She lifted the bloom to her nose and drank in its intoxicating fragrance.

'I will love wearing you in my hair tonight,' she told it.

Once more she returned to her toolbox. Gently, she placed the cut rose on the balcony beside it. Then she put away the pair of shears and searched through the box for the final tool she would need that evening.

She found the pocketknife quickly. It was small, but her toolbox was familiar and well ordered. Nothing could hide within it for long. Mikki opened the knife. The little blade was honed to a razorlike edge, which glinted dangerously in the fading light. Methodically, Mikki opened the bottom drawer of the box. Extracting a small packet, she tore open the alcohol wipe. First she swabbed the palm of her left hand, and then she cleaned the already-sterile-looking blade.

She could hear her mother's familiar voice speak from her memory, *You can never be too careful, Mikado. There's no need to get an infection.*

Satisfied that both surfaces were clean, Mikki discarded the alcohol pad. She glanced around her. Even though her balcony faced a busy street, the apartment's height and the thick foliage of her rosebushes coupled to prevent any passersby from catching much more than a glimpse of her. But on the evening of the new moon, Mikki wanted to avoid even the possibility of being glimpsed.

Nothing was stirring around her except the breeze.

Mikki held her left hand in front of her. The skin of her palm was mottled with slender white scars. She glanced at the palm of her right hand. Yes, she had remembered correctly. Amidst the little bone-colored lines on that palm was a more recent mark, still pink and newly healed, which assured her that this month it was her left palm she must use.

Without further hesitation, Mikki pressed the sharp blade against her left palm, and with a practiced, precise movement, cut herself.

Blood welled instantly, and Mikki was suddenly reminded of Sevillana's injury. It had been in exactly the same place, only deeper and wider. And then with a jolt, she realized what else she had seen on the old woman's palm. Bone-colored scars, slender, well healed, and familiar. Mikki felt a wave of dizziness and closed her eyes quickly on the spinning balcony.

How could the old woman have the same cutting scars as she? It was only the women in Mikki's family who practiced this ritual, and they had done so in strict secrecy for generations. And since her mother had died the year before, Mikki had thought she was the last of her kind, the only person left in the world who knew

35

the secret of blood roses. Mikki had to find out more about her. First thing Monday morning she would pull Sevillana's patient record and get her address. She must see the old woman again.

The vertigo-like feeling faded, and Mikki opened her eyes. Blood was pooling in her palm. Before it could drip onto the balcony, Mikki plunged her hand into the watering bucket. At first the cut stung, but the coolness of the water quickly turned soothing. Mikki swished her hand around, watching the water blush with her blood.

After a few minutes she pulled her hand from the water, shook it and wrapped it tightly in a strip of gauze she pulled from the open bottom drawer of the toolbox. She knew the bleeding would stop soon, leaving a narrow, unobtrusive scab she would cover for the next couple days with a flesh-colored Band-Aid. If the other volunteers at the Rose Gardens noticed it, Mikki would simply smile her way through their admonishments about being more careful when she pruned and making sure she always wore her thick leather gloves.

But few people ever noticed such a small, insignificant cut.

Carrying the bucket with her uninjured hand, she carefully divided the water among the five plants. She poured the blood-tinged liquid slowly over each plant's roots, whispering endearments to them and praising them for their beauty. As always, Mikki thought she could actually see the roses responding to the ritual. The cool breeze filtered through their thick leaves, causing the heavy blooms to nod their heads as if they were saying, *Yes, we are part of you . . . blood of your blood . . .*

And to Mikki, they were more than just plants. They were her legacy and the last vestige of her mother and her family. Without them, she would be alone in the world.

When the water was gone she smiled happily at her charges.

'I'd like nothing more than to pull my rocking chair out here, pour myself a glass of that new red I bought yesterday and spend the evening reading a good book.' But she had a date, she reminded herself, with a man who had a nice voice and a charming laugh. Mikki checked the time; it was 6:45. It would take her at least ten minutes to walk to the restaurant.

'Damn!'

Mikki grabbed the empty bucket and the toolbox and tossed them inside the balcony door. She'd clean up the mess when she got home. Rushing to her bathroom, she gave her makeup and hair one last check. She looked good – the black leather skirt was one of her favourites, and the rust color of the cashmere sweater was a lovely complement to her red-gold hair. Quickly, she chose a long, slender strand of antique black glass beads to hang around her neck and dug through her earring drawer until she found a pair of matching chandeliers.

She rushed from the bathroom, grabbed a sweater for her shoulders and was struggling to zip up her sassy new boots when she remembered the rose for her hair. She'd left it on the balcony. Grumbling to herself about being absentminded, she retrieved the cut flower, trimmed the leaves and the stem, and used the little decorative mirror in the living room to check herself as she positioned it snuggly within the curls over her left ear. Breathing deeply, Mikki smiled at her reflection. What better perfume could she choose?

Perfume . . .

Mikki narrowed her eyes thoughtfully and glanced at her purse. Deciding quickly, she unzipped the little side pocket that usually held only her lipstick, a compact and her keys. The glass stem was there, nestled among the more familiar items.

'Well, why not?' Mikki asked herself. 'Sevillana said it brought her luck. Maybe if I wear it tonight I'll be lucky enough to have a decent date for a change.'

Mikki pulled open the tiny cork and raised the vial to her nose. She inhaled and blinked in delighted surprise. The perfume was an earthy mixture of roses and spices. Mikki inhaled again. She'd never smelled any perfume like it. Along with the familiar scent of traditional roses, she thought she recognized cinnamon, ginger and clove, all blended together in a rich, sweet oil. She dabbed the perfume on the pulse points of her neck, throat and wrists before placing the vial back in her purse.

Humming softly to herself, she locked the door behind her and hurried to the sidewalk, loving how the evening breeze mingled the sweetness of her namesake rose and the earthiness of her new perfume. She certainly smelled good.

And suddenly she realized that she really was feeling very lucky.

Chapter Five

The Wild Fork was located in the heart of Tulsa's Utica Square – a beautiful area filled with lovely landscaping, mature trees, trendy shops and fine restaurants. As usual, it was a busy Friday night and all the outside tables were already filled with hungry patrons. Mikki glanced surreptitiously around her. No, she didn't see any solitary men. He was probably seated inside. She checked her watch again. It was 7:10. She hated being late. Sighing, she entered the restaurant.

The harried maître d' was taking the names of a party of six. He assured them the wait would not be too long and then with an effeminate flutter of his long, slender fingers, he waved the group into the waiting area. When his gaze shifted to Mikki his businesslike expression was immediately replaced with a welcoming grin.

'Mikki! Get yourself on in here. It's been ages since I've seen you.'

Mikki returned his smile, and they shared a soft, girlfriend hug.

'Blair, you handsome thing, when are you going to kick Anthony out of your bed and invite me in?' Mikki teased.

Blair giggled and pretended to blush.

'Hush, bad thing. Tony's working tonight. He'll hear you and turn positively green with jealousy. And you know green is his worst color.'

'As a striking redhead, I think it's tragic that some blondes can't wear green,' Mikki simpered, batting her eyes coquettishly at her friend.

Blair stepped back and studied her. 'And dahling, you *are* looking yummy tonight. That hot little skirt is just to die for! What's the occasion?'

Mikki's grin faltered. She had almost forgotten. Almost.

'I'm meeting a blind date here.'

Blair sucked air and clutched his pearls. 'Tragic,' he said. 'Let me guess. Nelly had something to do with this?'

Mikki nodded.

'Not another transient doctor?'

'Well, kind of. This one isn't a medical doctor. He's some kind of professor – an engineer or something. He's guest speaking at TU next week.'

Blair's eyes widened. 'Get out of town! Sounds dreadfully dull.'

'Be nice. I'm trying to be.'

Blair's shocked expression froze, and he lowered his voice. 'Wait . . . he must be Mr. Dark and Dangerous who's been here for about twenty minutes. Girl, he's not bad at all!'

Mikki felt a little skip of anticipation and tried to remember the description Nelly had given her of Arnold Asher.

'Is he medium height, kind of stocky build, shaved bald head with a small diamond stud in one ear?' she asked.

'That's him. Totally. And he has a yummy mustache. Tony and I were just whispering that he reminded us of a cross between a mob boss and that fabulously sexy Telly Savalas – may he rest in peace.' Blair hastily crossed himself.

'Stop it. You're not Catholic.'

'Girl, you know I believe in covering all bases.'

Mikki rolled her eyes at him. 'So what you're saying is that he's cute.'

'Cute?' Blair squeaked. 'He's simply delicious.'

She squared her shoulders. 'Well, good. I mean, I didn't expect anything else. You know Nelly wouldn't fix me up with anyone who was hideous.' Which was true. But there was a whole hell of a lot more to a man than appearance. 'Lead on. I'm ready to meet Mr. Delicious.'

Blair took a menu and turned. Over his shoulder in his most professionally snobby maître d' voice, he said, 'Follow me please, mademoiselle.' He started walking toward the section of the restaurant relegated to its far side.

'Hey.' Mikki tugged on his sleeve. 'This is the I'm-on-a-sexy-date seating area.'

'That's where he asked to be seated,' Blair said, eyes sparkling. 'Somewhere private.'

'Huh,' Mikki said.

'You may have gotten more than you bargained for with this one, little missy,' Blair said in his truly abominable John Wayne accent.

'Please. No John Wayne tonight. My stomach is already churning from nerves.'

'Oh, relax. I have a good feeling about this one.'

Mikki followed Blair through the restaurant to the dimly lit side room that held intimate little tables and couples who were close talking. Blair stepped to the side so she could be seen by all the tables. A solitary man wearing a tastefully expensive black jacket and pants with a silk knit sweater underneath that was a lovely shade of cool green looked up from the book he was reading. His head was shaved, and the light caught a small diamond earring in his left ear. Nelly had been honest in her assessment. She had described Arnold Asher as 'attractive, but not in a traditional way.' Mikki had to agree. The man was definitely interesting looking – a little dark and bad boy-ish, and decidedly masculine. She felt a stab of unexpected pleasure. She wasn't attracted to traditionally handsome men – there was something about them that she found too much. After spending time with a 'handsome' man, she often felt like she'd eaten too many rich desserts. And all too often she'd discovered that their inside was as empty as their outside was full and attractive. But an unusual or interesting-looking man . . . Mikki watched as he recognized the rose in her hair and waved a hand at her.

'Bingo!' Blair said.

Mikki smiled and strode purposefully forward to meet her date. He stood as she approached his table.

'You must be Mikki Empousai,' he said as his eyes slid appreciatively down her body.

'Yes I am, Arnold. It's nice to meet you.'

They shook hands. His grip was strong and warm, and as welcoming as his smile.

Blair held her chair out for her, and she sat.

'Wow . . . I . . .' Arnold stumbled over his words, sounding shocked and a little nervous. 'I'm sorry, I just suddenly had the overwhelming impression that we've met before, even though I know that's not possible.'

'Really?' Mikki laughed a little, enjoying the appreciation that was clear in his eyes. 'Do you usually dabble in the psychic? I don't remember Nelly saying anything about that.'

His smile stayed warm. 'I like to call it being intuitive and willing to be open to new possibilities.'

Feeling her face flush with the obvious interest he was showing in her, Mikki's eyes dropped to the book he had been reading. The title was *My Losing Season* . . .

Mikki gasped, reaching for the hardback. 'Pat Conroy! You like Pat Conroy?'

'He's one of my top ten favorite writers,' Arnold said.

'Mine, too. I love him! *The Prince of Tides; The Great Santini, The Water Is Wide . . .*'

'*Beach Music, The Lords of Discipline,*' he continued for her.

'I adored *Beach Music.*'

'So did I. Almost as much as *The Prince of Tides.* I hated that it got some bad reviews,' he said quickly.

'I couldn't agree more! Pat Conroy's prose is magic. I cannot understand how anyone could give him a bad review.'

They sat and smiled in happy surprise at each other, and Mikki felt a rush of something she hadn't felt for a long time on a date – hope.

Blair's romantic and totally exaggerated sigh changed into a contrived cough when Mikki glared at him.

'Oh-mi-god, excuse me,' Blair said. 'Something tickled my throat.'

'Blair, honey, you can bring me a glass of my usual chianti.' She glanced back at the still-smiling Arnold. 'Are you hungry? I skipped lunch and would love an hors d'oeuvre.'

'Sounds good to me.'

'Fantastic. How about the olive bread? It always makes me think of Italy.'

Arnold nodded and Blair hurried away.

'So you're a Conroy fan,' he said. 'Which is your favorite?'

'Probably *The Prince of Tides,* but I love them all.' Mikki stroked the cover of the book before passing it back across the table. 'I haven't read that one yet.'

'You have to! He gives amazing insight into his life.'

'I'll be sure to get it.' They shared a look of complete understanding, and Mikki felt another lovely flutter of hope. 'You said

43

he was one of your top ten favorite authors. Who are some of the others?'

Arnold leaned forward, obviously warming to the subject as only a true booklover could. Mikki studied him as he talked. No, he was not traditionally handsome, and she did tend to prefer her men taller – and younger. But there was definitely something about him, something intelligent and experienced and sexy.

'It's hard to narrow them down to ten. I suppose with Conroy I'd have to add Herman Wouk.'

'*The Winds of War*. What a fabulous book!' Mikki said.

'And don't forget *War and Remembrance*.'

'Couldn't do that.'

'Then I'd have to go from there to James Clavell,' he said.

'*King Rat, Tai-Pan* and the best, *Shogun*,' she said, barely nodding at Blair as he brought her wine and their olive bread.

'I didn't like the miniseries, though.'

'Richard Chamberlain as Blackthorne? Please. No, no, no. I really hate it when a great book is turned into a cheesy miniseries.'

'Unlike one of my other top ten picks – Larry McMurtry's *Lonesome Dove*.'

Mikki paused mid-bite of her olive bread. 'I loved the book *and* adored the miniseries.'

And from there they launched into a lively discussion of the settings depicted by their most beloved authors, from McMurtry's West to Wilbur Smith's Africa and Egypt. Somewhere in the middle of their conversation they managed to order and eat dinner. Mikki felt like she wanted to pinch herself. She couldn't remember the last time she'd had such great dinner conversation with a man. With girlfriends it was the norm to have easy, interesting discussions. With men it seemed – at least to Mikki – almost impossible. Yet before she knew it, she'd killed three glasses of chianti, eaten an excellent meal and was just ordering an Irish coffee for dessert instead of the Death by Chocolate Cake that had been tempting her. She was nicely buzzed and having a great time – and was completely surprised when she glanced at her watch and saw that almost two hours had passed.

She sipped her coffee and felt his eyes studying her. The question on his face was so clear she smiled and said, 'What?'

'It's just so amazing.'

'Actually, I was thinking the same thing,' she said a little shyly.

'I can't believe I found a woman who has actually read, and can appreciate, more than a trashy romance novel.'

Mikki felt the beginning of cold water being dashed on her warm, happy buzz. Had he actually said 'trashy romance novel'? As in the wonderful Nora Roberts, and the ever-delightful MaryJanice Davidson, Susan Grant, Gena Showalter, Sharon Sala, Merline Lovelace, and a host of other fabulous women authors who had kept her company on long nights and made her laugh and cry and sigh happily?

'What do you mean by that?'

Oblivious to her change in tone, he went on enthusiastically. 'I mean that it's unusual that an attractive, available woman has read and comprehended some interesting books.'

'I've made it a point to read a wide range of authors and genres. I think it gives an important added perspective to what might be an otherwise narrow view of life,' she said carefully, trying to keep her tone neutral. 'I was wondering, Arnold, have you ever read any of Anne Tyler's work?'

'Tyler? No, I don't think so,' he said.

'She won a Pulitzer for *Breathing Lessons*, you know.'

'Did she?' He flashed his smile again. 'Good for her.'

Mikki cringed internally at his patronizing tone. 'How about *The Historian* by Elizabeth Kostova?'

'No.'

'I thought you liked historicals,' she said.

'I do.'

'Hmm. Then how about *The Mists of Avalon* by Marion Zimmer Bradley?'

'The Arthurian myth told from a woman's point of view?' His laugh was sarcastic and condescending. 'I wouldn't consider that historical.'

'Did you read it?'

'No, of course not. I choose to stick with Tennyson or T.H. White.' His hand rubbed his forehead as if she was causing his head to hurt. 'I like things that are tried and true.'

'Okay, then what about any of Nora Roberts's books? I read a statistic once that said that every sixty seconds someone buys a Nora Roberts novel. Sounds as if she is definitely tried and true. And statistically, at least, you might have read her – maybe even on accident.'

'Nora Roberts? Doesn't she write those bodice rippers?'

Blair fluttered up to the table. 'I'll just leave the check here.' He put it next to Arnold's arm. 'But there's no rush for you two, take . . .' Blair's words trailed off as he recognized the look of narrow-eyed annoyance Mikki had trained on her date. He cleared his throat. 'What I meant to say is that I'll be happy to take this for you whenever you're ready.' With a worried glance at Mikki, he retreated to watch from the waiter's station.

Blair's abrupt departure made Mikki realize that she needed to fix the expression on her face, but when she glanced at Arnold she saw she needn't have worried. He wasn't looking at her. He was frowning over the bill.

'Is there a problem?' she asked.

He looked up at her and then slid the bill over so she could see it. 'No. No problem at all. I was just figuring up my part of the bill.'

'Excuse me?'

'Well, you were the one who ordered the appetizer. You had one more glass of wine than I did, and that Irish coffee certainly wasn't cheap.'

Disbelieving, Mikki blinked and tried to find her voice.

He reached into his wallet and got out a twenty and two tens. 'That should take care of my part, plus a tip.' Then he looked expectantly at her. 'Are you paying with cash or a credit card?'

Mikki burst into laughter. 'You want me to pay for my half of dinner?'

'Of course,' he said with a perfectly straight face. 'Times have changed. Today's women want to be treated equally and with respect. I'm just showing you the respect you want.'

'Perfect,' Mikki said, still laughing. She could feel the lovely red-headed fit brewing just under her breastbone. This was going to be truly delicious.

'This is just perfect. Okay, here's the deal Dr. Asher – that is how one formally addresses you, isn't it?'

He nodded, looking vaguely confused.

'Good. I want to be sure I get this right. Here's the deal, Dr. Asher. It's not showing me respect to use rhetoric about what today's women want as an excuse to be cheap. It's actually showing me the opposite. I don't care what year it is. If this is a date – and I was under the impression that it was – then it should be a point of pride and good manners for a gentleman to pay for a lady's dinner. That's being respectful. But you wouldn't understand that because you clearly do not respect women.

Your attitude about what you believe women read is as patronizing as your obvious disdain for female authors.' Mikki reached into her purse, pulled out three twenty-dollar bills and plopped them on top of the check. 'And here's a newsflash for you – those so-called trashy romance novels outsell all other genres of writing. Many of the authors are insightful and well educated. They create worlds filled with strong, passionate women and honorable, heroic men. You should try reading some of them. Those female romance authors you disdain could definitely teach you a thing or two about being a man.' She stood up and put her purse over her shoulder. 'Good night, Dr. Asher.' He started to stand, clearly struggling to say something. 'No, please. Don't get up. I want to remember you just like this – confused and speechless. It's a good look for you; it certainly beats patronizing and chauvinistic.'

Grinning wickedly, she turned and sauntered lazily out of the dimly lit room.

She was still grinning as she strolled down the sidewalk. God, she was glad she'd told him off and walked out! She had never been a wimpy, doormat kind of a woman; she had an extraordinarily low bullshit meter. God, didn't it just figure! He had seemed interesting and sexy at first. But like most men, he had turned out to be a disappointment.

Whispering through her subconscious was the thought that no man had been able to get close to her because she had never been able to allow herself to share the secret that pulsed through her blood . . . but the thought was fleeting, and she quickly stifled the stark honesty of it with a tipsy laugh and a little impromptu twirl in the halo of light under a streetlamp.

She'd never actually walked out on a date before.

It was exhilarating!

Her steps slowed. Lately, she'd been thinking more and more that maybe she wasn't meant to have a permanent relationship. Maybe tonight had been the final sign she needed. Something like a modern omen. She *was* different, and it was becoming more and more clear to her that there was no 'right' man for her. He didn't exist. Oddly enough, the thought didn't make her feel sad or lonely. Instead, it made her feel wise, like she had come to a realization that her friends weren't mature enough yet to understand. It gave her a sense of release that was almost overwhelming.

Mikki walked past McGill's, a popular local pub, and considered ducking in for a quick drink. But the door opened and a current of noise rolled out, changing her mind. She didn't feel like dealing with shouting above a din of music just to order a drink. Plus, she'd probably had enough – not that that was a bad thing. She wasn't driving – she was flying! Mikki laughed and walked on, breathing in the cool October air.

As she left the business district and got closer to Woodward Park and her apartment, the buildings changed from posh shops and restaurants to the stately old oil mansions that surrounded the park. Mikki loved this part of Tulsa. It made her wish she had lived during the 1920s. She would have been a flapper. She would have cut her hair short, worn loose beaded dresses that shimmied when she moved, had too much to drink and danced all night. Between parties she would have crusaded for equal rights for women.

Kind of like she'd done tonight, she thought happily. Well, minus the dress, the haircut and the dancing. She did a happy little skip step under the next light and laughed at herself. Maybe not minus the dancing. She'd have to go back to the restaurant tomorrow night for dinner and get all the gory after-she-left details from Blair and the gang.

The sidewalk was interrupted by the road forking in front of her. Mikki was at the juncture of where the mansions gave way to Woodward Park. Here was where she usually crossed the street to her apartment. Hesitating, Mikki looked into the park. She didn't detect any strange shifts in perception that might signal one of her episodes. Actually, until that moment she'd forgotten about the weirdness that had crept into her life with her recent dreams.

'Just goes to prove dumping a man is good for what ails me,' she said pleasantly to herself.

And everything did look utterly normal. The free-standing antique streetlights scattered throughout Woodward Park speckled it with pools of creamy light. The wind whispered through the well-tended oaks, calling softly the change of seasons and causing a cascade of leaves to scatter like mini-tornados that had been taught to heel. And smack in the middle of it she could see the soft illumination of the stage lights for the Performance in the Park rehearsal. Faintly she could hear the actress speaking her lines . . .

'A little love is a joy in the house,
A little fire is a jewel against frost and darkness . . .'

She started to cross the street toward home but hesitated, looking longingly at the park, awash in light and sound. It was so lovely. It looked like a magical oasis in the middle of the night – a special little sub-city of her very own. A teasing breeze whisked from the park and twirled around her body, enticing her forward with the cinnamon scent of autumn leaves.

Why not?

Mikki checked the time. It was only nine. The park and the rose gardens didn't close till eleven. Nelly had specifically told her to go on with her normal life. It was definitely normal for her to walk through the park and visit her roses. She'd make her way around the rehearsing actors and then take a quick stroll through the gardens. She really should check on the roses that surrounded the construction site. She'd been concerned that all the tromping of the workmen's booted feet with their clumsy comings and goings was overstressing the roses.

Mikki glanced up at the darkening sky, reminding herself that it was the night of the new moon. If the roses needed help, what better time could she choose to give it to them?

She'd make one pass through the central tier and be sure the workers had cleaned up their mess and not manhandled the roses. Then she'd go home, pour herself a glass of bedtime wine and curl up with a good book . . . by a female author!

Or, her errant thoughts whispered enticingly, she could just go to sleep. Wouldn't she rather revisit her dream lover than do anything else?

With a supreme effort of will, she steered her mind away from that line of thinking. She couldn't start living life around her fantasies. Then she really would be crazy.

Chapter Six

Mikki stepped into the crossroads between the park and the street and then onto the sidewalk that twisted past the lovely waterfall-fed ponds that framed the north edge of Woodward Park. At the next fork in the walkway she headed up and away from the northern street side, walking toward the central area of the park, which was currently abuzz with activity around the raised stage that had only just been erected the night before. Bits and pieces of poetic lines drifted around her, teasing her with snippets of the play.

'The holy fountains flow up from the earth,
the smoke of sacrifice flows up from the earth,
the eagle and the wild swan fly up from the earth, righteousness
    also
has flown up from the earth to the feet of the goddess . . .'

Intrigued, she searched her memory for details of *Medea*'s story. She vaguely remembered that the play was an ancient Greek tragedy and that the plot centered around Medea, who had been jilted by her husband, Jason, for . . . Mikki scrunched up her face as she tried to sift through the dregs of long-forgotten high school English.

. . . *But women will never hate their own children.*

Floating to her on the soft wind, the line jogged her cobwebby memory. Medea had been pissed at Jason because he had dumped her for a younger woman, the daughter of the king of wherever it was they had fled to after she'd betrayed her homeland to save Jason.

'Figures,' she muttered to herself. 'Just like a man . . .' She slowed as she approached the busy group of people who were rearranging lights and hauling pieces of freshly painted plywood setting here and there. Several actresses were onstage, but they had fallen silent. Three grouped nervously together on stage left. Another woman was standing by herself opposite them stage right. They were wearing drapey toga-like outfits, and their hair flowed long and loose down their backs. All of them were looking around as if they expected someone to materialize from the shadows at the edge of the stage. Mikki stopped to watch, wondering why they seemed so uncomfortable.

'Where in the hell is Medea?'

The voice boomed from a little open-ended tent not far from her, causing Mikki to jump.

'She . . . she said she had to take a break,' the lone woman said sheepishly.

'That was half an hour ago!' the shadowed voice yelled, clearly annoyed. 'How are we supposed to finish the sound check without Medea?'

Mikki's eyes slid to where the voice was coming from. All she could make out from the interior of the tent was an illuminated soundboard that had lights and switches blinking away on it, in front of which the dark figure of a man stood.

'I could wear two mikes and read her lines as well as mine,' one of the three women said, shielding her eyes from the spotlights trained on the stage as she peered toward the man who Mikki decided must be the director.

'That won't work. We can't get an accurate check that way. Goddamnit! I'm tired of Catie's theatrics. The little twit thinks she *is* Medea.' The man paused, and Mikki could hear him pacing irritably back and forth over the leafy ground. Then, as if her gaze had drawn it, his head turned in her direction. 'Hey you! Would you mind giving us a hand?'

Mikki looked around. No one was near her. The guy was actually talking to her.

'Me?' She laughed nervously.

'Yeah, it'll just take a few minutes. Could you go up onstage, let them key a mike to you and say a few lines?'

'I don't know the lines,' Mikki said inanely.

'Doesn't matter.' The man gestured at a worker who was standing near the stage. 'Get the lady a script, and tell Cio to mike her.' Then he turned back to Mikki. 'How 'bout I give you a couple tickets to opening night for helping us out?'

'O-okay,' Mikki stammered. What the heck? Nelly loved this kind of stuff – she'd take her.

Feeling only a little foolish, she let two men lead her to the stage. One thrust an open script into her hand, and the other guy, the one the director had called Cio, pushed back her hair, fitting a neat little mini-mike into her hairline.

'Hey,' Cio yelled back at the director. 'Her hair's as thick as that wig Catie wears.'

'Good, it'll give us an accurate test.'

'There's your mark,' Cio told her, pointing to a line duct taped on the floor of the stage. 'All you have to do is stand there and after the Corinthian women say their lines, I'll point to you and you read Medea's invocation of Hecate.' He paused, took a pen from his shirt pocket and circled a paragraph in the script. 'That stanza right there. Face the audience and try to speak as slowly and clearly as possible. Got it?'

Mikki nodded.

'Great.' He patted her shoulder absently before exiting the stage.

'You'll be fine,' one of the three ladies said, smiling at her. 'This is easy-peasy.'

'I don't know,' Mikki whispered back at her. 'I've never invoked a goddess before.'

'Hey, don't worry about it. You won't invoke one tonight unless you really are Medea,' the friendly looking woman said, still grinning.

'Or unless you're one of Hecate's blood priestesses,' another lady chimed in.

'Or have delusions of grandeur and diva yourself into believing you're both.' All of the actresses rolled their eyes at the first woman's comment. Clearly the absent lead actress had let the part go to her head.

'Ready, ladies?' the director called.

The four women sent her looks of encouragement as Mikki moved center stage to her mark.

'All right, let's get this done so we can go home. First Corinthian Woman, start us out please.'

The First Corinthian Woman's voice was strong and clear as she repeated the lines Mikki had overheard earlier.

'The holy fountains flow up from the earth
the smoke of sacrifice flows up from the earth,
the eagle and the wild swan fly up from the earth . . .'

A little thrill tingled through Mikki's stomach, and her nervousness was suddenly replaced by excitement. The actress's words seemed to fill the space around her, chasing away her trepidation.

The Second Corinthian Woman spoke her lines earnestly to Mikki.

> 'Women hate war, but men will wage it again.
> Women may hate their husbands, and sons their fathers,
> but women will never hate their own children.'

Mikki's eyes followed the lines on the script as the First Woman's voice trembled with emotion.

> 'But as for me, I will do good to my husband,
> I will love my sons and daughters, and adore the gods.'

From the edge of the stage Cio pointed to her, and like a horse goaded by spurs, Mikki plunged into Medea's lines.

> 'You will be quiet, you women.
> You came to see how the barbarian woman endures betrayal;
> watch and you will know.'

On the script were written the words (*Medea kneels and prays*). Mikki glanced questioningly at Cio. He nodded and gestured to the stage floor. Drawing a deep breath, Mikki knelt and began reading the invocation.

> 'Not for nothing I have worshipped the wild gray
> goddess who walks in the dark, the wise one,
> whose dominions are the crossroads of man, wild
> beasts, and ancient secret magicks,
> Hecate, sweet flower of the ebony moon.'

As Mikki spoke, her voice gained power and the small electric thrill that had lodged in her stomach when the First Corinthian Woman began to speak swelled throughout her body. Excitement rushed, adrenaline-like, into her throat, so that when she continued the invocation, her voice strengthened and magnified. Had she been looking at the director, she would have seen him frantically adjusting switches and turning dials. Had she glanced at the actresses onstage with her, she would have seen their mildly amused expressions change to confusion and shock. But Mikki looked nowhere except the script before her and the words that suddenly appeared, glowing, on the page as if her voice had called them alive.

'Queen of Night, hear your errant priestess's prayer.
Forgive me that I have forgotten your ways.'

Mikki faltered. The small, Band-Aid-covered cut on her palm throbbed painfully. There was a great rushing sound in her ears that reminded her of the ocean. She felt the night wind, which had only moments before been gentle and cool, whip in a sudden heat around her, lifting her hair as if it, too, along with her body, had been electrified. Caressed by the wind, the unusual scent of the perfume she'd dabbed on her pulse points lifted with the breeze to fill her senses. She breathed deeply, inhaling rose and spice and heat. Overwhelmed by the exquisite beauty of the rich oil, the glowing words on the script blurred until Mikki could no longer see them. But it didn't matter. Unbelievably, she heard the lines within her mind, and with a sob, she opened her mouth and cried the words that were echoing through her head.

'I call upon you now Hecate, by the blood that runs thick in my
veins and ask that you help me to return to your service and your

realm so that I might once again remember the use of the blood magick and the ancient beauty that is the Realm of the Rose.'

A great roar split the night, ringing in Mikki's ears with an intensity that washed her in dizziness. She blinked tears from her eyes, looking around her as if she had just awakened from a dream.

Ah, hell! I'm having one of those damn episodes! Mikki frantically tried to make sense of the bright lights and the women who were staring open-mouthed at her. *The play! Crap! Crap!* Mikki looked down at the script she still clutched in her sweating hands. The words printed there in ordinary black and white made no sense. They weren't the lines she had just said. What the hell had happened to her?

Three single claps came from the rear of the stage.

'Lovely job of ad-libbing. Truly moving.' The voice was filled with sarcasm.

Mikki managed to get awkwardly to her feet as an attractive petite woman wearing a gold toga and a long, dark wig stepped up to her.

'But the star has returned. So I'll take my mike and my stage position, and you can run along.'

Mikki felt frozen with humiliation as the actress reached up to yank the neatly hidden microphone from her hair.

'Ouch! Fuck!' the diva shrieked, pulling back her hand and sucking on her bleeding finger. 'The damn thing stabbed me.'

Woodenly, Mikki raised her hand to touch the rose that still sat behind her ear.

'Sorry,' she muttered, quickly pulling the mike from her hair. 'Mikado Roses don't usually have prominent thorns.'

'Catie, darling, it's all right. She was just helping us out with the sound check.' Cio rushed onstage.

Catie snatched the mike from Mikki and turned her back dismissively as the sound manager hastily began working the tiny microphone into the hairline of the star's wig.

'Someone get me a Band-Aid before I bleed to death! And my God! What is that smell? Who has on too fucking much perfume? It's like I'm standing in the middle of a bordello, not a stage. For Christ's sake! I leave for half a second and everything goes to shit!'

Two more people hurried onstage, and Mikki sidled off, ignoring the director when he called insincere thanks and reminded her that she could pick up her tickets opening night at the Garden Center.

Chapter Seven

It took several minutes for Mikki's cheeks to cool down. She could easily imagine the blazing red of her blush. Jeesh, what a humiliating experience! She left the sidewalk and retreated up the side of the gently sloping hill that would lead her to the uppermost entrance to the rose gardens. Shuffling her feet through the dry leaves that browned the soft grass of the park, Mikki tried to make sense of what had just happened. Everything had seemed fine – even fun – when she'd gone up onstage. Then she'd started reading her lines and . . . she looked down at the script that she had forgotten to leave behind. The light was too dim, and she couldn't make out the words, but she didn't have to read them to know that what had come out of her mouth had definitely not been what had been written on the script. She remembered all too well seeing the lines glow and then hearing them ring in her mind. She ran a shaky hand through her hair.

What was happening to her? She should go home. Maybe she should call Nelly. If having a totally embarrassing hallucination in front of multiple people didn't constitute an emergency of enormous girlfriend proportions, she didn't know what did.

Just then Mikki topped the little rise and came to a halt. The Tulsa Municipal Rose Gardens stretched before her like a familiar dream, comforting her frayed nerves. Just what exactly was so terrible about what she'd just done? What had really happened had probably more to do with three glasses of wine and being freaked out by suddenly being thrust onstage than with psychosis. She shoved the script into her purse. When she got home she'd reread Medea's words. What she had said was probably close to the original text. She needed to quit being so hard on herself. It was ridiculous to focus on every little mistake she made and every little daydream she allowed herself. She grinned suddenly. She'd even pick up the free tickets and consider heckling diva Catie on opening night.

Mikki felt the pull of her beloved gardens dissipate the last of her nervous stress as she gazed out across the expanse of roses. The gardens had been built in the shape of a gigantic tiered rectangle that always reminded Mikki of a huge, Italian wedding cake. There were five sections of terraced gardens, which climbed almost 900 feet from street level. Each tier was filled with row after row of meticulously tended roses. The gardens were styled after the gardens made popular during the Italian Renaissance, and amidst the more than 9,000 roses and imported statuary were Italian junipers, sheared by hand into formal, conical shapes, southern Magnolias, as well as deciduous holly and mugo pines.

Each level also held its own distinctive water element. The gardens boasted everything from peaceful, deep reflective pools and ancient-looking spouting wall fixtures to the graceful, cascading fountain situated as the garden's water showpiece in the magnificent center of the third and largest level.

It was fully dark, and, unlike Woodward Park, the rose gardens didn't have freestanding lights. Instead, each water feature was lit from underneath. The effect was spectacular. The gardens seemed to glow, suspended in the flickering illumination of rose-scented water. A whimsical breeze lifted Mikki's thick hair, pulling her forward. Eagerly, she crossed the boundary between the two parks and drew in a deep breath. Roses filled her senses.

'Heaven couldn't smell any better,' she whispered.

As if her feet made the choice for her, Mikki started down her favorite walkway, working her way slowly toward the center most garden area. Some nights the grounds remained filled with people almost until closing. They brought chairs and picnic baskets, books and sketch pads. That night Mikki was relieved to see that the only other human activity was a couple of lovers who were making out on a blanket at the edge of the top tier. She ignored them, and they ignored her. Mikki preferred it that way. She loved to have the roses to herself. She walked lazily through the gardens, pausing often to visit beds of her personal favorites. The night was quiet, and except for the wind playing through the trees, the hypnotic tinkling of water and the muffled tap-tap of her boot heels against the pebbled cement of the pathways, there was little outside noise. It was like the roses created a sound barrier between their gardens and the rest of the world.

The disappointing date in the past and the *Medea* fiasco forgotten, Mikki was thoroughly enjoying herself once again as she chose the wide stairway that ran down the right side of the third tier. Hurrying, she almost skipped down the steps that led to the heart of the gardens. The bottom of the rocky stairs was framed by a large archway made of heavy rock. She stepped through that amazing arch of stone and, as always, she felt like she was entering another world. Mikki smiled and glanced to her left.

'And you know you're a big part of the reason why.' She spoke to the enormous statue that perched imposingly between the archway she had just walked beneath and the second stone archway, which framed the set of steps to its left – a mirror image of the stairs she had just descended.

She walked to the statue and looked up at it, breathing in the scent of the profusely blooming Double Delights that surrounded it.

'Hello, old friend,' she said softly.

The flickering light from the large, circular fountain situated a few yards from them threw a strange, aquatic glow over the statue, illuminating it with an eerie, ever-changing light. For a moment Mikki felt a tremor of unease; the thing looked almost alive in the blue tinged light. Its marbleized skin seemed to borrow a glow from the water that pulsed, giving it the façade of living flesh. The ancient statue appeared to breathe. Then she mentally shook herself.

'Don't be ridiculous,' she said firmly. 'It's the same statue that's always been here. And it's supposed to be scary-looking, that's why it's called the Guardian of the Roses.'

As Mikki spoke, the statue settled into the familiar marble lines she had known since she was a child. Local legend said that the statue had been a gift from an eccentric Greek heiress in 1934, the year the gardens were christened. No reason had ever been given for her largess – the local assumption was that she had visited and had fallen in love with the design of the gardens.

Mikki drifted forward and let her fingers play over the raised words of the plaque that proclaimed it: *Beast of the Greek Goddess of Night – This statue is a restored copy of one found in the Parthenon and is thought to have been the inspiration for the Cretan myth of the Minotaur.*

Mikki's lips twisted in a crooked smile. The beast had never looked like the Minotaur to her. Yes, he had always evoked exotic images of fantasy and myth, reminding her of late, sleepless nights and the shadowy fairy tales her mother used to read to her throughout her childhood, but she just didn't see that much similarity between the statue and the mythological creature who was supposed to have had a man's body and a bull's head.

'It's more like you're from another world than ancient mythology,' she told the marble creation. Actually, Mikki admitted to herself as she studied him for the zillionth time, the statue was a wonderful, frightening mixture of raw male power and beast.

He was huge, at least seven feet tall, and more human than Minos's Minotaur, but the fact that he was manlike didn't make his appearance any less imposing. He crouched on the top of a wide, ornately carved marble pedestal. His rear legs were thick, much like a world-class sprinter's, except that they were covered with a coat of fur and ended in cloven hooves. His hands were massive, and they curled clawlike around the top of the pedestal. The thick muscles in his arms, shoulders and haunches strained forward. His face had been carved with indistinct lines, almost as if it had been half finished. It gave the appearance of a man, though he was decidedly fierce and bestial. His eyes were wide, empty marble under a thick, bestial brow. Mikki cocked her own head as she studied him. A beast, yes, but in a man's skin. Not really a bull, yet vaguely Taurean. On his head were thick, pointed horns, and an impressive mane of hair cascaded around his enormous shoulders. The sculptor had carved the creature's mane so it was swept back, making it appear as though he was straining against a raging wind.

Mikki felt a jolt of recognition. That's right, the statue had horns! Like the creature in her dream last night. She narrowed her eyes. Maybe this was where her fantasy had originated. She wanted to smack herself on the forehead. Talk about too much imagination! Was the answer to her supposed obsession as simple as that? She had always loved the rose gardens, especially this particular tier. And as her mother would have reminded her if she had still been alive, she did have a tendency to be overimaginative. How many times had her mother admonished her to quit daydreaming and get her room cleaned up . . . or her homework done . . . or the dishes washed?

Nelly had been right. Again. Her recent dreams were probably nothing more than a reflection of her obsession with roses and all that surrounded them. And the rest of her hallucinations were nothing more than daydreams from a sleepy, daydreaming (and clearly horny) mind.

A mind that had no one else to fantasize about, she reminded herself. She'd faced the truth tonight – her real life was decidedly void of men about whom she wanted to fantasize.

So the dreams had just been an elaborate fantasy she had created to amuse herself.

Mikki felt a wave of disappointment, which she quickly squelched.

'Would you rather have had a basketball-size brain tumor?' she chided herself as she absently kicked at a loose pebble. 'And if it wasn't a brain tumor, what did you think? That you were actually having some kind of magical experience? That a fantasy lover was going to step from your dreams into your life? How pathetic. Get a grip, girl. And try to remember why you're here.'

Mikki turned her back on the statue and marched toward the roped-off construction area, shaking her head in self-disgust. Already annoyed, she approached the construction site with determined steps. That particular part of the terrace wall had begun to crumble, so masons had been hired to repair it, with explicit instructions *not* to mess up the roses that had lived happily in the beds around the wall for decades.

Mikki let out her breath in a huff of disgust. Just as she'd suspected, litter had been left all over. She bent under the yellow construction tape and entered the rose bed, picking up the garbage that dotted the otherwise neat rows of bushes and shoving it into an empty plastic bag she'd untangled from the thorny trap of two rosebushes. When she found the small plastic cooler lying on its side in the middle of the bed, she felt her temper snap.

'This is just bullshit!' she exploded.

Tomorrow was Saturday, so the master gardener wouldn't be on the premises, but first thing Monday morning Mikki would call her and make a full report about the workmen's negligence. And tomorrow she would be sure she was there all day to supervise those Neanderthals and keep them from creating any further havoc.

She finished picking up the trash and then focused her attention on the roses themselves.

'Oh, no!' She felt her stomach clench as she examined the stressed-out bushes. She had thought they had looked wilted yesterday, but she had hoped it was just her overprotective nature rearing its maternal head. Today she knew she had been right to worry. The normally thick, shiny foliage looked markedly dull, even in the subdued light from the fountain. And the blooms were in bad shape. The blossoms were limp, and prematurely loose rose petals sprinkled the ground like sad feathers from dying birds.

Mikki shook her head slowly. 'What incredibly bad timing,' she told the damaged bushes. 'After all this, you won't be strong enough to fend off much cold weather. If the winter is too harsh, we could lose this entire bed.' Mikki clucked and fussed with the bushes like an irate kindergarten teacher.

The possible loss of the bushes tugged at her heart. Mikki knew most people wouldn't understand her love of roses – her girlfriends had certainly told her enough times that they were only plants, not people or even pets. But whenever Mikki touched a rose or breathed in the heady fragrance of the gardens, she was reminded of her mother and her grandmother; through the roses, if only for a moment, she could feel their love again. Mikki was tired of losing those she loved.

She had to do something. She stopped and looked around her. The tier was empty. Nothing stirred except the water and the wind. Absently, Mikki picked at her already chipped finger-nail polish.

Just do it! she told herself. *No one will know.*

The empty cooler beckoned. Mikki made her decision.

'Okay!' she said to the nearest wilting bush. 'Just don't tell anyone.'

She grabbed the cooler, ducked back under the construction tape, and walked quickly to the fountain. She dipped the empty cooler in the water, and with a grunt, pulled it out. Filled with water it was heavy, and she had to strain to lift it. Water sloshed around her feet when she set it awkwardly on the ground beside her.

It only took a second for her to work the Band-Aid free from her left palm. The cut was already scabbing over, but her flesh was still pink and tender from the knife wound. Mikki rested her right thumbnail against the little slash line. Holding her breath, she closed her eyes and pressed her nail into the wound, forcing it open again.

Mikki sucked her breath in at the sudden pain. But when she opened her eyes, she was relieved to see the darkness of fresh blood flowing into her palm. With a grimace, she dunked her hand into the pool of water held by the cooler.

She certainly had a lot of disinfecting to do when she got home.

Trying not to think about how much her palm ached, she began dragging the full cooler across the stony path back to the bed of sick roses. Once inside the construction area, she straightened, unsure of her next move.

'There are so many of you,' she told the bushes. It was obvious that she couldn't pour the usual amount of blood-tinged water on each bush. She felt her lips twitch in a sarcastic smile. She'd have to open a damn vein for that – and that was probably not a very good idea.

Assuming a businesslike stance, Mikki put her hands on her hips and addressed the roses. 'How about I just sprinkle you guys with some of this water?' The bushes didn't answer, so Mikki counted that as a yes. Bending, she used both hands and began scattering the blush-colored water over the roses that surrounded her. Snapping her wrists and flicking the liquid off her fingers soon became a game. The cool evening breeze mixed with the darkness and the sweet scent of roses and earth. Mikki laughed and sprinkled the blood-kissed water all over, pretending she was a garden fairy raining magic on sleeping children.

Mikki was breathless and smiling by the time she had finished. She studied the damp bushes. It might just be her overactive imagination, but she was sure they were responding already. In the dim, watery light, she swore she could see the limp leaves straightening and the wilting blooms healing. There was more water in the cooler than she had anticipated, and she bent to pour it out onto the nearest bush when a flicker of light caught the corner of her eye as it danced over the guardian statue.

Why not? Mikki thought. Glancing around to make sure she was still alone, she carried the almost-empty cooler quickly to the marble statue.

'Your roses deserve a little extra boost, too,' she told the silent beast. 'After all, you've been watching over them a lot longer than I have.'

Grinning, she dunked her still bleeding hand into what was left of the pink water. With practiced motions she rained drops over the roses that surrounded the statue. When she was finished she stashed the cooler near the wall next to where she had left the full bag of garbage. Noticing that she had inadvertently sprayed some of the water on the statue, she patted one of the creature's big hands.

'Oops. I didn't mean to get you wet,' she said fondly. 'But I'm pretty sure you understand. I mean, please. We, more or less, have the same job. You watch 'em – I watch 'em.'

Digging into her purse, she retrieved a Kleenex, which she wrapped around her left palm, wincing at the tenderness of the reopened cut. She didn't really care about the pain. It had been worth it. She was certain now the roses would survive the winter to thrive and bloom again next spring.

With feet that felt light, she retraced her path out of the third tier, passing under the stone arch and climbing up the stairs. With languid, lazy steps, she walked through the second tier, staying close to the side of the path so she could occasionally reach out and brush her uninjured hand gently over a delicate bloom.

The gardens were absolutely deserted, and Mikki imagined that they were hers – that she was a great lady who lived in a huge mansion and whose only job was to tend to and enjoy her roses.

The night seemed to agree with her. There was no noise at all, not even any echoes of the actresses from Woodward Park, which relieved her because it meant they must have finished and gone home. Thankfully, she wouldn't have to face them again.

It was so silent that Mikki imagined a soundless bubble had been formed around her made of roses and cool October air.

The silence lent itself to listening, so Mikki noticed the noise immediately. It began as a strange, shattering sound, and it came from somewhere behind her – somewhere on the third tier. The sound made her jump in surprise. It reminded her of the crack of faraway thunder. She even glanced up at the sky, half expecting to see clouds announcing the coming of a storm.

No, the night was clear. Thousands of stars spattered the thick ink of the sky; there was not even a hint of clouds above her. Mikki stopped and listened carefully. When she heard nothing more she decided the sound must have been caused by a rabbit or maybe a wandering cat.

'Probably knocking over some of the construction workers' garbage,' she told the rosebush nearest to her.

Mikki walked on, ignoring the fact that her feet were carrying her forward more quickly and the hair on the back of her neck felt prickly and on edge.

The other noise started as soon as she reached the middle of the second tier. At first she thought it was the echo of her boots bouncing back from the rock wall that framed one tier from the next. Two more steps forward were enough to assure her that she wasn't hearing an echo. She was hearing independent foot-steps. They crunched on the pathway with a decidedly heavier tread than her neat little boot taps.

But it wasn't the footsteps themselves that were odd. Lots of people liked to walk the rose garden paths, even after nine o'clock on a cool fall night. It was the distinctive noise that went along with the steps that caught Mikki's attention. She heard it once and discounted it.

She heard it a second time and halted, pretending to stop and smell a particularly lovely Princesse de Monaco. Actually, she was listening with every fiber of her being.

The third time she heard it she was sure. It was an achingly familiar grunt . . . a deep, rumbling exhalation that was somewhere between a growl and a snarl. It passed through her body in an intimate wave that caused her to shiver. Mikki's eyes widened in shock. There could be no other noise like that, and no other being could make such a sound except the creature from her dreams. And it was coming closer to her with every heavy step.

No fucking way! her rational mind screamed. *That's utterly impossible.*

It's just a delusion, she reminded herself firmly. *Nothing more than a symptom of my overactive imagination.*

But no matter what common sense told her, Mikki knew that what she was hearing was real – at least to her. At this moment what was happening had become her reality.

Her heart was beating erratically. *Get out of the gardens and into the park where I'll be surrounded by lights and people!* Her mind nagged at her, belying the rush of sexual excitement that stirred low in the pit of her stomach.

She wasn't dreaming. She was not safely asleep in her apartment or retelling an erotic fantasy to her girlfriend, or even mixing up lines on a script because of nervousness and too much chianti. Something out there was stalking her. She had to get to safety. As soon as she left the rose gardens, she would be away from the shadowed darkness of their paths and the night-shrouded privacy they afforded. Then she could scream for help. Even if the actors and stagehands had all packed up for the night, someone was always within hearing range in Woodward

Park. Plus, she would be well illuminated within the park's free-standing light fixtures. Easy for rescuers to see her.

And easy for *him* to see, too, that 'other' part of her whispered seductively.

Mikki quickened her pace.

A muffled grunt – a mighty burst of breath that sounded as if it came from a blacksmith's bellows rather than a living being – came from the path that ran parallel to the one on which she was walking. Separating them was only a neat bed of profusely blooming Tiffany roses. Mikki sent a furtive look across the pink-faced flowers.

She wasn't close enough to the park for the city lights to help her see him very well. She only caught the flash of glowing eyes before he spun away from her. Size – she gasped – the creature was immense. Against her will, her body flushed with a wild rush of excitement.

A sudden, violent snarl made the hair on the back of her neck stand on end. He was flanking her. He meant to cut her off from the lights of the park.

Faster! her rational mind warned. *Get out of the gardens and into the light of the park and then scream for help!* Fear overshadowed excitement, and in a frightening parody of her dream, Mikki ran.

WHEN he felt her presence, he thought he was dreaming. Again. He didn't understand them, but he welcomed the dreams as rare gifts. They relieved the unending darkness of his entombment. They almost gave him hope . . . almost.

But the fabric of this dream was different. At first that didn't surprise or alarm him. He'd been there generations and had only infrequently been allowed the wisp of a thought . . . the enticing

72

aroma of the living world . . . any living world. Each time it had been a little different. Over the years he'd strained to hear the sound of a voice, the touch of a soft hand, the scent of roses and spice. Sometimes he'd be rewarded; most of the time he had not.

Until recently. The dreams had come to him. That was when she had entered his prison and he had begun to live again.

He had reveled in the dreams, inhaled her until he felt drunk on her essence. Dreams . . . who better than he knew what magic they held?

Perhaps he would dream of touching her skin again. Perhaps . . .

Then her blood had spattered against the cold stone that entombed him, and the pain that jolted him shattered the past two centuries like ice cast against marble.

He hadn't believed he had been freed. He'd thought it was just a cruel delusion. It might have taken a decade for him to attempt even a small movement of one of his massive muscles if her scent hadn't begun to wane.

She was leaving him. Escaping from him.

No! Not again!

Embracing the pain, he flexed his great muscles and broke the barrier of shrouding darkness.

He scented the air. Yes, there, layered within night smells of roses and blood, was the anointing oil. He commanded his stiff body to move, and he followed the fragrance he knew too well through the dark, unfamiliar garden. With an enormous effort of will, he did not crash through the few rosebushes that separated them and seize her. He forced himself to wait until he was able to more carefully control the beast within him. The creature had been penned too long . . . his needs were too raw . . . too brutal. It would not do to rend her flesh with his claws. That

73

would solve nothing. He must capture her gently, as he would a delicate bird, and then return her to the destiny she had thought to escape.

Controlling the ferocity within him, he stalked her. He could not see her well, but he did not need to. The anointing oil drew him; she drew him. And she was aware of him. He could feel her panic. But there was something else – something unfamiliar that radiated from her. He frowned. Something was wrong. He picked up his pace as she left the rose gardens and burst into a small pool of light. He stopped abruptly.

This was not the priestess he sought. Disappointed and confused, he stood frozen, watching as she struggled with the opening of the leather satchel she carried, clearly looking for something. A weapon? Her eyes frantically searched the dense shadows behind her – the shadows in which he stood.

'Come on! Where is that damn cell phone?'

He heard her unfamiliar voice and saw that she was trembling as she searched through the satchel – trembling so badly that the slick leather of the bag slipped out of her hands and fell to the stone path with a sickening crunch.

'Shit! Shit! Shit!' the stranger said.

She dropped to her knees and slid her hand into the purse, and he heard her breath rush from her lips, as if in response to a sudden sharp pain. She jerked her hand back. He could see that her fingers were sticky with blood.

The scent hit him hard in his gut – blood mixed with the anointing oil of a High Priestess. She was not the betrayer, but she had clearly been marked by the goddess. And he must obey the goddess's will. He began moving toward her again, this time using his newly freed powers to call the darkness to thicken about him so his body would remain cloaked with night. Still, her head jerked up and she stared wide-eyed in his direction.

'Do not fear,' he murmured, attempting to gentle his powerful voice.

She gasped. 'Who are you? What do you want?'

He could feel her terror, and for a moment he regretted what he must do. But only for a moment. He knew his duty. This time he would fulfill it. Before she could dart away from him, he used his inhuman speed to reach her where she still crouched on the leafy ground. She stared up at him, unable to see through his mantle of darkness.

She was so small . . . so very human . . .

With a gruff command, he ordered the darkness to cover both of them, and for a single breath he wrapped his great arms around her, engulfing her in a tide of vertigo. The cool breeze that earlier had been friendly and inviting suddenly beat against them in a frenzy of scent and sound. They were caught in a vortex of confusion. The ground seemed to open to swallow them. It trembled . . . shifted . . . rocked. The world around them faded and then disappeared altogether, and the shimmering air was rent by a tremendous roar.

Like a snake slithering into its hole, darkness and the beast retreated, carrying Mikado Empousai with it.

Part Two

Chapter Eight

Softness . . . she was surrounded by softness. Curled on her side, her face rested against a pillow. Mikki rubbed her cheek against its sleek surface. Silk. It had to be silk. She snuggled more deeply into the thick comforter, breathing in the rich scent of expensive, down-filled bedding.

While she lay there, someone combed through her hair with a wide, soft-bristled brush. Mikki sighed happily and rolled over on her stomach so the someone could have better access to more of her hair. Dreaming . . . she had to be dreaming.

And, she told her sleeping self, her dreams had certainly been wonderful lately. She should just relax and enjoy.

The person hummed a wordless tune while she brushed Mikki's hair. Her voice was a gentle waterfall of notes that blended with the soft strokes of the brush lulling Mikki into an almost hypnotically relaxed state.

Mikki sighed with perfect contentedness.

Somewhere in the lullaby-like humming, the whispered words *Welcome, Priestess* echoed in her sleep-heavy mind.

Mikki breathed another dreamy sigh; she was definitely going to have to do more sleeping.

Another pair of hands touched her. These new hands focused on rubbing her feet. With the confidence of a master masseuse, the hands drew firm, soothing circles across her insteps.

Mikki felt like she was liquefying. Well, she certainly deserved an excellent dream, especially after the night she'd had. Her mind traveled languidly back. The crappy blind date . . . humiliating herself by screwing up the lines of that play . . . then being stalked by some terrible imaginary beast through the rose gardens . . . cutting her fingers on the broken perfume bottle . . . the deafening roar and the horrible sense of suffocation . . .

Memory tried to break through the dam of contentment her dream had built. She had to be dreaming, but how had she gotten home? Just what exactly happened before the weird dizzy spell that had overwhelmed her in Woodward Park? A silver of unease skittered spiderlike through her body. She needed to wake up.

Mikki opened her eyes.

A flutter of activity sounded behind her. Mikki spun around. Two women stood next to her bed.

No – it wasn't *her* bed.

Mikki snapped her eyes shut.

No. No. No. This wasn't right. It was the bed from her dreams. The *huge* canopy bed in the *enormous* bedroom, to be precise. Mikki pressed the palms of her hands against her closed eyes. Then she rubbed her face vigorously. She could feel her body, too damn well. The feeling was distinct, not like the sweet, erotic fog that filled her dreams. With her eyes still closed, she slapped her own cheek. Hard.

'Ow, shit.' Mikki flinched. It definitely hurt. She was certain she was awake now.

She opened her eyes.

Sticky tendrils of fear laced their way through her stomach. Nothing had changed. The bed was still there, as was the bedroom and the two women. They were wearing long shimmering robes that wrapped toga-like around their bodies and brushed the lushly carpeted floor. They were young and beautiful, especially silhouetted against the wall of mullioned windows behind them.

'Shit on a shingle!' Mikki automatically used her favorite curse as her breath left her body and her heart slammed against her chest. 'Who the hell are you?' she squeaked. Fear clenched her. Had she been attacked in the park and killed? 'Am I dead? Are you ghosts?' she blurted.

The women's eyes widened, and the brunette held out a delicate hand in a gesture that was probably meant to have been reassuring, but the fact that she was there at all, and that she could respond to Mikki's question, was definitely not comforting. Mikki immediately shot backward, crablike, over the bed until she was pressed firmly against the headboard.

'My Lady! We are of the living. You have nothing to fear.' Her voice was soft and melodic, and Mikki recognized it instantly as the one that had recently been humming the lullaby to her. 'We are here to welcome and to serve you, Priestess.'

The other woman, the one with the lion's mane of wheat-colored hair, nodded in agreement. 'Yes, Priestess. We are all very much alive.'

Clutching the comforter to her chest, Mikki tried to control the shaking in her voice. 'Wh- where am I?'

'You are home, Priestess!' The brunette smiled magnanimously.

'And just exactly where is "home"?' Mikki asked, feeling numb around her mouth, like she'd eaten a Popsicle too fast and was having a hard time making her lips work.

'You are in the Realm of the Rose,' the blonde assured her.

'I have finally done it,' Mikki moaned. 'I have finally gone stark raving, totally fucking crazy.' She buried her face in her hands.

Instantly, the two women rushed to her, patting her shoulders and stroking her hair. Mikki jerked back from them.

'Don't touch me!' she yelled. 'You're only making it worse. I can damn sure feel you when you touch me, even though I should be sleeping and this should all be a dream, and . . .' She broke off her babble. Breathing hard, she just shook her head at the women. 'No. Stay back. You're just giving me more proof of how kooky I am!'

The women took nervous little half-steps away from her.

Obviously the leader, the brunette spoke quickly. 'Let me assure you, Priestess, you are of your right mind. We are not imaginings, nor are we deranged fantasies.' Her smile was hesitant but sweet. 'I know this must seem very odd to you' – she glanced at her partner, who mirrored her smile – 'but you truly are in the Realm of the Rose, and we are your handmaidens.'

The blonde nodded her head, the waves of her hair bouncing in perky agreement.

Mikki felt her right eye begin to twitch.

'Maybe I'm drunk,' she muttered, trying to remember how much she'd had to drink before she'd dumped her date. Three, or had it been four glasses of that fabulous chianti? Oh, Lord . . .

'We would be happy to bring you wine, Priestess,' the blonde chirped.

'Oh, be quiet and let me think,' Mikki snapped. 'And stop calling me priestess. It's not my name, nor is it my job title.' Then she rolled her eyes at herself. What a totally moronic thing to say. Not her job title? Being a kook was bad enough. Being a stupid kook would be completely humiliating.

But the handmaidens seemed oblivious to her idiocy. They were busy exchanging startled glances.

'But,' the brunette began hesitantly, 'you must be our priestess. You awoke the Guardian.'

Mikki made an exasperated sound in her throat. 'The only thing I *must be* right now is crazy.'

The women went on talking to each other as if she had not spoken.

'She is beautiful,' the blonde said. Studying her carefully, she sniffed in Mikki's direction. 'And she has been properly anointed.'

The brunette squinted at Mikki. 'But she is not as young as the other priestesses who were Chosen.'

Her partner nodded silently, her brow wrinkling in concern. 'Perhaps that is for the best.' Her voice dropped to a whisper, and Mikki had to strain to catch her words. 'You know how badly the last one turned out.'

'Silence!' the brunette snapped.

The blonde paled and clamped her lips together.

'You are a maiden, are you not?' the brunette asked Mikki matter-of-factly.

'That's it!' Mikki swung her legs over the side of the bed and stood up so abruptly that the two women each took a startled step back. 'It's bad enough that I'm having some kind of psychotic break with reality, but I really have to draw the line when my delusions begin talking about my age and questioning my sexual history.' Mikki made little shooing motions at them. 'Go on. I prefer to sink into psychosis by myself.'

'We did not mean to offend, Priestess,' the brunette said, instantly contrite.

The blonde nodded again – vigorously.

'You didn't offend me. My mind, or more accurately, my lack of it, offended me.' The women blinked at her like Kewpie dolls. 'Oh, just leave me alone for a while. I have a lot of thinking to do.'

'You have only to call for us if there is anything you desire,' said the brunette. 'Of course, Priestess, we will return when the sun has set to prepare you for the goddess's evening ritual. We all hope that once again—'

Mikki's raised hand cut off her gushing words. 'No! Nothing else right now. To quote an idiot accountant I once had the misfortune to date, "My bucket is too damn full right now to deal with anything else." Just leave.' At their hurt looks she added, 'Please.' They were fabrications of her mind, but (as she was sure her mother would have reminded her) there was really no reason to hurt their feelings and be impolite. They couldn't help her kookiness.

Reluctantly, they walked gracefully across the room. Mikki expected them to pass through the wall like proper figments of imaginations, but the blonde opened the large, ornately carved door, which clicked closed softly behind them. Even her hallucinations didn't behave properly.

'Insane,' Mikki said firmly. 'You are completely insane.'

Her legs felt weak, and abruptly Mikki sat back down on the bed. The thick down comforters billowed around her like clouds of hand-spun gold. Unable to help herself, she ran her hand over the rich, silk surface of the duvet.

'Unbelievable,' she muttered. The bedding was sumptuous and incredibly beautiful, richer than even the linens from The Blue Dolphin, the expensive boutique she liked to browse through at Utica Square. And *browse* was the key word – she could never have afforded to buy her bedding there. Now she was surrounded by material that made The Blue Dolphin look like K-Mart.

At least she was having an expensive delusion.

Actually, *expensive* didn't begin to describe the room. It was more like obscenely *RICH*. Definitely spelled with capital letters.

The stuff of fairy tales, her mind prodded.

Mikki ignored her mind, which had already proven totally untrustworthy, and looked around. She knew the room. Her fantastic dreams always began in this very room, but the images her sleeping mind had retained had been fleeting. Typically, when Mikki awoke she could only remember that she had been in 'the room' again and that the room had given her a sense of comfort, setting a pleasurable stage for the rest of her dream experiences.

What was it the brunette had said? *You are home, Priestess!*

Impossible. Home was a nice little apartment in a great location, not a room fit for a princess. Mikki's admiring gaze took in her surroundings. Princess, hell, the room had been made for a goddess. The light from the wall of windows was dim, but three huge crystal chandeliers hung suspended from the ceiling on golden chains. Their many candles mixed with the freestanding candelabrum that perfectly accented the corners of the room, as well as the enormous fireplace in which a fire crackled and popped cheerily – the entire effect was to cast the chamber in the warm glow of living flame. The gold and scarlet color scheme of the bed linens was reflected in the rest of the room. The carpet was plush, incredibly soft, and the color of untouched snow. The marbled walls were the color of clouds streaked through with delicate veins of gold and hung with ornate tapestries. Their intricate designs were all – Mikki grinned in pleased surprise – roses! Each tapestry was a woven marvel. Not able to stop herself, Mikki drifted over to the closest of the works of art and sucked in a sudden breath.

The tapestry rose was the Mikado.

Her eyes went from wall to wall. Each hanging was filled with artistic renditions of roses so real Mikki almost expected to be able to smell their delicate bouquet. And each and every one of them was of the Mikado Rose.

'Consistency should count for something, even if it's delusional,' she said firmly.

Intrigued by what her mind was concocting, Mikki explored the room. Beautifully carved wardrobes rested elegantly between wall hangings, and a huge mirrored vanity was placed not far from the canopied bed. It seemed to be waiting for a fairy princess or goddess to sit before it and primp. The tinkling light of the closest chandelier caught Mikki's eye, and she looked up. The walls stretched to an incredible height. Mikki had to tilt her head back to see the domed ceiling far above, which was painted with delicate frescos of blood-and-gold – colored Mikado Roses.

Incredulous, Mikki muttered, 'Where the hell am I?' How could her mind have fabricated such an amazing 'reality'? *Maybe I didn't fabricate this . . . maybe this is real and my old, boring, uneventful life was the dream.* The thought, more elusive than smoke, drifted through her bedazzled mind.

Trying not to feel like an interloper, she stood, wiggling her bare toes into the lush carpet.

Bare toes?

She looked down at herself. She was wearing a long, white robe that V-ed deeply to expose a generous amount of cleavage. The sleeves were trimmed in lace that circled her wrists. The entire garment was embroidered with tiny scarlet roses. Mikki rubbed a finger against the material; she had never felt anything like it. It wasn't exactly silk, but it was too soft and slick to be cotton. Expensive linen? Whatever it was, it was certainly flattering. It flowed in a diaphanous wave down her body, showing just enough flesh to be seductive without being sluttish. Mikki swung one long leg out in front of her, loving the richness of the fabric against her naked skin.

'Naked?' She froze. Then, holding the top of the dress away from her chest, she peered down at her body. 'Very naked,' she whispered, feeling her cheeks warm.

How had she gotten that way? Or more to the point, *who* had gotten her that way? Probably the little handmaidens, she told herself (*please, oh please*, her mind shying away from the memory of the beast that had so doggedly pursued her). Even though they were strangers, they were definitely female. Having talked herself into feeling relieved, she let one hand absently caress her sleeve. The tangible touch of the fabric soothed her frayed nerves. She lifted her hand to look more closely at the filigreed lace, and she noticed the pad of her hand was scabbed over but still sore when she pressed on it.

She clearly remembered cutting them when the perfume bottle had broken last night. Mikki pressed the healing scabs again and winced. The cuts were real. She breathed deeply and, sure enough, the scent of the exotic perfume she'd dabbed on her pulse points, as well as smeared all over her hand, wafted distinctly to her nose. Surely a hallucination couldn't include so many of her senses. Could it?

Mikki sighed and walked to the wall of windows. As she got closer to them, she realized that the middle panes had marble handles and opened outward to an enormous balcony. She pressed her face close to the glass, trying to see through the fading light. All she could make out was the distant outline of the balustraded balcony. Beyond that, she could only see vague, dark shapes. And then the glass fogged over with her breath.

'Don't be such a sissy,' she told her reflection. Ignoring the fluttering of her heart, she turned the handle and stepped out into the cool evening.

The balcony seemed to stretch on forever. It was a smooth

pane of pearl-colored marble that curved gracefully in an elliptical shape. On either side of her it wrapped out of sight around that section of the . . .

. . . Castle!

Mikki gulped and turned to face the imposing structure behind her.

'Ohmydearlord!' Stunned, she stared wide-eyed. The building was made of the same opaque marble as the balcony, and, on closer inspection, looked more like a huge palace than a traditional castle. It rose above her like a man-made mountain and stretched to either side of her as far as she could see. It appeared to be elevated, as if it had been built on a cliff. Mikki gawked, totally amazed. From where she stood, she could tell that there were several rounded wings that climbed above what appeared to be the basic palace structure. Through huge picture windows she glimpsed flickers of light. She gazed at the palace and a key turned within her.

'I couldn't have made this up,' she said, letting the sound of her own voice reinforce her words. 'If I was going to dream up a palace or a castle or whatever, I would have made up something like Cinderella's fairy-tale castle, and I mean straight out of Disney.' She shook her head. 'Not this – I could not have fabricated this.' Her hands lifted and then fell helplessly. 'I don't know where I am, or what has happened, but this can't be taking place only in my mind.'

Behind her a sputtering, popping noise drew her attention, and she turned. Past the edge of the balcony, lights flickered. Swallowing hard, she started forward. It took her more than thirty steps to reach the carved balustrades that supported the balcony's edge. The flat marble top reached just above the level of her waist, and with a catch in her breath, she leaned against it as she gazed down upon the grounds.

'Roses!' Mikki cried in delight. The palace was surrounded by an enormous circle of mazelike rose beds intermingled with ornate trees, hedges, fountains and statuary. In the heart of the gardens she thought she saw the dark outline of another structure, but fading day had not left enough light for her to distinguish anything clearly, even though sprinkled throughout the grounds were winking sconces of open flame that were either suspended from branches of trees or held by thick torches that sprang from the ground. The muffled sputtering noise sounded again, and Mikki watched as the wispy outline of a silk-draped girl lit one of the torches. Soon, Mikki noticed many such girls moving soundlessly along the garden paths and, cometlike, leaving flickering tails of flame in their wake. Staring out at the unbelievable sight, she felt a rush of nausea.

'See!' Mikki waved her hand in a frustrated gesture, fighting back the dizzying sickness. 'There's another thing I don't think I could have made up – little nymphlike servants lighting tiki torches.'

'You are not fabricating what you are seeing, nor are you going mad, Mikado Empousai.'

Mikki sucked in a breath and jumped as a woman's strong, throaty voice surprised her. Shock chased away the weird vertigo feeling that had gripped her. She turned quickly to a woman who had suddenly materialized and who no doubt reigned supreme over them all. Overwhelmed, Mikki couldn't find her voice. She could only stare at the woman like an awestruck child.

She was tall and wide shouldered with a statuesque, appealing body and a strong, intelligent face. Her lips were full and crimson, and her wide, watchful eyes were a startling, piercing gray. She wore a gown that was layer upon layer of shining black silk, draped to flowing perfection around her body; the curve of

89

her waist was girdled with a chain of silver roses linked together by stems of rubies. Through a slit in the shimmery gown Mikki could see part of her long, slender leg – so perfect it appeared to be carved from living marble. Her feet were covered with golden sandals, and beside them reclined two of the most enormous dogs Mikki had ever seen. The black creatures unblinkingly met her gaze with eyes that glowed an unearthly red, and Mikki hastily looked away, her startled gaze skipping from the flaming torch the woman held in one hand, to the gleaming headdress that was wrapped around her head. Nestling in her dark, intricately braided hair was a waterfall of shining pinpoints of light. They twinkled like miniature stars in the night of her hair.

Then the woman spoke again, and the power that filled her voice sent a thrill of fear through Mikki.

'I am the Goddess Hecate, and I welcome you to the Realm of the Rose.'

Chapter Nine

'Hecate?' Mikki's mouth felt numb again. There was something unnamable about the woman that caused her knees to go to liquid as she automatically moved back until she was pressed against the marble railing 'Medea's Hecate?' she rasped, her voice barely above a whisper.

'Indeed, I am Medea's goddess.' Hecate spoke in hard, sharp words. 'If you faint like a typically weak woman, I will be very displeased, Mikado.'

'I've never fainted before.' Mikki blurted the first thing that came to her amazed mind.

'Do not start now,' the goddess said.

Mikki could only nod with a jerky motion of her head.

Hecate studied Mikki silently. Her strong face was inscrutable, and Mikki had a childish, nerve-filled desire to wring her hands and fidget, but she forced her arms to her side and stood still, even though the goddess's gaze was so sharp she imagined she could feel its touch.

'I am not simply Medea's goddess.' Hecate broke the silence suddenly. 'I am Goddess of Beasts, Magick and the Ebony Moon. I have dominion over the dark of night, dreams and the crossroads between the known and unknown.' The goddess's words rang with authority, and Mikki felt the power of them slide over her skin like hungry, searching snakes. Then Hecate's voice lowered dangerously, and Mikki had to work hard not to cringe away from her in fear. 'I knew your mother, Mikado, and her mother before her, and hers before that . . . for generations I have watched the women of your family. I continued to watch and stay faithful to them, even after the women all but forgot me.'

Complete surprise had Mikki crying, 'My mother! My grandmother! How? I don't understand any of this.'

Almost imperceptibly, the goddess's expression softened. 'Have you never wondered at the origin of the gifts you've been given, Mikado?'

'Gifts?'

'Yes! Think!' the goddess snapped. The dogs at her feet growled restlessly. 'Do not stand there stupidly as if you are a man and can think with naught but the flesh that hangs between your legs! Acknowledge your gifts, Empousa!'

Mikki responded automatically to the goddess's command with a voice that shook only a little. 'My blood makes roses grow. I mix my blood with water and during the new moon . . .' She paused, eyes widening as she realized what the title, Goddess of the Ebony Moon, implied. 'During the new moon I feed my roses with my blood.'

'And your roses always grow,' the goddess finished for her.

'Always,' Mikki whispered.

'That is one gift. The other is also something the women in your family have carried with them from generation to generation,' Hecate said.

Thinking, Mikki frowned. Then her face cleared. 'My last name! All the women in my family always keep their last name, Empousai. We never change it – no matter what. It's tradition, an unwritten rule that we've followed for generation after generation. Even when it was unheard of for a woman to insist that she keep her own name and not automatically take her husband's, the Empousai women stuck to their tradition. Trust funds have been set up and whole wills have been written under the strict provision that the Empousai women always retain their name. My mother told me stories about Empousai brides who broke off engagements when men refused to follow the tradition.' Mikki clamped her mouth shut suddenly, certain that she was babbling like a hysterical fool.

Hecate dipped her head in brief acknowledgment. 'That is because within the veins of the women of your family runs the rich blood of the Empousa – my most cherished priestesses. It has been a long wait, but it gladdens my heart that finally you have rekindled the goddess flame within you, anointed yourself, mixed blood and water, and called upon my name.' For an instant the goddess's formidable face almost looked kind. 'You can see that I rewarded your faith. You awakened my Guardian, and you have returned to the Realm of the Rose.'

'But it was an accident! I didn't do any of it on purpose.' Mikki felt like sobbing.

'Explain yourself. How could you possibly have anointed yourself and invoked me *accidentally?*' The goddess spat the word like it had a foul taste.

The marble of the balcony railing felt like cold iron as it pressed through the back of Mikki's sheer nightdress. The huge dogs at the goddess's feet pricked their ears at her, as if they, too, were curious about her answer. Mikki wondered semi-hysterically if Hecate would command them to eat her when she found out that this whole thing had been nothing but an insane mix-up.

Mikki drew a deep breath and met the goddess's icy gray eyes. 'You say I anointed myself – by that I assume you mean the perfume I'm wearing.'

Hecate raised both brows. 'Perfume? Indeed. And how did you manage to acquire a perfume that is the exact fragrance of my High Priestess's ceremonial oil?'

'It was given to me by an old woman I met earlier today . . .' She paused. Had it been earlier today, or had several days, or for that matter years, gone by? She couldn't think about that now; it really didn't matter. The only thing that mattered was that Hecate understand that she didn't belong here. Or none of this mattered at all because she was wrong about this place being her new reality, and she had really gone stark raving mad and was curled up in a fetal position in the middle of the Tulsa Rose Gardens drooling on herself.

'I told you before that you are not suffering from hallucinations or delusions, Mikado. Nor are you mad,' Hecate said firmly.

'Can you read my mind?'

'I always know the deepest fears and the most passionate desires of my Empousa. Now, Priestess, continue to explain this *accident* to your goddess.'

Your goddess . . . an unimaginable thrill shocked through Mikki's body when Hecate spoke those two simple words. It was as if a memory, long forgotten, had begun to stir, restless with the possibility of new life.

Your heart remembers, Empousa, as does your blood. The goddess did not speak, but the echo of Hecate's voice whispered through Mikki's mind.

A voice in her mind? Mikki shook her head, suddenly afraid again. She spoke quickly, hoping the sound of her voice recounting events she knew had happened in 'the real world' would anchor her shifting sense of reality.

'An old woman gave me the perfume. She and I hit it off because she had been named after a rose, too.'

'And what was this crone's name?'

'Sevillana Kalyca,' Mikki said, noting how Hecate's eyes immediately narrowed. But the goddess didn't interrupt her again, and Mikki continued. 'I had a date that night, so I thought I'd wear the perfume.' She grimaced, remembering the arrogant Professor Asher. 'But the guy turned out to be awful. I left and walked home.'

Hecate nodded thoughtfully. 'Few men are worthy of an Empousa.'

Mikki looked into the goddess's eyes and was surprised to see understanding there. She smiled tentatively at Hecate. 'I've definitely not been lucky in love.'

Hecate snorted. 'Men are inconsequential.'

Mikki felt some of the tension in her shoulders relax. They had certainly been inconsequential in her life. 'Well, I decided not to go straight home, so I cut through the park because I wanted to walk in the rose gardens.'

'You live near rose gardens?' the goddess asked.

Mikki nodded. 'Right across the street from the city's rose gardens. I volunteer there year round.'

Hecate looked pleased. 'It is proper. As Empousa, your most important duty, after honoring me, is to care for your roses.'

'I have always cared for roses. So did my mother and my grandmother—'

Hecate's impatient gesture cut off her words. 'The women of your family are tied by blood to the roses. I know that. What I do not know is how you invoked my name.'

'It really was an honest mistake. I was walking through the park to get to the rose gardens, and they were rehearsing the play *Medea*. They needed someone to step in for the actress who was supposed to play Medea at the same time I happened by. The

95

director asked if I would read a few lines, and I did . . .' Mikki's words trailed off as she remembered how the lines on the script had blurred, glowed and then seemed to be spoken of their own accord. 'It was like once I said the goddess's name, everything changed.'

She hadn't realized she'd spoken the thought aloud until Hecate's stern voice answered her.

'Your soul and the very blood that pounds through your heart know my name, and they called for their goddess, even though your mind has forgotten me.'

'It seems so impossible . . .' Mikki shook her head and wiped a shaky hand over her face.

'But there was no blood sacrifice made. The wind would have stirred at your words, the earth would have trembled, and the waters wept as flame blazed, but you could not have awakened the Guardian and been carried to my realm without the letting of your blood.'

'I fed the roses,' Mikki said faintly, remembering the cacophony of sound that had swelled around her as she had read the goddess invocation. Wind . . . earth . . . water . . . fire . . . had they really all responded to her? The thought thrilled and overwhelmed her. Then the goddess's impatient frown brought her quickly back on track. 'Some workers in the gardens had trampled the roses. It was the night of the new moon, and I'd already fed my roses – the ones on my balcony at home. It was a simple thing for me to reopen the cut in my hand and help them, too. I guess I went a little overboard, because I was sprinkling water everywhere. I even got some on the Guardian statue—' Mikki sucked air and stared at Hecate. 'The statue. That creature. It . . . It . . .'

'*He*,' Hecate corrected her. 'The Guardian is male. And, yes, your call to me – coupled with the sacrifice of your blood

– awakened him. He brought you here. It was his duty to return my priestess to her proper place.'

Mikki's eyes darted from the goddess to the shadows that were lengthening with the thickening of night.

'He is not near. He has been absent from his charge for too long. There is much that he must correct; many things are amiss to which he must attend. You are not to concern yourself with him. And you have nothing to fear from him. The Guardian's only purpose is to protect the Realm of the Rose, to make sure the threads of reality are woven into dreams and magick.'

Mikki shook her head. 'Threads of reality? How does he—'

The goddess cut her off. 'It is not important that you understand his purpose. Just know that he is not a danger to you. He guards all who reside within my realm.'

'If he's your Guardian, then what was he doing being a statue in the Tulsa Rose Gardens?' *And*, Mikki's mind shrieked, *what was he doing seducing me in my dreams?*

Hecate's gaze shifted from Mikki, and the dark goddess stared out over the flame-lit gardens that stretched in a seemingly limitless expanse of beauty before them. When she spoke, it was more to the shadows than to the woman who stood beside her.

'I am a goddess, but I am also fallible. It was through an error of my own judgment that my Guardian was banished. It is my desire to correct that error.'

Mikki didn't know what to say. If she had thought about the ancient gods and goddesses before today, her basic assumption would have been that they were powerful, omnipotent beings who were immune to simple mistakes in judgment. And now she was standing before a being who proclaimed herself Hecate, who radiated power and authority, and this same goddess was

97

admitting to having made a mistake? It made no sense. But then, none of what was happening to her made any sense.

Again Hecate spoke without looking at Mikki. 'Yes, a goddess can err. I have a heart and a soul. I have passions and dreams. I love and I hate. How can I be a wise goddess, worthy of worship, if I do not intimately understand the mistakes of humanity? To understand those mistakes, I must experience some of them,' she concluded in a somber voice.

'I'm sorry,' Mikki said softly.

Hecate's gray eyes returned to rest on her. 'I have missed the presence of my Empousa in the Realm of the Rose. Even though your return appears *accidental*,' this time she added a touch of humor to her voice when she said the word, 'I am pleased you are here. I have grown weary of waiting.'

'But I still don't know why I am here.' Could she really be priestess to this amazing goddess?

'You are here for the roses!' Hecate spread her arms in a magnanimous gesture to include all the gardens before them. 'You will reinstate my rituals and bring health and life renewed to my realm.'

'Hecate, I don't know how,' Mikki said.

'Of course you do!' she said fiercely. 'The knowledge has been written in your blood. All you need do is turn your eye inward and learn to read what my hand printed there generations past.'

The patter of slippered feet running on marble interrupted Mikki's reply. She and the goddess peered down on the gardens as four women hurried up the nearest path to the staircase that led to Mikki's balcony.

'Your handmaidens approach.' Hecate glanced at the darkening sky. 'I see that at least they haven't forgotten the proper order of things, though the Realm of the Rose has suffered with the absence of its Guardian and my Empousa.'

Like a wave lapping eagerly on a thirsty beach, the four women rushed as one onto the balcony and instantly fell into deep, graceful curtseys, heads bowed, with their long, unbound hair falling forward to shade their bright faces. The handmaiden who wore buttercup yellow silks, a perfect complement to her golden hair, spoke first. She lifted her face to the goddess and cried in a voice filled with gladness, 'Hail Hecate! Great Goddess of the Ebony Moon!'

Next spoke the girl dressed in brilliant red whose fall of glossy scarlet hair blazed like fire. 'Hail Hecate! Wise Goddess of Beasts!'

Mikki realized that she recognized the two remaining girls when the handmaiden dressed in sapphire blue with the waves of sea foam-colored hair lifted her head.

'Hail Hecate! Beautiful Goddess of Magick!'

Before the sound of her sweet voice had faded the brunette, who was tonight dressed in moss green silks the color of her large, dark-lashed eyes, lifted her head, face glowing with obvious joy.

'Hail Hecate! Goddess of the Crossroads between reality and dreams and mighty protectress of the Realm of the Rose.'

'Rise, daughters. Come! Kiss my hand. I have missed you.'

The handmaidens rushed to Hecate. Mikki realized that they were much younger than she had at first thought – really, they looked little older than teenagers, especially as each of them pressed her lips to the goddess's hand, giggling and cooing like happy children. Hecate touched their heads and greeted them, clearly pleased to see the youths. The enormous dogs at her feet wriggled, totally (and shockingly) puppylike, sniffing enthusiastically at the girls, accepting kisses and caresses from each as was their due. Then Hecate raised her torch high, and the handmaidens fell instantly silent.

'Handmaidens of Hecate, I bid you welcome the return of my Empousa!' At her proclamation, the torch blazed, sending a cascade of sparks falling in a whirlwind around the goddess.

The handmaidens gasped, whispering excitedly to one another as they curtseyed to Mikki. She was sure she heard the brunette hiss a clear 'I told you she had returned!' to the others.

Hecate raised her hand for silence.

'Go within. There you will prepare the Empousa for the self-initiation ritual, which will be performed in the heart of my realm.'

Once again Hecate lifted her torch, only this time she faced outward, looking over the vast gardens.

'Let the Temple of Hecate be lit once more!'

At the goddess's command, lights suddenly blazed from deep in the gardens. The handmaidens reacted with exclamations of excitement and joy. Wide-eyed, Mikki watched the silhouette of a columned temple suddenly illuminate.

'Go now,' Hecate told the handmaidens gently. 'The priestess will join you shortly.'

The girls curtseyed deeply to the goddess and then scampered across the wide balcony and into the bedroom in which Mikki had awakened.

'You must do two things tonight, Mikado,' Hecate told her sternly. 'First, cast a sacred circle. The handmaidens will aid you in this until you learn to listen to the knowledge that sleeps within your blood. Second, you will perform a self-initiation ritual. In that ritual, you will dedicate yourself to a new life as my Empousa, a Priestess of the Blood of Hecate.'

'But I don't know how to perform an initiation ritual! I don't know how to perform any ritual,' Mikki said, exasperated at how inept she felt.

'Mikado!' Hecate's gray eyes pierced her. 'You invoked my presence. You awakened my Guardian. There lives within your blood the knowledge of generations of my priestesses. If you do not have the courage to partake of that knowledge, cast the sacred circle and then choose to step from within it. I give you my oath that the moment you leave the circle, you will return to the life you left in that mundane world at the far side of my crossroads.' The goddess's lip curled in disgust, and the flesh on Mikki's arms prickled in response as Hecate's divine anger sizzled around her. 'Perhaps you shall marry . . . perhaps you shall not. Doubtless, you will produce a daughter, another Empousai, as you have come to call yourselves. You will live and die an ordinary life. And I will look to other generations for the return of my priestess. But if you do not break the sacred circle and instead choose to complete the ritual, know that as surely as your heart beats and your lifeblood flows you will forever after be my High Priestess, Empousa in the Realm of the Rose.' Hecate lifted her blazing torch once again. 'Decide tonight, Mikado Empousai, and know you will never receive another chance at changing your destiny!' Sparks showered from the torch, and with a great roar of wind, Hecate disappeared.

Chapter Ten

Thoroughly confused, Mikki stood alone, blinking away the bright spots of the goddess's light from her eyes. She was supposed to cast a circle? Wasn't that witch stuff? And if she managed to bumble her way through that, without being struck by lightning or swallowed up by Satan or who/whatever, she was supposed to listen to her blood to know how to perform a self-initiation ritual because she was an Empousa, a Priestess of Hecate. How?! What the heck was she going to do?

Girlish laughter drifted from the open doors of her room. Mikki sighed. She was also supposed to be getting dressed. And deciding on her destiny.

'Damn, my head hurts.' She rubbed at her throbbing forehead. The newly illuminated temple tugged at her gaze, and she found herself staring across the dimly lit gardens at the domed building. A little rush of excitement fluttered through her stomach. If this was real . . . if all this was actually happening, then she was being offered the opportunity to be High Priestess of a powerful goddess – a goddess who had watched over the women in her family for generations. Mikki couldn't deny that the possibility fascinated her.

And if none of this was real? If she had fabricated all this and the world and the goddess were nothing more than figments of her delusion?

If that were true, then it didn't matter whether she chose to stay or return. Either way she was screwed – figuratively speaking.

So why not ride it out? Why not choose to become High Priestess of Hecate over being a psych patient?

She thought about the goddess. Hecate was powerful and intimidating. What would it be like to be her priestess? The thought was like a bright flame, and it drew her with its exotic warmth. Hecate had said that her first duty as Empousa would be to care for her roses. Mikki stared out across the dark expanse of gardens. The soft night breeze swirled around her, carrying with it the compelling and familiar scent of roses. She closed her eyes and drew a deep breath.

It smelled like home.

The thought startled her. Could it be possible that she belonged here? Was she brave enough to consider believing this was her reality ... her future ... her destiny? She was many things – stubborn, opinionated, too cynical but she was not a coward. Resolutely, she crossed the wide balcony and entered the beautiful, rose-themed room.

Like a small school of exotic, silk-finned fish, the young women turned to her and bobbed down and up in quick curtseys.

'Empousa! Your ceremonial dress awaits,' said the brunette. She gestured to a fabulous length of glittering purple silk that cascaded over the edge of Mikki's bed.

'Thank you,' Mikki said automatically and then her mind caught up with her words. 'But before we go on, I think introductions need to be made. My name is' – she paused for only an instant – 'Mikado. As you probably already know, I've been brought here by rather unusual circumstances, and all of this is new and more than a little overwhelming to me.'

The brunette frowned. 'Are you not Empousa in your own land?'

'No,' Mikki said.

The four young faces registered mirrored expressions of shock.

'If you were not Empousa, then what did you do?' the brunette asked.

'I was . . .' Mikki hesitated, carefully choosing her words. 'I was an assistant to a very important woman. She made sure sick people were cared for.'

The brunette's frown deepened. 'This woman could not have been as important as Hecate.'

'No!' chorused the others.

They had her there. 'Maybe working for a less important, uh, goddess' – Mikki's lips twitched at what her boss would think of being called a goddess – 'was preparing me for this job.'

'Job?' the flame-haired girl tittered. 'Empousa is not a job; it is a destiny.'

'A divine privilege!' added the handmaiden dressed in buttercup silk.

'Yes, I'm beginning to understand that.' Mikki felt like she was futilely trying to hold the reins on a runaway horse. 'But where I'm from, things are a lot different. It's going to take some time for me to get used to my destiny.'

The brunette suddenly gasped, green eyes bright with understanding. 'You are from the mundane world!'

'Yes, yes I am,' Mikki said.

Clearly horrified, the handmaidens stared silently at her. The golden blonde pressed her hand against her mouth as if to hold back a sob.

'It's really not that bad there,' Mikki said, feeling the need to stand up for, at the very least, Tulsa. 'It's filled with interesting

104

people and things. Like the Internet and' – she grasped at straws – 'and some really excellent restaurants. Especially around Utica Square.' Far from convinced, they continued to stare at her. 'So,' she said, purposefully changing the subject, 'how about you tell me your names and then I'll get dressed and you can give me some pointers about how to handle the rest of the night.'

'How incredibly rude of us, Empousa!' the brunette said quickly giving the other three girls a hard look. 'I am Gii.'

'I am known as Floga,' said the striking redhead.

'You may call me Nera,' said the blonde who had been there to welcome her with Gii.

'And I am Aeras,' said the final girl.

'It's nice to meet the four of you,' Mikki said, smiling warmly at them and mentally crossing her fingers that they would become her allies as she took in the unusual names.

'Shall we dress you, Empousa?' Gii asked.

Mikki wanted to say 'Thank you very much but *no*.' Then she looked at the long length of silk and realized she had not one clue about how to put it on. Did it wrap like a toga? What held it together? (And where were her panties?)

'Fine. Let's get me dressed.'

'I cannot go out in public in this. Really. There has to be another piece to it.' Mikki stared at herself in the full-length mirror. The royal purple silk was caught in a braided silver tie over her right shoulder. From there it swept down her torso in a graceful drape, leaving her left boob and her right leg, from waist to ankle, completely, utterly, totally bare.

Gii's frown was back. 'But Mikado, this is the traditional dress for the Empousa's ebony moon ritual.'

'Why would you want to add anything to it? You look quite lovely,' Nera said, confusion wrinkling her smooth brow.

Mikki pointed at the reflection of her bare breast. 'I'm half naked!'

Like those little bobbing-headed figures that sat on the dashboard of tacky cars, the four handmaidens nodded at her.

Mikki sighed and tried again. 'How can I walk around with one of my breasts exposed?' Not to mention her entire right leg and part of her pantiless butt. 'It just can't be right.'

'Of course it is right,' the redheaded Floga said, clearly disconcerted by Mikki's negative reaction. 'It is how Hecate's Empousa has always dressed for this ritual.'

With a sudden flash of understanding Gii said, 'Is it not normal in the mundane world for a priestess to perform rituals with her breast bared?'

'Actually, in the mundane world it's very abnormal to be seen in public with a bare breast – at least in my part of the world.'

Gii shook her head sadly. 'Women must be horribly restricted in your old world.'

Mikki opened her mouth to set Gii straight – to tell her that women in modern, albeit mundane, America had equal rights with men and . . . But the image of the last rape victim she'd read about in the *Tulsa World* surfaced in her memory. The girl had been young, only twenty-one or twenty-two, and she had been attacked while she had been clubbing downtown. The newspaper report had made several slanted references to the seductive way she had been dressed, vaguely implying that she had caused her own rape. Hot on that memory came the voice of the newscaster she'd listened to as she'd dressed for work that morning. Seems a serial molester had attacked yet another Tulsa woman. As in the other instances, he'd come in through the woman's open bedroom window. Police and the media advised the public – the female public – to be more careful about locking their doors and windows. Mikki felt the stir of anger low in her gut. Women had been lectured, judged, and warned. Neither of the men had been condemned as the animals they clearly were. She met Gii's gaze.

'I think you might be right, even though on the surface it doesn't appear that way.'

'Like hidden thoughts, it is the world beneath the easily seen one that most often controls us,' Gii said.

Mikki nodded slowly. Then she turned back to her reflection in the mirror, straightened her shoulders and lifted her chin. The woman who stared back at her looked exotic and incredibly feminine draped in liquid purple with her hair hanging free around her shoulders and her bare skin flushed a delicate blushing peach in the flickering candlelight. On an impulse, she swung out her bare leg, pointing her naked toes. The soft material of the ceremonial dress fluttered attractively in response. Sexy . . . she was definitely sexy – and that ten pounds or so she always seemed to battle with only added to her sensuous look. She was curvy and full-bodied and more beautiful than she had ever thought possible.

'I'm ready,' she said firmly, more to herself than the four women who were watching her so intently.

Gii's smile was instantaneous. She grabbed Mikki's hand and tugged gently toward the open doors to the balcony. 'Come! Hecate's Temple glows with light once more. Let us hurry and fill it with life, too!'

On a tide of silk and laughter, Mikki let herself be led across the balcony and down the pearl-colored stairs that emptied into the gardens. Another odd wave of dizzy sickness engulfed her as she followed the handmaidens. She gritted her teeth and did her best to ignore it, thinking that it was logical that changing worlds would be hard on one's system. Wide-eyed, she tried to take in everything as the girls hurried her along one of many curving marble paths that wound between row after row of roses. She could make out bubbling water features and benches, but everything was gently cloaked in night and shadow and the warm light of the fragrant oil lanterns that hung from the limbs of ornamental trees.

Then everthing left her mind as the temple rose like a dream before them and Mikki stumbled to a halt. Torches blazed inside and out, illuminating tall, slim columns supporting the dome of a raised, open-air temple. In front of the temple sat a huge, multi-basin-shaped fountain. Crystal water cascaded from it, spilling all around its edges and into four marble troughs that appeared to carry the musical water out into the gardens.

The temple itself was elegant in its minimalist design. There was nothing inside the building except a single flame that burned brightly from the center of a broad, circular expanse of slick marble floor.

'Hecate's torch has been lit,' Floga said in a voice choked with emotion. The beautiful scarlet-clad handmaiden was the first to ascend the stairs and enter the temple. 'I felt it in my soul, but to see it once again makes my heart leap with gladness!' And then to Mikki's astonishment, Floga walked straight to the fire and caressed the flame as if it was a beloved child. Instead of burning her, the fire appeared to rejuvenate her. Her hands glowed where it touched her, and her red hair crackled around her as if it was alive.

'She's touching the fire!' Mikki gasped. 'But it doesn't burn her.'

'Of course it doesn't burn her,' Gii said. 'She is Flame.'

With an effort, Mikki pulled her gaze from the scarlet hand-maiden, turning her attention fully to Gii. 'What do you mean "she is Flame"?'

Gii studied her carefully. 'Empousa, do you not recognize your own handmaidens? I know you did not act as if you understood who we were when Nera and I welcomed you, but surely you know who we are now that you have seen the four of us together.'

'Gii, I've never had handmaidens before. How could I recognize you?'

'You truly don't know us?' Nera said sadly.

Mikki had the sudden urge to shout that she didn't even know herself anymore – how the hell could she know four women who were total strangers! But the hurt in their eyes made her check her words.

'In my old world I didn't worship any goddess.' Mikki carefully met each young woman's eyes. In the silence that followed her words, she heard Floga approach. Without speaking, the handmaiden rejoined her friends. Mikki continued, slowly and distinctly. 'I have never cast a circle. I have never performed any ritual. I had no idea I was a Priestess of Hecate until the goddess told me so herself. So it's not just that I don't recognize the four of you, it's that I don't recognize anything in this world.'

The women stared at her, wide-eyed and shocked.

'There are no goddesses in the mundane world?' Gii finally said in a hushed voice.

Mikki considered her words carefully before answering. She remembered that Hecate had told her she had been watching over the women of her family for generations. And there was no doubt that the Empousai women had a magical something in their blood. *Goddess touched* . . . the thought flitted through her mind. The women in her family were goddess touched, which means that, acknowledged or not, goddesses must exist, even in Tulsa, Oklahoma.

'I think goddesses exist in my old world,' Mikki said, thinking of the women in her family and letting instinct guide her words. 'But most people – most women – have learned to live without them.'

'How terrible,' Aeras whispered.

'So if you don't want to call me Empousa, I won't blame you,' Mikki said. 'I don't really deserve the title.'

'Hecate named you her Empousa. It is the goddess's right to do so, and only she can remove the title,' Gii said. 'If the goddess acknowledges you as such, then so shall we.'

The other three women nodded, but Mikki thought they did so less than enthusiastically.

'And do not forget,' Gii added, looking sternly at the other handmaidens, 'Mikado awakened the Guardian. That is something only Hecate's Empousa has the power in her blood to do.'

At the mention of the Guardian, Mikki felt a chill move across her skin. She'd almost forgotten about it – *him* – she corrected herself. The statue. Only he wasn't a statue anymore. He was out there somewhere, alive again because her blood had touched him. What part did he play in all of this? Why had he visited her dreams? And suddenly she was truly sick of unanswered questions.

'Gii, you said Floga didn't get burned by the fire because she is Flame. Please tell me what you meant by that.'

But Floga didn't give Gii a chance to answer her. Instead the fire-haired handmaiden stepped forward so she stood beside Mikki. She raised her hand, palm up, and then, smiling, Floga blew a small breath, much like she was blowing a kiss, onto the palm of her hand. Mikki felt the unusual heat of her breath even before the rust-colored flame spouted from her palm.

'Gii meant what she said literally, Empousa. Your personal handmaidens are carefully chosen by Hecate from all other women in the Realm of the Rose. Each of us was selected because we carry within us a special affinity for one of the four elements. My element is Flame. I can conjure it; it will never burn me; when the thread of my life has been followed to its end, I will return to it.'

'Unbelievable . . .' Mikki breathed. Hesitantly, she reached a finger to the fire that burned steadily in Floga's hand. It was like touching the flame of a candle. She could bear it for an instant, but she knew it would burn her if her finger stayed too close for too long. Then Mikki's gaze slid to the other three women.

'I am—' Gii began but Mikki shook her head sharply, interrupting her. 'No, don't tell me. If I am really Hecate's priestess, I should be able to figure out some things for myself.' She squinted her eyes, thinking . . . *The four elements . . . Floga already said she is Flame. So what's left?*

As she considered, her eyes remained on Gii, at first unconsciously, and then more purposefully. She took in her moss-colored robes that matched the rich green of her eyes, accenting the thick length of her mahogany hair. And she knew.

'Earth!' Mikki said. 'You have to be Earth.'

Gii's smile was a brilliant reward. 'Yes, Empousa. Floga is Fire. I am Earth . . .' She paused and nodded encouragement.

Mikki turned her attention to the two remaining handmaidens, Nera and Aeras. Nera was wearing blue and had hair so light it could be reminiscent of clouds, but Wind just didn't seem to fit her. Nera was too voluptuous. Her body was lush; the blue silk lapped around her like translucent waves. Petite Aeras wore butter-yellow robes that seemed to move gracefully around her in time to a secret breeze of their own. Her long, straight hair was the golden color of summer sunlight.

'Nera is Water, and Aeras is Wind.'

The handmaidens clapped their hands happily, making Mikki feel inordinately proud of herself.

'You see, Empousa,' Gii said. 'You did recognize your handmaidens.'

'With your help I did. Now with your help maybe I can figure out how to cast a circle, too.'

'You have everything here you need to cast the sacred circle, Empousa,' Gii said. 'You have the spirits of the four elements, and you have your own affinity.'

'My own affinity? But there are only four elements. What could I represent?'

'You represent the heart of the circle – its spirit,' Gii said. 'That is why you wear sacred purple. It is the color of Spirit. And that is why your position will be in the center of the circle.'

'We will show you, Empousa,' Aeras said, skipping up the stairs into the temple. 'We each have our positions.'

Mikki squared her shoulders and moved with the handmaidens into the temple. Aeras walked purposefully to a place a few feet away from the ever-burning flame which was in the center of the temple. She turned to face Mikki. 'Wind is always positioned in the east.'

Floga moved around an invisible circle to Aeras's left. 'Flame is allied with the south.'

'Water prefers the west,' Nera said, taking the position directly across from Aeras.

'Earth's place is always in the north,' Gii said, completing the circle. 'And your place – Spirit's position – is in the center of the circle near the heart of the goddess's flame.'

Not giving herself time to hesitate, Mikki moved into the center of the circle made by the elements personified and stood beside Hecate's flame. Then, feeling a little lost and a lot foolish, she moved her shoulders restlessly. 'I don't know what to do next.' She whispered the words, but her voice carried eerily in the stillness of the temple.

'It is a simple thing, really,' Gii said gently.

'A natural thing,' Nera added.

'A wondrous thing,' Floga said, with barely suppressed excitement.

'You always begin with me,' Aeras said, smiling brightly. 'Greet me and call Wind to you, welcoming my element. Then move deosil around the circle and call the other elements to you.'

'Deosil?'

'This way,' Floga said, moving her hand in a clockwise motion. Mikki nodded. 'Okay, I've got that.'

'As you call each element, think of the energy you beckon forth to protect and support you, Empousa,' Gii said.

'Will a circle really appear?' Mikki asked tentatively.

'That depends on you, Empousa,' Gii said.

Mikki's stomach fluttered with nervousness. *Just do it!* she told herself. Mikado Empousai lifted her chin and approached Aeras.

Chapter Eleven

'Hello, Aeras.'

'Empousa.'

The handmaiden sank to the marble floor in a graceful curtsey, and Mikki's mind frantically searched for something, anything, to say. She was supposed to focus on the elemental power as she called it. She drew another breath to calm herself. She drew a breath . . . air . . . which was really wind . . .

'I call to the circle the element Wind,' she said, mentally crossing her fingers that she wasn't totally messing up. 'It is what we breathe in when we are born. Without it we would all die.' As Mikki had begun speaking, Aeras had risen from her deep curtsey. The handmaiden lifted her slender arms, closed her eyes, and tilted her head back. Mikki swallowed around the nervous dryness in her throat and continued. 'When I think of Wind I think of movement and invisible power. It is a contradiction – a paradox. It cannot be contained, but it can be harnessed. It can gently fill a newborn's lungs, and it can destroy cities.' Suddenly, the ethereal yellow silk that clothed Aeras began to lift and stir, and then, in a rush of white sound, wind whipped around the handmaiden like she stood in the vortex of a magick tornado. Wind moved against Mikki's skin, too, but not as violently. It felt caressing, causing her bare nipple to harden in response. Surprisingly, Mikki didn't feel embarrassed or exposed. Instead, the nakedness of her body seemed natural, and the fact that the element had come at her call and touched her body so lovingly, bolstered her confidence. She smiled and met Aeras's shining eyes. 'Welcome, Wind!'

Then she turned to the right. Her steps were much surer as she approached the scarlet-clad handmaiden.

'Hello, Floga.'

'Empousa,' she said. And she, too, sank to the floor in a respectful curtsey.

'I call to the circle the element Flame.' As Aeras had, Floga stood, lifting her arms and closing her eyes. Mikki thought the handmaiden's face look rapturously expectant, as if she was prepared to greet a lover. Inspired by the element's personification, Mikki continued, 'Fire is passion and heat. It consumes, but it also feeds and warms. Without fire our nights would be dark and cold.' Floga's glossy scarlet hair began to lift, and in a whirl of heat the girl's body became outlined by a luminous glow. Mikki could feel the heat radiate from Floga. It licked against her skin, too, causing a fine sheen of dewy sweat to glisten over her body. 'Welcome, Flame!'

When she turned to her right again she thought she caught a glimpse of a delicate silver thread of light stretching between Aeras and Floga.

'Hello, Nera.'

'Empousa.' Nera dropped to the floor. Her thick, blond-white hair covered her face like a wave.

'I call the element of Water to the circle. It surrounds us before we are born, and it nourishes us during our life. It cleans and purifies, feeds and soothes.' Nera stood slowly, and Mikki watched as the voluptuous outline of her body appeared to liquefy. And then her hair really was sea foam and waves, and the blue of her silk robes rippled like the changing tide. Mikki was engulfed in a misty coolness that smelled of spring rains and warm, tropical beaches. 'Welcome, Water!'

Mikki's feet felt incredibly light as she hurried to where Gii waited. And this time she clearly saw the sparkling silver ribbon that connected Aeras to Floga and now also Nera.

'Hello, Gii.'

'Empousa.' She curtseyed as had the other handmaidens.

'I call to the circle the element Earth.' Mikki smiled fondly at Gii as the handmaiden stood, lifting her arms and awaiting the approach of the spirit of her element. 'Earth is really our mother. It's as fertile and nurturing as farmland, as moist as soil and as dry as sand. It's home for all the other elements.' Gii's mossy robes shifted and changed until they were more ivy than silk. Her dark hair seemed to lengthen, blanketing her shoulders and falling down her back with the richness of a newly ploughed field. Mikki's senses were filled with images of Earth. She smelled the sweetness of cut hay. She tasted ripe fruit and berries. She felt cradled in warmth and security, as if her mother's arms were once again around her. With a catch in her voice, Mikki said, 'Welcome, Earth!'

'And now, Empousa, you must greet your own element,' Gii said, pointing to the place at the center of the circle beside the sacred flame.

Mikki moved to the center of the circle. She closed her eyes and raised her arms, mimicking the other women.

'I call to the circle the element Spirit.'

Then the handmaidens' voices flooded her thoughts and senses until Mikki couldn't tell if they were actually speaking or if they were only voices within her soul.

'Spirit is present everywhere,' Aeras said in her sweet, clear voice.

'It is the great alchemist.' Floga's voice was filled with passion.

'Spirit is the element that unites all others.' Nera spoke with the sound of a cascading stream.

'It has the power to shape the very nature of all things,' said Gii, in a loving mother's voice.

'Welcome, Spirit!' Mikki cried. There was a crackling snap, and the air within the temple sizzled with energy. Mikki opened her eyes to see that she stood in the middle of a circle ringed by four women who were bound together by dazzling gossamer threads of silver woven to create a boundary that pulsed with light and power. The flame burning beside her had taken on a lovely violet tint.

'Wow! It worked!'

The handmaidens laughed, filling the temple with sounds of feminine happiness. Their laughter was like music, and Mikki wanted to twirl and dance.

Dance, Empousa . . .

The silent words settled into Mikki's mind like a remembered dream. She didn't stop to question her next impulse or hesitate until she could second guess herself. Mikki danced. Within the circle she twirled and swayed. The handmaidens took up the tempo of her movements and began humming a seductive melody. She felt beautiful and powerful and utterly joyous. And she knew what her decision for the rest of her life would be. She would choose this world – this magickal life – and not because she was afraid of snapping out of it and finding out she was crazy. She chose this life because it had awakened a joy deep within her that she had never before experienced. Reality be damned! This was real enough for her.

Speak the words that will bind you to me, Empousa, commanded the voice within her head.

Automatically, Mikki answered the goddess. As she spoke, her own voice grew stronger and more confident.

'Hecate, Goddess of Crossroads, Beasts, and the Ebony Moon, I have cast your sacred circle and been given a chance at a new life – a new destiny. I stand on the threshold between my old life and my new . . .' Mikki hesitated, but only long enough for her to turn to face the violet-tinged flame. 'My decision is that I am willing to become your Empousa.'

'What two perfect words do you offer your goddess to bind you to me?' Hecate's somber voice hung heavy in the midst of the sacred circle.

Mikki stared into the spirit flame. She had no idea what words to speak. What could bind her to Hecate? What did her instincts tell her? She wasn't sure, but she knew what her heart was telling her. There were only two words that should ever bind one person to another . . .

'Love and trust,' Mikki said.

'Then it shall be, Empousa. You are bound to me through blood and by love and trust!'

The violet flame leaped, shooting almost to the ceiling of the temple's dome.

'Blessed be your feet that have brought you on this path,' Aeras said. The Wind spirit held her hands out to her Empousa. Mikki grasped them, feeling a surge of energy swirl into her.

'Blessed be your sex, source of love and power,' Floga cried.

Mikki retraced her path inside the circle to the spirit of Flame. When she took Floga's hands, power filled her with a rush of heat.

Nera's voice called her farther around the circle. 'Blessed be your breasts, and the heart that beats within.' The Water spirit's hands were a wash of cool energy that reminded Mikki of a deep, clear well.

Gii's blessing had her moving to the head of the circle. 'Blessed be your lips that will speak the rituals of the goddess.' Mikki clasped hands with the Earth spirit and felt the strength of ancient trees and ripe meadows enter her body.

Then, without needing to be prompted by anything except an innate feeling of rightness, Mikki returned to her place beside the spirit flame and whispered, 'Blessed be my eyes that will see clearly the new path before me.'

'The Empousa is mine, and I am hers – body, mind and spirit.' Hecate's powerful voice filled the temple. 'The ritual is complete; so mote it be!'

Suddenly Mikki was aware of a multitude of voices cheering in celebration. She looked beyond the circle to see what must be hundreds of women, young and old. They crowded the gardens around the temple and were all clapping and waving her way.

The watching crowd began to hum a wordless melody, and soon the seductive beat of drums joined the voices. Then the gathering of women danced, barefoot and exuberant, in the torch-lit garden of the goddess.

Intrigued, Mikki watched them frolic. In the shadowy gardens, they looked like beautiful night flowers waving in the breeze. Briefly, she wondered at why there were no men present, but the thought was fleeting and Gii's voice chased it completely from her mind.

'Close the sacred circle, Empousa, and we will join the people's celebration!' Gii said.

Before she had to ask, Aeras's soft voice lifted above the noise of the crowd like a warm summer breeze. 'Walk in reverse order around the circle. Touch each of us in turn, and visualize the web of light fading away.'

Smiling her appreciation, Mikki retraced her steps, lightly brushing her hand over each woman's head as she sank into a curtsey at the approach of the Empousa. She watched the woven thread of light unravel, and eventually, as she returned to her place in the center of the circle, it disappeared completely, leaving only the goddess's flame to burn a bright, but ordinary yellow.

Then Gii took one of her hands and Aeras another, and flanked by Earth and Wind, the newly christened Empousa was led to her people and the celebration that awaited its priestess.

THE Guardian watched from beneath an ancient oak. The lighting of Hecate's temple had drawn him. When it blazed again in the heart of the realm, he had been pulled to it unerringly, even though his body was wracked with the pain of newly awakened muscle and sinew. He had wanted to kneel beside the flame – to again beg the goddess's forgiveness and to ask that he be allowed to resume all the duties that had been his before he had broken faith with Hecate. But before he could move, the night breeze shifted and brought her scent to him. His nostrils had flared and his bronze skin quivered.

The priestess approached.

He knew it was she by her scent – spices and roses distilled by the heat of her soft skin. He recognized it because he drank the fragrance of her in his dreams, and, waking, he had touched that skin when he held her in his arms as the power of the goddess transported them to Hecate's realm. He closed his eyes and leaned against the tree. He had frightened her then, though he had not meant to. His awakening had been abrupt, and the beast within him that seemed at constant war with his humanity had been too strong, too eager to capture and possess. Remembering, his body shuddered and his heart ached.

He should go, retreat to his lair and prepare himself for tomorrow. He had long been absent from the Realm of the Rose, and he could already tell that all was not as it should be. He must be diligent – focused – he must resume guardianship of the realm as was his duty; and, if the goddess was merciful, he would also be allowed to use all his magickal gifts again.

But he stayed.

When his keen hearing detected the light tread of her feet, he spoke a command in a language long dead, and the lanterns that hung from the massive tree's limbs instantly extinguished, wrapping him in shadow. Under the thick ridge of his brow, his expressive eyes opened in time to see Floga rush into the temple. He paid little heed to the Fire spirit though, or to any of the other handmaidens. Like a bewitching Siren, *she* commanded his attention.

He watched her.

Her awkwardness was obvious to him, as he was certain it was to the handmaidens, too. They were accustomed to an Empousa who moved with practiced confidence, who knew each ritual of the goddess so well she could perform them as if it was as natural to her as breath and heartbeat.

This woman was different.

The handmaidens had to prompt her on how to cast the sacred circle. He saw her overcome her initial hesitation as she moved from element to element, calling Wind, Flame, Water, Earth, and Spirit alive again within the goddess's temple. Despite her inexperience, her power was evident in the tightly woven thread that bound the circle together.

She danced.

His breath went thick. A low growl rumbled almost inaudibly in his throat. Lust surged, hot and insistent through his body in time with the beat of his heart. His inhumanly keen eyesight became blessing and curse. Because of it he could see the sweat-slickened flush of her naked skin as she moved in a seductive dance around the circle. The nipple of her exposed breast was tightly puckered, elemental and alluring. He turned his massive head away from the tempting sight, pressing his forehead into the rough skin of the oak until the tips of his ebony horns rested against the tree. The betraying breeze flirted around him, once again bringing him the scent of her – woman and roses, oil and spice, now heightened by the heat and sweat of her. He snarled a curse, damning his preternatural senses.

Goddess help him, the longing was still there.

Why? He raised his hands. They became claws as razor-edged talons dug into the thick bark of the tree. Why hadn't his long imprisonment cured him of this terrible, futile desire?

He heard Hecate's voice commanding the new Empousa to bind herself to the goddess with ritualistic words.

'Love and trust . . .'

She spoke the words, and the night took them and carried them to him so he felt the power of her oath fold over his skin.

Why had she chosen those two words? For countless generations, Hecate's Empousa had always chosen words such as *knowledge* . . . *power* . . . *beauty* . . . *strength* . . . *success* . . . to bind herself to the goddess. Yet to complete the self-initiation ritual, this Empousa had chosen *love* and *trust*.

The Guardian bared his teeth. What did a priestess know of love and trust! What did any mortal woman know of such things!

He sensed the crowd approaching the temple and commanded more shadow and night to surround him. The women of the realm could not see him as they passed the great oak, but they sensed his presence and averted their eyes from the darkness that hid him, nervously making a wide path around the tree. When they shouted with joy at the completion of the ritual and began to welcome her with song and dance, the Guardian felt as if he had become a great island of misery amidst an ocean of rejoicing.

And still he could not stop himself from looking at her again. She was closing the circle. The changing light of the goddess's flame caressed her naked skin. Her body enticed him as she acknowledged each of the elements and bid them depart. Without conscious thought, his claws tightened on the tree, slashing deep grooves into the ancient bark.

In response to the flexing of his muscles, pain shot through his arms and chest. He welcomed it. The pain reminded him of his banishment and the reason for it. He had been bespelled for generations because of his weakness. What perfect irony. He was a beast. He had physical strength that no mortal man could match, yet weakness had caused him to betray his duty, and, ultimately, himself.

Not again. I will not allow it to happen again.

Then his mind cleared as a new thought formed. Perhaps all of this – the dreams of her, the awakening and now the return of the agony of his desire – perhaps it was all part of the goddess's test.

Yes . . . he straightened, sheathing the daggers that were his claws. It did make sense. Hecate was providing him the opportunity to regain her sacred trust. He was being tempted so he could prove to her that it would not happen again.

Never again would he betray his goddess and his realm.

He would perform his goddess-appointed duties as Guardian of the Realm of the Rose. And when it was time for Beltane's

Spring Ritual, he would complete his charge, sending this new Empousa to meet her destiny.

With a mighty effort of will, the Guardian repressed the longing within him. He would not give in to his weakness again. For countless generations he had protected Hecate's magickal realm. He had been ever vigilant. He had been tireless in his devotion. And he had been alone, even during the brief moments when he had imagined that his solitude might come to an end.

He remembered the pain of discovering just how wrong he had been and knew that the misery of that rejection had been greater than all the years of loneliness that had preceded it.

What the last Empousa had said had been true. He was a beast. A woman might become fond of him, might treat him with compassion, as she would a favorite cat or an especially loyal hound, but a woman could never truly love a beast. It mattered little that the goddess had gifted him with the heart and soul of a man. The heart and the soul were within the body of a beast. It was his destiny to be alone, and destiny could not be changed.

With one last look at the new Empousa, he turned away. Duty. That must be his life.

But part of my duty is to ensure the Empousa's safety . . . to make certain she is well cared for . . . The man within him whispered temptation. *Would any of the handmaidens remember that the Empousa must eat and drink after the ritual to ground herself? Of course not. And she . . .* He paused and glanced over the corded muscle of his shoulder at where laughing women surrounded her. *She was so inexperienced she had to be led in the casting of a circle. She would not know that she must ground herself and use food and drink to replenish her strength.* Again, he forced his gaze from the Empousa. Snarling a hasty command, he drew darkness closely about him and made his way unseen from the temple celebration. When he was clear of the crowd, he picked up his pace, clenching his teeth against the pain that radiated from leg muscles that had just the day before been dead stone. *It is only another part of my duty as Guardian to order her meal prepared and to be certain that she partake of it. Yes, only another part of my duty . . .*

His cloven hooves thudded against the soft ground with a shy, secretive voice that seemed to echo the word *liar . . . liar . . . liar . . .*

Chapter Twelve

It was only when she stopped dancing that Mikki felt the return of her sick dizziness. So many women . . . she put a hand to her sweaty forehead and brushed back a mass of tangled hair. And every one of them had a word of welcome for her, just as they each wanted to dance and twirl and laugh with her. She was breathing hard and her legs felt wobbly. She was definitely all danced out.

'Empousa?' Nera peered into her face. 'Are you well?'

'I'm just tired. It's been a long day.'

'Come with me.' Gii was suddenly beside her, tucking a steadying hand into her elbow. The handmaiden began to lead her in a weaving path between the revelers, heading back in the direction of the palace.

'Do you wish the other handmaidens to accompany you, Empousa?' Gii asked when Nera, Floga, and Aeras noticed they were leaving and paused in their celebration.

'No!' Mikki said hastily, gesturing at the young women to stay. The last thing she wanted right now was to be fussed over. Actually, solitude and something to drink sounded perfect. 'And you don't have to leave, either, Gii. I'm sure I can find my way back to my bedroom.'

'It is my honor to accompany you,' Gii said firmly. Then she smiled and spoke the Empousa's regrets to the women who would have drawn Mikki back into the celebration, smoothly extracting the High Priestess from the throng. Mikki sighed and resigned herself to Gii's mothering.

The well-lighted palace looked warm and inviting, and Mikki was incredibly glad to see it grow quickly closer. She wrapped her arms around herself. Now that she wasn't dancing, she was all too aware of the chill of the night air as well as her hunger. When was the last time she'd eaten a real meal? Had dinner at The Wild Fork only been last night? How did time work in this magickal realm? Little wonder she was starving and felt so sick and shaky inside . . .

Mikki stumbled up the marble stairs that led to her balcony. Gii halted suddenly, almost causing Mikki to trip and fall over her. The handmaiden was staring at a lovely little table someone had placed near the open doors leading to her room. It sat invitingly in a pool of light on the otherwise dark balcony. A thick blanket was draped over the back of the single wrought iron chair, and a pair of slippers was placed strategically in front of it. The table was, blessedly, laden with food.

'Oh, man! Whoever did this is my new hero.' Ignoring Gii's reticence, Mikki hurried across the dark balcony to slide her cold feet into the slippers. Then she groaned aloud with the pleasure of a woman who truly loves her food. There were several platters on the table, each filled with delicacies. Aromatic cheeses, olives, thin slices of meat, and a loaf of bread that was still warm from the oven. Before she fell into the food like a starving fool she remembered Gii, who was still standing near the entrance to the stairs. Oddly enough, it appeared that the handmaiden had forgotten her. Gii's attention was focused on the deepest of shadows that nested at the far side of the balcony. Mikki cleared her throat to get the girl's attention. The handmaiden jerked, as if Mikki had startled her and, though she was too far away for

Mikki to be sure, she thought Gii looked almost frightened when their eyes met. She smiled at the handmaiden, wondering what was bothering her. Had she committed some kind of cultural faux pas by rushing to the food without inviting Gii to join her? She certainly hadn't meant to be rude to the person who had shown her the most kindness in this world. So even though she preferred to be left alone to eat and relax, she gestured to the table.

'I know there's only one chair, but we can pull another out here from my room.' Her mouth already watering, Mikki looked back at the table. 'And there's plenty for two. Why don't you join me?'

Slanting one more nervous glance at the shadows, Gii returned her smile but shook her head. 'No, Empousa. You are weary. It is best that you are given the privacy to eat and then sleep.' The handmaiden started to depart. Then, changing her mind, she turned back and took a few hurried steps toward Mikki until her delicate face was more clearly visible. 'Mikado, please forgive my impertinence, but I cannot remain silent.'

'What is it, Gii?'

The young handmaiden closed the distance between them and knelt beside Mikki, taking her hands in her own. Though her voice was hardly louder than a whisper, she spoke with quiet intensity that demanded Mikki's attention. 'Your destiny and that of this realm are now woven unalterably together. The choices you make affect more than you know.'

Though she was feeling like a fish out of water, Mikki did recognize Gii's concern as real.

'I'll remember, Gii.' Not knowing what else to say she added, 'I'll be careful. Promise.'

Looking relieved, Gii nodded and squeezed her hands before letting them go. 'You did well tonight, Empousa. Welcome to your destiny.' She curtseyed deeply and then padded softly to the stairs and disappeared as swiftly and silently as if she really had been only a dream.

Finally, she was alone. What had that been all about? Too damn tired to give Gii's weird behavior and cryptic advice much thought, Mikki stretched and then rolled her shoulders. Her neck was killing her, and her body felt stiff and sore. What the heck was wrong with her? She should spend more time in the gym (who shouldn't?). But she didn't think she was in such bad shape that frolicking about for an hour or so should make her feel like an old woman, or like a young one who had just taken a beating.

Her hands shook as she forked cheese and meat onto her plate, but as soon as she'd swallowed a few bites of the delicious fare she began to feel more settled. Mikki shivered and pulled the blanket off the back of the chair and wrapped it around her shoulders. Warmer, she broke off a hunk of bread and sighed happily as she bit into the soft center. She imagined that it somehow fed her soul as well as her body. A beautiful candelabrum sat across from her place setting, like a silent dinner partner who came to the table just to illuminate. Its light danced off a crystal goblet filled with dark red wine. She lifted it, admiring the elaborate rose design etched into its surface and appreciating that someone had already filled her glass as well as left an entire pitcher of wine for her personal use. If any occasion called for wine drinking – lots of wine drinking – tonight was one. Mikki glanced around her, trying to see if there was any movement in the deepening shadows of the balcony. Everything was still; it seemed she really was completely alone.

Raising the goblet to her lips, she paused, brows drawn together in confusion. Floating in the middle of the tiny scarlet sea was a rose blossom, so deeply red that it appeared almost black.

What the heck was a flower doing in the middle of her glass of wine? Not sure of the correct protocol for extracting a rose blossom from wine, Mikki glanced from the table to the crystal goblet. Should she pull it out with her fingers? Or was she supposed to use a fork? Maybe a dessert spoon would be more appropriate?

'I can't even call for a new glass,' she muttered, thinking that finding a rosebud in her wine was a perfect punctuation mark to a truly bizarre day. 'What would I say? Hey, waiter, or in this case, handmaiden, there's a rose in my soup, uh, glass, uh, wine.' She shook her head and laughed aloud. 'Doesn't it just figure?'

'The Ancients believed that a glass of wine could not be fully enjoyed unless there was a rose blossom afloat within it.' The deep, powerful voice rumbled from the area of the balcony that was shrouded in the darkest shadows, washing around her and causing the hair on her body to prickle. 'It is a belief to which I adhere.'

Mikki jumped and fumbled with the glass, almost dropping it.

'Forgive me for startling you, Empousa.'

'I just wasn't expecting a . . .' Mikki faltered, trying to see through the shadows. She could discern only darkness within darkness, but she didn't need to see him. She knew to whom the voice must belong. Her stomach tightened. She took a deep breath and pulled the blanket more securely around her shoulders, suddenly very aware that she hadn't changed from the ceremonial dress that exposed far too much of her body. 'I thought I was alone,' she said, amazed that her voice sounded so normal.

'I did not mean to disturb you. I came only to see that you grounded yourself after the ritual.'

Mikki stared blankly in the direction of the faceless voice. Ignoring the rose blossom, she took a long drink of wine. *It was him – the statue – the beast from her dreams – the creature who had stalked her through the rose garden.* Unlike her voice, her hands could not hide their emotions so easily and she had to wrap both of them around the goblet so their shaking didn't clatter the crystal against her teeth.

When she didn't respond, he continued speaking in that preternaturally powerful voice that was at such odds with his civilized words.

'Again, Empousa, I ask that you excuse my lack of judgment. I thought only to see that all was acceptable to you so your grounding could be completed. I did not intend to disturb or to discomfort you.'

She stared into the dark space from which the voice originated. 'You did all this?'

'I directed the servants, yes. Empousa, you must always remember to eat and drink after you cast the sacred circle and perform any ritual. In that way you will once again be grounded to this world. If you do not, you will feel weak and sick at heart.'

Mikki had to swallow down a hysterical bubble of laughter. She was conversing about post-goddess ritual rules with the living statue of a beast who talked like a college professor in a voice that could have belonged to Godzilla.

It was totally fucking Loony Tunes.

Mikki took another long gulp of wine. This time the scent of the rosebud tickled her nose and she noticed the way its elusive sweetness heightened the richness of the wine. She put down the goblet and looked out across the table. Fine linens. Beautiful

131

porcelain china. A crystal goblet and pitcher etched with a rose design. Plates heaped with carefully chosen delicacies. A blanket and warm, comfortable slippers. He had ordered all of this for her?

Mikki glanced at the corner of the balcony and then hastily averted her eyes and poured herself some more wine. His silence was making her even more nervous than his inhumanly powerful voice. Had he left? Was he sneaking up on her? Stalking her?

The erotic chase scene from her last dream teased through her memory, causing her cheeks to flush and nervous words to rush too loudly from her lips.

'I didn't know about the grounding. And everything is delicious. I guess I owe you my thanks.' She wanted to bite her lip at her idiocy. She *guessed* she owed him her thanks?

'You owe me no thanks, Empousa. I am Guardian of this realm, and as such it is my duty to see to the welfare of those within the realm, which includes Hecate's High Priestess,' he said gruffly.

'Oh, well,' she mumbled, feeling awkward and not knowing what to say, but wanting to be polite. 'Still, I appreciate—'

'Do not!'

She felt the force of the command against her skin. It battered her and made the flush that had heated her cheeks drain white and cold. Hecate's assurance that the beast wouldn't harm her seemed only weak, faraway words. Mikki pressed her hands into the arms of the chair and bunched her legs under her, preparing to sprint for her room. Maybe he wouldn't come inside the palace. Or maybe she could call for help and . . .

'Forgive me. It seems I have again frightened you. That was not my intention. It is just that your appreciation is not appropriate.

What I did for you is out of duty. It is why Hecate called me into her service. Do you understand?'

He was clearly trying to modulate his voice to a softer, less-intimidating timbre. She recognized the attempt, even though he was being only partially successful. Instead of answering right away, Mikki took her death grip from the chair handle and, two-handed, lifted the wineglass to her lips. After she'd had another fortifying drink she stared into the darkness again. This was ridiculous and twice as scary because she was talking to a disembodied voice and letting her imagination fill in all the gory details of his appearance.

'I'm trying to understand, but it's not easy. Especially when I can't see who I'm talking to.'

There was a long pause. And then he stepped from the darkness. The crystal goblet slid from between her numb fingers and shattered against the marble floor. He made a movement like he was going to approach her, and with a rush of adrenaline, Mikki surged to her feet, knocking over her chair with jerky, panic-laced haste. Shards of broken crystal crunched under her feet.

Instantly, he halted. 'Have care where you step. The glass can cut through the soles of your slippers.' The words were meant to be gentle, but the voice that spoke them rumbled with an inhumanly thunderous warning.

Mikki couldn't breathe. She couldn't make her vocal cords work. She could only stare at the creature. Then he sighed, and it was in that lonely, wordless sound that she heard the echo of a familiar roar. That one small thing pushed through her panic, allowing her to draw a gasping breath.

'I did not come to you tonight to harm you. You have my oath that you are in no danger.'

Her lips felt cold and numb, but she forced herself to speak. 'You're the statue. The one from the rose gardens.'

He nodded his massive head. 'Yes, you have known me only as I was in your world, entombed in marble amidst the roses. Now that I have awakened, I have resumed my rightful position as Guardian of the Realm of the Rose.'

Mikki brushed a shaking hand across her forehead, trying to clear her mind.

The creature took a step closer to her, his hooves thudding inhumanly against the silent balcony.

'No!' she blurted, blood pounding in her ears. 'Stay away!'

As if to show that he meant no harm, he raised one huge hand toward her, palm up. Except for its size it appeared normal, but Mikki was sure she caught a flash of the candlelight glinting off something sharp and deadly. She stared at his hand without blinking.

He closed the hand and let it fall to his side, where it was enveloped in shadow. 'I was only concerned that you might faint.'

'I'm fine,' she said automatically, but she did pick her way carefully among the pieces of broken glass, righted her chair and sank into it before her legs gave way. 'I don't faint.' She forced herself to sound as normal as possible. He said he wouldn't hurt her. Hecate said he wouldn't hurt her. And, anyway, if he was going to attack her, it would do no damn good for her to hyperventilate and freak out. She clasped her hands together to stop them from shaking. 'Really, I'm fine,' she repeated, more for her own assurance than his.

'You should eat,' he said. 'It will strengthen you.'

She just stared at him. How the hell was she supposed to eat with him standing there?

She was surprised to easily recognize comprehension on a face that was so alien. And at the same time she recognized something else, something that clouded his powerful voice like fog. Sadness . . .

Did he really sound sad, or was she just imagining it?

'I should leave you to your meal. First allow me to . . .' He broke off and spoke a sharp, unintelligible command. He held out one large hand, and instantly a crystal goblet, identical to the one she had broken, appeared in midair. His hand closed around it.

A noise, somewhere between a sob and a scream, squeaked from Mikki's lips.

'Did you not desire another glass?' he asked.

Mikki could only nod. Her swarming thoughts semi-hysterically said that what she really wanted was a valium to go with the wine.

He was watching her closely, and she thought his expression might have softened, but his face was so fierce that it was hard to tell. 'May I bring this glass to you?'

She hesitated and then nodded again with a quick, slight movement.

Slowly, he stalked forward with an athletic grace that was as powerful as it was feral. His ebony hooves echoing against marble sounded unnaturally loud in the silence of the balcony. Mikki couldn't look away from him. As he moved closer to her, she couldn't help pushing herself against the back of her chair, where she sat rigid and unmoving. Her heart was pounding hot and loud in her ears, and for a moment, she thought she might make a liar out of herself and actually faint.

Would he catch her if she did? The thought of him touching her shivered through her body.

When he reached the broken glass he made a dismissive gesture with one hand and muttered a word under his breath.

The shards instantly obeyed him, blowing off the balcony in a tiny crystal tornado.

Then he stood beside the table. This close the light from the candelabrum flickered over him, illuminating the hard, inhumanly muscular lines of his body. He kept very still, allowing her time to study him and to become accustomed to his nearness.

The statue in the park had not been clothed, but the living Guardian was. He wore a black leather breastplate over a short tunic. The outfit reminded her of something Russell Crowe would have worn in *Gladiator*, except had the two stood side by side, the Guardian would have made the Aussie actor look like a boy in dress-up clothes.

The creature was huge. He had to stand almost seven feet tall. His hair was the unrelenting black of a new moon night. It fell thickly around his massive shoulders. Two dark horns protruded from his head. They curled forward and tapered to dangerous-looking points. His face . . . Mikki's breath caught in her throat. The face of the statue had been roughly hewn and indistinct, but the living Guardian was no unfinished rock; he was powerfully masculine, with a thick brow; high, distinct cheekbones and a square jaw. Taken by itself, his face reminded her of ancient images she'd seen stamped on foreign coins or carved into statues of warriors long dead, but mix his classic features with the horns and the sharp glint of a carnivore's teeth, and it was obvious that the man did not completely dominate the beast that lay so close to the surface.

His breastplate and tunic left quite a bit of his muscular body bare. The skin that covered his torso was dark and looked like living bronze in the candlelight. She let her eyes travel down his body. She knew what she would see, yet still she sucked in a shocked breath at the reality of it. His thick legs were covered in dark fur. Instead of feet, the flickering light glinted off cloven hooves.

He was the personification of animalistic power, and though he did not move to threaten her, the aura of feral viciousness that surrounded him was almost palpable. Mikki shivered and pulled the blanket more closely around her shoulders.

'The night is getting cold,' he said as softly as possible. 'I should have had them set your dinner within by the hearth.'

'I–I like it out here,' she stuttered.

'Do you? Or are you just being polite?'

'No, I often eat dinner on my balcony at home,' she said, feeling a tremor of homesickness. There wasn't a lot she'd miss about her old life, but her comfortable apartment and her view of Woodward Park was something that would always be a bittersweet memory.

'Then I am pleased that I chose to set your dinner on your new balcony, Empousa.'

Slowly he placed the goblet on the table and, with a gentlemanly gesture that was in direct contradiction to his bestial appearance, he poured her another glass of wine. Each of his movements was unhurried and carried with it a catlike grace.

Like a predator, she thought.

When he was finished pouring he took a step back from the table and nodded at the full glass.

'Drink. It will soothe you.'

Mikki did as she was told, barely tasting the excellent red. Her body felt detached and unreal, but the wine warmed her and helped anchor her senses. She drank deeply, for the moment not caring if it made her tipsy or muddled her thoughts.

Her thoughts, after all, were highly suspect. Perhaps they could use some muddling.

'I dreamed of you. Back there, in your old world . . . at your old home. I dreamed of you often.'

His words jolted through her, and she put down the goblet before it, too, broke. Mikki raised her eyes to his. They were almond shaped and as dark and bottomless as a quarry.

'I know,' she whispered. 'I dreamed of you, too.'

'It was a shock,' he said, pulling his gaze from hers to look out into the darkness. 'After all those countless years of nothingness . . .' He shook his head and his mane moved softly around his shoulders. 'It seemed impossible that I was aware again. At first I sensed you, but I could not see you. I only knew your presence.' His voice was deep with a low, hypnotic sound, but his face remained expressionless, as if part of him had become stone again. He did not meet her eyes. 'Then the dreams changed. They became more real. I could see you and feel you. Finally you called to me and I awakened completely. I knew you were Hecate's Empousa; only she could have awakened me. My mastery over magick returned to me, and so I brought you here.'

'I thought I was going crazy,' Mikki said, wishing he would look at her or give her some hint about what he was feeling. But he only stared, stone-faced, into the night.

'No, Empousa. You are not mad. You are fulfilling your destiny.'

Chapter Thirteen

'You know that's not really my name,' she blurted. Now why the hell had she said that?

He turned his head and finally looked at her again.

'Of course not. Empousa is a title of respect, not a name.'

'Well, it doesn't really seem like it's me yet,' she said. 'Like just about everything here it seems foreign . . . odd . . .' Mikki stifled a sigh, wondering how it could be that she was talking so easily with this man-creature.

'If not Empousa, then what shall I call you?' he asked.

'Mikki,' she said.

His thick brow furrowed, and for a moment she thought she caught the glint of humor in his dark eyes.

'Mikki? That is a name?'

'It's not my given name, but it's what everyone calls me.'

'What is your given name?'

'Mikado,' she said.

'Ah.' He nodded, and the candlelight glinted off a quick flash of too-sharp teeth as he smiled. 'The Mikado Rose. It is appropriate.'

Mikki took another drink of wine. With its spread of warmth through her body came a sudden, delicious sense of heady courage. She cleared her throat and spoke quickly before she changed her mind. 'What is your name?'

'I am Guardian of the Roses.'

Mikki frowned. 'But what do I call you?'

'I have always been called Guardian.'

'Guardian?' Mikki said doubtfully. 'That sounds like Empousa – a title, not a name.'

'It is what I am. Title or name, there is no difference for me.'

His face changed again, and this time Mikki was sure she saw sadness there before his expression settled into an unreadable mask. He was such a mass of contradictions. One second he was scaring the breath from her, and the next he was making her feel pity for him. Her head was a little woozy. She was definitely more relaxed – not exactly grounded, but relaxed enough to allow the next question to spill from her mouth.

'Am I making you up? Is this all happening just in my mind?'

'No. We are real, you and I. As is the Realm of the Rose and the goddess we both serve.'

'So I'm not asleep and dreaming this?'

'No, Mikado.' He enunciated her name carefully. 'Not this time.' His eyes caught hers, dark and expressive with the knowledge of what their dreams had become. 'You are very much awake, as am I. Finally.'

'Sometimes my dreams of you felt more real than the world around me.'

Slowly, not taking his eyes from hers, he moved closer to her and lifted his hand so his fingertips brushed lightly over her cheek. 'You broke the spell that entombed me. For that I will eternally owe you a debt of gratitude.'

The heat of his brief caress made her shiver, and he quickly dropped his hand and stepped back.

'But why me?' Her voice was rough, as equal parts of fear and fascination struggled within her. 'How could I have broken a spell I didn't know anything about?'

'You carry the blood of Hecate's priestess within you. None other could have broken the spell and awakened me.'

'I awakened you . . .' Mikki repeated. 'And I'm here because you needed a spell lifted from you.'

'No, Empousa,' the Guardian said firmly. His words were stone, and the power that he had been keeping in check roiled between them once more. 'You are not here for me. You are here for the roses.'

Inadvertently, she cringed away from the force of his voice, once again fearful of the monstrous creature who stood before her.

The Guardian sighed wearily. When he spoke, he had tamed his voice so it was no longer overpowering.

'I will leave you to finish your meal in peace. If you have need of anything, simply call and your handmaidens will attend you. I bid you good night.' He bowed neatly to her, turned and blended back into the shadows from which he had emerged.

When she was sure he was gone, she unclenched her hands and wiped them across her face.

Breathe. Be calm. Breathe. Be calm. She let the words sink from her mind into her body. Instead of reaching for the wineglass, she began to methodically eat meat and cheese. She needed to be able to think clearly. Food made her feel more normal, so she ate and let the simple act of refueling her body rejuvenate her mind. She didn't take another drink or think more about the impossible conversation she had just had until the edge of her hunger was gone and the woozy feeling in her head had cleared.

Mikki slowed her eating and sipped the wine. The food worked exactly as he had told her it would. She was full, and she felt normal again – if she could use the word *normal* to refer to anything she was experiencing in this fantasy world.

The creature . . . how could anything so terrible and powerful walk and speak like a man? As a statue she had always thought of him as more man than beast, but seeing him alive – hearing him speak – had made her understand all too well that he was not, *could not*, be only a man.

You are not here for me. You are here for the roses. The words seemed to echo on the empty balcony, accusing and mocking her. She remembered the sadness that had shadowed his face. Did beasts feel sadness? Would a beast think to have a sumptuous table set for a woman and then float a rosebud in her wine? Could a beast enter a woman's dreams and fantasies? And why would a beast touch her face with such gentleness?

He was not, *could not*, be only a beast, either.

Mikki tried to wrap her mind around the things he had said. He wasn't a dream. He wasn't a hallucination. He was all too real.

You are here for the roses. He had told her that, and so had Hecate. But what did it mean?

'Tomorrow,' she said aloud. 'Tomorrow I'll find out.'

She drank the last of the wine and then with a groan of protest at her stiff muscles, she dragged herself from the balcony and into her bedroom. While she had been busy circle casting and conversing with a living statue, someone had blown out the chandeliers and all but one candelabrum. The fire was banked, but the room was pleasantly warm after the coolness of the night. The thick bed linens were pulled back in preparation for her and a nightgown, a twin of the one she had been wearing earlier, lay across the foot of the bed.

Before she changed into it, Mikki nervously closed the doors to the balcony and drew the thick velvet drapes. Then she hastily peeled off her scanty ritual dress and gratefully slid on the soft nightgown. As she curled up in the middle of the opulent down comforters she thought about how much she'd like a warm soak in a bath. Man, her body was stiff. She sighed. She could tell she'd be sore as hell tomorrow. Her eyelids felt weighted. It was impossible to keep them open.

Her final thought before she slipped into sleep was to wonder if he would visit her dreams that night . . .

THE Guardian paced back and forth across his lair's sleeping chamber. He should be pleased. He should be celebrating his release. At last, after all those silent, frozen years, he lived and breathed again. And she was here. It mattered little that she was inexperienced or that she was from the mundane world where he had been entombed for so many centuries. She had Hecate's blessing. Mikado was the new Empousa. The Realm of the Rose would, once more, be set aright.

He remembered the fear in her eyes when he had stepped from the shadows, but he had watched as that fear had changed, as it had become tempered with fascination, even while his power had intimidated her. He knew what she was feeling. It was fascination for her that had awakened him. He had known it before, when she had invaded his mind as his consciousness had been trapped within the marble body. He had not wanted to admit it, not even silently to himself. But now that he'd seen her . . . talked with her . . . smelled her living fragrance and touched the warmth of her skin . . . he could not delude himself any longer. His desire for her was like air – it filled him, sustained him, and he only felt truly alive when he breathed her in.

'*Why?*'

He growled while he paced. A test. That was the only answer for it. Hecate had given him this burden to bear, and by all the immortal Titans he would bear it!

Spring came early to the Realm of the Rose. Surely then the goddess would relieve his agony. Then he could return to the loneliness that had been a comfortable enemy. Until that time he would keep busy with his duties, which, he admonished himself, did not include watching the Empousa eat. It had all been a lie his mutinous desire had rationalized into temporary truth. He hadn't needed to stay and watch, nor had he needed to speak with her. The ritual had made her hungry and thirsty. Her body would have shown her naturally what it needed to be grounded, and even the empty-headed Elementals would have eventually gotten around to explaining such a basic concept to the inexperienced priestess.

He must not delude himself. Staying away from her was the wisest choice. And that would be easy. He didn't need to see her to know when she was near; he knew her scent. His hands curled and he quelled the urge to smash them into the smooth walls of the cave. Her scent would warn him if she was near, as would the sun glinting off the rich copper of her hair. He had touched that hair in his dreams. He had run his hands along the length of her smooth skin, reveling in its softness. And she had touched him in return, stroking his body as if they were lovers. He had seen the memory of that touch reflected clearly in her eyes. He had longed to respond to it, just as he had longed to respond to her body as it had shuddered beneath him in the last dream.

'No!' he roared.

He could not allow it to happen again. He had one chance to right his past wrong. He must not love her. He could not. And this time he would not delude himself into believing that there was any chance she could love him in return, though in reality her feelings mattered little. She was Hecate's Empousa; therefore, she must die.

144

The Guardian sank down on the thick pallet of furs on which he slept and buried his face in his hands. He wanted to weep, but he felt empty of everything except pain and despair. There were no comforting tears within him.

'Are you sorry that I allowed her to awaken you?'

The Guardian's head snapped up and he beheld his goddess in her full regalia – headdress of stars, cloaked in the veil of night, with her torch blazing in one hand and the other resting on the head of one of her massive hounds. He fell to his knees before her, supplicating himself with his head bowed so low that his horns touched the ground at her feet.

'Great Goddess! I rejoice that I am in your presence once again.'

'Arise, Guardian,' Hecate said.

'I cannot, Goddess. Not until I beg you to forgive my crime.'

'You did not commit a crime. You simply succumbed to the humanity I placed within you. I was mistaken when I punished you so harshly for a weakness that I was ultimately responsible for gifting you.'

His shoulders shook with the effort it took for him to maintain control of his turbulent emotions. 'Then I beg that you forgive my weakness, Great Goddess.'

Hecate bent and touched his bowed head. 'I demonstrated that forgiveness when I allowed my new Empousa to awaken you. Now arise, Guardian.'

Slowly he stood. 'Thank you, Goddess. I will not disappoint you again.'

'I know that. We will not speak again of a past which is dead. You have finally returned to me. The realm has felt your absence keenly, as have I.'

'I am prepared to resume my full duties, Goddess, if you will grant it so.'

'I do.' Hecate scooped her hand through the air, gathering invisible power until her hand glowed. Then, with a quick throwing motion, she tossed the brilliant pile of light on him and said, 'I hereby return to you dominion over the threads of reality.'

The Guardian's head bowed again as the magickal power resettled into his body, filling him with its familiar warmth. When he was able, he met his goddess's gray eyes.

'Thank you, Hecate.'

'There is no need to thank me. I return to you what is yours. In all the time you were gone, the handmaids never got the knack of it, not even the Elementals were as adept at turning reality into the threads that bind the garment of mortal dreams as you.'

'I am eager to begin again, Goddess,' he said.

'I expect no less of you. But tonight I command that you rest. Tomorrow is soon enough to begin.'

'Yes, Great Goddess,' he said. He bowed his head again, expecting that she would disappear as she normally did in a shower of stars. When she didn't, he glanced up, curious as to her hesitation.

'Goddess?'

'As you know, my Empousa has returned.'

Silently, he nodded his head.

'She is . . .' Hecate paused, choosing her words carefully. 'She is not like the other Empousa. She is, of course, from the mundane world. This realm is strange and new to her.'

'And she is older than the other priestesses,' he said. Hecate's quick, knowing gaze made him silently curse himself for speaking at all.

'That is true. It is also true that she is inexperienced in the duties of my High Priestess. Keep a watchful eye on her, Guardian. She has much to learn and very little time in which to learn it. Beltane is not far away.'

He bowed his head. 'I will do your will, Goddess.'

When she glanced up at him, her gray eyes were piercing. 'This time I have taken steps to ensure that you will not be so easily tempted to err. With the return of your power over the threads of reality, I have given you a' – she paused and her lips tilted up in a humorless smile – 'let us call it a special thread of reality of your own. I know your body burned for my Empousa and that she used that desire against you as you sought the impossible. So you will never be tempted to betray yourself for lust again, know that I have made it impossible for you to consummate your desire for a woman unless that woman loves and accepts you for the beast you are, as well as the man who lurks within the creature's skin. Henceforth, you will be safe from your own impossible dreams. Do you understand, Guardian?'

Awash in shame, he bowed his head again. 'I do, Great Goddess.'

Her voice softened. 'I do not do this to be cruel. I do this as protection for you, as well as the realm. For what mortal woman could ever truly love a beast?'

Awaiting no response from him, Hecate raised her torch and disappeared in a whirlwind of light, leaving her Guardian as he was before, alone and filled with despair.

Chapter Fourteen

Unlike the first time, there was no confusion or lingering sense of displacement when she woke up. Mikki knew exactly where she was. She opened her eyes to the perky light of full morning shining in a golden wave through the wall of windows. Someone had drawn back the curtains, and she could see that the table she'd eaten dinner at the night before had been reset for breakfast.

Had *he* directed that breakfast be prepared for her? Was he out there again, watching? Mikki's stomach gave a sickening lurch as she wondered what it would be like to see him in the full light of day. Last night he had belonged to the darkness, like the boogey monster or a nightmare creature. *Or . . .* her imagination murmured *. . . a forbidden lover.*

'Get a grip on yourself.' Mikki sat up, shaking her head as if the physical movement would clear the ridiculous thoughts from it, and she was struck again by the beauty of the room that was now hers. Pushing the Guardian from her mind, she intended to leap out of bed and glide gracefully to her balcony, as should any woman lucky enough to live in a room this incredible, but the leap turned into a stagger, and the glide became a stiff limp accompanied by a groan when she made her body straighten fully.

Oh baby, she was sore! She hobbled to the door. When the handmaidens had first met her, they had seemed to think she was unusually old for an Empousa. Maybe that was because it took a damn teenager to withstand the hidden torture of casting a circle and dancing around with a gaggle of women. Who knew? Even her hair hurt. She sniffed at herself. And she needed a bath. A long, hot one.

She opened the door and was met by a cool, rose-scented breeze. It pulled her attention from the waiting breakfast, her sore muscles and the mysterious Guardian, and drew her across the wide balcony so she could look out over the vast gardens.

Mikki was awestruck.

The land that stretched before her was filled with bed after bed of roses. They blazed clouds of color in the green sky of their branches. White marble paths circled labyrinthine around the beds, connecting them to trees and shrubs and an occasional water feature. She could see the creamy marble of the domed roof of Hecate's Temple and the dancing reflection of the sun off the great central fountain that stood near it.

It was so beautiful that it weakened the disbelief and cynicism she had learned from a very young age to carry as her shield. She could be happy here . . . she could belong.

'It is your charge, Empousa.'

This morning Hecate's presence did not startle her. The goddess materializing beside her felt comforting – a reinforcement of the miracle that lay before her.

'This is where I belong,' Mikki said without looking away from the gardens.

'Yes, it is your destiny.' The goddess sounded pleased by her acknowledgment.

Mikki turned to face Hecate and flushed with surprise. Last night the goddess had appeared an indeterminate age, anywhere from thirtysomething to fiftysomething. This morning Hecate wore the same night-colored robes and star-studded headdress.

The gigantic dogs lounged by her feet, as they had the night before. But the goddess had shed decades. She had the fresh face and tight figure of a teenager. Her smooth cheeks were kissed with a blush of youthful peach.

Hecate frowned and raised gracefully arched brows. 'You do not recognize your goddess, Empousa?'

Mikki swallowed hard. She might look like a teenager, but Hecate had certainly not lost any of her powerful aura.

'It's not that I don't recognize you; it's just that you're so young!'

'Of my triple forms I simply chose the Maiden today. But do not be fooled by the facade of youth. You should already know that the exterior of a woman does not define her interior.'

'It may not define her, but it certainly affects her. I'm old enough to know that,' Mikki said automatically. Then, appalled at the brusque tone she had inadvertently used, she added, 'I didn't mean any disrespect.'

Intelligent gray eyes looked unnaturally mature and out of place in the goddess's smooth young face. 'I rarely find it disrespectful when an Empousa speaks honestly to me, Mikado. And you are correct. Too often our exterior is what we are judged by, especially in your old world, one that has largely forgotten the lessons of the goddesses.' Hecate shrugged her smooth shoulders. 'Even in my realm where a woman's appearance should not be the basis on which she is judged, my daughters too often forget the lessons of the three-faced goddess.' Hecate's wise gray eyes sparkled. 'For instance, some would say that an Empousa of your advanced years is too old to assume the role of my High Priestess. They would not say it in my presence, but they would say it. And how would you answer their impertinence, Mikado?'

Mikki ignored the stiffness in her back and her sore muscles and met the goddess's steady gaze. 'I'd say that I may be older, but that also means I've lived through more experiences, so I suggest they watch their silly young selves. Age and treachery usually triumph over youth and exuberance.'

Hecate laughed, and as she did so, her appearance shifted so she was, once again, the beautiful, middle-age woman Mikki had met the night before. 'I will tell you a secret, my Empousa. Of the three, this is the form I prefer. Youth is often overrated.'

'Especially by the young,' Mikki agreed.

The two smiled at one another, and for a moment, they were not goddess and mortal. They were just two women in perfect agreement.

After a short, compatible silence, the goddess said, 'I imagine this' – she gestured with one hand to take in the gardens and the palace – 'all seems quite unusual to you.'

Encouraged by the goddess's approachability, Mikki smiled crookedly. 'It is strange and unusual, as well as more than a little overwhelming, but I do feel drawn to everything here.' She hurried on, not wanting Hecate to know included in that 'everything' was her cloven-hoofed late-night visitor. 'When I cast the circle and performed the initiation ritual I felt more beautiful and powerful and *right* than I've ever felt in my life.'

Hecate nodded. 'The Empousa blood runs thick in your veins, Mikado. You could not have felt true belonging in the mundane world. Part of you longed to take your proper place in my realm. I suspect even your mother and her mothers before her knew the unease of not quite fitting in.'

Mikki thought about her mother, remembering how she had always seemed to prefer to be alone – or to spend time working in her garden with her roses – than to socialize. How she hadn't ever seemed to miss her father's presence and when Mikki asked about him she only said that he had been an indulgence of her youth, but that she would always be grateful to him for giving her the most important gift in her life – her daughter.

Her grandmother, too, had not been a woman who had many friends outside her daughter and her granddaughter. She rarely spoke of the man who was her grandfather, except to smile surreptitiously and say that they had had two different viewpoints on marriage – he had enjoyed it; she hadn't. Men had not been important in either her mother's or her grandmother's life. Not that either of them hadn't been wonderful, loving women. They had been, and Mikki missed them both desperately. Her grandmother had died of an unexpected heart attack five years ago, and breast cancer had stolen her mother four years after that. Mikki thought of both women as beautiful and ageless, like they'd stepped out of one of the fairy tales her mother used to read to Mikki when she was a young girl. They had been otherworldly . . .

'They are at peace now, Mikado. Even from the mundane world across the far edges of my crossroads, their souls were able to find the paradise of the Elysian Fields, and, finally, true belonging. You need not weep for them.'

Mikki reached up, surprised to feel the tears wetting her cheeks. She looked at Hecate. 'They belong here, too. That's why they didn't really fit in back there.'

'Part of them belonged here, but the magick in their blood was not as strong as the magick within you. If it had been, they would have awakened the Guardian and returned.'

Mikki wiped her cheeks dry. 'The Guardian . . . I met him last night.'

The goddess cocked her head, studying her priestess. 'And what was your reaction to him?'

'He scared me,' she said quickly. And then more slowly she added, 'And he made me sad.'

'Sad?' Hecate's brows lifted into her dark hair.

Mikki moved her shoulders restlessly. 'I don't know . . . there's something about him that feels so alone.'

'There is no other creature like him in existence, so by his very nature he is alone. Ages ago, when I took dominion over this realm, I knew I needed a guardian to stand watch over it. This is the realm from whence all the dreams and magick originate; it must be protected. So I called upon the great beasts of olde – the immortal offspring of the Titans. Though I am Goddess of the Beasts, I do not hold dominion over them. Even I could not force one of their kind into my service. The creature you met last night bound himself willingly to me. He took up this eternal burden when it was not his own. I have gifted him with some powers that are unique to this realm, but the Guardian has an ancient magick of his own – he ties the threads of reality to that of this realm.'

'Has he always been as he is now?'

Hecate's sharp gaze seemed to look within her. 'The Guardian has never been a man, nor will he ever be. Do not ever make the mistake of believing otherwise.'

With effort, Mikki didn't flinch at the goddess's anger, but she quickly changed the direction of her questioning.

'He's called the Guardian, and you said he is needed to protect the realm. From what does it need protection?'

'Dream Stealers and those who desire to possess the fashioning of magick for themselves. Dreams and magick belong to all of mankind, even those who live in the mundane world. No one has the right to steal such things for himself.'

Mikki didn't really understand what the goddess was talking about, but she was damn tired of sounding like a blundering idiot. As she had implied to Hecate, she was old enough to figure things out for herself. So she'd keep her eyes open and learn. And she wouldn't ask too many personal questions about the Guardian – clearly that made the goddess angry, and a pissed-off goddess couldn't possibly be a good thing.

But there was one question she needed to ask, whether it made her look moronic or not.

'Where do the roses fit in to all this?'

Hecate smiled as she gazed out at the expanse of dream-colored flowers.

'Roses are beauty, and beauty is at the heart of all dreams and magick; it is its foundation, its support. Without beauty, the mind cannot reach beyond the corporeal to grasp the ethereal.'

Mikki's brow furrowed as she frowned. But hadn't the goddess just talked about the exterior not defining the interior? Now she was saying that beauty was everything.

Hecate laughed softly. 'There is more than one kind of beauty, Empousa.'

Mikki said the first thing that came into her mind. 'Well, you wouldn't know it by the tastes of the majority of the men in my old world.'

'Why should you sound so cynical? Your form and face are pleasing, Mikado.'

'That's just it. I'm pretty. I have good hair, nice boobs, and decent legs. And that's all men see. They don't bother to look deeper.' Her conscience reminded her that she hadn't often given any man the opportunity to look deeper ... to discover her secrets ... the truth of which only made her scowl harder.

'I think there is much you can teach this realm, Mikado. And it has much it can teach you in return. It will be an adventure for you, as well as your destiny.'

Mikki sighed softly. She'd only been here for a day, and already she was sick of mysteries.

'I'm here for the roses,' she said, unconsciously mimicking the Guardian's words.

'You are. They are the foundation on which dreams and magick are built, as well as the boundary between worlds.'

'The boundary between worlds? Do you mean that literally?'

'I do, Empousa. Roses fill this realm, and the strength of their beauty gives life to dreams and magick. Their strength also forms the border of my realm.' Hecate pointed out across the gardens and made a sweeping motion that encircled them. 'The edges of the gardens are bound by a great wall of roses. Past that wall is a vast forest, a kind of netherworld, which is the crossroads between reality and magick. On one side of the forest rests the ancient world where gods and goddesses are still honored; on the other your old world can be found, that of the mundane. The rose wall is what defines the boundaries between that world and ours. See to the health of the roses, and, in turn, all else in my realm will prosper. If the roses sicken, so, too, will this realm. You should know that this realm has long been without its Empousa. The roses need your care, and you do have other duties, too. You are High Priestess of Magick, and as such the people of this realm will come to you for advice, spells, and rituals. Be wise, Mikado, for you stand as my Incarnation. When you speak, it is my power that answers.'

Mikki felt the blood drain from her face. 'Hecate, I don't know anything about spells and magick and rituals!'

The goddess's serene expression remained unchanged. 'Your mind doesn't know, but your spirit does. Look within, as you did last night, and you will find what you seek. No matter how things appear on the surface, follow your instincts. They will not fail you. And use your experience, Mikado. I believe I will enjoy having an *aged* Empousa.'

'So just trust my gut?'

'Crude, but correct,' Hecate said. 'Your handmaidens are here to aid you, but remember – you alone are my High Priestess. They personify the Elements over which I lend you dominion. Befriend them if you will; use their powers as you need them. Just as the handmaidens are at your disposal, so, too, is the Guardian. He is a magickal creature whose powers have been pledged to protect the Realm of the Rose. If there is a problem in the realm, do not hesitate to call upon him.'

Mikki felt a little jolt of excitement at the mention of the Guardian. Guiltily, she said, 'But if I think the realm is in danger, shouldn't I just call you?'

'My duties are vast! I do not have time to answer your summons as if I were a mere handmaid!'

Mikki took an involuntary step back, surprised by Hecate's sudden burst of anger. 'That's not what I mean. I—'

Hecate cut her off with a brisk wave of her hand. 'I forget that you are inexperienced in the ways of an Empousa. I do reign as supreme goddess over the Realm of the Rose, but you and the Guardian have been given the task of caring for and protecting it. I would like to spend much of my time here, but my duties do not allow me that luxury.' Hecate studied Mikki carefully. 'You must not fear the Guardian. I have told you that he will not harm you.'

'I know.' Mikki bit her lip. Avoiding Hecate's eyes, she stared out at the gardens. 'It's just that he's like nothing I've ever imagined before.'

'Is he?' Hecate's voice was soft. 'Didn't you tell me that you spent much of your time tending the roses in the gardens in which he slept, frozen in the form of a statue?'

Mikki nodded her head. 'Yes.'

'Well then, how could he be like nothing you've ever before imagined?' Hecate said matter-of-factly.

'I suppose when you put it like that . . .' Mikki's words trailed off doubtfully as she turned back to the goddess.

'There is no other way to put it,' she said briskly. 'He stood silent watch over your roses then. He does the same now, only not so silently. If it is easier for you, simply forget that he is a beast – think of him only as a Guardian.' Not giving Mikki time to answer, Hecate continued, 'Excellent. I must leave you now. Break your fast and then call the handmaidens to you so you can be dressed and begin the day's duties. The roses have gone too long without the touch of an Empousa. They are in need of your care. Remember, follow your instincts, Mikado. Allow your spirit and the knowledge held in your blood to guide you, and you will do well . . .'

The goddess raised one elegant hand, and she and the dogs disappeared in a shower of star-colored sparks.

Shaking her head, Mikki walked to the table that was laden with fruit and bread and cheese. 'It might be easier if I really was kooky,' she muttered. Pouring herself fragrant, rose-spiced tea from a steeping pot, she wished desperately for a couple aspirins and some BenGay.

Chapter Fifteen

The food really was delicious, especially the cheese. Mikki took one last bite of a creamy white cheese she'd spread on a slice of chewy bread. She'd been carrying on a passionate love affair with cheese for as many years as she could remember – as her curvy butt could certainly attest to – and the selection someone had laid out for her breakfast was even more extraordinary than last night's feast.

Was that because the Guardian knew what she liked best? Could he, like Hecate, read the passions and fears in her mind? Had he plucked her favorite foods from her subconscious? If he had, then that would mean he would also know that she was thinking of him . . . and that she was intrigued as well as intimidated at the thought of seeing him again.

I am here for the roses!

She jumped guiltily. He was a beast. A creature from a strange world who had sworn an oath to guard Hecate's realm. Clearly, something had happened a long time ago and he had screwed up, Big Time, and ended up a statue in Tulsa.

What had he done? Whatever it was, she'd bet he wouldn't do it again. Mikki sighed. There were so damn many mysteries and unanswered questions here it was overwhelming. No! She shook her head and took a last sip of tea. She'd take things one step at a time and figure them out as she went. She just needed to think of this as a new job. It might be daunting to learn all the new . . . well . . . procedures, but not impossible.

And the Guardian? If she thought of him at all she should think of him like she would any security guard. For a moment the image of the Tulsa Rose Gardens' night watchman, Mel, flashed into her mind. He was short and round and very gray. Actually, he reminded her of a balding Santa Claus. Mel couldn't have been more different from the magnificent creature who had turned from stone into living flesh. Her lips curved up at the comparison. The Guardian and Mel? She really was crazy if she started thinking of the two of them as similar.

Mikki bit nervously at her lip. She didn't know how she was supposed to deal with the creature, the roses, the magick . . .

Before she could get overwhelmed – again – she stood and stretched carefully, focusing on working the stiffness out of her muscles. Her body had definitely felt better. Then she made her way slowly back into her bedroom. Busy. She needed to get to work and keep busy. It would help her muscles loosen up and her brain not to obsess on horns and hooves. And she was anxious to check out the roses. Her roses. Hecate had said that she was in charge of caring for them, that it was her destiny. She was no longer just another volunteer who daydreamed about making the gardens her own.

Eagerly, she looked around the room. Hecate had said to call the handmaidens to help her get dressed. Did that mean there was some kind of bell/rope system in her room? Isn't that how they did things in palaces 'back in the day'? But this wasn't a scene from some old English movie with castles and such; this was a realm of myth and magick, something her personal life experiences hadn't exactly prepared her for.

'Maybe I should try calling a messenger owl. Talk about Hogwarts,' she grumbled to herself. 'Okay, you're being ridiculous.' Mikki put her hands on her hips. 'It can't be that hard.

Hecate said to call them. So I'll call them.' Actually, she thought she'd just call Gii. She felt the most connection with her, and, quite frankly, all four of the girls at once were a little more than she wanted to deal with so early. She cleared her throat. 'Gii?' she said tentatively and then a little louder, 'Gii, could you come here, please? I could use your help.'

Nothing. Nada. Zip. The handmaiden didn't suddenly materialize. No pitter-patter of little feet were heard rushing across her balcony.

'Okay, there must be another way to do this.' Mikki paced while she thought. She was supposed to call the handmaidens . . . she came to an abrupt stop. The handmaidens were really the personification of their element. She'd called each of their elements into the circle last night. Maybe she could do something like that now. She closed her eyes and thought about Gii . . . the element Earth . . . last night the element's presence was preceded by scents that invoked the fertility of the earth and the harvest . . . the sweetness of newly cut hay . . . the ripeness of fruit and berries. Mikki could almost smell and taste the richness of a green and growing Earth.

'Gii,' she said softly. 'Come to me.'

Almost instantly two quick knocks sounded on the far wall of her room. Mikki opened her eyes in time to see a door open seamlessly into the opulent bedroom, giving Mikki just a glimpse of a wide, moon-colored hallway as Gii hurried in. The handmaiden's arms were filled with several lengths of amber and cream and gold cloth.

'Good morning, Empousa.' She curtseyed gracefully.

'I did it!' Mikki grinned. 'I called and you came.'

Gii's smile was warm. 'Gladly, Empousa! It is a true pleasure to once again have Hecate's High Priestess within our realm. We

160

have been idle too long.' She paused and looked around her. 'Did you not call the other handmaidens as well?'

'Actually, since I'm not used to having any handmaidens, I'd like to start with just you for today. Is that okay with you?'

'Whatever you wish, Empousa. It is an honor to be chosen to serve you.'

The young woman's exuberance made Mikki feel a lot less nervous about not knowing what the hell she was doing. She was where she belonged. Everything else would fall into place. She nodded at Gii's laden arms. 'I was going to say I needed you to help me find something to wear, but it looks like you already have that taken care of.' Mentally Mikki crossed her fingers that today's outfit would cover both of her breasts.

'Naturally, Empousa. I knew you would be eager to oversee your gardens. When you summoned me I made certain that I was prepared.'

Gii began helping Mikki out of her nightdress, and with the words *your gardens* echoing delightfully in her imagination, Mikki shrugged her way out of her clothes and held very still as the handmaiden took the long, rectangular length of gold fabric and wrapped it once around her body. With gold pins that appeared from the voluminous folds of her own robe, Gii fastened it at the shoulders. Thankfully, it formed a full bodice, covering both of her breasts. Then she unwound one of the elaborately braided belts from around her own waist and hung it low on Mikki's hips.

'Gii, I don't mean to complain, and I think this' – she hesitated, trying to think of the right word for the rectangle that had become a flowing, toga-like garment – 'this dress is flattering and very feminine, but don't you have something else that's better suited to working in the garden?'

Gii straightened and gave Mikki a confused smile. 'How could any garment be better suited than a chiton?'

'Well, it's an awful lot of material. Won't this' – she pointed at the length of golden fabric that hung gracefully to her feet – 'just get in the way?'

'Not if you tuck it here and here.' Gii demonstrated tucking her own lovely mint-colored chiton up into her belt so her long, strong legs were left mostly bare. The Earth Elemental held out her arms. 'Our arms are not hindered by cumbersome sleeves, but if you feel chilled, you can easily wrap your palla around your shoulders.'

'Palla?'

Gii wrinkled her forehead at her High Priestess. 'Empousa, have you never before worn a chiton with a palla?'

With an effort, Mikki didn't shriek her frustration. 'Gii, I explained to you last night that my old world is totally different. There I didn't know about priestesses or goddesses, and we don't dress anything like this. If I was going to work in the garden I would wear jeans' – here she mimicked stepping into a pair of pants – 'and a short T-shirt that I'd pull over my head, and it would cover the top half of my body.'

Gii looked horrified. 'I do not mean to speak ill of your old world, Priestess, but it sounds barbaric! Why would a priestess, or any woman, choose to dress in such an unflattering, uncomfortable manner?'

Mikki meant to say that she'd never thought of jeans as unflattering or uncomfortable, but her eyes were caught by her reflection in the full-length mirror and the words stopped before she could form them. She looked like a queen from an ancient world. She walked slowly forward, studying herself carefully. The fabric was soft and unbinding, feminine and alluring. She had nothing on under it to crawl up her butt or to bite into her shoulders and leave red marks at the end of the day. Compared to this outfit, a bra, panties, jeans and a T-shirt were barbaric and uncomfortable.

'Teach me about this, Gii. You called it a chiton?'

'Yes, Empousa. It can swathe the female form in almost endless ways, especially when you add a palla or various other types of mantles.' Taking a wide, soft brush from the vanity dresser, Gii fussed with Mikki's hair as she spoke, brushing it back and then tying it in place with a gold thread. 'We believe our clothing should idealize a woman's body, rather than attempting to conceal its natural shape. Or bind it unnecessarily.'

'There's no doubt that it's beautiful, but can I work in it?'

'Shall we see, Empousa?'

Mikki took the amber-colored palla from where it lay like a spilled treasure across the end of her bed and wrapped it around her shoulders. 'Absolutely.'

Mikki knew something was wrong as soon as she approached the rose bed that had been planted so close to the stairs that led from her balcony that the roses brushed against the marble railing. It was the same sick feeling she'd had the night before, only this morning it was far stronger. Her stomach clenched, and she had to fight a bizarre impulse to be sick. The smile that had lit her face when she recognized the Old Garden Rose, Blush Noisette, faded along with the color in her cheeks. The bed was large and the plants well spaced, but the closer she got to them, the more obvious it was that they were not as healthy as they had appeared to be from above. She hurried down the rest of the steps. She ignored the sick feeling that had hit her as soon as she approached the roses and left the marble path, ploughing directly into the bed, muttering under her breath while she touched leaves and lifted canes to get a better look at the heart of the plants.

'Empousa?'

'They look terrible!' Mikki said without pausing in her inspection. 'The leaves are yellow and limp. The canes are spindly. The blossoms, which seem fine from a distance, are really undersized and several don't look like they're going to open at all. When's the last time they were fertilized?'

Mikki didn't look up from the roses until she realized that Gii wasn't answering her. The handmaiden was staring uncomfortably at her tightly clasped hands.

'Gii, what's the problem? I just asked when was the last time the roses were fertilized. It's something that should be done regularly enough that . . .' Mikki's words trailed off as she realized that Gii was becoming more and more obviously upset.

'The Empousa cares for the roses,' Gii blurted, without looking at Mikki.

'Are you telling me that for the entire time you've been without an Empousa no one's taken care of these roses?'

Gii finally lifted liquid eyes to Mikki. 'It is the Empousa's sacred trust to care for the roses. Without their Empousa, Hecate bespelled them. They slept.'

Just like the Guardian.

Mikki's mind whirred. Nausea rose in her throat again, and she was hardly able to concentrate on what else Gii was saying.

'There was nothing we could do for them. The roses wouldn't respond to us. They had stopped blooming.' She lowered her voice to a whisper. 'We believed they were dying.'

'And none of you thought to mention this to me while we were frolicking around last night?' she cried, exasperated with herself for being so starry-eyed that she hadn't noticed how sick the seemingly beautiful gardens really were. And where the hell was her intuition last night? Today just getting near the beds made her feel like she was going to throw up her breakfast. Wait . . . maybe her intuition had been firmly intact. Last night she had just attributed it to nerves and lack of food, but she'd definitely been light-headed – her stomach had clenched and she'd felt sick. And then this morning she'd felt like she'd been beat up. It hadn't been because she was having a nervous breakdown or because she danced too much. Her body was reacting to the sickness in the roses.

Why hadn't Hecate warned her about the sorry state of her roses? Mikki frowned. What was it the goddess had said? *You should know that this realm has long been without its Empousa. The roses will need your care . . .*

Need her care? Mikki let her eyes sweep over the beds nearest to her, recognizing more Old Garden varieties, Eglantine and La Ville de Bruxelles. She narrowed her eyes at them. They looked sickly as hell, too! They definitely needed a lot more than a little of her care.

'We thought all would be well now that you are here. We even knew the moment you arrived because the roses suddenly began to bloom again.'

'Gii, these roses aren't getting well. They're underdeveloped and anemic! And these pathetic things aren't normal blooms, they're . . . they're . . . they're more like final death throes than healthy blossoming.'

Then, as if Hecate was still standing beside her, she heard the goddess's voice replay through her mind. *The edges of the gardens are bound by a great wall of roses . . . The rose wall is what defines the boundaries between that world and ours . . . If the roses sicken, so, too, will this realm.* A chill swept through Mikki, and she felt the warning in it pound with her blood.

She had to call the Guardian.

Chapter Sixteen

'Gii, do the roses in the rest of the realm all look like these?'

The handmaiden nodded and then, sounding childlike, she repeated, 'We thought everything would be well now that you are here.'

Mikki put on a smile she hoped didn't look too fake. 'I think it will be, but it'll take some work. The first thing I want you to do is to gather all those women we were dancing with last night. Have them meet me at Hecate's Temple. And get the other three handmaidens, too.'

'Yes, Empousa.' Gii curtseyed and then hesitated before she turned away. 'You do not come with me?'

'No, go on. I'll be at the temple soon. I have something I need to take care of here first.'

Gii flashed a relieved look at her before hurrying away. Mikki waited until the girl disappeared around the corner of the path that curved between two more beds of sick roses. Then she straightened her shoulders and walked purposefully back to the wide marble stairs that led to her balcony. Was she doing the right thing? She thought so. No, she knew so. When she'd realized how sick the roses were – *all* the roses were – she felt the unmistakable chill of danger deep within her.

Mikki climbed up two of the steps, stopped, reconsidered, and climbed up one more. There. That should make her tall enough.

She closed her eyes. Just as she had called Gii to her earlier, she called him. She thought about the strength of his body . . . the power in his voice . . . the care with which he had directed dinner be made ready for her . . . the slippers and the rosebud that floated in the crystal goblet . . .

'Guardian,' she said softly, 'come to me.'

The air seemed to thicken and press with an angry hum against her skin.

'Why have you summoned me?'

For the length of one breath Mikki pressed her eyes more tightly closed. *These are my gardens now. He is a security guard. Think of him as nothing scarier than a difficult employee.* She opened her eyes.

He was standing only a few feet from her. How could any living creature be so massive? She'd been smart to move up that additional step. In the revealing light of morning he looked less manlike than he had the night before. He was dressed the same, in the short, military-looking tunic and leather breastplate, but the clothes seemed to extenuate the bestiality of his cloven-hoofed legs and horned head rather than dress him up as civilized . . . controllable. Mikki's mouth went dry, and she had to swallow twice before she could find her voice.

'I called you because Hecate told me that was what I should do if I thought the realm was in danger.' She had to fight to make herself speak, and the result was that her voice was unintentionally loud and angry. When the Guardian's black eyes widened in surprise, she decided that her new (albeit unintentional) firmness might be a good thing.

'What is the danger, Empousa?' he rumbled.

With an effort, she kept herself from biting nervously at her lip. 'I don't know exactly. All I know is that the roses are sick, which means the rose wall that surrounds the garden is probably sick, too. My intuition tells me that possible weakness is somehow dangerous.' She held her breath, waiting for his snarl. Instead, he surprised her by bowing his head slightly to her.

'You were right to summon me, Empousa. I should not have questioned your authority. If the boundary between the worlds is weakened, I must guard against those who would use it as an opportunity to slip into our realm.'

'So as I try to heal the roses, I need to focus on the rose wall first?'

'That would be wise, Empousa.'

Mikki nodded and said, more to herself than to him, 'That's what my gut was telling me. Good thing I listened.'

'Your gut?'

'Yeah,' she said hastily. 'Hecate said I should follow my gut and I'd do the right thing.'

He snorted. 'The goddess said *gut*?'

Was it possible his dark eyes were glittering with humor?

'That's not exactly how she put it.' Surprising herself, Mikki smiled at him. His eyes locked with hers, and Mikki could feel the sudden weight of his stare as if his look could bridge the space that separated them and touch her with its intensity. And she felt something else, something that she recognized from her dreams. Mikki felt the stir of desire. He was dangerous and frightening, but he was also a powerful, overwhelmingly masculine being. As in her dreams, she was drawn to him by a hot chain of fascination. Holding his dark gaze, she said, 'Hecate told me to follow my instincts, and that's exactly what I intend to do.'

As if he had become tethered to her gaze, the Guardian moved to her until he stood near enough that he could easily touch her. 'And what is it your instincts are telling you right now, Mikado?'

Mikki's breath caught. She could feel the heat from his body. Standing up several steps had brought her almost eye level with him, and she was, once again, struck by the impossible contrasts that made up his face . . . handsome and fascinating . . . bestial and dangerous.

He's not part man, part beast. He's more than that. He's part god . . .

Slowly, he lifted his hand and took a thick strand of her hair that had escaped from its golden tie between his thumb and forefinger. While Mikki stood frozen, he let her hair slip like water through his fingers. His deep voice rumbled intimately between them.

'Can you not speak, Mikado? Where is the brave priestess who commanded me into her presence? Is my nearness enough to frighten her away?'

'I'm frightened, but I'm not going anywhere,' she said resolutely and was pleased to see his eyes widen with surprise at her honesty. Purposefully mimicking his gesture, she reached up and touched a shiny length of dark mane that spilled over his shoulders.

As if her touch was an electric charge, the Guardian jerked back from her. His voice was raw and hoarse. 'Have a care, Empousa. You might find the beast you awaken is not as tame as the roses that are yours to pet and pamper.' Then, with a growl, he whirled around, his hooves biting into the marble pathway. He was leaving, abruptly and without warning . . .

'Wait!' she yelled after him.

The great creature froze, his broad back turned to her. With a jerky motion his head swung so he glared over his shoulder.

She met his eyes again and could almost see herself reflected there – a weak, indecisive woman who, like an inexperienced young girl, had called him back to her without knowing for sure what she wanted to say.

The image angered her.

Hecate had chosen her as High Priestess, Empousa of the Realm of the Rose. *She* had summoned *him*. It had been her instincts that had alerted them to a possible danger. It didn't matter that she didn't totally understand the danger. She was doing what Hecate had chosen her to do. And damnit! He had touched her first! What the hell game did he think he was playing, and by what right did he think he could dismiss her? She was no girl child dressed up in the robes of power. She was a grown woman – independent and intelligent. She didn't tolerate patronizing men, with or without hooves and horns. Mikki slitted her eyes at him and spoke slowly and distinctly.

'There are things I need to know before you run away.'

'I do not run—'

'No!' She shouted the word, ignoring the warning in his voice. 'I speak with Hecate's authority. This time it's your turn to listen and answer.'

His face was alien in its mixture of man and beast, but she was certain she saw approval register in his dark eyes.

'What is it you wish to know, Empousa?' he said. Turning, he walked the few paces back to her.

She felt his approach as if he changed the pattern of the air around them. She swallowed hard, careful to keep her voice businesslike and her mind from wandering.

'I need to know if there is one area of the rose wall that is more easily penetrated than the rest of it. Maybe a place where there is a break in the roses, like around a door or a gate.'

He considered, then nodded, his shaggy mane spilling over his broad shoulders with the movement. 'Yes, there is a gate in the roses, and it makes sense that that is where the barrier might be most easily breached.'

'Do the handmaidens know about this gate?'

He nodded again. 'Yes, Empousa.'

'Then I'll have them show me where it is after I have them collect fertilizer.'

His thick brows shot up. 'You expect the handmaidens to tend the roses?'

She looked at him like he was totally nuts. 'How do you expect me, all by myself, to tend this many roses? They need to be fertilized, pruned and deadheaded, and that's just for a start. I'd kill myself trying to do all that alone, not to mention that I wouldn't get it all done. That's not smart or productive.'

His face had hardened again into an unreadable mask. She blew out a burst of frustrated breath.

'Are you telling me that the other Empousas did all that by themselves?'

'I do not recall an Empousa commanding the women to do anything to the roses except to cut bouquets to decorate her room.'

'What about the fertilizing and pest control and the general care roses always need?'

'These roses have never before needed that kind of care. They simply required the presence of the Empousa to thrive.'

'They've never been sick before?'

'Never.'

'And before the, um, time you spent as a statue, you'd been here a long time?'

'I have been here since Hecate claimed dominion over the realm.'

Which, Mikki guessed, had been a damn long time ago. So for literally eons the roses had been healthy, without needing any care except for the presence of Hecate's High Priestess. Until now, when she had suddenly become Empousa. Great. The news just kept getting better and better.

'Well, it looks like times have changed, or I'm a different type of Empousa, because the roses need care now. I can't do it on my own, so the women are going to have to help me.'

He looked at her silently for what felt to Mikki like a long time before saying, 'I believe you are a different type of High Priestess.'

'Is that good or bad?'

'Neither,' he said gruffly. 'It is simply a fact.'

'I think it's good,' she said firmly, determined to be undaunted by his cynical attitude. She knew from her personal propensity for cynicism that the attitude usually hid feelings that were too painful to let the world see. Her cynicism had hidden the fact that she never felt like she truly belonged. She wondered what his was covering. Did it have something to do with what he had done to cause Hecate to turn him to stone and banish him? She realized she had been standing there gawking at him, and she hastily continued. 'But I suppose changing worlds has made me more likely to think different is good.'

'Odd,' he said, his deep voice edged with sarcasm. 'It did not have the same effect upon me.'

'I imagine if I'd been turned to stone I wouldn't be so willing to think "different" was synonymous with "good," either. But at least you know I can't cause you to turn into a statue,' she said and wanted to cover her flapping mouth with her hand and stop her stupid words as she watched his face go rigid with tension.

'Is that all you wish to ask me, Empousa? I should go to the rose wall and inspect the boundary.'

173

'Yes, I'll get the women and meet you at the gate.' Mikki had to shout the last part of her sentence at his swiftly departing back. 'You're welcome,' she muttered. God, he was confusing! One second he was all smoky-eyed and erotically dangerous – talk about the classic bad boy! And the next second he was withdrawn and cynical. It was like he was two people.

'What the hell am I thinking?' She shook her head at herself. 'He's not two people; he's a person and an animal, and I need to quit having delusions of a young Marlon Brando (with horns) and remember He Is Not Human.' Interracial dating was fine. Interspecies dating? 'Please, Mikado. Just please. Relocate your common sense and take care of the roses.' With a sigh she started down the path Gii had taken to the center of the gardens, heading into what she was sure would be the continuation of a vastly difficult day.

THE gathered women parted like a sea of delicately colored flowers to make a path for Mikki to join the four handmaidens who were standing within Hecate's Temple. Many of the women called greetings to her, but they were decidedly more subdued than they had been the night before. Mikki hoped they were in the mood to work. She climbed the temple steps, smiled a quick hello to the Elementals and then turned to face the crowd. *Please don't let me sound as nervous as I am*, she thought. Immediately, Hecate's stern voice spoke from her memory. *When you speak, it is my power that answers.* The memory boosted her confidence. She ignored the lingering soreness in her body and the vague nausea she seemed unable to get rid of and looked out at the crowd, purposefully meeting the eyes of several of the women as she spoke.

'The roses are sick.'

Frightened murmurs ran through the group, and Mikki had to raise her hand to silence them.

'But that's why I'm here. I understand roses. I know what they need, and with your help, we can make them healthy again.' Mikki was pleased at the attentive expressions of the listening women. 'The first thing we must do is fertilize them. So I need you to gather things that roses need to thrive.' She paused, ordering the thoughts in her head. She'd already realized the obvious – that she would have to depend on wholly organic methods of fertilizing and pest and disease control, and that wasn't all bad. Many times the natural ways were the best. Last night she'd eaten meat that tasted like prosciutto. That was pork, wasn't it? Which meant they had to have pigs somewhere. It was a start . . .

'Hog manure,' she said, and the bright, attentive expressions dropped into frowns. 'You do have pigs, right?'

A few heads nodded hesitantly.

'Good. I want you to fill baskets with pig manure.' Hardly taking a breath, she turned to Nera. The Water Elemental was watching her with large, round eyes. 'Nera, is there a lake or sea nearby?'

'Yes, Empousa, there is a large lake within the realm.'

'Excellent.' She turned back to the crowd. 'I'll need fish heads, entrails – anything you'd normally throw away instead of cooking. Actually,' she continued as if the group of women wasn't staring slack-jawed at her, 'I need dead organic matter, both plant and animal. Gii, I'm assuming that the forest outside the rose wall is dark and dense?'

'It is, Empousa.'

'Then the forest floor should be rich with loam. Bring buckets or baskets or whatever, along with something to turn over the ground around the roses so we can mix the fertilizer into the soil.'

'But bring them where, Empousa?' Gii said.

'Oh, I'm sorry.' Mikki spoke so her voice carried out over the crowd. 'Bring everything, empty baskets and those filled with the fertilizer I've mentioned, along with gardening tools, to the gate in the rose wall. We'll start there.'

No one moved.

'Now would be good,' Mikki said firmly. 'The roses have been ignored too long.'

Still no one moved.

Floga cleared her throat and moved closer to Mikki. 'Empousa, this is highly irregular.'

'What is? That I've told you we need to fertilize the roses or that you're refusing to do as an Empousa asks?'

Floga paled. 'I would not refuse your bidding, Empousa.'

Mikki looked at her other three handmaids.

'None of us would refuse you, Priestess,' Gii said quickly, and the girls nodded agreement.

Mikki swung her gaze out to the crowd and raised her voice, making sure she sounded well and truly pissed. 'Then is it only the women of the realm who refuse to obey Hecate's Empousa?'

The crowd stirred restlessly. One woman, who was probably about Mikki's age, stepped forward and curtseyed quickly.

'My sisters and I will gather the baskets for the forest loam, Empousa.'

Another woman moved to the front of the group. 'I will bring the fish offal.'

'As will I.'

'And I.'

'We will see to the hogs,' a young girl said from the middle of a group of teenagers.

Mikki wanted to weep with relief and thank them all profusely. But her gut told her that was not the reaction the people expected, or deserved. So instead she simply said, 'Then I will meet you at the gate. You'll need to hurry. We have a long day ahead of us. The quicker we get started, the better.' She turned her back to the dispersing crowd and caught Gii's eyes. 'I'll need you to show me where the gate is,' she whispered.

Gii smiled her approval before bowing her head and dropping into a deep, respectful curtsey. 'As you wish, Empousa.'

Chapter Seventeen

'There! This is the rose wall. The gate is just around that bend in the hedge.' Gii pointed a little way ahead of them at an area of the wall that curved back toward the gardens.

'Multiflora roses – that figures.' Following the imposing boundary that seemed to materialize out of the air, Mikki shook her head. 'Well, they have been called a living wall, but I've never seen them contained in such an orderly way.'

She'd seen multiflora roses take over pastures and completely destroy them in less than a couple of years, but stretching before her was a huge wall of the wild roses that had apparently been tamed. She and Gii turned with the curving wall. Mikki gazed up. The mass of climbing roses had to be at least twelve feet tall. 'Do they ever spread and threaten to take over the forest?' *Or the rest of the realm*, she mused silently.

'The rose wall obeys Hecate's command.'

Mikki felt Gii's body jerk in response to the Guardian's deep voice, and she was profoundly grateful that she, too, hadn't jumped out of her skin when he spoke. But then, she'd known he was going to meet her at the wall. Subconsciously, or maybe not so subconsciously, she'd been waiting for him to appear. Her gaze shifted from the roses to the Guardian. He was standing on the other end of the curve they had been following, framed by what looked like an immense gate made entirely of multiflora roses. As per usual, his strong face was somber and his expression unreadable, but his eyes . . . his eyes seared her. *He is not going to intimidate me. He's a security guard – a big, grumpy security guard. I'm Empousa, which would translate at the very least to his supervisor.* Mikki smiled pleasantly.

'I know more than a few ranchers in my old world who would pay just about anything to have Hecate command roses like these to behave themselves.'

He frowned. 'Hecate is not a merchant who can be—'

'I didn't mean that literally. I was just kidding,' Mikki interrupted, working hard not to roll her eyes. She glanced at Gii. The Elemental had her lips pressed tightly together in a thin white line, and her eyes darted nervously back and forth from the Guardian to Mikki. *Huh. I guess no one kids with the Guardian. Or maybe the Empousa has never had a sense of humor before – the others were probably too young to have acquired one. Yet another* thing she was going to have to change.

'Okay, well, obviously this is the gate.' Mikki ignored both of them and marched over to stand not far from the Guardian. From the corner of her eye she noticed that Gii followed her but was careful not to get too close to the man-creature. Mikki moved nearer the gate, observing that the roses that made up the wall looked only marginally healthier than the sickly plants in the gardens. The leaves of the multiflora roses were still mostly green, but there was a disturbing amount of yellowed foliage mixed in with healthy growth. There were a few half-hearted light pink buds, but none of the blooms had opened. She touched leaves, turning them over and looking in amidst the mass of plant that made up the body of the hedge, checking automatically for black spots and insects.

'I don't see anything specifically wrong with them – no obvious disease or insect infestation.' She sighed and chewed her lip. 'Like the rest of the roses in the gardens, they just look sick.'

The Guardian moved closer to her. He, too, was studying the rose wall. 'Can you make them well?'

'Of course,' Mikki said with much more confidence than she felt. 'I've never met a rose that didn't like me.' Of course she'd also never met a wall of multiflora roses that listened to the commands of an ancient goddess, either, but she thought it'd be counterproductive to mention that. 'We'll just start at the beginning and work our way forward from there. Step one – make sure the roses are well fertilized. It doesn't get much more basic than that.'

At that moment a little breeze carried to them the sound of chattering women. The Guardian cocked his head and drew a deep breath. Then he looked down at Mikki and raised his eyebrows.

'You must smell our approaching fertilizer. What is it, fish heads or pig manure?' Mikki said.

'Pig waste.'

This time it didn't matter that his face was like no other living creature; Mikki easily recognized the glint of humor in his eyes.

'Good!' she said brightly.

'You are, indeed, an unusual Empousa if pig waste causes you happiness.'

She grinned. 'I am and it does. Now it's time we get to work.'

He flashed a smile that showed very white, very sharp teeth. Then he bowed to her. 'I am yours to command, Priestess.'

Ignoring Gii's sudden surprised intake of breath, Mikki tilted her head in what she liked to think was a goddess's acknowledgment of his goodwill before turning to begin giving directions to the approaching women.

*   *   *

THEY weren't doing a half bad job for women who had never worked with roses. Mikki stood and stretched, carefully circling her shoulders to try and relieve the tension that always found a way to rest between her shoulder blades. She wiped her hands on the outside of one of the tucked-up edges of her chiton and surveyed her surroundings.

The women were spread out along the rose wall for as far as she could see. Those she had stationed at the wall had three jobs – one group dug shallow trenches up and down the area near the roots of the roses. Another group covered the fertilizer with the freshly dug dirt after yet another group of women dumped the baskets of organic matter into the trenches. A steady stream of women carried baskets back and forth from wherever the pig poo and fish guts came from to the hedge.

There was also a chain of women who passed baskets filled with the loam of the forest floor from outside the rose gate back through to the women waiting to mound it snuggly around the base of the living wall.

Mikki glanced toward the open gate. Sure enough, she had only to wait a couple seconds to see the Guardian. All morning he had paced restlessly back and forth on the forest side of the gate. The playful goodwill that had begun to exist between them had dissipated when Mikki had insisted that the women be allowed to go into the forest to pile the rich loam into the baskets. The Guardian had been, quite simply, thoroughly pissed at her.

'It is not wise that the gate be left open,' he'd growled when she'd explained how she intended to fill the empty baskets.

'The roses need the nutrients that are found in the organic matter that makes up the forest floor. So the gate has to be open because the women need to go into the forest,' she'd told him, in a clear, unafraid voice right in front of all the women.

'The forest is not safe,' he'd said stubbornly.

'Isn't that why you're here?'

He growled something unintelligible at her that made her skin prickle, but she'd refused to look away from him, just like she'd refused to back down in her insistence that the women go into the forest. She knew what the roses needed, and some of it could be found out there. Mr. Grumpy would just have to deal with it; he wasn't going to scare her out of what she knew was the right thing to do. And anyway, what could he do to her in front of the women in the realm? Eat her? Bite her? Pick her up and shake her? Please. She was Empousa – he was supposed to make sure she was safe. He couldn't very well be what caused her damage. She figured the worst he could do would be to throw a fit and stomp away. If he did that she'd just have to listen within and figure out how the hell to open a gate made of roses that didn't have a handle or a latch or a . . .

'I insist none of the women leave my sight.'

'Whatever you say. Security is your job, not mine.'

He'd cocked his head and sent her a black look.

'Well, I mean whatever you say as long as the women go into the forest and collect the loam,' she'd amended sweetly.

'I still do not like it.'

'And yet I am still insisting.' Mikki had felt the weight of the women's staring eyes when she contradicted the Guardian. It was as if they were shocked that she stood up to him, and it made her wonder how the other, younger Empousas had handled disagreements with the intimidating Guardian. *It doesn't matter*, she told herself firmly, *I'm Empousa now, and he needs to learn that I'm not some virginal infant he can bully.*

'Huh,' he'd snorted. But he'd gone to the gate, raised his hands and spoken words Mikki could not understand but the power of which rippled like warm water over her skin. The rose gate opened slowly, and only far enough for the bulk of the Guardian to pass through. She'd followed him, and the women, led by Gii, had followed the beast and their Empousa into the edges of the dark forest.

The forest was dark – and it should be. The trees were enormous, ancient oaks, so thick at the trunk that even the Guardian's wide reach couldn't have wrapped around one. The interlocking branches formed a canopy of lush green, through which very little sunlight managed to escape. But it seemed perfectly normal. Birds chirped. Squirrels scolded. Mikki even thought she caught sight of the rear end of a startled deer as it bounded away.

The women who scooped the leafy loam from the forest floor and into the baskets were unusually silent, and none of them wandered very far apart, but no boogeymen or monsters jumped out at them. And all the while the Guardian paced, his sharp eyes focused past the women and into the depths of the forest.

Gii's sweet voice interrupted Mikki's musings. 'It is midday, Empousa,' the Earth Elemental said after delicately wiping the sweat from her brow. She pointed to a line of women who were approaching from a different direction than the chain of fertilizer had arrived. 'I see that women from the palace come bearing food.'

'So late already?' Mikki hastily took her gaze from the Guardian's ever-vigilant form and smiled at the handmaiden.

'Yes, Empousa, and several of your rose workers must eat and then be allowed to change places with the Dream Weavers within the palace.'

'Dream Weavers?'

183

'I forget that you are new to this realm and its ways, especially today, after watching you work so easily with' – Gii paused and her gaze slid to the open gate and the grim guard who stood beyond it – 'the roses,' she finished.

Mikki ignored her reference to the Guardian because she was not sure what to make of it. She was dying to ask questions about him and about the High Priestesses who had come before her – for instance, where were they now? Did the women retire? If so, couldn't one of them be called out of retirement temporarily to . . . well . . . train her properly?

But intuition told her that asking a bunch of personal questions about the Guardian and the previous Empousas would make her look even more inexperienced and insecure than she already was. She'd gained a measure of respect from the women today. She didn't want to lose ground. And there was something else, too. Something in the way the women averted their eyes from him and avoided standing too near him.

'May I, Empousa?' Gii was saying.

'Oh, I'm sorry, Gii. Yes, it is time we took a break. Then I'd like to hear more about these Dream Weavers.' Which, she decided, should at least be a safe topic. As Gii sent a couple young women who were working close by to inform the other three Elementals that it was time to break and refresh with the midday meal, Mikki retreated to one of the many marble benches placed in lovely rose alcoves all around the gardens. She sat, realizing how tired her achy muscles were now that she'd stopped moving, and was sincerely grateful that Gii was so capable and able to quickly call the women to order. They broke into little groups, clustering around benches and fountains, and the soft sound of their conversation mixed with the ever-present scent of roses, creating an atmosphere that Mikki found soothing, despite her tired muscles and the general feeling of sickness that clung to her.

She breathed deeply, thinking how wonderful the gardens would be when they were healthy again. Letting her mind wander with her eyes, she imagined the beds and the rose wall in full, magnificent bloom. Her daydreamy interlude was interrupted when her gaze landed on the frowning Guardian as he ushered the last of the women back through the rose gate. He looked so damn serious and gloomy. Why? What was it about the forest that made him so uptight? Hell, maybe he was always uptight. No . . . she remembered the glint of humor in his eyes and the touch of his hand on her hair . . . clearly he wasn't always uptight. Still, she needed to have a frank talk with him. No mysteries, no evasions. If the forest was that dangerous, she needed to know the specifics.

The Guardian spoke a terse command and the wall closed seamlessly. Mikki yawned and stretched and tried not to be obvious about watching him. One of the palace servants approached him and offered him a basket of food. He ignored it, but he did accept a floppy skin, which he raised to his mouth and drank deeply from. He handed it back to the woman, and she hurried away. Then he paced over to a tree that grew near the rose wall and seemed to disappear within the shadow of its trunk.

Gii hurried up with a basket of her own, which was filled with tempting smells, and sat beside Mikki, placing the basket between them.

'Is the food not to your liking, Empousa?' she said when Mikki made no move to begin eating.

Mikki hastily looked away from the shadow under the tree. 'No, everything is wonderful.' She broke off a piece of bread from the long, thin loaf and added a slice of cheese to it. Nonchalantly, she said, 'I was just wondering why he doesn't eat.'

Fixing her own sandwich, Gii said, 'I have never seen him eat.' The Earth Elemental shrugged. 'Not that he doesn't. He must. The food that is left at the mouth of his lair disappears and must be replaced.'

'Lair?' Mikki sputtered, almost choking on the piece of cheese she'd just swallowed.

'Yes, his lair.' Gii paused, looking confused at Mikki's surprise. 'The place in which he sleeps – where he goes when he is not out amongst the roses.'

'I guess I assumed he lived in the palace, like I do.'

'Oh, no, Empousa, he is a beast.' Gii sounded appalled. 'It would not be proper for him to live in the palace.'

Mikki studied Gii, trying to read the handmaiden's face as well as her words. The Earth Elemental was kind and compassionate. So much so that Mikki naturally sought out Gii's company more often than the rest of the handmaidens, and she already felt as if the two of them were becoming friends. Yet here Gii was, sounding cold and unfeeling. The Guardian was an animal. Period. So he didn't deserve the same luxuries or consideration the rest of them did, yet he was the being who protected their realm.

Deep in her gut it felt wrong – terribly, hurtfully wrong.

But she didn't correct Gii or question her further. Mikki didn't know enough about what was going on here. Not yet. Something wasn't right, and it had to do with the Guardian. She'd already learned from getting close to the roses that everything in this realm was not as it first appeared. She'd keep her eyes open and watch the Guardian. Her instinct told her that if she got close enough to him she might discover what was hidden beneath his facade, too. That is, if he let her – or if she dared. Until then she would watch and learn, and follow her gut.

'Tell me about the – what did you call them – Dream Weavers?' She purposefully changed the subject.

Gii brightened. 'The Dream Weavers have the ability to take the ordinary – and the not so ordinary – and weave it into dreams and magick, which they then send from this realm out into the other worlds. It is from what is created here that all the dreams and magick of mankind are born.'

Mikki struggled to take it all in. 'And by "the other worlds" you mean?'

'Your old world, that of the mundane. And then there is also the ancient world, where the gods and goddesses are still revered. It is the ancient world from where the women of this realm and I were chosen.'

That was what Hecate had said when she'd talked about the crossroads between the worlds. It had confused Mikki then, but today her mind felt more able to absorb the seemingly impossible details of her new home. And she realized that at least one of the questions she had been pondering had been answered. The other Empousas had obviously come from the ancient world, and that must be where they retired to. In a slightly crazy way, it did make sense.

'You said the women had to go back to the palace to take their turn as Dream Weavers. So they're doing that – creating dreams and magick – right there in the palace?'

'Yes, Empousa.'

'I'd like to see that. Is it possible that I could watch?' Mikki asked eagerly.

'You could do more than watch. As Empousa, you have the ability to weave dreams and make magick, too.'

187

Chapter Eighteen

SHE had the ability to weave dreams and make magick . . .

Gii's words remained with her all the rest of the day, circling around and around in her imagination, which stayed as busy as her hands. Just the concept that dreams came from somewhere other than a sleeping subconscious was bizarre enough. But to think that she had the ability to create them! It was the most extraordinary thing she'd ever imagined.

'Empousa.'

The Guardian's deep voice startled her, but she was careful to cover her jumpiness with a show of wiping her hands briskly on her muddy chiton while she straightened from crouching under an unusually large cluster of a Felicite Parmentier shrub. He was standing so close that his shadow seemed to engulf both her and the rose on which she'd been working, making her feel flushed and nervous. Buying time to steady herself, Mikki said briskly, 'Oh, Guardian. Just a moment.' Then she called to Gii, 'Gii, the roses in this bed will need to be staked. Would you remind me that tomorrow we'll need to have wood cut and brought out here?'

'Yes, Empousa,' Gii called back.

Then, composed again, Mikki turned to face the Guardian. 'Sorry about that. Now, what can I do for you?'

'Dusk approaches. The women cannot be in the forest after dark.'

Mikki squinted over his shoulder at the sun that was, indeed, beginning to settle into the massive canopy of the forest. 'I've really lost track of time today. I keep being surprised at how late it is. You're right; it is time we stop.'

'You have accomplished much, Empousa.'

Mikki smiled softly. It looked like he'd gotten over being pissed at her. 'That sounds like a compliment.'

He bowed his head in slight acknowledgment. 'Indeed.'

Since he seemed to be in an agreeable mood again, Mikki said, 'It would really be a help if you would check out the rest of the rose wall and let me know if there are any other parts of it that look weak. The thing is huge; it seems to stretch on forever. I want to make sure it's fertilized, but I also feel like it's important that we begin working on the roses in the gardens.'

'It is logical. The garden must have your care, too. I will inspect the wall at first light.'

She tried not to stare at the way the setting sun glinted red off the gleaming tips of his dark horns. 'Thank you. That would definitely save me time.' Then since he showed no sign of leaving, she added, 'I was thinking that it would be smart to have Gii or someone draw me up a map of the gardens and then I'd divide the area up into fourths – north, south, east, west – and have each of the Elementals take their direction and a group of women, and that would be the section of the gardens they'd be responsible for fertilizing and anything else I can see they need. I'll still go from section to section supervising, but at least dividing up the area might help organize things.'

'The idea has merit.' He seemed about to say more and then looked away as if he changed his mind.

'What is it? Hey – I'll take any advice I can get about this. Don't worry about stepping on my toes.'

His broad brow wrinkled as he looked from his thick cloven hooves to her slippered feet. Mikki burst into laughter, calling curious looks from several of the women. 'No! I didn't mean that literally. It's just a saying – stepping on my toes would be you offending me because you're giving me advice when I didn't ask for it.'

'Oh,' he snorted. And then, amazingly, the beast laughed. It was a full, rich sound that had the women of the realm staring openly at him.

'You're not laughing because you're actually considering stepping on my toes, are you?'

'Not now that you agreed the women should leave the forest.'

A joke? Was he actually kidding around with her? Well, wonders would never cease.

'Gii,' she called, not taking her gaze from his. 'Would you please tell the women that we are done for the day? Be sure you call the women in from the forest first. The Guardian would like to close the gate as soon as possible.'

'Yes, Empousa,' Gii said, sending the Guardian a nervous, sideways glance.

'Thank you, Mikado. I can never consider the realm safe while the gate remains open,' he said.

Wondering if this was the right time to ask him about the specifics of the dangers in the forest, Mikki bent to reach a pair of shears she had been deadheading roses with and the slim shoulder strap of her chiton slipped down her arm. Before she could shrug it back into place, she felt a prickle of heat run the length of her arm. As if in slow motion, the beast tilted his great head and deftly hooked the tip of one slender, ebony horn beneath the linen strap and then lifted it back to its proper place over her shoulder.

Their eyes met and held.

'I'm . . . I'm not used to wearing a chiton yet,' she stuttered.

'It becomes you.'

'Th-thank you,' she said breathlessly. Though her voice was little more than a whisper, the intensity of his dark, sensuous eyes compelled her to ask, 'Is that just more of you being the Guardian and doing your duty?'

His face, which had seemed so readable just a moment before, suddenly closed down. As if remembering himself, he took a quick step away from her. His voice was clipped and he didn't look at her when he spoke. 'My duty . . . yes. Caring for you is my duty.'

Mikki frowned. What the hell was up with him? His mood swings were wearing her out. So was the uncomfortable silence that had settled between them. She was searching for something . . . anything to say when he finally spoke.

'I could draw the map for you, Empousa.'

His voice was deep and as unreadable as his expression, but he looked at her and then quickly away, as if he had become suddenly, inexplicably nervous.

'A map?' she said stupidly and then she remembered. 'Oh! A map of the gardens so I could divide the area up among the Elementals. That would be great,' she said quickly. 'Why don't you give me time to get things wrapped up here and get cleaned up and then you meet me on my balcony? We can discuss the map while we have dinner. You could even bring your drawing supplies and sketch something out for me.'

'No!' The word rumbled from him, causing several heads to turn in their direction again. He lowered his powerful voice. 'No,' he repeated. 'It would not be proper.'

'I don't know why not,' she said easily. 'I have to eat; you have to eat. We need to talk about this, and the sooner the better so

I can give the new directions to the handmaidens first thing in the morning.' She wondered briefly at the certainty with which she felt she must push him. Did it have something to do with the callous way Gii had talked about him earlier? *It's time I stopped questioning myself and followed my gut!* she told herself firmly. 'But if you really don't want to come to my balcony – which I don't understand at all because you were just there last night – I could always have dinner brought to wherever you live. We could eat there while we dis—'

'I will come to your balcony!' he said hastily.

'Good.' She was careful not to show the rush of exhilaration she felt when he gave in. 'But don't forget that I have to finish up here and then take a bath or something because I am definitely a mess and—'

He held up one powerful hand to cut off her words.

'Would you rather I just called for you when I'm ready?' she asked sweetly.

'Call and I will come to you.'

Then he turned and stalked back to the gate.

'I think that went well,' she told the Felicite Parmentier shrub.

'I would give just about anything for a long, hot soak in a whirlpool bath,' Mikki said to no one in particular as the four tired handmaidens walked slowly back to the palace with her.

'Empousa, can you describe what you mean by "whirlpool bath"?' Nera asked.

'Absolutely – and you'll like this because it definitely has to do with water.' She grinned at the Water Elemental, who giggled in response. 'A whirlpool bath is a large tub of warm water that bubbles around you and almost magically soothes dirty, tired muscles,' Mikki sighed wistfully. 'It's possible through technology, which is my old world's version of magick.'

'I believe your new world can do better.' Gii smiled knowingly at the other handmaidens.

Nera added, 'We can certainly provide more for our Empousa than a tub of bubbling water.'

'It's true,' said Aeras.

'And if you would like it hotter than merely warm, I can arrange that,' the Fire Elemental said mischievously.

Gii took one of her hands and Nera the other. With renewed energy, the handmaidens hurried Mikki around the side of the palace that held her chamber and the curving balcony. They walked on a path that led between two rows of ornamental shrubs that had been trimmed into cones. The path turned and almost immediately fell away to reveal a wide staircase that spiraled gently to the right. Before they had reached the bottom, Mikki felt the temperature of the air get warmer and she smelled something that was vaguely familiar . . .

The stairs emptied on a white marble landing. Mikki stepped out onto it and gasped in pleasure. 'It's a hot spring!' But it was like no hot spring Mikki had ever seen. It was two levels. The first held the smallest pools – five of them, Mikki quickly counted. Each was roughly double the size of a modern whirlpool bathtub, and it was like each one had been hollowed out of the lumpy white rock by a giant ice-cream scoop. They were filled with lazily bubbling water so blue it was turquoise. From the lip of the tier, steaming water cascaded down to a larger pool. Mikki walked over to the edge and peeked down. The pool was deep and ringed by more of the white rock, and she could easily see through the clear water to the white sand of the pool's bottom.

'The upper baths are hotter than the large pool below,' Nera said. 'They should be perfect for soaking away your aches.'

'Amazing . . .' She breathed the word on a sigh. 'The only thing that would make it more perfect would be soap, clean clothes and lots of wine.'

The words had no more left her mouth than the patter of feet were heard on the stairs behind them. Wordlessly, Mikki watched several young women hurry onto the landing. Some of them were carrying trays of goblets and pitchers of wine. Others' arms were filled with clean lengths of fine linen, and still others had baskets packed with delicate glass bottles, soft sponges and brushes.

Gii laughed at Mikki's expression. 'Empousa, if you wish for a thing, it will appear. These women are palace servants whose sole responsibility is to be certain that Hecate's Empousa is well cared for.'

'Like magick,' Mikki whispered.

'Not *like* magick. It *is* magick. Your magick,' Gii said, gently unpinning the brooches that held her dirty chiton precariously at her shoulders.

'So my wishes are actually commands?' Mikki asked, feeling numb with shock as the servants placed their treasures on the landing, curtseyed and disappeared back up the stairs.

'They are,' Gii said.

'Good lord, what if I wish for something inappropriate?'

Gii looked searchingly into her eyes. 'I believe you are too wise for that, Empousa.'

She certainly hoped so. Good thing she'd be busy with hard physical labor for some time to come. Wishing for triple fudge cake late at night might not be classified as dangerously inappropriate, but without exercise, it would definitely be unwise.

Lost in thought, Mikki let the Earth Elemental unwind her from her chiton and, with a moan of pleasure, she slipped, naked, into one of the bubbling pools. Nera, Aeras and Floga had already poured five goblets to the rim with white wine the color of sunlight and dragged baskets filled with bottles and sponges over to within reach of each of the pools. Gii passed Mikki a goblet before she began to take off her own clothes.

'I'm so glad you chose this cold white instead of a red!' Floga said from the pool on Mikki's left. 'I was dreaming of this very wine all afternoon.'

'But I didn't . . .' Mikki began and then closed her mouth as she realized that, yes, she had been picturing in her mind a cold, refreshing white wine when she'd spoken. *Unbelievable . . .*

The icy wine was a wonderful contrast to the hot, bubbly water, and Mikki shivered in pleasure. She rested back against the smooth side of the pool and gazed at the beauty that spread before her. The springs were situated on the rear of the cliff on which the palace had been built. The view was spectacular. Mikki looked out across an area of the gardens filled with what appeared to be all the same type of rose. They had been planted in beds that each formed a spiraling circle, and even though Mikki knew that they, too, had to be sick, it seemed that these roses were greener and healthier than those in the rest of the realm. Beyond the beds of roses, she could see the thick multi-flora hedge, and past it the forest. The sun had already sunk beneath the leafy horizon, but the sky still held its dying colors. Mikki sipped her wine and let her eyes linger on the circular rose beds, appreciating the symmetry and style of the unique beds. She could just make out the hint of some blossoms, and it even seemed that a few of them had bloomed. They were scarlet, with a touch of gold at the base . . .

Mikki sat straight up, causing water to slosh over the smooth, white rocks around the pool.

'I wondered when you would notice,' Gii said softly.

'Have these beds always been filled with the Mikado Rose?'

'No. They change with each new Empousa. This area of the gardens is sacred to Hecate's High Priestesses. If you look carefully, you will see that in the middle of the central bed there is a small temple. It is your private shrine, a place in which you will never be disturbed.'

A sudden thought drifted through Mikki's mind like smoke, and almost without meaning to, she asked the question. 'Where is the Guardian's lair?'

'The entrance is beneath these springs. Hecate fashioned it there so his protection would never be far from her Empousa.'

Mikki could hear the frown in Gii's voice, and she turned to look at the handmaiden. 'You don't like him.'

'It is illogical to like or dislike him. He is a beast. It is simply his duty to protect the realm – his sole purpose for being.' Gii sounded unusually terse.

'She's worried that he will err again and cause the realm to become bespelled once more,' Floga said.

Mikki noticed that the Fire Elemental's expression was as cold and disapproving as her voice.

'You sound like you're worried about that, too,' Mikki said.

'I am.'

'And are the rest of you?' She looked from Nera to Aeras. Both Elementals nodded quick agreement.

'Okay, what exactly did the Guardian do that made Hecate so angry?' Mikki asked, wondering why she felt so damn annoyed at the handmaidens and so damn defensive of the Guardian.

When no one answered, she turned back to Gii. The hand-maiden squirmed and wouldn't meet her eyes. Mikki sighed. 'Will you please tell me what in the hell is going on? I mean, how terrible can it be? Hecate did finally let him return.'

Gii's gaze rose to meet Mikki's. Her eyes were bright and round with unshed tears. 'I cannot tell you, Mikado.'

'You've got to be kidding! Why in the world can't you tell me?'

'Forgive me – forgive us, but we are not permitted to speak of it. We shouldn't have said as much as we did.' Tears spilled down the little Elemental's cheeks.

'Please don't be angry, Empousa,' Nera said.

'She tells you only the truth, Empousa,' Aeras cried. 'We have been forbidden to speak of it.'

'Gii is right; I should never have mentioned it. Hecate commanded that it remain in the past. We may not speak of it ever again,' Floga said.

'Well, how about the Guardian? Will he talk about it?'

'Oh, Empousa, no!' Gii's face, which had been flushed from the bath, suddenly drained of its color. 'You must not speak of the past with him!' The other Elementals echoed her with horrified No's of their own.

'Okay, okay! I won't ask him. It's all right, Gii, please don't cry. Let's just forget I said anything about it,' Mikki hastily assured her, hating that she had caused the young women to become so upset. 'Here, help me figure out which of these bottles holds what. I don't want to accidentally pour oil instead of shampoo on my hair.'

Sniffing and wiping her eyes, Gii pointed out the soaps and oils in Mikki's basket. Mikki only half listened to her. Her thoughts kept circling around unanswered questions. Even after the warnings she still wanted to ask the Guardian what had happened. Not tonight, of course. Not so soon. But what if she got to know him better? Today he had actually smiled and joked with her. And touched her . . . she shivered, remembering how his horn had prickled the skin of her arm and how his eyes had seemed to see into her soul.

Admit it. He totally intrigues you.

It was true, but she squelched the thought, pulling her mind from the beast to the mystery that surrounded the realm he guarded. Hecate couldn't honestly expect her to live here and *not* want to find out what had happened that caused the sequence of events that led to her becoming the goddess's Empousa. Maybe the truth was that Hecate didn't want her to hear about it secondhand, like common gossip, and that was why she had forbidden the handmaidens to talk about it. Gii hadn't specifically said that the Guardian had been forbidden, too; she'd just freaked out and said not to ask him about the past. Well, it was obvious that the handmaidens, as well as the other women in the realm, tip-toed around the Guardian, vacillating between treating him like a rabid dog and a god.

She didn't think of him as either.

Mikki uncapped the cork from the bottle Gii had said was shampoo and poured a generous amount of it into her hair. As the night cooled, steam from the pools lifted in thickening waves, veiling each bather in warm mist. In a world of her own, Mikki inhaled deeply, noting that the soap was the same fragrance as the exotic perfume the old woman had given her. She finished washing and rinsing her hair and uncapped the other bottles, too. All of it – the soap, shampoo and oil – were the same rich fragrance.

'It is the anointing scent of the Empousa. None other may ever wear it.'

As each woman sipped wine and bathed herself, the pools had grown still, and Floga's voice startled her. Mikki peered at her through the steam and noted that the Fire Elemental's expression was odd – it was almost as if she looked angry.

'Do you wish you could wear it, Floga?' Mikki asked pointedly, lowering her voice so her words were for Floga alone.

The handmaiden instantly looked chagrined. 'No, Empousa! Of course not,' she whispered.

But as the handmaiden turned away, avoiding her eyes, Mikki wondered . . .

Chapter Nineteen

'No, thank you, Gii. I'll be fine. I'm going to eat a quick dinner and go straight to bed. I'm totally exhausted, and tomorrow will be another busy day.' Mikki smiled brightly, telling herself she wasn't really lying to Gii. She was just failing to tell her everything.

'But, Empousa, are you quite sure you wouldn't like me to help you into your nightdress?'

'No need.' Mikki glanced down at the simple yet elegant butter-colored dress. 'I think I'm finally getting the hang of the way these chitons wrap.'

Gii smiled. 'Did it serve as proper work attire for you today?'

'Actually, it did.' And Mikki meant it. After some initial awkwardness at getting used to tucking in the trailing skirts, she found that the outfit was comfortable and easy to work in, even if it had required some help from the Guardian to stay on straight. Actually, maybe it was because it had required his help that she liked it so much . . .

'So you like it better than the . . . jens?'

'Jeans.' Mikki laughed, forced her thoughts back to the girl beside her and gave Gii an impulsive hug. 'You know, I think I do like chitons better than jeans.'

Gii returned the hug with an affectionate squeeze. 'Then rest well, Empousa.'

'You, too, Gii. Why don't I call you and the other handmaidens as soon as I wake up, and we'll all have breakfast together? I have some new ideas I want to discuss with you.'

'As you wish, Empousa.' Gii curtseyed, and then skipped lightly to the balcony steps and away into the night.

Alone at last, Mikki had time to be nervous about the next part of the evening. As it had been last night, the little table was placed just outside the glass doors to her bedroom. It was, again, laden with meats and cheeses, bread and wine. Only one place had been set, but tonight there were two chairs instead of one.

Mikki frowned. He wasn't going to get away with this. She'd invited him to dinner, and dinner it would be.

She closed her eyes and thought about the servants who had magickally appeared when she'd wished for wine and soap and clean clothes. 'I need another place setting. Please,' she said.

In less time than she could count to ten, she heard two sharp knocks on her bedroom door. She stuck her head inside her room and called for them to come in, and one of the women she recognized from the hot spring hurried in, carrying a tray on which was another complete place setting. Mikki met her halfway across the room.

'I appreciate you coming so quickly.' Mikki held out her hands for the tray.

'I apologize, Empousa. Had I know you were not dining alone, I would have made certain the table was already set for two.'

'Don't worry about it. Actually, these are last-minute plans,' Mikki said quickly, hoping the servants could just tell when she wanted something and not when she was lying. 'I'll take it from here.'

The woman looked confused, but she nodded. 'Of course, Empousa. Shall we bring you more food and wine?'

'No. There's plenty. No need to bother.'

'It is never a bother to serve you, Empousa.'

Mikki reminded herself not to sigh. It might not be a bother for them to serve her, but she could already tell that such diligent service could very easily become bothersome.

Changing tactics, Mikki asked her, 'What is your name?'

The servant blinked in surprise. 'Daphne.'

'Daphne – that's pretty.'

The servant blushed.

'Daphne, I'll be fine carrying this to the table myself.' She took the tray from the disconcerted Daphne. 'But I'll definitely need you in the morning. I'm going to have breakfast with the four Elementals. Could you be sure to bring enough for all of us?'

'Yes, Empousa.'

'Wonderful! Now, you and, um, the rest of the women can relax tonight. I won't need anything else.' Daphne opened her mouth for what Mikki felt sure would be a protest, so she added firmly, 'Good night, Daphne. I'll see you in the morning when I call for breakfast.'

Reluctantly, Daphne curtseyed and left the room.

'A pain in the ass . . .' Mikki muttered to herself as she set the table. 'All this "Yes, Empousa, what can I do for you, Empousa?" might sound like a good idea in theory. In practice it is a pain in the ass.' *Of course it probably wouldn't be if I wasn't sneaking around like a teenager meeting a thug boyfriend against her parents' rules.* 'I'm not a teenager,' she told her reflection as she brushed through her drying hair. 'And he is not my boyfriend. This is no different from a business dinner.' She pressed a hand against her fluttering stomach. 'So stop being so damn nervous!'

The table was ready. She was ready – or as ready as she was going to be. Mikki walked to the balcony and sat down. She put her hands in her lap, closed her eyes, and thought about the Guardian . . .

. . . The way he had kept such careful watch over the women today . . . his laugh . . . the heat of his body when he was near her . . . his touch . . . and how alone he'd looked disappearing into the shadow of the tree instead of being included in one of their groups at lunch . . .

'Empousa, you look sad. Is anything amiss?'

She opened her eyes. He was standing, just outside the pool of light cast by the candelabrum that sat on the table.

'I'm not sad. I was just concentrating. I'm not used to calling someone by just thinking about him.'

'It is a gift given to each Empousa by Hecate.'

'Oh, I appreciate it – it'll just take some getting used to.' She motioned to the chair at the other end of the table. 'Please, join me. I don't think I realized how hungry I was until just now when I smelled this food.'

He stepped from the shadows slowly, as if giving her time to readjust to the sight of him. Mikki realized that she shouldn't stare – that she was being rude. But he was such an incredible being she couldn't just smile and make polite conversation and pretend like each new sight of him didn't send shockwaves through her mind. In the silence, his hooves rang against the marble, pulling her gaze down. He was wearing another short, military-looking outfit, which left much of his muscular legs bare. She noted that except for the fact that they were covered with a coat of slick fur, his legs were fashioned more like a human man than an animal. The leather breastplate molded to his chest and abdomen so it clearly outlined the definition of his muscles, which were completely manlike. *No*, Mikki mentally corrected herself, *no normal man could have a chest like that. He's not stone anymore, but he looks like he could have been carved from marble.*

She realized he'd reached the table and stopped and was just standing there, letting her study him. Mikki felt her face heat with an embarrassed blush.

'What is that called?' she blurted, trying to cover for her rude staring.

'Empousa?' His wide brow wrinkled in confusion.

'That leather top you wear. I'm new to all of this.' She lifted an edge of her own clothing. 'It was just this morning that Gii taught me that this is called a chiton. So I was curious about what yours is called.' She didn't think she sounded too terribly moronic. Maybe.

He looked down at himself and then back at her. 'It is a warrior's cuirasse.'

'Cuirasse,' she repeated the word. 'Is it over a chiton?'

'No, this is a short tunic. A warrior would not wear a chiton into battle.'

Because his expression seemed to tell her she was amusing him, she pointed to his bare legs. 'I'd think you'd need more covering for battle.'

His face hardened. 'I would, were I a man. For protection, Greek men go into battle with leather enemides strapped on their legs from ankle to knee.' He lifted one massive hoof and set it down with a heavy, dangerous sound. 'I do not require such protection.'

A little tremor that was fear mixed with fascination shivered over her skin. She looked into his dark eyes and was immensely proud that her voice sounded perfectly normal. 'Huh. Built-in protection like that must come in handy in your line of work.'

'Being Hecate's Guardian is not my work; it is my life.'

Mikki forced a little nonchalant laugh and started to lift a slice of cold meat onto her plate. 'You have no idea how many men in my old world say that about their jobs.'

'I am not a man,' he growled.

This time Mikki did sigh. Deliberately, she put down her fork and met his gaze. 'I'm well aware of that. Just like I imagine that you – as well as the rest of the inhabitants of this realm – are well aware that I'm not like any other Empousa. But am I all prickly about it? No. Do I feel the need to constantly remind you that I'm probably a good twenty years older than the norm, and that I'm totally confused by almost everything surrounding me? No. For two reasons: one, because it's annoying and, two, because bemoaning the fact won't change a damn thing. I mean, I could complain constantly about wanting to be taller or thinner, but that wouldn't ever change the fact that I'm five-seven and weigh' – she hesitated and reconsidered – 'ten pounds more than I wish I did.' She pointed to the chair with a sharp, frustrated motion. 'Now would you please sit down and have some dinner. I'm hungry, and when I'm hungry I get grumpy. So let's eat.'

To her surprise, he didn't snarl at her or whirl away. He sat.

Mikki picked up the fork and resumed loading her plate with a variety of the delicious selection of meat and cheese. Tonight they had added dark, flavorful olives and roasted sweet peppers as well as fresh, plump figs. She glanced up when she realized he was still just sitting there. Mikki raised one brow at him.

'I am unaccustomed to eating in the company of others,' he said slowly.

She didn't have to ask him why. Gii had already answered that question for her. The rest of the realm saw him as a beast, little more than a walking, talking animal. Even the goddess herself

205

had reminded her sternly that he had not ever been, nor would he ever be, a man.

Well, Mikki was different. No, he wasn't a man, but he wasn't an animal, either.

'Where I'm from it's mean-spirited to make someone eat alone while everyone else excludes him.'

'And you are not mean-spirited, Mikado.'

He didn't phrase it as a question, but she answered anyway. 'No. Sometimes I'm selfish and stubborn, and even cynical, but I can promise you that I've never been mean-spirited.'

As she spoke, something in his face changed. It was like she had somehow peeled away a protective layer that he kept wrapped around himself, leaving him terribly, unexpectedly, vulnerable. She remembered that awful, lonely roar she'd heard echoing from a dead statue all the way through a modern world and into her dreams. Mikki wanted to reach out and touch him, to tell him that everything would be okay, but she was suddenly afraid, and not of the fantastic beast who sat so awkwardly across the table from her. Mikki was afraid of herself.

She looked away from the raw emotion revealed in his eyes and busied herself arranging the food on her plate. Soon she heard the clanks and rattlings of cutlery, which told her that he, too, was filling his plate. Mikki filled her goblet with the cold white wine that was beading its pitcher and was pleased that it was the same excellent wine she'd had earlier at the springs. She glanced up at the Guardian.

'Wine?'

He nodded, and she poured. Then she lifted her own goblet and smiled.

'To the roses,' she said.

The Guardian hesitated. He made a small gesture with his hand and spoke a single word under his breath. Then he, too, raised his goblet. His powerful hand engulfed the delicate crystal, and he held it awkwardly, as if he was afraid of crushing it.

'To our new Empousa,' he said.

When she lifted the glass to her lips, she saw the perfect white rose blossom floating in the sea of wine. It hadn't been there before; he'd made it appear – for her. Mikki closed her eyes and drank, inhaling the sweet perfume that was the perfect accompaniment to the crispness of the liquid.

Later, she would remember it as the moment she began to fall in love with the beast.

Chapter Twenty

SHE'D wanted dinner to be easy and casual, but in truth, there were several awkward moments. The Guardian was silent and clearly self-conscious and uncomfortable. Which made total sense. He always ate alone. The entire realm considered him an animal, an outsider. How was he supposed to know anything about polite dinner conversation?

She was careful not to stare at him, because whenever she looked his way, he quit eating. Trying to make him more comfortable, she dispensed with the niceties of using knife and fork and picked up the meat and cheese with her fingers, purposefully chewing more noisily than was her norm. Still, he sat stiff and silent, eating little and drinking only when her attention was elsewhere.

Mikki glanced across the table and awkwardly met his eyes, then looked away quickly, for what seemed like the thousandth time. Too bad they didn't have a TV they could sit in front of or, at the very least, other diners they could eavesdrop on. He needed something to get his mind off the fact that he was sitting at dinner with her. And then she had it!

'The map of the gardens,' she said. 'While we're eating, you could sketch one for me.' Her mind was racing. 'I'll bet those little servants who bring dinner and such could scare up some paper and a pencil.' She'd stand by the door and not let them come in her room. They wouldn't even know he was here.

'I created it while I awaited your call.' He held out one massive hand and spoke a word that sounded like a growl mixed with vowels, and a rolled-up parchment burst into being in his hand. He offered it to Mikki, and she took it from him gingerly, half afraid it would disappear at her touch.

'You know, it's amazing the way you can make things appear like that.' She cleared her throat and, only half kidding, added, 'Could you teach me to do it?' It didn't seem possible, but in this world, who knew?

'I'm afraid you must be born the child of a Titan to have the ability to conjure inanimate objects.'

'That's too bad. It'd come in handy to be able to conjure up a hoe or pruning shears whenever I needed them instead of lugging them around.'

His lips tilted up in the hint of a smile. 'But I do not have the ability to call the Elements to me, or to cast Hecate's sacred circle.'

She smiled. 'There are definitely good things about being Empousa.'

'Agreed.' He lifted his wineglass to her again, and this time seemed more at ease holding the crystal goblet.

Mikki pushed some of the dishes to the edge of the table, making room for the wide parchment paper. She unrolled the Guardian's map and placed four of the smaller plates at each of its corners so she could study it. It was all done in what looked like quill and ink. He'd drawn a thick, wide, spherically shaped circle, which clearly represented the rose wall boundary. Within the boundary, created with amazing attention to detail, was the garden's blueprint. The palace was placed in the north. He'd even sketched in the southern-facing balcony on which they sat, as well as the cliff behind the palace where the springs were located and the unique beds of roses it looked out on, which were Mikki's private gardens.

Hecate's Temple was drawn in as a domed shape, with the enormous fountain beside it, which Mikki could see was, indeed, situated in the geographical center of the gardens. Spiraling out, like spokes on a wheel, he'd drawn bed after bed of roses nestling within a labyrinthine series of interwoven pathways.

She had expected the crude map equivalent of a stick-figure drawing, but he'd created something filled with detail and rich with beauty. Completely caught off-guard, she looked from the map to the creature who had drawn it with such obvious care and unexpected talent.

'Guardian, this map is wonderful! Not only does it have everything on it, so I can easily divide it into fourths and show the handmaidens exactly which area of the gardens I want each of them to be responsible for, but it's a great resource for me. Now I don't have to worry about not knowing my way around.' She couldn't help looking at his hands, which more closely resembled massive paws than an artist's delicate tools. 'How did you do it?'

For a moment he didn't answer and then, slowly, he lifted his left hand. It was man-shaped, but bigger, with thicker, more powerful fingers than even what she imagined would be normal for a pro football linebacker.

'They're really more dexterous than they look,' he said. 'I have spent centuries learning to wield them.'

Spreading his fingers, his hand quivered, and from each fingernail bed a long, pointed, talonlike claw extended.

'Shit on a shingle!' she gasped.

He barked a rough laugh. 'Is that a curse?'

She drew her spine up straight. 'Yes. A very bad one. I should watch my language, but you . . .' Her words ran out and she could only gaze at the five dangerous knives his fingers had become.

'I frightened you,' he finished for her.

'No,' she said quickly. 'You didn't scare me, you just surprised me.' She met his eyes. 'May I touch them?'

'Yes . . .' The word rumbled from deep within his chest.

She touched one of the gleaming claws. 'You're like Wolverine.'

'I'm like a small, mean-tempered animal?'

'No.' Fascinated, she stared at the claw. It felt cold and hard against the pad of her finger. 'It's the name of a fictional character who was created for something called comic books in my old world. Actually, he probably was named after the animal. He's a man who has special abilities. One of which is that he can make claws come out of his hands, like you can.'

The Guardian didn't take his eyes from his hands, where she was still tracing his claw with the soft warmth of her finger.

'And is this Wolverine a demon, shunned and rejected by the rest of the comic book characters?'

'He seems to get himself in more than his share of trouble, but he's really a man with a good heart who tries hard to do the right thing.' She finally raised her eyes to his. 'After you get to know him you understand that the only demon within him is the one he imagines in his own imperfections.' Mikki couldn't look away from him. His dark eyes devoured her sense of reason. Reality bent until it wasn't important what he was, as long as he kept looking at her like that – like she was his world.

With a little tremor, she felt his claws retract and she realized that her hand was resting within his. With a nervous laugh, she pulled her hand quickly to her side. 'So you actually use your claws as quills?'

'Yes, Empousa.' His expression hardened into unreadable lines again.

Mikki's stomach clenched. She didn't want him to retreat from her, so before she sat back down she reached over and placed her hand gently on his forearm. His eyes shot to hers, but he didn't speak, nor did he pull away from her touch.

'Thank you for this beautiful map. It is exactly what I need to organize the women tomorrow.'

'You are most welcome, Empousa.'

She smiled and then returned to her chair. 'I wish you would call me Mikki. I like being High Priestess, but there are times when I just want to be me.'

'If you would not mind,' his deep voice rumbled between them, 'I would prefer to call you Mikado. It is a lovely rose, and I find that it reminds me of you.'

She felt a thrill of pleasure at his compliment. 'I don't mind. I like the way my name sounds when you say it – like there's some kind of secret hidden within the word.'

'Perhaps there is,' he said.

'Perhaps . . .' she said. She was falling into his gaze again, losing herself . . .

'I should go,' he said abruptly, breaking their gaze and beginning to stand.

'Not yet!' Leaning forward, she caught his hand and felt the jolt that went through him when their flesh touched. 'Stay a little longer and have one more glass of wine with me.' When he relaxed back into his chair, she reluctantly released his hand and then busied herself refilling both of their wine goblets. 'I know I should be exhausted, and my body is, but my mind keeps going around and around with all the things I need to do tomorrow and all the things I should have gotten done today.'

'You accomplished much today. You should be pleased.'

I am. I'm just impatient to get to work on the rest of the gardens.'

He nodded. 'It is important that the roses heal and thrive. They are the foundation of our realm and its strength. It is dangerous for them to be unwell.'

'Can you tell me what it is in the forest that you're so worried about?' she asked quietly.

'Dream Stealers.'

'That's what Hecate called them, too, but I have no idea what that means. All I know is that you and she, and by the way the women who went into the forest stayed quiet and frightened looking, everyone in this realm believes they're dangerous. I get that, but I don't get what they are.'

'Dream Stealers take different forms, depending upon their victim. That is one reason they are so dangerous. The face they would show you would be different from the one they would show one of your handmaidens.'

'So they're physical beings?'

'They can take physical forms, yes.' He paused and studied her carefully. 'In your old world, there must have been Dream Stealers. Perhaps they just chose to personify yet another form there.'

She thought about the young gang members who were regulars in the ER until they inevitably ended up in the morgue or the state penitentiary – about the statistics that reported Oklahoma as one of the states with the largest number of teen pregnancies, as well as reports of child abuse – and about the ridiculously high number of Oklahoma women who lived in poverty.

'You're right. There are Dream Stealers in my old world. Young men throw away their lives; girls repeat cycles of abuse until they can see no way out; terrible things happen every day.'

'And what causes those things to happen? What is at the heart of those tragedies?'

'Hatred, ignorance, apathy,' she said.

'Exactly. And those are just some of the Dream Stealers that lurk in the forest of the crossroads between worlds. If they would enter our realm, they would be able to not simply destroy people's lives, but the dreams on which generations survive.'

'You'll keep them out, won't you?'

'I have sworn a life oath to do so.'

'You should have told me all this earlier.' Mikki shivered, feeling sick at the thought that she'd insisted he open the gate and let the women go into the forest. 'No, it's not your fault. You tried to tell me that it was dangerous; I should have listened to you.'

'You did what you believed was best for the roses. No harm was done; I was there to guard the gate. I will always be there to guard the gate.'

'But if those things are in the forest, why is there a gate at all? Shouldn't we seal it up and be sure it's never opened again?'

'We cannot. Mikado, not everything in the forest is evil. You should know that even dreams must be tempered with reality from time to time. Our reality comes from the forest and the threads of reality that drift there from the worlds beyond.'

'First thing tomorrow you'll check all the rest of the hedge to be sure no other area has been weakened by the roses being sick?'

'I will. You may rest easily, Mikado. The realm is safe under my protection.'

She knew what he said was the truth – she knew it because she felt it deep within her blood. All her intuition told her that this incredible man-beast would give his life to keep the Realm of the Rose, and its Empousa, safe.

'Thank you.'

This time instead of bristling at her appreciation, he simply bowed his head slightly.

For a while they sipped their wine, each lost in their own thoughts.

'May I ask you another question?' Mikki said.

'You may.' He was looking at her with an open, interested expression.

'When I asked you if you could teach me to conjure things, you said you couldn't because only someone born of a Titan had that ability. Just exactly who were your parents?'

He didn't respond to her question for a long time, weighing whether he should tell her his story, or whether he should stay silent and remain a mystery to her – a mystery that she would eventually tire of trying to solve.

The thought made him feel crushingly alone.

When he began to speak, his powerful voice was unusually subdued, and he could not look at her. Instead, he stared blankly out into the night.

'My father is the Titan Cronos. One day he visited the ancient island of Crete and was struck by more than the beauty of the land amidst sea. He saw and instantly fell in love with the fair Pasiphea. But she was no mindless maiden. Pasiphea knew that mortals who become lovers of the gods usually come to tragic endings, so she refused the Titan. Cronos was not dissuaded by her rejection – he waited and watched. When Minos, king of Crete, chose Pasiphea as his bride, my father saw his opportunity. On Minos's wedding night, he drugged the king and took his likeness, as well as his bride's virginity. Minos was fooled, as was Pasiphea. But Cronos's wife, Rhea, was not. She suspected her husband's infidelity and confronted Cronos. He denied loving Pasiphea. And in truth, he did not lie. Once he'd sated his

215

desire for the mortal woman, his love faded. Still, Rhea was not satisfied. She watched Pasiphea, discovering that the new bride was pregnant. In a fit of jealous anger, Rhea cursed Pasiphea's child. If, indeed, it was the son of a Titan, the child would be born not man or god, but an abomination, a creature like none other in the ancient world. That is how I came into being.'

'You *are* what the myth of the Minotaur was based on!'

Bottomless and empty, his eyes found hers. 'That is the name Minos gave me. He loathed me from the moment I was born.'

'And your mother?'

'Pasiphea was kinder than her husband. She even used to secretly visit me, and I remember when I was young, she sometimes sang me to sleep.' He paused, struggling to control his emotions.

'Your mother loved you.'

He flinched and felt as if her words physically hurt him. 'I like to believe that she tried to love me. She named me Asterius, refusing to call me by the name Minos had given me, but even in her kindness she could not forget that I was a beast. She knew that because of my monstrous form, Cronos had somehow been successful in entering her bed, the very thought of which was abhorrent to her. The sight of me was a constant reminder that the Titan had tricked her and invaded her body. So she persuaded Minos to build an enormous labyrinth, saying that in the center of it was where he should hide the fortunes of Crete, and that I would guard it for him. The labyrinth on Crete is where I lived, away from my mother's eyes and those who would hunt me for sport. It is where I would still be today if not for Hecate.'

'My God! They tell stories about you. Stories that say maidens and boys were sacrificed to you.'

The stunned expression on her face made him feel hot and cold at the same time.

'You should know that I have not always been as I am now. Before I answered Hecate's summons, I was as Rhea cursed me to be – an abomination, of both body and soul. When I pledged myself to the goddess, she lifted Rhea's curse and gave me the heart and soul of a man, though there was nothing even the Great Goddess could do to alter my physical form.'

His hand was resting on the table near the open map. The Empousa reached out and put hers on top of his. He looked down at her hand.

'I don't see an abomination when I look at you,' Mikki told him.

'Perhaps you should look deeper. There is still a beast within me.'

'I'd like to believe in the man, if you'll let me, Asterius.'

'The man . . .' His words were barely audible. He looked from her hand into her eyes. 'The man hears you, Mikado, even if it seems your voice is speaking from his dreams.'

'Maybe I am.' She smiled softly. 'You and I have been in each other's dreams before.'

He turned her hand over in his and let his thumb trace the delicate lifeline that bisected her palm, following it until it met the pulse point at her wrist. Then, with a caress softer than the brush of a butterfly's wings, he smoothed his thumb in sensuous circles over her pulse.

'I can feel the beat of your heart,' he murmured.

'Can you feel that it's beating faster?'

He lifted his eyes to hers. 'I can.' Her face was so close to his that he could feel the warmth of her breath on his skin. Her eyes had gone soft and her lips were parted. He wanted to taste her! He wanted to drink her in and lose himself in her sweetness. With a low growl he bent his head, replacing his thumb with his lips. He could feel her life's blood pulsing, and he tasted the salt of her skin. She shivered under his touch, and he let his lips move to the delicate indentation of her elbow. Then he lifted his head. Her breathing had deepened, and she was staring at him with wide, liquid eyes. Before reason and common sense could make him change his mind, he leaned forward and touched his lips to hers. She made a little gasping sound that seemed to call to his soul, and he deepened the kiss.

Pain lanced through his body. His blood had turned to white-hot lava, and it pounded with ferocious intensity within him. For a moment he was so disoriented that his claws automatically shot from his skin and he bared his teeth in a snarl, ready for the stealthy enemy that had attacked him. Then he understood. Hecate's spell!

The Empousa did not love him; therefore, her passion would not be allowed.

He raised tortured eyes to hers. Mikado looked pale and shocked, and she had scooted back in her chair as far away from him as she could get.

Abruptly, he stood, knocking over his chair and causing the little table to rock dangerously. 'This was unwise. I should not be here with you.'

'What's wrong? What's happened? You look like you're in terrible pain.'

She reached one hand hesitantly toward him, but he lurched away from her, not able to bear her gesture of kindness.

'You must not touch me!'

'Okay!' She dropped her hand shakily to her side. 'I won't touch you. Just sit down and tell me what's going on.'

'No.' He took another step back. 'I should have obeyed your command to create the map, delivered it to you, and returned to my lair.'

'I didn't command you to make the map. I asked you to, just like I asked you to have dinner with me. You didn't do anything wrong – *we* didn't do anything wrong,' she said, looking utterly confused by his sudden change.

'That is where you are mistaken. You did nothing wrong, but I did. Today I began to twist the threads of reality into a waking dream, something that, even in this realm of dreams and magick, is as impossible as it is dangerous. This cannot happen again.'

The Guardian flung himself from the balcony. With the agility of a beast and the power of a god, he distanced himself from her, and as he did the pain in his body subsided, leaving him exhausted and empty.

So this was what his life had come to. This was what it was to be. He was a man within a beast, tethered by a goddess. He was to know desire but not surcease. Like Tantalus, he was to live in torment – his relief in sight, but unattainable. Asterius stumbled to a halt, threw back his head and roared his agony to the deaf heavens.

Chapter Twenty-one

Mikki woke up with a headache and puffy, red eyes. Yawning and stretching, she walked to the wall of windows and opened the door. The sun was just starting to peek over the horizon, and the morning was so cool she could see her breath. Someone had already cleared away all the dishes from dinner. It made Mikki sad, as if the night before, the good along with the bad, had been wiped away without a trace. She walked over to the chair in which he had sat, her fingers lingering on the back of it.

Asterius . . .

He'd never be just the Guardian to her again, not after what he'd told her last night, and not after what she'd seen in his eyes – a soul-deep loneliness, and, for just a moment, a longing that struck an answering chord within her.

But it didn't matter that he'd given her a glimpse of his soul. Nothing could come of it. And not just because of the obvious – that he was a beast, or, more accurately, he was a creature, a mixture of mortal and god, a being like no other, as he had explained last night. *Asterius . . .* No. It wasn't because of the obvious; the obvious mattered less and less to her. If she was honest with herself, she'd have to admit that, even back in Tulsa when he'd first begun to seduce her in her dreams, his appearance hadn't been a deterrent. The truth was quite the opposite. His appearance had been a fascination from the beginning.

It was impossible between them because he was making it that way. It was as if there was some kind of unwritten rule that no one was allowed to get close to him. He'd touched her – kissed her – clearly desired her. Yet he'd run from her as if she was the one who was dangerous. His behavior was confusing and just plain annoying.

Mikki rubbed at her eyes again. Okay, maybe it *was* a rule. Maybe no one was allowed to be close to him. The smart thing to do would be to talk to Hecate about him. To ask the goddess about . . . about . . . about what? Did she really want to ask the imposing Hecate if it was okay that her new Empousa had a crush on the man-beast that was her Guardian? Please. Mikki wasn't an idiot. It wasn't okay. Asterius had made that clear. If she asked the goddess outright and Hecate commanded her to stay away from him, then what would she do? She'd have to keep her distance from him. Wouldn't she?

Better not to ask at all.

Was she actually considering pursuing him, even after what had happened between them the night before? Yes. Yes, she was. Mikki had no idea where it would take them, but she couldn't forget the physical jolt that passed through his body when she'd touched him. She rubbed her wrist absently, remembering the heat of his lips. And beyond his physical magnetism, she'd seen the vast loneliness that seemed to shadow his every unguarded expression, even as he rejected her touch. *But he's so used to being treated like an abomination that maybe his rejection is more about fear and habit than the desire to push me away.*

She needed to think more about where she was heading. She needed to think more about Asterius. Mikki shivered as the early morning breeze whipped through her sheer nightdress. The hot springs would be all dreamy and steamy on a cool morning like this . . . what better place to think?

Before she started down the balcony stairs to follow the path around the side of the palace, Mikki closed her eyes and sent Daphne a quick thought.

MIKADO was thinking about him as she bathed. He could sense it – feel it. Not because she was calling to him. It was nothing that specific. She was just *thinking* about him. He shouldn't be able to sense it. He shouldn't know. But he did.

This had never before happened. In all the eons he had been Hecate's Guardian, and all the generations of her Empousas who had presided as High Priestess within the realm, he had never felt the thoughts of one of Hecate's chosen.

Just as he had never felt the gentleness of any Empousa's touch. Not even the priestess he had loved ... and who he thought might possibly have loved him in return. No woman had ever touched him caressingly. He only had a vague recollection of his mother sneaking into the labyrinth a few times. One of those times he thought he remembered her touching his cheek. But it had been so long ago and such a brief caress. Yet this woman, this mortal from the mundane world, had not just touched him willingly. She had accepted his caress in return; she had shivered beneath his lips.

The touch of a woman ... such a small, ordinary thing, really. Mortals and gods alike thought little of it. They touched on greeting and on parting. They touched as they laughed and talked. They touched when they loved. Yes, such a small, ordinary thing ... unless it had been a thing denied. How he had longed for the kindness of a woman's touch to soothe the beast within and without.

Mikado's touch had undone him.

His moan of frustration changed to a rumbling growl as he propelled himself from his sleeping pallet. She had called him

Asterius and said she believed in the man within the monster. Then she had allowed him to kiss her! Surely she meant nothing more than kindness. She couldn't realize that her touch and her words were seducing the man as well as calling the beast to her. His hooves cut into the marble floor of his lair as he paced. She couldn't know how desperately he had wanted to kneel at her feet and beg her never to stop touching him . . . thinking of him . . . talking to him as if she truly did believe in his humanity.

And then what? In the spring she must be sacrificed. In despair, he looked down at his hands as his claws extended. He could still feel the softness of her skin against their razorlike tips. Would he allow her to escape, as he had the deceiver who had come before her? No. He could not. The roses were sick, and he had little doubt as to why. Their last Empousa had fled without completing her destiny. What would happen to the realm if this one did the same?

He knew what would happen. It wouldn't survive.

If he would be the only one to pay the price, he would gladly do so. He knew it for truth, even though the thought shamed him. It meant he was willing to betray his goddess again. But no matter how desperately he longed for Mikado, he would not allow his own desires to cause the destruction of the Realm of the Rose.

His growl deepened, and he had to fight against the urge to rend and tear. The man within him held the beast at bay, but only just. The ache and yearning for the impossible that caused his emotions to be in turmoil also roused the monster within. She might believe in the man, but he was joined with the beast – they were one in the same. If she stirred the man, the beast roused. He had to remember that no matter how sweetly she may speak his true name, or how sweetly she might touch him and let him touch her, she would be imagining the man. What would happen when she realized that she was seducing the beast, too?

She would reject him. Anything else was only a dream. And he, of all creatures, knew how insubstantial dreams really were. He must forget the dream and deal in reality, which was what he did best.

And none of this mattered. He could not love her – he could barely touch her without feeling the raging pain of Hecate's spell.

Asterius's head suddenly lifted and his eyes widened. That was it! He didn't have to hold the beast at bay. The goddess had tethered the monster for him. He could stay as close to Mikado as she would allow; the goddess's spell would ensure that he never went too far . . . all he need do would be to bear some pain. When it became too much, too unendurable . . . he remembered the feel of her skin against his lips and her small hand within his. Yes, he could endure a taste of the goddess's punishment for the miracle that was the touch of Mikado's skin.

If she allowed him near her again. He resumed his frustrated pacing. After the way he'd left her last night it would be understandable if she avoided his company completely.

But perhaps she would not always avoid him. She was so different, so unlike any of the other women. She had asked him if he would seal the gate! No other Empousa would ever have asked such a thing. Of course, she didn't know her fate. Didn't know that her only escape from it was through the rose gate and back to the world of the mundane that lay beyond the forest. Part of his mind whispered that even if she knew, she might still choose to stay for the roses . . . for him . . .

He went to the mouth of his lair. The sun was calling the sky awake with young tendrils of light. He could feel Mikado's thoughts slide away from him as she left the baths and then he could no longer feel her at all. He imagined that she was preparing to summon the Elementals and begin her day. He, too, must begin his. She had asked him to inspect the rose wall, and her request had been a wise one. He left his lonely lair and began his solitary trek along the boundary between worlds.

Choosing to remain invisible, Hecate watched her Guardian. His powerful stride was weary, and she clearly saw the strain of conflicted emotions in his dark, expressive eyes. The goddess smiled and let her hand absently caress the head of one of her great hounds.

'It goes well . . .' she whispered.

'SEE how I've divided the gardens into fourths?' Mikki had hated to tamper at all with Asterius's map, but it was necessary that everything be clear for the Elementals, so she'd had Daphne bring her a quill and some ink, and she'd drawn her own considerably less-attractive lines to quarter the blueprint. 'As I said before, each of you will take the area that corresponds to the direction of your element. Nera, you'll be west; Aeras, east. Gii and Floga will, of course, be north and south. You'll each have your own group of women. Start by fertilizing the beds, like I showed you yesterday. I'll make my way through each area, checking to see if the roses need any other special attention. Do you have any questions about your areas?' Mikki asked the four Elementals. As she'd done the night before, she'd pushed the dishes aside and spread Asterius's map out on the dining table. The handmaidens were gazing at it raptly.

'This is a lovely map, Empousa,' Gii said, touching the delicate sketch that represented the realm's central fountain.

'And accurate, too,' Aeras said. 'I think every one of the paths have been duplicated here.'

'Your baths are even drawn in,' Nera said, obviously delighted with the squiggly water lines that represented her element.

'Who did this for you, Empousa?' Floga asked.

Mikki lifted her eyes from her own contemplation of the map to meet the Fire Elemental's sharp gaze.

'The Guardian drew it for me,' Mikki said, careful to keep her voice casual, her expression placid.

'The Guardian!' Gii exclaimed. 'But how could he have—'

'She commanded it,' Floga interrupted the Earth Elemental. 'He would do whatever she commanded.'

Unruffled by her odd tone, Mikki said, 'Actually, I didn't *command* him. I just asked.' She lifted a shoulder. 'That's all. Apparently it wasn't that big of a deal. He has claws that he can extend and use as built-in quills. And he's been here for ages. No wonder he knows all the nooks and crannies of the realm.' She gave Floga a tight smile. 'But thank you for reminding me. I do need to command him to come here. I asked him to inspect the rest of the rose wall and make sure there are no other weakened parts of it we need to pay special attention to.' Mikki didn't need to close her eyes to concentrate on him. After last night, he never seemed to be far from her thoughts. She turned her back to the handmaidens and looked across the gardens. 'Come to me, Asterius,' she whispered into the wind.

She only had time to wonder if he minded that she called him by the name his mother had given him, before the pressure of the air on the balcony changed. It felt heavier and thick against her skin. Then she heard his hooves pound forcefully on marble as he climbed the balcony stairs. Though his stride was powerful, that unmistakable mixture of animal and man with which he moved, Mikki thought he looked tired and was almost as annoyed as she was disappointed when he bowed and spoke formally to her without meeting her eyes.

'You commanded that I come to you, Empousa?'

'Yes. I was hoping you'd had a chance this morning to inspect the rest of the rose wall.'

'I have, Empousa.'

'And?'

'I see no area that appears particularly weak except that which surrounds the gate.'

'So you agree that we can focus on the roses within the garden?'

Finally, he met her eyes. 'Yes, I am in agreement with you.'

'Good,' she said briskly, ignoring the fluttering he caused deep in her stomach. She turned to the handmaidens. 'So each of you collect your group of women and set up your own line of fertilizer baskets. Prepare the beds just like we did the area around the roots of the multiflora roses. I'll visit each area, and we'll go from there.'

'Yes, Empousa,' the Elementals chorused. They curtseyed and began to leave the balcony, along with the Guardian.

'Floga, Guardian – I need to see the two of you,' Mikki said.

Mikki thought that though the Fire Elemental had carefully arranged her face into a blank expression, her eyes gave away her uneasiness at being singled out. *She doesn't trust me.*

'Floga, your area of the garden is the section that is most southerly. This happens to include the rose gate. I know it would be quicker for your women to go to the forest and use the loam for fertilizer as we did yesterday, but I'm concerned about having the gate open again today.'

Floga looked surprised, and Mikki couldn't really blame her. Just yesterday she'd insisted, in front of everybody, that Asterius keep the gate open, danger be damned. Mikki looked at him. 'What do you advise?'

'I believe you are wise to be concerned about reopening the gate so soon,' he said.

'So we are agreed that maybe in a day or two Floga can allow the women to collect more loam, but right now it's not a good idea?'

'Yes, Empousa. We are in agreement.'

'Good.' She knew the smile she gave him was obvious in its warmth, and she could feel the handmaiden's eyes watching her every expression, but she didn't care. Let them all know she valued the Guardian's judgment. She would not treat him like an animal when he was not one, and neither would they. Not while she was Empousa. There was a new boss in the realm, and they'd better get used to it. Still smiling, she turned to Floga. 'Do you understand what I need you to do?'

'Yes, Empousa.'

'Good. Then you're free to get started. The Guardian and I will be along shortly.'

Floga's eyes widened, but she said nothing as she curtseyed and then hurried from the balcony, leaving the priestess and the beast alone.

'Good morning, Asterius,' Mikki said softly.

And that was it. The sound of his true name on her lips undid him. He could not fight his desire for her and his need to be in her presence. Despite the spell Hecate had placed upon him and the pain it would cause him, come spring or come the very gates of the Underworld, for as long as they had together he had to hear the sweet sound of her voice and, if fate granted it, feel the touch of her hand again.

'Forgive me, Mikado.'

'For what?'

'For the way the night ended. I have no practice in . . .' He paused, struggling for words he'd never before spoken.

'There's nothing to forgive,' she said. 'It's hard to know the right thing to say or do, especially when you're faced with a completely new situation. Sometimes it's easier to run away.'

'That makes me sound like a coward.'

She smiled. 'No, it makes you sound human.'

He looked shocked, and then, slowly, his lips turned up into a smile that eventually reached his eyes. 'You are an extraordinary woman, Mikado.'

'Well, let's see if you still think so at the end of the day.'

He raised a questioning brow.

'I'm going to put all those muscles of yours to work. Tonight you'll be too tired not to sleep.'

His dark eyes caught hers. 'You knew I didn't sleep last night?'

'Don't be too impressed by my powers of observation. It doesn't take a goddess to figure it out. You look pretty rough this morning.'

'And I am usually so handsome,' he said dryly.

She gasped. 'Do not tell me that you just made a joke!' Mikki's laughter floated musically on the breeze as the two of them made their way from the balcony. Neither noticed the women who peered wide-eyed from the palace windows, watching them go.

Chapter Twenty-two

MIKADO hadn't been exaggerating when she'd said she was going to put his muscles to work. Asterius had never lifted so many baskets or dug so many holes in all the long centuries of his immortal life.

And he'd never been so happy.

He'd been working beside Mikado all day. She actively supervised, which meant she did not shy from even the dirtiest of jobs. He could tell that the women of the realm were not pleased with the messy, tiring tasks she had given them, but they were visibly pleased that their Empousa was right in the middle of the mess with them. She worked twice as hard as they did; she seemed to be everywhere at once. And perhaps most surprisingly, she was cheerful about the work. The High Priestess appeared to actually enjoy getting her hands in the dirt as she demonstrated exactly how the earth needed to be worked around the roots of the bushes. She didn't shy away from the rank fertilizer; she did the opposite. The Empousa helped scoop it into the dirt and even laughed and made jokes about the irony that such a horrid smell could make sweet roses thrive.

He ignored the looks the women gave him. He was used to it. No matter how often he walked amongst them, the women of the realm were always uncomfortable around him. More so now than ever before. They all knew what he had done and the rage his actions had evoked from their goddess. They, too, had paid for his error. They hadn't been encased in stone and banished from the realm, as he had. They had only to wait . . . without aging . . . without changing . . . unable to do more than watch time pass around them for all the centuries he slept. He could only imagine how disturbing it must be for them to see him beside their new Empousa, especially when she made it clear that she appreciated his opinion and she treated him like . . .

Mikado treated him as if *he were a man.*

What a true and wondrous miracle she was. And she did stay in his presence – or rather, he stayed in hers. She began the inspection of the roses in the east, and after thoroughly examining all of the beds, with Aeras promising to follow each of her directions, she had moved to the south.

He would never forget how he'd stood there pretending to be busy piling empty baskets easily within the women's reach as Mikado waved a bright farewell to the little Wind Elemental. He thought he would stay there in the east and continue working, that perhaps later in the day he would catch a glimpse of her as she moved amongst the plants, but she'd had other ideas. When she'd realized he wasn't leaving with her, she'd marched right back to him and said, 'I need you to stay with me. I would very much appreciate your help today.'

'Of course, Empousa,' he'd said formally, but the joy that had rushed through him hadn't been formal and he hoped she could see its reflection within his eyes. As they'd hurried away from Aeras and her women, Mikado's palla had fallen from her shoulders and snagged on a nearby rosebush. Deftly he had extricated it and then placed it back around her, letting his palms rest against the roundness of her shoulders until he felt the stinging burn of pain.

But when she smiled up into his eyes, he forgot the pain and remembered only the warmth of her skin against his hands. Little wonder the handmaidens' eyes followed them wherever they went. He couldn't keep his hands from her, and she . . . she *smiled* at him, often taking obvious pleasure in his company.

It had taken Mikado longer to inspect the southern section of the gardens. The roses were more ill there, though he didn't need to look at the plants to know that. Watching Mikado become grim faced and pale told him more than inspecting the rose-bushes ever could.

Midday came quickly. He was readying a bed of wilting, multicolored roses called Masquerade for their baskets of fish entrails fertilizer when he caught the scent of food. He didn't look up when the women from the palace arrived with the midday meal. He kept working. The most uncomfortable part of the day before had been at exactly this moment. The women had separated into their little groups to talk and laugh and eat together – things that were denied him. He could guard them, but he would not be accepted by them, not enough to share a simple meal with them. Last night Mikado had granted him a great gift when she'd shared her table with him, and he silently cursed himself for ruining the evening.

He could hear the women breaking for the meal. They grouped around the fountains in the area, letting the garden's clear water wash their hands free of dirt. Their laughter came easily, and it mixed musically with the sound of the tinkling fountains. He wondered where Mikado was – probably in the middle of the laughter. She laughed readily, and the women of the realm responded well to her. He hoped she was busy, distracted enough that she would not notice him and see how they shunned him. He did not want her pity.

He knew one of the palace servants would soon find him and offer him food and drink – not because she wanted to, but because it was her assigned duty. Without looking around, he slipped from the rose bed in which he'd been working and headed toward the rose gate. A large tree sat near it, under which he could call its shadows to him and attempt to cloak himself from prying eyes. There he would rest and perhaps drink some of the wine the servant would offer him. Of course he was hungry, but he would not eat. He could not stand their stares. It was as if they expected him to fall to his haunches and tear at the food with his teeth. Perhaps he should! That would cause quite a stir amongst them. No . . . he stifled a weary sigh. It would cause nothing more than a reinforcement of their belief that he was, indeed, a mindless, heartless beast.

'There you are!' Mikado hurried up to him, a little out of breath. 'Good thing you're so tall or I would never have found you out here.'

He stopped and looked down at her. She was carrying a large basket. Her hands and face were wet, as if she had just washed, and as she smiled up at him she used a fold in her dirt-speckled chiton to wipe a trickle of water from her cheek.

'I completed readying the bed of Masquerade. What is it you would have me do next?'

'I'd have you eat!' She grinned, nodding at the well-laden basket. 'I made sure this one had enough for both of us.'

He wondered if she could hear the blood rushing in his veins, pumping shock and disbelief through his body. He drew a deep breath. When he spoke, he struggled to keep his voice low and for her ears alone.

'You should eat with the women, Mikado.'

'No. They've already formed their little cliques. If I butted into one, it would just be awkward, kinda like eating with the boss who crashed a workers-only party. And as many orders as I've given them today, I'm sure they need a break from me. Plus, I'd rather eat with you,' she finished simply.

'But it has never—'

'Stop!' she interrupted, causing several of the women's heads to turn their way. In a more sedate, but no less firm voice, Mikado continued. 'I'm tired of hearing what hasn't been done before. I'm Empousa now and things are going to be different, and not just with the roses.'

'As you wish, Empousa,' he said, using comfortable formality to cover his turbulent emotions.

'Good. Let's go eat under that tree you disappeared beneath yesterday. I want to take another look at the gate anyway.'

'As you say, Empousa.' He began to walk toward the ancient tree that shaded the area near the rose gate, careful to shorten his stride so she didn't have to struggle to keep up with him.

When they got to the tree, he felt a rush of relief when he saw that no group of women had chosen to eat nearby. With a long sigh, Mikado sat and leaned her back against the wide trunk of the oak and gazed at the rose gate.

'It doesn't look any better than it did yesterday,' she said.

'It also does not look any worse.'

'I suppose that's something. You know, I don't sense anything horrible coming from the forest. If you hadn't told me about the danger there, I wouldn't have thought the forest was anything more than an old, dark woods.'

'Dream Stealers choose their time carefully to appear. Remember to be on your guard always when you are near the gate or in the forest itself.'

'But you'll be with me, won't you? I mean, I can't open the gate.'

He raised a brow at her. 'Of course you can, Empousa.'

Her eyes widened as she looked from him to the gate and back to him again. 'I'll be careful,' she said. Then she turned her attention to the basket of food. 'Let's worry about the forest later. Now, let's eat.'

Hesitating only a moment, he sat and made an almost imperceptible gesture that caused the shadows around them to thicken. He wanted to be able to watch her without schooling his expression, and that was not something he would do if the other women could easily see them.

'You look tired,' he said.

'So do you,' she countered as she pulled a wineskin from the basket and then took a long drink.

'Your face is pale, Mikado.'

'That doesn't surprise me.' She tossed him the wineskin and then began taking cheese and bread from the basket. Mikado glanced up at him. 'Drink,' she ordered.

He drank, thinking that he could taste the essence left by her lips, and that lingering touch was more intoxicating than wine could ever be. Then he realized what she had said and commanded himself to stop daydreaming.

'Why is it that you are not surprised by your pallor?'

'The roses in this part of the garden are sicker than the ones in the east,' she said between bites.

'Yes, I thought so, too.'

'Somehow I'm connected to them. They make me feel sick, too.'

'I guessed as much. You seemed to change when we entered this part of the gardens.'

'Do you know if this has happened to any other Empousa?'

'Each Empousa has a special bond with the roses,' he said slowly. 'It is in the blood of Hecate's High Priestesses.'

'I already know that. Even back in Tulsa I had a connection to roses, and so did all the women in my family. We always have. It's – it's a kind of family tradition.'

He thought she looked uncomfortable. Perhaps she missed her family? Or her old world? The thought made his chest feel tight. Could there be a man for whom she was pining? Is that why she suddenly sounded so awkward when she mentioned her old life? Before he could consider asking, Mikado continued.

'But what I want to know is have any of the other Empousas felt things because of the roses?'

'They may have, but I would not have known. The other Empousas rarely spoke to me.'

She looked surprised. 'But you're Guardian of the realm. Didn't they need to talk to you about' – her hand fluttered in the direction of the rose wall – 'protection and whatnot?'

'Each Empousa knew I would do my duty. None felt the need to speak with me about it. If an Empousa felt that any danger approached, she would call for me. Other than that, we rarely had the need to speak together.' He thought of the Empousa who had come before Mikado and realized, again, shame at the ease with which she had fooled him into believing she might care for him. That for generations the Empousas had shunned him, taken his guardianship for granted, had been precisely the reason her ruse had worked so easily on him. One or two kind words and he had been blind to anything except the chance that she might show him another kindness.

Could that be what was happening with Mikado? Was he still so desperate for a woman's gentleness that he was becoming lost in yet another game?

But what game? Mikado did not know her destiny, so she had no reason to falsely seduce him.

'Asterius?'

The sound of his true name broke into the turbulence of his thoughts. 'You must not call me that when any of the women might overhear you.' His voice sounded rougher than he had intended, and he hated the hurt that was reflected in her eyes.

'I'm sorry. I should have asked if you minded that I call you by your given name.'

'I do not mind.' He met her gaze, willing her to read within his eyes all that he was feeling and all that he could not find words to say. 'It is just that to the rest of them, I prefer to remain Guardian.'

'I understand,' she said.

'Do you? Do you know what power there is in a true name?'

'No,' she said softly, 'tell me its power.'

'When you speak my true name, I hear it not with my ears, but with my soul. With that one word, you touch my soul, Mikado.'

'The soul of a man, Asterius.'

'So the goddess tells me,' he said.

'You don't believe her?'

'I would never lack belief in Hecate,' he said quickly.

'Then it's yourself you don't believe in,' Mikado said.

He looked away from her too-knowing gaze and didn't answer for several moments, during which he unconsciously flexed and contracted his claws over and over. Then, reluctantly, he said, 'Perhaps it is the man inside the monster in which I have trouble believing.'

Then it was her turn to be silent. He could feel her thoughts. He couldn't actually read them, but he knew that she was thinking of him . . . considering . . . weighing her response.

'Maybe you need someone else to believe in the man, so you can quit seeing nothing but the monster.'

The meaning of her words jolted Asterius, and hope surged so sweetly within him that he felt the beast shiver in response. 'How can you see anything but the monster?' The depth of his emotions made his voice rumble with the force of a growl, and even though he noticed that this time she didn't flinch away from him, he struggled to regain control. Through gritted teeth he said, 'Look at me. Listen to me. I cannot even gentle my voice to speak soft words to you! There is little that is manlike in my appearance.'

'Then I suppose I'll just have to look deeper than your appearance.'

The smile that tilted her full lips made his heart beat painfully against his chest. He wanted to pull her into his arms and crush her to him. But he could not – not here and now, and perhaps not ever. But he could touch her. Just for an instant . . .

Asterius lifted his hand and let his fingers brush the side of her cheek. 'Mikado, you make me believe that I still dream,' he murmured as gently as possible.

She met his eyes. 'Sometimes I think that would be nice. Gii told me that I have the power to weave dreams. Maybe I'll figure out how to weave one for us.'

His fingers began to sting, and reluctantly, he took them away from her face. She sighed, as if she, too, was disappointed that he wasn't still touching her. Then she gave herself a little shake.

'Dreams are for later. Right now let's hurry up and eat. I'm still not done here, and I really do want to check in with Nera and Gii before it gets too dark.'

So amazingly, he and Mikado ate the midday meal together within sight of many of the women of the realm, who did often steal looks in their direction, trying hard to peer through the shadows of the ancient oak.

His inhumanly acute hearing caught the sound of the Elemental approaching before Mikado noticed her, and he surreptitiously motioned for the shadows under their tree to lighten. Then he stood and moved aside, purposefully giving the appearance that he might only be there to wait on the Empousa's next command instead of sitting close beside her, sharing an intimate meal.

'Empousa, the women have finished their meal,' Floga said after sliding a narrowed glance at the Guardian.

'Good! We're done here, too.'

Then, very deliberately, Mikado held out her hand to him. Asterius hesitated only an instant before taking it in his own and helping the priestess to her feet. She smiled and thanked him as if he were a man accustomed to the touch of a woman's hand. Then she turned to the staring Fire Elemental.

'Let's get back to work.'

Chapter Twenty-three

'I'M glad the palace is situated in the north so Gii and her group of women are in charge of the roses surrounding it,' Mikki told Asterius as they watched the Earth Elemental pass the word to her women that they were done for the day.

'It's obvious that you and she are becoming friends,' Asterius said.

'Yes, we are,' she said, thinking that it was just as obvious that the Elemental was uncomfortable with her Empousa's familiarity with the Guardian.

'It's not surprising that the two of you are compatible. Earth and roses fit naturally together.'

'You're right – they do.'

Gii would just have to get used to having Asterius around. Mikki didn't think it would be too tough for the Elemental to do that. All she needed to do was to quit thinking of him as a beast, and she'd soon see what Mikki saw – the man within. It hadn't been that hard for her. How difficult could it be for the rest of them?

'I should go now, Mikado. The handmaidens will want time alone with you, and there are duties to which I must attend.'

She looked up at him, surprised that she could be sad to part from him after spending the whole day in his company. She usually got sick of being around a man in less than half that time. 'Will you come back?'

Mikki watched his eyes darken and he said, 'If you call for me, I will come to you.'

'Then I'll call,' she said.

He bowed formally to her just as the four handmaidens approached them. Mikki noted how each of them looked obviously relieved when Asterius turned and disappeared into the shadows of the darkening garden. She pushed down the annoyance she felt. They had worked hard today; they were all tired. And it really would be unreasonable of her to expect the women to change the way they felt about Asterius in just a couple of days. The other Empousas had treated their Guardian like an animal; it was logical, then, that was how the women of the realm would treat him. Mikki would just have to lead by example. They were smart girls – they'd catch on.

'Are you four as ready for a long soak as I am?'

THIS evening was even cooler than the one before, and steam from the baths veiled everything in a warm, damp mist. Mikki leaned back against the smooth side of her private bath and fed herself another grape. She was pleasantly full and a little tipsy from the wine. She hadn't planned on having dinner with the women. She'd planned on taking a quick bath and then retreating to her room and another private dinner with Asterius, but the women had been hungry, and, after all, who could bathe quickly when the 'tub' was this spectacular and the company was so enjoyable?

And Mikki was sincerely enjoying the company. The handmaidens were tired after another long day, but they didn't whine or complain. Instead, they talked about the work they'd done in their separate areas and asked Mikki countless questions about rose care. Already plans for tomorrow were discussed.

The fertilizing would continue, but some women would begin deadheading old blooms or blossoms that looked like they were too far gone to ever open. Mikki agreed to show the Elementals examples of both in the morning.

'I think we've conquered the hardest part of what we need to do to coax the roses into recovery. Most of the fertilizing will be finished tomorrow. Then we'll focus on the deadheading and cutting off of any useless canes. After that, we just keep an eye on them and wait.'

'How long before they begin recovering?' Gii asked.

'It doesn't take long for a good fertilizer to start working, especially if all that's wrong with the roses is that they needed to be fed. We should see a change in them soon.'

'And if we don't?' Floga asked.

'Then I try something else. I have more tricks up my sleeve.' She raised her wet, naked arm and wiggled it around, causing the young women to giggle.

'Perhaps you should cast a health spell for the roses,' Nera said. 'You know, as you would if one of the women of the realm asked you to cast a spell to rid her of a persistent ague.'

'It is a good idea,' Areas said.

'It certainly couldn't do any harm,' the Fire Elemental said as she nibbled at a fig.

'And it might very well do a great deal of good,' Gii added.

Feeling totally out of her realm of experience, Mikki wished desperately that her new job/destiny had come with an owner's manual.

'It would be like the self-initiation ritual. The four of us will be there when you cast the sacred circle and then you simply follow your heart.' Gii's smile was filled with kindness. 'You'll know what to do, Empousa.'

'You may as well begin with a spell for something you know as intimately as roses; it will be easier that way. And anyway, it's only a matter of time before the women in the realm begin coming to you for the typical love spells and such,' Floga said.

'She's right, Empousa,' Gii said.

'Love spells and such?' Mikki sputtered.

Aeras sighed wistfully. 'Love spells . . . it has been so long.'

'Too long!' Floga said.

'Actually,' Nera began hesitantly, 'I have been wondering. If perhaps – well, if you might . . .' The little Water Elemental paused. She looked nervously at the other handmaidens, who nodded encouragement. She sank a little lower in the steaming water, as if drawing strength from her element, and then she finished in a rush, 'I wondered if you might agree to cast an invitation spell for me and, well, a few others.'

Mikki noted the pink flush that colored the Elemental's cheeks, and she didn't think it was from the warm water.

'I'd be happy to cast an invitation spell for you and your friends. But what are we inviting and where?'

'The what is men,' Nera said shyly, her cheeks turning from pink to red.

'And the where is here,' Floga purred.

'Huh,' Mikki said. 'I was going to ask about the absence of men.'

'There are no men in the Realm of the Rose,' Gii said.

'You mean except for the Guardian,' Mikki said.

Gii frowned. 'The Guardian is not a man. He is a beast.'

Mikki opened her mouth to protest, but Floga was already speaking. 'There are no men in the realm because they can only come here if the Empousa sends an invitation spell to the ancient world. There has been no Empousa in the realm; hence no men have been invited.'

Mikki stared at the Fire Elemental. 'Are you telling me that for as long as the Guardian was banished and the Empousa gone you have been here without any men?'

'Yes,' the Four Elementals said together.

'How long has it been?'

For a moment no one answered her. Then Gii whispered, 'It has been a very long time, Empousa.'

And she thought her love life sucked. She was queen of romance compared to these girls.

'Then I'll definitely do an invitation spell. A big one – right away.'

Gii laughed. 'Tomorrow will be soon enough, Empousa. Tonight we are too tired to have the invitation be of much use to us.'

'Then tomorrow it will be. How about we only work till midday and then I'll cast a circle and try a little spell work?'

'Just don't make my invitation little,' Floga gibed. '*Little* men do not interest me, even after all this time.'

Nera giggled and flicked her wrist at the Fire Elemental, causing water to spew from her bath all over Floga. Gii called her too hot-blooded, and Aeras joked that if Floga needed a breath of cold northern wind she could certainly provide it for her. Mikki smiled and watched their good-humored play, but her mind was not on the handmaidens. She thought instead of bronze skin, a deep, powerful voice, and how candlelight looked glinting off ebony horns.

WOULD she always be nervous before she called him? Mikki looked around the balcony, for the zillionth time checking that she was alone. The table was ready. It was set with a pitcher of wine and two goblets. She hoped he had not waited to eat with her. She hadn't asked him to. Had she? No – no, she remembered asking only if he would come to her – not come to her and have dinner again. She ran a hand down the soft material of her chiton. This evening it was made of some kind of fabulous material that hugged her body like silk, and it was the exact green of her eyes. She knew it flattered her, just as she knew Daphne had brought it to her at the baths because she had been wishing for something beautiful to wear. She wanted to look beautiful for him. For Asterius . . .

'Come to me,' she whispered into the night.

She could feel him approaching. Like an electrical storm, he was a great gathering of energy and force.

'Good evening, Mikado.'

'Hello, Asterius.' Still nervous, she gestured to the table. 'Would you like some wine? I hope you've already eaten. The handmaidens wanted to have dinner with me at the baths, and they'd worked so hard today I didn't feel like I could tell them no.'

'That is as it should be. Your Elementals need the presence of their Empousa. Do not be concerned, I ate as I awaited your call.'

'But you'll join me in a glass of wine?'

'Of course.'

Again, when Mikki lifted the goblet to her lips she found a rosebud swimming in the wine. She savored the delicate fragrance as they drank.

'You'll spoil me,' she told him with a smile. 'I won't be able to really enjoy a glass of wine unless it has a rose floating in it.'

'That is as it should be, too.'

She watched him sip his wine. Tonight he seemed more relaxed than the night before, and she was able to look at him openly. He was such a paradox – monstrous strength and a body that melded man and beast, yet he was humane enough to conjure a rose for her wine.

'What do you think when you look at me thus?'

Mikki jumped guiltily at the question.

'You need not answer that,' he said quickly, looking away from her.

'I don't mind. I just . . . well . . . I know it's rude of me to stare at you.'

'I am accustomed to women's stares.'

She felt a rush of anger for the kind of stares he'd had to endure. 'Then I will tell you what I was thinking. I was thinking that it's amazing that you're so powerful and at the same time so kind.'

'Kind?'

'Oh, don't sound shocked. Of course you're kind. Who ordered my dinner the first night I was here? And you told them to put a blanket and slippers out here for me, not to mention the rose blossoms you never forget to add to my wine.'

'That doesn't make me kind. That just shows that I'm fulfilling my duty in caring for the Empousa.'

She snorted. 'Please. You're not just kind to me. You're like that with all the women. I watched you today. Even though they act weird and skittish around you, you're completely patient with them.'

'Mikado, that is my duty. Nothing more.'

'Are you telling me that you never get frustrated or annoyed at them?'

'I do,' he said.

'Then why don't you show it?'

'That would be dishonorable, and it would . . .' He stopped suddenly, realizing he was saying too much.

'It would what?' she prompted.

'It would be wrong,' he said.

'Would it be wrong, or would it be proving that what they say about you is true?'

His dark eyes found hers, and she read her answer there.

'What they say about you is not true,' Mikki said softly.

'You don't know that.'

'Yes I do. I know it here.' She pressed a hand to her heart. 'And I know it here.' She reached across the small table and placed her hand gently on the leather breastplate that molded to his chest. Through the pliable leather she felt the strong beating of his heart and the way his breathing deepened at her touch. They stared at each other. Mikki wished he would return her touch, cover her hand with his own, do something that told her it was okay for her to touch him. But his only movement was the pounding of his heart and the drawing of his breath. Reluctantly, she took her hand from his chest.

'It went well today, Mikado.' His voice sounded unnaturally loud in the stillness that had settled between them.

'I think so, too. Tomorrow we're just going to work until midday. Then I'm going to try some spell work.'

His lips tilted up. 'That should prove interesting.'

'Especially because I have no idea what I'm doing.'

'You will. Just listen within. And remember, the Elementals are there to assist you. When you cast a spell, you can call anything within their power to aid you with the spell.'

Mikki perked up. 'For instance?'

He sipped his wine and considered. 'For instance, let us say a maiden comes to you because she has been cursed with terrible pains in her head. She asks for a spell to cure this pain. Lavender has long been associated with health, peace and relaxation. So you command Gii to provide you fresh lavender and Aeras to fill the breeze surrounding the maiden with the scent of the herb.'

'That does make sense,' Mikki said enthusiastically. 'So all I need to do is to think about what each Elemental can provide to support whatever spell it is I want to cast.'

'Then you complete it with your words and Hecate's power.'

'Wow,' she breathed. 'Incredible.'

'And, you'll find, very effective. Hecate's High Priestess wields great power. Your spells will be strong and binding.'

'In other words, I better think before I speak.'

'I have no doubt that you will be wise, Mikado.'

'I wish I was as sure,' she muttered. Then she sighed. 'There's just so much I don't know.'

'You will learn,' he said.

'Will you help me?'

'If I am able,' he said carefully.

'Good! There's something you can help me with tonight.' She ignored the way he instantly retreated behind his all-too-familiar expressionless mask. 'It's a little like drawing the map for me last night.' That seemed to reassure him, and when he nodded slightly, she said, 'You know the gardens so well, I assume you know the palace equally as well.'

He looked surprised but said, 'I do.'

'Well, I don't.' She jerked her thumb at the glass doors leading to her bedroom. 'The only way I've left my room is through there. I've not stepped so much as a foot into the hall outside my bedroom. I know there's some kind of fantastic dream making and magick brewing going on out there in the rest of the palace, though.' Unspoken between them was what she had said earlier – that she wanted to weave a dream for the two of them.

'There is, indeed.'

'I'd love to see it, but I also want to be able to understand it and weld it. Would you show me around, Asterius?'

His eyes were dark and they glittered with the fullness of the joy her request gave him. He smiled, showing a flash of sharp, white canines. 'I would be honored.'

Chapter Twenty-four

WALKING through her bedroom with him was an oddly intimate experience. Mikki saw his eyes go to her opulent bed. His long, powerful stride was suddenly thrown off, and, for the first time, she saw him move awkwardly. She had to force herself not to smile. If he wasn't thinking about getting her into bed, then why should the sight of said bed make him jittery? She thought it was an excellent sign. Then he opened the door and stepped aside so she could go through, and all bedroom thoughts fled her mind.

Her room was the last in the hall and her balcony wrapped all the way around the side of her bedroom, which also was the eastern end of the palace. To her left, the vast main hallway of the palace stretched on and on. The hall was wide, the ceiling incredibly high. Huge mullioned windows faced the south, showing a nighttime view of the torch-lit gardens. The north side of the hall held door after door, each ornately carved with mystic symbols and designs, and stretching as far as she could see. Torches blazed from wall sconces on either side of each door, as well as up and down the hall on both sides. Mikki's eyes were drawn to the long marble boxes that covered the area between the doors. The boxes were filled with flowers that were – amazingly enough – not roses.

The air in the hallway was filled with a sweet, delicate fragrance that reminded her of daylilies. Actually, the flowers did look a little like daylilies, only their leaves were too big and round, even though the huge, trumpetlike white blossoms were lilylike. But the blossoms were weird . . . they were . . . she walked closer. They were surrounded by a glittering haze, like mist that had been sprinkled with glitter. What the . . . ? Then something about those blossoms pricked her memory.

'They're moon flowers! We have them in Oklahoma. They only open up like this at night. During the day their blooms close tight and droop down so they look almost dead.'

'Yes, we call them moon flowers here, too.'

'But what is the foggy stuff that looks like it's coming out of the blossoms?'

'It's not coming out – it's being drawn in.'

'It's being drawn in? What is it?'

'The essence of dreams. Every night the moon flowers capture the essence of dreams and draw them into the rooms beyond, where the women of the realm take that essence and fashion it anew to send back into the world to create the magick that is born of dreams.'

'All that's happening behind those doors?'

'It is.' He smiled at her look of innocent wonder.

The smile she flashed him in return was brilliant, and when she squeezed his arm he thought his heart would burst from his chest and he had to remind himself that it was the magick of the realm that had excited her thus, not his presence. But no matter. Her happiness pleased him, whatever its source, and he was determined to enjoy it, as well as the joy being in Mikado's presence brought him, for as long as her destiny allowed.

'Lead on, Mikado, and I will follow you into the rooms of dreams.'

She nodded, drew in a deep breath and touched the knob of the first door. It swung inward. Mikki moved into the room and blinked, trying to make sense of what she was seeing.

The room was misty with the sweet scent of moon flowers. All the women were blowing glass bubbles – that much wasn't hard to understand. It was warmer there than in the hallway, though not as hot as the open ovens that stood in each corner of the room should have made it. The women looked up from their tasks when she and the Guardian entered. They ignored Asterius but dropped quick curtseys to her and greeted her cheerfully.

'Don't let me interrupt. Keep doing . . . uh, whatever it is you're doing,' Mikki said hastily.

'They are creating dream bubbles.'

Asterius was standing very close to her, and his low voice rumbled into her ear, causing the skin on her neck to prickle.

'See how, as each bubble grows, so, too, does the dream within it?'

She nodded, watching raptly as the women blew into long, slender tubes, turning and fashioning, until the molten lumps at the ends of the tubes were formed into bubbles that looked like delicate, iridescent glass globes of all different colors. As the bubbles got bigger and bigger, Mikki could see that there was something inside them. She moved closer and realized that she was looking at fantastic scenes. In one bubble, a young girl leaped off a cliff, but instead of falling, the child floated through a violet-colored sky singing to birds that looked like flying penguins. In another bubble, two knights jousted while scantily dressed women cheered them on. In yet another, an old woman was looking into a hand-held mirror, and within the mirror her face grew younger and younger, until she was a tight-skinned teenager.

'You're seeing the essence of dreams reworked.'

'So those are actual dreams that people will have?' she whispered.

'Yes.'

'How do they get from here to the people's minds?'

'Like that.' He lifted his chin toward a woman whose bubble had reached the size of a grapefruit. She stopped blowing into the tube and lifted the bubble to eye level. In the scene taking place inside, Mikki could see a woman dancing through a knee-deep sea of blue grass as the sky rained flowers all around her. The palace worker tapped the bubble once with her fingernail, and it broke off neatly from the tube. But it didn't fall to the ground and break, as Mikki expected it to. Instead, it floated. The worker blew one last breath of air on it, and the bubble lifted, eventually disappearing into the ceiling.

'Would you like to create a dream, Empousa?'

Mikki jumped as the woman who had just sent the bubble through the ceiling offered her the newly emptied tube.

'Oh, thank you, but no. Tonight I'm just watching.'

'As you wish, Empousa.' The woman smiled at her and went back to work.

Mikki grabbed Asterius's hand and pulled him toward the door. 'I want to see more!'

'As you wish, Empousa.' He tried to sound formal and aloof for the benefit of the women, who were watching and listening, but the small hand that nestled so easily within his was a treasure beyond price, and he could not conceal the happiness that lit his face when she touched him so easily. He didn't care that they were watching; he didn't care that pain sluiced through his arm. All that mattered was that she did not take her hand from his until they reached the next door, which she touched open. He followed her in, smiling at her little gasp of pleasure.

This room was much cooler and smelled like moon flowers and spring rain. A clear stream bubbled through the center of the room, coming from nowhere and disappearing into nothingness. On one side of the stream, women lounged on puffy cushions the color of blushes, talking and laughing while their hands trailed into the water. Every so often one of the women would pull something that looked like a coin from the water, study it carefully, then, with a snap of her fingers, the coin would disappear in a puff of pink smoke.

On the far side of the stream, women sat comfortably cross-legged, dipping round hoops into the water. A young woman caught sight of her and called, 'Greetings, Empousa!' and soon the rest of the Dream Weavers greeted her.

'Don't let me interrupt you; I just want to watch,' Mikki assured them. Then she lowered her voice and moved closer to Asterius. 'Okay, what are they doing?'

'The stream carries coins from all of the wishing wells in the mundane world. The women choose a coin, and if they like the wish, they turn it into a dream.'

'What if they don't like it?'

'It stays in the stream and eventually becomes the sludge from which nightmares are formed.'

'Can't they throw them away or something? I hate nightmares.'

'There must be balance, Mikado. Light–dark, good–evil, life–death. Without balance, the circle of life would collapse.'

'I still don't like nightmares,' she grumbled. Then Mikki pointed to the women with the hoops. 'What are they doing?'

'They're finding the right mixture of dreams, water, and magick to make scrying mirrors.'

'Scrying mirrors?'

'Mirrors used for second sight – for discerning that which cannot be seen with the eye alone.'

'Really? That's fascinating. You know, I think I'd like to get a closer look.' Mikki marched over to one of the women fishing for coins.

'I would be honored if you would join me, Empousa.' She smiled warmly at Mikki and scooted over to make room for her on the cushion.

Mikki sat and looked down into the water. It was clear, tumbling hurriedly over the white sand that formed the bottom of the magickal stream. Then a circle of silver rolled into view, and without letting herself think too much, she plunged her hand in after it. The water was pleasantly warm, a nice contrast to the cool room. Her fingers closed around the coin. Smiling triumphantly, she lifted it, dripping.

'Well done, Empousa.' Asterius's deep voice rumbled from beside her. 'Now look into it and see if the wish is a dream you will grant.'

Mikki narrowed her eyes and stared at the coin. With a little shock, she realized she was holding a quarter! The mint date stamped on it was 1995. It was just a plain, ordinary quarter. No different than the ones she'd been seeing, and spending, her entire life. How could there be any magick within—

The skin of the coin rippled, and she almost dropped it. She looked closer. It was like putting her eyes to one of those old view masters, only the scene within the coin moved like a video. A man and a woman lay on a sheepskin rug in front of a crackling fireplace. They were naked and making love. Mikki could hear him telling her over and over how beautiful she was and how she tasted of honey and love. Then, as the woman orgasmed, snow began to fall in the room all around the couple, without touching them or getting them wet.

'Do you grant that the wish be made a dream?' Asterius asked.

Mikki looked from the erotic scene to the beast who stood beside her. She licked her lips, letting her gaze travel up the muscular expanse of his chest to the fullness of his very human lips. 'Yes, I grant it,' she said. Without having to be told what to do next, she snapped her fingers and the coin exploded in a puff of pink smoke, which drifted lazily up and then through the ceiling.

'Will you choose another, Empousa?' the woman sitting beside her asked.

'I'd like to, but I want to visit more of the other rooms tonight.'

For the second time that day, Mikki held her hand out to Asterius. This time there was no hesitation before he took it and helped her to her feet. When she stood, he let go of her hand, but she didn't move away from him. Instead, she placed her hand in the crook of his arm, as if he was an old-time Southern gentleman escorting her from the room. 'Let's go see some of the other rooms.'

'As you wish, Empousa.'

His words were still formal, but there was no mistaking the way his expression softened when he spoke to her and how they leaned their bodies toward one another, sharing intimate smiles and whispers. They walked from the room, neither paying any attention to the shocked stares of the Dream Weavers.

Chapter Twenty-five

MIKKI's mind was a whirlwind, filled with the unbeliev-able beauty she'd witnessed in the dream-weaving rooms. Just when she thought she'd seen something so incredible it couldn't be topped, Asterius would lead her to another room and she would be amazed all over again. She wished her mother and grandmother could be here with her. Her mother, in particular, would love the room where women were painting tiny porcelain animals, which came alive as they floated up through the ceiling. Her grandmother would probably most like the dream weaving that had been devoted to magick, like the room where brightly colored scenes were painted on long rolls of parchment so fine it was see-through. When the scenes were finished, the filmy paper suddenly broke apart, and like dove's wings, fluttered up out of sight. Asterius had explained that the women had been creating the essence of Tarot cards. And then there was the room they'd entered where women had been using shining silver hooks to crochet diaphanous blankets ranging in color from buttercup to smoke. Moon veils, used for drawing down the moon, he had named them. And she realized that they were, indeed, all the colors of the different phases of the moon.

But her favorite room was the candle room. It had been filled, tier after tier, with thick, cream-colored pillar candles, on which women carved into the soft wax fantastic dream scenes. When a scene was finished, the candle was lit. As it burned, the dream scene was released and then carried to the waiting world on fragrant, snow-colored smoke.

'One more room,' Asterius said sternly as they left the candle room. Before she could protest, he shook his head. 'No, there are shadows beneath your eyes. You can continue your exploration tomorrow night.'

'Is this more of your duty to care for me, or are you tired of me dragging you from room to room?'

'Neither,' he said quietly as they approached the door to the next room. He cupped her face within his hands and let his thumbs trace the shadows under her eyes. 'It is only that I do not like to see you looking weary, even though if I could choose, this evening would never end.'

Mikki looked up at him, surprised and pleased at his words and the gentleness of his touch. She wanted to say she was sorry she had misunderstood, or thank him, or – hell! – tell she was having a wonderful time, too, but he was already opening the ornate door. Her eager attention shifted to the new room and the wonders it held.

Everything within the room looked normal. Women sat around in front of large frames of cloth, their needles flashing in and out as they created exquisite tapestries. As usual, the women greeted her, but this time they did not ignore Asterius.

'Guardian, did you bring more thread?' one of the older women said in a businesslike, no-nonsense tone of voice.

'I have none with me. This evening I have been escorting the new Empousa through the dream-weaver rooms,' he said.

'Empousa, please do not think I mean any disrespect, but it is important that the Guardian collect more threads for us – tonight, if you would grant him leave to do so. While he was' – the woman paused uncomfortably for a moment before plunging on – 'away from the realm, we had to make do with the threads the Elementals gathered. They sufficed but only just.'

'The tapestries are becoming frayed,' added a slightly younger woman with a thick mane of blond hair she had tied back in a braid. Several of the other women nodded in agreement.

Thoroughly confused – again – Mikki contained her frustrated sigh. 'Of course I'll give the Guardian leave to, um, collect threads for you. We were just finishing here anyway.'

'Oh! Thank you, Empousa!'

Mikki waved off their thanks and retreated from the room with Asterius close behind.

'All right, you're going to have to explain that,' she said.

'Did you notice anything different about the scenes in that room?'

She frowned at him, not liking it that he answered her question with a question, but she thought about the scenes the women had been embroidering. There had been one with a mother holding a newborn child. Another had shown a man speaking in front of a huge crowd of people. Yet another had depicted a woman sitting at a writing desk chewing thoughtfully at a pencil. Mikki shrugged her shoulders. 'I don't know. They all seemed totally normal.'

'That is because in that room the dreams woven into the tapestries are those that actually come true.'

'You mean they really happen! The things those women were creating in there actually happen in the real world?'

'Always,' he said.

'That's why the thread has to be different.' She spoke slowly, following her intuition carefully, as if it was a dimly marked trail. 'They can't get it only from the stuff that the moon flowers suck in. Dreams that come true need something else . . . something more real.'

He looked pleased. 'Exactly! Dreams that come true must be woven with threads gleaned from reality.'

'And you can do that?'

He nodded. 'I can.'

'Will you show me?'

He started to protest that it was too late and that she was over-tired, but she touched his arm gently and said, 'Please, Asterius.'

'Very well. Come with me.'

'Where are we going?'

'To the rose gate,' he said, leading her back along the hallway.

'We're going into the forest?' Her hand tightened on his arm.

'We must. Reality cannot be gleaned from the realm of dreams and magick.' Briefly, he covered her hand with his. 'Do not be afraid. I would not let anything harm you.'

She smiled up at him. 'I'm not afraid. Not as long as I'm with you.'

MIKKI thought the huge gate made of roses looked damn creepy at night. It didn't matter that there were torches nearby and lanterns hanging from the limbs of the ancient oak. It was still dark, and the rose wall seemed like something out of a book of fairy tales by the sublimely twisted British author, Tanith Lee. Mikki liked Lee's weird fairy-tale retellings, a lot actually, but she absolutely did not want to walk into one. Ever.

'You could stay here. I'll go into the forest, gather the threads and then return as quickly as I am able,' he said.

'No! I'm not staying here by myself. I'm coming with you.'

With Mikki's hand wrapped tightly within the crook of his arm, he took the torch planted in the ground near the gate. After speaking the command that opened the gate, the two of them walked out of the Realm of the Rose.

Mikki shivered. 'It's colder out here.'

He barked another command, and a royal purple palla materialized around her shoulders.

'You're really handy to have around,' Mikki said, trying to cover her nerves with a smile. Then she nodded toward the dark depth of the forest. 'We're going in there?'

'Do not be afraid,' he told her.

'Easy for you to say; you have the claws,' she muttered.

His smile flashed white in the torchlight. 'My claws are at your service, my lady.'

'You say the sweetest things,' she said with her best Southern accent, and Asterius's chest rumbled with a deep laugh.

They entered the tree line and were instantly swallowed in a blackness that completely blocked out the silvery light of the waxing moon. Asterius's torchlight cast eerie, moving shadows against the bark of the ancient trees. Mikki thought that if she hadn't been with Asterius she would have been scared shitless. As it was, she was just creeped out and looking forward to returning to the bright safety of the palace.

'This is far enough tonight. I need only collect a few strands to satisfy the women. Tomorrow I can return for more.' He stopped and shoved the torch back into the ground. Asterius glanced down at where her hand gripped his arm. 'I have to have both of my arms free,' he said gently.

'Oh, sorry.' She loosened her death grip and took a short step away from him, glad that one good thing the darkness did was to hide her blush.

'Do not be sorry,' he said gruffly. 'Your touch pleases me.'

She blinked in surprise. Had she heard him correctly? The words were nice, but the way he said them made him sound pissed off. It was confusing. Just like his hands were gentle, but his face always seemed to reflect something that looked almost like pain whenever he touched her. 'Really?' she blurted.

His sigh was like a storm wind. 'Really.' Then he enveloped her shoulders with his hands and moved her a couple of steps to the side. 'Stand here. This won't take long.'

Silently, he stretched out his hands. The firelight glinted off the claws that suddenly extended from his fingers. He closed his eyes and lifted his head, moving in a circle until he was facing into the slight breeze. Though he was half turned away from her, Mikki could see his lips moving, as if he was reciting a soundless prayer. He raised one hand and thrust it forward; it looked like he was clawing the wind. Then his hand twisted and closed in one inhumanly quick motion. And from the tips of his claws, the air began to glow, as long, thin threads suddenly took form, which he pulled, hand over hand, to pile in a glowing pool of luminous filigrees around his hooves.

Amazed, Mikki watched him work. He moved in a small circle, always staying close to her within the torchlight. But he didn't just pull the threads from the breeze. Sometimes he reached into the leaves of the ancient tree above them and plucked heretofore unseen threads from the leaves. Then he'd shift his focus and sweep his hands through the forest plants that pushed up through the verdant loam. All the while the pile of exquisite threads grew. She couldn't look directly at the threads for too long. They made her dizzy with their shifting and glowing. In the pile she thought she glimpsed the shapes of people, but they were all disjoined. It was like trying to study a Picasso through the warped glass of a carnival mirror.

So instead of the threads, Mikki watched Asterius. He moved with the grace of a warrior coupled with the strength of a big cat. Despite the horns and cloven hooves, he seemed more lion than bull-like, with his mane of hair; his dark, bottomless eyes and his feral grace. And suddenly those eyes were focused on her. He was breathing heavily, and his arms were damp with sweat.

'Of all the wonders you've shown me tonight, watching you pull the threads of reality from the darkness is what I think is the most incredible.'

'Would you like to try it?'

'Oh, yes,' she breathed.

'Then this time, you must come to me.'

With no hesitation, she walked to him.

'Do you trust me?' he asked.

'Yes.'

'Then turn your back to me.'

Mikki turned around. She felt him close the small distance that separated them. He bent so he could cup one of her hands in each of his. 'Open your hands and press them against mine, so my claws become yours.'

Mikki spread her fingers wide, fitting them against his much larger hands. Then she pressed her arms to his until she was molded against his skin. Their bodies met, and she felt the sharp intake of his breath and the shudder that moved through him – her own body answered with a heat that made the inside of her thighs tingle.

'Now, move with me.'

And she did. Her hands combed through the night air along with his. She felt the tingle of the threads against her palms. When his hands closed on them, so, too, did hers, and suddenly the scenes within the threads were no longer dizzying. They focused in her sight and became clear. It was like she was watching a movie tape unreel as she pulled it from the darkness. She saw a woman whose back was turned to a man, as hers was to

Asterius. The woman was naked, and the long, soft line of her back was only broken by her fall of copper-colored hair. *Like my hair . . . she has my hair . . .* Mikki thought dreamily. Then into the scene came two arms, thickly corded with muscles and covered with skin the color of burnished bronze. The arms cradled the woman, pulling her back so her body rested against his naked chest. The man tilted his head forward to nuzzle the woman's neck, and light glinted off his two ebony horns.

Asterius's growl fragmented the scene the thread was revealing. Mikki stumbled and almost fell as he lurched away from her. When she caught her balance and turned to him, he was standing beside the torch, with his head down, surrounded by piles of gossamer thread. She could see that he was breathing heavily, and as she watched, he wiped the back of his hand across his forehead. His hand was trembling.

'I need to take the threads back to the palace.' His voice had retreated to emotionless formality.

'Have I made you angry?' Mikki asked.

'No.'

'Then why are you being like this?'

He lifted his head and looked at her. Mikki thought she had never seen such haunted eyes.

'Did you see it, too? The scene in the thread?'

'Yes,' she whispered.

Suddenly, with choppy, violent motions, he started gathering the piles of thread. 'I do not understand what has happened. These are the threads of reality. They are to be woven into dreams that will come true.'

Silently, she unwrapped the palla from around her shoulders and spread it on the ground near him so he could pile the threads on it.

'And?' she prompted when he didn't go on.

'And it is not supposed to show fantasies and falsehoods!'

The force of his voice caused the torchlight to flicker, but Mikki didn't flinch. Instead, she closed the two steps between them. She watched him fall suddenly very still. She reached up and let the tips of her fingers briefly caress the side of his face. He quivered under her hand, but he did not pull away from her.

'Do you dislike it when I touch you?' she asked him.

'No!'

'Do you want to touch me, too?'

'Yes,' he snarled through his teeth.

'Then I don't understand why you say the scene we just saw is a fantasy and a falsehood.'

'Because I am a beast and you are a mortal woman!'

'Stop it!' She glared at him. 'You're the one making this impossible. I don't care about the beast! All of this' – she made two brusque gestures at his horns and hooves – 'didn't stop me from wanting you way back in Tulsa when you started coming to me in my dreams – and I didn't even know the man within you then. Why would it stop me from wanting you now?'

'Mikado, you do not understand. There is more here at stake than what may or may not happen between the two of us. You are only—'

'Here for the roses! Damnit, Asterius! I know that. Do you think I'm incapable of doing my job and loving you, too? Jeesh! The people in this realm have said some ugly things about my old world, and some of it is even true, but I'm beginning to wonder about the priestesses who came before me. Were they not able to multitask?'

'Please. I beg you not to say things to me you do not mean.'

Mikki thought he sounded as if his heart had been rubbed raw.

'What are you talking about? I'm being completely honest with you.'

'A mortal woman cannot love a beast.'

'Who told you that?'

He looked quickly away from her.

Mikki walked to his side and let her fingers brush his cheek again. He closed his eyes as if her touch pained him. 'Was it the last Empousa, the one who caused Hecate to get angry at you?'

His eyes shot open. 'Who spoke of her to you?'

'No one – no one would. But I'm not stupid. You made Hecate angry. The Empousa's gone. The roses are sick. I'm here, and it's you who brought me. Come on – it's just not that tough to figure out that something happened between the two of you.'

'I am forbidden to speak of the past.'

'I get that. You and everyone else around here are forbidden. But I'm not, so let me explain something to you. One – I am not her. I'm sure I'm quite a bit older, and, let's say for the sake of argument, quite a bit wiser. Two – I come from another world, which means I don't have the prejudices the women of this world have. For example, I don't have a problem getting my fingers dirty taking care of the roses. And I don't have a problem seeing the man within you. Now, I want you to answer one question honestly and clearly for me, and I don't want to hear any of this "I am forbidden to speak of it" crap.'

'Ask,' he said.

'Is there a rule that says Hecate's Empousa cannot love her Guardian?'

His dark eyes met hers. 'I know of no such rule, but there has never been any need for one.'

Mikki held her breath and said, 'There is now.'

'Mikado, you say you see the man within me?' His voice was strained.

'Actually, what I'm saying is that I might be falling in love with the man within you. I think I have been since you came to my dreams.' She wasn't touching him, but she was standing close enough that she could see that his body was trembling.

'That may be, and just hearing you say those words is a rare and wondrous gift, one I have never before been given. But you must understand that though I have the heart and soul of a man, I also have the passions of a beast. I force the beast to submit to me, but he is always present, and he is as ravenous as the man for love.'

Mikki felt a rush of emotion that made her heartbeat increase. But she wasn't afraid. She was fascinated. She took his hand and slowly raised it to her lips.

'I could not love the man without accepting the beast.'

'Does it not make you fear me?' his deep voice growled.

She rested her cheek against his hand. He cupped her face, and she kissed his palm. 'Does the beast within you want to hurt me?'

'No! He wants to love you, but he doesn't know how.'

'Then we'll have to teach him.'

They finished gathering the threads in silence, but their hands met often and their eyes spoke of dreams yet to be fulfilled. They retraced their path through the forest, too preoccupied with one another to sense the presence that lurked in the shadows, its red eyes ravenously following their every movement.

Chapter Twenty-six

ASTERIUS carried the threads wrapped in the silk palla, and they made their way quickly through the sleeping gardens. They walked closely together, with arms brushing. He welcomed the sizzle of pain that contact with her body caused him. It was a price he was gladly willing to pay for her closeness.

Asterius's mind was a blur of thoughts. *Her touch still pains me, so she does not love me yet, but could she be falling in love with me? Could it be possible? And if she isn't – if this is a sham or an odd impulse she designed to follow, but will regret . . .* His chest tightened. He should leave tonight with the gift of words and hope she had given him. It was enough.

It was not enough! The beast within him roared.

But it must be enough. Even if by some miracle she could love me, it wouldn't change anything. Her destiny must remain the same.

Asterius's mind and heart were at war, and he remained silent, fighting internal battles and savoring the soft brush of her arm against his.

Mikki tried not to think at all. Every so often she would steal a sideway glance at his strong profile – the square jaw, wide forehead, pointed onyx horns . . . A chill shivered through her – part trepidation, part fascination. She wasn't going to think. She was going to follow her instincts.

Both of them were preoccupied enough that together they were surprised when the stairway to Mikki's balcony was suddenly in front of them.

'I will take the threads to the Dream Weavers,' he said gruffly.

'That's a good idea. They're waiting for you.' She made a motion as if she wanted to touch the pile of gleaming thread but seemed to think better of it and dropped her hand to her side. She looked from the threads into his eyes and said, 'The dream that we were in – will the women see it and weave it into a tapestry, too?'

He looked thoroughly surprised by her question. 'I do not know. I have no personal experience with dreams coming true.'

Mikki tilted her head back so she could look up into his face more easily. 'You don't have dreams?'

'I do, but they do not come true. Since I swore an oath to be in Hecate's service, I have been watching the dreams of others come true without being granted any of my own.' He continued to look into her eyes. 'You already know I am the son of a Titan and I have lived for countless centuries, with more centuries stretching endlessly before me. I also want you to know I will remember today for as long as my heart beats.'

'You sound like today is over.'

He smiled, flashing sharp, white teeth, but his eyes remained sad. 'It was a pleasing day, but as with all things, it, too, must end.'

Mikki didn't want it to end, not yet. She wanted . . . she wanted him to . . . Her mind fumbled through possibilities. What did she really want him to do? Standing so close to him she was, once again, struck by his size and the powerful melding of man and animal – the cloven hooves and furred legs – the muscular chest and powerful shoulders – the face that looked like it should belong to an ancient warrior god and not a creature who was part beast.

In her dream she had been pursued by him and then had ended up in his arms. It had been erotic and exciting, but it had been a dream. Reality was much different. For one thing, he was definitely not pursuing her. For another, she had to remember what he'd said about the beast within him. She was no fairy-tale Beauty, and he was not going to turn into a foppish prince if she agreed to marry him. Hell, he hadn't even asked her. Who knew what his intentions were – half the time his expression was so masked that she couldn't even guess at what he was thinking.

But what were *her* intentions? She'd admitted to him that she might be falling in love with him. What did that mean? Just how hard and far was she willing to fall?

'If there is nothing else you require of me, then I bid you good night, Mikado.'

When he finally spoke, she realized she'd been standing there staring stupidly, speechlessly at him. She blinked her eyes, feeling a little like she was coming out of a trance.

'There is one more thing you can do for me.'

Mikki climbed quickly up three of the balcony steps. He started to follow her, but she turned so he had to stop abruptly. She was almost at eye level with him, and for a moment he just stood there, enjoying the exquisite sensation of being so physically close to a woman who did not shrink from him or treat him as if he was an errant hound. Then she put her hands on his shoulders.

'What may I do for you, Mikado?' Despite the instant pain that began to radiate through his skin at her touch, he tried to speak as softly as possible, mentally cursing his inhumanly powerful chest and the voice that boomed from it, afraid that he would frighten her again. Afraid that she would stop touching him . . . or that she would not.

'This,' she whispered.

She leaned forward and touched her lips to his. He could not move. It was as if her kiss had turned him back into stone. She pulled away, but only by a hand's width, so she could meet his eyes.

'Your lips are warm,' she said, still whispering.

'Yours – yours are unimaginably soft.' He somehow got the words free from where they had lodged in his throat.

'May I kiss you again?'

He knew she could feel his body trembling under the uncommon and bittersweet pleasure caused by the weight of her small hands. Not trusting himself to maintain control of his voice, he nodded.

This time her lips lingered. With a supreme effort of will, he pushed aside the white-hot jolt of pain and drank her in. Her scent filled his senses. Mikado was sweet rose spice and warm mortal woman, and she was touching him – kissing him – almost in his arms. It was more intoxicating than any of the magick he had at his command.

'It's better if you kiss me back,' she murmured against his lips.

As he had watched so often in other men's dreams, he opened his mouth slightly and tilted his head. When her tongue flicked briefly against his, Asterius's body responded automatically. With a growl that changed to a moan, he dropped the palla so the luminous threads spilled all around them on the stairs. His hands came up and circled the gentle curve of her waist. She leaned farther forward so her full breasts pressed against the leather of his cuirasse. He could feel the heavy heat of them, just as he could taste her. He wanted her with a lust that was as white hot as the agony that was coupled with his desire. His pulse pounded in his temples as his blood surged in streams of liquid fire through his body. There was nothing in the world except Mikado – her touch, her taste, her heat. He had to have her. Even if the pain destroyed him, he had to have her! He had to bury himself in her and pump an eternity of need into her seductive warmth. Her arms went around his shoulders, and the kiss deepened. He slid one hand up the smooth line of her back as the other dropped down to cup her irresistibly round ass and bring her closer, holding her tightly against his throbbing length.

Ah, Goddess! He'd never felt anything like the delicious pain of having her body pressed against his.

His pain-filled and lust-fogged mind didn't register her first cry. He only heard the second because she had begun to struggle to get away from him. Breathing hard, he forced himself to lift his mouth from hers. Then he smelled blood. Her blood. He stared at her lips. They looked swollen, bruised. One was cut and bleeding. Her eyes were wide and she, too, was panting for breath.

'No!' he growled. Releasing her, he staggered back a step.

She took a shaky step back, too, so her body pressed against the banister. When her back touched the marble, she winced.

'What have I done?' he rasped.

'Your claws . . .' she began, her voice sounding unnaturally shrill. 'You must have scratched me.'

He looked down at his hands. His claws were fully extended. His eyes shot to her. *Oh, Goddess! Please no! Please don't let me have harmed her!*

'Let me see your back,' he said, but when he started to move toward her, she jerked back another step away from him. He stopped, as if she had driven a stake through him, impaling him into place.

'It's fine. I'm sure I'm fine.'

Mikado's eyes were filled with fear – and something else. Something he was sure he recognized – loathing. He knew the look too well. He'd seen it the night the other Empousa had rejected him. Her eyes, too, had told him she feared and loathed the beast. Slowly, making no further move to touch her, he collected the spilled threads, gathering them into the palla. Then he straightened and walked down the staircase before allowing himself to look at her again. She was still standing with her back pressed to the banister, watching him with wide, stunned eyes.

'I did not mean to hurt you. I do not ask you to forgive me, because I know that is not possible, but I do ask you to try to believe that I did not want to hurt you. I would never want to hurt you.' With a choked growl, he turned and fled into the night.

When he was gone, Mikki wiped a trembling hand across her mouth and winced. She felt the cut on her lip with her tongue. She hadn't even known his teeth had done that. Her knees were wobbly, and she climbed the winding staircase slowly, but she didn't go to her room. She kept walking along the length of the balcony and down the stairs that hugged the eastern side of it. Thankfully, she didn't have to call for Daphne. As she'd ordered earlier that evening, the servants had begun leaving thick towels and extra chitons and nightdresses, along with soaps and oils and jugs of wine in large baskets near the baths. They had, of course, protested that it was their duty to attend to the Empousa's needs at all hours. But Mikki had insisted. She'd known she would want the privacy to bathe without being attended to and watched – she just hadn't known she'd want it this soon.

She unwound herself from the chiton, filled a goblet from a jug of red wine and gingerly lowered herself into one of the steaming pools, sucking in a breath as the mineral water covered her back.

It had scared the shit out of her. She'd been kissing him and liking it. He'd tasted like man with something musky mixed in – something as alien as it was exciting. And he'd felt . . . she shivered. He'd felt like stone, only his body was warm and unbelievably powerful. And he'd wanted her. Desperately. She could feel his muscles bunch and quiver under her touch. She reveled in the hard length of his erection as it pressed insistently against her, and her own body responded with an answering heat and wetness that felt so damn good it made the back of her teeth ache. She'd rubbed against him, teasingly erotic, loving how easily she could feel his body through the thin silk of her chiton. The low, rumbling growl he'd breathed into her mouth had thrilled her. She was doing that to him! It was she who had held that incredibly powerful beast in her arms and made him tremble for her. She'd molded herself against him, fitting her softness to him. It had been like her dream, only better. She didn't have to wake up alone and limp from an unsatisfying solo orgasm. He was right there. She could have him – all of him.

Then the pain had mixed with the pleasure. She'd known he hadn't meant to extend his claws. He had simply been lost in her and passion had triggered an automatic response. She'd tried to tell him – tried to push him away. He hadn't seemed to hear her at first, and then . . .

She sighed and closed her eyes. Then he'd been horrified. He'd seen the fear in her eyes and he'd run, especially after she wouldn't let him get close to her. He'd misunderstood. Of course he would. How many women had looked at him with fear in their eyes? That's probably what that other damn Empousa had done. When he'd said that Hecate had no reason to make a rule stating that the Guardian and the Empousa could not desire one another, he'd been intimating that there had been nothing between the two of them, but she knew he was hiding something. They were all hiding something they didn't want her to know. The other Empousa had broken his heart. Maybe that's why Hecate had sent him away, so he could get over her. And maybe she'd fired the other priestess because she'd rejected him. Who knew why? Who knew the why of anything in this strange realm of dreams and magick and desire?

Mikki thought about the hopeless look on his face as he'd left her. She'd broken his heart, too. She hadn't meant to. It was just that she'd been so shocked – shocked and afraid – when his claws had scratched the length of her back and she'd felt the raw rush of lust that had been her response. She'd wanted to sink her teeth into his lip and demand that he fuck her right there, rough and fast, over and over. To feel his strength fill her and to know that his lust, his passion, his barely controlled violence was hers . . . Mikki shuddered with the pleasure of remembering how it had felt to imagine that she could claim him whenever she wished and that he would respond with that same flame until she was finally sated as none of the inadequate men in her life had ever been able to do. It had overwhelmed and intrigued and shocked her to get a glimpse of what would finally satisfy her – and know that 'what' was not a man, but a beast.

The simple truth was that she hadn't been afraid of him; she'd been afraid of herself.

Chapter Twenty-seven

'I THINK we got a lot accomplished, especially for only working half a day.' Mikki wiped her hands together and surveyed the neat beds of newly fertilized roses that framed Hecate's Temple. If she didn't look too hard or think about the weird sick feeling she carried around in her gut whenever she was near the unhealthy roses, the gardens appeared almost normal, especially in this area of the realm closest to Hecate's Temple. Here the roses were all in shades of lavender and purple, and even in their sad condition, their sweet fragrance filled the space. Water flowed from the huge multi-basined fountain to trickle steadily into the marble troughs that stretched from its base outward and all the way to the four corners of the gardens. Nera had explained that the fountain carried water to all of the rose beds. Mikki had never imagined such a beautiful irrigation system.

'The work proceeds well. Many of the women were smiling and laughing today,' Gii said.

'That's just because rumor has it that I'm going to cast a spell to invite men into the realm.' But Mikki smiled back at the Earth Elemental. The women had worked hard and done so with good attitudes, especially today. She was keenly aware of it, because she had been struggling all morning with a decidedly surly attitude, which she had gone to great pains to hide.

Damnit! Asterius had shown not one hoof or horn or hair all morning. True, she hadn't called him. There hadn't been any reason for her to. Most of the heavy work had been finished the day before. Today the women were focusing on deadheading and clearing out weak canes. Neither task required his brawn. But he could have shown up to say good morning or check in or something – anything!

Logically, she understood that he believed she had thoroughly rejected him after he'd hurt and frightened her. But the sad truth was that love and lust were not logical. She'd wanted to see him – expected to see him. And she didn't want to have to force him to come to her or even ask him to come to her. She wanted him to come because he couldn't stay away.

'Empousa, shall I dismiss the women, or would you rather they stayed while you cast the sacred circle and invoked the spells?' Gii said.

'Oh, sorry. Yes, dismiss the women. I don't want an audience yet.' Mikki pulled her thoughts into line. 'And tell the other handmaidens that I want to do the magick work first. We can eat afterward.'

'Yes, Empousa.' The Earth Elemental hurried away.

Mikki frowned and chewed her lip. Instead of obsessing about Asterius, she should have been deciding exactly what she was going to do for the garden spell. She sighed. The man-drawing spell was easier to figure out – or at least she hoped she'd figured it out. For the other, she still had only half-formed ideas and confused musings. Crap.

Much too soon the four Elementals were waving and calling to her from their places around the ever-burning flame within Hecate's Temple. Mikki hooked her hair back behind her ears and brushed at a smudge of dirt on her violet-colored chiton. She'd been leery that morning when Gii had brought her the piece of beautiful material, thinking it would be damn awkward to work until noon with one boob exposed, but Gii had laughed and said that exposing her breast was only the ritual dress for rites during the dark of the moon. Otherwise, it was enough that she simply wore the color of the Spirit Elemental for spell casting. Well, that had been a relief. Or at least it should have been a relief, but part of her mind whispered that she would love to see Asterius's reaction to her wearing the more seductive garb – that is, if he had bothered to come to see her that morning.

Mikki climbed the steps and entered the goddess's temple. Its beauty soothed her nerves. She straightened her spine and walked with her chin up. She was High Priestess here, granted power by a great goddess. It was not appropriate that she moon over a guy (or a beast) when she should be focusing on the work of an Empousa.

Mikki took her place in the center of the circle. She closed her eyes and cleared her mind, breathing deeply and centering herself. Then she envisioned the threads of light she had seen the last time she'd cast the sacred circle and how they had formed a boundary of magick and power, linking the four elements together. When she felt ready, Mikki turned to the east and approached Aeras.

'Hello, Aeras.'

'Empousa.' The Wind Elemental fell into a deep, graceful curtsey.

Calling the elements to the circle was easier this time, and Mikki worked her way deosil through Air, Fire, Water, and Earth quickly and with much more confidence than she'd shown the first time. When she called upon Spirit, the protective threads that encompassed the circle's boundary were shining and clearly visible, even in the bright midday light. Then Mikki drew another deep breath and took a moment to listen carefully to her internal voice before she began the ritual.

'Hecate, Great Goddess of the Ebony Moon, I ask that you grant me the power and knowledge to call health and protection to the Realm of the Rose.'

The spirit flame in front of her leaped in response, and she felt a sudden rush of energy within her body. Following her instinct, she turned first to Floga.

'Floga, you are Flame, and I command that your element protect the realm. Each night when the sun sets I want torches to blaze all along the rose wall, sending light into the darkness and causing that which would hide in the shadows to look elsewhere for camouflage.'

Dancing flame licked the handmaiden's body as she ritualistically replied, 'This you ask of me; therefore, so mote it be.'

Next, Mikki approached the Water Elemental. 'Nera, you are Water. Your part in today's spell will be health and not protection. Every fourth sunrise I want soft rainwater to wash the gardens in a brief, refreshing shower. It isn't enough that the realm is irrigated; the roses need the touch of your element on their leaves to keep them healthy.'

Nera's pale blue chiton rippled around her body like waves lapping a shore. 'This you ask of me; therefore, so mote it be.'

Then Mikki stood between Gii and Aeras. She looked from one to the other as she addressed the personified elements. 'Gii, you are Earth. Aeras, you are Wind. I command that you join to nurture the health of the roses. Gii, I want you to summon ladybugs from the forest.' Mikki paused, picturing the kind little red-and-black-spotted insects in her mind. 'And Aeras, I want you to call the wind to carry them into the realm so they can find a new home here' – she smiled at the pretty Wind Elemental – 'just like I have.'

Together, Gii and Aeras intoned, 'This you ask of me; therefore, so mote it be.'

Then she returned to the place of Spirit and said, 'I thank you, Wind, Water, Fire, and Earth – powers of the elements – divine spirits of nature. With Hecate's blessing, I asked that you always be present in this realm of dreams and magick and beauty. So I ask of thee, and so mote it be.'

As she finished the spell she had a sense of completion, as if she had just cleared a rose bed of particularly nasty weeds. *One spell down, one to go . . .*

This time she started with the Wind Elemental, just as she'd begun casting the sacred circle there. She'd already thought about what she would ask of the elements, already planned out the words and practiced them in her head that morning, so as she spoke her mind wandered . . .

'Aeras, I command that men be allowed within the realm again, but only by a woman's invitation. If she speaks the invitation aloud, carry the words on the wind to her lover and then let him come to her.'

Asterius . . . that's the name I would call and the lover I would have the wind invite to me . . .

Mikki moved to the Fire Elemental. 'Floga, your affinity is with flame. Use the heat of your element to ignite the passion of any man who is desired by a woman of the Realm of the Rose. Let their passion burn as bright and hot as fire.'

I know he wants me. He proved that last night. I wish Asterius would burn for me so much that he couldn't stay away – couldn't let our differences separate us.

She stood before Nera. 'Let your element ready our bodies for the sweet intrusion of accepting a lover. Hot and wet and ready – that's what I wish for each woman who desires a man in her bed, so each will experience the physical thrill of the consummation of love.'

I want him in my bed. I want his body joined with mine, and I don't want to be afraid of my desire for him anymore.

Almost without knowing how she got there, she found herself in front of Gii. 'Earth is rich and wild, fertile and lush. Let your element fill the senses of the lovers. Let them know the fullness of love that is as deep as an ancient forest and as ripe as the sweetest fruit.'

Help me not to fear loving him so Asterius can finally know a love like this with me.

Back at the Spirit flame, Mikki's body felt flushed. Her nipples prickled against the soft fabric of her chiton, aroused and ready.

'Hecate, I ask that through your power and the powers of the elements that this realm be a place of passion and love, as well as peace and enchantment. So I ask of thee, and so mote it be.'

Mikki closed her eyes against the rush of liquid desire that slid through her body, and she had to bite her lip to keep from moaning his name aloud.

Asterius . . .

SHE shouldn't have been surprised at the speed with which the handmaidens made their excuses and drifted off to their separate rooms. By this time Mikki knew that the women of the realm lived in the west wing of the enormous palace, so far from her own room she could have gone ages without knowing they were there had Gii not told her. Mikki smiled to herself as she walked dreamily up her balcony stair. She could definitely imagine what was going to go on in the women's wing tonight. *I wish the same thing was going on in my room – only with more growling and biting.* A little bubble of laughter escaped from her mouth. She still felt hot and flushed – giddy. No. That wasn't right. She felt hot and flushed – horny. Mikki looked around her balcony.

Empty. She'd hoped he would be there. He was male. He had to have felt the spell, and he had to have known she was the only one who could have cast it.

What if he thought she was opening the realm to men so she could call someone else to her? But how could he think that? She'd used his name during the ritual; she'd thought only of him.

The truth had to be that he was staying away because he thought he'd hurt her. Or maybe because he was afraid he would hurt her if he came to her.

Just the thought made Mikki shiver with erotic pleasure. All that power – a beast barely harnessed by the soul of a man. It was delicious beyond belief. And so damn poisonously seductive.

Okay, she could call him to her. He'd have to come. But is that what she wanted? Of course not. She wanted him to come to her of his own free will and . . .

. . . And that was it. He needed her to come to him. If she did, she'd be showing him she wasn't afraid of him and she cared enough – desired him enough – *loved him enough* – to come to him.

Gii had said his lair was below the baths. Mikki didn't stop to primp or to think; instead, she followed her gut and her heart. She hurried from the balcony and down the path that led to the hot springs. From the top landing, she descended the stairs that connected the large bottom pool to the separate baths on the landing above. She hadn't been down on this level before, but it didn't take long for her to find a second stairway, one that clearly was not as well used as the others. It declined sharply, turning to the north. The end of the stairs emptied into a grassy area that hugged the side of the cliff on which the palace and the springs sat. To her right the grounds opened up to the labyrinth of Mikado Rose beds that were, by far, the healthiest roses in the realm. She knew her private temple sat in the middle of the spiral arrangement of beds; she'd been through the whole area with Aeras and Asterius the day before. So she also knew that there was no lair stuck out there.

Mikki studied the wide patch of grass. It ran along the base of the cliff, just like a path. She smiled and followed where her instincts led. Turning the corner, the cliff wall abruptly opened into a smoothed out entrance to a cave.

'Or better yet, a lair,' she whispered.

She held her breath, stepped inside and was instantly surprised. The entrance had only been a little larger than an average-size door, but inside magickally smokeless torches lent a warm, yellow light to the area, making it look very un-cave-like and welcoming. The cream-colored walls were high and smoothed like the baths of the hot spring. They were also covered with lush paintings. Awed by the talent of the artist, Mikki gazed at the walls. The scenes showed a rocky island surrounded by white sand beaches and water that was a brilliant turquoise. The only person in the landscape was the faint outline of a tall, golden-haired woman.

Crete – these have to be images he remembers from the island of his birth. And the woman? Is it his mother, or the Empousa who rejected him? Not sure if she really wanted to know, she turned away from the beautifully decorated walls. There was a large wooden table in the middle of the room. On it was a bowl filled with cold meat and cheese and a pitcher of wine. There were also several rolls of parchment and glass bottles filled with a thick, dark liquid. Intrigued, Mikki came closer and realized the liquid was ink. One of the parchments was unrolled and held into place with smooth stones. An almost-finished ink drawing was on it. She walked around the table to see what he had been sketching

– and gasped. It was her in the ritual dress she had worn her first night in the realm. She was standing in Hecate's Temple, in front of the Spirit flame. He'd somehow captured the aura of power she felt within the sacred circle, as he depicted her hair flying around her and the look of rapture on her face. It was a beautiful sketch, obviously drawn with loving attention to detail as well as a master's talent.

A beast didn't do this. A man did this, and one who might be very much in love.

'You should not be here!' he snarled.

Chapter Twenty-eight

THE power in his voice caused the torches to flicker madly, but Mikki didn't cringe or start in surprise. Slowly, she raised her eyes from the sketch. And then her stomach lurched. He was standing in a rounded doorway that led to another room deeper within the cave, and he was almost naked. The leather cuirasse was gone, as was the tunic. All he had on was something that looked like a short linen towel slung low and tied around his hips. She licked her lips and reminded herself that if she didn't speak he would assume fear had paralyzed her.

'You wouldn't come to me, so here I am.'

She could see his angry facade falter, and when she smiled, he seemed at a total loss as to what to say. She tried to ignore his almost nakedness, and instead nodded at the walls of the cave. 'The paintings are beautiful. Is that Crete?'

'Yes.'

'You're very talented. Just looking at these makes me want to go on a long Mediterranean vacation.' Before he could formulate a response, she pointed to the sketch of herself. 'And this is flattering. I didn't even know you were there that night.'

'It wasn't meant to flatter.'

'I didn't mean that in a bad way. I meant you made me look pretty and powerful, and that's flattering.'

'That is how I see you,' he said.

'Really?'

'I will never lie to you.'

'Some people would say evasion and omission are lies,' she said bluntly.

'Mikado, if the goddess has commanded me to do or not do something – or to say or not say something – I must obey her. I have given her my oath.'

'Okay, I understand that. I'm sorry. It's just extremely frustrating for me to be in a situation where I don't know all the facts.'

'If I could answer all your questions, I swear to you that I would,' he said.

'Well, that's something I guess.' She sighed and looked back at the walls of the cave. 'How about you show me around? This place is incredible.'

He didn't move from the doorframe. 'Is that why you came here, Mikado, to have me show you my lair?'

'No. I came because I wanted to see you.'

'Why?'

'Because you didn't come to me today. I missed you, especially after I cast the spell that would allow men into the realm.'

'I am not—' he began.

'Jeesh, enough! Didn't we go over this yesterday? I know you're not a man, but man or not, when I was casting the spell, you were who I thought of,' she said.

He looked away from her, and she could see the tension in his jaw and the way his hands kept clenching into fists.

'I know.' His voice sounded strained. 'I felt the spell, and I felt you thinking of me. I wish you would not.'

'Why?' It was her turn to ask.

'Because I cannot bear it!'

Mikki thought it sounded like he had to grind the words between his teeth to get them out.

'I wasn't afraid of you last night,' she said abruptly.

'I saw the fear and loathing in your eyes, but I do not blame you. I wanted only to hold you in my arms and kiss you, and I couldn't do even that small, ordinary thing without becoming a beast.'

'You didn't want to do any more than to just kiss me?' she asked, smiling seductively at him.

His eyes narrowed. 'If I show you my lair, will you leave me in peace, Empousa?'

'Probably not.'

'I thought you were not mean-spirited; I see that I was mistaken,' he said woodenly.

'I'm not being mean-spirited! I'm just doing a really awful job of trying to explain myself. I'm nervous, and I don't know how to put what I'm feeling into words.' She wanted to fidget or pace, but she forced herself to be still and look him in the eye. 'You didn't hurt me last night, and I wasn't afraid of you. I wanted you, even more so when it got a little rough between us. I liked it, Asterius. Your power – the strength in your body that you barely hold in check – is more passion than I've ever known in my life. Until I met you, men were inconsequential to me. And now I think I know why. They always seemed weak, especially when I compared them to the women who had raised me. You see, Asterius, I need someone who is more than a man. Last night when I realized that, the truth of my passion did frighten me. My fear had been formed by the voices I'd heard all my life – the voices of a mundane world that would be shocked by what I feel for you.'

Asterius didn't speak for a long time; he just stared at her as if trying to comprehend something she had said that was very important to him, but spoken in a language he barely understood. Finally, he said, 'Would you still like to see the rest of my lair?'

'I would.'

He stepped from the doorway. 'This is my bedchamber.' He gestured for her to precede him into the room.

She walked through the arched doorway and entered the room. She could feel him follow her. Her whole body was attuned to his presence, as if he was a cobra and she was attempting to charm him. Then the beauty of the room registered. It was smaller than the main room, and it, too, had torches that gave off no smoke. Only here there were fewer of them so the room was dimly lit. The floor was covered with thick animal pelts, in the middle of which sat a huge pallet covered with more pelts. *This is where he sleeps.* The thought sent a wave of wet heat through Mikki's body. She looked quickly from the bed to the walls and was amazed all over again. The walls were filled with scenes from a garden covered with tier after tier of magnificently blooming roses. Each level of the garden held a water element, and in the central tier sat a large statue of—

'It's Tulsa's Rose Gardens!' Mikki gasped. 'How could you have had time to paint this since you've been back?' She approached the smooth wall and touched it cautiously. It was completely dry. 'There's so much here; this should have taken you months, or even years to paint.'

'It did,' he said.

She looked over her shoulder at him, not sure she had heard him correctly. 'How can that be?'

'I painted this from images I saw in my dreams.'

Caressingly, she skimmed her hand over the wall. 'It's perfect. You got all the details right.'

'Does it make you long for your home?'

She could feel him getting closer to her, but she didn't turn around, afraid that if she moved, he'd shy away. 'No. The Realm of the Rose is my home now. I don't want to be anywhere except here, with you.'

'I ached to come to you today,' he said.

'And I couldn't stop thinking about you.' Mikki's hand was trembling, so she dropped it quickly to her side.

He was so close to her she could feel the heat of his body against her back. Then his hands were on her shoulders and his mouth was against her ear. 'When you cast the spell opening the realm to men, I felt you calling to me . . . beckoning . . . asking . . .' He growled low in his throat, and Mikki could feel the vibration through the depths of her soul. 'I thought it would drive me mad to stay away from you.'

'Then don't stay away from me. I don't want you to stay away from me,' she said breathlessly and she pressed back into him, feeling his erection push against the swell of her ass. His hot lips were on the side of her throat, and she could feel his sharp teeth barely graze her skin with his kisses. When his hands left her shoulders to cup her breasts, she arched to meet him. Her arms went up to pull his head down to her, and, just like in her long-ago dream, she felt his horns through the thick mane of his hair at the same time his teeth found the hollow between her neck and shoulder and teased her with a stinging bite. She moaned and pressed herself more firmly against him.

Suddenly he froze.

'No, don't stop,' she pleaded.

'It – it's gone!'

With the words his breath came out in a rush, and she could feel his body begin to tremble violently. Worried, she turned in his arms. He was staring at her with an expression of mixed joy and shock.

'What's wrong? What's gone?'

He took her face between his hands. 'You love me.' His voice broke on the words, and tears dripped silently down his cheeks.

She smiled. 'Yes. I love you, but what's gone?'

He closed his eyes, trying to contain the raw joy of his emotions. 'The last of the spell, my Mikado, and the last barrier between us. No matter what the Fates may bring, I will love you until the end of time.'

He bent and kissed her gently. Fisting her hand in his hair, she pulled his mouth more firmly against her. His growl moved through her already-aroused senses like a knowing caress. He lifted his head and opened his eyes. They were dark and fierce with desire. His bronze skin was already slick with sweat. She ran her hands down his body, from his shoulders over his chest, to the cords of his abdominal muscles, which quivered under her touch. When she'd begun touching him, he'd taken his hands from her face, and now they were braced against the wall on either side of her so she stood in a cage of his arms.

'Don't move. Just let me touch you,' she said huskily.

'I do not know how long I can keep my hands from you.' His chest rumbled, passion straining his voice.

'It won't be long.' She touched the side of his face and then traced his lips with her thumb. 'First I want to see you – all of you.'

She saw the automatic doubt that shadowed his eyes, but he nodded slowly, acquiescing to her need. Her hands slipped down his body again, this time not stopping until her fingers hooked in the linen wrap tied low around his waist. She pulled at the fabric, and it came free easily. Mikki stared at his naked body.

'Your father's wife meant to curse you, but she had actually created a creature of incredible beauty,' she whispered the words into life. 'You're not an abomination; you're a miracle.'

He was raw male power so perfectly blended with beast that it was difficult to tell where exactly the man ended and the beast began. His waist tapered to flanks and thighs covered with dark fur. From his waist down he was less thickly muscled than he had appeared to be when his body was clothed. Naked, his lean, powerful lines were visible. Mesmerized, Mikki stroked the place where the skin of the man gave way to the body of the beast. Asterius bowed his head and growled. She looked into his face. His eyes were tightly closed, and he was breathing heavily in an effort to control the creature within. Mikki felt a hot rush of desire as she watched the beast stir. Her eyes moved back down his body. He was fully erect and formed like a man. The skin that covered his shaft was the same bronze of his chest. Mikki took its heavy length in her hands, stroking with one, squeezing with the other. When she touched him, his eyes opened to find her watching him.

'You don't always have to keep the beast chained, Asterius,' she whispered. Still stroking him, she leaned forward, circling his nipple with her tongue. 'Let him loose, my love. I'm not afraid of him.' She took the hard nub of his nipple between her teeth and bit sharply down.

His snarl was a wave of thunderous sound. He lifted her into his arms. His hooves thudded heavily against the pelt-covered floor as he strode to his pallet. He laid her there, but before he could cover her with his body, she stood, causing him, once again, to pull back. In his pained expression she read too easily what he was thinking.

'You've got to stop believing that I'm afraid of you. I'm not. I didn't stand up to get away from you. I just thought you would like this off . . .' Mikki began to unpin the silver rose brooch that held her chiton together over her right shoulder, but her hands were trembling and she could not unclasp it. Frustrated, she looked up at him and then her expression changed to a seductive smile.'Would you do something for me?'

'Anything,' he rasped.

'Unsheathe your claws and get this thing off me.'

With a movement catlike in its grace, he silently extended the daggers from his fingers. Quickly and easily, he sliced through the material at her shoulder. She shrugged and the chiton fell from her body. His dark eyes gazed at her. He lifted a hand to touch her breast and then jerked it back when the still extended claw met her soft flesh. Mikki caught his wrist.

'Your control is so great that you can create beautiful art with these claws. Use that same control to touch me with them. Let me feel your power against my skin.' Unflinching, she pressed his hand against her breast.

Hesitantly, he let the sharp points graze the creamy smoothness of her skin as his hand moved from her breast to her stomach and slid slowly . . . slowly . . . over the wet, hot core of her. Mikki sucked in her breath and shivered.

'Don't stop,' she moaned.

His eyes never left her face as his claws trailed down her thighs and then around to rake softly over the voluptuous swell of her ass.

'Turn around. I want to see your back,' he said, his deep voice rough with desire.

Mikki turned. She felt his lips replace claws as he kissed the raised pink lines he had left on her back.

'I thought I had ripped through your skin.' His breath was hot against her skin.

'Of course you didn't. They're just scratches.'

His lips moved to the small of her back, and his tongue tasted her. 'I didn't think I would ever touch you again.'

She turned and wrapped her arms around his neck as he licked and teased her nipples.

'Don't ever stop touching me, Asterius.'

She sank down to the pallet, pulling him with her. He knelt beside her. Sheathing his claws, he touched her face gently. 'I could not stop now, Mikado, even if Hecate herself appeared and commanded it.'

'Shh.' She pressed a finger against his lips. 'I don't want to think about anything else except you.' Slowly, she lifted her hand until the same finger that had pressed against his lips traced the smooth line of one dark horn. 'You are amazing. I don't ever think I'll get enough of touching you.'

'Mikado, you are a rare and unexpected gift.' His deep voice trembled with the depth of his emotions. 'I have never known the love of a woman – never, in all the eons of my existence, has a woman touched me, accepted me, loved me . . .' He had to pause before he could continue. 'I will love you for as long as there is breath in my body, and beyond, if the Fates and our goddess will it.'

'Come to me, Asterius. Show me the power of your love,' she beckoned.

He worshipped her with his mouth and hands. He drank in her body as if he would never get enough of it. He explored her and, with the superhuman senses of a beast, he read the flushes and changes in her body, learning what brought her the most pleasure. And then, when he thought he could never know anything sweeter than watching the passion he had built within her, she pressed him to the pallet and began her own exploration.

When her tongue teased him and she whispered against his skin that the hard length of his body was magnificent and how much she desired him, Asterius thought he would die of such exquisite pleasure.

'I need to feel you inside me.'

Mikki opened herself to him. He trembled with the effort of controlling himself as she wrapped her legs around him and arched against him. Blood rushed painfully through his body, and the roar of the beast filled his mind. The beast wanted to pound violently into her, to bury his aching hardness in her wet heat. He clenched his teeth, sliding carefully in and out of her, trying to focus on her soft sounds of pleasure through the tumult in his mind. And then he realized that she was meeting his gentle thrusts with a fierceness that blazed in her eyes. When he bent to kiss her, she bit his lip. He growled. She smiled.

'Let the beast loose. I want him,' she said in a deep, sultry voice.

Her words ignited a flame of lust within him that he was afraid would consume them both. Unable to fight against the combined force of her desire and the power of the beast, Asterius grabbed her ass and lifted her up to meet him as he impaled himself within her, over and over again. Mikado didn't shrink from him. She answered his passion with a strength that was goddess-touched. The beast and the priestess blazed together, until finally the man within could no longer stop the raging force and he poured a lifetime of need into her as beast and man together roared her name.

Chapter Twenty-nine

HE couldn't stop looking at Mikado. She was asleep, her naked body pressed against him. She was using his arm to cushion her head. One of her long, smooth legs was thrown intimately over his inhuman one. Her hand lay limply on his chest. He drew a deep breath, letting her scent imprint upon his senses.

He'd never imagined this. Even when he'd wildly hoped that the other Empousa might care for him . . . love him . . . he'd only thought about the sweet softness of her hands touching him. It was only in his dreams that he'd allowed himself to imagine making love to a mortal woman. But his dreams never came true. Until now. Until Mikado. When he had touched her and realized that the pain of the goddess's spell had been lifted, and what that meant, she had spun reality into his dreams, and in doing so had healed the wound of loneliness that had been festering within him for an eternity.

What was he going to do? She had saved him. Could he do any less for her?

If he did not sacrifice her, the realm would die. It might not happen immediately. Hecate might find another Empousa, but irrevocable damage would already have been done. The betrayal of one Empousa had caused sickness in a realm that had never before known blight or pestilence or illness of any kind. Those things did not belong in Hecate's realm of dreams and magick. But betrayal and abandonment had caused the barrier to weaken. Asterius was certain that only Mikado's swift action had prevented further disaster.

So he must choose between destroying his dream or destroying the dreams of mankind.

It was really no choice at all. Only a beast could choose himself over mankind. He felt the agony of what he must do press against him like a flaming spear thrust into his entrails.

'I can feel you watching me,' Mikki said. Sleepily, she opened her eyes and smiled up at him. 'Don't you ever sleep?'

'I would rather gaze at you.' He brushed back a thick strand of hair from her face.

'I should have guessed that you'd be a romantic when you put the rose in my wine.'

'That is not romantic; it is civilized.' He tempered the gruffiness of his voice with a slight smile and caressed the graceful slope of her neck and shoulder, smiling again when she sighed happily and stretched like a contented feline.

'Don't burst my bubble. I prefer to think of it as romance.'

'Then, for you, I will call it romance, too.' Slowly, with a sweet hesitance and innocence that were at direct odds with the fierceness of his body, he bent and gently kissed her lips. 'When you came to me today, you offered me more than your body and your love. You offered acceptance. And that is something I never imagined knowing the joy of.'

She took his hand and threaded her fingers with his. 'That's something you and I have in common. In my old world, I didn't feel like I belonged.' She took a deep breath and made the decision. She wanted him to know. She needed him to know. 'Hecate explained to me part of the reason I felt so out of place – because I was meant to be her Empousa in this world, that I carry the blood of a High Priestess in my veins. But there's another reason. It's why I never let anyone, especially any man, get too close to me. It has to do with my blood, too.' She studied his dark eyes, silently pleading with him to understand. 'The women of my family are tied to roses through their blood. If we feed roses water mixed with our blood, they grow. Always – incredibly. In the mundane world, what I could do was unheard of – outside of the women in my family, no one would understand. It made me feel like I was a freak. I had to hide my secret.' Worried by how still and pale he had suddenly become, she felt herself shrinking inside. 'I wish you'd say something. I've never told anyone else.' When he still didn't speak, she started to move away from him, but with a low growl, he pulled her fiercely into the protection of his arms.

'You did not feel accepted there because it was your destiny to be Hecate's Empousa – to come here and to save the roses and their lonely Guardian. The blood that runs through your veins is this realm's life force, and it is your love that sustains us.' He closed his eyes and buried his head in her hair, willing himself not to tremble . . . willing himself not to think . . .

Mikki relaxed and fitted herself more comfortably against him. 'It still amazes me. If the exact sequence of events hadn't happened, I wouldn't be here.' She leaned back in his arms so she could look into his face and wondered, briefly, about why he still looked so pale. 'You know, it was my blood that woke you up.'

'I did not know.' His voice was gravely. 'I just know you roused me and that I could smell your scent and knew you were Hecate's Empousa.'

'Actually, that's one of the weirder aspects of what happened. Just that day an exotic old woman had given me some perfume. On impulse I wore it. As strange as this sounds, it is the same scent I'm wearing now. Gii calls it the Empousa's anointing oil.'

He frowned. 'How can that be?'

Mikki shrugged and nestled back against him. 'I have no idea, but she was really eccentric. And beautiful, even though she was old. She had the most incredible blue eyes. She was foreign, but I couldn't place her accent. She said she got the perfume . . .' Mikki had to stop and think about what the woman had said. 'Somewhere in Greece, if I remember correctly. What I do remember for sure is her name, because, like me, she's named after a rose – Sevillana.'

She felt the jolt of shock jerk through his body. She pulled back to find him staring at her with an unreadable expression on his unnaturally pale face.

'What is it? What's wrong?'

'It – it is . . . nothing. Nothing is wrong. I am only surprised that a woman in the mundane world would carry the anointing oil of Hecate's High Priestess. It is a mystery.' He wrapped his arms around her. 'Lie against me. Let me feel your body touching mine.'

Mikado lay on his chest, and as he caressed the long, graceful line of her back, his mind whirled unbelievingly. Sevillana . . . the name had sent shockwaves through his body. It was she! He, too, would always remember the cold beauty of her calculating blue eyes as well as her name. The last Empousa was still alive in the mundane world. How could it be possible? Time moved differently there, he knew that. But at least two hundred of that world's years must have passed. Perhaps the absent Empousa had taken more with her through the crossroads than a vial of anointing oil. Perhaps she'd managed to steal some of the realm's magick.

Then the enormity of the truth sifted through his shock. Sevillana lived! In the spring when an Empousa must be sacrificed for the realm it would be Sevillana and not Mikado who must die. All he need do was to find a way to return the absent Empousa to the Realm of the Rose. It had to be possible. Sevillana had escaped – she could certainly return. He held Mikado more tightly. That was his answer. He would not sacrifice Mikado. He would exchange her for the errant High Priestess, returning Mikado safely to her home in the mundane world. He would still be without her, but Asterius could live with that. He would miss her for all of eternity, but he could bear that. What he could not bear was knowing that it was by his hand she would die. If she left, he would lose his love. If he sacrificed her, he would lose his soul.

He wouldn't sacrifice his love, nor would he lose his soul. He had his answer, and he had the powers of the son of a Titan. He would turn that vast store of magick to achieving his end. But not now. Not tonight. Tonight he would revel in the miracle of Mikado's love, and he would not think about the endless empty dawns to come.

MIKKI leaned against the smooth entrance to the cave and gazed out at the misty morning while she chewed a piece of bread. Asterius came up behind her, and she leaned comfortably into him.

'Rain,' he said, sounding surprised. 'It does not often rain here.'

'I did it. It's what I commanded Water to do when I cast the health and protection spell yesterday. Every fourth morning it's going to rain for a little while. It's good for the roses, and it's good for the realm, too. Rainy mornings are restful – a perfect time to sleep in and rejuvenate the soul.' She turned in his arms. 'Unfortunately, I didn't think to tell the handmaidens yesterday that rainy mornings equate to taking the morning off. I imagine the four Elementals are wondering impatiently why I haven't called them to work. And because last night was the first time men could be invited into the realm in a long time, I would bet that at least a couple of them are tired and grumpy while they wait. I should go see to them. What are you going to do?'

'I will do the same thing I do every morning. I will follow the rose wall around the realm to be certain all is secure. Then I will collect more threads for the Dream Weavers.' He caressed the side of her face. 'Only this morning I go about my duties with your scent on my skin and the memory of your smile, touch, taste, in my heart.' He smiled. 'Some say rain is dark and dreary, but to me this morning is bright and filled with promise.'

'An incurable romantic. Who knew?' Mikki tugged at his cuirasse. 'Kiss me so we can be on our way.' She wondered if he would ever lose that look of startled happiness that was reflected on his face when she surprised him with a touch, or, like now, with a kiss. She sincerely hoped not. 'Can you take time to eat the midday meal with me?'

He kissed her again before he answered. 'Of course. All you need do is to call me to you.'

'And tonight?'

'Command me, Empousa, and I shall obey,' he said, dark eyes shining.

'You say that now, but let's see what you think of obeying my every command in a year or so,' she teased, raising an eyebrow at him cockily, and was surprised to see his look tighten and his eyes lose all their sparkling humor.

'I would never tire of you, or of your commands, Mikado, not if we had an eternity to share together.'

His words pressed heavily on her heart. How had she forgotten that he was an immortal? She would age; he would not. She would die; he would not. No! She wouldn't think about that now, not at the beginning of their love. They deserved time to savor the sweet, heady feeling of new love – in that way they were no different from any other couple. She wouldn't ruin the honeymoon of their love with dire thoughts of a future with her, shrunken and tottering around the gardens, leaning on his perpetually virile arm. Would he let her? Would he still want her then? *Stop it! I'm doing exactly what I just promised I wouldn't.* Mikki made her lips smile.

'I wasn't being serious; I was just kidding you, Asterius. But since you mentioned the whole command thing, I'll be happy to command you to come to me tonight.' She glanced over his shoulder at the cozy cave, as filled with his presence as it was with the exquisite art he created. 'Actually, I think I'd rather come to you.'

'I do not believe you received the tour you requested earlier.'

'Well, that's one of the things you'll be doing tonight, but only one . . .'

THE light rain changed the appearance of the gardens, washing them with a watercolor brush, turning reality impressionistic. Mikki decided she liked it. It went with the theme of the place – dreamy.

She meant to go straight to the palace and call the Elementals – the poor girls were probably going to be thoroughly pissed at her, especially if any of them had kicked someone scrumptious out of her bed – but she wandered, letting herself get lost in the misty magick of the roses. They felt better this morning. Even as she made her way slowly in a southerly direction, the sickness that had been pulling at her stomach whenever she immersed herself in the gardens didn't come. She even saw several hearty

Floribunda lavenders she recognized as Angel Face in full bloom, where yesterday they had just been weak buds. Mikki smiled. Inordinately proud, she dubbed herself *Goddess of the Rose.*

And she daydreamed about him. Her body felt deliciously sore in places she'd forgotten she had. It had been almost a year since the last time she'd had sex, but she'd never experienced anything like making love with Asterius. His body . . . the man/beast mixture had been intriguing . . . alluring, but what she'd found most seductive was the freedom she felt with him. She could let her own beast loose when they were together and trust him not to turn away from her. He matched her, passion for passion. And he knew her – he saw into her soul. Asterius, Minotaur, Guardian – he knew what it was to be an outlander. Well, they had finally found their home – together.

'The rain was a clever idea, Empousa.'

Mikki thought she'd stroke out at the sound of Hecate's voice. 'Good grief, you scared the bejeezus out of me!' Then she remembered to whom she was speaking, cleared her throat and turned around to face the goddess with a heart that pounded painfully in her chest. 'I'm sorry, Hecate.' Mikki curtseyed as she had seen the handmaidens do so often. The goddess was sitting on a marble bench just a few feet behind her. 'You surprised me. I shouldn't have spoken to you like that.'

Hecate waved her hand dismissively. 'My Empousa is allowed liberties few others will ever know.' She gestured beside her. 'Come, sit with me.'

Swallowing down her nerves, she approached the goddess. The enormous dogs were at their position by her side, and they ignored Mikki completely. Hecate was clothed in the colors of night – black, the deepest blue and gray. She had manifested as the striking middle-aged woman again, and the light misting of rain looked like jewels in her dark hair.

'The spell of protection and health you cast yesterday was well thought out. I agree with your instincts. The rain refreshes the roses and the realm. Also, the little insects you commanded Earth to provide were a lovely surprise, and Wind was delighted to carry them here' – the goddess paused and then surprised Mikki with a musical laugh –'although you cannot see their red-and-black bodies through this mist.'

'Ladybugs feed on aphids, and roses hate aphids,' Mikki said, a little overwhelmed by Hecate's effusive praise.

'The roses thrive again. I am pleased.'

'Thank you, Hecate.'

'It was also good that you instructed Flame to illuminate the rose wall, most especially at the gate. Now that men will be coming and going again, you must take special care with the gate.'

Mikki rubbed a hand across her brow. 'I didn't even think about that. Uh! I'm a fool. How did I expect them to get in and out of the realm?'

'It is not a bad thing that you have allowed men here again. You've made many of the women very happy. All night I heard the names of lovers whispered in invitation and carried to the ancient world where they were eagerly accepted.' Hecate's expression became sultry. 'Still this morning lovers are being called and enjoyed by my women, who have long been revered as some of the most beautiful and intelligent in the ancient world. Having males about means we will have new life in the realm. Girl children are a blessing, and I look forward to the births.'

'But Dream Stealers are in the forest. We have to be careful if that gate is opening and closing at all hours.'

'You are the Empousa, Mikado. You may place limits on when the men are allowed to come and go.' Hecate gave her a kind look. 'It is good that you understand the dangers that lurk on the other side of the rose barrier, but you need not worry yourself. The Guardian's strength will protect the realm. Couple his vigilance with your nurturing of the roses, and all will be well in the Realm of the Rose.'

Mikki tried not to think or react at all. She kept her mind blank and nodded respectfully.

'Excellent. Now, what I came to tell you is that I have matters to attend to which will take me far from my realm. You are not to be concerned if I do not visit here for' – she moved a round, white shoulder – 'some time. Within this realm my powers are always here if you have need of them. I sense that you are relying more confidently upon your instincts, and for that I applaud your wisdom. Let your intuition guide you. If your blood and heart and spirit tell you something, then you may always believe it. And remember, Empousa, I applaud what you have done for the roses, but it is not so much your actions that have begun their recovery. It is your presence, and the blood tie you have with them that assures they will thrive. Be wise, Empousa. The dreams of mankind depend upon you ...' Hecate raised her hand and disappeared in a glittering of mist.

Chapter Thirty

MIKKI couldn't say she wasn't relieved that Hecate would be gone for a while. Of course she'd have to tell the goddess about her relationship with Asterius. Telling her would be ever so much better than Hecate reading her mind or finding out on her own some other way. Mikki wanted to run and hide just thinking about it. So she'd tell her, but she sure as hell didn't want to do it soon. It wasn't that she was ashamed that she loved Asterius, and it wasn't that she was afraid of Hecate, though the goddess was definitely intimidating. It was just that Mikki wanted to keep Asterius to herself. Why couldn't they have privacy to discover the shared secrets of new love? Even had she fallen in love with a man back in Tulsa, Mikki would have wanted time for the two of them to get over the newness of love before she hauled him around and opened their lives up for everyone to poke and prod. She was private, and the more important something was to her, the more private she was about it. Asterius was very important to her.

When Hecate returned from wherever, she would have a conversation with her about Asterius. Then she'd deal with the goddess's response, whatever it may be. Until then she would cherish this honeymoon period they had been granted and thoroughly enjoy the fact that she had finally fallen in love.

Satisfied with her plan of attack, Mikki left the bench and checked the surrounding beds and fountains to make sure she was heading in the right direction. Hecate's comments about the men coming and going through the rose gate had worried her, and, no matter what the goddess said, she was going to keep that worry fresh. Right now her instincts were telling her to check the gate for herself – then announce a curfew, even though she loathed the thought of acting like a den mother at a naughty sorority. She'd like to talk with Asterius about it, but it only made sense to place some limits on when the gate could be open. And also, she needed to find out who exactly could open it. Asterius could, of course, and he'd said she could, too. The Dream Weavers had mentioned that the Elementals had collected the threads of reality while he had been bespelled, so they had to be able to open the gate. But who else? It would be a massive headache if every woman in the realm could wave her fingers and have the damn thing part like the Red Sea. Clearly, there was a lot of work for her to do.

Checking her mental watch, Mikki picked up her pace. She really did need to get a move on and call her handmaidens. She could, of course, call them right now and have them meet her out here in the gardens, but it seemed too Nurse Ratchet-like. She'd much rather get the gate checked, hurry back to her room, change out of her wet (and torn, then pieced back together this morning) chiton, have Daphne bring some lovely tea and eventually have a comfortable meeting with the girls over a late brunch. And anyway, it was still early. The handmaidens weren't stupid. They could certainly look at the weather and realize that there was little work in the gardens they could do in the rain. Maybe they would even climb back in bed. Mikki smiled to herself, hoping they weren't climbing back into lonely beds – tonight she certainly wouldn't be.

The rain had moved lazily from drizzle to mist to a moon-colored fog that drifted over the roses as if they were in the

Lake District of England. The fog thickened the farther south she walked, and Mikki was preoccupied with thoughts of the evening to come, trying to decide if she could sneak Asterius up to the hot springs for a whole new meaning to 'scrubbed clean,' when multiflora roses reared in front of her nose and she almost smacked into the wall.

'Remember, next spell tell Wind to blow away the fog after the rain,' she mumbled to herself while she scanned the gate for signs of wear and tear. 'You look good,' she pronounced, patting part of the foliage.

'Priestess! Can you help us?'

Mikki looked around, trying to see where the deep voice was coming from. It was unmistakably male, which seemed out of place in the gardens.

'Here, Priestess! We're out here!'

Mikki realized that the voice was coming from the other side of the rose wall. She bent a little so she could look through a less-dense part of the climbing branches, and her eyes widened in surprise. Four men stood just outside the gate, surrounded by thick gray fog. Three of them were dressed as she imagined ancient Greek men should dress. In toga-looking outfits, with one arm bare, and regal purple embroidered cloaks tossed over their broad backs. They were all tall, well built and youthfully handsome.

The fourth man was clearly their leader and the one who had spoken. He stood in front of the others and was dressed in much the same style she was used to seeing Asterius wear, with a cuirasse over a short, pleated tunic. But there is where his similarity to her lover ended. This man was beautiful, tall and golden. Even in the foggy morning he shined. His skin was tanned to that singular color only a few true blondes get naturally – a healthy, burnished brown that looked like the purest of honey. It covered a body that was perfection. He was athletically built, without being too heavily muscled and brutish. His hair was thick and wavy, cut short enough to be masculine, but left long enough to be endearingly boyish. His eyes were so blue that Mikki could feel them searching through the roses to find her.

She'd never seen a man that handsome in person. Usually such perfection was limited to Hollywood and the machinations of filmmakers and plastic surgeons.

'There you are, Priestess!' He smiled, and his incredible face lit with warmth. 'We're here. We answered your call.'

She smiled back (who wouldn't return a smile like that?). 'My call?'

'Well, Priestess, I can only pray to the Great Goddess that I could be lucky enough to be called by a beauty such as you.'

Ridiculously, Mikki felt her face flush. 'I've heard that blue eyes are weaker than brown or green. I think you've just proven the rumor true.'

He laughed, and the sound was as catching as it was seductive. 'Ah, I see my prayers have been answered! The goddess has granted me a priestess who has wit as well as beauty.' He took a few steps toward the rose gate. His friends followed.

Mikki watched him move with a natural confidence that was easy and attractive – and so unlike Asterius's inhumanly feral grace that the comparison was jarring. She didn't desire the golden man, but she did feel a sliver of envy for the woman who had called him, followed instantly by a rush of guilt. What the hell was wrong with her? She'd just left Asterius's bed after proclaiming her love for him! And here she was gawking all calf-eyed at a handsome stranger? Maybe the rain had seeped through her head and into her brain, waterlogging it.

'Priestess, will you open the gate for us, or shall my comrades and I woo you through the prickly wall?'

'No!' she said a little too loudly. And then, feeling like an idiot, she added, 'I didn't call you, so you don't need to woo me at all.'

His expression showed honest disappointment. 'I must apologize, gracious lady. I assumed you were one of the Elementals – Flame perhaps, with your wealth of fire-kissed tresses and your extraordinary beauty. It was, after all, Flame who called me here. I would have been a fortunate man had you been she.'

'Sorry, I'm not an Elemental.' Mikki smiled. She wasn't being unfaithful to Asterius by being polite to him – she was doing her duty as Empousa. After all, she was the one who cast the spell to allow men within *her* realm. 'I'm the Empousa.'

The man's aquamarine eyes crinkled endearingly at the edges with his joyous smile. 'Empousa!' He bowed with a lovely chivalrous flourish, which the other men copied, each calling gallant greetings to her. 'What a fortunate coincidence that you were passing at this moment. There is word that a new Empousa reigns in the Realm of the Rose. We are honored to meet you.' His smile was boyish with good humor. 'Though the meeting was shouted through a barrier of roses.'

'You say Floga invited you?'

'She did, Empousa.'

'Did she invite your friends, too?' Mikki tried to keep the mischievous grin from her face, but she failed miserably. She could all too easily imagine the Flame Elemental needing four men to extinguish her passion – even if one of them did look like Adonis.

For an instant Mikki felt a stab of jealousy as she thought about the Elemental's freedom and the ease with which she could walk side by side with any man she chose.

'She did not, Empousa,' said one of the toga-wearers who had thick, dark hair and a well-defined face, bringing her thoughts back to their conversation. 'The Earth Elemental is the priestess whose call I answer.'

'Water called me, Empousa,' another man said.

'I am fortunate to be summoned by Air,' said the fourth man, who had long, auburn hair and remarkably green eyes.

Damn, but they were four deliciously handsome men! Her Elementals definitely had made good choices. Mikki made a mental note to ask Gii just exactly how this whole man-inviting thing worked. It was a little weird that they had been called by the girls this morning, but then again, maybe it wasn't. She hadn't called them to work – it was rainy – they'd decided to busy themselves in their own way. Clearly they were as smart as Mikki had given them credit for being.

'I'm sure the Elementals will be here any second. I'll be happy to let you guys in.'

Their leader's eyes lit, and he bowed again to her. 'To be invited within the Realm of the Rose by its Empousa is truly an honor we do not deserve.'

'Oh, it's no problem. We can walk back to the palace together. I was just going to head in that direction.' And being escorted by four to-die-for-handsome young men was definitely not a hardship. Neither was it wrong. She felt an unexpected surge of anger. Hell, no! It wasn't wrong. She was in love, not dead. And all she was doing was taking the men to her handmaidens. The only ulterior motive she had was maybe to engage in some harmless flirtation. And why not? She felt amazingly pretty and completely loved. But that didn't mean she wanted to be controlled and caged! Asterius could just think again if he expected to put his brand on her and treat her like a prize heifer! Is that what Asterius would expect from her? To allow him to own her every movement? She was suddenly afraid that he might. He was, after all, a beast. She couldn't expect him to know how to treat a woman.

Somewhere in the depths of Mikki's mind a warning tried to cry its way through the cacophony of unnaturally defensive thoughts that bubbled and brewed like a rancid stew. But they could not be heard over the hatred and envy, selfishness and fear that were shouting so loudly.

Feeling totally pissed off, she moved to the middle of the gate and frowned at it. No doorknob. No latch. No bar to slide back. Frustrated, and especially annoyed at the massive headache that pounded in her temples, she raised one hand and pressed her palm against the gate.

'This is your Empousa speaking. Open the hell up,' she muttered angrily.

The living gate instantly swung open. The four men stepped out of the swirling fog, smiling at her as if she had just given them the key to paradise. Mikki smiled absently back at them, wishing they'd hurry and get inside. She didn't like the looks of the gray-cloaked forest, and she wanted to get the gate shut right away. The second the last man was through, she raised her hand again and whispered for the gate to close, breathing a sigh of relief when it obeyed her. Then she turned to the men.

'Okay, the palace is that way.' Mikki gestured to the widest of the marble pathways.

'After you, Empousa,' the golden man said.

Mikki began down the path but stopped abruptly when the dark-haired man stepped in front of her to block her way.

'Uh, it's that way,' Mikki said, pointing over the man's shoulder and thinking that he may be handsome, but he definitely wasn't the brightest Crayola in the pack.

311

'Perhaps you would like to know our names before you lead us to the palace, Empousa.'

The golden man's voice came from directly behind her. He was standing so close she could feel his breath on her hair. The other two men stepped in to close the tight circle so they had her neatly surrounded, and in that instant her mind cleared – the pain in her head stopped, as did the deafening emotions that had been seething in her mind.

Mikki was suddenly, horribly afraid. They were Dream Stealers, and she had opened the rose gate for them.

Instincts that had been silenced from the moment she had begun talking with the golden man screamed at her not to show fear. Mikki swallowed the bile that had risen in her throat, drew herself up regally and turned to face the golden man.

'What is this all about?' she snapped.

'We're simply saying that we would like to introduce ourselves to you, Empousa. You see, we already know you. We've enjoyed watching you. Now we'd like for you to know exactly who you have so graciously invited within your realm.' His voice had changed from charming to sarcastic. His lip curled at her, and his handsome face twisted in disgust.

'I don't like your tone, and I don't like how close you're standing to me,' Mikki said sternly, trying to imitate Hecate's intimidating tone. 'I think it's time you left. I've decided my handmaidens wouldn't like you.'

'Too late! You opened the barrier to us, and you will see that once invited, we are not so easily banished.' He reached out and lifted a strand of her hair that had fallen over her shoulder. Mikki tried to jerk away from him, but hard hands grasped her shoulders and held her in place as the golden man bent and sniffed at her hair. Mikki struggled. Fisting his hand in her hair, he jerked

312

her head to the side. Like a snake tasting the skin of its prey, his tongue flicked out to graze the side of her neck.

'Ah, the sweet taste of an Empousa. It has been centuries since I've sampled this particular delicacy.'

'Stop it!' Mikki cried. 'Let go of me!'

Surprisingly, the golden man let loose her hair. He smiled at her, but it was a baring of teeth, not an expression of humor. 'We're going to enjoy our visit with you, Empousa. And we do appreciate the weather change you commanded – all the better to cloak our little rendezvous, though it looks as if someone has already had the pleasure of your company this morning.' With reptilian grace, he lashed out and ripped the brooch that held together the torn pieces of her chiton.

Mikki was frozen with fear. She clutched at her chiton, trying not to vomit as the men crowded closer around her, grasping her with hungry hands and watching her with ravenous eyes.

'Come now, Empousa. Don't be shy. You can't say you don't recognize me.'

'Or me,' the dark-haired man breathed into her back.

'Or me.'

'And me.'

'Look into my eyes, Empousa. I'm sure you've seen me before. Can you not guess my name?'

She stared into the golden man's blue eyes – and they changed. The pupils shifted and became slits. The color faded and washed from brilliant blue to the red of old blood. Mikki did know him. Who he was seared through her mind, and with his naming came a fury that burned away her fear.

'Get your fucking hands off of me!' She jerked violently. Surprised, the dark-haired man holding her from behind stumbled and lost his grip on her, and she was able to back several steps away from them.

The golden man laughed and followed her with smooth, serpentine grace. 'Good . . . we like it when they struggle. It makes it more interesting. What do you see when you look within my eyes, Empousa?'

'I see an asswipe who needs to invest in color contacts.' She kept backing away. He and the other men followed her.

'Ha! I will have to teach you better things to do with that sharp tongue of yours. But for now, tell me, Empousa, what name would you give me?'

'Hatred,' she said without hesitation.

His smile was fierce. 'Ah! You are a quick study. Perhaps I will take you with me when we leave here. Would you like that? I am a man who knows intimately the hidden desires of women.'

'Man?' She laughed sarcastically. 'You're not a man; you're a creature. A carrion eater that feeds on the carcasses of dreams. I don't care what kind of skin you wrap yourself up in! You're no man.'

He lunged forward and grabbed her arms. 'Not a man? I'll show you how much of a man I am!'

As the others closed on her, Mikki screamed the one name that filled her heart and soul, 'Asterius!'

'Your lover, whoever he is, will not save you now, and if you truly care for him, I suggest that you remain very quiet. No mortal man could look upon us without losing a part of his soul.' Hatred breathed stinking breath in her face as he grasped the front of her chiton and ripped it from her body. 'Cover her mouth, and be certain she does not make a sound. In this fog there is no chance we will be discovered until it is too late for her, and too late for them.'

They dragged Mikki off the marble path into a bed of Salet roses. She struggled, kicking for groins and insteps and using her fingernails to gouge any flesh they came in contact with, as every damned self-defense class in America taught, but the four of them easily overpowered her. They pushed her to the ground, and she saw that the newly worked dirt was covered with the pink petals of destroyed roses, as if blushing snow had fallen to the ground with her. One of them was choking her. She could not scream, so within her mind she shrieked over and over *Asterius! Come to me!*

'And now, I will show you that I am, indeed, a man,' Hatred said, pushing aside the front of his short tunic and taking his engorged flesh in his hand. 'Then Fear, Envy, and Selfishness will have their turns with you.' His laugh was thoroughly mad. 'It is an interesting irony that Selfishness chooses to take you last. Or perhaps it is not. Perhaps he will choose to keep you to himself while we visit the women in the rest of your pathetic realm, Empousa.'

Mikki caught a blurred movement from the edge of her darkening vision and then Asterius burst out of the fog. His roar of rage was deafening. Hatred whirled to face him. As the Dream Stealer moved, his body rippled and reformed until he was, as Mikki had accused, not a man, but a creature, and one that should exist only in the realm of nightmares. His skin was scaled, and his snakelike eyes bulged from a head shaped like a cobra's flared hood. His body had remained humanoid, but he crouched on all fours, hissing black froth from his open mouth like an evil reptile. Asterius's hand whipped out as he charged past the creature, slicing a bloody trail across Hatred's chest.

Mikki heard angry hisses from the creatures who were holding her and then she was suddenly free as Fear, Envy, and Selfishness hurried to stand beside their leader. They were truly a horrifying group. Each had retained something of his man form, but with monstrous mutations. Fear was a rotting corpse, with long, filthy claws and misshapen features. Envy's all-too-human body was covered with a sickening plant whose spikes burst through his skin like deadly thorns. He crouched, hissing, reminding Mikki of a poisonous swamp creature. Selfishness's body had elongated, and he had grown several sets of snakelike tentacles. He gnashed gruesome teeth while his arms writhed independently of one another.

They all faced Asterius as the Guardian charged them. Fear went down first, disemboweled neatly by the great beast's claws. The Dream Stealer's body crumbled and then dissolved, turning into scarlet smoke that hovered in an oily cloud over the rose beds.

Mikki scrambled to her feet.

'Aeras! Come to me!' she cried.

Moments later the wide-eyed Wind Elemental rushed up to her Empousa.

'Oh, Goddess! Save us from—'

'Hecate's not here. We have to save ourselves. Aeras, I command your element present. Blow in a mighty wind from the north and rid us of the smoke of Fear. Now, Aeras!'

White-faced, Aeras flung her arms wide. When she lifted them, a blast of cold wind hurled past them, carrying the morning fog as well as the red smoke over the rose wall and into the forest.

A scream of agony wrenched Mikki's eyes from the dissipating cloud and back to the battle. Asterius's dark eyes flashed, and he roared his fury as he dealt blow after powerful blow against the evil creatures. Each movement he made was controlled by a grace that was as beautiful as it was deadly.

She thought Asterius was the most magnificent thing she had ever seen.

He lunged and struck, and Selfishness was writhing on the ground, sliced tentacles spurting dark blood in a scarlet arch across the roses. Envy clinging to his back, Asterius lowered his head. With one blindingly swift movement, he impaled the fallen Dream Stealer, and at the same moment he reached around, plunging his claws into the base of Envy's spine. Both creatures' bodies shivered and then they, too, disappeared into clouds of blood-colored smoke.

'Again, Aeras!' Mikki commanded.

Aeras called the north wind, which banished Envy and Selfishness far into the ancient forest.

'You interfering bitch!' Hatred shrieked at Aeras.

Like a viper, he struck at the Wind Elemental, but Mikki was quicker, shoving Aeras out of the way. The Dream Stealer collided with the Empousa instead of her handmaiden. Mikki felt a searing line of pain explode across her shoulder and arm as she went down beneath him.

Then Hatred screamed. His body bowed as Asterius clawed his back to scarlet ribbons. With a terrible snarl, the Dream Stealer wrenched Mikki from under him. He spun around, holding the Empousa before him like a shield.

Instantly, Asterius checked his attack.

Hatred hissed evil laughter. 'Why do you hesitate, Guardian? I am shielded from your rage by only a weak, mortal woman. Are you not willing to sacrifice your Empousa, even to rid the realm of hatred? I supposed that's hardly surprising. I seem to recall you have a weakness for Hecate's High Priestesses.' The creature rubbed his groin against Mikki. 'Not that I blame you. Her fruit is ripe and sweet.'

317

Asterius's growl lifted the hair on her arms and the back of her neck. His voice was that of a deadly predator. 'I will make you suffer for an eternity for touching her.'

'I think not, Guardian. Instead, you are going to open the gate for me, and I am going to pass through it unharmed.' The creature began pulling Mikki before him as he backed toward the rose wall. 'If you get too close, I will play Destiny and slice her throat right now.' He pressed the point of one jagged claw against Mikki's neck.

'This is not finished between us,' Asterius snarled, moving carefully with the Dream Stealer and his hostage to the gate. 'If it takes an eternity, I will make you pay for touching her.'

'Hatred is never finished, Guardian. You should know that by now.' He halted, his back to the gate. 'Now open it for me, and I will return your Empousa to you, though I would enjoy having her entertain me for a while.' Hatred bared his teeth at the Guardian as he bent so he could flick his tongue out and taste the High Priestess's salty-sweet neck.

And that was it. Mikki had had enough. More than enough.

'Oh, hell no!' she yelled, driving her thumb into the bulging, insectlike eye that he had been foolish enough to get close to her.

The Dream Stealer's scream of pain was deafening, and he hurled her from him, but not before Mikki felt his talon pierce her skin and the rush of wet heat that followed the wound. She grasped her neck and fell to the ground, watching through a haze of pain as Asterius picked up the writhing creature and bent his evil body back farther and farther until the Dream Stealer's spine was broken with a sickening crack. Asterius lifted Hatred and threw him over the rose barrier.

Then he was on his knees by her side, crying her name, touching her face, stroking her hair.

She tried to smile at him. *It's okay. It's not your fault. I let them in.* Mikki thought she was saying the words aloud, but she couldn't seem to make them come out. Then her four hand-maidens were suddenly there, too. They were crying – even Floga, who Mikki thought hadn't liked her at all. She wanted to comfort them, to tell them she wasn't afraid and to ask them to please treat Asterius nicer because she knew, without any doubt, that she was dying.

Chapter Thirty-one

ASTERIUS refused to lose her like this – not to Hatred – not when Mikado had brought love, desire, kindness and acceptance, everything that was Hatred's opposite, into his life. He lifted her in his arms and faced the distraught Elementals.

'Let us take her to the fountain, Guardian. There we will wash her clean and then lay her in Hecate's Temple, where we will offer prayer to the goddess for her soul,' Gii said through her tears.

'She is not dead,' he said and snarled a warning as Gii tried to approach him.

'Not yet, but her wound is mortal; soon her spirit will be in Hades' Realm,' Nera said brokenly.

'No! It is not her destiny to die today!'

'The Fates have deemed otherwise,' Aeras said softly.

'Then I defy the Fates!'

'Guardian, what will you do?' Floga asked.

'I will claim my birthright.' Carrying Mikado's limp, bleeding body, he began to brush past them, but Gii's soft hand on his arm made him pause. When he glared at her, she met his eyes unflinchingly and said, 'How can we help you?'

He hesitated only a moment. 'Come to the temple. Perhaps the power of the elements will help my plea reach Cronos's ears.'

Without waiting to see if they followed, Asterius rushed to Hecate's Temple, his hooves striking thunderously against the white marble path. He tried not to think about how still Mikado was and how much of her blood soaked their bodies. The beast simply ran.

He took the temple steps three at a time and then drew himself sharply to a halt in front of Hecate's sacred flame. Asterius dropped to his knees and gently placed Mikado beside the flame. He heard the handmaidens hurry into the temple after him. They quickly took their places, surrounding him in their familiar circle.

'Does she still live?' Gii asked.

Asterius looked down at his love. Her eyes were closed and her face was colourless. Blood still pumped freely from the long, slender slash that dissected her neck while her chest rose and fell in shallow pants.

'She does,' he said.

'Then do what you can, Guardian. We do not want to lose another Empousa before destiny requires it,' Gii said.

He lifted his eyes to meet hers. 'Then summon your elements and form the sacred circle.'

'You love her, don't you?' Floga said suddenly.

His gaze swiveled to Flame. 'I do.'

'And are you going to save her just to steal her away from us?' the Fire Elemental asked.

'On Beltane the realm's Empousa will meet her destiny. I give you my oath on that,' he said.

'Even though you love her?' Aeras asked.

'Not long ago you watched me battle Selfishness. It is not the first time I have faced that particular Dream Stealer. This time I was victorious. I will not sacrifice the dreams of mankind for my own needs ever again.' He looked back at Mikado and gently touched her cheek.

321

'You are not a beast,' Gii said softly.

'I am,' he said without looking at the Earth Elemental, 'but I am also a man, and Mikado's love has made the man the stronger of the two.'

'Then the four elements will help you save your love.' Gii nodded at Aeras. 'Begin, Wind.'

The Elemental threw her arms wide. 'I call Wind to the sacred circle!' Instantly, the air began to stir.

Like an electric chain reaction, Floga flung wide her arms, embracing her element. 'Come to me, Flame!'

'Water! I call you to attend me!' Nera cried.

'Earth! I call you to complete the circle and to magnify the powers of our Guardian who we shelter within,' Gii said.

Asterius felt the power of the elements sizzle across his skin. He bowed his head and raised hands stained with his lover's blood. In a voice magnified by Wind, Fire, Water and Earth, as well as by the beast within him, he shouted to the faraway reaches of the heavens.

'Cronos! Great God of the World and of Time – Titan divider of the heavens and Earth – Father! I call you by your ancient names as well as by the one my blood has earned me. I have lived for ages, and never before have I asked anything of you. Not acknowledgment or power. Not love or acceptance. But today I call upon you by right of birth and ask that you grant me the power to save this mortal. Her life's thread has been cut before its time – her string is not yet unwoven to its end.'

The sacred flame stirred, and within its flickering light a man's face appeared – ageless, but well lined, as if it had been chiseled from young rock by time and experience. It was a face he would have recognized anywhere, for it mirrored his own so completely.

'Father,' Asterius said, bowing his head.

The Titan did not acknowledge Asterius. Instead, he jerked his chin at Mikado. 'Is this the mortal you would save?'

'It is.'

'She is Hecate's Empousa?' Cronos said.

'Yes.'

'Then her salvation will be only temporary.'

'She has not lived her allotted time. It is not yet Beltane,' Asterius said.

'What did this to her?' the Titan asked.

'The leader of the Dream Stealers, Hatred. I would not have her die from that creature's touch.'

Cronos shifted his attention to his son. 'Hatred has killed her, and you want love to save her?'

Asterius's jaw tightened, but he nodded. 'I do.'

'Love . . .' Cronos chuckled. 'I am surprised by your weakness, Guardian.'

'I have learned that love is only weak when it is selfish,' he said, a clear challenge in his voice.

Surprise flashed over the Titan's face. 'You remind me of your mother.'

'That is probably because she, too, understood the weakness of those who love selfishly.'

Cronos frowned. 'I am not accustomed to being insulted when my aid has been asked.'

'I meant no insult. I only spoke the truth,' Asterius said quickly.

'Regardless, I grow weary of this conversation.'

'Cronos! Forgive me. I did not—'

'Silence!' The flame flickered madly, and the floor of the goddess's temple shook. 'I have not finished. I grant your request. You may share a piece of the immortality that lives in your spirit with the priestess. A very small piece, mind you. It will steal her from Hades' realm only this once. But know that there is a price for the spark of immortality you share with her. Even after she dies, she will carry that piece of your spirit. You will only feel whole when she is beside you, and your spirit is whole. When she no longer walks this realm, your heart will be empty and your days filled with loneliness. Think carefully before you make this choice.'

'I have already made my choice. The cost is something I knew I would pay if I allowed myself to love her. I accepted it then. I do not mind accepting it again for her life.'

'Very well then, it is your birthright to ask a boon of me, but do not trouble me again. You chose Hecate, and it is the goddess you must beseech in the future.' Without another word, the Titan disappeared from the flame.

Asterius looked down at Mikado. His father had granted him the ability to save her, but how? He had to give her a piece of his immortality – a piece of his spirit. And then he knew. Slowly, he bent forward and touched his lips to hers. As he kissed her, he willed her to live – to share what he offered her and to accept him all over again.

Mikado stirred and sighed softly against his mouth and then she opened her lips and their kiss deepened. When Asterius finally pulled away, her eyes were open and she was smiling up at him.

'She lives!' Gii cried.

And then the handmaidens were laughing and crying together as they closed the circle and rushed to their Empousa's side. Mikki sat up and blinked in confusion, not sure where she was or why Asterius knelt beside her and was holding her hand right in front of the Elementals. She looked around. They were in Hecate's Temple? That wasn't right. She wasn't supposed to be here, she was supposed to be checking the rose wall to make sure that—

And it all came rushing back to her.

'The Dream Stealers!' she gasped, trying to get to her feet but finding that she was so light-headed that any abrupt movement made the temple pitch and roll sickeningly around her.

'Shhh,' Asterius reassured her. 'All is well. The Dream Stealers have been banished from the realm.'

'I'm so sorry.' She looked frantically from Asterius to the handmaidens.

'Empousa, you need not apologize. Dream Stealers are masters of manipulation. We should have prepared you better,' Gii said, crouching to take her other hand.

'Yes!' Nera nodded her head a little frantically, as if that could convince her Empousa. 'How were you to know the cunning games they play?'

'But I let them in. They told me that – oh, God! The things they made me think and feel! It was horrible.'

Aeras smiled through the tears that washed her cheeks and touched Mikki's hair reverently. 'You were very brave, Empousa. You took the blow Hatred planned for me.'

Mikki had forgotten all about that. She frantically looked down at herself. She was covered with blood. How could anyone lose so much blood and live? She remembered the pain in her shoulder, but when she looked, she saw nothing but bloody skin. And there had been something else . . . something much worse . . .

Her eyes widened, and she felt a wave of dizziness. He'd slit her throat. She had been dying. But now she was very much alive. Slowly, she lifted her eyes to meet her lover's.

'It's over now,' Asterius said.

'I was dying,' she whispered.

'No. I could not let that happen,' he said.

'He saved you,' Gii said with a little sobbing hiccup.

'He saved all of us,' Aeras said, wiping her face.

'We will never forget it,' Floga said.

'Never,' said Nera.

Mikki smiled at the Elementals. 'He did what any honorable man would do to protect his home and those he loves.' Then she wrapped her arms around his neck and whispered into his ear, 'Take me home.'

Chapter Thirty-two

Asterius carried her through the garden. Mikki wouldn't normally like being carried around as if she was a child, but she wasn't sure she could walk on her own. Her insides felt weak and sick. And she needed to be in his arms. She needed to feel his heartbeat against her own to reassure herself that she really was alive.

'Hatred tricked me,' she said faintly, her head resting against his shoulder.

His arms tightened around her. 'That's what Dream Stealers do. They infect mortals until their poison actually twists thoughts so that dreams sicken, and eventually, die. Do not punish yourself for falling prey to that which has been destroying mortal dreams for uncounted ages.'

'I thought awful things. I was filled with . . .' She shivered convulsively, not able to continue.

'You were poisoned by hatred, envy, fear, and selfishness. They weren't your thoughts, Mikado, they were sick shadows of your infected imagination. You must not punish yourself for their evil, for that is a type of a victory for them. If they can taint your life, even after they've been banished, then they haven't truly been defeated.'

'I'll never let them fool me again. And I'll never go into that damned forest again, either.' She raised her head and stared at him. 'How do you stand it? How can you go out there and collect the threads of reality and know they're out there, too, watching and waiting for a chance to attack?'

'It is my destiny to battle them. Many of them are old, familiar enemies.'

'Aren't you afraid?'

'Only when I think about what would happen if I failed and allowed them to have their way with the realm.'

'But you won't ever fail,' she said.

'No. I cannot.'

She thought he sounded incredibly tired, and she hoped desperately that he wouldn't have reason to battle the Dreams Stealers again until he was well rested and – 'Oh, God! Put me down! You have to go back and make sure the rose wall is okay and that no part of those things stayed in the realm.'

'The realm is safe. The north wind blew the last vestiges of their evil deep into the forest.'

'But shouldn't you go back and make sure everything's really okay?'

'All is well, Mikado. When Dream Stealers have been faced and defeated, they are loath to attack again soon. They know that once they have been recognized for what they are, their power to taint lives is drastically weakened. They must retreat to lick their wounds and plot a new attack for another day.'

'I remember Hatred said he is never finished.'

'He isn't. We must always guard against him.'

Something she had read once surfaced in her mind, and she spoke the words softly aloud. 'Good defeated is stronger than evil triumphant.' She touched the side of his face. 'You fight on the side of good.'

'And I will not allow evil to triumph.'

'I won't let them taint my life; they won't defeat me.' She lay her head back on his shoulder and then said, 'How did you save me from dying?'

'I beseeched a boon from Cronos,' he said quietly.

Her head snapped up again. 'Your father?'

He nodded.

'You talked to your father?'

'Briefly.'

'How long has it been since the last time you talked to him?' she asked, wondering at the odd, wooden expression that had hardened his face.

'I have never before spoken to him.'

She studied him, feeling angry as hell at the arrogant Titan who had so cavalierly created and then discarded a son, wishing that she could erase the centuries of pain and loneliness in his past. Not knowing what else to do, she kissed him gently on the cheek.

'Thank you for saving my life,' she said.

His face softened into a smile. 'I was just returning the favor, Empousa. Remember, you brought me back to life once, too.'

'That's right.' She nipped his jaw. 'And I like you better this way.'

'Because you find that you are weary of walking, and you enjoy being carried about by your beast?'

Mikki laughed. 'Well, the myths do say that the Minotaur was half bull, but I don't think bulls make very good beasts of burden. Rumor has it they're not docile enough.'

'In this case, the rumor,' he said, giving her a quick, hard kiss that ended in a growl, 'is true.'

*　　*　　*

By the time they reached Asterius's lair, Mikki was tired of being carried, even though when he finally put her down the cave rocked a little under her feet. Especially after she realized that her chiton was hanging in shreds from her body, which was sticky with drying blood.

She groaned through clenched teeth. 'I'm going to puke my guts up if I don't get this stuff washed off me.' She glanced up at Asterius. 'You may have to carry me up the stairs to my baths.'

He swung her into his arms again, but instead of leaving the cave, he strode to his bedroom.

'Okay, I realize that my head is truly screwed up right now, but I do believe you're going in the wrong direction. Not that I don't want you to take me to your bedroom, but *after* I've washed this mess off of me.'

'We keep forgetting to finish your tour of my lair.'

'We don't forget; we get interrupted,' she said.

'Then allow me to show you the rest of my lair without interruption.' He carried her through his bedroom and then to a rounded doorway that fit neatly within a corner Mikki hadn't noticed before. It opened to a torch-lit tunnel, at the end of which was another rounded doorway, which, Mikki noted with surprise, was framed in sunlight.

'You know, this place isn't really very lair-ish. I mean, it's actually comfortable and beautiful. I think you should call it . . .' She paused, thinking, while he took them closer and closer to the light. Then he stepped from the tunnel and into a large round room, the ceiling over the center of which was open to show the clearing morning sky. And also to allow the rising steam from the contained hot spring bath to escape. 'I think you should call it paradise!' she breathed.

He laughed and put her down. In seconds, she'd stripped off what was left of her chiton and, with a satisfied groan, walked down the smooth steps and sank into the deliciously hot water. From behind her, she heard him speaking quick, sharp commands in the magickal language he used to call things to him, and she turned her head in time to see two baskets burst into being. One was filled with soaps, clean towels and lengths of soft chiton material. The other – she sighed happily – was full of food.

Asterius lifted a crystal bottle from the first basket and then smiled at Mikki. She grinned back, wondering at why he suddenly looked so shy.

'What is it?' she asked.

'Your soap,' he said, holding up the bottle.

'I didn't mean the bottle. I meant what's that expression on your face about?'

'I would like to ask you something.'

'Okay.' Then she laughed. 'You look a little mischievous.' Feeling much revived by the warm mineral water, she gave him a sexy smile. 'Are you feeling like being a little bit naughty?'

'I – I would like to bathe you,' he said in a rush. And then he thoroughly shocked Mikki by flushing a deep red against the bronze of his skin.

'I would love that.'

He walked to the edge of the rock pool and put down the crystal bottle. Then he took off his leather cuirasse and the short tunic he wore underneath. She loved looking at his body, watching as more and more of it was exposed. He was so physically powerful, such an amazing blending of extremes – man and beast, just as his mind was a blending of extremes, too. He was fierceness and compassion – childlike innocence and ancient knowledge mixed together to form a being truly unlike any other who would ever exist in any world. She was so distracted by her happy contemplation that it wasn't until he entered the pool that she realized the blood that spattered his body had come from more than her wounds. His arms were covered with slashes and bite marks.

'They hurt you!' She pulled him down so she could begin soaking the wounds in the hot water. 'I'm such an idiot! Do you have bandages? Ugh – some of these look like they need stitches. There has to be a doctor in the realm. Let's get these cleaned up and I'll call for her, and—'

Asterius caught her wrists. 'I do not need the healer.'

She frowned at him. 'Look, I worked at a hospital. Just take my word for it. You need a doctor.'

He smiled and kissed her gently. 'Your care for me warms my spirit.'

'Lovely. I'm glad it does. It would warm *my* spirit if we'd get the doctor in here.'

'Mikado, I am an immortal. I do not require a healer. The wounds already heal themselves.'

Still frowning, Mikki lifted his arm and stared at it. 'You're right! They are healing.'

'Are you satisfied?' he asked.

'I'm dumbfounded,' she said. 'But definitely relieved.' She splashed water over his arms, touching the newly healed bite marks, watching as the flesh knit itself together. 'Is there any wound you can't recover from?'

'If you said you no longer loved me, it would destroy me.'

She met his eyes. 'Then you will live forever.'

Asterius took the crystal bottle from the edge of the pool. 'Let me show you how much I cherish you, Mikado.'

She stood so the pool's water covered her only to her waist and then took the bottle from him and poured a generous amount of the heavy liquid over her neck, arms and breasts before putting it back on the ledge. The heady fragrance of the Empousa's anointing scent mixed with the heat of Mikki's skin, subtly changing it and making it unique to her.

Slowly, Asterius slid his hands over her slick skin. He caressed her neck and shoulders before moving to her breasts and the seductive flesh of her stomach. His hands dipped below her waist, carrying the rose-spiced scent to her thighs. Mikki felt as if she had turned to liquid heat as his hands slicked over her skin. His fingers found their way briefly between her legs, where he used his thumbs to stroke her with quick, circular motions, but then those knowing fingers would glide away, to tease her stomach or breasts before returning again to her core. She felt as if his touch was calling awake sleeping parts of her body that the warmth of the water continued to caress even when his touch had moved on. He turned her, and this time took the bottle himself and poured the soap in a thick line down her spine. Weak-kneed, Mikki leaned forward against the edge of the pool while his hands caressed her back and then dipped down to knead and cup her ass.

'Remember the last time I came to your dreams?'

She felt his breath hot against the middle of her back as he stayed on his knees and worked his clever hands across her skin.

'I remember,' she said huskily.

Both of his hands slid around her body. She leaned back against him as they caressed their way slowly up her thighs.

'We were in a pit of roses.' His deep voice rumbled across her skin, sending little ripples of pleasure through her body. 'I was on top of you. You opened your legs to me.' His fingers found the center of her excitement. The tempo of his caresses increased. 'I was engorged, and when I pressed myself against you, rubbing and stroking, I could feel your wetness and heat and how your body gathered itself and then exploded with release.' With a choked cry, Mikki climaxed, hard and fast.

And then he turned her to him, and in one swift motion lifted her through the water and impaled her while her body still pulsed and throbbed. Mikki arched to meet him, using the edge of the pool as support. His hands gripped her hips, and with a throaty growl, he extended his claws. His sex plunged in and out of her, exquisite in the barely controlled strength of his thrusts. Mikki didn't close her eyes. She wanted to see him, to watch the terrible beauty of his face as he loved her. Her skin was tight and overly sensitive, and jolts of pleasure were sensual shocks every time his claws shallowly pierced her skin. The liquid sound of him moving in and out of her coupled with his growls and the husky way he moaned her name, and it became an erotic symphony, the crescendo of which broke through her body with pleasure so intense it verged on painful.

She collapsed against him, breathing hard and feeling limp and replete. She was smiling contentedly against his chest until she realized it wasn't just his breath that was causing his chest to shake. He was trembling violently. Mikki pulled back to see that his eyes were closed and tears were slowly tracking their way down his face.

'Asterius?' She put her hand against his cheek. 'What's wrong?'

He opened his eyes and kissed her palm. 'It is only that I have been alone for so long – I find that I am unprepared for the happiness you bring me.' He reached up and felt the tears on his face as if he hadn't realized until then that he was crying. 'Does this make me appear foolish and weak to you?'

'No, my love. It makes you appear human.'

Chapter Thirty-three

THEY didn't leave his lair. They ate and discussed more changes Mikki wanted to enact in the realm – like a specific limit to the time the rose gate would be opened to allow men into and out of the realm. And the fact that the weather was growing colder as winter approached, so it would be prudent if Mikki commanded Flame to warm the gardens, even if just briefly during the darkest part of the night. Black spot, she explained to Asterius, liked to creep out in cold weather, and it was hard to get rid of once it spread.

Mikki loved talking with him, and it didn't take long for her to realize why. Asterius listened to her. Truly and completely, he heard what she said. She tried to think of the last man she'd known who had actually listened to her, and she couldn't remember one. Not one man had ever shown her the quality of respect and sincere interest Asterius showed her. It was supremely ironic that a being who wasn't literally a man knew instinctively what so many 'real' men didn't seem to be able to grasp: women want to be heard and respected. It was really that simple.

His power thrilled her. It was a seductive lure of which she didn't think she'd ever get enough. She loved the exhilaration she felt just to be able to touch him, to stroke that incredible body and know he was hers.

That night they made love on the fur pallet, tenderly discovering more of the secrets their bodies held. Mikki delighted in the fact that his skin was so sensitive and that a light caress could leave him engorged and ready for her. Satiated, they fell asleep in each other's arms, secure in their love and the knowledge that tomorrow would be another day they would spend together.

'Empousa! You must come!'

Mikki thought she was dreaming. She knew she was in bed with Asterius – she could feel him tense and surge from their pallet – but she also clearly heard Gii's frantic voice. What was the handmaiden doing in Asterius's lair? Then her sleep-clouded mind cleared and understanding burst in.

'What is the danger?' Asterius boomed, pulling on his tunic and buckling his cuirasse.

'The roses . . .' Mikki's mouth had gone dry, and her stomach clenched. 'Gii, what has happened to the roses?'

Gii hurried to her Empousa's side, quickly wrapping the chiton she'd carried with her around Mikki's naked body while she spoke in quick, short sentences.

'The Elementals and I went to the rose gate at dawn. We thought to be certain no trace of yesterday's violence was left to disturb you.' Gii's voice shook, and her face was deathly pale. 'They're dying, Empousa. All of them.'

'The roses!' Mikki said.

Though it wasn't a question, Gii answered, 'Yes.'

'The wall – is the barrier still intact?' Asterius said.

'Yes, and there are no Dream Stealers in the realm. No one is in the realm who shouldn't be. We made certain all the men departed yesterday, and none have been invited to return.'

'I must go,' Asterius told Mikki.

'Yes – go, go quickly. I'll be right behind you,' Mikki said.

He paused only long enough to touch the side of her face in a gentle caress before the sound of his hooves echoed from the cave walls as he thundered from his lair.

'Hurry,' Mikki said. 'I need to get out there, too.'

Minutes later, the two women rushed into the gardens. Mikki felt the change the instant she left the cave. Her head ached, and nausea rose in her throat.

'Show me the quickest path to the gate,' Mikki told Gii and then neither woman had breath to waste on talking. They ran.

Women were crowded around the rose beds that ringed the gate, milling like frightened sheep. And Mikki understood why. It was worse than she had imagined. She pushed her way past them, taking only a cursory look at the dying beds. She needed to get to the heart of the disease that had suddenly afflicted the roses, and she knew she would find its center at the gate. She broke through the last group of women and staggered to a halt. Asterius was already at the gate, his keen eyes studying the forest as he paced back and forth before it. The other three Elementals weren't watching him; they were staring at the roses in the beds adjacent to the gate. Their faces were strained and pale. When they saw Mikki, they rushed to meet her.

'Empousa, it is terrible,' Aeras whispered.

'What has happened to them, Empousa?' Nera said, keeping her voice low.

'I don't know. I can't tell yet. Give me room and let me examine them.' Mikki felt the press of the women's fear almost as much as she felt the roses' sickness. 'Have the women move back.'

All the Elementals except Gii hurried off to speak to the watching, waiting groups of women.

'Do not ask me to leave, too,' Gii said quietly. 'You look as if you might faint at any moment. I want to stay with you. If you fall, I'll be there to catch you.'

'As will I,' Asterius said, joining them.

'The Dream Stealers?' Mikki asked.

He shook his head. 'There is no sign of them. Not within the realm, and not as far as I can see or sense in the forest.' He looked around at the roses. 'But it seems they need not be present to destroy.'

Mikki drew a deep breath. 'Okay, then let's see what I can do to fix it.'

The Elemental and the Guardian shadowed her as she moved slowly from bed to bed, examining rose after rose, but soon she forgot they were anywhere near her. The roses consumed her. She'd never seen devastation so horrible. They looked like they had been afflicted with a mixture of Botrytis Blight and Brown Canker and then burned from the inside out. The leaves were shriveled and covered in a dirty-looking fungus, but it felt like no fungus she'd ever encountered. It was sticky, and it smelled like rotting flesh. The canes of the bushes were blackened, with swollen places that looked like an old arthritic woman's knuckles. The buds were shriveled and a deep, bruised purple color.

Mikki straightened from inspecting another dead bush and gazed out into the gardens. Like a poisonous wave, she could see that the sickness was spreading, and she felt a bone-deep chill of fear. This blight wasn't natural. It had been brought to the realm by the evil of the Dream Stealers. Intuition told her that the disease had been in the oily cloud of evil each creature had dissolved into. They hadn't really been dead. She didn't imagine that creatures like that could ever really be killed. Hatred, envy, fear, and selfishness were emotions that would always slither around the fringes of mankind, waiting for their chance to strike and destroy dreams.

It was true they had been banished from the realm, but not soon enough. And Mikki had no idea how to battle something that had infected her roses through creatures of nightmares.

'Empousa,' Gii asked timidly. 'What would you have us do to save them?'

Mikki looked from the Earth Elemental to her lover. Both were watching her with expressions that were concerned, but she could also see the hope in their eyes and the confidence they had in her.

'I – I have to think! Just stay here and leave me alone for a second.' Abruptly, Mikki walked away from them. She left the dying beds and went down the wide marble path that led to the rose gate, thinking she'd sit under the ancient oak and try to come up with a plan – any plan.

A splash of color caught at the corner of her vision, and she stopped and stared. Pink blossoms, in full and healthy bloom, filled two plants that sat in the middle of an otherwise blighted and dying bed. She hurried to the bushes, breathing their sweet scent and caressing the vibrant green of their leaves as if they were prodigal children newly returned. Salet Roses – she recognized them easily. They were one of her favorite Old Garden varieties, with their double blooms and abundant midseason and fall repeat blossoming. But why had these two bushes been spared from the killing blight?

She looked around, searching for spots of brightness within the ocean of rot and disease. She found a splash of red in the bed closest to the rose gate. Quickly, she made her way there. Three bushes there, all at the edge of the bed, were in full bloom. Their color and the deep, true rose fragrance of the blooms identified them as Chrysler Imperials.

What did the two types of roses have in common? Chrysler Imperial was a Hybrid Tea Rose; Salet was of the Old Garden variety. One was red; the other pink. And they weren't even near each other. Mikki stared at the healthy pink where it sat, blooming contentedly, seemingly unfazed by the death around it. Mikki shivered. Hadn't the Salet bed been the one the Dreams Stealers had forced her down in the middle of? They'd meant to rape her there. Thankfully, Asterius had arrived in time and—

Mikki's breath caught. She knew why these roses lived, thrived even in the midst of others that had succumbed to death and disease; she knew what all five bushes had in common. Her blood had touched each of them.

Mikki walked unsteadily to a nearby bench, making it just in time for her to sit as her knees gave way.

She had been in the Salet bed when she had taken the blow on her shoulder. Absently, she touched her shoulder, remembering how freely it had bled. Then near the gate – that was where Hatred had sliced through the vein at her throat. She vaguely remembered lying there, half in the bed, half on the marble path, as blood pumped from her body.

Her blood had saved the roses, had protected them from the Dream Stealer's poison. She put her face in her hands and tried to understand the enormity of her discovery. Over and over the words *my blood saved them* played in her head.

'Mikado, the women await your command.'

She looked up, blinking her vision clear. Asterius knelt beside the bench and wiped the tears from her cheeks.

'Trust yourself, my love. You will find a way to heal them.'

She stared into his dark, expressive eyes and knew what he said was the truth. She knew how to heal the roses, and she did trust herself. Now all she needed to do was to find the courage to act.

'I'm going to Hecate's Temple to speak to the women. Have the Elementals gather them and meet me there.'

'Yes, my Empousa,' Asterius said. He bowed to her and then took her hand and kissed it gently.

MIKKI stood within the raised temple. The four Elementals had formed a semi-circle behind her. Asterius stood behind them, near the goddess's ever-burning flame. Mikki looked out at the large group of women. They were silent, their faces set with worry and fear, every particle of their attention focused on their Empousa. She lifted her chin and drew a deep breath, projecting her voice into the crowd.

'We have a lot of work to do. We need to move fast, and we need to be focused. The disease that is killing the roses must be stopped, and I give you my word that I know how to stop it.' She paused as a sigh of relief rippled through the crowd. 'They'll be no dividing into the four groups this time. All of us need to focus on the area closest to the rose gate and work our way out from there. First, I want buckets of the strongest wine we have brought out to the gardens.' She saw the looks of surprise on the women's faces, and it almost made her smile. 'What you are going to do is to cut the diseased roses down to the ground. Then take the canes and pile them outside the rose wall, where Floga will burn them. As you move from bush to bush, be sure to dip your shears in the buckets of wine. It will help stop the disease from spreading to parts of the plants that have not been infected. Your shears must be razor sharp, and you need to make each cut at an angle.' Her eyes passed around the group, looking confidently into the women's eyes. 'Are there any questions?'

No one spoke.

'Then let's get to work.' The women hurried off in groups to gather cutting tools and wine, and Mikki turned to face her handmaidens. 'I wasn't exaggerating. We have to work hard and fast. The disease is spreading at an unnatural rate.' Her eyes found Asterius in the shadows. 'Asterius, as much as I don't like the idea of opening that damned gate, my instincts tell me that burning the sick roses inside the realm would be a terrible mistake.'

'Then we follow your instincts, Empousa,' he said. 'And I will be there to guard the open gate.'

'I know you will. That's why I'm not afraid to open it.' She smiled at her handmaidens and had to work hard to keep the tears from her eyes. 'And I know each of you will do whatever it takes to help heal the roses. I'm proud of you, and I believe in you. The Realm of the Rose will thrive again, I promise.'

'We believe you, Empousa,' Gii said. She walked to Mikki and kissed her gently on the cheek before curtseying and hurrying out to the roses.

'We trust you, Empousa,' Aeras said. She, too, kissed Mikki before dropping into the familiar, graceful curtsey and departing.

The Water Elemental walked forward to take her turn kissing the High Priestess, but Mikki's question made her pause.

'Nera, I seem to remember that someone told me that the fountain' – Mikki nodded her head in the direction of the massive water feature that bubbled and frothed beside Hecate's Temple – 'is the main source of irrigation for the realm. Is that true?'

'Yes, Empousa.'

'So water in those troughs actually reaches all the rose beds?'

'Of course, Empousa.' Nera smiled and continued. 'Before you commanded my element to visit every fourth morning, it rarely rained here.'

Mikki made herself return Nera's warm smile. 'Thank you. That's good to know.'

'We support you, Empousa,' Nera said. She kissed Mikki and then departed.

'We love you, Empousa,' Floga said. The last to kiss Mikki, Floga hesitated before curtseying. A tear trailed slowly down her smooth cheek as the Elemental said, 'Forgive me for doubting you, Empousa. As my element, I am sometimes too rash and my thoughts burn too brightly.'

Mikki hugged her. 'There's nothing to forgive,' she whispered.

When they were alone, Mikki went to Asterius and stepped into his arms. For just a moment, she let herself absorb his strength and his love, knowing the peace that comes with finding that one person to whom you were meant to be bound. But she didn't allow him to hold her for long. She couldn't.

TIME surprised Mikki by passing slowly. Maybe it was because the work of cutting the rotting, diseased roses and dragging them outside the wall to their pyre was so damn hard and depressing. Or maybe it was because Mikki's mind couldn't stop thinking about what the future held. Either way, it seemed that several eternities had passed in that one, endless day. Mikki had fallen into a hypnotic rhythm of cut–dip–cut–dip, so she was surprised to look up and see that, finally, the sky had darkened enough for Floga to light the torches up and down the rose wall.

'Gii,' she called to the Earth Elemental, who hurried to her side, smiling even though her eyes were bruised with shadows and her arms were pink with thorn scratches. 'That's all we can do today. Have the women finish dragging what they've cut through the gate, and let's call it a day.'

'Yes, Empousa,' Gii said, looking relieved.

Mikki didn't blame her. Her own shoulders were aching and her hands were bruised and sore from the shears. Thankfully, they were razor sharp – a group of women had spent the day doing nothing but sharpening and re-sharpening blades. Mikki glanced down at the shears. Carefully, she dipped them in the bucket of wine and then cleaned them in the grass before hiding them at the base of the rose she'd just finished pruning.

'The women are finishing their tasks as you commanded, Empousa.'

Gii's voice made Mikki jump guiltily, which she covered with a small laugh. Then she took the handmaiden's arm and said, 'Walk with me a little?'

'Of course,' Gii said.

They walked together silently, taking a meandering path back toward the rose gate. Mikki was satisfied by what she saw in the rose beds. The diseased bushes had been purged. It looked stark now, but she knew that in the spring they would grow back and be healthier and hardier than before. Roses were survivors – not the delicate fainting flowers too many people believed them to be. Mikki knew better. She knew about hidden strength and resilience. Too often people had misjudged her, discounting her as a pretty face and nothing more, or worse, considered her opinions inconsequential because she was 'only' a woman. She thought about Asterius. He, too, had been misjudged, solely on his appearance. Little wonder they fit so well together.

'You were wrong about him,' Mikki said softly.

Gii glanced at her, surprised by the High Priestess's words. 'Him, Empousa?'

'The Guardian. He's not a beast, and he doesn't deserve to be treated like one.'

Gii stayed carefully silent.

345

'I don't know what happened before. I don't know what he did, and now, I don't want to know. But let me tell you what I do know. He saved this realm yesterday when my mistake could have destroyed it. He would do the same today and tomorrow – or for every tomorrow until eternity. He's honorable, Gii. And he's kind. Did you know that he's an artist?'

'No,' Gii said.

'He is.'

'He loves you,' Gii said hesitantly.

'I know. I love him, too.' Mikki drew a deep breath. 'And that's why I want you to promise me something. I want you to promise me that you'll treat him better. Don't ostracize him. He . . .' She paused, struggling against a wave of emotions. 'He gets lonely, and I don't want him to spend eternity alone. If you change the way you react to him, so will all the handmaidens who come after the four of you. Would you do that for me?'

Gii stopped and gazed into the High Priestess's eyes. What she saw there made her breath catch. Then, slowly, she nodded. 'Yes, Empousa. You have my oath.'

'Thank you, Gii. Now, let's get out of here. It's been one damned long day,' she said with forced cheerfulness.

They reached the rose wall in time to see Asterius closing the gate, much to Mikki's relief. For a little while the four Elementals, the Guardian, and the Empousa stood with the women of the realm and watched the diseased roses burn at the edge of the forest. Then the women began to move off in little groups, calling tired farewells to Mikki, until only the Elementals were left.

'You did well today,' Mikki told them, meeting each of their eyes in turn. 'I want you to know how proud I am of you.'

The handmaidens smiled wearily at their Empousa.

'Tomorrow I want you to sleep past dawn – we'll all need the rest. Then eat breakfast and meet me at Hecate's Temple. We'll start again then, doing the same things we did today – pruning and burning the disease from the roses. But I believe they will be better tomorrow.'

'Is that what your instinct tells you?' Gii said, grinning at her.

'That's most definitely what my instinct tells me.' Mikki smiled through the tight, hot feeling in her chest. Then, impulsively, she hugged each of them before saying, 'If you need me, you can find me in the Guardian's home.' She enunciated 'home' distinctly, deciding then and there that she would never call it a lair again. 'Good night,' Mikki called, turning to join Asterius where he waited in the shadows.

'Sleep well, Empousa.' Gii hesitated only a moment and then added, 'Good night, Guardian.'

Mikki was facing him, so she saw the look of pleased surprise that crossed his powerful face.

'Fare you well, Earth,' Asterius said somewhat stiffly.

Then each of the other three handmaidens called similar good nights, leaving the Guardian to gaze in wonder after them.

'In all the centuries I have been Guardian of this realm, that has never before happened.'

'I told you I was going to change things.' Mikki linked her arm through his. 'Let's go home.'

Chapter Thirty-four

MIKKI stretched out on the pallet beside Asterius. The softness of the thick pelts was soothing against her flushed, sweaty skin. Absently, she traced a finger along the ridges of his abdominal muscles, prominent even as he lay there completely relaxed with his eyes closed. They'd made love twice. Once in his bathing pool again. It had been rough and fast, and Mikki knew her skin still showed raised marks where his claws had shallowly pierced her ass during the climax of their passion. The second time had been long and slow and incredibly gentle. He'd brought her to climax with his tongue twice before he'd entered her and slowly, slowly, rocked them to repletion.

Mikki couldn't imagine leaving him. Couldn't imagine never feeling his touch again – never talking with him again, or never seeing the uninhibited joy and wonder in his eyes when she reached for him. She couldn't imagine it, and so she refused to think about it. She would do what she had to do when the time came. Until then, she wouldn't waste the hours she had with him mourning the future.

'I want to paint you.'

Mikki jumped and made a little 'squee' sound.

Eyes still closed, his chest vibrated with his low laughter. She smacked his belly. 'I thought you were asleep.'

'I cannot possibly sleep with you touching me like that,' he said.

'Oh, sorry. I didn't realize . . .' She started to pull her hand back, and he caught her wrist.

'I do not mind.' He let loose her wrist and smiled when she continued to trace a soft path over his stomach. 'I still want to paint you.'

'You already sketched me.'

'Yes, but I want to paint you, too. Just as you are now. I want your image on the walls of my bedchamber.'

He didn't say 'so I can remember you when you're old and/or dead,' but Mikki's mind shouted the words in her head, along with words that whispered that he might need the painting to remind him of her much sooner than either of them expected. She pushed down her morbid thoughts, but suddenly she wanted desperately for him to paint her – for him to capture even just a piece of what they had so he would remember . . .

'Would you do it tonight? Now?' she asked.

Asterius opened his eyes and studied her. 'Yes,' he said slowly. 'I will paint your portrait tonight.'

Mikki watched as he left their bed and began gathering bowls and brushes from niches that had been carved into the walls of the cave and lighting more torches until the bedroom was alive with warmth and light. He hadn't bothered to get dressed beyond the linen wrap he'd slung haphazardly around his hips. She was struck again by the raw power and untamed beauty of his body. He was beast, man, and god, all mixed together to form a miracle, and there was only one thing she wanted more than to spend her life by his side.

When he had readied the paints and had a brush in his hand, she sat up and smiled at him. 'Okay, how do you want me to pose?'

He walked over to the sleeping pallet and gently pressed her back so she was lying on her side as she had been when he'd been beside her. He spread her hair out around her so it made a copper veil on the cream-colored pelt. He positioned her hands so one was draped over her head and the other lay, palm down, on the pallet next to her, as if she had just caressed him. Then he pulled the blanket that had been covering her from her waist down off her, leaving her naked. She raised an eyebrow at him.

His lips tilted up. 'Are you cold?'

'If I am, will you warm me up?'

His laugh rumbled between them. 'When I am finished. For right now, just lie still and close your eyes.' He went back to the clay pots and brushes.

'Do I have to close my eyes? I'd rather watch you.'

He looked over his shoulder at her. 'It will forever be a surprise to me that you enjoy looking at me.'

'I like to do more than look.' She smiled seductively.

'Do not move,' he chided, but his smile was clearly indulgent.

He began painting, working with bold, fast strokes, which he painted right over the top of the Tulsa Rose Garden scene, causing the garden to be cast in the background, as if he was superimposing one view of reality over another.

'Can I talk to you while you do that, or do you need to concentrate?' Mikki whispered, a little awed by the beautiful, glistening version of her that was taking form.

'You may talk. I may not answer, though. Sometimes I forget where I am when I paint.'

'In my old world they call that The Zone. I read an article on it once. It happens to artists and authors and athletes. Something about brain endorphins. It's supposed to mean you're doing something right if you can find The Zone.'

Asterius grunted.

'Do you always get in The Zone when you paint?' she asked.

'Yes. Usually.' He squinted as he studied her and then turned back to the cave wall and drew the long, curving line of her waist, hip and leg.

She watched him paint and thought about his talent and the beauty he seemed to so easily create, even though he had, for centuries, been an outcast. *Please, Gii, keep your word.* Then she pulled her mind from the handmaiden's promise, afraid Asterius would study her face too closely and be able to read her melancholy thoughts.

She needed to think of him instead. As he was then   as he had been earlier – passionate, tender, loving and full of surprises like the exquisite paintings he could produce. Which reminded her . . .

'Asterius, who is the woman you drew on the wall of the front room?'

His hand stilled mid-stroke. Without looking at her he said, 'It is Pasiphea, my mother.'

'I thought so,' she said. And she had. Asterius wasn't adding her picture to his wall as he would a trophy. He wouldn't do that – he wouldn't even think that way. 'She's very beautiful.'

'That is how I remember her.'

Mikki wanted to ask him to please remember her as beautiful, too. To please forget her faults and the pain of their parting after she was gone. To just remember how much they loved. But she knew she couldn't. All she could do was to hope that when the time came he would forgive her for being mortal. Mikki closed her eyes, afraid if she kept looking at him she would blurt out what she was thinking – admit everything and beg him to help her find another way out of this mess.

*   *   *

SOMEHOW, Mikki slept. She only knew it because the next time she opened her eyes the room was much dimmer and Asterius was sleeping beside her. She lay there for a few moments, listening to him take deep, regular breaths. Then, tentatively, she eased up from their bed. Quietly, she wrapped herself in a length of chiton she'd discarded earlier. She didn't look at the wall until she had the material fastened at her shoulder. Then she stared, pressing her hand to her mouth to stop her gasp. He had made her look like a goddess! Her painted image was sleeping, with a slight upturn to her lips, as if she had been having a lovely dream. Her skin looked touchable, her body lush and inviting. And he hadn't painted her lying on his pallet. He'd painted her sleeping on a bed of rose petals – specifically, Mikado rose petals.

She turned back to the bed and looked at him, wishing she could wake him up and make love to him. But she couldn't take the chance. She had to check on the roses. *If my instincts are wrong*, she promised herself, *I'll come back and wake him up and make love to him all morning*. Without looking at him again, Mikki padded on bare, silent feet from the room.

The sun hadn't risen yet, but the eastern sky was starting to turn from night's black to a gray that would soon welcome dawn. The grass was cold and damp under her bare feet as she followed the path around the base of the cliff to the stairs that would lead her up past the hot springs baths, around to her balcony, and then down into the heart of the gardens. Mikki didn't allow her mind to wander. She hurried up the stairs, barely glancing at the steaming baths, not wanting to remember how wonderful it had been to soak there in the company of her handmaidens and how much she had been looking forward to doing so again. Her balcony was empty, as was her room, but she could see a welcoming fire burning in the hearth and a candelabrum tree still lit beside her bed. She bit her lip and turned away from the homey sight.

Mikki descended her stairs and stepped into the garden proper. She chose the path that would lead her most directly to the center of the realm and the temple and fountain that awaited her there. She was careful to keep her thoughts on the roses and away from the Elementals or Asterius. She didn't want them to misunderstand and think she was calling them. What she needed to do she could only do alone. And it was easy to keep her thoughts on the roses. They seemed to be consuming her.

Sick . . . God, she felt sick. The closer she got to the center of the realm, the worse she felt. Two or three times she stopped and inspected beds of roses that just hours before had been already responding to the care and feeding she and the women had given them. Now they were black with the Dream Stealer blight and smelled of death.

Her instincts had been right, but it was even worse than she'd imagined. The blight had spread at an impossible rate. No mortal sickness could have decimated a garden like this. But the blight wasn't mortal. It was the manifestation of evil, and intuition told her there was only one way to combat it.

Hecate's Temple was like a torch-lit dream, and the sound of the huge fountain's flowing water was the accompanying magickal soundtrack. But Mikki didn't pause there. She kept walking until the lights illuminating the rose wall blazed before her. It was easy to find the bushes her blood had touched. They were the only color in the midst of darkness, death, and disease.

I was right. I wish I hadn't been, but I was right.

Mikki retracted her path back to the temple, pausing only long enough to find the newly sharpened shears she'd hidden at the base of a rosebush. She climbed the steps to the temple and stood before the spirit flame.

'Hecate,' she said softly, looking into the yellow-orange flame. 'I know you're far from your realm, but I'm hoping you're still attached enough to it ... to me ... that you will somehow be able to hear me. I need to talk to you before I finish this. I want you to know how much I have loved being here. For the first time in my life, I know I'm where I belong. The four Elementals are good girls, especially Gii. If you could, please tell them that I appreciate everything they've done for me.'

She drew a deep breath and wiped silent tears from her cheeks.

'I love Asterius. You probably don't like that, but you did tell me to follow my instincts, and everything inside of me led me to him. He's not a beast, you know. And he needs what we all need – acceptance and someone to love.' Mikki had to stop and press her hand against her mouth to stifle a sob. When she had her emotions under control, she continued. 'He's why I'm doing this – him and the girls and the Dream Weavers. I finally know the real reason I'm here, and it *is* for the roses. I can save them. I don't really have any choice. I've seen what waits in the forest, and I can't let those creatures destroy everything I love.'

Mikki stared into the fire, wishing she was more articulate, wishing she had more time to learn the special words to prayers and rituals so she could do this right.

'When I pledged myself to you, I did so with two words, "love" and "trust." And it's those two words that bring me full circle here. What I do next I do willingly because I want to preserve the love I've found within this realm, and I believe I'm doing the right thing, because through that love I've learned to trust myself – to believe in my own instincts, intuition and judgment. So if you can, Hecate, I ask that you be with me for what comes next. So mote it be,' Mikki whispered.

Resolutely, she left the temple and approached the fountain whose water fed the realm. The graceful fountain was really very beautiful. It had been formed by a series of huge marble dishes that eventually ran from a pool-size basin to a series of troughs that spoked off into the gardens. Mikki dipped her hand in the water and was surprised at its soothing warmth. *An odd coincidence*, she thought as she took off her chiton and folded it neatly on the ground beside her. *No. There are few coincidences here. I'll just consider it a parting gift from the goddess.* Naked, with nothing except the shears in her hand, Mikki stepped into the fountain.

The water welcomed her and she sat, settling comfortably on the bottom of the basin, which was deep enough that she was covered almost to her shoulders with clear, warm liquid. *Get it over with. Do it quickly. It's only going to hurt for a second.*

Mikki lifted her left wrist. She opened the shears and pressed the blade against her skin. She shut her eyes and sliced – quickly – sucking in her breath at the sudden pain. Then, she changed hands. This time it was more awkward but no less effective. Mikki dropped the shears over the side of the fountain. She winced as she submerged her wrists, but she had been right. The pain wasn't bad, and it didn't last long. Mikki rested her head back against the lip of the basin. Gazing up at the sky, she thought how right it felt that the moon had set and the sun had not yet risen. Hecate . . . Goddess of the Ebony Moon . . . perhaps the absence of light in the sky was a sign that the goddess approved of her sacrifice. She had done the right thing. The roses would live. The dreams of mankind would be safe, as would her love. Mikki closed her eyes. She was so sleepy, and the water was so comfortable . . . soft . . . like a big feather bed . . . a warm raft on a summer lake . . . her mother's arms when she was a small, frightened girl who'd had a bad dream. She sighed. There shouldn't be any bad dreams . . . there should only be love and beauty and roses.

She wasn't afraid. But she would miss Asterius. As her mind blackened softly, Mikki's final thought was of how much she loved him.

ASTERIUS woke up suddenly. Something was wrong. He shook off sleep as he always had – instantly – and sat up, already reaching for his clothes. Then, thinking he should wake Mikado, he turned and . . .

She wasn't there. At first that didn't trouble him. She could be in the bathing chamber. He pulled on his tunic and strode through the tunnel. She wasn't there, either. Foreboding had him lengthening his stride as he made his way back to the bedchamber and the room beyond. Still, she wasn't there. He buckled his cuirasse as he left his lair. The sun had risen, but it was still early morning. An unusually warm breeze was coming from the gardens, bringing with it—

Asterius stopped, testing the wind. Yes, he'd been right. The wind brought with it the rich and heady scent of blooming roses. He picked up his pace, and soon he burst into the gardens.

They were abloom. Clouds of color filled the beds, like the goddess had taken a divine brush to the realm and painted in life and health. But instead of feeling relief and happiness, worry broke over Asterius, and he ran, letting his instinct guide him.

Hecate's Temple was in sight when he heard the first cry of lamentation. The sound of it was an icy fist closing around his heart. Then another cry met the first, and another and another, until the gardens echoed with mourning.

356

His mind was screaming *No!* even though he knew what he would discover. Asterius thundered up to the temple. The four Elementals were standing beside the fountain, clinging to one another and weeping openly. Between them he caught sight of wet copper hair and the side of her colorless face. Slowly, as if he was moving through a bog of sinking sand and mud, Asterius approached the fountain. She was there, of course.

Mikado was dead.

Asterius, Guardian of the Realm of the Rose, fell to his knees and roared his grief over and over and over. One by one, the Elementals, led by Gii, moved to him and placed their hands on his shoulders, until the five of them, connected by their grief, mourned their Empousa.

Chapter Thirty-five

GOD, her mouth was dry. And she felt like shit. Mikki tried to roll over, but she was too weak. All she did was twitch and make a muffled moan.

'Oh, fuck! Call 911 – she's alive!'

Huh? Call 911? There weren't any phones in the Realm of the Rose. Nor did anyone besides her say 'fuck'. So what the fuck? She tried to move again, and this time she felt the strong hands that held her in place.

'Don't try to move, ma'am! It's going to be okay. I've called for help.' Then he yelled, 'Over here! Bring the EMTs over here!'

Mikki could hear the hurried tread of heavy feet, accompanied by a vaguely familiar voice.

'Oh, Christ! It's Mikki. Ah, shit, look at all that blood!'

Mikki's breath was coming in panting gulps. She placed the voice. It was Mel, the security guard at the Tulsa Rose Gardens. But it couldn't be Mel – she couldn't be at the rose gardens. She was . . .

Oh. She'd forgotten. She was dead.

'Mikki, hang on. The EMTs are here. You're going to make it.'

She tried to say that she didn't want to make it. That her intention had been to save the roses, and the only way she could do that was to give them her blood. Unfortunately, it was a damn big realm, and a few drops in a bucket weren't going to do it.

But she couldn't speak. Her mind was working, but her body felt heavy and not her own. And she was wet, which made sense, because she was supposed to be in the fountain.

'Okay, on three roll her over.'

They rolled her from her stomach to her back. Mikki blinked, trying to clear her blurred vision. It was morning. From what she could see of the sky over the EMTs' shoulders, the sun hadn't risen long ago. Then her gaze shifted to a blob to her right. She managed to let her head flop to the side to bring it more fully into her view. It was a massive stone pedestal, and it was even more familiar than her old friend the security guard. It was the base that had supported the great Guardian statue. Only now it was empty.

Mikki screamed soundlessly inside her head. Then everything went blissfully black.

'You look better today, Mikki. How are you feeling?'

'Is that a professional question? A test? Or are you showing genuine concern?' she said sarcastically.

Nelly flinched. 'I don't deserve that, Mikki, and you know it.'

Mikki chewed her lips and reached out to quickly squeeze her friend's hand. It was dead wrong for her to take out her shitty mood on her girlfriend. It wasn't Nelly's fault that nothing she could do or say would ever come close to making it 'better' for her.

'Sorry. I'm just in a wicked bad mood today.'

'Did something happen? Have the dreams returned?'

Mikki couldn't meet Nelly's eyes. She didn't want her friend to see the desperation she carried around with her every day.

'No. My dreams have been completely normal, which is to say I don't remember them. Everything else has been normal, too. I

362

don't know what the hell's wrong. I guess it's just the weather that's gotten to me. I'm tired of the rain and the cold.' She tried not to remember that once she'd commanded the rain to appear every fourth day, and that the first day rain had obeyed her it set up the circumstances that had brought her into Asterius's bed . . .

'Mikki?'

She turned her eyes and thoughts back to the present and lifted her cappuccino, trying half-heartedly to work up a thirst. 'Just daydreaming. Sorry again. I'm not very good company today, Nelly.'

'You're my friend; you don't have to entertain or amuse me. You know that.' The psychiatrist sighed. 'Honey, what happened to you was traumatic. The men who attacked you and stole the statue from the rose gardens left you bleeding to death – and they have never been caught. It's normal to go through stages of anger and depression and resentment during your healing process, especially when you have no closure for the crime.'

Closure for the crime . . . Mikki had the insane urge to laugh, which she quickly stifled. She didn't want to do anything that might make her appear nuts. She didn't want her story questioned too closely.

'I know. I just—' Mikki rubbed her hand across her forehead. For the zillionth time, she wished Nelly was right, that what she was feeling was just a part of a healing process. 'I just wish I felt normal again.'

'You will, Mikki.' Nelly glanced at her watch. 'Oh, hell! I'm going to be late.'

Mikki managed to summon up a smile. 'Is this a real kooky appointment, or just a kinda kook?'

Nelly laughed, standing and collecting her briefcase and purse. 'Totally, absolute kook.'

'Good job security.'

'Exactly,' Nelly said. 'Hey, call me later if you need to talk.'

'I will. Promise. See you tomorrow morning. Same time – same coffee place.' She grinned at Nelly and then proceeded to feel guilty as hell at the relief she felt when her girlfriend walked out the door. It was so damn hard to talk to Nelly! She couldn't tell her the truth: 'Hey, girlfriend. I wasn't mugged, cut up by criminals who ripped off the statue from the Tulsa Rose Gardens and left to die. I actually committed suicide, although I like to think of it as a sacrificial act – I'm not big on suicide, which should prove that I'm not really nuts. Anyway, I had to do it because the magickal Realm of the Rose in the crossroads between worlds was in danger and only my blood could save it. It was my duty as Empousa. So really, you shouldn't say I committed suicide because I was just fulfilling my destiny. And by the by, I'm desperately in love with a man-beast and the reason I'm so damn depressed is that I'm stuck here without him.'

Uh, no. Nelly was her best friend, but even she would be sure to have her locked up in a lovely, yet totally exclusive, padded cell if she babbled the truth. She'd realized that as soon as she woke up in the hospital and *they* – social services and the police – had started to question her. The story that had evolved had come about more out of omission and accident than anything vaguely resembling the truth. But it still made her nervous to tell it, especially to her friend who just happened to be a savvy shrink who knew her too damn well.

Mikki checked her watch. It was only seven thirty. She didn't have to be at work until eight. She did have time for another cup of cappuccino before heading off to work. As she stood for a refill, she caught her reflection in the glass of the picture windows of Expresso Milano. Thin . . . she looked thin. And she could have done something with her wild hair besides pulling it back in a haphazard ponytail.

The problem was she just couldn't work up the energy to care.

Well, at least there were still plenty of her favorite, the giant orange sugar cookies that the coffee shop bought freshly made every morning from the popular Pani Del Goddess bakery just a few doors down the street. Mikki ordered two to go with her cappuccino and then changed her mind and ordered a third. She needed to put on weight, and the sugar rush added with the caffeine high might be enough to get her ready to face another meaningless, endless day at work. She grabbed a copy of the *Tulsa World* and made herself comfortable at one of the plush, silk-covered chairs while she waited for the multiply pierced coffee girl to bring her coffee and cookies on the café's elegant little silver trays. When she heard approaching heels on the tile floor, she didn't look up from her paper.

'Just go ahead and put it on the coffee table. Oh, and keep an eye on me. I have a feeling this is going to be a three-espresso morning.'

'Is everything not well, Mikado?'

Mikki almost dropped the paper in surprise. 'Sevillana! I'm sorry – I thought you were the coffee girl.'

The old woman's amazing aquamarine eyes sparkled. 'I have not been mistaken for a girl in a very long time.'

Mikki smiled, and for a moment it felt genuine. 'Would you join me?'

'Yes, I would like that.' The old woman settled herself gracefully into an adjoining chair and rearranged her beautiful pale blue pashmina shawl around her shoulders.

'I didn't think you lived here.' As on the first time they'd met, Mikki felt a little intimidated by the woman's presence. She was just so grand – in the old European fashion. There was an air of grace and culture about everything she said or did. And then, with a jolt, Mikki remembered, and in the remembering she wondered how she could have ever forgotten. 'The perfume! Where did you get the perfume you gave me that night?'

Sevillana smiled, but the waitress's delivery of their coffee and sweets kept her from saying anything. Then, even when they were alone again, Sevillana took her time emptying the coarse sugar into her cappuccino and stirring carefully with the tiny silver spoon before she spoke.

'There is only one place you can find such perfume, and it is in a realm that is far from here.'

Mikki felt a dizzying rush of an emotion she'd been missing for three months – hope. 'You're talking about the Realm of the Rose.'

The old woman nodded her head slightly.

'Oh, God,' Mikki gasped.

'I believe, Mikado, that it would be more appropriate for you to exclaim "Oh, Goddess."'

'How? How do you know about it? How did you get there, and how do I get back? What are you doing here? Why did you—'

Sevillana's raised hand cut off Mikki's torrent of words.

'Everything has its order and its time. Drowning me in questions will not change that.'

'I'm sorry.' Mikki pressed her hand against her chest, afraid that her heart would pound out of her body. 'I just – I need to know . . .' She ran a trembling hand over her face and began again. 'I have to get back.'

'I know, child,' Sevillana said softly. 'I know.' Then the old woman's gaze went past Mikki, and when she spoke again her voice reminded Mikki of a sad little girl. 'Did no one speak my name while you were there? Did they not remember me at all?'

'Your name? No. Why would they—' Mikki's eyes widened with realization. 'It's you. You are the last Empousa.'

'No, I *was* Empousa. I am no longer. Hecate's High Priestess. I discarded that position when I was young and foolish. But I have paid for my betrayal. For two hundred years I have been separated from my realm and my goddess and have walked the mundane earth, restless and unsatisfied – a true outlander.'

'Two hundred years!' Mikki could only stare at her. 'But how?'

'I have never fully understood it myself. Obviously, I age, but I do so slowly. I used to believe it was Hecate's way of punishing me – extending my life long enough that I was well and truly sorry for my selfish actions. Then, in my travels decades ago I visited Tulsa and happened to attend the unveiling of its new rose gardens . . .' She paused, her expression pained. 'I recognized the Guardian statue, and I knew it had been placed here for a reason, so I always circled back to Tulsa, waiting and watching . . . And then I met you, and I began to hope that perhaps Hecate had allowed me to live for so long for another reason.' Sevillana's blue eyes returned to Mikki. 'I hoped the Great Goddess had meant for me to give you the anointing oil so you could awaken the Guardian and return to the realm – and fulfill the destiny I left undone.' Sadness filled the old woman's beautiful eyes. 'Why did you make the same mistake I made? I did not mean for you to run away.'

'But I didn't!' Mikki cried. Then she lowered her voice when several heads turned in their direction. 'You know about the blood, don't you? Somehow you understand.'

'Yes, your blood nurtures the roses. How could I not know it? We carry the same blood in our veins, Mikado.' Sevillana touched her hand lightly in a caress that reminded Mikki so much of her mother that it made her breath catch. 'At the hospital that day I told you my name was Sevillana Kalyca, and it is. But that is only part of my name. I rarely use my family name – it is too difficult for me to hear it and to know that I forsook it, even though the deed was committed long ago. My true name is Sevillana Kalyca Empousai. I was the first Empousa to flee from the Realm of the Rose. I had hoped when I met you and felt the strength of the blood within you that I was also the last.'

'I didn't run away,' Mikki said numbly, staring at the woman who was her ancestress. 'I died.'

'Time runs differently there, but still it could not yet have been Beltane in the realm.'

'It was just starting to be winter.' Confused, Mikki frowned. 'But the weather didn't have anything to do with it. Dream Stealers got into the realm.'

Sevillana's hand flew to her heart in a gesture that oddly mimicked Mikki's earlier one. 'Oh, Goddess, no!'

'It was me. They fooled me. I let them in. Asterius killed them – or, I suppose they can't actually be killed, so that's not the right word, but he got rid of them, sent them back into the forest.'

'Asterius?'

Mikki studied Sevillana, her mind beginning to catch up with her racing emotions. This woman was the one they'd all been forbidden to talk about. She was part of why Hecate had bespelled the realm and Asterius. Well, Mikki was no longer in the Realm of the Rose, and she damn sure wanted to know, once and for all, what had happened.

'Asterius is the name given to the Guardian by his mother.' Watching carefully, Mikki saw the flash of surprise and unease that passed through Sevillana's eyes. 'I want to know what happened between the two of you. All of it.'

Sevillana stared out the window as she spoke, and her voice took on a faraway sing-song cadence, as if she was retelling a story that had been passed down from generation to generation. 'I was young and worse than foolish. I was selfish. I loved the power of Empousa, so much so that I was not willing to relinquish it. As the days drew closer and closer to Beltane, I convinced myself that it was only right that I escape the destiny planned for me. That I was different. But I knew I could not cross through the forest without protection. I convinced the Guardian to betray his duty and escort me through the forest to the entrance to the mundane world.'

'You seduced him?' Mikki felt very cold.

'Only with words. I would not bed a beast, but I made him believe I would. It was not a difficult thing to do. He had little experience with women. It was odd, though, that he allowed me to escape even after I rejected him.' Sevillana shook her head. 'I have long wondered about that. He should have turned on me and, at the very least, forced me back to face Hecate's wrath. Instead, he said one small thing and then stepped aside and let me go free.'

'He thought he loved you,' Mikki said woodenly.

Sevillana finally met her eyes, and Mikki could see the surprise there. 'That is the one thing he said – that he loved me. But it made no sense. How could a beast love a woman?'

'He is not a beast!' Mikki hissed under her breath, anger making her face pale. 'And you're not good enough for his love if you couldn't see the man within him.'

'You love him!'

'I do.'

369

Sevillana stared at Mikki for a long time without speaking and then she bowed her head slightly to the younger woman. 'Forgive me for speaking so cavalierly. I was a young girl then. I have come to understand since that I was wrong about many things, this, then, is simply one last lesson for me. You have my admiration, Mikado, as well as my respect. I have never known such courage as yours.'

Mikki took several deep, calming breaths. There was absolutely no point in getting so pissed off at the old woman. What she'd done had happened two centuries ago. It was over. Finished. And she didn't want to alienate her. Sevillana Kalyca Empousai was her ticket back to Asterius.

'I forgive you. I think Asterius does, too. And what I did wasn't that courageous. I didn't have any choice. Asterius had gotten rid of the Dream Stealers, but it was too late. They'd already poisoned the roses – all of them except the ones I'd bled on. I tried to stop the blight another way, but nothing worked. I knew it wouldn't. The only way to save the roses was by my blood.'

'And you do not think it courageous that you went to your lover and allowed him to sacrifice you? It was not even Beltane, yet you met your destiny early and saved the realm.'

Mikki frowned. 'Asterius didn't sacrifice me. He didn't even know what I'd planned. I knew he'd try to stop me, so I snuck out. And what's this you keep saying about Beltane? That's in the spring, right? What does that have to do with anything?'

'You truly do not know?'

'No!' she said, exasperated and thoroughly sick of mysteries.

'They must have been afraid to tell you. Afraid that you, too, would leave them. Mikado, the Empousa serves one true purpose. She is there for the roses.'

'Yes, yes, yes! I know that.'

'You also know that Hecate's Empousa is bound to the roses through her blood. What you do not know is that every Beltane night the Empousa is sacrificed by the Guardian, because her blood insures that the realm thrives for another year.'

Mikki felt everything within her go very still. 'They were going to kill me?'

'Not they. He was. It is the Guardian's duty to protect the roses.'

It all made horrible sense. Asterius's behavior when they first met and were attracted to each other . . . how he had said they could not be together . . . how he had struggled against loving her. It had been more than disbelief that she could ever see him as a man – more than the rejection of Sevillana. He'd known he would have to kill her.

The thought made her physically ill.

Sevillana's warm hand on her cold, numb one was a physical shock.

'He had no choice.'

'And Hecate, she meant all along for me to die,' Mikki said.

'Life and death is different for the gods. Hecate is stern and powerful, but she is also a loving goddess. She would see your sacrifice as just another link in the great circle of life. The goddess would not forsake you, Mikado, even in death. Had you met your destiny at Beltane, Hecate would have made sure you spent eternity in the endless beauty of the Elysian Fields. The goddess cares for those who belong to her; she only turns away from those who betray her.'

'It's a hard concept for my mind to grasp. Everyone I cared about, everyone I loved, they all knew I was going to die.' She paused as the enormity of it hit her. 'So even if you could help me figure out a way to get back, I'd just be returning to die again.'

'Yes. Do you still wish to return?'

371

Chapter Thirty-six

Dɪᴅ she still want to return? It was already the end of February. Wasn't Beltane the same day as May first? So she'd have a couple of months and then Asterius would kill her.

The thought was impossible to believe. Yet even in the middle of her disbelief, intuition told her Sevillana was speaking the truth. It all fit, and she suddenly felt like the piece outside the jigsaw puzzle. She knew where she belonged, and it wasn't in Tulsa, Oklahoma.

'I want to go back, but I don't know if I'm brave enough.'

'Listen to your instincts, Mikado. Trust what they tell you.'

'They tell me that I don't belong here.'

'Then perhaps you should return home,' Sevillana said.

'Do you know how to get me there?'

'I can give you the anointing oil, but the rest you already hold within you. You sacrificed yourself for the Realm of the Rose, and you were selfless enough to love its Guardian. You were, my dear, the exact opposite of the realm's last Empousa. I believe Hecate will hear your call, and honor it.'

'But how—' Mikki stopped herself. She knew what she must do. She had to listen to her intuition and follow her instincts. She glanced at Sevillana, who nodded approval at her introspection. *Calm down and think. I'm Hecate's Empousa. There has to be a way for me to return.* Suddenly Mikki smiled. 'That's it! I'm still Empousa. Hecate said I carry her power – that can't have completely gone away, not even here. I mean, look at you! You've lived two hundred years, and you walked away from the goddess.'

'Her power should still be yours to wield,' Sevillana said. 'Even in the mundane world.' The old woman reached into her leather clutch and pulled out a glass rose stem, exactly like the first one she'd given Mikki. 'This is the anointing oil of Hecate's Empousa. It is the one step in the invocation ritual with which I can aid you.'

'Thank you, Sevillana.' Mikki took the stem, carefully folding it in a napkin before sliding it into her purse.

'I ask only one thing of you, Empousa,' the old woman said. 'I ask that you petition Hecate's forgiveness for me. I know I cannot return to the realm, but I am weary and I would like to be allowed to shed this life and embrace my eternity in the Elysian Fields. I cannot do so without Hecate's forgiveness.'

'I'll ask her. But why not ask her yourself?'

'I wish I could, but I cannot return. I have tried, many times over the long, silent years. The goddess will not hear me. She has turned her face from me.'

'But Hecate hasn't turned her face from me!' she said in a rush of understanding. 'Why do you think I'm not a ghost in the Elysian Fields? I died. I should not have woken up back in Tulsa – unless there was a damn good reason Hecate wanted me to return here.' Remembering, Mikki sat straight up. 'She knew you were here. I told her your name when she asked me how I'd "accidentally" gotten my hands on the anointing oil of an Empousa. I remember the look on her face now – she knew it even then.'

'The Guardian Statue – the goddess did put it here so I would find it – and find you,' Sevillana said through a voice thickened with tears.

'Hecate meant for me to come back so I'd see you.' This time it was Mikki who took the old woman's trembling hand in hers. 'Hecate's forgiven you, Sevillana.'

'Oh, my dear, if only that was true . . .'

'Let's find out. Tonight is the night of the new moon. Come to the rose gardens. Stand inside the sacred circle with me. Let's try to go home, Sevillana.'

Mɪᴋᴋɪ was glad for the rainy night. It was cold and miserable, but it was also so dark that even the illuminating lampposts in Woodward Park cast only the smallest halo of weak, iridescent light in limited bubbles around the park. It was easy for someone who knew the park well to avoid the lights. And Mikki knew the park well.

She clutched her briefcase in one hand and held tightly to Sevillana with her other, helping maneuver the old woman through the darkness. They didn't speak; they didn't need to. Mikki kept up a running commentary in her head that prayed over and over that no one would be in the park or the gardens. By the time they'd reached the boundary between the park and the gardens, Mikki had relaxed a little. Clearly no one was crazy enough to venture out into the park on a night like this, especially a couple of hours past midnight. Still, Mikki didn't say anything until they passed beneath the rock archway and stepped lightly onto the third tier of the gardens.

The illumination from the fountain lazily lit the area surrounding it in a watery light that, coupled with the drizzly mist that hung in the cold air, washed the tier with dreamlike color.

'It's appropriate,' Mikki said softly.

'Yes. The lighting evokes dream images,' Sevillana said in perfect understanding. 'It is a good omen, Empousa.'

'Let's hope so,' she muttered. Then she looked at the empty pedestal. She hadn't been back since that horrible morning they'd found her. She couldn't bear it. Mikki hadn't quit as a volunteer; she'd asked for a leave of absence, which was granted immediately. Everyone said they understood how hard it must be for her to come back into the gardens where she'd been attacked and left for dead. But of course, they didn't really understand. How could they? They'd never know the truth.

'Mikado?' Sevillana touched her arm gently.

Mikki turned her back to the empty pedestal. 'You're right. We need to hurry. This will definitely be impossible to explain if we get caught.'

'Then we must not get caught,' the old woman said firmly.

'Agreed. Let's get busy.'

Mikki chose a place near the fountain. She opened her briefcase, and Sevillana helped her place a candle in each of the four Elemental positions of the circle: yellow in the east for Wind; red in the south for Flame, blue in the west for Water; green in the north for Earth and, finally, purple in the center of the circle for Spirit. Then she took the long, narrow fireplace matchbox from the briefcase as well as the little razor-sharp knife that usually stayed hidden in her apartment, and placed them beside the spirit candle.

Stepping outside the ring of candles, Mikki took one last thing from the briefcase before she placed it in the shadows beside the empty pillar. She pulled free the cork that closed the end of the delicate glass stem and then applied the perfumed oil liberally to the pulse points at her neck, wrists and breasts. Then she handed it to Sevillana. With only a small hesitation, the old woman took the bottle and applied the perfume to her own body. The scent of roses and spice was heavy in the damp air, and Mikki's stomach clenched with remembrance.

This had to work; she had to return.

'Are you ready?' Mikki asked.

The old woman nodded and tugged two long hair pins from her elegant French knot, setting her waist-length fall of silver hair free. Then with a flourish that showed grace and beauty that belied her years, Sevillana whirled off her long raincoat, under which she was wearing a beautiful silk chiton the color of lilacs.

Mikki discarded her own coat and ignored the cold as she, too, was now dressed in a violet-colored chiton. The only difference between her chiton and Sevillana's was that Mikki's was a shade darker, and, as was proper for a new moon ritual, it left one of her breasts bare.

'One thing you can say about chitons is that they are definitely easy to make,' Mikki said.

'I have missed them dreadfully.' Looking down at herself, Sevillana smiled. Then she glanced at Mikki and dipped into a fluid curtsey. 'Shall we continue, Empousa?'

'Absolutely.'

Together the two women walked to the center of the circle. With the purple candle between them, they faced north. Then Mikki picked up the box of matches, thinking how much she missed the company of the Elementals, especially tonight. Shaking off doubts, Mikki approached the yellow candle and lit the match.

'Blowing winds, strong and everywhere, even in the realm of the mundane, I summon you, Wind, as the first element in the sacred circle.' Mikki touched the match to the candle and held it there until it lit. Without letting herself worry about whether or not the element actually heard her and would answer her call, Mikki moved quickly to the red candle. 'Blazing force of cleansing fire, dancing flame of light, even in the realm of the mundane your power is rich and true. I summon you, Flame, to the sacred circle.' When the match touched the red candle's wick, the flame burst into being and Mikki felt a surge of hope. Without hesitation, she moved to the blue candle. 'Sparkling, glimmering tide of life, you bathe us, cool us, quench us, even in this realm of the mundane you cover more than half our world and give us life. I summon you, Water, to the sacred circle.' Through the lit wick, Mikki thought she saw the blue candle waver and shimmer like waves. Then she was facing the green candle. 'Lush and fertile, familiar and wild, even in this realm of the mundane you hold us and care for us. I summon you, Earth, to the sacred circle.' Mikki moved back to her place beside the purple candle. 'I summon you, Spirit, to the sacred circle with the two words that bound me to my goddess – "love" and "trust."' She lit the purple candle and then dropped the match. Staring around her, she was disappointed that she saw no luminous threads weaving together to bind the elements to the circle.

'Do not despair that you cannot see them in this realm,' Sevillana said as if she could read Mikki's thoughts. 'See them within your mind. Believe they are there. The power of an Empousa's belief is a magick all its own.'

Mikki nodded, and within her mind she imagined the gossamer threads outlining the circle.

'Now, let's finish it,' Mikki said resolutely. She bent and picked up the knife. She looked at Sevillana, and the old woman gave Mikki her hand, palm up. With a quick, practiced movement, Mikki pressed the sharp blade against Sevillana's thin skin and drew a long line across her palm. As her blood welled, Mikki handed the knife to Sevillana. The ex-Empousa took Mikki's hand firmly, and with one quick stroke, cut a similar line in her

377

palm. Then she dropped the knife and the two women clasped their hands together, palm to palm, mingling the blood of generations of Hecate's High Priestesses.

Mikki closed her eyes and cleared her mind. When she spoke, she gave no mind to lowering her voice. If it worked – if the goddess was really invoked – the circle would hold and no mortal would be allowed to intrude. And if it did not . . . if it did not, then Mikki didn't care what happened to her.

'Hecate, Great Goddess of the Ebony Moon, Crossroads of Mankind and Beasts. I am Mikado Empousai, High Priestess and Empousa of the Realm of the Rose. In a land far from you I have anointed myself, cast your sacred circle and by the right of my blood I call upon your name. We have a pledge between us, an oath sealed with love and trust. And by the power of that oath I invoke your presence and ask that I be heard.'

Suddenly, wind whipped around them, causing the candles to shiver madly. The mist swirled, and as Mikki watched, it became filled with glitter until from the center of the vortex of wind and sound and light, Hecate appeared. The goddess was dressed in full regalia – robes of night, the headdress of stars and the golden torch. At her feet the massive hounds snarled and snapped at the misty garden.

Mikki started to cry the goddess's name, but Sevillana's tearful voice interrupted her. The old woman pulled her hand from Mikki's and fell to her knees.

'Great Goddess! Forgive me!' Sevillana sobbed, tears falling freely down her well-lined face. 'What I did was wrong. I have spent lifetimes trying to atone for my unforgivable error. The foolish, selfish girl who betrayed you no longer exists.'

Hecate's face was unreadable, but her voice was soft. 'What is it you have learned, Sevillana?'

I have learned that there are things more terrible to lose than my life.'

'And what are those things?'

'My honor . . . my name . . . and the love of my goddess.'

'You never lost the love of your goddess, daughter.'

Sevillana pressed her hand to her mouth, trying to stifle her sobs. Mikki put her hand on the old woman's shoulder, lending her strength through touch.

'Will you forgive me then, Hecate?' Sevillana was finally able to say.

'Child, I forgave you long ago. It is you who have not been able to forgive yourself,' said the goddess.

Sevillana bowed her head. 'May I rest now, Goddess?'

'Yes, Sevillana. All you ever needed to do was to ask. I would never turn my face from my Empousa – even an errant one. Behold!' Then Hecate swept out her hand and a section of the mist opened, like a door made of night. Suddenly a lovely scene came into view. It was a beautiful meadow, filled with clover and ringed by tall pines whose needles looked like giant feather dusters. As they watched, a lithe figure skipped and danced into the meadow, followed by a group of young, beautiful women. Their flowing chitons were draped alluringly around their bodies, which looked strong and young, even though each of them had an odd, semi-substantial look.

And then Mikki felt a jolt of shock as she recognized one of the women.

'Mama!' she cried.

Before Mikki could rush forward, Hecate said softly, 'It is not your time, Mikado. Your destiny is not complete yet.'

Through streaming tears, she stared at the goddess. 'But it is my mother, isn't it?'

379

'It is, indeed. And look closely. You will see your grandmother, as well.'

Mikki watched breathlessly. Yes – she did recognize the stunning young woman who danced holding her mother's hand. She had looked into that beautiful face countless times, only when she'd known her it had been lined by life and wisdom.

'Where are they?'

'The Elysian Fields,' Sevillana said, her voice filled with awe. 'There they will be eternally young and happy and free.'

'Take your place beside them, Sevillana. Your banishment is over.'

Slowly, the old woman stood. She turned to Mikki and hugged her tightly. 'Have a blessed life, my dear,' she whispered.

'Tell my mother and grandmother that I love them,' Mikki whispered back to her.

'I shall. They will be as proud of you as I am, daughter.'

Sevillana walked through the boundary of the sacred circle to the goddess. She stopped before Hecate, and, sobbing again, she curtseyed deeply. The goddess reached out and embraced her, kissing each of the old woman's cheeks.

'Enter Elysian with my blessing, Sevillana.'

The old woman walked through the door the goddess had opened to paradise, and as she did her body changed. Old age fell from her like a discarded cloak, until with a shout of joy the beautiful young Sevillana took her place with the group of dancing maidens. Then the door faded and was once again nothing more than rain-heavy mist and darkness.

'I am pleased to see you again, my Empousa,' Hecate said.

Mikki wiped the tears from her face and smiled at the goddess. 'I'm unbelievably glad to see you, too. If I had known I could do this – invoke you here – I would have cast the circle and called you months ago.'

'Ah, but then you would have been missing one piece in the invocation – the anointing oil of an Empousa. You needed Sevillana for that.'

'You're right – you're right. I don't know . . . I've learned so much today that my mind can't seem to hold it all. I'm so glad you forgave Sevillana.' Then Mikki blinked in surprise, as more of the pieces of the puzzle fit together. 'The first night I was in the realm – you said you'd made a mistake and you wanted to fix it. That mistake was about Sevillana and Asterius, wasn't it?'

'It was.' Hecate sighed, a sound that Mikki found amazingly mortal and fallible. 'I should not have punished them as I did. Sevillana was young and selfish – I knew that when I chose her as my Empousa. I mistakenly hoped the power in her blood would mature her. It did not.'

'And what about Asterius?' Mikki asked, feeling like she should hold her breath.

'That was my biggest mistake. I gifted him with the heart and soul of a man and then refused to truly acknowledge that he was, indeed, more than a beast. In that respect I was even more selfish than his mother, who could not see more than her own mistakes whenever she gazed upon him. I was wrong to disallow him a mate – to believe he was a creature who needed no more than duty to exist. It was my fault his need drove him to choose unwisely when Sevillana tempted him. It was anger at myself that caused me to banish her and bespell him. Unfortunately, I understood that too late. Then all I could do was to wait for the right mortal to be born. One who could see the truth and have the courage to act upon it.'

'Then you'll let me love him, if only until Beltane?'

'No, Mikado.'

381

Mikki's body went cold and still. 'Please, Hecate. I love him. Let me make him happy, even if it's only for a little while.'

'The roses thrive, Mikado.'

Confused at the sudden change in subject, Mikki said, 'Good. I did what I felt had to be done.'

'You sacrificed yourself willingly, calling upon the oath of love and trust with which you were bound into my service.'

'Yes, Hecate.'

'That has never before happened in the Realm of the Rose. Oh, yes, for generations Empousas have given their blood to nurture the realm, but they did so because they had to, because it was the thread of life Fate and Destiny had together woven for them. But you, Mikado Empousai, a mortal woman from a land almost completely bereft of magick, willingly sacrificed yourself to save something as nebulous as the dreams of mankind. And you also saw the man within the beast and let yourself love him, breaking his spell of loneliness and isolation.'

'I – I just did what my instincts told me to do. I loved the realm. It was my home, and protecting it, and everyone in it, was worth dying for,' Mikki said quickly, feeling completely overwhelmed by the goddess's praise. 'Asterius wasn't hard to love.' She smiled and moved her shoulders nervously. 'Isn't there always something of a beast within every strong man? It's part of what makes them so deliciously different from us.' She took a deep breath. 'Can't you please let me return to him? I give you my word that I will willingly go back to the fountain on Beltane night.'

'What you have done has changed the fabric of the realm, Empousa. Your sacrifice was pure – unsullied by the bonds of duty or force or fear. There need never be another Beltane sacrifice; your blood has ensured that.'

When Mikki began to speak, Hecate raised her hand to silence her. 'But simply returning is not that easy. You have also been changed by your sacrifice. As long as you stay in the mundane world, you will live a normal lifespan. But should you return to the Realm of the Rose, your blood ties you to it irrevocably. Which means you would be an immortal, reigning in the realm eternally as more than my Empousa – you would become Goddess of the Rose.'

Mikki heard Hecate's words, but they were almost drowned out by the dizziness and disbelief that hummed through her mind. Did Hecate just say that she would never die? That she could become a goddess?

'But you should know that a goddess's path is not an easy one to tread, Mikado. Eternity is a daunting companion – sometimes he is glorious – sometimes he is melancholy and petulant as a spoiled child. Think carefully, Empousa. I give you a choice, but that choice is irrevocable. You may stay here, in the mundane world, and live out your mortal life's thread – at the end of which I will not desert you and will welcome you to the Elysian Fields as I did your mother and her mother before her.'

'But Asterius—' she began.

'Because I regret the mistakes I made, I will grant him a boon. If you so choose, I will gift him with a mortal man's body.' The goddess smiled and her eyes glittered mischievously. 'I will gift him with a mortal man's body, but for you, my favorite Empousa, I give you my oath that his new form will be more pleasing to look upon than Adonis. But it is impossible, even for my powers, to change his form in the Realm of the Rose. I will have to bring him here, to live out his mortal life by your side. You will have children and grow old together and find solace in each other's arms when your lives are finished.'

'Or I can return?' Mikki prompted, when it didn't seem like Hecate was going to continue.

'Yes. You may return as Goddess of the Rose – I will relinquish the realm of dreams to you eternally. But remember, in that realm I cannot change Asterius's form. He will remain eternally a beast, but with the heart and soul of a man. Make your choice, Mikado.'

Mikki started to consider and then realized that she actually had no choice. She knew exactly what she had to do.

'I choose the Realm of the Rose and my beast. I don't want to live anywhere else, and I would not ask Asterius to change. I love what he is, not what others would have him pretend to be.'

Hecate's smile was radiant. 'Then let us return you to your realm.'

Chapter Thirty-seven

THE forest had certainly not changed. It was still dark and creepy – especially now that Mikki knew what lurked out there. Of course now she was a goddess, so the Dream Stealers would have a whole new ball game to play if they tried to trap her again. And they would – Hecate had already warned her about that. Just because she was an immortal now, it didn't mean she wasn't still fallible and able to be manipulated by darker emotions. Hecate herself had been proof of that. Mikki shivered and wrapped her purple palla around her shoulders more tightly. She'd be careful.

Weird that she didn't feel any different. Or at least not that much different. She'd felt the roses when she'd returned. Really *felt* them. Embarrassingly enough, they had rejoiced when she entered the realm. Although now that she knew they had real emotions and bright little spirits, she felt decidedly less ridiculous about all those years she'd talked to her bushes. Still, it was a wonderful yet odd sensation that she'd have to get used to.

The handmaidens would be really glad to see her, and Mikki was looking forward to surprising them in the morning. But not tonight. Tonight there was only one person she wanted to see – only one place she wanted to be – and that was in Asterius's arms.

Mikki could feel that he was out here somewhere, gathering the threads of reality to take to the Dream Weavers. She could have waited for him in his home. She could have called him to her bedroom in the palace. She hadn't wanted to do either. She would come to him because she loved the innocent joy he so obviously felt every time she chose him. And she wanted him to know she would keep choosing him for all of eternity.

A flicker of light drew her to the right. She followed it, and the flicker became a torch. Holding her breath, she made her way slowly and silently toward it. He was standing with his back to her, combing the limbs of the ancient tree above him. Glittering threads appeared within his hands, and he pulled and spun them into a luminous mound of magick on the forest floor.

She moved closer and then stopped when he made a low moan. He turned to the side with a sudden flinching movement, as if the thread he was weaving had caused him pain. But he didn't drop it. Instead he stared at it with an agonized expression filled with despair and longing.

Mikki looked within the thread and saw herself. She was heavy with child, which was truly a shock, but her shock shifted to joy as she watched Asterius enter the frame and pull her into his arms. He kissed her and then dropped to his knees, placing his lips gently against her swollen belly. In the dream vision, Mikki saw herself smile contentedly and reach out and stroke her finger down one of his ebony horns, just as she had done long ago.

With an anguished cry, Asterius hurled the thread away from him. 'Why do you torment me?' he roared.

Mikki stepped from the shadows. 'It torments you to think of me being pregnant? I think I'm the one who should be tormented. I mean, the whole horns and hooves issue in utero is a little daunting.'

Asterius didn't move. He only stared at Mikki with eyes filled with hatred. 'Begone apparition! I will not fall prey to your evil lies.' Growling menacingly, he started moving stealthily toward her, holding his deadly claws before him like blades.

'Asterius! It's me! I just wanted to surprise you.'

His look darkened. 'I said begone, nightmare creature!' He closed on her.

Mikki squealed and stepped back, blurting the first thing that came in her mind. 'The first night we met you put a rose in my wineglass!'

As if he'd run against a wall, Asterius halted.

'Mikado?' he said tentatively.

'That's what I've been trying to tell you.' She sighed when he still didn't seem to thaw. 'You know, as often as you've rejected me, it's a wonder we've ever gotten together at all.'

'Mikado!' He lunged forward, pulling her into his arms.

His powerful body was trembling so hard he didn't seem to be able to do more than just hold her and repeat her name over and over again. She held him in return, touching him and murmuring wordless endearments, until his shaking stopped and he was able to loosen his grip on her.

She looked up into his beautiful, terrible face, which was wet with tears.

'How did this happen? How can you be here?' he asked.

'Hecate gave me a choice.'

'But the realm – your blood – it is safe, eternally. The goddess said that after your sacrifice, no other Empousa's blood would be needed to make the realm thrive, not for an eternity.'

'I know. I chose the eternity, and I chose to spend it with you.'

At first his eyes were blank and then understanding flashed joyously across his face. 'We will never be parted?'

'Never,' she said.

'Then the threads – they were not tormenting me. They were showing . . .' He broke off, unable to speak through the swell of emotions.

'They were showing you our happily ever after. And, yes, my love. That particular dream has finally come true.'

Slowly, he bent and kissed her, cupping her face between his massive hands. Mikki wrapped her arms around him and held on to their future – their eternity.

In the shadows, Hecate smiled and patted one of her great beasts on his dark head.

Pea felt a wash of relief, which was quickly followed by embarrassment when she heard the fire siren getting closer. Crap crap crap! What a way to start Saturday morning.

'They're almost here, Chlo-chlo-ba-bo!' she yelled up at the tree.

The pitiful whine that replied from the middle of the winter-bare branches squeezed at her heart, but Pea shook her head sternly at the dog, refusing to give in to Chloe's manipulation.

'Okay, look! How many times do I have to tell you? You. Are. Not. A. Cat.'

A black nose appeared from a top branch of the tree. Behind it Pea could see the glint of bright, intelligent eyes staring down at her.

'Hrumph!' Chloe barked the strange, deep growl sound she made when she was highly annoyed.

'Whatever! You can love cats. You cannot be one.'

Chloe had just *hrumph*ed indignantly at her again when the fire engine glided to a smooth stop at the curb. Pea sighed and gave Chloe one more glare. Then she started to walk toward the men who were climbing out of the traditional shiny red fire truck. Instantly Chloe erupted in a pathetic chorus of whines and yaps. Forgetting all about embarrassment and doggie manipulations, Pea rushed back to the tree.

'Chlo-chlo! It's okay, baby girl. I'm right here.'

'Bring the ladder over here, Steve,' a deep male voice called from close behind her. 'This is the tree.'

'Hurry!' Pea yelled without taking her eyes from the frightened dog. 'She's really scared, and if she falls she's definitely going to break something.'

'Ma'am, cats rarely hurt themselves when they jump from trees. The whole land-on-their-feet myth actually has quite a bit of truth to it,' the voice over her shoulder said.

Chloe whined again.

'Hey, that's not a cat.'

Pea turned to the fireman, an annoyed frown on her face. 'I clearly told the dispatcher that my *dog*—' she began, putting her fists on her waist and letting the worry she felt for Chloe shift over to irritation, but one look at the man had her anger fizzling and her tongue stammering. She felt her cheeks flame with heat. Quadruple crap! It was *him*. Griffin DeAngelo. The most gorgeous man she had ever seen. Ever. Even on TV. He was also the guy she'd been crushing on for the entire past year – ever since she'd walked Chloe by his house (which was just down the street from hers) and seen him mowing his yard. Without a shirt on. And here he was. Standing in her front yard like he'd walked right out of one of her very graphic dreams.

Naturally he wasn't looking at her standing there in her baggy sweatpants and sweatshirted glory, and he hadn't noticed her sudden pathetic inability to speak. He was peering up at Chloe with a quizzical smile tilting his delicious-looking lips.

'How in the hell did he get up in that tree?'

'She's not a he, she's a she. And she climbed,' Pea said.

'Oh, pardon my language, ma'am; I forgot you were there. I'm Griffin DeAngelo, captain of the Midtown Station.' He tapped his helmet in an archaic and adorable gesture of a gentleman greeting a lady.

'I know!'

'You know?' He raised an eyebrow as if to punctuate his question.

'Yeah, you live down there.' Pea pointed down the block directly at his house. Like a stalker. 'Remember, we met at the fourth of July block party last fourth of July, and also at the summer weenie roast and again at the pre-Christmas light hanging neighborhood meeting,' she babbled, sounding exactly like a stalker.

His beautiful forehead wrinkled in confusion. 'I'm sorry, ma'am. I don't remember.'

Of course he didn't. No one remembered meeting her. 'No problem, I'm um . . .' She paused as she stared up into eyes that were so big and blue and beautifully dark lashed that she suddenly and moronically forgot her name.

'Ma'am?'

'Dorreth Chamberlain!' she blurted, holding out her hand like a dork. 'And the dog caught in the tree is Chloe.'

He took her hand gently, like he was afraid she might explode at his touch. And why wouldn't he think that? She'd just told him that they'd met three times, none of which he remembered, and she was still standing there gawking at him like a kindergarten kid in a bubble gum factory. And her hair! Pea forced herself not to groan and pat manically at the frizzy mess she'd tied back in her favorite scrunchie.

'Check it out. It's a dog,' said a young fireman who had joined them with two other men carrying an extension ladder.

'How the hell did it get up there?' said another fireman, with a laugh.

393

Griffin cleared his throat and gestured at Pea.

'Sorry, ma'am,' was mumbled in her general direction.

Pea laughed gaily, gesturing up at the tree, trying hard to sound perky and interesting. 'She climbed!' As usual, none of the men so much as glanced at her.

'Climbed? She must be twenty feet up in that old oak,' one of the unnamed guys said.

'She's a good climber. She's just not a good climber downer,' Pea said, and then wanted to dissolve into the sidewalk in embarrassment. *Climber downer?* God, she really was such a dork.

'Well, let's get her down,' Griffin said. The men went to work extending the ladder, and Chloe started growling.

'What kind of dog is she, ma'am?' Griffin asked her.

'She's a Scottie, but she thinks she's a cat. See, I have a cat named Max, and Chloe is totally in love with him, hence the fact she is clueless that she's a Scottie *dog*. Chloe is in denial. She believes she's a Scottie *cat*. I'm not sure whether to get her another dog, get her some Prozac or take her for a visit to the pet psychic.'

Griffin laughed, a deep, infectious sound that made Pea's skin tingle with pleasure. 'Or maybe you should just invest in a safety net.'

Pea giggled and tried to have one of 'those moments' with totally, insanely gorgeous Griffin the Fireman – one of those eye-meeting moments where a man and a woman share a long, sexy, lingering, laughter-filled look.

Naturally the moment did not happen.

First, her coquettish giggle turned into – horror of all horrors – a snort. Second, blonde and beautiful appeared on the scene.

'Pea! Don't tell me Chloe got caught in a tree again!'

394

Griffin immediately shifted his attention to her neighbor, who was hurrying up to them, her six-year-old daughter in tow. 'Hi, Griffin,' she said.

'Good to see you again, Stacy,' he said, and tilted his hat to her, too.

Pea sighed. Of course he remembered Stacy – tall, sleek, always together-looking Stacy – even though Pea knew for sure that Stacy had only made *one* of the neighborhood meetings in the past year. With Stacy there was no way in hell gorgeous Griffin would give her another thought. If he'd ever given her a first thought. Even with a kid at her heels, Stacy was ridiculously attractive.

But, surprisingly, the fireman's eyes slid back to her. 'Pea?' he asked with a raised brow.

'Yeah,' she said, shrugging and launching into the short version of her all too familiar explanation for what everyone called her. 'Sadly, Pea is an unfortunate childhood nickname that stuck.'

'Oh, come on! There's nothing wrong with your nickname. Pea's adorable,' Stacy said, grinning at her.

'Yea for Pea!' Stacy's daughter Emili chimed in. 'I like your name. It's cute. But it's not as cute as him.' Emili pointed up at Griffin. 'Are you married? Pea's not married. Maybe you could marry Pea. She doesn't even have a boyfriend and my mommy says that's a shame because she really is cuter than people think she is 'cause—'

Pea sucked in air and felt her face blaze with heat while Stacy clamped her hand over Emili's mouth and tried unsuccessfully not to laugh.

Thank the sweet weeping baby Jesus that Chloe chose that moment to snarl a warning at the young fireman who was positioning the ladder against the tree.

'Chlo! It's okay.' Pea hurried over to the trunk of the tree and looked up at the black snout and bright eyes. Chloe whined. 'Sorry, she doesn't like men,' she said to the fireman. 'I really don't think she'll bite you. But she will complain. Probably a lot.'

'I'll get her,' Griffin said.

'She's all yours, Captain.'

Griffin started up the ladder and Chloe's low, rumbling growl intensified.

'Chloe! Manners!' Pea called up to the perturbed Scottie. *Please, God, please don't let her bite him*, she mentally telegraphed over and over . . . Until Griffin did something that made Pea's thoughts, as well as Chloe's growls, come to an abrupt halt. He was calling Chloe, but he wasn't calling her like someone would call a dog. He was, unbelievably, kitty-kittying her.

'Come here Chloe, kitty-kitty. It's okay, little girl. Come here, kitty-kitty-kitty . . .'

Dumbfounded, Pea watched her dog's ears lift and her head tilt toward the approaching man.

'Good girl,' Griffin murmured. 'Good kitty-kitty, kitty-kitty.' He held his hand out slowly and let Chloe get a good sniff of him. 'See, you smell her, don't you? That's right, kitty-kitty-kitty, come on down.'

Pea could only stand and stare as Griffin reached into the tree crevice and pulled Chloe, who was still sniffing him curiously, into his arms and began the descent down the ladder.

'Amazing,' Stacy said with a deep breath. 'How did he do that? Chloe hates men.'

'He's too pretty to hate, Mommy,' Emili said.

'Honey, let's keep that for our inside thoughts, shall we?' Stacy said. Then she glanced at Pea and whispered, 'Even though it's totally true.'

Pea pretended not to hear either of them, which was easy. Her entire being was focused on her dream man striding toward her with her dog – who was actually wagging her tail – held firmly in his arms.

'Here ya go, ma'am.' He handed Chloe to Pea.

'Th-thank you,' Pea stuttered. 'How?'

'How?' he repeated.

'The kitty-kittying. How did you know to do that?'

'Just makes sense. You said she thinks she's a cat, and you have a cat, right?'

Pea nodded.

'That's how you call your cat. Right?'

Pea nodded again.

'I figured she'd recognize the call.'

Griffin scratched Chloe on the top of her head, and Pea watched in astonishment as her dog – her man-hating dog – closed her eyes and sighed happily.

'That's just part of it, though,' Griffin said. 'I was counting on Chloe smelling Cali.'

Pea suddenly understood. 'Your cat?'

'My cat.' Griffin gave Chloe one last scratch, then turned back to his men. 'Okay, let's get this loaded up. Have a good day, ma'am.' He nodded politely to her and then to Stacy. He winked at Emili, and then he was gone.

'Em, honey, go on inside and wait for Mommy. I'll be there in just a second,' Stacy told her daughter.

'Are you and Pea going to talk about how pretty that fireman was?'

'Of course not, honey. Now go on.'

''Kay! Bye, Pea.' Emili skipped off to her house, singing a song about lemon drops and unicorns.

'Okay, I'd forgotten how drop dead Mr. Tall Dark and Fireman is. I can definitely understand why you've had a thing for him for ages,' Stacy said.

Pea put Chloe down and the dog trotted over to the tree and began sniffing all around the trunk. 'Do not even think about climbing up there again,' Pea told her sternly. Chloe glanced back at her and snorted. 'I swear that dog understands every word I say,' Pea muttered.

'Hello! Sexy, incredible man. We were talking about him and not your insane Scottie.'

'She's not insane,' Pea said automatically. 'And yeah, he's gorgeous and I might have a little crush on him.'

Stacy rolled her eyes, which Pea chose to ignore. 'But now he's gone. I don't see the point in going on and on about him.'

'Like you haven't gone on and on about him before?'

Pea silently chastised herself for the one or two – okay, ten or twelve – times she'd mentioned to Stacy how hot she thought their neighbor was. 'Whatever,' she said, trying to sound nonchalant and dismissive. 'He's still gone, and there's still no point in talking about how gorgeous he is.'

'The point is, Ms. Totally Single, that he seemed interested in you.'

'Get real, Stacy. He wasn't interested; he was polite. There's a world of difference.'

'Bullshit.'

'Stacy, he didn't even remember me, and today makes the fourth time we've met. Men like him are not interested in women like me.'

'So he has a crappy memory. Lots of guys do. And women like you? What does that mean?'

Pea sighed, and didn't feel up to mentioning that Griffin's memory hadn't failed when she'd walked up. 'Women like me short, plain, forgettable. He belongs with a model or a goddess. He doesn't belong with me.'

'You know, that's your problem! You defeat yourself before you even start. I've told you before that all you need is a little self-confidence. You're perfectly fine looking.'

Perfectly fine looking. Didn't that just sum it all up? There was sexy Stacy giving her what she really considered praise and encouragement, but the best she could come up with was perfectly fine looking. She studied Stacy – tall and blond with her great curves, fabulous boobs and those cheekbones that made her face look like someone should carve it out of marble. How could she possibly understand what it was to be so average that you went through life being invisible? She'd never walked into a room and not turned heads. Pea would bet the great raise she'd just got that gorgeous Griffin had already forgotten her. Men always did, but she would also bet that the firemen were discussing her hot blond neighbor all the way back to the station. And then someone might say something like: 'Oh, yeah, that *other* girl was there, too.' Pea was the other girl. The forgettable girl.

'So will you do it?'

'Huh?' Pea said, realizing Stacy had been talking and she'd not heard anything she'd been saying.

Stacy sighed in exasperation. 'I said, it's not even noon yet. You have plenty of time to go into that fabulous kitchen of yours and bake a big plate of your to-die-for brownies and deliver them to gorgeous Griffin at the station as a thank you.'

'Let me think about that.' Pea paused for half a blink. 'No.'

'And why not?' Stacy didn't give her time to continue. 'Because you have so many men beating down your door to go out with you tonight? Because you're in an incredible relationship with your dream man? Hmm? Which one is it?'

'You know I'm not dating anyone, and thanks for reminding me,' Pea said through her teeth, and then thought *for the zillionth time*.

'Okay, so is it because you don't find Griffin attractive?'

'As you very well know that's definitely not the case.'

'Then is it because you're hateful and rude and you don't believe in thanking the man who just saved your weird Scottie cat's life?'

'Chloe isn't weird and she wasn't about to die,' Pea said.

'She definitely could have broken something if she'd fallen out of that tree.'

'Stacy, it's stupid and pathetic to bake brownies as an excuse to see a man who has no interest in me.'

'He smiled at you and asked about your nickname,' Stacy countered.

'He was being polite.'

'Maybe. Maybe not. If you don't bake the brownies, you'll never know.'

Pea opened her mouth to say no. Again. But Stacy interrupted. Again.

'Take a chance, Pea. Just one small chance. The worst that can happen is that a bunch of overworked firemen will get a treat. On the other hand, maybe your brownies will work magic and you might actually live out one of those fantasies you usually only dream about . . .' Stacy waggled her brows at Pea.

'Fine!' Pea surprised herself by saying. 'I don't have dance class till this afternoon. I'll bake the damn brownies and drop them off on my way to class.'

'Finally I'm victorious with the Pea-and-men issue! Okay, look, be sure you write a little thank you note, too. On the stationery that has your new work title and letterhead.'

'Huh?'

Stacy rolled her perfect eyes. 'It serves two purposes. He'll know how amazingly successful you are, and he'll also know how to get in touch with you.'

'Great. Yeah. Okay. Whatever.' Pea called Chloe and started to retreat up the steps to her homey porch.

'You'll write the note?' Stacy called.

'I'll write the note.'

Watch out for other titles in
PC Cast's Goddess Summoning series

Coming soon from Piatkus

GODDESS OF SPRING

Lina's trendy bakery in Tulsa, Oklahoma, is proving to be less than lucrative and she must come up with a plan to save it. When she stumbles upon an Italian Goddess cookbook, she can't help but think she's found the answer to her problem – even if it means invoking a goddess to save her business. Soon enough, Lina finds herself face-to-face with Demeter, who has a plan of her own. She proposes that Lina exchange souls with Persephone, the Goddess of Spring, who will breathe new life into the bakery. In return, Lina must set order to the Underworld.

Before all this, Lina's problems mostly involved dough and second dates. Now that she embodies the enchantingly beautiful Persephone, Lina has weightier things on her mind – like the formidable task of bringing Spring to a world of spirits. But when the handsome, brooding Hades kindles a spark in her heart, Lina wonders if this Lord of the Underworld might be the man of her dreams . . .

978-0-7499-5371-3

GODDESS OF LIGHT

Tired of dating egomaniacs, interior designer Pamela
Gray has nearly given up on men. She wants to be
treated like a goddess – preferably by a god. As she
whispers her wish, she unwittingly invokes the goddess
Artemis, who has some tricks up her celestial sleeve . . .

Twins Artemis and Apollo have been sent to the
Kingdom of Las Vegas to test their mantle. Their first
assignment: make Pamela's wish come true. So Artemis
volunteers her golden brother. After all, who better
than the handsome God of Light to bring love to this
lonely woman? It might be a first but here in Sin City,
where life is a gamble, both god and mortal are about to
bet on a high-stakes game of love.

978-0-7499-5346-1

GODDESS OF LOVE

Pea Chamberlain needs help. Her shoes, hair, clothes,
make-up are all disasters and she really needs a
makeover – especially if she wants to attract sexy
fireman Griffin DeAngelo at the firemen's masked ball.
And who better to coax Pea out of her pod than the
Goddess of Love, whom she invokes when she gets her
hands on a book of enchantments.

Sure enough, Venus works her magic on Pea, which is
what she has been doing for eons – helping others find
love. But who will help the Goddess of Love when she
finds herself falling head over heels for the same sexy
fireman she is trying to land for Pea? Could it be that
Venus needs a love makeover herself?

978-0-7499-5356-0

THE CHIMNEY SWEEP'S SISTER

Emma Hornby

PENGUIN BOOKS

TRANSWORLD PUBLISHERS
Penguin Random House, One Embassy Gardens,
8 Viaduct Gardens, London SW11 7BW
www.penguin.co.uk

Transworld is part of the Penguin Random House group of companies
whose addresses can be found at global.penguinrandomhouse.com

First published in Great Britain in 2023 by Bantam
an imprint of Transworld Publishers
Penguin paperback edition published 2023

A CIP catalogue record for this book
is available from the British Library.

ISBN
9780552178129

Typeset in 12/14.5pt ITC New Baskerville Std by Jouve (UK), Milton Keynes.
Printed and bound in Great Britain by Clays Ltd, Elcograf S.p.A.

The authorized representative in the EEA is Penguin Random House Ireland,
Morrison Chambers, 32 Nassau Street, Dublin D02 YH68.

Penguin Random House is committed to a sustainable
future for our business, our readers and our planet. This book
is made from Forest Stewardship Council® certified paper.

For Lou Sutton, with best wishes.
And my ABC, always x

Rightly understood, Manchester is as great a human exploit as Athens.

Benjamin Disraeli

Chapter 1

THE LAST OF the coal had been fed to the fire hours ago. Hands on hips, Jenny scanned through narrowed eyes the sparse, single room of their cellar dwelling – and not for the first time – in search of an alternative to sacrifice for fuel.

She hadn't two farthings to rub together until her brother arrived back from his toil later and would hand over his meagre daily wage, therefore buying in fresh supplies was out of the question. And she must have a fire if she was to cook – young Noah would be ravenous upon his return. Furthermore, the temperature outside was cruel and only set to worsen with the hours; numbers would be into the minuses by nightfall, she'd bet. Without warmth, they would surely catch their deaths from pneumonia before a new dawn rolled around. *Think, think.*

Again, she took stock of their belongings, such as they were: the small battered table and two rickety stools set beneath the strip of high window. Two tin bowls, two mugs and two spoons stacked on the bare floor by the hearth beside the solitary, black-bottomed cooking pot. The lumps of straw-filled sacking in the far alcove, atop which were folded neatly several threadbare blankets and matted shawls, which served as their bed. However, there was nothing they could afford to part with; every item was a necessary one and would only need replacing, meaning the loss of vital and precious pennies.

Shrugging, her mind made up, she went to collect the small hatchet from the mantelpiece.

The weapon swinging loosely in her hand, Jenny crossed to the steep set of wooden stairs to her right that led up to the front door. There had been eight steps at one time; now, but five remained. She bit her lip and contemplated whether the loss of a few more would hamper greatly their passing in and out of the home. Then desperation had her throwing caution to the wind and taking aim, she lifted the hatchet above her head.

A fire was burning merrily in the grate, and the evening meal of scrag-end stew was bubbling away nicely in the pot suspended from a hook above the flames, when footsteps from outside filtered down. Jenny craned her neck in readiness to welcome her brother, hastening to add as he opened the door, 'Oh, lad, mind yon steps. There's a couple more gone.'

Noah accepted this news with an easy nod and deftly jumped the distance into the room. He hurried to the fire and held out his soot-encrusted hands to it gratefully. 'By, it's cowd out.'

'Aye.'

'I'm fair clemmed, our Jen.' As though to cement

2

the fact, his stomach released a low growl of hunger. 'How long will the grub be?'

She motioned to the table. 'Not long, lad. Sit thee down and pour yourself a sup of tea whilst tha waits.'

Noah did as she'd bid him, and as she stirred the food with a long ladle she cast him a sidelong look across the space. He'd removed his filthy and too-large flat cap and had run his hands through his startlingly bright ginger hair, and it was sticking up in all directions. Yet the soft smile of fondness that appeared at her lips at the sight soon vanished when her stare dropped further.

The dirt covered face that had been peeking out from his headgear was now on full show and more pinched than ever, she saw. But it was the pure exhaustion reflected in his dull green gaze that really had the all-too-familiar guilt creeping in. She gave a soft sigh. How it tore at her conscience to see him like this, to know what he was forced to do from dawn till dusk, to earn them a crust.

For a fortnight now he'd been employed as a chimney sweep's boy, and Jenny had fretted herself silly throughout every minute of it. The terrible conditions of his trade seemed to have aged the lad overnight; the new lines at his brow and deep-set shadows beneath his eyes were those meant for someone in their middle years at least, not a child of only nine.

However, what choice had they? she asked of herself again, as she'd done at least a dozen times daily since. None, that's what. He was too stunted and scrawny for most fetching and carrying jobs, and too

3

weak and sickly to withstand the hellish conditions of the cotton mills. Besides, she wouldn't have chosen that life for him, no way. Deaths and mutilations in the factories that choked their city were all too regular. You heard about folk having their lives cut short, or witnessed the effects with your own two eyes all the time: it was commonplace around here to see both adults and children minus fingers and even limbs, chewed clean off by the jaws of the deathly machinery. It was merely an accepted occupational hazard.

All else he'd have been fit for would have been to join the masses of other raggedy orphans and urchins who scraped a miserable living begging on those mean streets out there. However, that alternative certainly wasn't without its dangers. Nor would Noah have stood a chance of out-running the workhouse van should it have trundled by; he'd have been bundled inside and carted off to the much-feared institution in half a heartbeat.

Never would Jenny see that happen. Nothing and no one would take him away from her, or come between them. Hadn't she vowed to her dying parents the previous summer that she'd do all within her power to care for him, keep him safe? So long as she had breath in her lungs and a beat in her chest, that's exactly what she would do.

Nonetheless, when Noah's cough started up to hack through the stuffy room, his older sister couldn't refrain from saying with bitterness, 'They'll be the finish of thee, will them bloody chimneys, damn it.'

'I'm all right, Jen.'

'How's your knees?'

Hesitantly, and biting back soft whimpers of pain, the boy ruched up his trouser legs to show her.

Taking in the bloodied gouges scoring the tender flesh, she tore her gaze away with a muttered curse. 'Good God.'

'Aye, they're bad – but the master promised they'll soon settle down once I've got used to the job.'

The master: Mr Vincent Tottington – Totty to his cronies. Professional chimney sweep, expert ale glugger and well-practised evil blighter when the mood struck. Jenny's hands bunched into fists by her sides.

'He ain't touched you yet, has he?' she demanded 'I've heard the rumours about him, know how he can be with the boys in his employ—'

'Nay, Jen. Honest.' Noah was quick to assure her. 'He's not raised a hand to me once.'

For now . . .? She'd kill the varmint with her bare hands if he laid a finger on the lad.

'You must tell me if he does, d'you hear me?' Taking Noah by the shoulders, she stared deep into his eyes. 'I'd sooner we starved than have you stop on some place being thumped about. Promise me.'

Her brother nodded. Then: 'Is it time to eat now?'

Her anger trickled away at his uncomplicated nature, his innocence. Smiling and rolling her eyes, she motioned to their waiting bowls. 'Aye, all right, three bellies. Pass them over here and I'll dish up.'

They were midway through their food when she remembered the money.

'Tip up your wages, then, lad.' Jenny held out a

hand with a smile. 'I want to get in what we need afore everywhere closes for the night.'

'Oh. Er . . .' Noah refused to meet her gaze.

'What's to do?'

He shuffled uncomfortably on his seat. 'The master, well he said as how he were a bit short the day, and—'

'He never paid thee?' Her eyes were like slits. 'That rotten, swindling . . .!'

'The morrow he will. He promised.'

Doing her utmost to stem her bubbling fury for Noah's sake alone – this wasn't the lad's fault, and he did so worry when her short temper threatened to ignite – she forced herself to nod. But this wasn't done with. Oh no, not by a long chalk. 'Aye, all right,' she said. 'Let's leave it at that. Eat up.'

Placated, her brother returned his attention to his meal. However, Jenny's appetite had flown in light of the news. She'd have found it impossible to squeeze another morsel past the lump of injustice and anger clogging her throat – *damn that Totty!* – and she pushed her bowl aside.

The wood shifted in the grate and the firelight dimmed. Jenny swallowed a moan. The thing would burn itself out completely in a handful of minutes, she knew; they would be plunged into darkness and the cold would creep in to settle inside their bones before they could blink. She must do something.

'Where you going? You'll not seek out the master, will you?' Noah wanted to know when his sister rose to don her woollen shawl, tying the tasselled ends together tightly beneath her breasts.

Attempting to appear convincing, she smiled, shook her head. 'Nay, course not. Don't fret none.'

'He'll not be best pleased and might think to give me the shove if you have a go at him. Please, our Jen.'

Reaching across to ruffle his mop of hair, she clicked her tongue. 'I'm away to our Coral's, that's all, to see if I can't cadge a bit of coal. I'll not be long, lad, but if the fire goes out whilst I'm gone, you be sure to get yourself into bed and wrapped up well. It's perishing, and you know how your chest gets. You hear?'

He waved her off with a nod; satisfied, she hauled herself up over the broken stairs and let herself out into the dark and dingy lane.

The smile she'd plastered in place inside for her brother fell away the instant she was alone, to be replaced with a hard thin line.

Hands on hips, her promise to Noah and visiting their elder sister's home far from her thoughts now, Jenny scanned the corners of the street with murder in mind, contemplating which direction to try first. Then, the decision cemented, she turned left towards the main thoroughfare of Jersey Street and the many inns and taverns that thronged it.

A low moon hung like a wheel of cheese just above the rooftops and she followed its jaundiced glow towards the grimmer and seedier watering holes, which were frequented by the dregs of society in all its forms, knowing here she'd be more likely to find her man. Sure enough, the first door she pushed open revealed to her irrefutable proof of the chimney sweep's presence: his guffaws were unmistakable. *Where are you, you swine?*

Eyes steely, mouth set, she followed the source of the noise through the smoky, oil-lit room with her gaze. Her search didn't take long.

A hulking frame by the small open fire up ahead snared her attention – and her building fury erupted to spy him motioning to those in his company as to whether they each fancied a refill. *Throwing his money around as though it was going out of fashion, when all the time . . . Skint my foot! Filthy, lying pig!*

Before she could stop herself, Jenny was striding through the mass of sweating and stinking bodies, barging aside anyone who refused, or was too slow, to move from her path quickly enough.

She halted behind an unsuspecting Totty, thrust out an arm and shoved him hard in the back. ''Ere, I want a word with thee.'

His dark frown when he whipped around melted slowly into an expression of surprise tinged with mild amusement. He looked to his friends, who were gawping back in clear astonishment at the scene playing out, then turned once more to look her up and down.

Having recently turned sixteen, Jenny was as tall as any man and afraid of none. She took after her father in that respect. He too had been of good height – and handy with his fists when need be, it must be said. Her mother, a dainty little thing, had passed her delicate features on to Noah and Coral only – a fact that sometimes rankled Jenny the older she got, when the desire to be a little more feminine like other lasses struck. However, in moments such as this, she was glad of it. Now, as she'd been forced to countless times, and in particular this past year, when standing up to chancers and bullies, she used the fact to her full advantage.

'Did you hear me?' She ground out the words through her teeth. 'I said I want a word.'

'Oh, tha does, eh?'

His tone had been low, almost menacing, and although even she was no match for his brawn, she lifted her chin and met his stare head on.

'Aye. You've some explaining to do. How tha can stand in here, knocking back ale – buying drinks for all and sundry into the bargain – whilst we're sat at home without even a lump of coal for the fire . . . you make me sick!' By now, the inn had fallen deathly silent – you could have heard a flea sneeze. 'That poor lad back yonder works his knuckles to the bone – aye, his shins, an' all, come to that! – up your rotten chimneys. And you don't even have the decency to pay him an honest wage? Well shame on you, you owd bugger!'

'Eeh! Bold young bitch!' an inebriated customer called out incredulously, although with not a little admiration.

Jenny ignored them, her attention on Totty unwavering. 'The brass owing to my brother.' She thrust her outstretched palm beneath his nose. 'I want it. Hand it over.'

'The morrow.'

'Nay, *not* the morrow. Now.'

The chimney sweep's hairy nostrils flared whilst a

muscle at his jaw rippled in evident rage – for a brief moment, Jenny thought he might strike her. Nonetheless, she stood her ground. Her hand as steady as rock, she held his gaze.

Seconds felt like hours as they played out this public power struggle. Finally, and to her sheer relief, Totty broke eye contact.

He fished in his pocket, brought out a fistful of coins and counted through them. Then without a word, he handed her a small mound. He nodded once and she returned it.

'Now, if you don't mind . . .'

'Aye. Fret not. I got what I came for and now I'll leave you to your drinking.' All eyes were on her as she turned and coolly walked across the room. At the exit, she paused to glance over her shoulder. As she knew he would be, the chimney sweep was watching her. A definite smirk played about his mouth. 'Oh, and Totty?' she called out. 'Don't ever think to pull a stunt like that again or next time, I'll not be so friendly. No one puts on me or my family. No one. *No* bleeder takes advantage of us . . . not without living to regret it, anyroad. D'you hear?'

Without waiting for a reply, and leaving her audience with mouths flapping, she swung the door wide and swept out into the freezing night.

Alone, she leaned against the crumbling bricks of the building and closed her eyes for a moment. She'd taken a mighty risk there, of course – she knew this. That man could have felled her with one swipe of his beefy hand, and there would have been no one to stop him or come to her aid. But she'd been desperate. Besides, she raged inwardly as she walked on, why should people like him get to tread all over folk, treat them just as they chose, anyway? It wasn't fair, blast it, and she'd had a bellyful of it, of this life in general. Someone had to stand up and be counted – why not her?

Several minutes later, with her heart beating a normal rhythm once more and her anger dissipated, she put Totty from her mind and reminded herself that the most important thing was she had Noah's wage. She allowed herself a smile. They wouldn't freeze to death this night at least – well, so long as she caught the local coal yard before closing, at any rate. The merchant might even throw in a few extra cobs if she asked nicely enough ... With a quick glance to the pitch-black sky and biting her lip, she quickened her pace and hurried on.

'Please, you're not done for the day, are you?' she asked breathlessly of a familiar figure standing nearby as she reached the iron gates. Every visible inch of the long-time employee was grime-covered, as always. It was as though the dust he was forever in contact with had burrowed deep into his flesh and become as one with him – Jenny hoped fleetingly it wouldn't happen to her brother. She held out her hand to show the man her money and bestowed upon him her most winning smile. 'Oh, mister, say you're not.'

Before answering her, he hawked up a globule of sooty phlegm and spat it on to the cobblestones. Then opening his mouth, his teeth standing out starkly in his blackened face, he yawned loudly. It was clear his had been a long hard day. 'You're just in the nick of time, lass.'

Oh, thank God. Jenny heaved a grateful sigh. 'Eeh, ta, mister.'

'The usual?'

'Aye.'

'Hang about whilst I weigh it out.'

She waited patiently and a minute later he was back. He placed a small grubby sack in her arms and, flashing him another smile, she dropped the relevant coins into his hand. Yet it soon slid from her lips when, having checked she'd given him the correct amount, he lifted his eyes back to meet hers. The pale blue pools were full of accusation:

'What in the hell . . . is this some sort of lark?'

'Eh?' She blinked, nonplussed. 'What d'you mean?'

'This, what you're for palming off on me. It's bloody counterfeit.'

Jenny shook her head. 'Nay . . . Nay, it ain't—!'

'Listen, I know fake brass when I sees it – and this ain't even done well, neither. It's lighter than it ought to be and you can clearly see the white metal showing through the plating. And 'ere, look, you look at that.' He held up a coin between his thumb and forefinger to show her. 'If I were in any doubt, which I ain't, then that proves it right enough: the queen's bleedin' head's not even facing the right way, for Christ's sake!'

A hasty check of the rest of the money and her worst fears were realised: not a single farthing of it was real. *Dear Lord . . . Totty, the devil.* She'd have him for this. By God she would!

'Nice try, aye. Now sling your hook.'

'Nay, wait, please, I . . .' She was desperately close to tears. 'I didn't know, you have to believe me—'

'Tripe. Now go, go on.'

'Please,' she beseeched him. 'Please, I *must* have coal.' However, her words were falling on deaf ears, she could see it. The man thought her a swindler and wanted no truck with her. She would receive no understanding from him – no precious fuel, either. The fight left her veins. Dropping her chin to her chest, she fell silent.

'Well, what are you waiting for? Get gone and don't come back.'

Jenny nodded. Gulping back the lump in her throat, she dragged her feet in the direction of home.

There would be no point in confronting the chimney sweep again, not this night. She believed she'd bested him but it had been one big ploy. He'd emerged victorious after all – she felt a first-rate dolt. Never would she endure a second confrontation and the public humiliation it would bring. She didn't have it in her. Tomorrow, however . . . Well, that was another day entirely.

Calling in on Coral after all, and begging from her what they needed, flitted into Jenny's mind as she neared Carruthers Street; however, the notion was a fleeting one and she was quick to dismiss it.

Their sister – or more to the point, her husband Martin – were not exactly accommodating at the best of times. Turning up at this hour and possibly disturbing their children at bed would do her no favours whatever. Besides, she was tired of scraping to them and tolerating their false grandeur ways. Their sniffs of exasperation at having to regularly bail out the 'poor relations', the private looks that passed between the pair when they thought she wasn't looking, which screamed irritation and was mounting almost to the point of apathy, set her teeth on edge and had her hackles rising. She hadn't the strength for their disapproval, not right now.

Noah was sleeping when she arrived back at the cellar. Doing her best not to disturb him, she slipped off her clogs and slid into bed fully dressed, shawl and all. Still, there was no blocking out the brutal cold; teeth chattering, she moved closer to the lad to instil warmth into him as much as herself.

Was this it, their lot for ever? she asked of herself, watching through a film of tears the thick strands of shadows, slithering along the ceiling, that the meagre light from the stub of candle still clinging on to life was unable to chase away. Clawing and scratching for the very basic of necessities, day in, day out? Would life, this never-ending fight for survival, really always be so damn hard? Did she even want to battle on if the answer was yes?

Just where, at all, was the point? But no, she wouldn't cry, refused to. She was a near-grown woman now; tears were for babbies, after all. *Eeh, but I could do with a reet good bawl, though, sometimes, if truth be told . . .*

'I miss you, Mam, Father,' she whispered into her

brother's back. 'I ain't up to this, nay; can't even keep us warm most days, never mind owt else. I'm trying but it's hard. I want youse back. I want things to be like they were. I want my family.'

'Jen?'

Noah's sleepy voice cut through her lamentations and she checked herself immediately. She couldn't allow herself to wallow in his presence, she reminded herself. She was the strong one, always, had to be for him. 'Sorry, lad, did I waken thee?'

He nodded. Then: 'Sing to us, our Jen.'

'Eeh, lad, nay . . .'

'Go on. Do that one I like. Please?'

Singing was her first and only passion. Noah's too, for that matter – to hear it at any rate. From the moment she could string a sentence together, her love of the art form had been born. The same could be said for her brother. Amongst his very first words had been to beg from her a song. Now, smiling, she rolled her eyes, capitulating as usual, as he knew she would. 'Aye, all right.'

He snuggled into her and flopped an arm around her neck – the poor thin limb was like ice to the touch. Clicking her tongue, she reached up to chafe it and began, allowing her pure and faultless voice to embrace them.

The boy was breathing steadily once more before she reached the end of the old ballad. Stroking his hair, she hummed the remainder softly to ensure he wouldn't re-stir. He didn't, and she was left to ponder on the next day and the trials of life that would once again await her. By, but it was a bone-weary prospect. If not for the lad here beside her, she'd have welcomed in this moment not wakening in the morn at all. She was sick of it, the fight. *Sick* of it . . .

The wick spluttered and spat itself out. Cloying darkness enveloped the squat room like a shroud. With hatred in her heart for the world, the whole universe and everyone bar Noah in it – none more so, not by a merry mile, than Vincent Tottington – Jenny finally let her tears fall.

'Morning. By the Christ, you look awful.'

'Ta very much.'

The aged man cast Jenny a shiny-gummed smile. 'Come on then, come in.'

Owd Nobby, as people hereabouts knew him, was eighty if he was a day and wily as a young fox. A friend to everyone, his dwelling two doors down was a hub to all and never devoid of a warm welcome.

'So what's the story, then, lass?'

Reaching up to pat with her fingertips her somewhat swollen under-eyes, Jenny shrugged. 'Oh, nowt much – I didn't get much sleep last night, that's all.'

'How so?' he pressed, hobbling across the room and reaching for the teapot. 'You sickening for summat, are thee? A fella, is it? You been losing rest from mooning over some handsome young bucko, aye?'

She hooted with laughter. 'Don't talk so bleedin' daft! Anyroad, chance would be a fine thing. I ain't got time for nowt, not even myself, never mind lads.'

16

Chuckling, Nobby motioned to the brown vessel. 'Sup of tea, lass?'

'Er . . . aye, all right, go on,' she replied as nonchalantly as she was able. Truth was, she was dying for a cup.

Not a thing had passed her lips since the stew the previous day. The last of the leaves had only just stretched far enough earlier for Noah's morning brew, and the remainder of the bread had gone the same road. No way would she have seen him off to face a full day's toil with an empty belly. Of course, she'd been forced to lie to her brother when he'd enquired over her not joining him at his breakfast, had assured him she'd already eaten before he roused, was loath to have him feel guilty, which she knew he would, kind and considerate soul that he was. However, she wouldn't let her desperation show, not even to Nobby; she hated folk knowing how difficult things were at home.

Her old friend, retired long since as a blacksmith at the nearby steelworks, and who now scratched by a living selling newspapers in all weathers in the city centre, had bailed her out since her parents' passing, when she'd been reluctant to run to Coral yet again, more often than she cared to count, and always with a smile on his craggy face. Nonetheless, every time, the shame of it churned her guts into knots. How she despised relying on others to keep Noah fed and warm; it was meant to be her job after all, no one else's. And it was for him and him alone that she would swallow her pride and accept the help in leaner times. Left with just herself to worry about keeping body and soul together, she'd have sooner gone without.

Nobby passed a piping drink across and motioned to a bowl of half-finished porridge he'd evidently been eating upon her arrival. 'My appetite's not what it was the older I get – you're welcome to finish that off.'

Jenny hesitated, but a firm nod from the man coupled with her twisting hunger saw her relenting and, murmuring a thank you, she shovelled it into her mouth gratefully.

'So?' he asked when she'd finished and was sipping her cup of tea. He took a long puff of his clay pipe and blew the smoke towards the damp-riddled ceiling. 'What did keep thee from tha slumber, then?'

Her rage from the previous evening sparked once more at the memory and she bunched her hands into fists. 'Bloody Totty, that's what. He never paid the lad his wage.'

Click-clicking his tongue, Nobby shook his head. 'Why?'

'I'll tell thee for why: 'cause he's a dirty rotten sod. I sought him out last night, ought to have thumped the bastard when I had the chance. Aye, see how he'd have liked that! I will, too, if he tries the same act with Noah the night.' As for the counterfeit coins . . . Surely the nasty trick the sweep pulled had simply been his way of showing her who was in charge. He hadn't taken kindly to being given orders and decided to teach her a lesson. He'd cough up everything that was owed, however, this evening. Wouldn't he? He must. Aye, and he'd better.

'Careful, Jenny.' Nobby's tone was serious. 'He ain't the kind to trifle with.'

'And neither am I,' she retorted with force. 'One more stunt like the last from him and I'll have the bugger, I mean it.'

With a small sigh, he fell silent. 'Anyroad, what's your plans for the day?' he enquired at length, his voice convivial once more.

'The usual: on the hunt for work.'

'Ah.'

'Aye, exactly.' Jenny pulled a face. 'I'm that fed up with it.'

'Well, 'tain't nobody's fault but your own, lass . . .'

'I know, I know.'

Over the past year, Jenny had had more jobs than the man before her had had hot dinners. Trouble appeared to follow her about like a bad odour; she'd never managed to hold down a position for longer than a few days. At least that's what she'd convinced herself. The truth of the matter was, her temper was at the root of her getting the shove time and again.

One wrong look or word from someone and she was away with her gob, ready to do battle in a heartbeat – and to hell with the consequences. Of course, she always regretted her actions later but by then it was too late. She just couldn't seem to help herself, however hard she tried.

'Worst of it is, it's because of me that our Noah's having to do what he's doing,' Jenny whispered,

19

lowering her head to conceal the blush that had bloomed to stain her cheeks. 'If only I were earning regular brass, he'd not have to toil for swines like that Totty – he'd not have to toil at all, nay. It's my fault, all this. I do know that and I hate myself for it, I do. Why can't I ever just turn the other cheek? Why am I like this, Nobby – hot-headed and so full of anger?'

'It's the way you're made, lass, is all.'

'But I don't want it to be. I want to be different.'

Peering at her over the stem of his pipe, Nobby took another long suck, then picked at the lonesome stump of brown tooth at his lower jaw. 'Try, then.'

'I *do*, honest.'

'Try harder. No one can do it for thee. Look, you've had a lot to cope with this past year, ain't that right? Losing your mam, then your father as well so soon after . . . it's enough to make anyone feel at war with the world.'

She sniffed loudly and brushed her sleeve across her nose. 'It's just not fair. I miss them.'

'It's not, nay, and of course you do. Thing is, it's life. Things occur, people get sick and then they die. We just have to pick ourselves up, brush ourselves down and push through it. Ain't no other way.'

Heaving a colossal sigh, Jenny bobbed her head. 'Aye, I know. And what you said is right enough: I could try more, I reckon.'

'There you are, you see? We got there in t' end, eh?' he told her, winking.

A smile crept across her lips. 'Don't you ever grow tired of being right all the time?'

'Oh, it's both a blessing and a curse, lass, a blessing and a curse.'

Shaking her head, she joined in with his gravelly laughter.

'I'd best be on my way, then, Nobby,' Jenny announced brightly some ten minutes later after another cup of tea. With a bit of something in her belly and his sage advice to draw upon, she was feeling a lot more hopeful than she had done half an hour before. 'Wish me luck, eh?'

'My best be with thee. Remember,' he reminded her at the door, cupping her shoulder with his gnarled fingers in a supportive squeeze, 'just bite that tongue of yourn and keep on biting it till it learns its lesson, the nowty bugger. You can do it, I know you can.'

'For Noah.'

'For youse both,' he corrected her softly.

Taking a deep breath, she nodded. Then she turned and headed west towards the centre of town.

Upon reaching the bustling stretch of Oldham Road, she paused and glanced about. The surrounding cotton works were out of the question: she'd been dismissed for varying reasons from almost every mill and factory in the district; she'd have no joy from that quarter. Besides, she hadn't the stomach for it if truth be told. No, what she reckoned would suit her best was solitary work. Something that didn't put her in close company of others, aye. That way, she'd have less opportunity of being drawn into a ruckus and finding herself out on her ear. But what? And where?'

Biting her lip, she wracked her brains. There was

always cleaning. She'd had numerous scrubbing positions in the past, and though each had ended in the same way as everything else, she really ought to try that route again, she reckoned. She enjoyed it for one. What's more, she was good at it. Better still, she was left alone to get on with the job in hand, hadn't the need to converse much with anyone bar her mistress or master. Her hopes rose further. Crossing her fingers, she picked her way across the traffic-choked road.

Two butchers' shops, a clockmaker's and a cobbler's workshop later, she was beginning to grow a little disheartened. Each had answered in the same vein to her polite enquiry: sorry but no, her services were not required, they already employed a daily cleaner. Nonetheless, she refused to be put off. She *had* to find work – must, for the sake of her brother. The sooner she could get him away from those treacherous chimneys and that holy terror Totty, the better for all concerned.

A slight drizzle gradually grew into full, harsh rainfall and after an hour of tramping the grey and miserable streets without success, she was soaked to the marrow and nearing the very end of her tether. Eyeing a small baker's on the edge of the row of buildings up ahead, she asked herself just where was the point: she'd never find a place. Then a stern voice in her head told her to shut up and shape up – she wouldn't get anywhere, nay, not with that attitude! – and she straightened her shoulders. Lifting her chin, she set forth with renewed purpose.

'Yes? Can I help you?'

Plastering on a smile, Jenny nodded. 'I do hope so, missis. I'm looking forra position – scrubbing, like. I'm a good toiler and don't cut corners. You'd be happy with my work, I'm sure of it.'

The portly woman, swamped in a snowy white apron and frilly mobcap, surveyed her with a definite air of interest. 'You've got experience, then? Cleaned in a baker's before, have you?'

Jenny hesitated for only half a second, then: 'Oh aye, aye,' she lied. 'A few, missis, actually.'

'Really? And why did you leave these other premises?'

'I . . .' She scrabbled around inside her brain for something to say. 'I had to leave one because the owner sold and shut up shop. And another, well, erm . . . it erm . . .'

'Are you hoodwinking me, girl? Is that what you're doing?'

Though the woman was frowning, her tone wasn't altogether unkindly, and Jenny took a chance on honesty being the best policy. Dropping her gaze, she nodded. 'I am, missis, I'm sorry to say. But it's only 'cause I'm desperate. Mind, it's true what I said about being a good worker, every word. You'd not find none better than me, I swear it.'

'You've got spirit, girl, I'll give you that,' the woman said on a chuckle. 'Took some guts, that did, to own up. It just so happens that our usual cleaner recently left our employ, so there is a vacancy open—'

'Oh! Sorry,' Jenny added quickly in the next breath,

hadn't meant to interrupt the woman, had let her excitement run away with itself. 'Please, go on.'

'How's about I take you on on a trial basis? Say . . . a week? If I'm happy with you, we'll talk about it becoming a regular thing.'

'Eeh, missis.' Jenny had to stop herself from doing a happy dance. 'Eeh!'

'Would that suit thee?'

'Aye. Aye, it would. Ta, thanks.'

'Right then. Here's what your duties will be . . . Oh.' The woman broke off to motion behind Jenny. 'Here's my husband.'

She turned with a ready smile to greet the person in question who had appeared from a back room. However, it was swift to melt from her face. The weedy, pock-scarred and severely balding man she was met with immediately put her on her guard. He was scouring his gaze over every inch of her body with open and blatant lechery. Her breathing quickened in disgusted outrage.

'Actually . . . forget what I said.' The woman was speaking again and it was quite obvious that her husband's behaviour hadn't escaped her notice, either. 'We're not looking to take on anyone new just now after all.'

'But . . .!' Jenny was crushed. 'You said—'

'Yes, but I was wrong. Sorry.'

'Sorry my left eye!' To have her dreams dashed this way, just as she'd thought her prayers had been answered and things might go her way after all – and without doing a single thing wrong to boot – was devastating. Her voice rose. She brought her fists down on to the counter with force, making the woman flinch. 'You're not sorry, you cow, norra bit. I bet I can guess why your last cleaner scarpered, aye. You've no right to punish me and all because that filthy beast you call a husband can't control his roving eye. No right at all!'

'Get out! Go on, you young slut, get gone.' Puce with clear mortification at the truth of things, the woman thrust a finger towards the door and stamped her foot. 'And don't you ever darken this step again, d'you hear?'

'Ah, get shitted on, you bleedin' bitch. You can stick your cleaning where the sun don't reach – right up your flabby arse!' Jenny added, just in case the woman might have been in any doubt, before marching off.

Outside, Jenny squeezed shut her eyes and sucked in some ragged breaths. *Blast and bugger it!* She was so angry she could spit. What was the use at all? No matter what she did or however hard she tried, it got her nowhere in the end, did it? Just why did she ever bother? She was fit for nothing, and everyone knew it. Well, she'd had enough. Being nice got you nowhere, evidently, so why even try to change? From now on, she'd stick to what she did best – to hell with them all!

'So, lass? How did you get on—?'

'Not now, Nobby,' she cut in harshly shortly afterwards, storming past the old man when he made to accost her as she neared her dwelling.

'Jenny?'

'I *said* not now.' Eyes gritty, her face like thunder,

25

she let herself into the cellar, slamming the door behind her.

'Well, lad?' It was late and Noah had just arrived home. Filthy black and almost dead on his feet with exhaustion, he was a pitiful sight. Jenny held her breath: 'Did Totty pay thee the night?'

'Oh. Nay. He said—'

'Said what?'

'The master, he's still short of brass, you see, and—'

'Right. That's *it*.'

'Jen, where you going?'

She was trembling, so up was her dander. No way on God's green earth would that man do this to them, not again. 'Lad, listen, don't worry. Now I want you to go into Nobby's forra bit—'

'But why?'

'Because I have to go out and you can't stop here. We've no candles or coal, and it's dark, and perishing again. We've norra scrap of grub in t' house, neither. Go on, now. Tell the owd man I'm sorry for snapping earlier . . . ask him if he can please spare thee a bite of summat – I'll make it up to him.'

'Aye, all right.'

'Good lad. I'll come and collect thee when I get back.'

There would be no defeat this night. Vincent Tottington wouldn't walk away as victor a second time. Their very lives depended on it.

Throwing on her shawl, Jenny stalked from the house.

Chapter 2

A SERIES OF whoops and brays went up around the
grotty drinking den as she entered – clearly, those
present remembered her and the performance with
Totty from the previous night. Grinning like imbe-
ciles, the gathering parted, making a path for her,
ready to enjoy the spectacle to come. Well, Jenny
wasn't going to be a means of cheap entertainment,
wouldn't give them the satisfaction:

'Mr Tottington, I'd like to talk to thee. Outside,'
she added, much to the onlookers' obvious dismay.

The man blinked in surprise at the level way in
which she'd delivered her request – clearly, he too
had been expecting another explosive tirade. For an
age, he peered down at her through hooded eyes.
Without a word, he brushed past her and led the way
into the street.

'Well?'

'What d'you mean "well"?' Jenny began, then
quickly checked herself. If last night had taught her
anything it was that going into this all guns blazing
would get her absolutely nowhere fast. Instead, she'd

decided to change tack, choose her words – for once in her life – wisely. Though whence she'd drawn the strength to hold her calm this long was a sheer miracle even to herself. For two pins, she'd have set about him and clawed the skin from his bones . . . Taking a deep breath, she dragged back control. 'What I mean is, I thought you'd have guessed why I'm back. Noah's wages – we need them. We need 'em reet bad.' Another intake of air, then: 'Please.'

'Say it again.' His words were spoken slowly, concisely, and it was painfully apparent to her that he was relishing every moment. 'Go on, like you mean it.'

'Please,' she forced out.

'Now, then. That weren't so hard, was it? You see, a bit of grovelling goes a long way.'

You bastard, bastard . . .

Totty unfolded his meaty arms and in imitation of their previous set-to reached into his pocket. Again, he counted through his money. Then he stared her straight in the eye and threw several coins at her feet. 'Well, pick them up, then. After all, scavenging about in the gutter is all you're fit for.'

Jenny was incensed. 'Why, you spiteful—!'

'Careful, careful.' Quick as a flash, he caught the hand she struck out with which to slap him and gripped her by the jaw. He brought his face close to hers and grinned when she turned her nose from his ale-soaked breath with a grimace. 'That temper of yourn shall get thee into hot water one day.'

There was no room for fear. Her fizzing anger

blocked all other emotion. 'Get your stinking hands off me or, by God, you'll regret it.'

He released her harshly, sending her stumbling, and half-turned back towards the inn. The resolve it took her not to run at him with a scream and pummel her fists into his ugly phizog was almost unsustainable.

'You're fortunate I never told the brat this morning to take a running jump, after your antics last night. Lucky for thee, he's a sound little worker. But remember this well, you little whore.' He pointed a finger at her, and with each word stabbed at the air between them: 'I pay my lads when I'm good and ready and not afore. D'you hear me? Now get gone, skedaddle, and don't ever make me have to set eyes on you again.'

Jenny waited until he'd disappeared inside the building before dropping to her heels and covering her face with her shaking hands. Never before had she known this level of hatred for another living soul. How she'd have loved to tell him to shove his job, as she'd done with the baker's wife earlier. However, she couldn't, *she couldn't*, damn it. The consequences were just too great – with not a penny coming into the house, it would be the poorhouse for them, and that was a fact. What's more, the chimney sweep knew it. Why, *why* did he have to treat her brother so? What pleasure did he derive from acting such an odious monster, belittling them like this? It made no sense to her and never would.

Her gaze swivelled to the scattered coins. She glanced about her. Then tentatively, and swallowing what little pride he'd left her with, she moved forward to retrieve them.

'Are you all right?'

The voice startled her; blushing scarlet to be caught indeed scrambling in the muck, she whipped around with an angry frown. 'Who goes there?'

'Sorry. I didn't mean to fricken thee.'

Taking stock of the young man who had stepped out of the shadows to stand before her, Jenny stuck her chin in the air. 'Frighten tripe,' she announced with her trademark boldness restored. 'I ain't afeared of no bugger.'

To her surprise, the stranger laughed.

'What's funny?'

'You are. You're a reet little alley cat and no mistake. That your brass, is it?' He nodded to the money. 'Here, let me—'

'I can manage.'

'Don't be daft. Let me help thee.'

She watched whilst he picked them up then held them out to her.

'Well?' he asked, his dark blue eyes deepening with interest, when she made no attempt to take them. 'Do you want 'em or not?'

'I need them. There's a difference.'

He didn't press her for an explanation, simply handed them over.

Jenny counted the money. Two days' wages, all present and correct. What's more, she saw, scanning each piece in turn, no forgeries here – this time, they were the real deal. That was one small mercy at least. 'Well, I'd best be on my way.'

'Aye. Goodnight.'

'Goodnight. And ta,' she added, feeling suddenly awkward. 'It were a kind offer, that were.'

'Nay, don't mention it.'

'All the same . . . Most would have pounced on that brass, aid being the last thing on their mind, and pilfered it from under my nose without a by your-leave.'

'Aye, well. I'm not most people. Anyroad, you're welcome.'

Silence hung between them. Jenny was first to break away. Nodding once, she turned and made off for home.

Nobby answered her soft knock with a sigh of relief. 'Thank the Lord for that. I worried you might not return in one piece.'

Having followed him inside, she flopped down into the ancient sagging chair by the hearth and closed her eyes. 'What a bleedin' to-do.'

The old man lowered himself into the seat opposite. 'What occurred?'

'Let's just say that bastard Totty will rue the day he thought to cross me. I mean it, Nobby – I'll have that swine one way or t' other, you see if I don't.'

He gave a soft click of his tongue. 'Whatever happened to what we spoke on this morning, then? You know, about you knocking that temper of yourn into touch?'

Jenny filled him in on her disastrous attempts at

finding employment and the cruel way in which she'd been treated at the baker's. 'It got me nowhere, Nobby, so where's the point, eh?' she finished dully.

'There's allus a way, lass. Don't be for giving up afore you've even properly begun.'

'Aye, we'll see.' Though she nodded, smiled, more to placate him than anything, in theory she held out next to no hope. Tiredness seemed to swoop upon her suddenly; smothering a yawn with the back of her hand, she looked to the ceiling. 'The lad in your bed, is he?'

'That's right. Fast akip, he is, poor beggar. I gave him a bit of broth and that was him, out for the count. Couldn't keep his little eyes open. Done in, he were.'

'Ta, Nobby. I'd best get him up and back home. I'll see thee the morrow?'

'If the good Lord don't summon me home, lass, afore I waken, then aye, you will that.'

Though the reply had been spoken in jest, Jenny felt fear's fingers grip her heart. He wouldn't last for ever, it was true – the prospect of life without him was an unfathomable one. He'd been a part of her life since the day she was born, was more like a grand-father than a mere neighbour or friend. Please God that He spared him for a good few years to come.

Noah, groggy with sleep, allowed her to guide him out into the frostbitten street without protest. Indoors, she shepherded him to the wall where their sacking beds were propped and, after dragging them on to the earth-packed floor, eased him down and covered him up. He was asleep once more before his head had even touched the bunched-up shawl that served him as a pillow. Shivering, she hurried to follow suit.

The day's events played through her mind again as she lay in the pitch dark, the only sounds the harsh raindrops whack-whacking against the thin window-panes. The hurt and unjustness she'd suffered during her job search had been bad enough. Totty's treatment of her shortly before had been crucifying. Just what was with him, at all? He'd had absolutely no reason to treat her and her brother as he had. And what of next time, when Noah's wage was due again? Would they have to endure this self-same rigmarole day in, day out? It didn't bear thinking about.

She had to think of something, *must* find a position. That was the top and bottom of it. They just couldn't go on like this, relying on the whims and fancies of that sod for evermore, not knowing whether they would eat some days depending on what mood he was in and if he would hand over what he owed. The unpredictability of it would be her undoing – it was a fate worse than death.

'I'll do it, lad, I promise thee. I'll make ours a better life somehow.'

Snuggling into the boy, Jenny meant it with everything she had. Closing her eyes, she prayed with all that she was for a miracle.

The smell of toasted bread and freshly brewed tea was a blessed one. It was clear Noah was appreciative of the small luxuries, too.

'Eeh, our Jen. It's nice in here.' Skipping to the fire, he held out his hands to the leaping flames.

Hands on hips, she gazed about the room and smiled. She'd been up with the larks and had been the first customer of the day when the nearby shops opened. She'd purchased a small loaf, tea and milk, candles and fuel for the fire, and had had their dwelling looking and feeling like a home again before Noah woke. 'It is that, aye. Come on to the table and fill your belly, lad.'

'Was it our Coral what gave thee the brass, Jen?' he asked through a mouthful of food, which he quickly washed down with a large gulp of his brew.

She shook her head. 'Nay, lad. Totty.'

'The master?'

'Aye, he . . . he saw me, by chance in t' street last night, and he handed over your wages.' The lies tripped easily from her tongue. She'd rehearsed what she would tell her brother, knew he would ask, and was well prepared. 'Now then,' she followed up with, keen to change the subject lest he guessed there to be something off with her explanation and began fretting, 'get another slice of toast down thee and I'll refill our cups.'

He left for work shortly afterwards and she watched him go from the top step with a false smile at her lips and an ache in her heart. Then shaking herself, she nodded firmly and returned indoors. She'd put plans in place in her mind last night before falling to sleep, and she was determined more than ever to see they bore fruit.

34

Today marked the start of her quest to change their circumstances for the better. The real start this time – she wouldn't be swayed again. By hook or by crook, she would do it. She'd show them, the whole shower out there, what she was made of.

After clearing away the breakfast dishes and banking down the fire, she plucked down her shawl from the nail in the wall and left the cellar.

A snappy wind accompanied her on her walk to Carruthers Street and by the time she reached number forty and her sister's house, her fingers were an unholy shade of mauve and her toes had lost all feeling. She knocked at the door. Blowing into her cupped hands and stamping her clogs, she awaited the familiar figure with a bellyful of nerves.

Coral answered her call with customary dourness. Her expression barely altered to see who her visitor was.

'Alreet?' Though she didn't expect it would be returned – it rarely was – Jenny flashed a smile anyway. 'Cowd, in't it?'

'Aye.' Without offering anything more, the older woman turned and disappeared along the tiny dark hallway, leaving Jenny to follow on.

She entered the living room and looked about. Though inexpensive and far from new, the various pieces of furniture and knick-knacks never failed to interest her – and fill her with mild envy. Bar the extreme basics, every possession her cellar had once boasted had gradually found its way to the pawnshop in lieu of life's staples. It was difficult to take pride in your home, as her sister evidently did and who could blame her, when it was far from feeling like one.

Tin candlesticks on the mantel top were as ever polished to a high sheen; the geranium on the side table in its brass pot, that was pruned with military regularity, sporting not a leaf out of place; the curtains at the sparkling window, freshly laundered and crease-free as usual . . . Spick and span as always, no matter the time of day. Jenny reckoned nothing would have dared to move an inch from its rightful place, nor a single speck of dust to have the audacity to settle, not in Coral's house.

The woman inclined her head to a chair before perching her tightly corseted frame on one nearby. Head high, spine ramrod straight, she patted her mousy brown hair bound severely in a neat bun at her nape, then folded her slender hands in her lap. She eyed Jenny in silence and waited for her to begin the reason for her visit.

'So, Coral. How's tha been?'

'Fine, ta.'

'And the kiddies, Martin?'

'All well.'

'Good, good.'

'You and the lad? You're all right?'

'Aye, aye.'

A somewhat awkward silence set in – they both glanced around trying to think up further small talk.

'Weather's turned, ain't it?' Jenny offered finally.

'Oh, bleak, aye.'

Again, another long silence. Jenny sighed inwardly. Reasoning that she may as well hurry this on and thus draw the visit to a merciful close, she got straight to the point: 'I'm on the hunt for employment.'

'Again?'

Her sister had delivered the remark on a soft snort – Jenny's back stiffened in automatic defence. 'That's right, aye, again.' She kept her tone as even as she could, despite the struggle. 'Thing is, I might need your help.'

Coral's eyebrows lifted in clear surprise. '*My* help? I don't know where they're taking on folk, I'm sure.'

'Nay, it's not that.'

'Then how so?'

'Well, I've got that desperate that I'm just about ready to accept owt what's offered me. That includes night work. So you see, if I am for finding summat requiring me to stop on long hours, I were wondering whether . . . well, if you might . . .'

'You want to know if I'll keep an eye to Noah whilst you're out?' Coral finished for her. 'Is that it?'

'Well, aye. I can't very well leave him at home on his lonesome late at night.'

'Plenty do.'

'Aye, well, I'm not them, am I? Owt could happen, young as he is, and I'll not take the risk. Go on, our Coral,' she wheedled, gentler now, banking down her annoyance and giving her what she hoped was her most beguiling smile. 'You know how the lad is – he's good as gold, would be no bother.'

The woman hesitated for a moment, then: 'Nay.'

She shook her head. 'I'm sorry but I've enough on my plate with my own family.'

'*He's* your family, an' all, unless you've forgot!'

'You know what I mean. Then there's this house – it don't clean and keep in order itself, you know. Anyroad, besides owt else, Martin wouldn't like it—'

'Ah, there we are. There's the truth of things, I get it now.' Jenny threw her hands in the air.

'Meaning?'

'Martin. It's what it allus boils down to, in't it: that bloody husband of yourn.'

Twin high spots of crimson sprang to Coral's cheeks. 'You hold your tongue. You don't know what you're talking about.'

'Aye, I do. He says shit, you jump on the shovel – ain't it allus been the same?'

'To speak of him so!' The woman's eyes were spitting steel. 'After all he's done for youse!'

'Oh aye, yeah. Saint bleedin' Martin, that's him. Truth is, he just loves seeing me grovel – you, an' all, I reckon. Pity the poor soddin' orphans, eh. Chuck 'em a few scraps from your table now and then, a penny here and there for good measure, and watch them bow and scrape with gratitude. That's what youse expect, am I right? Well I'm tired of it, d'you hear? Sick and bloody tired! I didn't ask for this.' Jumping to her feet, she beat at her chest, tears bursting forth to stream down her cheeks.

Still, the tirade ran on. Now the dam had broken, the torrent seemed unstoppable on its course for release. 'I didn't ask for Mam to die, for Father to follow her lead,' she cried. 'I didn't ask to grow up overnight, run a household on my own, be a parent to a lad I should see only as a brother. I didn't ask for this worry – real worry, aye, the terrible frightening kind what keeps me awake at night – over keeping Noah safe, finding grub and coal and rent, and everything else in between, day after day after miserable bloody *day*. I didn't ask. I didn't ask for none of it!'

Coral, her face now devoid of colour, her gaze wide and bright with emotion, rose slowly from her seat. She extended her arms as though to reach for Jenny's hands, but Jenny stepped away.

'Jenny . . .'

'Forget it, eh? Forget it all. Just pretend I never came.'

'But—'

'Goodbye, Coral.'

'Lass, wait.'

Jenny refused to listen. She picked up her skirts and without looking back ran from the house.

She'd been walking aimlessly, shoulders hunched, face taut with fury, her chest aching and eyes burning with suppressed tears, when a touch to her arm had her bolting around, fists poised for battle. The man who had stopped her held up his hands.

'Sorry. I meant thee no harm . . .'

'You again?'

'By gum.' He grinned. 'I thought for a minute you were going to clock me one, then.'

'I was.'

Throwing back his head, he roared with laughter. 'You're a tonic, you, d'yer know that?'

Jenny eyed him with a mixture of caution and intrigue. In the better lighting, she took in his appearance now fully. Eighteen or nineteen was where she'd have put his age to be. Tall and stocky, with collar-length auburn hair framing a fresh and open face, he wasn't altogether bad on the eye, she had to admit. His looks then, it would appear, matched his nature. After all, he'd seemed nice enough when coming to her aid with the coins last night, hadn't he? But well, you never could be too careful, she reminded herself. Her guard, therefore, remained firmly in place: 'Did you want summat?' Then, keen not to appear rude, she added, slightly softer now, 'Only I'm in a bit of a rush, you see.'

He stroked his brow and shook his head. 'Not really. Just fancied saying hello.'

'Oh. Hello.'

'Hello.'

'Goodbye.'

'Hang about.' He tugged at her sleeve and stopped her as she made to turn. 'Bloody hell.' Again, he laughed heartily. 'You're not one for standing on ceremony, you, are yer? Right to the point and to hell with propriety.'

A smile peaked the corners of her mouth. She pulled a face. 'Sorry.'

'Don't be. I quite like it.'

'Huh! You're the first person I've met what does.'

Two women, shawls drawn over their heads,

tut-tutted and skirted past the couple. They stared back over their shoulders to throw Jenny and her companion dark looks, and the man grinned.

'We're getting in folks' way idling about here. What say we nip across the road forra drink? My treat?'

Jenny was sorely tempted. Nonetheless: 'Eeh, I don't know that I ought.'

'Why not?'

'Well, because . . . I don't even know thee. Tha could be a raving madman for all I know.'

'Oh, I am, but only on weekends. As it's but Wednesday the day, you've nowt to fret about.'

The quip, coupled with his deadpan expression, were her undoing; she giggled. 'Daft beggar.'

'So . . .?'

'Aye, go on. Only the one, mind. I really do have business to be getting on with.'

They chose a quiet corner in a nearby run-down tavern – few better class of places wouldn't be seen dead allowing admittance to a member of the fairer sex – and Jenny took a seat on the scuffed bench running along the dark, wood-panelled wall, whilst the man went to the counter to order their drinks.

'What's your name, then?' she asked when he returned.

He took a sip of his ale. 'George.'

'George what?'

'Sixsmith. You?'

'Jenny. Jenny Brodings.'

This basic formality out of the way, they sipped their ale in silence until George said, nose in the air,

41

'So what is it that you're about, then, the day, Miss Jenny Brodings?'

She smiled at his poor attempt at a gentrified accent, yet it soon fell from her face in remembrance. She sighed. 'I'm on t' hunt forra position.'

'Oh?'

'Aye. Only I can't seem to catch a break. There's just nowt about.'

'You tried at places, then, aye?'

'Well of course I have.' She bit her lip. 'Well, some. Thing is, I don't really have much luck with jobs, you see. Keeping hold of them, anyroad. That's my problem.'

He listened without interruption to her explanation of her past experiences with employers and how she'd allowed her quick temper to get in the way in each instance. 'And you reckon things'll be different next time, aye?'

Jenny was resolute. 'Oh they will. They have to be. My brother . . .' She glanced away and cleared her throat. 'He's had to start toiling as a sweep's boy to put grub on t' table, and I hate myself for it. He's gorra cough on him lately summat chronic, and as for his poor little legs . . . I have to do summat, find a place and begin earning a wage of my own so I can get him out of it. If something should happen to the lad – well, I'd never forgive myself.'

George's face had turned serious. He folded his arms. 'Got hisself a swine of a master, has he, this young brother of yourn?'

42

'Oh, has he! Don't even get me started on that per-isher Vincent Tottington—'

'Totty?' He ground out the name on a growl. 'Is that who you said?'

Jenny nodded. 'You know of him?'

'Know of him? Oh, I do that, all right. I can't believe he's still at it; thought he'd have packed all that in by now.'

'Nay – well, you know what sweeps are like, eh? They care naught for the law so long as they're mak-ing their brass.'

Parliament had passed an Act in 1840 forbidding the climbing of chimneys by those under twenty-one years of age. Here they were now, almost three dec-ades later, and the move had made little impact. Even the threat of receiving a fine – this only owing to the introduction of a further Act just five years ago – wasn't enough to curtail sweeps using boys at will and to cull the practice. Still they went about with their business as they had always done. Nor did it look as though anything was set to alter anytime soon.

Naturally, the children under their employ would never have passed for an adult; however, this posed little bother. All were versed in lying, should anyone query whether he was a sweep's boy, from the moment they were taken on – Noah included – and few ques-tioners were inclined to press the matter. Some chimneys were far too narrow to allow a grown man passage, and so the customers who hired out their services simply turned a blind eye to the truth of things. Better to keep quiet than risk rocking the boat when you needed your chimney regularly cleaned.

'Course, it's the government what are the real culprits in all this, you know. At least it's them what forced this about, anyroad,' George was saying now.

'How d'you mean?'

'Well all this, the need to use children as sweeps because of the narrow chimneys: it stems from the seventeenth century hearth tax, or so I've heard said. When Charles II restored the monarchy following his father's beheading by Parliament, the nation was in crippling debt thanks in the main to the English Civil War. He needed a regular source of income to build the country back up, and so he introduced the new tax based on how many hearths a property had – a chimney money, essentially. As you can imagine, folk begrudged paying this twice a year, and so many began constructing buildings differently, with twisty and turny interconnected flues, as a means of cheating the system. This meant now, though, that the passages became impossible for grown men to squeeze through to sweep ... boys had to be used instead.' George spread his hands wide and shrugged. 'So there it is.'

Jenny thought she'd grasped at least a little of what the man had just imparted to understand the basics; however, she remained steadfast on one thing: 'There's still no call for these master sweeps to act so downright bloody evil with the youngsters, though, is there?'

'Nay,' George readily agreed. 'And that Totty is the worst of a bad lot. I ought to squeal on him to the police, see how he'd like that—'

'Nay!' She was horrified. 'Nay, you can't do that.'

'You give me one good reason why.'

'I'll give you two. For a start, I've had more than one run-in with him this week. Should the law suddenly start questioning him or haul him before the courts, you can bet whose blood he'd be baying for: mine. He'd think it were down to me without a shadow of a doubt. And second . . . as much as I hate admitting it, we can't afford for our Noah to lose that job. Not yet, at least, not until I'm in employment and can support us both. You understand, don't yer?' And at George's reluctant nod: 'You'll keep your counsel, then? Eeh, say you will.'

It was clear that it took effort to agree to it. Nonetheless: 'Aye, all right.'

Jenny took a long draught of her drink to calm herself down before asking, her curiosity getting the better of her, 'How is it you know Totty?'

Again, that stony look took possession of his countenance. 'I, well, I swept for the bastard as a little 'un.'

'You?'

'Aye. And let me tell thee now, he made my life a living hell.'

She chewed the inside of her cheek. She knew she shouldn't, knew she'd learn things she'd rather not, but couldn't help herself and asked anyway: 'What happened? What did he do?'

'You don't want to know.'

'You're likely right, aye, but I want to hear it all the same. Tell me.'

'Aside from the beatings, you mean? The punchings

and kickings he's not shy of doling out when the mood strikes?' George's tone was harsh.

'Noah swears he's not laid a finger on him,' she whispered.

'Aye, well, all's I'll say is the lad should enjoy it whilst it lasts. Totty ain't one for changing – it'll surface sooner or later, that evil streak what runs right the way through him, you mark my words.'

'You said aside from the beatings . . .'

'Aye.'

'Well, what else?'

'Totty had a game he liked to play with his climbing boys called beat the needle.'

She didn't like the sound of that. The fine hairs rose on the back of her neck.

'I say *he* liked to play it,' George went on. 'Can't say we garnered all that much pleasure from it.'

'Tell me.'

'Sewing needles. He'd jab the things right in deep in our feet if we weren't fast enough climbing the chimneys. Jesus, the pain . . . Used to like that one, he did; it was one of his favourites. And the more you cried, the harder he'd stab—'

'Mother of *God*.'

It was commonplace in the chimney trade for sweeps to 'teach their boys a lesson' when they felt the need by sticking sharp pins into their bare soles – everyone had heard talk of that. It was usually done to new recruits, who when faced with the pitch dark and narrow chimneys for the first time became paralysed with fear and refused to climb any further. And

46

rarely did it prove ineffective. Few could bear such agonising treatment; their terror of the chimneys was soon inclined to pale in comparison to the brutality from their masters if the work wasn't completed.

The practice was a heinous one and something Jenny had been dreading happening to Noah. This, however, what George was relaying . . . this didn't sound like an act of misguided necessity but rather a sadistic sport from which Totty derived actual pleasure.

She'd felt the blood drain from her cheeks in devastation, and it was evident George had noticed it too – he paused. 'D'you want me to go on?'

'Nay. Please.' To imagine even for a second her dear sweet brother suffering such cruelty made her want to scream. 'No more.'

Reaching across, George pressed her hand. His voice had lost its edge now; he spoke softly, soothingly. 'I'm sorry, Jenny.'

'Don't be. I did ask.'

'Happen Noah will have a fairer time of it . . . who can say?'

The line had sounded hollow in its truth, she was sure even to himself. Desperate to believe it, however, she nodded nevertheless. 'Aye, mebbe.'

'As for his cough and legs . . . there's not much to be done with the first – it's the soot, you see, burrows reet down deep in the lungs, it does, nasty horrible stuff. It affected me, an' all, although it were my eyes what suffered from the effects the most. Rubbing at them to clear them of the dust, which is a natural reaction, does you no favours, nay. My sight were never the same; even now, I can barely see further than a few feet in front of me. Warn your brother of it, will thee? As for his legs, mind, there is a solution of sorts: strong brine. That's the answer.'

'Brine?'

'Aye. It's the salt; it helps toughen the skin to leather. It'll protect him a bit in the chimneys, stop the flesh from tearing so easily when he's shimmying up the things. Get yourself a bucket filled at the fishmonger's and try it. A rag doused in the stuff and rubbed on his knees and shins of a night in front of the fire will do the trick.'

'It shan't harm him none, nay?'

George shook his head. 'When I were a lad, folk swore by scraping the skin from the knees first, reckoned the blood helped in the process, sped things up, like. And aye, that were torture, let me tell thee – I bear the scars to prove it. Me, I don't believe the cutting makes a difference. So nay, it'll not cause him no pain done how I said. The smell's enough to turn your stomach inside out, mind.'

'Aye. Ta. I'll do that.'

He nodded, sighed, then picked up their empty glasses and slipped from the bench. By the time he returned with fresh drinks, he'd resorted to his earlier light-hearted mood and cheery smile. Jenny was relieved of the lift in tension.

'So what is it you do with yourself these days, George?' It was obvious he was in regular employ, mustn't be short of pennies if he could afford to chuck away his money on ale.

A grin lit up his face. 'I sing.'

'Sing? What do you mean sing?'

'What d'you think I mean?' He laughed. 'I sings and people pay me for the privilege.'

Raising an eyebrow, she stared at him keenly. She was suitably impressed. 'Where?'

'The Balloon Inn on Rochdale Road. It's nowt grand, I grant thee, but it suits me and helps me put bread on t' table. So you see, there's hope for your brother,' George continued. 'He'll not be a sweep's lad for ever, Jenny. I got through it in one piece and he will, an' all, I'm sure.'

Touched by his attempts to reassure her, she smiled. 'Ta, George.'

'Is tha feeling a bit better?'

'Aye.' And queerly, she was. 'Aye, I am.'

'You know, come to think on it . . .' He tapped at his chin. 'I reckon there might well be a position going for thee at the inn, you know.'

Her lips parted. She gasped. 'Really? You mean it?'

'Hyacinth Harewood, the landlady, she's run off her feet at the minute since her daughter wed and gave up working. It might only be clearing up and wiping down tables and the like, but well, if you're not too proud to skivvy—?'

'Oh nay,' she cut in eagerly. 'I ain't too proud for that at all.'

'I'll put in a word for thee, then, see what occurs, shall I? She can only say no.'

Once again, Jenny could have leapt to her feet and done a jig, so pleased was she. *Please God that, unlike the baker's, this wouldn't fall flat.* Eeh, but meeting this man here might very well turn out to be the light at the end of the dark and worrisome tunnel she'd been prisoner to for so very long. If George came through for her . . . if he snagged her a position and she was earning an honest crust once more, it would change everything, *everything,* for the better – for Noah as well as herself.

She wouldn't mess up, not this time. She'd see that she stuck to it, come hell or high water, no matter what it might bring. By, she would.

Chapter 3

'REMEMBER, YOU'RE TO go straight round to Nobby's when you're done.' It was the following morning and Jenny was seeing her brother off to work. Easing back his cap so she could see into his eyes properly, she tapped the tip of his nose with her fingertip. 'No dawdling on t' walk home, d'you hear? The owd fella will only fret if you're late back.'

Noah nodded, smiled. 'All right, Jen.'

'Good lad.'

'Jen?'

'Aye?'

'Will you get taken on, d'you reckon?'

She'd told him last night all about her conversation with George Sixsmith. Giving the words life to another had bolstered her enthusiasm further still. In her excitement, she'd blurted to the lad that if she was fortunate enough to land the job then he wouldn't have to continue with what he was doing, that he would be free to leave the chimneys behind him for good. Noah had been utterly delighted, which at the time had warmed Jenny's heart something lovely to have pleased him. Now, though, she wondered whether speaking as she had done might have been the wrong thing to do. What if she wasn't successful after all; it was a possibility, wasn't it? She'd be forced to snatch back from him the sliver of happiness – how? He'd be crushed.

Now, more than ever, she must hold fast to her vow of securing this – and holding on to it for all she was worth, she knew. She couldn't let him down again. She just couldn't. The weight of responsibility was a hefty one.

When he'd left, she pottered about the cellar washing the breakfast pots and tidying up with only half her mind on the task. A hundred and one things that could go wrong later that evening plagued her brain, allowing her little respite. Therefore, when a knock came at the door, she barely registered it. Frowning, she paused and cocked her head, unsure if she'd heard correctly.

'Jenny?'

Coral. Her brow furrowed deeper. What on earth could she want?

'Jenny, it's me.'

She hesitated and pondered on whether she should just ignore her. The disastrous meeting the previous day stung still – she hadn't the energy for another fight, had far more pressing matters on her mind right now.

'Are you in there?'

Hell's teeth. The woman was persistent if nothing else. Heaving a sigh, Jenny went to open the door.

'All right?'

Unsmiling, Jenny nodded.

'Ain't you going to ask me in?'

She stepped aside to let her pass. 'Oh aye, mind your step.'

'Good Lord, Jenny . . .' Assessing the missing stairs and shaking her head, then muttering to herself as she lifted her skirts, Coral hopped awkwardly into the room. 'What occurred?'

'The usual: I had nowt to feed to the fire.'

'So you ripped up the staircase? Should the rent collector spy what you've done when calling for his brass, he'll have your guts for garters. It's out on your ear you'll be, I'll be bound.'

'He'll not see: I'm allus mindful to block his view at the door. And well, anyroad, it were either this or freeze to death . . .' Breaking off, she screwed up her eyes, her patience wearing thin. 'Sorry, did tha just come here to cast judgement?'

'Nay, I—'

'Then what *is* it you're doing here? What d'you want?'

Coral crossed to the table and sat upon a stool. She removed her shawl, folded it neatly and placed it on the table. A quick pat of her immaculate hair, then she turned to face Jenny. 'I wanted to see how tha were, that's all. Norra crime, is it?'

'Nay, but . . .'

'What?'

'Well, we didn't exactly part on friendly terms, did we?'

The fire crackled and spat. Coral watched a tumbling lump of coal settle in the grate then shrugged her shoulders. 'It don't matter. It's forgotten.'

Well of all the . . .! Jenny was dumbfounded. Her sister might have evicted from her mind what had passed between them, but she hadn't – couldn't. To her, Coral's lack of support *did* matter, a lot. She gave a harsh sniff.

'Let's not row no more, eh? We'll put it behind us and no harm done.'

'You just can't fathom how hard this is, can yer? I came to thee because I were desperate for your help. Never afore have I spilled my guts as I did yesterday – does that not tell you summat? I'm trying to be better, don't you see it? Me and the lad, we've no one left in this world but you. Well, bar Owd Nobby, and we can't keep putting on him at his age, 'tain't right. We *need* thee, Coral.'

She lowered her gaze. 'I'm sorry.'

'Not enough to help, though, still. Am I right?'

'Jenny, tha has to understand . . . Martin—'

'Oh, Coral, just go, will yer. Go on, get back to your precious family and leave us in peace.'

The older woman's face was pained. Nonetheless, her voice was firm: 'Don't speak to me like that, Jenny, I'll not have it.'

'What, 'cause I'm your sister?'

'Well . . . aye.'

'And sisters are meant to be respectful of each other, kind, *there* for one another. Is that it?'

'Now look here—'

'Nay, Coral, you look! From day one, ever since our parents went, you've seen me and the lad as nowt but a burden. I've tried so hard not to bother you unless I absolutely needed to, have gone without grub some days myself when our provisions ain't stretched so as to feed Noah. You dread me coming round; I've seen your faces, yours and Martin's, and youse hate it.'

'That's not true.'

'Just what has that husband of yourn got against me, anyroad? Eh?'

'Nowt. Nowt, really . . .'

'Well he's gorra funny way of showing it,' Jenny interjected harshly. 'And you – you allus take his side, every time. D'you know, we feel like strangers to thee, me and Noah. You're thirty come your next birthday and aye, that's quite an age gap betwixt us, I know, but still . . . Why ain't we like other siblings, Coral? Why can't you support us, love us?'

'Eeh, lass.' Coral was on her feet. She made to step towards Jenny then, as though remembering her last attempt and the girl's rejection of her, she paused and dropped her hands to her sides. 'I wish I could do more, really I do . . . it's just, there's matters you know nowt about, nor could you understand.'

'Like what?' Jenny was frowning.

'Don't you think I'd have given owt to take youse in when Mam and Father died? Imagining you both scraping by alone, living in this God-awful hole in the ground? But I couldn't. I *couldn't*.'

Seeing the tears glistening on her sister's dark lashes, the clear tremble of her lips, Jenny was taken aback. Nothing usually ever cracked the woman's iron-firm exterior – she hadn't expected this, didn't know how to react.

'Martin has his reasons for how he behaves, Jenny. Tha must believe me, though, when I tell thee it's not personal; you're in no way at fault. Promise me you'll remember that.'

'I . . .' She hadn't time to say anything further as on a quiet sob, Coral rushed past her, pulled herself up the remaining stairs and hurried from the cellar.

It was as though Nobby had been waiting in the street; seconds later, his wizened old head appeared around the door: 'Jenny? How's tha fettling?'

'All right . . . I think. Wait there,' she told him distractedly. Her mind was filled with questions. Just what had Coral been talking about just now? It made no sense to her, none at all.

'What's that, lass?'

'I said wait there,' she repeated, louder now so that his aged ears could catch her words. 'I don't want you breaking your skull trying to jump in – I'll come to thee.'

Nobby led the way into his house when she'd joined him. He left her to take a seat and headed for the table where sat the teapot. 'You'll take a sup?'

'Aye. Ta.'

'So what's afoot now, then?' he asked when their mugs, cracked and chipped through age and use, were filled and they were sitting facing one another. 'You and your Coral had a set-to, did youse?'

'You heard?'

'Not what were said, nay, but I caught wind of raised voices as I were passing your door. When she flew past me like the hounds of hell were on her heels, I reckoned I'd best call in on thee, see how tha fared.'

'We argued yesterday. She'll not help out with Noah should the need arise when I'm working. That's the top and bottom of it. Then she turns up here the day as though nowt were amiss – I lost my rag.'

'Jenny . . .'

'I know, I know.' Resting her cheek in her hand, she sighed. 'She just gets me so mad at times, Nobby. She don't want us cluttering up the place, making her perfect little world untidy, that's the truth of it. I just wish I could rely on her a bit more, that's all.'

'Mebbe she don't realise how she's behaving. Did you explain to her how yer feel, like?'

'I did, but you know what she's like. That poker she's got rammed up her arse, what makes her all high and mighty, it blinds her to all else but herself. I might as well be talking to the chimney back; nowt gets through to her. Well, mebbe that's not true,' Jenny was forced to admit, 'for today . . . she seemed different.'

'How so?'

'Well, she showed herself to be almost human at one point. Mind you, she didn't half spout some queer things.'

Nobby eyed her over the rim of his mug. 'Oh?'

'Aye, about Martin. She says he's standoffish with me for reasons I'm not to blame for. Which must mean the fault lies with him, eh? What d'you reckon?'

'I'm sure I don't know. Besides, it's no business of mine.'

Releasing a long breath, Jenny shrugged. 'Let's forget about that now, anyroad. I've had enough of it for one day.' The ghost of a smile tugged at her lips and moments later she was grinning. ''Ere, guess what? I've a bit of news.'

'I'm guessing it's good going by your phizog?'

She nodded.

'What's that then?'

'I might have got myself a position.'

'Aye?' His smile matched her own. 'Doing what and where?'

She relayed to him her meeting with George. 'Thing is, Nobby, if they do offer me the job, it being in a public house, like . . .'

'You'll be required to work nights?'

She dropped her gaze. 'Aye. Only what with my sister refusing . . .'

'Tha wants to know if I'll keep an eye to your brother whilst you're gone? Well course I will, daft lass. I'm only too happy to help and it's not like I've owt else on. Anyroad, he'll be company for me. 'Tain't half lonely rattling about this place on my own.'

'I do so hate to ask . . . Eeh, Nobby. You'd really not mind?' Emotion had thickened her words. She reached for the old man's hand.

'I'd not. So that's that sorted. All that remains now is to see whether you get the job.'

At his meaningful look, Jenny had the grace to blush. 'I'll try my very hardest to secure it, I will. And aye, if I do, I'll not lose it through this infernal tongue of mine, honest. I have to do this. And I can, I know it.' George's revelation regarding Totty and the terrible ill treatment he'd received at his hands came back to her with painful remembrance, and her chin went up. She squared her shoulders determinedly. 'I'll not let Noah down.'

She'd been waiting in eyeshot of the Balloon Inn for but a handful of minutes when she caught sight of George turning the corner of the street. Her insides did an uncomfortable flip and she swore beneath her breath. She'd been half hoping he'd be a little late in arriving. That way, she'd have had more time to prepare, compose herself. And by, did she feel she needed it. Her nerves were in ribbons, her palms clammy, and her rapidly beating heart was threatening to break from her chest – could she really do this?

'All right?'

'Nay,' she admitted.

He chuckled. 'Don't tell me plucky ol' Jenny Brodings is scared?' he teased.

'It's not funny, George. So much depends on this going right. I'm shaking like a leaf, here.'

'Come on, you'll be just fine.'

Before she had a chance to say anything further, George had pushed open the navy-painted door and was beckoning her inside. She licked her dry lips. Then on legs that felt like melting wax, she forced herself forward and shadowed him into the inn.

The hour was early still; the place had only opened

for the night shortly before and there were but a few customers present. George led the way to the high counter and signalled to a tall stout woman in her middle years, dressed all in black and busy filling a tankard with ale.

'Evening, Hyacinth. There's someone here I'd like thee to meet.'

'H—hel—hello.' Jenny brought to her lips what she prayed was a smile, although in her current state she suspected it might be more of a grimace.

'All right, lass.' Hyacinth nodded politely then turned her attentions back to George. 'What's all this about, then? A friend of yourn, is she?'

'Aye, that's right.' He paused to give Jenny a supportive wink. 'Her name's Jenny, Jenny Brodings, and she's after work. She'd fit in well, Hyacinth, you have my word on it.'

To Jenny's relief, her eyes lit up. Placing her elbows on the counter, she leaned across and said excitedly, 'She's interested in t' position, then, aye?'

'Ask her for yourself. Jenny's gorra tongue in her head right enough.'

'Are you, lass?' Hyacinth asked, swivelling her head to face Jenny. She smiled. 'George here's explained what your duties shall be, aye?'

'That's right.'

'Eeh, you'd be saving my life and no mistake. Miss Drummond – that's the last lass I employed – well, she upped and went without a by-your-leave. Aye, left me in t' lurch good and proper, Daisy did. My daughter, Lord love her, she helped out, but she's gone an' all just lately, so things have gorra bit desperate. I'm powfagged trying to run this place single-handed; can't be in two places at once, you see, and there's that much to do. Never get a second's peace, I don't. So what d'you say?'

Jenny couldn't keep the grin from her mouth. She bobbed her head rapidly. 'Oh aye. Eeh, I'd like nowt better, Mrs Harewood.'

'Nay, you just call me plain owd Hyacinth.'

'Ta, Hyacinth. Eeh, thanks ever so.'

The woman slapped George good-naturedly on the back, her gratitude in who she clearly deemed her saviour this night clear. 'Can tha start this evening, Jenny?'

Her answer came without hesitation. 'Aye.'

'Gradely. Right then. Give me one minute whilst I see to this thirsty customer and then I'll talk you through your chores proper, like. All right?'

Jenny opened her mouth in ready agreement. However, her chance of giving the words life was snatched from her. Before she could speak, a hard slap to her backside stole the wind from her lungs. She spun around in disbelief.

A burly young fellow stood facing her. Slack-jawed from the copious amount of ale he'd consumed, he raked his eyes up and down her. 'All right, sweetheart. Fancy a—?'

Whatever he'd been about to suggest never reached his lips – a wave of fury coursed through Jenny's veins and before she knew what she was doing, she'd drawn back her arm and punched him square in the throat.

Wearing an expression of utter surprise, the man fell backwards. He landed on a table, which splintered beneath his weight, and he was sent sprawling across the sawdust-strewn floor. Spreadeagled, he gazed up at the ceiling, stupefied.

The room had fallen deathly silent. Jenny closed her eyes in despair. *Good God above, what have I done?*

'Whey!'

'Ha-ha!'

'Good on thee, lass.'

'That's a fierce left hook you've got yourself there, young 'un!'

'Aye, that showed the randy bugger!'

The myriad of different voices that burst forth dragged her back to the present. Slowly, she opened her eyes again and, frowning in confusion, looked around. The whole pub was on its feet; there wasn't a customer not cheering.

'My bleedin' windpipe,' the man she'd laid out flat croaked. 'She's severed the thing, she has!'

'Oh shurrup whinging, you mardy arse.' It was Hyacinth. To Jenny's astonishment – and sheer relief – she had tears of mirth running down her cheeks. 'Get thee up and take a sup; you'll be reet, I'm sure. And ay, let that be a lesson to thee: keep your filthy paws to yourself in future.'

'Eeh, Mrs . . . Hyacinth. Eeh, I am sorry, I . . .'

'Don't be.' The landlady squeezed Jenny's shoulder reassuringly. 'That dirty git got what he deserved – you did right, aye. Anyroad, no harm done.'

She could barely believe it. 'You mean yer still want me working here? You ain't changed your mind?'

'Nay, nay.' Laughing, Hyacinth plonked a fresh glass of ale in front of the man with the wandering hands, who looked to have made a full recovery at the promise of free alcohol and had slinked up to the counter. 'Get that down thee,' she told him, 'and behave yourself from hereon in, d'you hear?'

Shooting wary glances in Jenny's direction, he nodded and took himself, his drink and his dented pride off to a quiet corner with his tail between his legs to lick his wounds.

'You don't need to ask whether the lass can handle herself against rowdy patrons at any rate,' George told the landlady. There was a definite twinkle in his eye. 'Told you she was a good fit for the job, didn't I?'

'Aye, you did. And by gum, lad, does it favour you were right!'

Jenny's first shift proved nothing like her introduction: the hours passed in ease without a hiccup. She'd been a little disappointed when George had told her shortly after she'd begun that he wasn't working tonight and would be leaving soon – she'd been looking forward to hearing him sing – however, the hours sped by and before she knew it, Hyacinth was announcing last orders.

'Come on, you 'orrible lot, let's be having thee,' the woman bellowed good-humouredly, banging on the countertop with two tankards to get the drinkers' attentions. She stifled a yawn with the back of her wrist. 'I want my bed – aye, and it favours the new lass, here, does too. Toiled like a Trojan, she has, the night.'

'I'm all right really,' Jenny hastened to assure her. 'Besides, I like hard work when I can get it.'

'Huh! Well, you're in the right place, my girl, let me tell thee. You think this evening was busy, you just wait until the weekend. They're the divil's own holiday. Fellas' wages shall be burning holes in their pockets – it'll be all go here. Not that I'm complaining, mind; oh nay. I'm more than happy to relieve them of their hard-earned brass! Anyroad, go on, you get your shawl on and take yourself off home. Aye, and take my thanks along with thee.'

Jenny felt she was walking on air as she passed the short distance to her house. To think she'd kept hold of her job after her shocking display! She could barely believe it. She'd struck pure gold snagging herself a position at the Balloon, there was no doubt about it. The landlady was a fine woman, a real no-nonsense type and how Jenny preferred folk to be, just like herself. Not only that but the work was enjoyable. Even the customers were all right once you got to know them – and you were willing and ready to put them in their place if they did try something they shouldn't.

For the first time in her life, she felt she could be herself and not hold back. No hiding herself away or struggling to bite her tongue, no fear of being dismissed for sticking up for herself. All in all, she was as pleased as punch.

'So? How did it go?' Owd Nobby wanted to know the moment she was through the door.

Jenny's smile said it all, she was sure: 'Good. Really good.'

'Aye?'

She regaled him with all that had transpired. By the end of it, the old man was in fits of giggles and she herself was wiping tears of laughter from her eyes. She nodded. 'I tell thee, Nobby, it's the God's honest truth, every word. That bloke's face when I thumped him one; it were like summat from a comic show. I'll never forget it.'

'I don't reckon he's likely to in a hurry, neither, lass. Bloody hell fire; what's tha like!'

'I stuck to my promise, eh, Nobby.' All trace of amusement had left Jenny's face now; she felt tears sting her eyes. 'I said I'd secure a place, and some-how, with the Lord's help, I have. This is just the start, of summat new, summat better, aye. For Noah.'

'For youse both,' he reminded her once more.

The Balloon was in full swing the following evening when Jenny arrived for her shift. Oil lamps dotted along the emerald-and-gold-tiled walls threw their lurid light on the grinning, florid faces of the revellers, and her mood perked instantly – the jovial ambience was intoxicating. Pausing and looking around, she returned a smile or two from people with whom she'd made acquaintance the previous night and sighed contentedly.

'Alreet, lass?'

Glancing across the room towards the source of the bawled greeting, she caught the eye of Hyacinth, who beckoned her across. Jenny waved and made her way over.

'You look happy with yourself.'

Leaning her elbows on the counter, Jenny nodded. 'I am, aye,' she admitted. 'I like being here.'

The woman chuckled. 'What, even when randy owd sods try their luck getting a grip of thee?'

Recalling again the run-in, her cheeks immediately grew hot in a deep blush. She shook her head. 'Hyacinth, eeh, I am really sorry about that—'

'I know, lass, I know; I'm just teasing, that's all. Anyroad, he looks to be behaving hisself the night – see for yourself.'

Jenny followed her gaze towards the window where, sure enough, the man certainly did seem to be on better form this evening. Arms akimbo and head thrown back in laughter, he was dancing a lively ditty and looked to be thoroughly enjoying himself, much to the amusement of fellow bystanders.

'He's harmless enough,' Hyacinth said. She swept her arm to encompass the pub. 'They all are, aye. Well, most of the time. You just keep being you, and put the buggers in their place should they need it, and you'll not go far wrong. All right?'

'Ta, Hyacinth.' Jenny winked. 'And aye, don't you fret, I will!'

'Now then, let's get to work. Give them tables over there a wipe over, will you, lass, whilst I serve these fellas just coming in? 'Ere, and George shall be making an appearance shortly. That's summat to look forward to, eh?'

Jenny went about her duties with a smile. Indeed she *was* looking forward to seeing him – not to mention his performance. What with singing being almost an obsession of her own – a secret one, mind you; only those closest to her, Noah in particular, were privy to her efforts – she knew a sense of excitement to have found someone who shared her interest and understood how it could make you feel when lost in the wonder of song. The drabness of life and all the trials that came with it ceased to exist for just a few short minutes, leaving only a beauty she hadn't the vocabulary to describe. It was there, though, all the same. She knew it instinctively, felt it deep within her bones. She really had struck lucky meeting George.

At eight o'clock on the dot, the door opened and the man she'd been awaiting at last entered. He made a beeline for her and bestowed upon her a wide smile.

'All right, Jenny?'

'I am, George. And you?'

'Can't complain, lass. Well, I could, I suppose, but no bugger would listen.'

Seeing him wink, she laughed. 'You're right enough there, mind you. Folk, well, they have problems aplenty of their own, aye, without letting theirselfs get bogged down with everyone else's woes. Sad, but that's the truth.'

'I'd listen to thee.'

The lopsided smile, as she searched his face for a sign of him being sarcastic or poking fun, slowly melted into an O of surprise – it was nowhere to be found. He was being genuine, she realised. She lowered her lashes, felt suddenly choked with emotion.

'I mean it, Jenny,' he went on, his quiet tone as equally sincere as before. 'If ever you're in need of an ear to bend . . . owt, owt at all . . . you've got it in me.'

'Ta, George.' *Even if it's just polite you're being . . . never will you know what it means to have you say that,* she added with her eyes. *And you a near stranger, too – you wouldn't think I have family, would you? It's them what should be saying stuff like that to me but nay, they care not a fig. Neither use nor bloody ornament, our Coral ain't. And oh, how I do need someone, lad. I've been that lonely for such a long, long time. Eeh I have.* 'I'll remember that,' she murmured.

He nodded once. Then scanning the room, he breathed in deeply and grinned. 'We've a decent-sized crowd in, eh? Should be a good night.'

Jenny quickly brightened. 'When will you be singing?'

'In about ten minutes' time. I'd best oil the owd pipes first,' he added, stroking his throat. He motioned towards Hyacinth who was handing out drinks to a group of customers. 'I'll see thee later, Jenny.'

She watched him stroll off to down a tankard of ale then returned to her duties. All the while, her gaze would occasionally flicker towards him in anticipation – she could barely wait for him to begin his own work.

Eventually, a sudden hush fell on the pub and she turned to see the singer had taken up position beside the open fire. All eyes were on him and he took the time to nod or smile to the patrons in turn. Then he closed his eyes, cleared his throat and began.

The strains that burst forth to strangle the air were a shock to her senses at first – it was something she really hadn't been expecting. Booming in volume yet screechy to the point of unbearable in its pitch, coupled with each single note being slightly off kilter . . . she couldn't believe it, was bitterly disappointed. In a word, George's voice was terrible.

Chest pumped out in evident self-pride, he shot Jenny winks across the room as he blasted out the chorus – it took all the strength she possessed not to openly wince or cover her ears and to force back a smile. In sharp contrast, the revellers and even landlady Hyacinth looked to be lapping up every second of the cringeworthy performance; Jenny was utterly baffled. Were they really not hearing this? she wondered in amazement, gazing about at the expressions. But surely, *surely* . . . Christ, it was enough to make your lugholes bleed! Happen they were merely being polite? But no – looking around again, she could see only genuine enjoyment etched in the faces. It didn't make sense to her.

Finally – mercifully – the war ballad reached its crescendo then drew to a close. Jenny heaved a none-too-discreet sigh of relief.

'So?' Having sauntered his way amidst much roaring cheers and backslapping from his adoring audience, George leaned against the table she'd been wiping down and folded his arms. He was openly preening. 'What did tha make of that?'

'Well . . .' She gave an awkward laugh and did her utmost not to meet his eye. 'It were summat else, George.'

'Aye?' A grin split his face.

She blew out air slowly. 'Oh aye. I can honestly say I ain't never heard nowt like that afore in all my born days.'

She'd told him no word of a lie which, she knew, she would never have managed had she ever attempted to – the fib would have stuck in her throat. Thankfully – the last thing she wanted was to hurt his feelings; he'd been a good friend to her, after all – he took what she'd said at face value, was mighty pleased with her assessment.

'Lucky for thee, lass, there's plenty more where that came from.' He nodded, smiled, as though bestowing upon her some great gift. 'I'll just get myself another drink – thirsty work is singing, aye – then I'll get back to it. Any requests?'

Just the one, she answered inwardly, *though I doubt it's summat you'd like to hear.* She shook her head, saying instead, 'Not just yet, George, but thanks all the same.'

For the next hour, Jenny was audibly assaulted with rendition after awful rendition of popular local songs. If she never heard them ever again it would be a day too soon. With no way to drown out the painful racket, it was almost like a torture from which she couldn't escape.

By the time it was over, she had a thundering headache and was nearing the end of her endurance. Just how in God's name would she cope with this every night? She wouldn't do it, couldn't; she'd go stark, staring mad!

'Eeh, he loves entertaining, does our George,' Hyacinth said to her as they were clearing away the glasses, the last of the customers having just left.

The woman's face gave away not a hint as to his inabilities, however. Nothing – she was being completely genuine. She was, it was true. Jenny blinked back at her wordlessly.

'Reet sought after, he is,' Hyacinth went on. 'The keeper of the Rose and Thistle not far from here has been after him for ages, aye. Offered him a shilling a night over whatever I give him, they have, are that desperate to steal him from under my nose, cheeky sods. But George, he's the loyal sort and won't be tempted. Will thee, George?' she asked of the man, patting his shoulder.

'Nay, Hyacinth, I'll not. Brass ain't the be all and end all. You were the first to give me a chance when I were desperate and out of a job, and I'll not forget that. I'd not want to work anywhere else, and that's the truth.'

'Eeh, lad.'

He turned to Jenny and pulled on his flat cap. 'Shall I walk thee home?'

'Oh.' It was the last thing she desired. Right now, she wanted nothing more than to be alone in blessed silence; dreaming of it had been all that had got her through the evening. 'Er . . .'

'It's no skin off my nose,' he assured her. 'Besides, I don't like the thought of you wandering these streets on your lonesome at this time, young as you are. This city's riddled with all sorts – I'd not forgive myself should harm come to thee.'

He had a point. Much as she was able to look after herself – she'd had to learn to, had had no choice – and much as she hated to admit it – she was big tough Jenny Brodings after all, wasn't she, and apparently, at least outwardly, afraid of no one – there were many dangerous and desperate people out there. Grown men – rough, tough northern specimens at that – born and bred here and who knew the place like the back of their hand, would think twice before walking around Manchester alone once daylight fell. Even the police were known to go about their beats in twos in certain districts. She'd be a fool not to take George up on his offer. She nodded. 'Aye, all right. Ta, thanks.'

The temperature was unforgiving, the wind coming in from the river brutal, and they passed through the gaslit cobbled streets at a good pace. At the corner of her road, Jenny slowed to a halt.

'I'll be all right from here.'

'You're sure?'

'I am. Ta again.'

He flashed her a smile. 'See thee the morrow, lass.'

'Night, George.' She waited until he'd disappeared up the street. Then groaning, she picked up her skirts and ran the short distance to Nobby's dwelling.

The elderly man opened the door to her with a gummy smile then held a finger to his lips. 'The lad's fast akip; dead to the world, he is, poor divil.'

'Eeh, Nobby, what a night!' Jenny removed her

shawl then lowered herself into the fireside chair. 'My poor head's pounding.'

'Why, what's to do? Oh, what's occurred this time, what's tha done?'

She couldn't help but laugh. 'Nowt, Nobby, honest! I told thee, I'm going to do all in my power to keep hold of this position. I'll not risk messing it up. Nay, it's nothing of my doing, It's just . . . ech, I feel mean even saying it.'

He listened whilst she explained about the young man's terrible performance, then he cocked his head. 'It were that bad, eh?'

'Oh, worse! Honest, Nobby, I felt rotten for George but he just couldn't hear how God-awful he is! And the others, they don't help – clapping and whooping like things possessed, they were. Happen they're all as tone deaf as he is, or mebbe they were that muddled with ale they couldn't tell the difference . . . I don't know. I couldn't fathom it. How am I meant to bear it every shift? He'll finish up sending me mad, I know it.'

'And that's all what's bothering thee? You look . . . I don't know, lass: disappointed almost.'

'I am, aye, if truth be told,' she confessed. 'I thought we . . . well.' She cleared her throat, her cheeks flushing. 'I thought we had a connection, you know? I've never known no one what loves singing as much as I do, and it felt nice. Special, like. George, though, hearing him the night, it's spoilt things somehow.'

Owd Nobby nodded slowly. 'Handsome, is he, this young fella?'

'I . . .' Jenny's blush deepened. 'Can't say I've really noticed—'

'Ha!'

'What? I ain't!' She glanced away to stare into the fire. 'Anyroad, as I've said afore: it'd make no odds, would it, for I'm never going to wed. No lad would look twice at me, what with the way I am, and having Noah to care for. Not that I want them to anyway,' she hastened to add, her chin rising with her legendary pride. 'Oh, just forget I said owt.'

'Don't be losing your rag, lass. I'm teasing, is all. And anyroad, what's all this about "what with the way I am"? There's norra thing wrong with thee, and don't tha forget it. As for young Noah, he's no trouble, is he? Any bloke would be fair lucky to have you as his girl, and don't you go convincing yourself otherwise, all right?'

She pulled a face then laughed to hide the emotion his words had evoked. 'Eeh, fancy me saying all this, though, about George when he's been nowt but kindness itself to me. I'd not even have a job if not for him. By, but I can be a reet bitch at times, can't I?'

'Huh,' he chuckled, patting her cheek. 'You show me a wench what ain't!'

Rising from her seat shortly afterwards, Jenny motioned to the decrepit horse-hair sofa, upon which her brother lay curled up fast asleep. 'I'd best get him indoors, now, Nobby. Ta for having him. What?' she added to see that a frown had furrowed the man's already deeply lined brow at the mention of Noah. 'What is it?'

'It's likely nowt . . .'

'Spit it out.'

'Well, the lad, he were limping when he arrived here from work earlier and complaining about his little leg. He's gorra few fresh and nasty scrapes on his shins – looked sore, they did. I bathed them best I could, lass.'

Closing her eyes, Jenny sighed. 'Ta, Nobby.'

'It was the bricks, lass.'

She nodded. It had been an ongoing problem for the lad since the day he'd started the job. Making his way up the inside of the chimneys in the dark, it was difficult to navigate the bricks sticking out and which he used to climb and pull himself higher on his elbows and knees. He'd missed his hold and slipped a number of times, taking several layers of skin from his legs in the process. One mass of scabs had barely begun to heal before they were torn away, to be replaced with the next lot to take their place.

With her hopes of him shortly leaving the chimneys behind him for good, she hadn't taken up George's suggestion of applying brine, thought it a waste of time – now, oh how she wished she had. Happen it wouldn't have made much of a difference in just a few days, but it may have at least alleviated her guilt a fraction, to feel as if she'd at least tried *something*, some way in which to help him, however small. The pain must be excruciating. Jenny could have cried for him.

'Sorry,' Nobby was saying now, dragging her back to the present; she scrubbed the tears that had dripped to her cheeks with her sleeve. 'I know how you worry. I just thought it best you knew so's you can keep an eye to the cuts, make sure they don't turn bad ways, like.'

'Aye. I'll do that.'

He helped her to waken the boy and to guide him, insensible with exhaustion as usual, to the street.

'See thee the morrow, lass.'

Jenny returned the farewell, then, as though leading a drunkard, shepherded Noah inside. She got him into bed, where he immediately fell back into a comatose sleep, and went to sit at the table.

Keen to save on candles, she made no attempt to add life to the wick, making do instead with the slim ribbon of moonlight filtering through the window to keep at bay total darkness. Coal was more precious still; no way would she fritter a single cob on herself. Her shawl would have to suffice.

For how long she'd been hunched on the stool, a prisoner of her savage thoughts, she couldn't say. Straightening her aching back, she winced and knuckled her tired eyes. A draught had cast its icy fingers beneath the ill-fitting door to touch every corner and crevice of their humble abode; she shivered. However, the chill inside her breast cut far deeper than anything that the elements could produce. Guilt still thrashed in her guts like a sack full of eels.

There was she, griping to Nobby over how she'd endure work at the public house owing to something as trivial as George's singing, when all the time . . .

God above, she didn't know how fortunate she had

it, did she? Her place of employment was friendly, bright and well ventilated, her boss kindly and welcoming. Moreover, it was safe. Poor young Noah had none of those qualities to look forward to when he stepped out of that door of a morning en route to *his* job, did he? The conditions *he* faced were nothing short of monstrous. He was suffering a living hell every waking moment of his miserable existence. What's more, much to her unbearable shame, he never uttered a single word of complaint, unlike her.

'You're a cow, Jenny Brodings,' she spat to herself in disgust, bunching her hands into fists until her nails dug painfully into her palms. 'A foolish, brainless, selfish young cow, that's what.'

Lord help the child get through the following days. Clasping her hands together now beneath her chin, she prayed for all she was worth. *A few more days, aye, that's all it ought to be. I'd have him gone from that awful bloody job right here and now, you know I would, God, but we must eat, and how can we do that without the brass he fetches in? Just as soon as I receive my first wage from the Balloon, Noah can tell that Totty to kiss his arse. He can leave the chimneys behind him for good. I'll look after him then – always. I'll not let him down, I swear it.*

'A few more days.' Jenny whispered the words out loud to the small hump that was her brother's slumbering form, rising and falling steadily beneath the bedcovers. 'Just stay strong, lad. Just forra little while longer. Please . . .'

Chapter 4

'Evening, George.' Having striven last night to make a concerted effort at being grateful with her lot from hereon in, Jenny greeted him warmly. 'I'm looking forward to hearing you sing again the night.'

'Ta, Jenny. I'm up in a minute. Any requests this time?'

She nodded slowly. Since the dawn of time, she was sure, stories relayed around firesides had been put to tunes and retold in song form throughout every corner of the world. It was a unique and deeply intimate social activity, passed on from generation to generation, and enjoyed by all ages. Surely then it was vital when singing to a crowd that the tone and theme of the songs were fitting to that particular situation and the mood you wished to portray?

From what she'd heard the previous night, George seemed to sing about only war and tragedy. Stirring and patriotic indeed the numbers may well be, but in Jenny's opinion they were horribly heavy and depressing – certainly not in keeping with the merry-humoured audience at the Balloon.

Her friend could be forgiven, however, for his choices. Since the invention and rising accessibility of the printing press, songs relating to events of the day appeared regularly on broadsheets and were hugely popular – everyone knew them. Every disaster, be it wrought by nature's hand or that of man, was inclined to find its way into print and sold on the streets, to be sung in taverns and inns across the land. From social and political clashes to floods and battle tales of loss and heroism – the Crimean conflict and even more recent American Civil War, which affected Lancashire towns and cities execrably owing to cotton being prevented from reaching their mills, leading to appalling hardship, were particularly prevailing subjects – the material was endless.

They tended to share, however, a common trait: oversentimentality bordering on maudlin and scarcely any fun. A soldier's farewell to his lover or mother, and stories of death and destruction were, surely to goodness, the last thing folk wanted to recall or be dwelling upon whilst partaking of a couple of relaxing ales after a hard day's toil? Wouldn't they much prefer to forget their troubles and strife for a short time in laughter and lively verse instead? Jenny thought so.

She put her suggestion to him tactfully: 'I reckoned, George . . . well, how's about summat a bit brighter, mebbe?'

'Oh?'

'Aye, you know; more comical, like?' *Something more entertaining might well divert somewhat from his terrible voice, make it just that little more tolerable, please God.* 'Tha must know a few?' she almost begged.

His brows drew together with uncertainty. 'I'd not want to be doing owt too coarse, Jenny? 'Tain't my style, that.'

'Nay, nay. Mine neither.' She shook her head. 'Nay, what I were thinking was tongue-in-cheek. Suggestive without being distasteful, you know? Summat we can all have a reet good chuckle to, cheer us up a bit. What d'you say?'

'I'm not sure as to whether I know any.'

'*I* do!' She grasped his arm in her excitement and grinned. ''Ere, I know a reet good one about the boggart Jinny Greenteeth – make you laugh your clogs off, it will. Then there's one my father used to sing to us about Dick Turpin. It didn't half make mine and our Noah's ribs ache when he did that. Ooh, and there's—'

'But I don't know them, lass. Anyroad, I thought tha liked the ones I do? You seemed to enjoy the Ashton Famine Song especially – least you said you had when I did it yesterday.'

> *We have come to ask for assistance*
> *For at home we've been starving too long;*
> *And our children are wanting subsistence,*
> *Kindly aid us to help them along . . .*

Jenny shuddered inwardly in remembrance. 'Oh aye, I did, really. It's just . . . Oh, never mind, George.' She shrugged, unable to think up further excuse and unwilling to risk offending him. 'It were just an idea, is all.'

'And it weren't a bad 'un.'

Jenny glanced back up in relieved astonishment. 'Nay?'

'I'm up for trying owt, why not?' He nodded. 'D'you think you can teach me quick them songs you mentioned?'

Within ten minutes, George knew three or four off by heart and looked to have thoroughly warmed to the prospect of performing something different. Jenny was smiling from ear to ear.

'Right then. Let's see what the mob makes of it.'

'They'll lap it up, I'm sure. Eeh, good luck.'

It was clear to see that the first strains of his opening song took the whole room by surprise. Chatter paused, heads turned and several mouths fell wide. Then people were exclaiming approvingly, and some began to clap along to the tune. George seemed delighted.

'Ay, that's more like it, lad!' Hyacinth shouted across the pub, tapping her toes in time to the beat.

'Aye – I love this one, I do!' a customer cried in agreement. 'Go on, lad, stretch yon lungs and give it all you've got. Gradely, it is!'

Laughing and stamping her feet, Jenny was in her element. When George broke into a warbling rendition of the hilarious classic The Old Woman of Wexford, she lifted her voice above the rest and sang with gusto:

There was an old woman from Wexford
In Wexford town did dwell,

She loved her husband dearly
But another man twice as well . . .

'Here, listen to this! Bleedin' hell!'

So lost was she in the merriment, Jenny failed to realise that the burly man standing close by was referring to her. Before she could blink, he'd enveloped her in his muscular arms and whisked her off her feet.

Gasping, she struggled to be set loose. 'What the . . .? Leave go of me, right now!'

Yet her words fell on deaf ears. Grinning, her assailant stood her in the centre of his table on full show and yelled over the noise, 'Listen, everybody. Just you listen. Go on, lass,' he continued, giving her a friendly shove. 'Sing like what tha did just then. I've never heard nowt like it in all my born days.'

Every eye was on her. She swallowed hard. 'I don't . . .'

'Sing! Sing! Sing!'

The entire pub picked up the mantra; her ears were ringing and a deep blush was creeping up her neck. She looked towards Hyacinth, who nodded and smiled encouragement. Shrugging, she began the next verse:

One day she went to the doctor
Some medicine for to find,
Saying, 'Doctor give me something
That'll make me owd man blind.'

As she became lost in her performance, the music soon overtook Jenny. As it was wont to, the world and everything in it vanished, leaving only her and the wondrous exquisiteness it evoked. Eyes closed, shoulders swaying, she raised her face to the wood-beamed ceiling and sang her heart out.

The last notes melted into an expert finish on the fuzzy air.

Silence.

Her heart was banging painfully. The seconds stretched on as she slowly floated back to reality. Finally, she forced herself to open her eyes.

The audience, standing completely motionless, were staring right back at her. Then as if of one body, they erupted. The thunderous roar of applause and cries of, 'More! More!' were deafening; blinking in stunned confusion, she took a step back, almost overturning the table and falling headlong to the ale-stained floor.

The man who had brought attention to her shortly before was swift to catch her before she tumbled and he set her back on the ground. 'Well done, lass. Three cheers!' he added to the room. They readily obliged.

'Good on thee, aye!'

'Bloody marvellous, that were!'

'Ay, tha should be on t' stage with a set of pipes like that, lass!' yet another punter shouted out.

Drunk on the moment and intoxicating praise, Jenny made a slightly unsteady journey to the counter. The landlady was waiting with a glass of small beer – Jenny gulped it down gratefully.

'Eeh, I'm shaking!'

'You're excitable, lass, and your emotions are all of a jumble. You'll be right as rain in a minute, nice deep breaths.'

'I were never expecting that to happen, Hyacinth.' A smile piqued the corners of her mouth. 'Eeh, but I did rather enjoy myself, I must admit. Love singing, I do, allus have.'

George appeared at her side. His expression was unreadable but Jenny sensed instinctively his displeasure. She swallowed a sigh. She hadn't meant for things to turn out like that, had only wanted tonight's performance to go well for his sake, hadn't meant for a second to steal away his thunder. 'George, I'm sorry—'

'Don't be. They loved thee.'

'Aye but—'

'It's fine, Jenny, really.'

She could tell that it wasn't. Figuring it would be best to let the matter drop and allow him to smooth his ruffled feathers in his own time, she nodded. 'It'll not happen again, mind.'

Over the next hour, George performed a number of different songs but it just wasn't the same. Something was missing now; the spark had gone. Jenny could have kicked herself. Just as everything had been going so well, too.

'Do Jone's Ramble, lad, if tha knows it,' shouted a customer as the night was drawing to a close. 'One of my favourites, that is.'

'It were once sung to George III, that was, so I've

heard said, and 'ere, if it's good enough for royalty then it's good enough for us!' stated another.

'Aye,' called out a third fellow, 'and let the new lass join thee. Go on, George lad, do a duet!'

Jenny thought she saw her friend wince a little at the request, although he tried to hide it. She shook her head emphatically, saying to the crowd, 'Nay, sorry, I ain't doing no more.'

'Ay, come on. Tell her, George!' The customer's tenacity to have his way would not be quelled. 'End the evening on a bang, eh, go on!'

She cast George a helpless and apologetic look. To her relief, he took a deep breath then smiled. He held out his hand for her to join him and, hurrying across, she took up position by his side.

Said Jone to his wife one hot summer's day
'I'm resolved that in Grinfilt no longer I'll stay,
But I'll go to Oldham as fast as I can
So fare thee well Grinfilt and fare thee well Nan . . .'

It was a private struggle not to have George's tuneless voice lead her off course, but somehow Jenny managed it. Her singing was intentionally subtle; for the most part, her partner drowned her efforts out. However, not wanting him in any way to think she was taking over, this suited her just fine and, before she knew it, it was working well. George was thoroughly enjoying himself. The Balloon was spellbound.

They ended the song on a whoop and a cheer – the

audience went wild, almost bringing down the roof. George was grinning widely.

'You were brilliant,' Jenny told him. Lost in the moment, she forgot herself; reaching out, she took hold of his large hand and squeezed.

'Ta, lass. And so were thee.'

Feeling his fingers tighten around her own, she glanced down at them then up again to meet his eye. He stared at her for several seconds. Then he leaned in and brushed his lips across her cheek in a soft kiss.

'I, I think I'd best . . .' Her face was on fire. 'I've tables to wipe,' she stuttered before bolting from him and the confusing feelings his touch had evoked.

When the last of the stragglers were glugging down the remainder of their drinks, George came to find Jenny. Spying him making towards her, she pretended she hadn't seen; she felt queer in his proximity now without having the words to explain to herself why. Embarrassment, that's what it was, she surmised. She'd never known the kiss of a man before and, truth be told, she wasn't sure how to feel about it now she had. He watched as she put the glasses she'd collected on to the countertop, then he sidestepped her and took hold of her hands. She blushed furiously once more, much to her chagrin.

'There's no reason to avoid me, you know.'

'I ain't,' she shot back, inwardly cursing herself for how immature her tone sounded to her own ears.

Releasing her, George laughed. 'It were but a friendly peck on the cheek, Jenny, that's all. There were nowt in it. You're nobbut a girl yet; I don't see thee in that kind of way, nay.'

Something akin to a boulder slammed inside her guts and settled there, suffocating in its weight. For reasons she couldn't fathom, hot tears scorched her eyes. She wanted the ground to open wide and swallow her whole.

'Eeh, lass . . .' Seeing her discomfiture, George's face fell. He made to reach out for her again but she smacked his hands away savagely. 'I'm sorry—'

'Leave me the hell alone, you sod.'

'Jenny, lass, I didn't mean to—'

'You think a lot of yourself, don't yer?' Crushing mortification had ignited her temper and now there was no holding back. 'As if I'd ever want a gormless swine like thee slobbering all over me, anyroad – near knocked me sick, it did. Your breath stinks worse than a dead dog's arse. And another thing, I ain't mithered in the slightest what you think of me or don't; your opinion matters naught. Now get out of my road, I'm going home.'

Letting out air slowly, George held up his hands in surrender and stepped aside.

'See thee the morrow, Hyacinth, I'm off,' Jenny threw over her shoulder on her way to the door. Without a backward glance, her heart in ribbons, she slammed from the inn.

She was midway home when she realised she'd left without her shawl. Spitting out an obscenity – well, she wasn't going back for it, that was for sure – she

87

wrapped her arms around herself and quickened her pace.

Just who the devil did that man think he was, at all? she asked herself. However, her anger was dissipating fast. She tried to cling to it, for it was the one emotion she was used to, felt comfortable with, but it wasn't to be. Fresh tears were clogging her throat and her chest was heaving; she was going to cry, damn it.

Hurrying into the shadows of a nearby shopfront, she sucked in a ragged breath. Then clinging to the bricks, she dipped her head and gave the silent sobs release.

After that scene just then, he must think her a complete . . . child. Aye. She'd proved his assertion right by acting out as she had. *Foolish, foolish idiot.* Truth was, despite what she'd spewed back there, she did care how he perceived her. Why, she still didn't rightly know, but the feeling was there all the same. If only George knew how she'd struggled this past year and what she'd had to endure. He'd see, all right, that she was far from being just a girl. She felt ancient if truth be told, like someone thrice her age. Her childhood had ended long ago and there would never be any getting it back.

She took a moment to compose herself before knocking at Nobby's house. The moment he opened the door, however, she was off; her tongue ran away with itself as usual, and she broke into an angry tirade: 'You'll never guess what occurred the night, Nobby. Honestly, that fella—'

'Lass, sit down a minute, will thee?'

'But—'

'Please.'

The old man's expression, as she took in his face properly in the dim candlelight, killed her speech in an instant. Foreboding gripped her. She swallowed hard. 'What the hell's happened?'

'Sit down . . .'

'Just tell me, Nobby. I want to know right now.'

'It's Noah.'

She spun on her heel to scan the space but of her brother, there was no sign; the sofa was empty. She turned back to Nobby searchingly.

'I put him down to rest up yonder in my bed.'

Her voice was a whisper. 'What's going on, what's wrong?'

'He's in a bad way, Jenny.'

'Bad?'

'That master of his, he—'

'I'll bloody well kill him!' She'd begun to shake with unadulterated rage. 'What's that Totty gone and done?'

'It's the lad's feet—'

'Nay.'

Beat the needle.

She baulked at the notion. 'Not the pins? Don't tell me the divil's done that!'

'It weren't the pins,' murmured Nobby. 'Nor did you let me finish. It's his feet, aye – also his legs, his buttocks . . . God in heaven.'

'Eh? What d'you mean?'

'I think you'd best go up, lass, and see for yourself.'

Something in his tone turned the blood in her body to ice. She took the stairs two at a time and burst into the old man's bedroom.

'Lad . . .'

Noah was lying flat on his back in the narrow, iron-framed bed. He turned his head on the pillow to stare at her but there was nothing behind his eyes. They seemed empty, hollowed out.

Her heart hammering, she crossed to his side and dropped to her haunches. 'Lad?' she repeated tremulously. 'Can tha hear me? What's happened?'

His voice was a scratchy croak. 'Hurts.'

'What does? Tell me where you're in pain.'

'Everywhere. Everywhere, our Jen.'

Frowning, she gently peeled back the sheets. The sight of the injuries scoring his skinny frame were almost her undoing – a howl of pure horror ripped from her. 'Dear Lord . . . Nay!'

The normally pale flesh was scarlet with patches of livid burns. Blisters filled with amber-coloured liquid, some as large as a child's fist, had mushroomed on his legs, and he was trembling as though in the grip of a fever.

'I wanted to send for Mrs Bullock in the next street,' said Nobby, who had appeared in the doorway. 'She's good with traumas of the body, in't she, knows more than most medical men, I reckon, but Noah wouldn't hear of it. He said I was to wait for your return.'

Jenny could barely speak, seemed to have lost control over her faculties, so great was her shock and anguish. 'Why didn't tha send for me?' she rasped. There she'd been this evening, singing and laughing having a jolly ol' time – getting herself into a state over something as trivial as the opinion of her by a fellow she barely knew – when all the while . . . 'Someone should have fetched me right away!'

'The lad, he insisted we never—'

'I did, it's the truth,' Noah cut in. ''Tain't Nobby's fault. I were frickened you'd get the shove from your new position if we made you leave your work early.'

'Mother of God. You're more important than any rotten job! I should have *known*. Oh, lad. Eeh, my poor little love.' Dissolving into tears, she rested her head on his thin chest. 'Forgive me. I'm sorry, so sorry.'

'Don't say sorry. You've done nowt wrong, Jen.'

No, she hadn't, had she? This was Vincent Tottington's disgusting handiwork. A fury like she'd never experienced before burst through her every nerve and sinew to encompass her entire being. Bastard from hell, she'd murder him for this with her two hands . . . *Wait, wait.* A tiny voice inside her head spoke to her. *Retribution can come later. Right now, your brother needs you.*

A queer sense of calm washed over her. She wiped her eyes and straightened her shoulders. 'Fetch Mrs Bullock, please, Nobby. Tell her to come quick as she can.'

'Aye, lass.'

When his footfalls died away on the stairs, she turned her attentions back to Noah. 'Now, lad, you hold tight, d'you hear? You're going to be just fine.'

'The master won't have me back, now, will he? He said he's had enough of me, that I'm finished. What'll we do for brass? We'll not have to go in the work-house? Eeh we'll not, will we, our Jen?'

Wiping away the single tear that was making a track down his grubby face, she bit the inside of her cheek to stem her own emotion until she tasted blood. 'Nay, lad. I promise thee.'

'I didn't mean to defy him, Jen, the master. I wouldn't, honest.'

She must know. Dear God above, how she'd bear the telling though . . . 'What occurred the day, Noah?' she forced out.

'The last dwelling what we went to, it were a big fine house up Cheetham Hill way,' he began through small sobs. 'We were told to start in the library, but as soon as we got to the mantelpiece, I felt it right away.'

'What, lad?'

'The heat. The people of the house had had a fire lit in the room not long afore we got there, must have done, and it hadn't had time to cool. I bent down and put my hand to the metal grill – sure enough, it were red hot. I said as much to the master but he told me to shut my trap and stop skriking like a babby. I had no choice, didn't want to displease him, so I stripped naked, grabbed my set of brushes and got into the grate. My feet were burning in seconds. Eeh, it didn't half hurt, Jen.' He paused to sniff loudly. 'I were soon to find out, mind, that that were nowt to the inside of the chimney. The bricks were just too hot to touch. Not for owt could I bring myself to climb up them; it

92

were just too painful. I panicked and I started to cry. I begged the master to let me come out, but he turned raving mad and wouldn't allow it. Then he . . . he . . .'

Tears were flowing freely down Jenny's face. 'Tell me,' she mouthed.

'He got some old rags and matches out of his sack and he made a fire in the grate. He said he'd show me what real heat was, that I were useless, said I'd soon be up that chimney once the flames started nibbling at my toes.'

'Jesus Christ . . .'

'I were clinging to the bricks about that much from the ground.' The boy imitated a distance of around two feet with his hands. 'Now I couldn't go up and I couldn't come down – I didn't know what to do, Jen, were that scared. Finally, I couldn't hold on no more: I fell.'

'Into Totty's fire? The thing was still alight?'

He nodded then winced with pain from the movement. 'I were screaming and I tried scrambling out but he just kept kicking me back in, kicking me and kicking me and kicking me—!'

'All right, lad, sshhh,' she soothed as he broke down wailing. Inside, however, she wanted to thrash and curse and howl to the heavens. 'You're safe now. I'm here.'

'The mistress whose house it were,' continued Noah, 'she heard the commotion and came running to see what was afoot. She ordered Totty to stop and to leave her house, so we did. I were burnt and bleeding but the master didn't care. He told me I'd lost him a valued customer with my antics. He shoved me reet hard and told me to bugger off home, that I were finished.'

He'll be the one finished, all right, when I'm through with him. The evil, devilish old—

'Jenny?'

Nobby's voice sliced through her thoughts. Glancing round, she saw he was with the woman known to the children around these parts as Win the Witch.

'Step aside, lass.' Winifred Bullock bustled into the room with her mysterious cloth bag of potions. 'Wait downstairs with Owd Nobby whilst I tend to the youngster.'

'But—'

'Do as she asks,' Nobby said quietly, cutting short Jenny's protests. 'We'll only get in her road.' He put an arm around her shoulders – nodding reluctantly, she permitted him to lead her out.

The wait was torturous. Noah's soft whimpers, as the woman tended to him, travelled downstairs to wrap around Jenny's heart; it took all of her strength not to run to him. After what seemed like a lifetime but could only have been ten minutes, Mrs Bullock entered the front room. Jenny rose slowly from her seat.

'Right, now. That's that. I've done all I can.'

'Is he . . . will he be all right, missis?'

Winifred let her shoulders rise and fall. 'We can but pray, lass. Should infection set in, then . . . Well, let's wait and see what happens.'

Groping for Nobby's hand, Jenny nodded.

'His burns are second class, and so coating the area with flour to keep the air off, as I would normally with more minor burns, was out of the question. That wouldn't have helped at all. I treated him instead with a liniment of limewater and linseed oil. I took care not to break the bladders – best to let them burst and heal naturally.'

'Is he in great pain still?' Jenny made herself ask.

'He is, and likely will be forra while yet. If it gets too much for him to bear, feed him laudanum; it's the best cure for restlessness. Oh and I've give him a mixture of lemon juice and cream of tartar in water, to aid with the fever. He drank the lot down, good lad, so there should be no worries on that score.'

'Ta ever so, Mrs Bullock. You've been a godsend.'

'You're very welcome.' She patted Jenny's head and smiled. 'Try not to fret, eh, for there mightn't be cause to yet.'

'I'll try,' Jenny lied. How on earth would she ever manage not to?

'Right, I'd best be away home. I'll be back in a few days to apply fresh dressings. In t' meantime, keep your brother well rested.'

Whilst Nobby saw the woman out, slipping her some coins for her services on the way, Jenny hurried up to the bedroom.

'Noah?'

The boy, sleeping soundly, didn't stir. Mercifully, he looked peaceful now at least. She cast him a soft smile and padded back down to the front room.

'You will let your Coral know what's occurred?'

95

'I suppose I'll have to, won't I?' *For all the use she'll be.*

'You'll leave the lad here, won't you, the night at least? It'd not do to disturb him.'

'You don't mind, Nobby?'

'Nay, norra bit. I'll take the chair here, shall be comfy enough.'

'D'you know, I don't know what we'd do without thee.'

He shook his head. 'It's me what's the grateful one, and I don't reckon tha even realises it.'

Sitting down facing him, Jenny asked, 'How d'you mean, Nobby?'

There was a catch in his voice. 'You and the lad up there are like my own grandkiddies. It's youse what make my life worth living, and that's the truth.'

'Eeh, Nobby.'

'That's why I don't want thee doing owt daft where Vincent Tottington's concerned,' he finished grimly.

Her face hardened. She glanced away. 'Don't ask that of me . . .'

'I shall and I am. Stay away from him.'

'And let that demon from hell get away with what he's done? Never! I can't do it. What he's done to my brother the day . . . Totty may as well have dug his own grave whilst he were about it. He'll know suffering, all right, once I'm through with him.'

'Jenny—'

'I'm sorry, Nobby. That's my final word on it.'

The old man sighed deeply and let the matter drop.

Staring into the yellow flames of the fire, Jenny allowed her burning hatred to soak into every crevice of her brain and put her plan for vengeance into action.

Chapter 5

CORAL, IT WAS clear to see judging by the dirty marks streaking her hands and apron, had been busy black-leading the range when Jenny arrived at her house. She opened the door on a sigh of irritation, then blinked in surprise. 'Oh, it's thee.'

'I'm not disturbing you . . .?'

'Nay. Come in.'

The small room, as ever, was as neat and clean as a little palace. Jenny turned her gaze to her sister and got straight to the point: 'That Totty assaulted our Noah the evening last. He's in a bad way.'

'Assaulted?'

'He burnt him. You should see the state he's in, Coral.'

Her face stretched in incredulity. She shook her head. 'Wha . . .? *Burnt?* Why in God's name . . .?'

Jenny relayed all that their brother had told her, adding on a growl, 'He'll get what's coming to him for this, by he will.'

'You've informed the police, then?'

'And where would be the point in that?' she retorted with a snort of derision.

'Well, the authorities, they'll see he's punished as he deserves to be—'

'Oh aye? What, with a paltry fine? Mebbe a few months' hard labour thrown in if we were really lucky? Nay. It's not enough. Anyroad, besides owt else, who is there to back Noah's claim up? The lady what caught Totty red-handed ain't likely to act as witness, is she? Using lads as chimney boys is illegal now, remember – she'll not want her name dragged through the mud for allowing the practice to go on beneath her roof, will she? I'm telling the law nowt of this, and I don't want you to neither.'

Coral threw her arms up in exasperation. 'Then what? That man gets away with it scot-free? Huh, I'm surprised at thee, Jenny. 'Tain't like you to let things lie.'

Jenny shook her head. 'Course he'll not get away with it. What d'you take me for? Didn't I just say he'll get what's coming to him?'

'Oh, I see. I get it.' The woman closed her eyes. 'You're for thinking you can sort this out your way, ain't yer? All guns blazing and to hell with the consequences. Just when will you ever learn to grow up?'

The last question was like a slap to the face; Jenny stepped back, wounded. 'What is it with folk this week accusing me of being a child? First George, now you—'

'George? Who's George?'

'It don't matter . . .'

'Jenny?'

99

She sighed. 'He's just some fella I work with, that's all. Aye, that's right,' she went on when Coral's eyebrows rose. 'I've gorra position now.'

'Where?'

'The Balloon on Rochdale Road.'

'A pub? Never a pub! Saints preserve us!'

Here we go . . . 'And what's wrong with that?'

'What's right with it! Females with an ounce of respect for theirselves don't spend time in public houses, Jenny. It's not proper.'

'And neither's starving to death, for that's what would happen if I weren't doing this job. It's all I could find. Besides, I enjoy it, believe it or not.'

'And the lad?'

'Owd Nobby keeps an eye to Noah – you know, seeing as you wouldn't consider it.'

'Oh, please don't start.'

'Start? Start what?' Jenny asked with mock innocence. What did Coral expect her to do? Stand here and take her pouring scorn on her every attempt to get by the best way she knew how? Not likely. She'd give her just as much back and then some. She'd show her. 'I'm not starting nowt, not me.'

'Jenny . . .'

'Well I ain't. It's you what—'

'Why is it whenever we meet it allus turns into a slanging match? I hate it, Jenny.'

The sincerity and regret in Coral's tone brought Jenny up short. What anger she'd been feeling slowly fizzled; she lowered her head. 'Me an' all,' she grudgingly admitted.

'Aye?'

'Well you are my sister, ain't yer?'

'Lass . . .'

'Of *course* I wish we could rub along a bit better. It's just . . . You just . . .'

'I know,' Coral murmured. 'I'm sorry.'

'Then I suppose I am, too.'

They shared a lopsided smile.

'I'll brew a pot of tea, shall I?'

'Aye, all right.'

When they were sat sipping their piping brews, Coral asked, 'Can I nip round and see Noah later on?'

'Aye. He'd like that.'

'He'll be up to a visit, won't he?'

Jenny nodded. 'He had a good night last night all things considered, slept right through without any trouble.'

'What is it you're scheming up for that Totty, Jenny?' The dread-filled question was a whisper. 'You'll not do owt . . . daft, will thee?'

'Coral, don't—'

'Promise me.' She reached for Jenny's hands and squeezed. The desperation in her eyes was palpable. 'You need to stop away from him. I don't know what I'd do should owt happen to thee, lass.'

Torn between telling the truth and placating her sister – she felt quite emotional seeing her this worried for her welfare – Jenny bit her lip. Then: 'Don't fret none,' she heard herself say. 'I promise.'

She left Carruthers Street with an odd sensation of

equability. That she and Coral had parted company on sound terms was a novelty – truth be told, she quite liked this feeling she carried. If only it could be this way between them all the time, she thought to herself as she turned back in the direction of home. Their parents would want them to get along better, she was sure of it. Pity Martin was how he was. He was the fly in the ointment so far as Jenny could see, and the main cause behind the sibling disputes – just what was his issue at all? He seemed of late to find her very existence a great trial. It flummoxed Jenny no end; she hadn't been able to fathom it.

After spending some time with Noah, who despite his discomfort was a lot perkier today than she'd known him to be in a good long while, and whom Nobby had insisted must stay at his dwelling for another night to save the upping and toing from house to house, Jenny headed off for her shift at the inn. She wondered if Hyacinth would be cross with her for leaving so abruptly the previous night, what with it having been a little before she was meant to finish, but hoped not. There was something Jenny must beg of her and she prayed she wouldn't turn her request down. God alone knew what she and her brother would do if she did.

She found Hyacinth was already hard at work with the wooden barrels behind the counter. Mercifully, it appeared George hadn't yet arrived.

She acknowledged Jenny's entrance with a nod. Taking a deep breath, Jenny made her way over. 'Evening, Hyacinth. Hyacinth, about last night . . .'

Hyacinth's face was glistening with perspiration; dabbing at it with the hem of her apron, the landlady frowned. 'Last night?'

'Aye. I left a bit sharpish, didn't I . . . sorry. I'll make up the minutes later tonight if tha likes?'

'I didn't notice, to be fair, but your offer's a kind one all the same. By, I'm fagged.'

'Here, let me.'

As she took over the task, Jenny watched through the corner of her eye as Hyacinth plonked herself on to a stool and downed a glass of small ale, finishing with a burp of appreciation. When she surmised that the woman was relatively rested, Jenny licked her lips, then, 'There's summat I wanted to ask thee, Hyacinth, if it's all right?'

'Go on, lass.'

'Well, I wondered if I might . . . whether you'd consider . . .' Another deep breath. 'Could I please have some of my wages early?' she plucked up finally.

'Course tha can.'

Jenny couldn't believe it. It had really been that easy? 'Oh, well, thank you. Thank you very much.'

'That's all right. You're a sound little worker and I'm thankful to have thee. How much does tha need?'

'I . . . I . . .'

'Lovey, what's to do?' Hyacinth cried, leaving her seat to hurry to Jenny's side as she bent double, arms wrapped around her middle. 'Eeh, lass!'

'Why did I wait?' she wept. 'It didn't feel right asking thee what with me only having been here forra few short days. You're just so kind, Hyacinth. *Why*

103

didn't I come sooner? Our Noah and all he suffered yesterday . . . I made him stop on with Totty for the brass. Just a couple more days, I told myself, then he could chuck the job in and he'd be free of that demon. This, it's my fault. It could have been avoided, all of it!'

'What's happened?' a voice asked, snuffing out Jenny's garbled lamentations.

Looking up, she saw George standing in the doorway, his face wreathed in concern. *Dear God, not now* . . . The vitriol she'd thrown at him last night, born from her embarrassment at his assessment of her, slammed back to her mind and she winced inwardly. She wanted to apologise but knew that even if she could pluck up enough courage, the right words would never have come to her. Mercifully, he didn't look to be holding a grudge.

'Jenny?' he pressed.

'It's nowt, honest.'

'Come with me.' Before she could refuse, he took her elbow and led her to an empty table in a quiet corner, saying over his shoulder, 'Two ales over here, please, Hyacinth, when you're ready.'

'George, I haven't the time for this,' Jenny tried when he eased her into a chair, 'I have work to do . . .'

He killed her feeble protests with a click of his tongue. 'Hyacinth can spare thee for a minute or two, I'm sure. Now. What's afoot?'

As she'd done earlier that day with Coral, she once again found herself explaining the terrible occurrence.

He listened without interruption. Finally, he released a long breath. His expression was a mask of stone. 'I knew he'd never change.'

'It's not the first time he's done this, is it?'

George shook his head.

'To thee . . .?'

'Nay, not me, but other climbing boys what have been under his employ. That was another of his favourite tactics, aye, lighting fires – still is by the sounds of it. I know of a few that he caught sleeping on the job due to pure exhaustion that he did this to. And another poor sod, can't have been much older than four or five years old at the time, he got stuck in a chimney one day. Lodged tight in a twisting section of the flue, he was, with his knees wedged up under his chin and no way of freeing hisself – the terror he must have felt you can only imagine. Totty's solution was simple: smoke the youngster out. Course, it didn't work. The boy was unconscious and very close to death's door when he was finally hauled out, hours later, with ropes. How in the world he never suffocated, as plenty more had done afore him, is nowt short of a miracle.'

'How could a body be so downright *cruel* and to a child?'

'Because he's evil, Jenny, right through to the marrow.'

'I'll never understand it.'

'And d'you know why?' George's eyes softened as he ran his gaze over her face. 'Because you're a decent person, lass. Unlike him, you have only goodness in your heart and mind.'

'Not always,' was her automatic response. *And certainly not in this instance. Right now, she carried only murder inside.*

'I wish you'd not do that.'

Brought back to the present, Jenny frowned. 'Do what?'

'Sully yourself, put yourself down all the time. There's no cause to – you don't deserve it.'

She glanced away. What answer could she give to that? What he'd spoken was true, every word. However, it was a habit she'd developed unconsciously and one she doubted she could break from. She did dislike herself, believe herself worthless a lot of the time. Life, circumstances, had made her that way and though she recognised it to be an unhealthy trait, she was at a loss how to rectify it.

'Your hair's the exact colour of fine whisky in the right light, d'you know that?' He took hold of a loose tendril hanging by her face and wound it through his fingers. 'Very bonny.'

'Huh, don't be so—'

'What?' he asked almost challengingly, raising an eyebrow.

She opened her mouth and closed it again. She *had* been about to call him a daft so-and-so for saying what he did – as if anything about plain old her could be described as something as grand as that. She took a deep breath. Then squirming with awkwardness at the unaccustomed action, she forced herself to accept the compliment, for his sake if not her own: 'Ta, thanks.'

He grinned slowly. 'You see? That weren't so hard, was it?'

A smile stretched her own mouth. However, moments later, remembering Noah, who was never far from her mind, she was instantly grim-faced once more. She bunched her lips together tightly. 'Well, ta, George. I'm feeling better now,' she lied. 'I'd best get started on my work.'

He looked as if he'd say more but didn't. Instead he nodded, leaving Jenny free to escape and lose herself again in her broodings.

The evening was well under way and Jenny had been kept sufficiently busy, which prevented her from being swamped with her relentless thoughts, much to her relief, when Hyacinth instructed her to empty the pail of slops outside. Jenny did as she'd been bid and after tossing the contents on to the cobbles of the road, she stood wiping her hands on her apron, the empty bucket by her feet, allowing the cold to soothe her flushed cheeks.

A solitary star winked down from the jet sky and she watched it for a moment, wondering if it might be her mother or father visiting to say hello, as Owd Nobby had once told her that's what it meant. To be honest, she didn't really believe it but, nonetheless, in such instances, she was always sure to blow to the heavens a quick kiss. You never could be too sure after all, could you?

Harsh whispering met her ears before she saw the speakers. Lowering her hand from her mouth, she squinted around through the darkness. The silhouettes of a couple – a man and a woman she'd surmise, going by their heights and statures – were conversing by the corner of the road, and it was clear to see that whatever they were talking about was serious in nature. Heads drawn close together and arms folded, they faced one another as though they were opponents preparing to do battle.

Likely man and wife having a spat, Jenny thought idly, turning her back on them and reaching down to retrieve the pail. No doubt the husband had failed to come home, and his long-suffering wife had gone on the hunt for him to beg his return before he could spend the entirety of his wages in the inns and taverns – she'd seen it a number of times over the past week since working at the Balloon.

'Poor cow.' Jenny spoke to herself beneath her breath as she made towards the door. 'Fancy lumbering yourself with an ale-riddled wastrel, who cares naught for his kiddies starving at home. Sod that for a lark! I'd sooner be an owd spinster and alone for evermore than—'

'I *mean* it, Totty.'

Jenny's speech lodged in her throat at the hissed demand that had reached her. She stopped dead in her tracks. There was no room for doubting what she'd heard; the name had definitely been correct. Neither could the subject be anyone else, surely? It just *had* to be the sweep. Slowly, noiselessly, she moved towards the wall and pressed herself against the bricks out of possible sight. Then cocking her head, her heart beating fast, she listened harder.

'Tha knows me.'

The hairs on Jenny's arms leapt to attention. There could be no mistaking that voice. He was speaking loud and clear, now – it *was* that bastard. Her jaw tightened in fury. Drawing on all her strength not to spring for him and pound his face to mush, she forced herself to remain where she was.

'Aye, I do that, all right – only too well!' the sweep's female companion was growling back now.

'Then you'll also know I'm not someone what likes to be crossed.' Totty's words carried a threatening edge to them, but his partner wasn't to be cowed. Though she spoke in a whisper still, her anger was palpable; she came back with a retort without losing a beat:

'I've never been frickened of thee, lad, you know that. Nor am I about to start now, so don't you come the big man act with me. Just you do as I ask and we'll leave it at that.'

There followed a long silence. Holding her breath, Jenny inched a few steps nearer.

Then: 'All right, Coral.'

The flagstones seemed to sway under Jenny's feet. *What?* It couldn't – it couldn't be . . .!

'I have your word?'

'Aye.'

With that, they parted company and walked away in opposite directions.

For her part, Jenny remained exactly where she was, completely immobilised with shock.

Through wide eyes she watched the woman, shawl

pulled up over her head obscuring her features, melt away into the night. Not a sound could have left her lips even if she'd attempted it.

After what felt like an age, she drew into her lungs a large intake of air. Dazed and shaky, she returned to the Balloon.

George was in the middle of a song when she entered but followed Jenny with his eyes as she deposited the pail and went to wipe down some tables. Though feeling in a queer sort of dream, she was aware of his scrutiny and did her utmost to appear natural – an impossible task, however, given what she'd just learned.

Her sister and Vincent Tottington . . .? And that's who it had been, without a shadow of a doubt, she was certain of it. She hadn't needed to hear her voice fully or see her face to be sure. The name alone was sufficient enough. After all, how many women around these parts shared such with her, unusual as it was? And yet . . .

Jenny's brain was in a quandary. Could it really be true? Was there a chance after all, however minuscule, that she was mistaken? For the whole thing made not a jot of sense. How in the world would her sister, prim and proper and the epitome of respectability as she was, be on familiar terms with a drunken, violent, good-for-nothing wastrel like the chimney sweep? And know him well she must, judging by the way she'd spoken. *How?* More to the point, why had Coral never mentioned it to her?

The whys and what ifs continued to plague Jenny

and she was no closer to understanding any of it when she spied George crossing the floor towards her, the first half of his musical repertoire over.

He smiled, and she did her best to return it; however, her efforts were clearly not convincing, for he said, 'Talk to me.'

Feigning ignorance, she asked, 'About what?'

'You're not for letting Totty get away with what he did, are you?'

'What do you think?'

George nodded. 'I thought as much.'

'Well, can tha blame me?'

'Not a bit. What's more, I want to help thee.'

She shook her head emphatically. 'Nay, George.'

'What? Why?'

'Because I don't want thee involved.'

'But—'

'This ain't your fight, George. Whatever's gone on in t' past with you and him is your concern. This, with our Noah . . . this is my business. My battle. I'll be the one to make Totty pay for what he's done here, and me alone.'

'You're afraid I'll get hurt and you don't want to risk that because you're fond of me. Am I right?'

His superlative perception left her stupefied. She made to deny it; however, a blush was creeping up her neck to flood her cheeks – he must surely see it, so where was the point in pretending otherwise? With great reluctance and feeling mightily self-conscious, she shrugged. 'You've been a good friend to me, it's true enough.'

'I'm tougher than I look, you know.'

'Even so . . .'

'Then what *do* you have in mind?'

She'd concocted an idea last night that she was certain she could pull off. Now, though, contemplating uttering the details out loud, she knew a stab of uncertainty. Would he laugh at her, view her scheme as outlandish, foolhardy, try to talk her out of it? Or worse still, would he doubt her ability to succeed? Her pride rising to the fore, she brought her chin up determinedly: 'I'm going to burn his home to the ground. That's right,' she went on when George's eyebrows rose. 'Fight fire with fire, so to speak. Destroy all he holds dear as he very nearly did to me. He likes playing with matches, does he? Well let's see how he likes my game.'

'You know where he dwells, then?'

'Nay,' she admitted, 'but it shouldn't be too hard to find out.'

A lengthy silence followed. Finally, George released a long breath. 'I knew you were a bolshy piece, Jenny, but bloody hell . . . I were thinking more along the lines of jumping him in a dark alley and giving him a damn sound thrashing.'

'You don't think I have the bottle for it, nay?'

'Oh, I do, make no mistake about that.' He shook his head. 'You worry the hell out of me, d'you know that?'

She turned her attention back to the table she'd been cleaning as indication that the conversation was over. Picking up on the hint, George left her be to collect himself an ale.

Later, when their shifts drew to a close, George sought Jenny out once more and offered to walk her home. She thanked him but refused. Though she didn't tell him so, her night wasn't finished with just yet. She had an important call to make before heading back to Nobby's.

After bidding the landlady goodnight with reassurances she felt better now, along with an apology for getting upset as she had upon her arrival, which the woman was quick to pooh-pooh and insist she was always there if ever she needed a chat, Jenny set off into the night. A portion of her wages, sitting snuggly in her underskirt pocket, was a comforting feel pressing against her thigh. She and Noah would be all right for a few days, glory be to God – and kindly Hyacinth.

Despite her hunger for answers, the nearer she got to her destination the more her resolve receded. Upon reaching Carruthers Street, she knew she would have to wait to hear them.

She couldn't confront Coral, not now and at her home. Not only was the hour late but Martin would be present, and that was one thing she wished to avoid. Whatever was going on between Totty and her sister, Jenny would have betted a pound to a pinch of snuff that her brother-in-law wasn't aware of it. Never would he approve of the acquaintance. It would seem she wasn't the only person Coral was keeping secrets from.

No, it would do no one any favours to go in there shouting her head off and demanding to be told the truth. Far better to leave what she had to say until tomorrow when the children were out and Martin was at work.

Even so, still she stood for several minutes staring at the front door and biting her thumbnail, itching inside, knowing she'd never snatch a second of sleep tonight with so many questions swirling inside her head. Finally, the elements won out. With thoughts of a hot cup of tea awaiting her at Nobby's, she heaved a last sigh, tore her gaze from Coral's house and set off in the direction of home.

Noah was up and all smiles when she walked through the door, which warmed Jenny's heart something lovely to see. Now that he spent his days relaxing inside with Nobby, the gruelling toil that had slowly been destroying his small frame as well as his spirit a thing of the past, he'd blossomed. His eyes were brighter, his demeanour likewise. It was as if welcoming back a long-lost relative that she hadn't seen in a while. He was gradually returning to his old self, despite his injuries, and Jenny couldn't have been happier.

'All right?' she asked, removing her shawl and standing with her back to the fire to warm her behind. 'Did Mrs Bullock call round to change your dressings like she said she would?'

'She did. She says my burns are doing gradely, Jen.'

'Thank God for that.'

Her brother nodded. ''Ere, guess who else came earlier as well?' His eyes were shining. 'Our Coral.'

She'd forgotten all about the woman's promise to

114

drop by. Bringing a smile to her lips, she asked, 'Did she indeed?'

'Aye, and oh our Jen, she fetched me a muffin she'd baked fresh. I ate it, sorry.' He laughed sheepishly. 'Reet nice, it were. Oh but look, there, by the hearth: there's crumpets. Coral brought them, an' all. I saved them for you coming home. Three, there is: one for each of us. What a treat, eh?'

She murmured agreement. All the while, the urge to know details of what she'd witnessed earlier had resurfaced stronger than ever. However, she did her best to hide her tumult for the lad's sake. 'Shall we have them now, then?'

Noah eagerly agreed and whilst she bustled about Nobby's fire, spearing each crumpet on the toasting fork and holding it before the flames to brown them off before spreading them with a thin layer of butter, the old man scalded the pot for a cup of tea. All the while, she kept up the general chit-chat – anything to avoid thinking about her sister.

The feast had been over some twenty minutes when she noticed the youngster's eyelids were drooping. It was a contented tiredness, though, she realised, not the half-dead fatigue in which she'd grown accustomed to seeing him. Again, she marvelled anew at the change in, or rather return of, him. By but she loved the little soul, more than anything else in this world and beyond.

'Come on, you,' she said, feeling a tad choked with emotion. 'Let's get you home and into bed, eh?'

'You're all right?' Nobby asked of her discreetly at the door as she made to follow her brother into the street. He scrutinised her more closely. 'You seem like you've summat on your mind.'

'I'm fine.' She hadn't the energy now for explanations. Tomorrow was a new day and would be here soon enough. *And so much rested on it, in more ways than one.*

'You're certain?'

'I am. Ta ever so for keeping an eye to Noah these past days, Nobby,' she added with feeling, slipping her hand into his and squeezing. 'You're a godsend to us and kindness itself, aye.'

'I'm allus here, lass, should tha need me. You know that.'

'I do. Oh, and here.' Reaching into her pocket, she pulled out some coins and placed them into his palm.

'What . . .?'

'For Noah's keep and Mrs Bullock's services.'

'Nay, nay—'

'Go on, take it,' she ordered. 'You've barely two pennies to rub together as it is – I'll not take advantage of your good nature, Nobby. Besides, I need to pay our way. Let me do this. Please.'

With reluctance, he accepted. 'Goodnight, God bless, lass, lad.'

'Goodnight, God bless,' they echoed. 'Sleep well.'

Sleep well . . . Jenny was to reflect on her words hours later as she sat staring into the dying fire, images of Coral and Totty running on a vicious loop

116

in her brain. To all intents and purposes, the old man likely was at least. Her brother certainly was; his soft snores were testament to the fact. As for herself: impossible. She knew she'd never hope to rest again until she got her answers.

Chapter 6

'JENNY. HELLO.'

'Morning, Coral. Can I come in?'

The hour was early. Having seen to Noah's needs, cleaned the cellar and everything in it at least twice and even bought in provisions in readiness for the evening meal, Jenny had run out of things with which to occupy herself. Unable to stand the thought of watching further time crawl by before confronting the woman – her nerves would never have withstood it – she'd admitted defeat and hurried over. She simply *must* hear what Coral had to say.

Gesturing to the table, the woman made to turn in the direction of the fire for the kettle, but Jenny stopped her: 'Forget the tea; I ain't thirsty.'

'Well, I am. It'll not take a min—'

'Please, Coral, sit down. There's summat we need to talk about.'

Frowning at the serious tone, Coral complied. 'Is everything all right?' she asked, lowering herself into the seat opposite. 'Noah? He's not took a bad turn or owt?'

'Nay, it's not that.'

'Then what? Spit it out, will you? You're beginning to worry me.'

Eyes narrowing, Jenny folded her arms. 'How do you know Vincent Tottington?'

'What?'

'You heard. Don't think to deny it, neither. I saw the pair of youse last night with my very own eyes, whispering together in the road.'

Coral's hand snaked to the oval brooch pinned to the high neck of her collar. She cleared her throat: once, twice. 'You're mistaken—'

'Don't *lie* to me, Coral! I saw thee!'

A mammoth sigh seemed to lift Coral from her chair. Hands on hips, she paced the rag-rug in front of the hearth – back and forth, back and forth, eyes wild, as though possessed.

'Coral?'

'I . . . I don't . . .'

'*Coral.* Oh for Christ's sake, sit down, will thee? You're making me dizzy.'

Coral plopped, wringing her trembling hands, back into her seat.

'What the hell's going on? Just tell me, please.'

The woman refused to meet her eye. 'He's . . . just someone I know.'

'Someone . . .? But why have you never mentioned it afore? All the time Noah was working for him – even yesterday, when I told thee what he'd done to the lad . . . you never uttered a word.'

'That's my business!' she cried. Fat tears were

wobbling on her lashes. 'I don't have to run every single aspect of my life past you, do I?'

Jenny was flummoxed. None of this was making sense. 'Now that's daft talk and you know it. What you get up to and with who is no concern of mine . . . but Vincent bloody Tottington? Come on! I had a right to know of that. I did; surely you see it!'

'All right, all *right*.' Coral dropped her head in her hands. 'Just give me a minute to pull my thoughts together . . . I'll explain.'

'Aye?'

She nodded. 'I'll tell thee what tha needs to know.'

Whilst she gathered herself, Jenny poured them out a cup of tea. Watching her sister over the rim of her cup, she took tiny sips of her own drink, her stomach churning with anticipation, and forced herself not to press the woman. The last thing she wanted to do was risk her clamming up altogether and refusing to speak. Thankfully, her equilibrium paid off. Her sister finally raised her eyes to meet hers.

'This ain't easy for me to say . . .'

'It's all right. Take your time.'

'I'm not that person any more, you see. I've tried so hard . . . You'd not believe *how* hard.' Another deep breath, then: 'Me and Totty were friends. Good friends – the best. He . . . We . . .'

'Were youse lovers?' Jenny croaked. *Please, not that!*

'What? Course not, nay!'

'Thank God.'

'I were wicked, Jenny. When I were a lass. The group of friends I got mixed up with, well, they

120

weren't good. I drank, got into bother with the law, caused merry hell in the city—'

'You?' Jenny's mouth was flapping wide. 'I don't believe it.'

'Do, for what I'm saying is truth.'

'But you're so . . . so . . .'

'Straight-laced?'

'Well, aye.'

'I weren't made that way as I think you believe. Nay, I trained myself to be like this. It's the best thing I ever did.'

'Go on.'

'I had to change, you see, were determined, for Mam and Father's sake as much as my own. The stress and worry I caused them . . . I don't know how they bore it and I find it harder still to understand how they put up with all they did from me and managed to ever forgive me.'

'Does Martin know of all this?'

Coral dropped her gaze. 'Aye. He were my saviour, Jenny. I know things between you two are strained, but you have to understand what he did for me . . . he gave me the chance of a new life. A respectable one, aye. That's what I craved. I'll allus be grateful to him for that.'

'Is that why he don't like me?' Jenny mused the question more to herself than to the woman. 'I remind him of you – the old you?'

'How d'you mean?'

'Wild, impulsive, with a gob as big as a train tunnel.'

She looked decidedly uncomfortable, was practically squirming in her seat. 'In a way . . . aye,' she murmured.

Jenny was beginning to understand things a little better now. 'Oh, don't feel guilty, there's no love lost betwixt me and him and never shall be, it's all right—'

'Nay, it ain't all right,' Coral cut in fiercely. Leaning forward, she peered deep into Jenny's eyes. A world of pain was reflected therein. 'He punishes thee for my sins . . . I'll never forgive him for that.'

Feeling a sense of awkwardness at the intensity, Jenny turned the conversation. 'So Totty . . . he were in your gang of friends?'

'That's right. He were a bad 'un even then as kiddies, but never did me no harm. He'd not have dared.' She raised her fists and smiled lopsidedly. 'I were incensed when you told me of our Noah. I never wanted him working for Totty in the first place, couldn't believe my ears weeks ago when you mentioned who the lad had been taken on by.'

'You should have said summat, *warned* us—'

'I should, aye I know, but I couldn't. I couldn't tell thee of my past, were too ashamed. I wouldn't be doing so now if I hadn't been forced to. I knew I were taking a risk confronting him in the street but I couldn't hold back, were that spitting mad. I were on my way back from Owd Nobby's after visiting Noah. Seeing the lad like that, the state of his injuries . . .' She took a ragged breath. 'And so when I spotted Totty sauntering across the road ahead of me, looking like he hadn't a care in the world, summat in me snapped. I couldn't hold back.'

'What did tha say to him? You made him promise summat?'

'Aye, to stop the hell away from the lad and you else he'd have me to answer to. He agreed.'

Leaning back in her chair, Jenny sighed. 'I thank you for it, Coral, but it ain't enough. Not by a long chalk.'

'Stay well clear of him, Jenny. I mean it.'

'He has to pay—'

'And he will one way or another, you can be sure of it. What goes around comes around, after all. But not at your hands. You promised me, remember?'

'I know but—'

'It's over, Jenny.' Her tone brooked no argument and, for the first time, Jenny spied a hint of what this woman used to be like – her steely demeanour was undeniably intimidating. Though Jenny never would have admitted to it, a new level of respect for her sister was born. 'Now he knows who youse are, who you're related to, he'll not bother you no more. Trust me on this.'

'Are you sure you've told me everything?'

'How d'you mean?'

Eyes narrowing thoughtfully, Jenny shook her head. For reasons she couldn't pin down, she had the distinct impression Coral was holding something back. 'I don't know, it's just . . . This don't feel like the whole story. I see it in your eyes. What ain't you telling me?'

Confirming her suspicions, Coral flushed to the

roots of her hair. She held up a hand as Jenny made to probe further. 'You know all you need to. Let's leave it at that.'

'But—!'

'Enough, Jenny.'

'You have summat on him, don't you?' She nodded slowly. 'That's it, ain't it? Is it some crime he committed when you were younger? Did you threaten to inform on him if he didn't do as you say—?'

'I've said all I'm going to. That's an end to it.'

Though Jenny was dying to know, she knew Coral wouldn't be swayed, could see it in the hard gaze, the stiff set of her jaw. With great reluctance, she rolled her eyes and let the matter drop.

'So this position of yourn,' her sister asked some minutes later, pouring them out another cup of tea. She'd reverted to her usual self; it was as if their earlier conversation had never taken place. 'How are you liking it? They're treating you well, aye?'

Jenny nodded. 'I really enjoy it if truth be told.'

'That's good.'

She arched an eyebrow. 'You've changed your tune. You near had a fit when I first told you where I were working.'

'Aye, well. So long as you're getting on and they're looking after you all right . . .' Coral shrugged. 'There's worse things you could be doing to earn a crust, I suppose.'

'Ta, Coral.' Jenny meant it. It was oddly reassuring to know she had the woman's acceptance. 'And guess what? You remember George, who I told you about?

Well, he performs in there most nights – and the other evening, he let me sing with him.'

'You sang? In front of an audience?'

Jenny laughed. 'Aye! D'you know summat, Coral? I bloody loved it.'

'Language, Jenny . . .'

'Sorry, but I did. I were shaking summat awful when I finished, but it were a nice shaky, if that makes sense? The punters said I were good.'

'You are, too. I remember you as a kiddy; you were forever at it. Never shut up, you didn't.' They shared a smile. 'So will tha do it again? Sing, I mean?'

'Nay, I don't think so. I don't reckon George were best pleased with me stealing his limelight. The Balloon's his domain, you see.'

'Then why not find your own?'

'I don't understand.'

'Find your own domain. Surely you don't want to be scrubbing tables and the like for evermore? If singing is what makes you happy the most then do it. Don't settle for summat just because it's easier. You'll look back on life in ten, twenty years' time and kick yourself, lass, if you do.'

When Jenny left Carruthers Street a little later, Coral's words were still spinning inside her mind.

That her sister had even made the suggestion was a shock to her senses. Since their talk about Totty, Coral seemed different somehow – or perhaps Jenny was viewing her in another light now? Either way, Coral opening up to her had shifted something in their relationship, Jenny felt it, and for the better. She'd felt almost as an equal, a friend, to the woman and not as she normally did: a daft child, an annoyance, that Coral couldn't wait to see the back of.

As for the idea itself . . . could she really attempt it? She didn't want to leave the Balloon; the thought pained her. She genuinely liked her time there. There was, however, the few days off during the week when she wasn't working that she might perhaps put to good use . . .?

Happen a few hours singing in another inn on those days? It would work out perfectly if it were possible. She'd still keep her position at Hyacinth's, George wouldn't feel she was putting his nose out of joint, and yet she'd be doing the one thing she loved above all else. Moreover, the extra money would certainly be welcome. It would improve things tremendously for her family.

Her excitement at the tantalising prospect mounting, Jenny quickened her pace. Did she really have the nous to try it, though? she asked herself, self-doubt, as ever, slithering to the fore. That was the question. Then her head went up and she stretched herself to her full height. She could and she would, had to. As Coral had pointed out, she'd only regret it if she let the chance pass her by. Now the seed was sown, she knew there would be no extracting it; there could be no going back, not now.

A conversation she'd had with the landlady days before flitted into her mind and she nodded slowly. Hyacinth had mentioned another pub that had been trying to get George to work for them . . . the Rose and Thistle, was it? She could try her luck there. Aye, why not? Her being employed there, if she was fortunate enough to be taken on, that was, wouldn't upset her friends, would it? George had said himself, had he not, that he hadn't considered it, would never leave the Balloon. And Hyacinth could have no qualms about the decision. She didn't employ Jenny as a singer so surely couldn't feel she was losing her services to a rival establishment.

Jenny knew where the pub in question was located and when she reached the turning to home, she dithered, biting her nails, her eyes flicking in the direction that would take her instead to the Rose and Thistle.

You know what to do, lass. Coral's voice came to her in her mind as though she were standing at her shoulder. *Strike while the iron's hot, there's no time like the present.*

'Aye,' Jenny said to the flagstones. Then with more conviction: 'Aye!'

Striding around, she set off purposely for the pub.

The proprietor was a mountain of a man with deep-set eyes, thick mutton chop whiskers and a frizzy beard that reached down to his midriff. Halting on the threshold, Jenny wondered if she'd done the right thing in coming here after all. He cut a formidable figure; she was immediately tongue-tied. She was just sure he'd tell her to sling her hook.

'And what can I do thee for, then?'

'I . . . hello.' Swallowing down her misgivings, she stepped forward into the gloomy drinking room. 'I heard you might be looking forra singer . . .?'

127

'Did tha now? And who were it told thee that?'

She pointed over her shoulder through the window. 'Hyacinth, landlady of the Balloon down yonder, mentioned it. I sing myself, you see, and I were wondering—'

'Go on, then.'

She blinked, puzzled. 'Go on what, mister?'

'Sing! I wants to hear thee.'

Shaking the shock fog from her brain – she hadn't been expecting the meeting to run this abruptly – she cleared her throat and belted out the first song that came to mind:

> *There was an old woman from Wexford*
> *In Wexford town did dwell,*
> *She loved her husband dearly*
> *But another man twice as well—*

'Nay, nay, nay.' The keeper cut her off with a flap of his hands. 'It's all wrong.'

'Oh, I . . . I could try summat else if—'

'It's not the song what's the problem.'

'Then what?' she whispered.

'It's your voice! 'Tain't right.'

A lump was forming in her throat; she willed herself not to cry. 'But why?'

'Well it's good. Very good, actually.'

What? 'And that's bad?'

'For this place it is, aye. You see, we only hire comic acts to perform here. The customers love it; it's what

128

they want and that's what we give them. So thanks but no thanks. You just don't fit the bill.'

Comic acts? Then that must mean George was only wanted here as a source of ridicule, had to be. Well of all the rotten, nasty . . . He wasn't aware of the real reason, surely not. *Pray God he wasn't.* And Hyacinth? Did she know?

'Now if you don't mind . . .' The keeper flicked his chin to the door. 'I'm a busy bloke.'

'A swine more like,' she threw back before walking out.

Pausing by the roadside, she folded her arms and looked about. She'd started now so she may as well keep going. She wasn't about to let one hiccup scup per her plans.

She'd try every watering hole in the city if that's what it took. And even if she didn't prove successful, well, it wouldn't be from want of trying. At least she'd be able to say she'd given it her all.

'A singer, eh?' asked the keeper of another tavern she enquired at. She tapped her lips with her finger contemplatively. ''Tain't summat I've ever considered, if I'm honest.'

'Would you consider it?' Jenny asked hopefully. 'I can sing you summat, show you what I can do . . .?'

'Nay, no point, lass, I can't afford to pay thee.'

'Oh.' She was crestfallen, though did her best to mask it. 'Ne'er mind, thanks anyway.'

'You'll likely get the self-same answer at most places you try. They'll not mind you entertaining their punters if you can carry a decent tune – myself included – but shan't be too willing to pay you for the privilege.'

'Well I can't do it for nowt – I need the brass.'

'Course you can't, nay,' the woman agreed, 'but there's more than one way to skin a cat.'

Jenny had been making her way to the door. Now, her curiosity piqued, she paused to look back. 'Oh?'

'How's about this: you call in here later on and sing some ditties. Then, when you're done, go round the tables with an empty tankard and ask folk to dig deep in their pockets if they enjoyed what they heard. You're best off making it later in the evening when folk have had a skinful; they'll be inclined to be more generous then. You can but try.'

That worked for her. It was her night off from the Balloon. 'You really wouldn't mind it?'

'Not me. That way, I ain't losing out on money by paying thee and I get to have my customers entertained into the bargain. Win win, so far as I can see.'

Jenny was warming to the idea. 'Will it work, though?'

'Who's to say? You might make a tidy sum, you might make just a farthing or two.'

'Or I might come away with nowt at all.'

'It's the chance you'll have to take. Anyroad, it's up to you, lass. Me, I ain't much fussed either way whatever you decide.'

She mulled the proposition over for a moment. Then, smiling, she nodded. 'Aye, all right, I'll do it. Ta ever so, missis.'

'Gradely. I look forward to seeing you then and I wish yer luck. And call me Margaret.'

Jenny left the premises with a lighter step. Not exactly the outcome she'd dreamed of but it had to be worth a shot, surely? She could always try somewhere else tomorrow if tonight proved unsuccessful.

Aye, she told herself, brightening further. Maybe things hadn't turned out so badly after all.

Time would soon tell.

'I feel sick to my stomach, Nobby, and I don't mind admitting it.' It was almost time to set off for Margaret's tavern and Jenny was a bundle of nerves. 'What if no one likes me?'

He tut-tutted aside her question. 'Now don't be silly. They'll be hallooing for more once they've heard thee.'

She gave him a less-than-convinced smile. He'd been amazed when she'd called in earlier to tell him of her news. Yet, true to form, he'd been generous in his encouragement and faith – and quick to bolster her steadily flagging confidence as the hours wore on. His efforts had, in the main, worked for a time. Now, though, as the appointment drew ever nearer, she was wondering again just what the hell she was letting herself in for.

'I bet you'll be the best everyone's ever heard, our Jen,' Noah announced from the fireside chair. Wrapped snuggly in Nobby's horsehair blanket, he gazed across at her and beamed. 'I'm reet proud to have a sister what's a singer.'

131

'Eeh, lad.' *Just you keep that bonny smile of his in your thoughts,* she added to herself in her mind. *That's why you're doing this remember: for the sake of the child here as much as yourself. So you give over with the moaning and the doubts, and you make the bloody most of it. You never know, Jenny Brodings, you might just enjoy yourself.*

'See you later, lass,' Nobby said as she took a deep breath then reached for her shawl.

'Aye – bye, Jen. Break a leg!'

'Aw, don't be saying that, lad. Knowing my luck, I ruddy will.' She laughed and dropped a kiss on to Noah's brow. A last smile and nod to Nobby then she let herself out of the house.

Margaret greeted her warmly when she arrived. She inclined her head to the swell of customers. 'Norra bad crowd in the night,' she shouted over the din of laughter and general conversation. 'How you feeling?'

'Scared bleedin' shitless,' blurted Jenny, adding, when the woman grinned, 'sorry, ignore me and my midden mouth. I'm nervous is all.'

'Don't fret none, I've heard worse! Right then, you ready?'

'As I'll ever be.'

'Knock 'em dead, lovey.'

Gripping on to the counter for dear life, Jenny half turned towards the room, closed her eyes and began to sing.

Though the noise dimmed, signalling that most people had stopped what they were doing to listen, which was surely a good omen, she didn't dare look around. The number reached its climax and a decent round of applause flooded the room – Jenny's heart was beating fit to burst. She allowed herself a quick glance about before closing her eyes once more and breaking into song again. This time, when she finished, the clapping was accompanied with cheers and the punters' expressions were those of surprise mixed with appreciation. She'd made an impression, positive at that, and she knew it. She could have whooped with glee. Not even if she lived to be ninety could she grow bored of this feeling. Never did she want it to end.

'They like thee, lass, and that can't be a bad thing,' Margaret said, leaning across to whisper in her ear. 'Do another, go on; you've whetted their appetites well enough.'

Jenny did. She belted out song after song and, slowly but surely, her confidence soared. By the time she reached what she'd decided would be her last performance of the night, she'd grown emboldened enough to face her audience head-on. Their acceptance had done wonders for her fledging self-belief and now she was keen to enjoy this to the finish and would remember it for ever. Putting her hands behind her, she felt for the wooden counter and pushed herself, hopping up to perch on its edge. Legs crossed, swaying softly from side to side, she let the flawless notes burst high to stroke the rafters.

The crowd, when she'd finished, moved forward to mill around her and shake her hands. Gazing into the happy faces, Jenny thought she might cry, so immense was her joy and relief.

'Right then.' The landlady had appeared again, only now she carried an empty beer jar. She held it aloft and addressed her customers: 'How's about you show the young 'un just how supportive of that heaven-like voice of hers youse really are – come on, cough up a penny or two for her efforts. She worked ruddy hard there.'

Murmurs of agreement went up. Then, to Jenny's astonishment, the punters duly obliged.

She watched, awe-struck, as coin after coin clinked into the tankard. The vessel was over halfway filled when a smiling Margaret handed it across to her. Scanning the mound of silver and copper, Jenny shook her head. 'Eeh, missis . . . I don't know what to say, I . . . eeh!'

'You earned it, lovey, fair and square.'

'Thank you, Margaret. *Thank* you.'

'Same time next week, aye?'

Nodding her head vigorously, Jenny laughed. 'You just try and stop me!'

She seemed to float through the dark streets shortly afterwards on a cloud of euphoria. She'd done it. She really had! She was a singer, a *singer*. A real one, aye, who performed to a real audience and got paid good brass for the privilege. It truly was a dream come true. Thank the blessed Lord and His holy angels that she'd listened to Coral.

Coral. Jenny's gaze flicked to the opposite corner of the lane. She smiled. In the next moment, she'd picked up her skirts and was running full pelt to Carruthers Street.

'Sorry, Martin, I know the hour's late, only I had to see our Coral to tell her—'

'You're damn right it's late.'

Locking eyes with her brother-in-law, who had answered her knock and was standing with folded arms in the doorway blocking her entrance, his face like thunder, Jenny's hands instinctively bunched into fists. She lifted her chin. 'Like I said, I'm sorry—'

'Nay you ain't,' he threw back, cutting her off once more. 'You've norra considerate bone in your body, girl, and that's your trouble.'

'Now hang on! Just who do you think you—!'

'Martin? Martin, who is it?'

It was Coral. Jenny craned her neck to see over the man's shoulder towards the main room beyond, whence her sister's voice had come.

She opened her mouth again to call to her, but Martin got in first: 'It's no one.' The emphasis he put on the description was painfully clear as he looked Jenny up and down. 'No one at all.'

'You nasty bloody—' However, she hadn't time to finish her sentence. Without further ado, and before Jenny had a chance to halt his action and put her foot in the hall, Martin shut the door in her face.

Her hands were shaking. She raised her fists, intent on battering the wood, but common sense stopped her. All hell would break loose if she woke her nieces and nephews and, besides, furthering the argument would only fuel Martin's temper, and Coral would suffer it the most. Best she waited until tomorrow to try again when he was away at his work. Oh, but what a swine! Why, *why*, did he dislike her so? Just what *was* his issue at all?

He hadn't the faintest idea why she'd come here tonight, hadn't given her even half a chance to explain; for all he knew, her call could have been with regards to Noah. The lad could have taken a turn for the worse, might have been on his deathbed with no time to lose, and yet he cared not a fig. God help him, she'd swing for him one of these days, she would.

Thoughts of her brother as she turned and stalked off in the direction of home soon dampened her anger. He and Owd Nobby would be glad to hear how her night went at any rate. She couldn't wait to tell them. Now, despite everything, a small smile tugged at her mouth. The feeling from earlier, that delicious golden warmth and all-consuming pleasure she'd experienced seeing those folks' faces when she sang, washed through her again; it was like a drug almost. She could get drunk off this sensation. She reckoned the addiction that was slowly but surely forming within her wouldn't be too dissimilar neither.

Sure enough, when Jenny regaled Noah and the elderly man on the events of the night, they were almost as delirious with genuine excitement as she was herself. She could have kissed them – and did – for their unquestionable love and unwavering support. They, at least, were sure to never let her down.

'Will tha sing summat now, our Jen? Just for me?' the lad asked sleepily some time afterwards, when they were snuggled against the chill in their sacking bed.

Just for you . . . *All of it, everything, is always just for you.* 'Course I will.'

Later, when Noah was slumbering peacefully, Jenny slipped from beneath the covers and padded across to the far wall. Running her fingertips across the lip of a slightly protruding half-brick midway up, she closed her nails on it and jiggled it until it loosened. Then taking care not to make too much noise and with her tongue poking out of the side of her mouth, she eased the masonry out of its hole.

The narrow cavern it had exposed held a grubby cloth secured at the neck with a scrap of twine. This she undid and carefully opened out the material on the floor. Pennies, half pennies and farthings, which she'd secreted earlier, winked back at her in the light from the candle stuck to the saucer on the mantel top. Astonishingly, there were even a few sixpences contained in the riches. Again, she shook her head in wonder.

All this in just a single night! Again, and doing her best not to disturb her brother, she counted it through and let out air slowly. Four shillings and thruppence ha'penny. She could barely believe it still. By but they would be in clover, all right, if she could keep this up. *Please God.*

Bundling the mound up, she stuffed the pouch in the wall once more and replaced the brick. Then with a smile in her heart, she returned to the bed.

'Just for you.' Jenny spoke the words aloud now in a gentle whisper to her brother. 'This is only the beginning, lad.'

Chapter 7

GEORGE AND HYACINTH were agog the next evening
when Jenny informed them of the bold new develop-
ments. Eyes wide, mouths agape, they stared back at
her as though she'd gone and spouted a second head.
At last, Jenny threw her hands in the air.

'Say summat then? Are youse angry? Is that it?'

Their responses mirrored one another – putting
back their heads, they laughed heartily.

'Angry?' Hyacinth spluttered.

'Aye, angry?' echoed George.

'Now why would we be that, you daft thing, yer?'
The woman put her arm around Jenny's shoulders
and drew her in close for a hug. 'It's a shock is all. A
good 'un, mind you.'

'You'll do gradely, Jenny. I'm that proud of thee.'

Tears pricked her eyes for these people she was
privileged to call her friends. She returned Hyacinth's
embrace then glanced up shyly at George. 'You mean
it? You do, really?'

'Well of course, lass! You've a belting voice, aye. I'm

only surprised you ain't been snapped up by some place afore now.'

The tension seemed to rise from her in a rush; she heaved a relieved sigh. 'Eeh, what I can do with the extra money . . . I'll not lie to youse, I'm fair walking on air and that's the truth.'

Already she'd begun to put ideas in place with what she'd do with the surplus income. Once the rent was paid and she'd budgeted for food and coal for the week, whatever was over would be added to the pot behind the brick. She surmised that in a few weeks she'd have enough put by to fulfil her quest: turning their run-down dwelling into a decent and comfortable home, as it used to be before her parents died.

Firstly, Jenny planned to have the cellar walls and ceiling freshly whitewashed. Blackened with soot and damp as they were, that was bound to brighten the room up no end. She could hardly wait to see the transformation. Next on her list would be the purchasing of a proper bedstead and mattress and more adequate coverings. She and Noah would share this for a time until she'd saved the funds to buy a second one. Imagine it, a bed each all to themselves! Finally, she'd scour the local pawnshops and pick up some inexpensive odds and ends to chase away the bareness: several ornaments, a rug for in front of the hearth, a cheap framed painting or two for the walls, that sort of thing.

It seemed such a marvel to picture it coming to fruition. After living such a dogged and grinding hand-to-mouth existence for so long it would be wonderful to have a little disposable brass to do with as she liked and improve the way they lived. It could only benefit Noah, too? He'd surely be much happier in cheerier surroundings. Aye, in time, they would be giving Coral and her enviable home a run for their money! Jenny was determined.

She'd called at her sister's house earlier before coming to the Balloon, but to her disappointment there had been no answer. She longed to tell Coral that her suggestion had worked, how well she'd done at Margaret's tavern. As with George and Hyacinth, Coral would be proud too, she was sure. She craved this, Jenny realised to her surprise. The older woman's approval was important to her, however much she might have told herself otherwise in the past. Since Coral had opened up to her, she'd begun to view her differently. The heart-to-heart had drawn them closer somehow. She wanted her attention, her company. She wanted her love.

Some half an hour later, the inn filled already with thirsty patrons, it was as though she'd conjured her up: Jenny, feeling a tap on her shoulder, turned to find Coral standing behind her.

'Hello, lass.'

'Coral! What's tha doing here?'

'I were just passing, thought I'd show my face. You all right?'

'I am.' She pointed to a nearby table. 'Can I get thee a sup of summat?'

'Nay, nay.' The woman appeared horrified at the

prospect. Though at one time, her act of superior derision would have annoyed Jenny, now she found herself smiling. 'I can't stop long,' Coral added. 'Thanks all the same for the offer.'

'So. You're all right, an' all, aye?' Jenny asked when they had moved to a less busy nook.

'Aye. And Noah, he's doing well?'

Jenny nodded. Her gladness at the unexpected visit was strong; in an unaccustomed display, she squeezed Coral's arm. 'I'm happy tha came.' She knew what it must have taken for the woman to act so, and just to see her, given Coral's stance on rigid propriety. 'I really am.'

'That's all right.'

''Ere, guess what?' Jenny couldn't stem the grin that had sprung to her face. 'I gorra job, singing.'

'Nay!'

'Aye! Just like you said I ought to. I performed last night for the first time. Eeh, Coral, it were magic.'

The woman's smile matched her own. 'Eeh, that's gradely, lass. It's all right though, is it, where you've been taken on? Decent like?'

'It is, aye, and Margaret, that's the landlady, she's ever so nice.'

'Well I'm that pleased for thee, Jenny. See, what did I say, eh, I told yer you could do it. You'll go far, you will, lass.'

Jenny preened, smiled. 'Ta, thanks.'

'I do wish you'd have come and seen me, mind, informed me of the good news sooner.'

'I tried to, earlier on.' Though she wasn't sure why,

she thought it best not to mention the visit before that and her set-to with Martin. Coral would likely only take his corner and attempt to dilute his horrible behaviour, as was normally the case, and right now Jenny didn't think she'd bear that. Besides, what would the admission achieve? What was done was done, after all. 'You weren't in.'

'Aye, I'd nipped across to a neighbour's house. Sorry, lass.'

'It's all right. You know now, eh?'

They shared another smile.

'Happen I could stop by this other place one evening and watch you in action. Would that be all right?'

Emotion balled in Jenny's throat. Unable to speak, she could but bob her head.

'Well, I'd best be making tracks. I'll be seeing thee.'

'Aye.'

'Goodnight, God bless.'

'Night, God bless, Coral.'

When Coral had gone, Jenny knuckled her eyes and returned to her duties. These last few days had been truly wonderful, some of the best of her life without question. She just prayed her run of good fortune didn't turn anytime soon.

George made a beeline for her the moment his repertoire finished for his midway break. 'Did that wench upset thee?' he asked. 'You look as though you've been crying.'

'Nay, norra bit – Coral's my sister. She just called in to say hello is all.'

The worry melted from his eyes. He smiled. 'I were

142

fretting it might have summat to do with your little brother . . . Noah, is it?'

'That's right. But nay, the lad's doing fine, glory be.'

'So . . .?'

Pausing in her task of wringing out into the pail hooked over her arm the ale-sodden cloth she'd been using to clean up a spillage, she frowned. 'So what?'

'Totty.'

Her mouth hardened instantly. 'What about him?'

'Has tha given further thought on what we were talking about? You know, about you burning—'

'I remember well enough – and keep your voice down,' she hissed, glancing from side to side for possible eavesdroppers. The last thing she wanted was for word to somehow get back to the chimney sweep and all hell breaking wide. 'And in answer to your question: nay. It ain't much been in my thoughts, to be honest.'

'You mean you've changed your mind? Eeh, thank God—'

'That's not what I'm saying . . . at least I don't think it is. It's just . . .' She shook her head. 'Oh, I don't know.'

Truth was, since she'd been getting along better with Coral, she was reluctant to go behind her back on this. She'd promised the woman she'd leave it in her hands now, that she wouldn't think to wreak revenge, and it pained her physically to think of breaking her word and jeopardising Coral's new-found trust in her. And yet . . . still, at the memory of

143

dear Noah and what he'd gone through at that beast's hands, she was engulfed with such an all-consuming, murderous rage that it left her shaking. She felt torn – to do right by one sibling meant failing the other. It was a horrible position to be in.

'Should summat go wrong . . .' George breathed deeply. 'Bastard or no, that man ain't worth hanging for, Jenny.'

'I spoke to my sister about it. By all accounts, Totty has had a warning to leave us be.'

'Well that's good, eh?'

'But is it enough? You see, I can't fathom how it can ever be after all he's done. He ought to suffer. Bad, like, aye. I want him to *pay*.'

George stared at her for a long moment. Though he didn't voice it, she knew by the expression in his eyes that his sentiments matched hers completely. 'He'll get his comeuppance, Jenny, somehow or another. You can be sure of it.'

'Aye?'

He nodded. 'Steer well clear and leave his punishment to God to deliver. All right?'

'We'll see.'

'For me?'

Watching Noah stroke the thin grey cotton shirt and dark fustian trousers and jacket with such tenderness brought an ache to Jenny's chest.

Purchased that afternoon from a stall on Smithfield Market, they were far from new – fourth, fifth or even sixth hand, she'd have wagered. However, the lad was over the moon and stars to have received them. She doubted whether he'd have been more grateful had she handed him the finest flannel shirt and a suit made of the best broadcloth. By, but he really was a little love with a heart as pure as new snow. She ruffled his hair.

'They're warm at least, shall keep the frost from your bones well enough, eh, lad?'

His head went up and down in ready agreement. 'They're great, our Jen, thanks. I'll look after them, I swear. You're the bestest big sister ever.'

She'd decided to rig him out last night. Sewing yet another patch on to the knee of his old trousers – a futile act at best when the things were rotten and falling to bits from his former toil – she'd pricked her finger on the needle for a third time before with a growled curse finally admitting defeat. Sucking at the droplets of blood, she'd dashed the garment to the ground in disgust. The rest of his meagre clothing, she'd soon realised, upon thorough inspection, was in an equally dreadful state of disrepair. Therefore, her decision to break into the pouch of money had been a necessary one, she reckoned.

Full winter weather would be breathing down their necks very soon. The child couldn't very well be walking about with the arse hanging out of his trousers and his too-small jacket, the cuffs already up to his elbows, but a few inches off resembling a waistcoat, could he? Besides, the pleasure on his face would have been worth the money she'd spent thrice over. Luckily, his clogs still held life in them yet.

'What did you get for yourself, Jen?'

The question threw her for a moment but she regained her composure quickly. Hugging herself to hide discreetly the shattered material of her bodice by her underarms, she tossed her head with a false air of nonchalance. 'Me? Oh nothing. There were nowt I needed.'

This placated him and with a swallowed sigh she turned her attention to preparing their meal.

This evening was to be her second stint at Margaret's tavern. Despite the wonderful reception last time, still her insides were in knots at the prospect of singing to a crowd again. Nerves – or was it excitement? She couldn't rightly differentiate, knew only that she would see the performance through no matter what. She'd begin to enjoy herself after a while, this she was sure of. It was what she loved doing after all. She could only pray that the appreciative listeners would again prove as generous.

Much to her overwhelming relief, her wishes were realised later. Once again, the punters were free with not only their praise but their brass. Jenny was cock-a-hoop. She'd have guessed she'd earned tonight around the same sum as before, if not a little more. She and Noah would be millionaires if she kept this up!

After bidding Margaret goodnight, Jenny donned her shawl and, with a spring in her step, set off. A man drinking alone near the tavern door smiled and touched his narrow-brimmed hat as she passed; without giving him a second's thought, she smiled back and stepped outside.

Jenny had reached the turning of the street when something, she didn't know what, made her look back. In the doorway of the tavern she'd just vacated stood a figure – and it was evident he was watching her. Brow creasing, she squinted harder in an attempt to identity him if she could. However, it was too dark to make out any features. Just then, he struck a match and held it to the pipe between his teeth. In the flash of lurid light, she caught clearly his illuminated face: it was the man who had doffed his hat to her as she was leaving.

For a few moments more, she continued to stare, her mind a muddle of questions. But he made no attempt to approach her, moved not an inch, simply looked straight back as he calmly smoked his tobacco. Jenny, however, wasn't mollified. His scrutiny and the unknown reason behind it unnerved her. Suddenly acutely aware of her vulnerable state, she pulled her shawl closer around herself. A last glance at him then she turned and hurried on for home.

The incident was still on her mind the following day when she arrived at the Balloon for her shift. Yet, for the same reason she'd held off from telling Owd Nobby upon arriving back last night, she now refrained from making mention of it to George: the pair would only fret. When all was said and done, it could all have been perfectly innocent. She might well be making something out of nothing. The man hadn't followed her, had he? She saw therefore no real point in worrying her friends unduly.

Nonetheless, when work was over and George

made his usual offer to walk her home, Jenny agreed. Better to be safe than sorry.

On the journey, she regaled him with how well her singing had again gone down the night before. 'I'm saving up, you see,' she added, turning to him to wink.

George laughed. 'Oh aye, what for?'

'I'm going to spruce up our dwelling. It's in a shocking state, George.'

'What needs doing, then?'

She explained about the painting. 'That'll be the first job. I plan to make a start the morrow.'

'You know what you're doing, then, aye?'

'Not really.' She shrugged. 'It can't be that hard, can it?'

'I could help.'

'Aye?'

He nodded. 'I'll be at yours in t' morning at say . . . ten o'clock? Have the whitewash ready for me. I'll have it finished in no time at all.'

'Eeh, nay, I couldn't . . .'

'Why not?'

'Well, your free time is yours alone. I'll not ask thee to fritter it on me.'

'You never asked, though, did you? I offered. Besides, if it needs doing as badly as you say, it'll be time used wisely, won't it? Productively, aye.'

A grin crept over her face. She stuck her nose in the air. 'Pro-duc-tive-ly . . .' she drawled. 'By, that's a mouthful. Very gentry-like, I must say.'

'I'm full of big words, me.'

Jenny was much enjoying the repartee. 'Go on then, tell me another.'

Screwing up his eyes, he thought for a minute and chuckled when she laughed. 'Hang about, let me pick a good 'un . . . Ah. Aye.' His face had cleared. He nodded. 'Pulchritudinous.'

'Pah! You're just making these up!'

'I am not.'

'Nay?'

'I learned it from a toff what came in the Balloon one time. Been on a supping spree, he had, and finished up wandering into the slums. He had a grand ol' day mixing with the lowly class by all accounts. Mind you, I don't reckon he made the mistake a second time. He'd been robbed blind by the punters afore he ever made it home, daft bugger. Aye, taught me a few nice words that night, he did. So there you have it.'

'Then what the divil does it mean?'

'Well . . . it's you. You're pulchritudinous.'

'Oh, thank you very much, I don't think! It sounds bleedin' awful.'

George's eyes were soft. He smiled. 'It ain't, lass. It's a compliment, trust me.'

It most likely meant bull-headed or some such, a trait which he seemed to find amusing in her, she surmised. Jenny could think of nothing else it could be, not when describing herself. 'Aye, well, anyroad . . .' She motioned to the door a few steps away. 'This is me. If you're sure about helping, we'll see thee the morrow then?'

'You will. I look forward to it.'

'Night, George. And thanks.'

He stroked her cheek, turned and walked away.

Reaching up to cup the spot where his touch still lingered, she smiled and headed inside.

'Hello, young man. I've heard a lot about you – it's very nice to meet yer.'

Noah's gap-toothed smile was wide. 'Hello, nice to meet thee too, Mr Sixsmith.'

'Oh, call me George, please.'

'All right, George.'

'Good lad.'

Watching from the bottom of the cellar steps, wearing her mother's old apron and a scarf wrapped around her head in preparation to protect her hair from paint splatters, Jenny felt a warmth seep through her witnessing the pair's introduction. They were going to get along just fine, she could tell.

'I've scrubbed down the walls and ceiling in readiness, George,' she informed him, sweeping the space with her arm. 'And I went out early and bought the whitewash; it's all ready.'

'You've got brushes?'

'A neighbour were kindly enough to lend me the use of a few. They're half bald but shall have to do.'

Giving the bristles the once over, George nodded. 'These'll do well enough.'

'Will tha take a sup of tea afore we start?'

'Aye, go on.'

The trio chatted about the room, pointing things

out and offering suggestions for improvements, as they sipped their drinks. Though she noticed George glance more than once at Noah's bandages, Jenny was grateful that the man didn't make mention of it. Her brother, excited at the notion of the task to come, appeared the most animated she'd seen him in many a long day; to mar his mood would have upset her tremendously.

For his part, George seemed wholly comfortable in his surroundings. She had initially known a throb of embarrassment at letting him see their dismal living conditions; however, she should have guessed that she needn't have harboured worries on that score. George wasn't one to cast judgement. He certainly wouldn't make a body feel bad, and especially for reasons out of their control, if he could avoid it.

They got to work soon afterwards and within minutes were well under way. Standing on the table, which he'd dragged into the centre of the floor, George began on the ceiling whilst Jenny and Noah made a start on the far wall. Whilst they painted, Jenny and George hummed songs that they sang at their respective works, with Noah joining in at the parts he knew. All in all, it made for a happy team.

Everything was going smoothly until Jenny lifted an arm to wipe perspiration from her brow. It was the hand in which she held the brush, and the motion caused a spray of whitewash to escape the bristles. The droplets sploshed in a horizontal line along her brother's neck. Letting out a screech, Jenny fell about giggling.

'Aw, our Jen!' Drawing back his arm, Noah flicked his brush in retaliation. His cheers, when his target hit its mark, rang around the room: 'Gotcha!'

'Why, you ruddy young . . . Right then! Watch this!'

'Come on, you two, that's enough,' George intervened, chuckling, as the siblings grappled with one another, daubing every inch of the other's skin they could find, helpless with laughter. 'There'll be none left for the room if youse carry on—'

'Cop for that!'

George gasped as Jenny swept her sopping brush the length of his face. For a moment, he gazed at her in dumb shock. Then he was grinning and rushing across the floor for his revenge.

'Eek! George, don't you bleedin' dare!'

So immersed were the three of them in their playful fight that none noticed the front door opening or that anyone else was there until a voice shouted over the melee: 'What on earth . . .?'

'Oh. Coral.' Breathless and with tears of merriment coursing down her cheeks, Jenny could barely get the greeting out. 'Hello.'

The woman made her way inside and looked about, open-mouthed. 'I thought I'd call round, see how Noah was doing . . . You're making improvements to the room?'

'We were, our Coral,' Noah chortled. 'But then our Jen got whitewash on me and then—'

'I think I can guess the rest, lad,' she interjected, shaking her head and smiling. Her stare came to rest on a rather sheepish-looking George and her expression turned curious. 'I don't think we've met, Mr . . .?'

'This is George, who I work with,' Jenny informed her. 'He offered his services.'

'Pleased to meet thee,' he said, running a hand through his dripping hair. 'Sorry about all this . . . we got carried away.'

'Don't be sorry. You're young people having fun; there's no crime in it, lad,' said Coral. She glanced around. 'Do you have another brush?'

Jenny thought her ears were deceiving her. She blinked in disbelief. 'You mean you're for helping us? You?'

Removing her shawl, Coral nodded. 'Aye, why not?'

Because you're the very last person in the world I'd have imagined getting stuck into something like this! Because you're not exactly one to get your spotless hands and clothing dirty, that's why! The thoughts ran through Jenny's mind whilst, doing her best not to dissolve into laughter again, she murmured, 'Oh nothing . . . ignore me. Aye, we'd be reet grateful for your help.'

An hour later, four tired and mucky but extremely pleased workers downed tools with nods and sighs of satisfaction. The space looked marvellous; it was now like a totally different room.

'Have I to brew a pot of tea?' asked Coral.

Pressing her fingertips into the small of her aching back, Jenny groaned with pleasure. 'Eeh, yes please.'

'In that case, my contribution will be a bite of dinner.' George donned his jacket and cap. 'A beef and tatty pie from that inn on t' corner do thee?'

'Sounds gradely!' Noah chirruped, whilst the women answered in the affirmative.

'On me – I insist,' George added when Jenny made to press coins into his hand. 'I'll not be gone long.'

'He seems nice,' remarked Coral, as her sister suspected she would, when he left.

Hoping a blush wouldn't surface, Jenny nodded. 'He is, aye.'

'Handsome, an' all.'

Jenny didn't respond to this. Instead, she busied herself with rinsing out the cups. Thankfully, her silence did the trick – in the next moment, Coral had changed the subject.

Owd Nobby called by as they were tucking into their hot feast. Jenny welcomed him in, growling as she hurried across to help him down the stairs, 'I must get these soddin' things fixed.'

'I can remedy that. I know a bloke what I reckon will let me have some wood on t' cheap.'

'That's kind of thee, George! Ain't that kind of him, Jenny?' Coral gushed.

Her sister's intentions at selling the man to her were painfully obvious – to Jenny, at least. She felt her colour begin to rise.

'It is, aye,' she said a little too sharply, her irritation with Coral spilling over. 'But I can't accept, George. You've done enough already.'

'Stuff and nonsense! It's no bother; I've hardly done owt. Besides, them stairs can't stay as they are. Take the shine away from the nice fresh walls, they do.' He tapped the side of his nose. 'Leave it with me.'

'Here, Nobby,' Jenny said, switching the conversation to something less awkward – she could kill their Coral for interfering. Breaking her pie in half, she passed a hunk across. 'Get that down thee.'

'Looks lovely in here, now, aye,' the old man announced through a mouthful of thick pastry. 'Done well youse have.'

'Aye, we make a good team ' Coral began. However, she hadn't time to finish her sentence. A thunderous knocking cut her off and she held a hand to her heart. 'Who the divil . . .?'

Jenny was equally mystified. Frowning, she went to answer the door.

'Where is she?'

'What? Who—?'

'Who the hell d'you think, eh?' Martin bellowed over her. He shoved her aside and stumbled into the cellar. 'Ah, here she is.' He stabbed an accusing finger towards his wife. 'Surprise sur-bloody-prise.'

It was clear to everyone that he'd been drinking. His eyes were mere slits in his ruddy face and he was swaying on the spot. Jenny stepped in front of him. 'I think you'd better leave. Now.'

Looking straight past her as though she was invisible, he let his shoulders rise and fall. 'Well?' he threw at Coral. 'Nowt to say for yourself, nay?'

'I'm sorry, Martin. I hadn't noticed the time . . .'

'Coral, you don't have to go,' Jenny told her sister through gritted teeth as she moved to collect her shawl, her eyes downcast. 'You've a right to visit us if you choose – and don't let no bugger tell you different,' she finished, looking with undisguised disgust at Martin.

'Why don't you keep your poky little nose out of other folks' damn business?' he yelled, rounding on her. 'Allus have to jump in, don't you, with that venomous tongue. You ought to learn when to shut tha trap.'

Jenny didn't flinch. Squaring her shoulders, she stared him straight in the eye. 'And who's going to teach me?' she murmured. 'What, you? Huh. I'd like to see thee try.'

His face turned mauve with fury. On a roar, he drew back his hand. Coral let out a strangled cry.

'I wouldn't do that if I were thee.' Having jumped between Martin and Jenny, George's tone was like granite. 'Get your ale-sodden arse out of here right now or I'll make you sorry, mister.'

The men stared one another out. It was Coral who broke the charged silence. On a drawn-out sigh, she crossed the room, saying with a note of weariness over her shoulder, 'Martin, let's go home.'

'Coral.' Having followed the couple to the street, Jenny was trembling with helplessness and tears of frustration burned her eyes. 'You'll be all right?'

Her sister flashed her the ghost of a smile. She nodded. 'Goodbye, lass.'

'Goodbye . . .'

'Well, what a—' Glancing to Noah, who had run to Owd Nobby during the argument and was sitting pale, his eyes huge in his pinched face, George stopped himself from uttering an expletive, asking instead, 'Is he allus like that?'

'Nay,' Jenny was forced to admit. 'I've never afore seen Martin so bad.'

'He wouldn't really have struck you, would he?'

'I don't know.' Truth was, the incident had shaken her. She couldn't be entirely sure any more. 'He's gone down with the madness, I reckon.'

'Your sister? She'll be all right with him in that state?'

Jenny nodded. 'Oh aye, she knows how to deal with Martin. Poor cow's had practice aplenty there.'

Later, when George had left, telling her he'd see her that evening at the Balloon, and Noah had gone into Nobby's to keep the old man company and enjoy with him a game of cards, Jenny sat and looked about. She watched in her mind's eye the scenes from earlier: the fun and laughter they had had with the paint fight, the sing-songs and lively chatter, and the sense of heartening accomplishment when the job was completed. The memories would remain, and the room still looked amazing. However, the happiness of the day was tarnished for her now. Martin's vicious and violent outburst had taken centre stage in her head and she was unable to banish it.

Something Jenny was in the dark about was playing out with him and Coral, and that something was both unnerving and disturbing. Martin was getting worse, it was clear to see. But what was the reason? What had changed recently that could make him switch from harmless indifference to downright unpleasant? It was fast becoming unbearable. She was nearing the end of her tether with the family friction. God only knew how much worse her sister was feeling. Yet what could Jenny do to try to understand, let alone attempt to help if she could, when Coral wouldn't open up to her?

Whatever the solution was, none of them could carry on like this for very much longer. Something would have to give, and soon.

Chapter 8

JENNY SAW NOTHING of Coral for three days. During the late morning of the fourth, and much to her relief, she opened the door to find her sister standing there, seemingly unaffected and wearing a smile.

'Can I come in?'

'Aye, course.'

'Oh.' Gazing with approval at the newly fitted stairs, Coral nodded. 'George came through for thee then as he said, I see.'

'He did. Come on down and I'll pour thee some tea. I've not long since brewed a fresh pot.'

Sitting facing one another at the table, they conversed somewhat awkwardly over the general mundanities of life: the children's health and the weather, that sort of thing. Finally, when all else was exhausted, Jenny gave voice to the one subject still unspoken but which was suffocating the room with its cloying presence.

'Coral, about Martin.'

Dipping her chin, Coral closed her eyes. 'Aye.'

'Just what the hell *was* all that last week? I've never seen him like that. Fair shocked me, it did.'

'He don't touch me, you know.' The woman shook her head emphatically and Jenny saw without question she told the truth. That was one consolation, she supposed. 'He's never laid even a finger on me during our marriage, he wouldn't do that.'

'But the bellowing and the nastiness . . . it's bad enough on its own, Coral.'

'I know. He don't mean it, it's the drink. He's allus sorry after the fact.'

Her sister had tears in her eyes. Leaning forward, Jenny chose her words carefully. 'Why *is* he supping enough to sink a small ship all of a sudden? Why's he changed so, what's the reason for it?'

'Lass . . .'

'You can tell me, Coral. I ain't a daft kid no more – talk to me. Happen I can help.'

A mirthless snort left her sister. She smiled sadly and patted Jenny's hand. 'You can't, but I thank thee for thinking it all the same.'

'You'll not tell me what's afoot?'

'Nay. It's a private thing betwixt man and wife. But know this: none of it is your fault. However horrible he is with thee, whatever words he might spew . . . he's the one in the wrong. You've done nowt to warrant it. You'll remember that, won't you?'

In response, Jenny nodded. What else was there to do? She couldn't very well pin the woman down and extract the truth from her with brute force, could she? If Coral wanted to spill her guts, confide in her about her troubles, then she would. Until then, Jenny had no other choice but to let the matter drop.

Brighter now, she asked, motioning to the cloth bundle in Coral's arms, 'What's that you've got there?'

'Oh aye, I nearly forgot . . . Here.' She placed it on the table.

'Eeh, Coral . . .' Having peeled back the material, Jenny scanned the contents in awe. 'For us?'

'Aye, for t' house. 'Tain't much I know, but well, happen they'll help cheer the place up further.'

'Oh no, they're lovely. Ta, thanks.' Jenny recognised them as being from her sister's own home. A vase in blue and white, two brown dog ornaments, a pretty glass dish with roses patterned along its base . . . 'I'll treasure them.'

'Right, well, I'd best be getting back.'

'Aye, all right.'

'Ta for the tea.'

'Anytime, Coral, you know that. 'Ere,' she added on impulse when the woman was climbing the stairs, 'it's my shift at Margaret's tavern the night. You said you'd like to see me sing . . . happen you could slip in forra bit later on?'

'Aye.' She smiled. 'Happen I could.'

When she'd gone, Jenny spent some time arranging and admiring her new pieces on the mantel top, moving them this way and that until she was satisfied. It had been such a kind gesture of Coral's; she was truly grateful. They made all the difference to the room.

She arrived at work later to find her sister there already and standing by the counter. Pleasure burst through her chest. Hurrying across to her, Jenny pulled her into a quick hug. 'Eeh, you came!'

'Aye and you'd better be good.'

Throwing back her head, Jenny laughed.

Coral stayed for three songs before making back for home, but not until she'd showered Jenny with much praise. Jenny had watched the woman as she sang and it had touched her in ways she hadn't anticipated. Coral had been transfixed, her eyes shiny with tears. It felt so good to know she had her support and approval.

The evening was drawing to an end when a figure entered the tavern.

Jenny was midway through one of her favourite ballads but she spotted him – and his identity – right away. It was the man who had been watching her outside the last time she'd performed here.

Why in the world was he back? However, now wasn't the time for speculating – she must concentrate on the task in hand. The last thing she needed was to trip over her notes or forget the lyrics – it might well make all the difference to her earnings. With effort, she pushed him from her mind.

Afterwards, when she was going around the room shaking her tankard collecting her money, she purposely made a point of avoiding him. He hadn't taken his eyes off her from the moment he'd arrived, watching her intently throughout every song. Something about him put her immediately on her guard. She'd have to have a word with Margaret, she decided. This wasn't mere paranoia as she'd previously assumed.

He was clearly here to see her and her alone. The fact he wasn't here to drink – he'd ordered but a single ale and had barely taken a sip of it – was proof enough.

'Excuse me?'

It was him. He was calling to her.

Jenny feigned ignorance and pretended not to have heard.

'Young lady, over here.'

People were beginning to stare. She couldn't ignore him for much longer without appearing rude to the onlookers.

With great reluctance, she zig-zagged her way through the tables towards him.

'Sublime. Absolutely outstanding.' He dropped a large coin into the tankard.

Giving it a cursory glance, then doing a double take – a whole crown? Ruddy hell! – Jenny gasped. 'Mister . . . that's too much, surely?'

'Nonsense. You deserve it and more.'

'Well . . . thank you.' Dizzy with joy – she'd never even seen a crown before, never mind been in possession of one – she was unsure what to do now. She shifted awkwardly on the spot. 'I'm pleased you liked my singing, mister. I must get going now—'

'Wait. Can we talk?'

'About what?'

He inclined his head to the vacant seat at his table. 'Please, sit. Don't worry, I'll not keep you from your hearth long.'

Jenny did as he'd bid, perching on the very edge of the chair. 'Well?'

'What's your name?'

'Jenny Brodings.'

'Sol. It's a pleasure to make your acquaintance.'

Her stare flicked to the hand he'd held out to her. Resisting the urge to roll her eyes, she gave it a quick shake.

'I've been watching you—'

'I noticed,' she cut in. 'Why was that?'

'I wanted to speak with you but haven't found the right moment until now. You see, Jenny . . . May I call you Jenny or would you prefer Miss Brodings?'

Despite herself, she couldn't help but feel flattered that he'd taken pains to ask. His manners were impeccable; she couldn't fault those, at least. 'Jenny's fine.'

'You see, Jenny, I think you have one of the most beautiful voices I've ever heard. I also think you're wasted here.' He took a swig of his beer and grimaced before continuing. 'I have a proposition for you. I'd like you to come and work for me.'

'Eh?' She shook her head in confusion. 'Work for thee? Where, what as?'

'As a singer of course! As for where: are you familiar with Solomon's, the music hall?'

She thought for a second then shook her head. 'Nay, I don't think . . . Hang on. Solomon's? As in Sol – you?'

He smiled.

'You own your own music hall?' Her eyes were wide and a funny sort of tingling was spreading throughout her body. 'Eeh, mister.'

'You catch on quick, young lady.'

Jenny could barely believe what she was hearing. This wasn't happening, couldn't be. Not to her. A position, a proper one, in a proper music hall, as a professional singer? God above, how? She was dreaming, had to be!

She cleared her throat and shook her head. 'Sorry, it's just . . . it's a shock, aye.'

'I understand. Take your time.'

'Mister, are you sure you want me?' she asked after some minutes. 'You've not made a mistake?'

'Definitely no mistake, Jenny. You've a remarkable talent.'

'I . . . have?' Her head was swimming. To hear such words from a man of his standing, a man who must work with dazzling and sensational performers every day of his life? He truly deemed her worthy enough to be on a similar par? Could it actually be true?

'You have and more, with plenty to spare.'

'I . . . *Thank* you, mister.'

Sol accepted her words with a half bow. 'Now then. Wages. Would, hm, let's say . . . three pounds a week suffice?'

Jenny's jaw almost hit the table.

'Does that suit you?'

Incapable of speech, she goggled back dumbly.

'I can see you need some time to mull over my offer. Go home, get some rest, and come and see me at Solomon's tomorrow afternoon. We can discuss all the details then.'

'Aye . . . Yes . . .'

Sol touched the brim of his hat, smiled and disappeared from the tavern.

For how long Jenny sat on, gazing unseeing at the door, she couldn't say.

Eventually, Margaret approached her. 'You all right, lovey? What you still doing sitting here? I thought you'd left a while ago.'

'I did, I ... I mean I am. I'm going now. Goodnight.'

'You sure you're all right?' Margaret pressed. 'An ungodly shade of white, lass, your face is.'

Jenny nodded. In a daze, she turned and wandered off for home.

'Get that down thee.' Nobby nudged a cup across the table. 'You favour you're about to flake out again.'

'I feel it.'

Having arrived back and stuttered out in fits and snatches through her tears the incredible offer to the old man and her brother, Jenny had promptly flopped back in her chair in a dead faint. Now, slowly regaining her senses, she took deep breaths. However, it did nothing to quell the thundering of her heart.

'Will you go, the morrow?' murmured Nobby.

'Oh do, our Jen, go on!' piped up Noah before she could answer. 'Performing on a proper stage in a music hall – by! Eeh, you are lucky.'

She smiled across at him with tenderness; his excitement for her touched her deeply. This was what it had all been about, hadn't it? she reminded herself. Everything she'd been striving towards was for the lad here. Had she at last done it? Still she found it hard to believe it might be within her grasp. But surely she must at least try? She had to give this opportunity a fighting go, must snatch with both hands the possibility of changing their lives for the better if there was even half a chance. Otherwise, just what the hell had it all been for? She couldn't pass this up.

'Sleep on it, eh, lass,' Nobby was saying now. 'See how tha feels in t' morn.'

'I don't have to.' Damping down her bone-numbing terror of the unknown, the stubborn flurry of misgivings and, most of all, her fear of failure, she nodded once. 'I've made up my mind already: I'm going. I have to at least try.'

Whilst Noah grinned from ear to ear and clapped his hands, Nobby said nothing. Sipping his tea, the man stared into the flames of the fire.

Jenny located Solomon's, after asking around, without too much bother. On Manchester's border with neighbouring Salford, it was well situated, and judging by its attractive exterior, at least, a decent-sized venue.

Now, Jenny knew of music and variety halls, of course she did, but she'd never set foot in one such before. She wasn't sure what to expect. For what seemed an age, she stood staring at the ornately carved double doors, paced the flagstones outside them for a time, then returned to her post chewing her thumb. At last, the fear of being late and scuppering her chances with Sol before they had even begun got the better of her tumbling emotions. Plucking up every ounce of courage she possessed, she lifted a hand and rapped at the wood.

The doors creaked open a few inches at her second knock and an elaborately moustached man stuck his nose through the gap. 'We're not open. Come back later.'

'I'm here on an appointment, mister.' She felt a little silly at the grand-sounding statement. 'I'm here to see Sol?'

The man's demeanour switched in an instant. He threw the doors wide with much exuberance. 'Forgive me! Come through, come through!'

She stepped past him into a dim entrance hall and, hands clasped tightly in front of her to stem their trembling, waited for him to secure the main doors. Then on legs that felt like warm wax she followed on a few steps behind into a sprawling auditorium.

The lighting in here was, in contrast, brilliant. Countless paraffin lamps attached to the walls threw their glares into every corner and crevice and lent a sort of ethereal shimmer to the air itself. Bedazzled, she blinked and stared about in wonderment.

Row upon row of seats, above and around which were balconies containing more chairs in crimson velveteen, spread out to her left. This place could seat up to two thousand people easily, she reckoned – God above! Yet her anxiety at the notion of performing before such vast numbers rapidly lurched into full-scale panic when she turned her head in the opposite direction towards the stage.

Festooned either side with magnificent gold curtains and deeply frilled pelmet above, it was the most astonishingly beautiful – and utterly petrifying – vision she'd ever encountered. She walked towards it slowly and running her fingertips along the edge of the wooden stage, imagined all the wonderful and talented people who had graced its surface entertaining the public. *Soon, she too would be joining their ranks* . . . The idea was unbelievable.

'This way, deary.' With a flourish, the man who had admitted her entrance motioned with a sweep of his arm towards a narrow-arched opening. 'Come along now, we don't want to keep Sol waiting.'

She was led through along a corridor flanked on both sides by doors towards a room at the extreme end – here, the man knocked twice then disappeared inside. Left alone, Jenny concentrated on controlling her breathing. She didn't have long, however; the door opened again and the smiling man hooked his finger at her and beckoned her inside.

The office was modest in both size and décor. Tall cupboards, their shelves stuffed to bursting with papers, ran along two of the brown walls, whilst positioned in front of the window facing her was a large mahogany desk that took up most of the floor space. Seated behind it in a wing-backed chair was Sol. Shuffling forward, Jenny smiled.

'I hope I'm not late, mister.'

'Not at all. Punctuality: that's what I like to see.' He inclined his head to a chair opposite him. 'Please. Sit.'

169

'Ta, thanks.'

'You may go, Doll,' Sol told the man hovering nearby.

Doll? Jenny nodded to herself. The nickname was certainly a fitting one given his flamboyant style of dressing and effeminate manner.

'Yes, sir.'

'Stay where I can find you, though.'

'Very good, sir. Good luck, deary,' he added to Jenny with a wink before breezing out.

'You're nervous?' Sol asked when they were alone.

'Aye, mister, a bit.' *A bit! Ha! That was the fattest lie ever told to man!* She cleared her throat. 'Well, a lot if I'm honest,' she admitted, then smiled when he chuckled. 'I thought my bleedin' heart might give out on me on t' walk here.'

'You were born for the music hall. You'll soon feel at your ease here, I have no doubt.'

'I hope so, mister.'

'Now then. Let's get down to particulars.' He leaned back in his chair and steepled his hands on his chest. 'I'll be frank with you: you're special, Jenny. Really special. A rare gem that I'm almost unable to believe my luck that I've discovered. I want you to be Solomon's main attraction.'

'Eh?' Her voice was a squeak. 'Me?'

'Yes. You see I was mulling over a fitting stage name for you last night, and an idea so terrific that it can only mean my meeting you was indeed fate, suddenly struck me: your own name couldn't be more perfect if we tried.'

170

'Jenny Brodings?' It didn't sound all too theatrical to her.

Sol shook his head. 'Do you know what an anagram is, Jenny?'

'Nay, mister.'

'Well, you see, if you shuffle the letters in a word, put them in different orders, you can make other words.'

'Aye?'

'Do you know what your name, what Brodings, is an anagram for?' His eyes were shining; he clapped his hands together in evident delight. 'Songbird. Songbird! Simply amazing. It's like it was meant to be.'

'Songbird . . .' She smiled. 'That's nice.'

'It's more than nice, it's wonderful – and a cast-iron selling point. Jenny Brodings, I'm going to make you a star.'

His enthusiasm was contagious, and excitement was popping and fizzing through every inch of her. The laugh that leaked from her was bordering on hysterical: 'Me, mister? Really?'

'You wait and see. When I'm finished, there shan't be a man, woman or child alive who doesn't know the name Songbird.'

The following minutes, as Sol went over more details, rolled by on a dream – Jenny took in only snatches of what he was saying. One statement, however, brought her head up sharply; her mouth dropped open:

'What was that you just said?' She'd misheard him surely, had to have done.

171

'I stated that, as my employee, you will be required to live in. Every entertainer that makes up my team here at Solomon's must adhere by this rule. That doesn't pose a problem for you, does it?'

'But, mister . . . it's not necessary. I live but a half hour's walk away, will be here on time every night—'

He held up a hand. 'That's beside the point. You see, Jenny, Solomon's isn't my only premises. I also own a successful hall in Bolton . . . you know of Bolton?' he asked. Then, when she shrugged: 'It's a town some ten miles from here. My acts split their time between there and Manchester, are constantly on the move, and so must be flexible and be able to drop everything and travel between venues at a moment's notice. It gives the paying masses more variety, you see. The public soon grows bored of the same performances night after night. My method of operating proves extremely successful. Rules are rules.'

To say Jenny found herself in a quandary was putting it mildly. She hadn't for a moment anticipated this. Suddenly, the magical opportunity didn't seem so graspable any more. She could have wept, so crushing was the disappointment.

She couldn't agree to his terms, wasn't free to up sticks, move around between places at the drop of a hat for whatever lengths of time. Her life wasn't her own – she had responsibilities. She had Noah to care for. And yet, to even consider passing up on this, such an incredible, once in a hundred lifetimes' chance . . . Oh, how would she ever bear it now? Sol had sold the position to her and what it might mean for her, for them all, utterly and completely. The prospect of having it all snatched away from her at this point was like a physical agony – she couldn't, *couldn't*, risk that.

All this was, by and large, for Noah in the first place. Might there be a possibility of her making this work? There had to be. But what?

'So, Jenny? What is your answer to be?'

An idea was forming; she licked her lips. 'This live-in rule . . .'

'Employee accommodation is situated but a stone's toss from here – would you like to see the rooms before making up your mind? Doll would be happy to show you around.'

'No, it ain't that,' she said quickly as he made to summon the man. 'I wondered if, well, would it be at all possible to fetch my brother with me here to dwell? He's only nine, I look after him you see, and—'

'Certainly not.' His tone was terse. 'Such things are not permitted. The accommodation is for employees, and employees only.'

'But Noah's a good lad, he is. He'd be no bother, mister, you'd hardly know he was there—'

'Jenny, it is out of the question. Now, do you accept my terms or don't you? Forgive my forcing you for an answer but I'm a very busy man.'

There was definite impatience reflected in his dark eyes now. She swallowed, fear that she'd pushed him too far with her impertinence and that he'd change his mind about the whole thing at any moment, bringing her out in a cold sweat. 'I . . .'

'Fame, adoration, respect. More money than to

know what to do with. They're all yours for the taking, Jenny,' he murmured, his gaze alive now with intensity.

Oh God, God . . . *What do I do?*

'A new life, better than anything beyond your wildest imaginings,' Sol pressed on, sitting forward across the desk to stare deep into her eyes. 'Jenny, you deserve this.'

'I . . .'

'If not for yourself then do it for your brother.'

'Noah,' she whispered.

Sol evidently knew he'd hit the right spot. He smiled. 'You'll be able to give him whatever his young heart desires.'

'I . . . I . . .'

'So?'

'All right.'

'I have you on board?'

Drawing a shaky hand across her mouth, she nodded. 'Aye, Sol. Aye, you do.'

'Yes. *Yes.* My special, special Songbird . . .'

'I didn't know what else to do, Nobby.' It was an hour later and Jenny was sitting in the old man's house, wringing her hands. 'I were that frickened Sol would deem me to have too much baggage and be too difficult to work with that I panicked. I couldn't let a chance like that slip me by, could I? I had to agree.'

Releasing a long breath, Nobby scratched his whiskers. 'This Sol sounds like he's got all the talk, all right.'

174

'It's just the rules; all his acts have to abide by them. Nobby, what am I going to do?'

'Coral ain't likely to say aye to taking the lad in.'

'But she'll have to. Anyroad, it's about time she started sharing some of the responsibility. Aye, it's long overdue.'

'But Martin, lass.'

Biting her lip, she nodded. 'He ain't bad with Noah, though, nay. He treats him all right – it's me he has the problem with lately.'

'If the pair don't consent then the lad can allus stop here with me, you know that.'

She did. The golden-hearted man here would never turn them away at least. Love flooded her breast for him. 'You're a kind body, Nobby – the best. But you never know, Martin, he might just allow it . . . I'll never know his feelings on t' matter till I try.'

'And what of your own feelings?' Nobby spoke softly. 'I know how much the lad means to thee. Could you really cope with not seeing him?'

Banking down her swelling emotions quickly – this was for Noah, all of it; she wouldn't let her own selfish wants get in the way – she broke eye contact to stare through the window. 'I'd have him by my side in a heartbeat if it were in my power, you know that. But it's long hours. I'll be working six days out of the seven. And what with rehearsing and travelling to Bolton town if I must . . . it just ain't possible, is it? Besides, I get Sundays off. I can spend the whole day with him then.'

'Jenny, I have to be honest with thee.' Easing his

aged body down on to a stool, he took one of her hands in his. 'All this . . . well, I've been ruminating: it all sounds a bit too good to be true.'

'Eh? How so?'

'Well, I mean, there's plenty of folk out there who like to take advantage of lasses – and especially them from the poorer districts—'

'Oh, Nobby, please don't.'

'I have to say it.'

'Nay, you don't,' she snapped. 'I ain't daft, you know. I can spot a wrong 'un when I sees one. Solomon's is the real deal, honest. Just think of what this opportunity could mean for me and Noah – you an' all for that matter.' Brightening, she nodded. 'You ain't growing no younger, you know. I'm going to take care of you in the winter of your life, just like you've done for me and my brother.'

'Eeh, lass . . .'

'I mean it, Nobby. All this . . . we could all benefit from it, don't you see? We'd never have to fret about brass again. Just support me on this, let me try it. I'll give it a few months and if I ain't happy, I'll pack it in and come back home. Nowt ventured, nowt gained, eh?' she wheedled. 'Please, Nobby.'

'I don't want you being hurt, getting dragged into summat unholy, Jenny.'

'I'll not. I'm not, really. Trust me.'

Though he looked far from convinced – worry was etched into every line of his face – he jerked his shoulders in a helpless motion. 'You've to go whichever route you see fit, I suppose. I ain't got no right to force

176

your hand, don't have no paternal claims nor any others over thee . . . Please, though, you be careful.'

A smile sneaked across her face. She winked. 'Ay listen, I can look after myself well enough. God help anyone who thinks to put that to the test.'

That night in bed, Jenny held Noah to her tightly. He'd been taking a nap earlier when she'd conversed with Nobby, and upon him wakening she just hadn't the heart or the right words to discuss the subject with him, was dreading his reaction. Now, though, she knew the time had come. She couldn't put off telling him any longer. Wheels would be set in motion tomorrow evening and she must give the boy time to prepare, get used to the idea. Her heart like lead, she turned him around to look into his face.

'Lad, there's summat you need to hear.'

Twirling a lock of her hair around his finger, he blinked back sleepily. 'Aye?'

'That music hall position I told thee about . . . well, I got it. That's good news, eh?'

His little face came alive with the most joyous smile. 'Oh! Ech, our Jen—!'

'Hold your horses, lad, let me finish,' she cut in gently. 'You see, if I do take it, well, it'll mean me going away forra while.'

'Away?'

His soft frown above his trusting, jade-coloured eyes tore her soul in two – she glanced away. 'I'll not be able to live with thee any more because the music hall master, he likes his workforce to live in, you see.

God willing, you'll stop on with our Coral. You'll like that, eh? Being around our nieces and nephews a lot more will be nice, won't it, give you someone to play with? You've been short of that for too long, lad, having kiddies around you to act the goat with, as you should at your age. But all this, it don't mean we'll never get to spend time together, don't be thinking that. I get Sundays off, will come and visit every week without fail, I promise.'

Noah was silent for a full minute. When he finally spoke, his speech was thick with tears – Jenny had to strain to hear him: 'I'll miss thee.'

'And I'll miss thee, an' all, lad. More than I can ever say.'

'But I'll be all right,' he continued. He nodded with conviction. 'I'm a big boy now and I must be brave. I know you want to do good at this, for the both of us, our Jen.'

'Oh, lad. Eeh, come here.' On a sob, she drew him into her arms once more. 'I want to give you everything, every little thing you've ever deserved and more. And I will, you just wait. Eeh, you should see Solomon's, Noah. There's shining orange and white tiles around the main doors outside, and as for inside . . . beautiful, it is. Ay, it's a gift sent from God above, this is. No more going hungry, no more being cold or worrying about the rent or walking around in bloody rags. Your new suit, my singing paid for that, remember – I can make us some serious brass with this voice, I can.'

'Will we be rich like the nobs?'

She smiled into the darkness. 'Huh! We'll be better than that. We'll be richer than Queen Vicky herself, lad.'

He laughed. 'You are funny, our Jen.'

'And you're a little cherub, and eeh I do love thee. You'll want for nowt, soon, Noah. I'm going to make sure of it.'

Somehow or other, she would. Whatever it took.

Chapter 9

Jenny felt sick with nerves the following afternoon when she knocked at the house in Carruthers Street. Yet she was also determined and set ready to go into battle if need be. Coral must agree to this, had to help her. Noah was her brother, too, damn it.

Sitting facing her sister minutes later across the table, she folded her arms and took a deep breath: 'I need thee to let our Noah stop here.'

Coral jerked back in clear surprise. 'What, why? What's occurred, what's wrong?'

'Nowt's wrong. Quite the opposite, in fact. I've found a new position, and this time it's live-in.'

'Live-in? What is it, servitude? You're to be a maid?'

'Nay, nay, it's not domestic work, nowt like that. I'm going to be a music hall singer.'

If a feather had blown in, it would have had the power to knock the woman flat. Mouth and eyes like saucers, she shook her head. 'Is it really true . . .? But how? *When?*'

Jenny explained her encounter with Sol at Margaret's tavern and went on to tell her all that had transpired during the meeting at Solomon's the previous day. 'It's a dream come true, Coral, eh? I can hardly believe my luck!'

However, Coral's enthusiasm waned the more she listened; it was reflected clearly in her eyes. When at last she spoke, she confirmed Jenny's suspicions. 'Nay, this don't sound right to me. All that money, and dragging you away from your kith and kin to boot . . .? You need to tell this Sol fella to sling his hook.'

'I will not!' Jenny was incensed, not to mention filled with crushing disappointment. 'I thought you of all people would be happy for me. It was you yourself what said but a handful of days past that I ought to grab my future with both hands. Don't let life pass you by else you'll live to regret it, that's what you told me – remember?'

'Aye, but Jenny—'

'Nay, Coral! I don't want to hear it. I'll not sit here and listen to you pour scorn on this. It's too important, means too much to me. For God's sake, Noah's the only one who really matters in all of this, and he's all right with it. Even Nobby supports me. Why can't you, eh?'

'I'll tell thee for why, because this Sol bloke sounds like a slippery owd bugger. And because, believe it or no, I care about thee, *love* thee—'

'Just stop. You're a liar, Coral. I know exactly why you'll not give your blessing to this.' Jenny was hurting and her temper was up too much now to turn back. 'You just don't want to take the lad in. I'm right, ain't I? And why would that be, I wonder? Because you don't want to upset that stinking husband of yourn by suggesting it. By, but you're a sad, pathetic bitch, d'you know that? And *selfish* – my God. Why can't you ever think of anyone but yourself, eh? Christ, to be you!'

The backhander that Coral delivered to her face on a shrill cry sent Jenny spinning in her seat. Spots of colour flashed behind her eyes – stunned, she held a hand to her cheek.

'You . . . You . . .!'

'No, you listen to me forra change!' Coral gripped her by the collar and shook her hard, sending her teeth rattling. 'After all I've endured, the sacrifices I've made, and you dare to sit there and call me selfish! You're one viper-minded article at times, Jenny Brodings, d'you know that?'

Twisting this way and that, Jenny fought for freedom. 'Leave *go* of me!' However, Coral's grip was like iron – the more she struggled, the tighter the woman held on. 'I mean it, let me be or else!'

'Aye, what? What you going to do, eh?'

Almost nose to nose, they glared at each other, their breathing ragged.

Suddenly, it was as though Coral had woken from a daze. Her expression completely altered. Confusion swiftly followed by horror passed across her face. She gasped. Releasing Jenny, she shook her head and tears gushed from her eyes: 'Oh. Oh, lass . . .'

'You struck me.'

'Lass!'

'Don't you touch me.' Jenny spoke in a rasp, was visibly shaking. 'You stay away from me.'

'I'm sorry, I'm sorry—'

Jenny, having bolted from the room, snuffed out the woman's pleas with the slamming of the door.

For how long she wandered around the city, locked inside the prison of her own tumultuous mind, Jenny neither knew nor cared. When at last the cold got the better of her, she took herself inside the next low inn she happened across and ordered bread and cheese and an ale.

Though the food went uneaten on the tin plate, the alcohol and its fuzzing effects was a welcome balm and her glass was empty in no time. She was soon requesting a refill, then another.

When eventually she rose to leave, her legs felt strangely unsteady and the world appeared to her in a filmy haze, like trying to see through frosted glass. Dragging her shawl across her shoulders, she set off into the darkness.

The Balloon was in full swing when she pushed open the door and lumbered inside. She squinted about in confusion, didn't rightly know how she was here or why. Then she spotted the landlady at the counter and her face spread into a slack grin.

'There she is, the lovely Hyacinth! Least I've still got one friend left – come here, wench, give us a hug.'

Laughing in surprise when Jenny drew her in a crushing embrace and dropped kisses on to her plump cheeks, Hyacinth shook her head. Then taking in the younger woman's inebriated state, she clicked her tongue. 'You're sozzled!'

'Sshhh.' Jenny tapped a finger clumsily against her lips. 'I am a bit, aye.'

'But lass, you're meant to be working. You're fit for nowt in that condition.'

Frowning, Jenny closed one eye, trying her best to remember. Then she nodded slowly and slapped a hand to her mouth. 'Oh aye, so I am! It went clear out of my head – sorry, Hyacinth.' She felt her way across the counter. 'Fear not, wench, I'm all right, will see to my duties right away—'

'You will not – you can't see a ruddy thing. Come here, lass, sit down. That's it,' Hyacinth soothed, helping Jenny on to a stool. Hands on hips, she stared down at her and sighed. 'What's occurred, then? This ain't like thee at all.'

'I'm celebrating.'

'Oh aye? What's your gladsome news then?'

Jenny gave an exaggerated wink then dissolved into raucous laughter. 'It's a secret. Oh sod it,' she screeched in the next breath, 'you may as well know, will find out soon enough anyroad: I'm going to be a star! You're happy for me, ain't you, Hyacinth?' Sudden tears filled her eyes. Her bottom lip wobbled. 'Say you are, go on, please. No bugger else is.'

'What on earth . . .?'

The voice was masculine. Looking up, Jenny saw that George had appeared, his blurry outline swaying. Feeling sickness swoop, she pressed a hand to his broad chest. 'Eeh, keep still do. You're turning my guts inside out doing that.'

'I'm doing nowt, it's your own eyes. Christ's sake, Jenny, just what have you gone and done this for?'

'She's celebrating, going to be a star, apparently,' the landlady chipped in drily. 'Don't ask me,' she added when George raised his brows for explanation. 'I couldn't make head nor tail of it.'

'My name is Songbird and I'm to be a sensation. My fans will adore me!'

'Course they will. Come on now, lass, that's it.' Taking her under the oxters, George brought her to her feet.

'You don't believe me neither, that I can be a success. None of you do.'

He responded in a levelled tone, as one would to a child being difficult. 'Aye, I do. Now, let's get thee home—'

'Take your hands off me.' Jenny swatted him away. 'I don't need you or your help. I don't need no one. No one, you hear? You can all bugger off to bleedin' hell! I'm done with this place. Gorra new job, I have, at the best music hall this city's got to offer. Solomon's it's called and—'

'What?'

'You heard.'

'You're leaving?'

'Catch on quick, you, don't yer – I don't think!'

'But . . .'

'But what? But nowt, George Sixsmith. You, you're just jealous, that's what.' She jabbed a quivering finger in his face, almost making contact with his eyeball, making him take a step back. 'You're nobbut a talentless sod and everyone knows it.'

Hyacinth took hold of her wrists gently. 'That's enough of that. I think it's time you went home now and slept this off.'

'Oh, you can shut your fat trap, an' all,' Jenny spat back, yanking her arms free. '*You're* nobbut a stinking liar.'

'Lass—'

'This man,' she cut in with a roar, 'him here.' She looked George up and down in disdain. 'He's but a figure of fun, and you all know it.' She spotted Hyacinth cringe at the vituperation; however, so up was Jenny's blood that she didn't care; her lip curled further. 'The Rose and Thistle have been after him, have they, desperate to take him on as a singer? Ha! They have that, all right: as a bleedin' comic act!'

'What?' George's face was ashen with mortification.

'Surely you ain't surprised. You couldn't carry a tune if your very life depended on it. Sound like a drowning cat, you do – aye, a stone deaf one with a sore throat!'

'Is it true?' George half-turned to ask Hyacinth, but Jenny got in before her.

'It's true, all right. Seems I'm the only one what's got the gumption, though, to tell it to you straight. But then you know that already, don't yer? So, George, how's that for pulchi . . . pulchi . . . pulchiturdo, or whatever the infernal word was!'

'Pulchritudinous.'

'Aye! Translated simply as a big-gobbed bitch, am I right?'

'Pulchritudinous means beautiful.'

The room ceased its spinning. In the instant, her world appeared to her in crystal-clear clarity. She swallowed a hiccup. 'Wha . . .?'

'It means beautiful,' George repeated quietly. He turned and disappeared through the curtained area that led to Hyacinth's private quarters.

The whole tavern was staring at her. Some were muttering, others were shaking their heads. All wore expressions of disapproval.

In the clogging silence, Jenny gazed around, her breathing heavy. Then letting out a sob, she charged past the landlady, on through the crowd and burst out into the street.

'Lord above. Deary, what's happened?'

Jenny collapsed, weeping, into Doll's arms. 'Oh, I hate them, I hate them!'

'Shush now, child. I've got you.'

Propping her up, he supported her through the entrance hall and into the auditorium. One or two people were milling about this time by the stage. Feeling their curious gazes turn towards her, she shrank back.

'I'm sorry, I shouldn't have come in this state . . .'

'Sol is expecting you?'

'Aye.'

'Then come with me.'

Doll led her into the same office as before. Sol rose

from his chair at their entrance, brow creasing, and Doll hurried to his side to murmur something into his ear. Jenny couldn't catch what was being said but noticed Sol nodding. He dismissed Doll then came to perch on the edge of his desk in front of her.

'Please. Sit.'

She did as he'd instructed then promptly burst into tears once more. 'Eeh, mister. It's all gone wrong.'

He didn't speak, instead let her emotions run their course. When she was sufficiently composed, he asked, 'You trust me, don't you?'

'Aye, mister.'

'Then tell me all about it.'

She explained the confrontations in what little detail she could recall. Her head felt muggy again and her crying had made her exhausted. She finished with, 'Oh, it were horrible. They're my nearest and dearest, are meant to care about me, and yet they've all turned against me. Can you believe that?'

'Yes, as a matter of fact. I've seen it countless times before.'

Wiping her nose with the back of her hand, she sniffed. 'You have?'

'Of course. Families are such fickle beasts. Sadly, for many, the moment someone they know gets a chance of bettering themselves, bitterness soon replaces love. Envy is an ugly thing, Jenny.'

Nodding slowly, she whispered, 'I never thought of that. You reckon that's it, then? They're all just jealous?'

'Undoubtedly. You're going to be a huge success, Jenny. Plenty cannot accept that. I'm afraid it's simply something you must learn to get used to.'

She sniffed again, smiled. 'Ta, mister, for listening.'

'Thank you for coming to me. I, at least, will always be here for you. Remember that.'

'I will, aye. Sorry,' she added, dropping her head into her hands as a wave of nausea took claim of her, 'I feel bad, I . . .'

'Wait there.'

Jenny heard him go to the door to summon Doll. The man listened to what Sol had to say then disappeared, to return again moments later with a tall, raven-haired woman.

'Cassandra, this is Jenny. She's feeling somewhat under the weather . . . take her across to your room to rest up, will you?'

She looked Jenny over and nodded knowingly. 'Aye, all right.'

'Good.' Sol turned back to Jenny. He placed a hand on her shoulder. 'Come along, little Songbird. Cassandra will look after you.'

Too ill and befuddled to think straight let alone argue, Jenny allowed herself to be led.

She remembered little of the short journey. The last thing she was aware of was being helped into a bed. Flopping back, she immediately fell into a deep sleep.

When next she opened her eyes, the sky visible between the gap in the curtains was a light grey.

Except they were not her curtains; her cellar didn't possess any. Neither was this her sacking, she realised, glancing down at the iron-framed bed she was lying in instead. What the devil . . .? Putting a hand to her thumping head, she blinked in puzzlement.

'Ah, you're awake,' a voice trilled from the opposite end of the room.

Jenny almost jumped clean out of her skin. Gasping, she hauled herself up. 'Who . . .? Where the hell am I?'

The woman, who, now Jenny came to think of it, looked oddly familiar, laughed. 'I'm Cassandra. The dancer? I brought thee here, remember? Skennin' drunk, you were. 'Ere, and you're a terrible snorer.'

Frowning, Jenny cast her mind back. Snippets of memory drifted like smoke into her brain – she closed her eyes with a groan. *Mother of God.* Her fight with Coral. The scene she'd created in the Balloon and the horrendous things she'd spouted. So acute was her devastating regret, she could have curled up and died.

'What have I *done*?'

'Don't fret none,' the woman said with an easy smile. 'Everything will work itself out, you'll see. Things never seem so bad in the morning.'

'The morning?' Jenny's gaze flicked to the window once more. Now, her senses more alert, she realised the shade of the sky she'd noticed shortly before was that of late sunrise. She slapped a hand to her mouth. 'Nay . . . Noah! Why didn't no one waken me!'

'We thought it best to let thee kip the ale off.'

'We?'

'Aye, me and Sol.'

God almighty, the shame. 'I'm sorry, I, I have to leave.'

'Wait, where you going?'

'Home. I have to see my brother, explain . . .' *He and Nobby must be going out of their minds with worry.* 'I'll be back.'

'You'd better,' Cassandra called after her as she made a dash for the door. 'Sol shan't be best pleased if you let him down again this evening!'

Jenny skittered along the narrow landing, down the staircase and through the hall, her thoughts in turmoil.

You're your own worst enemy, you are, you foolish bloody cow, she upbraided herself, bunching her hands into fists, as she pelted at top speed through the damp and dreary lanes towards home. *Funny creating merry hell at every turn then stopping out all night into the bargain – what a first-rate idiot. By, but you never learn, do you, eh? When will you ever know to keep your trap shut, stop being so ruddy selfish? Well, it'd serve you just right should everyone turn their backs on you after this, tell you to take a running jump, aye. Stupid, stupid.*

The destructive yet wholly justified beratement of herself continued the length of the journey.

When she reached Owd Nobby's house, her face instantly exploded in chastened colour; she moaned softly. Poor Noah. The lad deserved better than a wicked swine like her, oh did he! I'm sorry, sorry . . . Head lowered, eyes downcast, she knocked at the door.

'Jenny?'

'Coral!' This was the last thing she'd expected. 'What's tha doing here?'

'Eeh, lass.' The woman drew her to her breast in a crushing hug then pulled back to glare at her. 'What d'you think I'm doing here – I've been going clean out of my head with worry! Nobby sent word to me when you never came home, didn't know what else to do.'

She heaved a sigh. 'I'm sorry, I am. For everything,' she added meaningfully.

Coral's face slowly softened. She nodded. 'As am I, an' all—'

'Nay,' Jenny interjected adamantly, 'it were me, my fault. I provoked thee summat awful and I deserved that slap to the chops. D'you know, sometimes, I don't know how you put up with me.'

'I love thee, that's how,' the woman murmured. She stroked Jenny's hair. 'Let's forget all about it, eh?'

'Aye. I'd like that.'

'Come on in and face the others, put their minds at rest.'

Nobby closed his eyes in relief at her entrance; Noah hurried over to wrap his arms around her waist. Never had Jenny felt so terrible.

'I'm sorry,' she repeated. 'I'm a thoughtless dolt, I know.'

'I thought you'd run away, our Jen.'

Eeh, lad, lad. 'Nay, never.'

'Did you get lost?'

'Nay, I got drunk, I'm ashamed to say. I know, I

know,' she continued at Coral and even Nobby's expressions, 'it were stupid.'

'Not to mention dangerous,' the old man told her quietly. 'What occurred, where did tha sleep?'

'I finished up stopping at the entertainment's accommodation provided by the music hall. Sol insisted.'

'It weren't him what got thee sozzled, was it?' Coral demanded. 'Did he cause this, aye?'

Jenny shook her head. 'Nay, it were on me, all of it. I told you, Sol's decent, kindly. He wants only what's best for me.'

Though Coral and Nobby shared a look, they made no further comment.

'I've some apologising to do at that quarter as well, mind you,' Jenny went on, cringing inside. 'Fancy me turning up at the music hall in the state I did . . . What must they think of me? I'll be surprised if Sol don't tell me he's changed his tune about taking me on.'

'You mean to go ahead with this, then?' Coral asked, arms folded.

'With the job? Aye, course I do, if Sol will still have me.'

'I still think you're making a mistake, Jenny. Nobby does, too.'

Jenny glanced to the old man, who lowered his eyes, before turning back to face her sister. As per usual, an angry retort was bubbling up in her throat but she somehow managed to restrain it. For something she remembered from last night had flitted into her brain, something Sol had said. She nodded slowly. Envy was an ugly thing indeed. He'd been right all along. Well, she wouldn't give them the satisfaction of another set-to. Taking a steadying breath, she let the comment slide, saying instead, 'Your offer to take the lad in still stands, don't it, Nobby?' And at his response to the affirmative: 'Good, for I leave this evening.'

'Jenny—'

'Sorry to have caused you worry, Coral,' she cut in in the same levelled tone as before. Leaning across, she kissed the woman's cheek. 'You'd best go now. Your family will be missing thee.'

Though frustration and concern screamed from Coral's eyes, she didn't argue the matter further, simply sighed and shook her head. 'You'll make your own mistakes regardless of whatever I say . . . Well, good luck to thee, Jenny.'

'Ta, thanks. Goodbye for now.'

Another lingering look and sad shake of her head from the doorway then Coral was gone.

With forced brightness, Jenny switched her attention back to her brother. 'Now then, Noah, let's enjoy these last few hours together, shall we? What would you like to do, play cards?'

'Aye, our Jen.'

'Gradely. Well come and sit down then. You can shuffle and I'll deal.'

'We only want what's best for thee, lass,' Nobby murmured as she passed him on her way to collect the dog-eared deck from the shelf.

She paused. As she'd done with Coral minutes before, she dropped a kiss on to his cheek. 'Course youse do,' she said measuredly, her emotions controlled. 'Thank you for agreeing to look after Noah, I appreciate it, truly.'

'Lass . . . you're sure you're all right?'

'Perfectly, Nobby.' *At least she would be just as soon as she got herself away from these two-faced people wishing only to hold her back.*

The sooner she was free of this place, the better.

The wrench later, when saying goodbye to her brother, was even worse than Jenny had dreaded the parting to be.

Despite his best efforts, Noah was unable to hold back. Tears cascaded down his face, dripping from his chin to soak into his shirt. His skinny shoulders heaving, he clung on to her like it might be for the last time. 'You will come and see me, our Jen?'

'Course I will. I promised, didn't I?'

'I wish you'd not have stopped away last night. That were our last one together and it got wasted – we ruined it.'

No, my sweet darling, I ruined it . . . 'I know. I know. I'm so sorry.'

'Be happy, our Jen. I love thee.'

Oh Noah, Noah. He was breaking her heart in two. 'You an' all, lad, on both counts.'

Nobby held her hands at the door and pressed them. His shining eyes held the same negative emotions Coral's had earlier – not a trace of happiness for her in sight, much to her chagrin. 'Tha knows where I am should tha need me.'

'Aye.'

'Be safe, Jenny.'

Not happy, though . . . Even Noah had had the grace to wish her that. They would do well to take a leaf out of his book, all right. The child had more sense, more heart, than the lot of them put together. Just what was wrong with these so-called adults in her life at all? She smiled tightly. 'Goodbye, Nobby.'

'Bye, our Jen! Bye!'

She stood at the end of the road, waving back and blowing kisses to Noah, until he went inside. Once alone, and despite telling herself she wouldn't, that it would result only in disappointment, she scoured the end of the street. Sure enough, no sight of Coral presented itself. A minuscule part of her had believed that the woman might just come to tell her she was glad for her after all, wish her well . . . but no. Jenny's heart hardened further. She took a deep breath. Shoulders back, chin high, she spun on her heel and set off at a smart pace.

The route to Solomon's took her past the Balloon. It came into sight and her insides lurched uncomfortably. She was gripped by deep remorse. For a split second, Jenny was tempted to enter, beg from Hyacinth, and especially George, forgiveness. But she couldn't face it, she couldn't; her legs refused to carry her there. Besides, the attempt would only lead to further pain – how could it not? They wouldn't forgive her. George could certainly never forget the humiliation she'd caused him. He'd been nothing but good to her and, in return, she'd thrown his friendship back in his face in the cruellest way possible. She hated herself for that. She always would.

Bar Noah, everyone she cared for, *everyone*, was lost to her now. The truth was crippling. She'd never known such loneliness in her life.

Doll greeted her warmly when she arrived at Solomon's. His friendliness was almost her undoing. Swiping away a tear, she brought to her lips what she hoped was an equally gladsome smile. This evening would mark the start of a fresh beginning and a new and improved Jenny Brodings – she'd promised herself so upon approaching the music hall – and she was determined to implement it. She flashed him a confident wink.

'Sol waiting for me in t' office, is he?'

'That's right, deary. Come, I'll walk you there.'

'Ta, thanks, Doll.'

The man in question rose from his desk as they entered but before he had chance to speak, Jenny got in quickly with her apologies:

'Forgive me for yesterday, mister. I don't make a habit of that. My mind weren't my own . . . it shan't occur a second time.' And this she meant wholeheartedly. Not a drop of that devil juice would pass her lips from now on. Alcohol had unearthed a darkness in her she hadn't known was there. She'd heard of nasty drunks, of those who turned into demons when in their cups – clearly, that curse lurked within her, too. Never would she be that person, act that way, again. 'I know I were meant to come here yesterday to get a feel of the stage, rehearse, and I'm sorry I let you down. It were reet kind of thee to let me kip the effects off. Cassandra looked after me well.'

Sol smiled. 'We're none of us perfect, little Songbird. Think no more of it.'

'Really?' Weak with relief, Jenny closed her eyes. 'Eeh, you're kindness itself, that you are.'

'Shall we get started?'

'Aye, mister.'

Sol nodded to the man at his side. 'Get everything ready, would you, Doll? We'll be through presently.'

'Very good, sir.'

The door closed and Sol's smile appeared once more. He motioned to a chair. 'Sit a moment, Jenny. I want to show you something which I'm sure you'll like.'

Frowning curiously, she did as he'd bidden and watched him cross to a high cupboard by the window. From inside, he brought out a large bundle wrapped in white tissue and placed it into her lap. She blinked from it to him mutely.

'Open it.'

'Me, mister?'

'Yes, go ahead.'

Carefully, she folded back the paper. A gasp escaped her.

'The colours are to your satisfaction?'

'Eeh . . . It's *beautiful.*'

The gown, boasting a wide neckline and dropped shoulders, was made from smooth, lightweight silk

198

taffeta in subtle lavender. It fastened down the centre with mother-of-pearl buttons, the row ending at the bottom of the hooked bodice, which finished in a point and was edged in ribbon and piping in rich cream, as were the cuffs of the full sleeves. Yet it was the extremely wide, glazed-cotton-lined skirt with pleated waistline that really took Jenny's breath away. Here, running the complete length down to the hem, were woven delicate silver motifs depicting birds in flight. She ran her fingertips over them in wonder. Her gaze, when at last she brought it back to Sol, swam with tears.

'Mister . . .'

'You like it?'

She could only nod.

'I had it designed especially for you. Cassandra, at my request, measured you up for it yesterday as you slept – I hope you've no objections. I wanted it to be a surprise, you see. The dressmaker and her band of seamstresses worked throughout the night to complete it. Oh,' he said suddenly in the next instant, 'I almost forgot.' He rose to retrieve something else from the cupboard, a box this time, and as before placed it in her lap for her to open.

It held, she discovered, sateen shoes in the same shade of cream as that on the dress. 'Eeh . . .'

'All right?'

'Aye. *Aye.* I just don't know what to say, I . . .' In her overwhelming gratitude and joy, she forgot herself and on impulse threw her arms around his neck. 'It's better than perfect. Thank you. Thank you.'

'This is the start of something wonderful, my little Songbird,' he breathed into her ear.

'Aye, mister.'

'You must forget about those who can never be happy for you. Will you do that, Jenny? For me?'

His words were hypnotic, bewitching almost. Recalling her loved ones' disapproval, something within her hardened a little further. She nodded into his shoulder.

'Good, that's good . . . You don't need anyone else. Solomon's is your family now.'

'Come on, Jenny, shake a leg.'

Skittering through the corridors in Cassandra's shadow, she was a bag of nerves. 'Eeh, I hope Sol likes it.'

'Course he will. He spotted thee, didn't he, deemed you talented enough to offer thee a job here?'

'Well aye, but—'

'But nowt. Stop fretting – he'll love thee, I'm sure. Now come on. The music hall doors open for the evening in just over half an hour, so you ain't got long to practise. You must get a feel of the stage afore it's time for the real thing.'

Jenny could have kicked herself. Yesterday was meant to have been her chance to rehearse properly – however, that had proved an impossibility given the state she'd arrived in. What a wasted and much-needed opportunity, fool that she was. Now, through no one's fault but her own, she found herself rushing around struggling to prepare like a headless chicken, blast it. Pray God Sol approved of her practice run. Should anything go wrong, he might refuse to allow her to perform for real in tonight's show.

Thank the Lord it would be but a short repertoire. 'Just the one song for the first night,' he'd explained to her with a knowing nod. 'Whet the audience's appetite. If it indeed leaves them hungry for more, which I trust it will, then I plan to place you at the very top of the bill as the main act. I believe in you, little Songbird.' And though Jenny had been thrilled at the notion, the pressure to meet expectations had left her sick to her stomach, did still.

When they reached the auditorium, they found it bustling with people. Performers of every description and wearing magnificent costumes were preparing, too. Doll, red-faced with exertion, flitted amongst them directing and giving advice. The atmosphere was enchanting; smiling, Jenny soaked up the moment with a deep sigh.

'You look stunning.'

She turned to see Sol approaching her and her mouth stretched further into a grin. She did an awkward twirl. 'Will I do, then, mister?'

Cassandra had dressed her hair in coiled plaits and ringlets and applied to her cheeks a smattering of rouge to, in her words, 'chase the dullness away and fetch out her bloom', before helping her into her gown, and the results were impressive, it was true to say. The lend of one of the woman's corsets and crinolette petticoats had done wonders in enhancing her shape. Jenny had gazed in the dressing room's long looking glass in slack-jawed amazement at the vision of womanly beauty reflected back at her, hardly recognising herself.

'Oh, I'll say,' said Sol. 'Now, young lady, take your place.'

The dress's crisp and lustrous fabric made a pleasing rustling sound with each step and seemed to change hues with the movement; Jenny knew she looked good. Her confidence mounted. She found she walked just that little bit taller.

'On my signal, deary,' Doll instructed her, though where exactly he was, Jenny couldn't have told you. The lights, she discovered, now that she was up on stage, were blinding. 'Ready: one, two, three . . .'

Sol's applause, when Jenny's song came to an end, was the real music to her ears. She laughed in sheer relief. 'Ta, thanks, mister.'

'Bravo! Bravo!' Doll hurried over to pat her on the back. 'It's like an angel fell from heaven, on through Lancashire's smoggy air, through Solomon's roof and landed – thlump! – on to the stage. Such silken tones! Such control! The crowd is going to adore you.'

Jenny was grinning from ear to ear. 'By, you've a way with words, all right, Doll. I just hope you're right.'

'He is, I'm sure,' Sol told her. He stooped to smooth out her skirts then gave a quick glance to the pocket watch suspended on a chain attached to his waistcoat. 'Right, it's almost time to open.'

The announcement jolted her unceremoniously

back to reality. She swallowed hard. 'Oh, mister, I am nervous!'

'You'll be fine, little Songbird. Don't let me down,' he warned over his shoulder as he walked away.

Chapter 10

THE CLIENTELE WHO had streamed through the doors to cram into every available twopence and three-pence seats in the stalls, colloquially known as the 'pit', and the lower and upper galleries, wasn't at all what Jenny had been expecting.

Young people little older than herself made up the majority of the swell and, what's more, they were far from genteel, as she'd naively assumed the audience would be. She'd have been hard-pressed to describe them even as decent, if truth be told.

Now, it wasn't the fact they were lowly labourers and factory hands and dressed in rough clothing, shawls and flat caps. She herself was amongst their class, after all. Their standing in society didn't come into it – money and position didn't, of course, auto-matically equate to good morals. No, it was the way in which they chose to conduct themselves that set them apart from the general respectable working class. What's more, it was evident that most had partaken of more than a little tipple before their arrival. They were coarse and they were rowdy, bordering closely on unruly. Peeking out through the side slit in the stage curtain and taking in the situation, Jenny's heart dropped like a stone.

'It's summat you get used to. You'll learn to take it all in your stride,' Cassandra, who had come to stand beside her, said, noticing Jenny's discomfiture. 'It's all par for the course in this job.'

'What d'you mean?' Jenny whispered back. 'Is there likely to be trouble?'

'You'll see for yourself soon enough,' was the woman's dry reply.

The first act up was a twelve-man sack race, which went down a storm with the audience, who laughed and cheered and stamped their clogged feet in appreciation loud enough to make your ears ring. So far so good, Jenny thought, who had remained at her post to watch. Next was a dancing dog, which received a similar enthusiastic reaction. Then a male performer singing opera took his turn – he lasted all of fifteen seconds before he was booed and heckled from the stage. Jenny felt rotten for him, and her anxiety for herself turned to full-blown terror. Just what sort of reception would she receive – something much the same? *Dear God, she'd made a terrible mistake, couldn't do this . . .*

'Next up, we have a brand-new performer making her debut tonight at Solomon's.' Doll's voice rang through Jenny's head like the shrill pealing of a bell, making her gasp. 'Please give a warm welcome to . . . Songbird!'

From where she found the strength to walk out,

Jenny would never know. Her legs took her the short distance of their own accord, as though they belonged to someone else.

She stood, centre stage, her knees literally knocking.

'Get on with it then, pigeon!' someone bawled from the crowd, earning themselves a round of laughter.

Below her, at the side of the stage, she saw Doll nod – her signal to begin. She knew there was no turning back.

The opening lines of her song brought forth murmurs of mild surprise, much to her blessed relief.

Then the comments started.

'Show us a bit of leg!'

'Aye, don't be shy, love. Let's have a gander at what you've got!'

It was one or two at first, which a shocked Jenny did her best to ignore. Yet within seconds, it seemed the whole auditorium had taken up the call, and this rapidly spread into a deafening chant:

'Show us! Show us! Show us!'

She glanced about desperately. To her relief, she spotted Sol standing in the wings. Yet his response to her dilemma was the very last thing she was expecting. To her horror, he nodded sharply and mouthed, 'Do it.'

She shook her head.

'Do it,' he repeated. His Stygian eyes were hard, unyielding.

Tears of anger and humiliation, corrosive in their

truth, were building in her throat. Her voice began to warble. All the while, the demand blared on, relentless.

'Show us! Show us!'

'*Now*, goddammit,' she heard Sol growl out.

Taking hold of her skirt either side and hating herself for it, she lifted it mid-calf. Collective whoops filled the air – she squeezed shut her eyes.

'More! More!'

Please . . .

'Aye – more, more!'

Another look to Sol, who was smiling now, and Jenny knew that she must. She whipped them higher, revealing a flash of bare thighs, before dropping the skirts and bolting from the stage, the audience's delighted cheers stabbing at her brain like vultures pecking flesh from a carcass. Fitting, for that's exactly what she felt like: a grubby piece of meat.

Sol caught her wrist as she made to rush past. 'You did well, little Songbird.'

Her eyes wet, her chest heaving with a whole host of emotions, she glared up at him in mute silence. She had no words, none. How could he have let that happen to her?

'Take yourself off to your room, rest. You've earned it. And this,' he added, pressing a wad of folded white paper into her hand.

She didn't even look at what he'd given her. Spinning round, she took to her heels and ran from the music hall.

*

Cassandra knocked and entered Jenny's room some-time later to find her lying face down on the bed, weeping into her pillow.

'Go away.'

'Come on, don't be like that.' The woman sat her-self down on the counterpane and patted Jenny's back awkwardly. 'As I said, it's summat you get used to.'

'Well I don't want to get used to it,' Jenny snapped, springing to her knees. Tendrils of hair had escaped their pins – she swept them from her face impatiently. 'That were bloody . . . bloody . . .'

'Awful?'

'In a word, aye!'

She nodded. 'None of us love it, you know.'

'Then why do it? How can you sell yourself that way like a common streetwalker?'

'Oh, don't be so dramatic,' Cassandra interrupted.

'*Dramatic?*'

Sprawling out to lounge across the bed, Cassandra stifled a yawn with her hand. 'It's not nice, I grant thee, but it ain't as bad as all that.'

Jenny was enraged. 'Well that's where we differ then, eh, 'cause I think it is bad. Very bloody bad!'

'Aye? Then what are you still doing here?'

Jenny opened and shut her mouth then looked away.

'Go on? Why ain't you thrown in the job and scut-tled back to your family if all this is so beneath you – you answer me that.'

How can I? she wanted to scream. They warned me

about something like this happening, all of them back home, but I'd not listen. No, I reckoned I knew best like I always do – look now where it's got me . . .

'I can't,' she eventually choked. 'My lot, they'd not understand.'

'Tried talking thee out of starting here, did they?' Cassandra nodded sagely. 'Aye, mine too. Oh, they'd be cock-a-hoop at the chance of saying I told you so. It's half the reason I stop on here, you know: just to spite them. Well, that and the brass, of course.'

Lifting a hand to wipe her tear-streaked cheeks, Jenny realised she was still holding what Sol had given her in her bunched fist. Unfurling her fingers, her eyes grew wide to see three crisp pound notes staring back at her.

'See what I mean?' Cassandra said. 'You tell me that's not a gradely sight, Jenny.'

Smoothing out the fortune, she bit her lip, her mind in a quandary. It was a gradely sight. It *was*.

'You'll give up earning that amount every single week, will you, for the sake of showing off a bit of skin?'

'I don't . . . know . . .'

Oh, what was she to *do*?

'Don't decide now. Get some kip, see how you feel the morrow.'

'Aye. Mebbe I will.'

Cassandra smiled. She dropped a kiss on to the top of Jenny's head and breezed from the room, closing the door with a quiet click behind her.

*

Bleary-eyed through lack of sleep, the following morning Jenny went in search of Sol.

For most of the night she'd lain awake, whilst her thoughts thrashed it out amongst themselves. Still, she was no nearer to figuring out what it was she would do.

Of course, she knew what she *should* do; however, the battle raging on between her head and her heart was a complicated one for several reasons, and right now she was unsure which would prove the victor. Nor was it merely about the money. The prestige which she felt her new position gave her was a mightily strong pull, too. As Songbird, she felt noticed, counted, *worthy* for the first time in her life. The prospect of losing that, of going back to being faceless, no one, just dreary old gutter-dweller Jenny Brodings was a dreadful one. As indeed for the wages . . . Oh, what she could do with all that brass. If she stayed on, she'd never have to worry about destitution again.

But doing what she had yesterday evening, night after night after night . . .?

Would she be able to bear it? Did she possess the stomach for such a thing? She wasn't so sure. Sordid was what it was; aye, and dirty. And she did feel unclean to think back on those leering people ogling her exposed body like that. There wasn't enough soap in the city to scrub clean the sear of their eyes from her flesh, nor the memory of it from her mind, she was sure.

And yet, as Cassandra had pointed out, it was only looking. Wasn't it?

Pity the poor women forced to do much, much

210

worse to earn a crust. At least she didn't have to suffer things that far.

As for the possibility of her family discovering . . . no. Right now, she wouldn't dwell on that, couldn't.

Just why had things had to go and turn out like this, why? Only one short day ago she'd been delirious with happiness, so full of hope for the future, and now it all seemed tainted. Why did nothing ever run smoothly in her life, eh? Was a tiny bit of good fortune just for once really too much to ask?

'Sweet Jenny, darling.' Sol received her full of smiles. 'You slept well?'

'Not really. Mister, we need to talk. Last night . . .'

'Ah, yes.' He pulled out a chair. 'Please.'

'I hated doing that,' she told him, when they were sitting facing one another. 'Grateful for this position I might be, mister, aye, but I never imagined, never dreamed . . .' She shuddered. 'Your face when you said I must do it. You were different. Scary almost.'

'Scary, me? Dear oh dear.' Cocking his head, Sol clicked his tongue. 'That is the last thing I am. What you thought you saw must have been a trick of the lights.'

Scrutinising him now, amiable as ever, she wondered if that might well be a possibility? 'Aye, mebbe.'

'Now I understand how the events of last night could have come as a surprise. I do. However, my audiences hand over good money to be entertained, and it is my mission to ensure that wish is fulfilled. We must give the paying customers what they want, now, mustn't we?'

211

'But it's all so . . . filthy.'

'Nonsense. Harmless fun. Boys will be boys, little Songbird.'

'But mister, they weren't even listening. I sang my bleedin' heart out, standing there in my lovely new frock, and hardly anyone batted an eyelid. Nay, it weren't my gob they were interested in, I don't reckon—'

'No, no. Had they not deemed you talented, they would have had no qualms in letting it be known. You're good. Exceptionally so.'

Recalling the opera man who had been verbally chased from the stage, she was forced to admit to herself Sol did have a point. 'I suppose.'

'Trust me on this. You do still trust me, don't you?'

'I do.'

'No harm will come to you under my employ. You have my word on that.'

Again, she bobbed her head. She was special to him – valuable too, this she knew. He wouldn't risk anything happening if it might mean losing her.

'So?' he asked her softly. 'What will you do? I very much hope you'll stay, Jenny.'

'I'm not yet certain in my head, I . . .'

'Why don't you take the rest of the day off?' he announced suddenly.

'But mister, I'm meant to be helping out with costumes, I promised Doll. And then I have to rehearse for tonight's performance—'

'I insist. A few hours to yourself to clear your mind

will serve you well. Visit the shops, purchase something nice with your wages. Treat yourself.'

Jenny blinked, and a warmness she'd never experienced before coursed through her, making her catch her breath. Treat herself? Never in her life before had she done that. By, but it did sound nice. She smiled.

'Aye, mister, all right. Ta, thanks.'

'I'll see you this evening.'

With a nod and a grin, she dashed off to collect her shawl.

Outside, she looked left and right along the street. Did she have the confidence to brave the high-end stores the like of which Market Street and Piccadilly boasted? She'd seen the sort of customer who frequented those types of establishments, the well-heeled ladies in their fine dresses and gentlemen in top hats. That wasn't her world. She'd stick out like a sore thumb, might even be refused service. London Road, then? Again, she shook the idea from her head. Somewhat less impressive the premises there might be but still, she wasn't sure enough of herself to attempt it, hadn't the first idea how to conduct herself with the shop owners or know what questions to ask. Then where . . .?

Smithfield's it is.

There was comfort in habit – it was all she knew, after all. Besides, there was nothing wrong with second-hand clothing so long as you knew what to look out for. Maybe one day, when she was rich and famous, she'd possess the nuance to visit those other, better places, but not yet.

'Eeh, lass, there's no danger of you getting above yourself, is there?' she said out loud to herself, smiling wryly as she set forth for the bustling market.

An hour later, hugging the package of clothing to her chest and feeling mighty pleased with herself, she made the journey out to Ancoats and Nobby's house. Sol had said to have the day to herself after all, and there was no way she could have wasted some precious free time all on herself without coming to visit Noah.

When she reached the street, she headed first of all not for the old man's door but her own.

The rent was paid up on the cellar for the next fortnight – what she planned to do after that, she wasn't yet certain. A part of her had said she should keep the tenancy on until then, just in case, and now she was glad she had.

She'd decided on the walk to slip inside home and get changed into her new rig-out before going to see them. Eeh, their faces would be a picture. If this didn't prove to them how well she was doing for herself, nothing would.

It wasn't swanking, was it? she asked of herself with a bite of her lip, the thought occurring to her suddenly. Then just as quickly she dismissed the worry. She just wanted everyone to be proud of her, that's all – was that really asking too much?

The familiar room was freezing and dead as the grave. Staring about, she shivered. It felt different, somehow. Empty, that's what it was. No Noah, no laughter or chatter. Loveless, aye. Her chest constricted in sadness.

Was it only a few short days ago since they were here, living beneath this roof, with each other? It seemed a lifetime ago to her now . . .

Pulling herself together before remorse and regret could settle – that would do no one any good; what was done was done – she placed her buys on the floor and unpicked the knot in the twine holding the bundle in place.

Nonetheless, as she lifted out the contents and shook each piece out, she couldn't stop her eyes from straying around the space. Memories, both good and not so good, trickled then gushed through her mind on a tide. Sitting back on her heels, she hugged herself. The years growing up here, the happiness despite the hardship, her parents, the unquestionable love. Cooking for herself and Noah when later it was just the two of them, mopping up his tears when he came home with knees shredded from the chimneys, soothing him to sleep with song as they snuggled in bed.

More recent recollections were quick to sweep in next: whitewashing the walls and the fun they had had. George's hilarious expression when she'd run the wet brush down his face . . . No. She tried to shake the thought of him from her brain fiercely. However, her efforts made little impact: his image refused to leave her.

She saw him again, lengths of wood piled in his arms, smiling on the doorstep, having arrived to mend the broken cellar stairs. The tongue peeking out of the side of his mouth in concentration as he'd worked, all the while without a word of complaint and wanting nothing in return. The way his shoulder muscles rippled as he knocked and hammered the planks into position . . .

'No.' She spoke the word aloud now. 'Please, no more.'

Her plea had no impact.

His expression at the Balloon, the clear devastation etched therein, when she'd shouted at him what she had, for all the world to hear. His eyes, creased and shining with pain, when he'd revealed softly the meaning of that word. Beautiful. He thought her beautiful, despite her being ugly inside right through to the core as she was. *Oh George, George.*

She missed him. She missed him a lot, in fact. And she was sorry, so sorry . . .

Solomon's and all that came with it. Was it worth it? Doubt stabbed.

Was she really doing the right thing? Giving up all she knew and loved, the hurt it had caused to those around her already. The less-than-glamorous aspect of the job she'd rather not dwell upon . . .

Happen she ought to just pack the whole thing in, go back to how things used to be. Safe, contented. Decent, familiar. *Dull.* She nodded slowly. Worrisome most of the time and downright desperate often. Year following year of grinding struggle stretching ahead with little else to look forward to? Breaking her vow to Noah, him going without? Her heart hardened and her mouth did likewise. Give it all up? Not bloody likely.

'So, how do I look?' she asked Nobby minutes later when he answered his door. Raising her arms, she preened. 'I paid over the odds for the dress and hat – well, you have to, don't you, for quality? – but the boots were a steal. Well?' she almost demanded when he merely continued staring at her. 'Cat got your tongue?'

'We've missed thee. You're all right, lass?'

She gave an irritated nod. 'But what about the clothes, Nobby? Do I scrub up well or what!'

'Aye . . . you look very nice.'

Very nice? That was it? Her annoyance mounted. She looked spectacular, and he knew it.

Her tone was cool: 'Noah inside, is he?' Without waiting for a response, she brushed past the old man into the house.

The lad's face split into a grin upon seeing her: 'Jen!'

'Hello, love. Come here, give me a hug.'

'But why're you here, our Jen? It ain't even Sunday.'

Holding him close, she smiled. 'The music hall master said I was to take the day off, have some time to myself. Very nice like that, is Sol,' she added, more for Nobby's sake than anything, and was gratified when he dropped his gaze. 'Now, tell me how you are, lad. Been up to owt nice, have thee?'

The parting a little later was as painful as the last time but, once again, Jenny numbed herself to it, had to for sanity's sake. It had to be done.

'I'll come and see thee again on Sunday, lad, all right?'

'All right, Jen.'

'You be good for Nobby, now, d'you hear?'

'He allus is. Never a moment's bother, he's not,' the man said, coming to see her off at the door. 'You'll look after yourself, lass?'

Her earlier negative feelings towards him wavered before slowly melting. The familiar care and affection reflected in his eyes was almost her undoing, and she swallowed back emotion.

'Aye, Nobby, I will. You as well, eh? And thanks again for all you're doing with Noah. I'd be lost without thee.' She rummaged in the pocket of her skirt and brought out the two pound notes remaining from her wages. 'Here. Please,' she insisted before Nobby could protest.

'But—'

'But nowt.'

'Nay, nay – that's far too much!'

'Tripe. It's nowhere near enough what we've had in dribs and drabs off you this past year. Treat yourself and the lad. And the same again next week.'

'You'll visit Coral afore you head back, will you?'

She hesitated then shook her head. 'Nay, I don't think so. I don't want to run the risk of bumping into Martin, haven't the energy for it.' *Nor have I the strength for another round of her telling me what a mistake I've made. Why, why, can't you both just be happy for me? It's like you've turned against me and, because of it, I'm starting to turn against youse, don't hardly recognise myself or my own mind at times any more. And I hate it, hate it* . . . 'Tell her, though, if you see her . . . tell her I were asking about her.'

Nobby smiled. 'That I will. God speed, Jenny.'

She made her slow way back to Solomon's with a heaviness in her breast that refused to abate. Whether it was leaving Noah again or the thought of returning to Solomon's that had her feeling this way, she couldn't rightly say. Nor did it matter. Both were necessary evils, it couldn't be changed, and the sooner she got used to the fact, the better for everyone.

'Jenny? Jenny, lass?'

Mind still on her thoughts, she turned towards the source of the voice with only half her senses in the here and now. Yet they soon snapped back into focus, her guts spasming with dread in the process, to see the woman beckoning her forward. With great reluctance, she dragged herself across the road.

'Hello, Hyacinth.'

The landlady searched her face for a moment before saying, 'Eeh, you look awful, lass.'

'I'm all right.'

'Nice new outfit, I see – it suits thee.'

Despite her recent desperation to have herself be noticed, now it didn't seem to matter. The observation brought her no pleasure. She dipped her head. 'Ta, thanks.'

'You're getting on all right, then, in your fresh job?'

'Aye,' she whispered. Then: 'Eeh, Hyacinth,' she cried. Her words came out on a rush. 'Fancy me leaving you in the lurch as I did, and in such a nasty, cruel way. My behaviour at the Balloon that night, all them things I said . . . I were a bitch! You ought to have clobbered me one, cheeking you and spewing them hateful words to you as I did – I'd not have blamed you a bit. I'm that sorry, I am!'

'Hush now, no need for all that—'

'There's every need! I were out of line. You've been nowt but kindness itself to me and just look how I repaid you. As for George . . . God, he must detest me. You both must.'

'Do we hell. We don't, nay,' Hyacinth reaffirmed when Jenny gave her a less-than-convinced snort. 'It were the drink talking, not thee. He knows that as do I.'

Relief like no other coursed through Jenny and she sagged. 'Fancy me saying what I did about him, though, and in front of everyone . . . I didn't mean it.'

'Aye, you did.' Hyacinth shrugged. 'I'd rather you'd not said it to him, that I do, but well . . . the lad *is* a terrible singer, it's true.'

'What?' Jenny was gobsmacked. 'You know?'

'Well of course I do, and so do the customers. We ain't ruddy deaf. Thing is, he came to me desperate for work and I couldn't turn him away. He were due a bit of luck, poor bloke. Had a God-awful time of it, he had, so I thought: what the hell? He loves singing, allus has, and who am I to take that away from him? The customers, they don't say nowt about his ability. George has gorra good soul, they know that, and his heart's in the right place, bless him. Mebbe we've been wrong leading him along but it were done with the best intentions. Anyroad, the truth's out now, eh? He's not took it too bad really, I'm glad to say, and is still at the Balloon. He works the counter now, serving drinks.'

Jenny wanted the ground to open up and swallow her; she was utterly shamefaced. 'Oh, Hyacinth, I feel just awful, *awful*.'

'What's done is done, lass.'

'Aye, but still ...' Her eyes turned suddenly thoughtful. She frowned. 'You said he's allus loved singing – you've known him a long time, then?' She'd just assumed they had made one another's acquaintance but a year or two past when George began working at the tavern.

'Oh aye, aye. I've known him since he were a lad. Horrible time of it, he had, growing up. But well, it's no surprise with a father like what he's got. Divil of a fella, he is.'

And to think she'd thought she couldn't possibly feel any rottener than she did already. This just got worse and worse. 'I had no idea.'

'You'd not. George don't like to talk of it and I can't say I blame him. He's a good lad, you know, Jenny.'

'Aye,' she murmured.

'And he's reet taken with thee, you know.'

Though she made no reply to this, Jenny knew without question that the woman was mistaken. George had made his feelings concerning her perfectly clear. He thought her but a child – a bonny

221

one, perhaps, but a child all the same. What's more, he'd been right all along. She had a lot of growing up to do, she saw that now.

'He plans to visit yon music hall – Solomon's, is it? – on his next night off.'

'What?' *No* . . .

'Aye, he wants to come and watch the rising star in action. He's proud of thee, Jenny.'

'When will it be . . .?'

'The morrow.'

'Hyacinth, I, I've got to go now.'

'Well, don't be a stranger, now, will you? There'll allus be a warm welcome for thee at the Balloon, remember that.'

'I will, aye . . . Goodbye.' Blindly, Jenny turned and made her escape.

Oh Lord, oh dear Lord.

The panicked lamentations played inside her brain on a loop throughout the remainder of the journey.

He can't come to watch me. He can't discover . . . he can't!

The shame of it would surely kill her.

Just what in God's name was she going to do?

Chapter 11

'I've made up my mind. I'm leaving.'

Having burst into Cassandra's room, Jenny was almost half mad with panic.

'What's happened?'

'Everything! I'm going, I must!'

The woman took hold of her by the arms, forcing her to stop. 'Calm down, take a breath. Now, start from the beginning; what's occurred?'

'Someone I know, a, a good friend, he's planning on coming to Solomon's to watch me perform. He can't, Cassandra! No way on God's green earth can George see me doing . . . doing those terrible, mucky things—!'

'Is that all?' She chuckled. 'By 'eck, Jenny, you don't half get yourself in a tizzy over the daftest stuff.'

'Daft? This ain't daft – it'll ruin everything!'

Cassandra sighed theatrically. 'Look, I'll sort it. All right?'

'What? How?'

'I'll alert the doorkeeper as to the issue and get him to refuse this fella entry. Say he's a trouble starter or some such. Problem solved.'

Jenny dropped slowly into a chair. 'It'll work, aye?'

'Course. Now, sort out your face and go across to the music hall, get ready for tonight. Doll will be wondering where you've got to.'

Feeling marginally brighter now, Jenny nodded. 'Aye, all right. And thanks, Cassandra.'

'Anytime,' she chirruped, before disappearing from the room on a cloud of cheap perfume.

The following evening, true to her word, the woman came to collect Jenny shortly before opening time and walked with her down to the foyer. They took cover in a side alcove facing the octagonal pay booth and waited. Minutes went by and people arrived in their droves. However, of George there was as yet no sign. Jenny was beginning to think he wouldn't show after all. Then suddenly there he was.

The sight of him took her breath away for a moment and the strongest urge to go to him gripped her, but she refrained from doing so, had to. She tugged at Cassandra's sleeve. 'That's him.'

Her eyes widened appreciatively. 'Handsome bloke.'

'Quick, Cassandra, afore it's too late.'

Nodding, the woman shifted forward. Catching the doorkeeper's eye, whom it was clear she'd briefed earlier as to what would take place, she flicked her chin towards George. The doorkeeper moved immediately to approach his target, and Cassandra rejoined Jenny and guided her away.

'All done, let's go.'

'But . . .' Glancing back, Jenny saw that the doorkeeper had confronted George and the two were speaking heatedly. 'What if he talks him round, don't get removed after all?'

'He'll be shown the door, all right. Now come along, will you? I'm on in a minute. Sol will have my guts for garters if I cause a delay.'

Throughout the evening's show, Jenny was on tenterhooks. Shielded from the audience's view behind the gold curtain, she'd scanned and rescanned the faces of the braying crowd until they all began to swim into a smudgy mess – still, she kept up her vigil, couldn't afford to take anything by chance. Yet of George, there really didn't appear to be any sign, praise be. Finally, as it was almost time for her performance, she'd begun to relax a fraction.

For one more night, at least, her dirty secret was safe.

As usual, the majority of the acts – in particular those featuring women – from tragedies to comic skits, dances and songs, all shared one strong common theme: over-sexualisation. And, as she'd come if not to accept then to expect, Jenny's performance was to prove again no different.

She sang three songs and during each was forced to raise her skirts and even tease the neckline of her dress lower over her shoulders. Sending her mind elsewhere in a desperate attempt to block out the whoops and whistles and vulgar comments thrown her way did little to stem her burning shame. It took all her strength not to dash from the stage and never look back. All the while, but one thought, one minuscule consolation, remained her companion: thank God that George wasn't here to witness this. He would never have looked at her in the same light again, nor would she have blamed him.

It was as her repertoire mercifully drew to a close and she was receiving the crowd's appreciation that she saw him.

Despite the bright lights and the tobacco-smoke-filled air, despite the flat cap that he wore low at the front, partially covering his face, she knew, knew without doubt, instantly. It was him. She'd recognise him anywhere.

Good God in heaven above . . .

Martin.

Becoming aware that she'd spotted him, he tilted his headgear to lock eyes with her fully. Then slowly, slowly, he stretched his mouth into a self-congratulatory smirk.

Locked in total horror, she could neither move nor speak, possessing only the power to gaze back. He rose from his seat, his job evidently done, and made off towards the exit.

Still, Jenny could but watch. She tracked her brother-in-law's every step until he disappeared from view. Then she turned and, on legs that felt strangely detached, made her unsteady way off stage.

Ignoring her fellow performers and Doll, who were milling about in the wings as she passed them, seeing no one and hearing their words of praise even less, she headed straight for her accommodation and crawled fully dressed into bed.

Cassandra found her, still unmoved and staring at the ceiling at nothing, sometime later.

'Jenny?'

'It's finished.'

'Eh? What is?'

'It's finished,' she echoed in a monotone. 'I'm finished.'

The woman flopped down beside her and rolled her eyes. 'Go on, get it off your chest, what's occurred now?'

'I knew, you know, deep down, that this was a mistake. I were too pig-headed to admit it. I let pride get in t' way of what's really important. Just what have I become, eh?'

'I ain't gorra clue what you're talk—'

'Foolish, arrogant, head in the clouds, that's me,' Jenny murmured on, alone in her private and terrible new world. 'Too big for my boots, aye. It were all too easy, you see. Something like this when you're someone like me . . . it's too tempting not to be sucked in.'

'Hell's teeth, Jenny. Just what on earth are you going on about? I don't under—'

'I want to go home.'

'Then go. No one's stopping thee.'

'I want to go home,' she said again. Then: 'I'm *going* home.'

Cassandra watched in silence as she sprang from the bed and began pulling off her stage costume. She tugged on her own clothes, thrust her feet into her boots and snatched up her shawl from the back of the chair. Only when she was making a dash for the door did the woman finally speak. Her words stopped Jenny dead in her tracks.

'What did you say?'

'I said have a nice life,' Cassandra repeated. 'Oh, and don't forget to drop your wages into Sol's office on your way out.'

'But . . .' Colour rose up Jenny's neck. She licked her lips. 'I don't have them any more.'

'You've spent all the brass?'

'Well . . . aye.'

'Dear oh dear oh dear.' Cassandra clicked her tongue softly several times. 'Whatever will tha do?'

In that instant, something inside Jenny's head popped and her eyes sprang fully open. For the first time she saw it, what had been there all along, staring her right in the face, mocking in its truth, her stupidity . . . Everything, all of it . . . The whole thing was a smokescreen. It had been nothing but a well-practised ruse, planned through with expert precision – and she'd fallen headlong into it without a single clue. Sol, Cassandra and who knew who else: they were all in this together.

Devastation, mortification and bone-shaking fury, the latter aimed more at herself than anyone else – how could she have been so brainless? – slammed home with the force of a hammer blow; she staggered back against the wall. So acute was the awakening, Jenny thought she might vomit.

'Now, you have two options,' Cassandra was saying, her demeanour cool as a spring breeze. Jenny could barely hear past the sound of blood rushing through her ears. 'Number one, try and somehow claw back the three pounds.'

'I can't do that, can I?' she roared. 'The money's spent.'

'Aye well, that's your lookout. As the saying goes: a fool and their brass are soon parted!'

If it wasn't for the fact they were the only garments here that she owned – she'd left her old clothes behind at the cellar – Jenny would have wrenched the wretched things from her back and torn them to shreds. *Stupid, foolish, big-headed show-off, she was nowt else!*

She hadn't a chance of claiming the money back. Returning the items to the market was an impossibility; the stallholder didn't accept refunds. She might, at a push, buy them back from Jenny – at a fraction of the price she'd forked out for them, that is, which of course wouldn't be enough. As for the notes she'd handed over to Owd Nobby: how in the world could she ask for them back? And, anyway, even if she did, who was to say he hadn't already spent them? She herself had told him had she not, damn and blast her, to treat him and Noah. The lot could be gone for all she knew.

The last and only other choice left to her would be to borrow the amount from someone; but who? She didn't know of anyone who had anywhere near that kind of money to chuck around. And, anyway, how would she pay them back? No, there was no one to bail her out. She was well and truly stuck.

'What's the other option?' she asked Cassandra through gritted teeth.

'It's simple: work off the week you're paid up for.'

'Sol, he knew I were in two minds about stopping on here; that's why he gave me my wages early, in't it? He trapped me.'

The woman smiled. 'He's a wily one, all right.'

'Wily? He's downright wicked – and you, you're no better! Right up his arse, you are, and no mistake.'

Cassandra shrugged. 'I look after his interests and, in return, he looks after mine. What's wrong with that?'

'You get a bit extra in your hand at the week's end to bully and spy on his acts, see they don't leave – and damage his pockets in the process – more like. And there was me thinking you were my friend. Bitch, you're nowt else. Have you no morals left in you at all?'

'You don't get owt for nowt in this world, darling. Got to make your own luck, aye. The sooner you realise that, the better for you.'

'I'm off – today! – and that's that.'

'Silly, foolish little girl . . .'

Jenny rushed at her, intending to wipe off the smug smile for good, but Cassandra grappled with her wrists, managing successfully to hold her back.

'Temper, temper . . . You ought to be more careful, yer know. You don't want an assault charge on top of one of theft, now, do you?'

'What theft? What you blathering about?'

'If you so much as think of leaving here, Sol will have the law on you so quick you'll not have time to blink. Taking money under false pretences . . . that's fraud, Jenny. It'll mean prison for thee, you mark my words.'

'You set of bastards!'

'Oh, calm down, for Christ's sake.' Cassandra pushed her away from her. 'All this, it ain't so bad as all that. Just get through the week and you're free to go. You never know, by then, you might have even grown to like it and decide to stop on—'

'Aye, and there'll be a snowstorm in hell on the day! Not likely. It'll never happen. I'll *never* be like you, never!'

'You know, Jenny, you're so daft.' The woman shook her head pityingly. 'That piousness of yourn won't fill your belly or keep the rain from your head, not in this life. A sharp mind does, though. Aye, wits are what's needed. Get some – you'll thank me one day. You could do well for yourself if you'd only give it a try. Nor am I only talking about prancing about the stage here at Solomon's.'

Jenny frowned.

'That variety hall in Bolton town – Sol's mentioned it to thee, no doubt? Aye, I thought so. Well, that place ain't exactly like here, nay. That one's a bit more special, and so is the money. There, we don't have an audience as such. What we offer there . . . it's more what you might call private performances. If you get my drift.'

Jenny had a good idea, all right. Her mouth twisted. 'By God, just when I thought things couldn't get any worse . . . Just how was I ever pulled in by the lies? You're disgusting, all of you. Low I might well have fallen but, by God, I'd never sink that far, never!'

The woman was unfazed by her response. 'We'll see.'

'Oh, I've had enough of this, get out of my way.'

'And where d'you think you're going?'

'Out. There's someone I must see.'

'All right. With the show finished, the rest of the night's your own now, after all. But Jenny?'

She glared back over her shoulder.

'Don't even think of doing a disappearing act. Sol will get the police involved, believe that.'

'Happen I'll get the law on him, let them know all about his filthy practices, has tha thought of that?' Jenny threw back.

'You can try but you'll not get far. Sol's clever. You really think he'd be daft enough to leave a trace of his activities? Grow up.'

With a last, hate-filled look at the woman, Jenny slammed from the room.

The sky was snow-heavy, and the pregnant clouds surrendered their load the moment Jenny stepped outside. Tilting her face, she stood, motionless, for what felt an age, letting the fluttering flakes soothe her flushed skin.

The task ahead was a monstrous one but, strangely, she felt as though a great weight had been lifted from her. At last, the decision had been made for her and her time at Solomon's was drawing to a close. Still, she could scarcely comprehend how naïve she'd been. Stupid, too, by the bucketload. Sol had fed her lie upon lie, burrowed like the worm that he was into her mind, eating away at her sensibilities, until she'd blithely swallowed all he had to spout without a second's doubt.

Families are such fickle beasts . . . Envy is an ugly thing, Jenny.

Recalling his manipulation, she shook her head. Those good people of hers back home were not the ugly ones, were not in the wrong, never had been – Sol was. He was the foul one, all right. She saw it now as clear as day. What's more, she felt utterly ashamed.

Her treatment of her nearest and dearest, who were obviously far wiser than she and only ever wanted the best for her, was nothing short of appalling. Well, she'd put this right, by she would. She'd beg their forgiveness, plead to them on her two knees if she must. She had to set this right, whatever it took. And that started right now.

Jenny was but an arrow's flight from Carruthers Street when she spotted her brother-in-law leaning against the side wall of a neighbouring house.

It would appear he hadn't yet been home. Which also meant he couldn't have spoken to Coral. *She wasn't too late.* Inexplicable relief replaced her dread. On a soft cry, she rushed towards him.

'Martin? Martin, it's me.'

He raised his head slowly. To her surprise, she saw his cheeks were wet with tears. He screwed shut his eyes; tentatively, she put her hand on his arm.

'Martin?'

'It'll kill her, you know. Coral finding out about thee. It'll *kill* her.'

'Then please, don't say nowt. I've, I've give it up. Honest, Martin, I have.'

His eyes narrowed. 'Aye?'

'Really,' she insisted. 'Well, at least I will at the end of the week—'

'Oh, you snidy young . . .' He laughed mirthlessly. 'I actually didn't believe it, you know, at first. I've heard the rumours about Solomon's, all right. When Coral mentioned you'd been taken on there, that she were worried – by God, she don't know the half of it! – I reckoned I had to come and see for myself. Watching thee the night . . . you love every damn minute of it, don't you?'

'Nay! Do I hell, Martin. I hate it! Sol, the manager, he's got me over a barrel—'

'Huh!'

'Don't be so filthy minded,' she snapped. 'I mean he paid me up for the week – three full pounds – and like a fool, I went and spent it. Now I've no choice but to see the next few shows through. He'll have the law on me else. Don't ever think for a minute I like doing it, though. It's wrong, it is, I know it.'

He directed his next words to the wall. 'I never wanted this, you know. I never asked for it. I were tricked, Jenny. Now, I don't know how to cope with it, what to do . . .'

'Never wanted what? Tell me,' she urged. 'You ain't been yourself forra while, it's true. What's occurred?'

'*You* did.'

'What's that meant to mean?'

'I can't take to thee. I tried and I can't. I *can't* . . .'

'Aye well.' She shrugged. 'That's nowt fresh, is it? As far back as I can remember you never have liked me much, have you, not really. I know that well enough.'

234

'That's not true.'

'Aye? So what changed? For it *is* true to say you can't bear the sight of me these days. I'm right, ain't I?' And at his nod: 'Well? Why have I become such an issue to you now?'

'Because she's getting closer to thee,' he burst out. 'She is, I can see it. Never out of each other's pockets lately, you and Coral ain't. Soon, she'll not be able to pull back, and all will be ruined . . . She swore to me, *swore* it'd never get out!'

'What? What are you talking about?' However, her words fell on deaf ears; he continued to ramble.

'How will I hold my head up in public again, eh? I'll be a bleedin' laughing stock – and it's all your fault!'

Jenny was completely baffled. 'You're not making sense . . . have you been drinking?'

'Well, wouldn't you? It's all what's getting me through of late.'

'Go on, Martin, go home.' She sighed. 'You're sozzled, don't know what you're saying—'

'I do, damn it!'

'Go on,' she tried again, giving him a nudge towards his door. 'We'll pretend tonight never happened, eh? Please? It can be our little secret.'

'Secret? Oh, another one, eh? Christ, what is it with your family? Like mother like daughter—' He cut himself off to glance away.

'You what? Mam didn't have no secrets.'

'Huh!'

Jenny's eyes had turned to slits. She pointed a

finger in his face. 'Careful, Martin,' she murmured. 'Drunk or no, you don't ever speak ill of her. You mind your tongue—'

'Your mam's a harlot.'

'Evil-minded bastard!' Jenny struck him hard across the mouth.

Panting, watching him wipe the blood from his lip, she squared her shoulders in readiness of his explosion.

It never came.

Instead, he smiled twistedly. 'I'm the bastard?' he said at last. 'You need to take a long hard look in the mirror, Jenny.'

'Eh?'

'The woman I call a wife. She ain't your sister. Coral's your mam.'

Chapter 12

'My mam's sleeping in Philips Park Cemetery, you disgusting liar.'

Martin said nothing.

'D'you hear me?' Jenny growled. 'Annie Brodings, remember? *She's* my mam.'

'She ain't. Coral is.'

'Nay!'

'Jenny—'

'Get your horrible hands off me!' she cried, slapping away his attempt to reach out to her. Staggering around, she set off on a stumbling run across the cobbles.

'Jenny. Jenny, wait. I, I'm sorry . . .'

She hurtled around corners, pelted down refuse-strewn entryways and continued on, on through the poorly lit lanes and streets. Seemingly on instinct alone, when she came to a shuddering halt, her lungs ablaze, she found she was standing outside Owd Nobby's.

She lifted both fists and pummelled at the door. 'Nobby! Nobby!'

'Ay, what in God's name—?'

'Is Coral my mam?'

'What?'

She moved past him into the house. Ashen-faced, the elderly man followed.

'Martin said . . . he said Coral's my mam.'

'He never did. Eeh, Jenny lass.'

He wasn't denying it. Nor did he appear scathing. He didn't even scoff.

It was true?

'Nay.' She shook her head jerkily. 'Nay, it's a lie, it is, it—!'

'Eeh, Jenny lass.'

'Stop saying that! For God's sake, Nobby – I don't understand!'

'I'm sorry.'

The two words and the way in which he delivered them were all the concrete proof she needed.

Burying her face in her hands, she howled.

'I prayed you'd not find out, I did . . .'

'You knew.'

'Lass . . .'

'For how long?' she choked. Then when he looked away: 'Always? You've allus known? All of my life?'

'It weren't my secret to tell. I'm that sorry.'

'Stay away from me,' she whispered, backing towards the door. 'The lot of you . . . never speak to me again.'

'But where are you going? Don't leave in this state.'

She didn't listen. Couldn't. *Wouldn't.*

'Jenny, lass, lass . . .'

Her brain near to bursting point, she set off once more into the night.

'And what time did you get back yesterday, yer dirty stop-out? Out on the sauce again, were thee?'

Jenny pulled the blankets up over her head.

'Miss High and Mighty my foot – pah! You're no better than me at all, ruddy hypocrite.'

Leave me be. Please.

Cassandra laughed and left the room, slamming the door behind her. Curling into a foetal position, Jenny closed her eyes.

Nothing was real any more. Nothing made sense.

Throughout the agonisingly long night, she'd found herself going over every minute detail of her past, picking apart conversations, analysing looks and comments, but there was no tangible clue, no evidence pointing to this being truth. She'd sensed nothing from the couple who raised her, never not once, and even less from Coral herself. How, *how*, could this be real?

And yet it was; she knew it without question now.

Her sister was her mam.

Her mother and father were her grandparents.

The lot of them were foul and filthy liars.

By mid-afternoon, weak with exhaustion, her mind wound itself down. Now, if she once more attempted to revisit all she'd known up until this point, it was like wading through thick mud. Thoughts were disjointed, out of reach. Jenny was glad of it. She didn't want to think, to feel . . . not ever again.

An hour before the music hall opened for the evening, Doll came to see Jenny in her room.

'Deary? It's me.'

'Aye, what is it?'

'There's a man outside wants to speak to you.'

Her eyes opened. Slowly, she peeled back the bedcovers to look at Doll. 'Who is it?'

'He didn't give a name, but he says it's urgent.'

She nodded and when Doll had gone, lay for a handful of minutes more staring into space.

She didn't want to move, see anyone; what was the point? Whoever it was and whatever they had to say wouldn't change what she now knew. Why couldn't they all just leave her alone as she desired?

'He's still there, deary,' Doll called up at length. 'Will you see him?'

She muttered a curse. Knowing she'd get no peace until she faced the visitor, she forced herself up, and down the stairs.

'Jenny.'

'What do you want?'

Martin lifted his cap to run a hand through his hair. He sighed. 'How are you?'

'Oh, I'm gradely. Feeling great, aye. Top of the world—'

'Lass . . .'

'How the bleedin' hell d'you think I am, eh?' There was no screaming or shouting, no histrionics; she didn't possess the strength. She spoke in a harsh flat tone. 'Why are you here?'

240

'To say that I'm sorry. Telling thee how I did . . . It were cruel.'

'But nonetheless true.'

'Aye.'

She folded her arms. 'Is that all?'

'Jenny, we need to discuss this, proper like. Coral, she—'

'Lied to me.'

'She wants to see thee. Desperate to, she is.'

'You told her what you did?'

'Nay. Nobby. He called to ours this afternoon.'

'Coward.'

Martin glanced away. 'She's in bits, Jenny. She were going to come here to see you herself but I persuaded her to let me try first. I just . . . I want to put things right.'

'Why? To ease your own conscience?'

'I've done wrong.'

'You all have. Every one of you have betrayed me, lied to my face all my life.' She shrugged. 'Nowt can make this better.'

'But—'

'Goodbye, Martin.'

'Wait.' He rummaged inside his jacket pocket and brought out three pound notes. 'Here.'

Jenny was nonplussed. 'How . . .?'

'I've begged, borrowed and stole to scrape that together. Your old landlady, Hyacinth from the Balloon, she contributed the lion's share. Pay that swine Sol back and come home.'

241

Home.

Well that was a joke. What home? What family? It had all been torn asunder.

'I'm stopping here,' she heard herself say.

'But . . . you can't, you have to—'

'Don't come here again. None of you. Just leave me alone.'

'I need a drink.'

Leaning on the doorjamb, Cassandra looked Jenny up and down. Then she smiled, nodded. She stepped aside. 'Come on in.'

A chair festooned with clothes sat beside the wardrobe – Jenny dropped into it with a long sigh.

'I take it he weren't bearing glad tidings then, that male caller of yourn?'

'Summat like that.'

'Here.' The woman handed her a glass tumbler a quarter filled with amber liquid. 'Get that down thee.'

The first sip scorched Jenny's throat and caused her to screw up her face. The ones that followed proved marginally more palatable. She eased back in her seat, her vow of sobriety flown.

'D'you want to tell me about it?'

Eyeing Cassandra, Jenny frowned. She didn't even know what she was doing here but could think of nowhere else to go. 'Why should I? You were a real bitch to me yesterday, there were no need for it.'

'There were no need for me to let you in my room just now, neither, but I did.' She arched an eyebrow.

'Aye. Thanks.'

Perching on the foot of her bed and folding her long, shapely legs, Cassandra swirled the liquid in her own glass. 'So d'you want to tell me? It must have been summat bad for you to come to me.'

'There were no one else.'

She laughed. 'You're honest, lass, I'll give thee that. Oh come on, just spill – a problem shared and all that . . .?'

Jenny downed the rest of her drink, coughed, then nodded. 'I've found out that my sister's not my sister at all. She's my mam.'

Cassandra blew out air slowly. 'Bloody hell.'

'Aye.'

'What will you do?'

'Nowt.'

'Fair enough. Fancy a top up?'

Jenny couldn't help but chuckle. 'Giving advice ain't one of your strong points, is it?'

'Not really,' Cassandra admitted. She grinned. 'Sod it, eh? Let's just get sozzled instead, what d'you say?'

'I say aye. You're right: sod it. Sod 'em all!'

Jenny found the show that evening far easier to deal with than those that had gone before. She cared nothing this night for propriety, morality, did what the audience demanded with benumbed abandon. She knew only emptiness inside her heart – and the same could be said for her mind. With her senses dulled with alcohol, she found that her brain and all the terrible things scourging inside had torpefied her and it didn't seem to matter too much any more. She didn't have to think about a thing, didn't have to feel, and she was more than grateful of the fact. Brandy, it seemed, was her new best friend.

Sol was full of praise later. 'You were wonderful out there tonight, little Songbird,' he gushed. 'You're fast becoming the beating heart of this music hall, do you know that? I hope we'll be working together for a long time to come.'

Taking a swig from the bottle she'd left backstage, Jenny shrugged. 'Aye, why not?' After all, she didn't belong anywhere else any more, did she?

She spent her Sunday off the following day with Cassandra and a few more of her fellow performers, drinking in the dancer's room.

Cassandra explained that, for varying reasons, they too didn't get along with their families. She herself had severed all contact with her own long ago. 'They're more bother than they're worth, the lot of them.'

'You're right enough there, all right,' Jenny whole-heartedly agreed, emptying her glass once again and immediately heading for a refill. 'To friends instead!'

When on Monday morning she awoke to someone shaking her by the shoulder, Jenny genuinely thought she was dying – never in her life before had she felt so ill. 'Oh, dear God, my *head*.'

'Deary, you're wanted again.'

'Nay, Doll, please . . . I'm poorly. Tell whoever's calling to go away.'

'They're insisting they see you.'

Hell's teeth. Groaning, she hauled her body from the bed.

When she saw who the visitor was this time, she came to a juddering halt.

'George . . .'

'Lass. Finally.' He drew her to him in a strong embrace then pulled back, brow creasing. 'Jenny, you stink of stale ale.'

Seeing him again had awakened within her a whole host of emotions. She'd been on the cusp just now of spilling her guts, apologising for her behaviour the last time they were in one another's company, opening up to him about how very much she'd missed him. Now, though, at his remark, embarrassment had her hackles rising and all other feelings flying; she tossed her head. 'I were enjoying myself with friends – norra crime, is it?'

Though he was frowning still, he didn't continue the issue. Instead, he said, 'We've all been worried sick about thee. I tried to see you last night, but that bulldog they've got guarding the door of the music hall wouldn't permit me entrance. Twice, now, that's happened. Lord knows what his problem is.'

'He just mustn't like your face,' she replied nonchalantly.

'Martin said I'd have better luck calling here at the accommodation instead. Eeh, Jenny.' He shook his head. 'Why didn't you leave with him when he offered you the brass?'

Tears were forming, despite herself. She bowed her head. 'Why d'you think? I take it you've heard by now how matters lie?'

'Aye, lass. I'm sorry. It must have come as a shock.'

245

'Humph! You might say that, aye.'

George was silent for a few moments, then: 'Jenny, whatever else is going on back home, you can't stop on here. What that Sol's done, the way he operates, trapping thee . . . he's nobbut a villain. 'Tain't safe.'

'I'm all right—'

'You're *not* all right. Christ's sake, do you know what Martin's saying, what else he's told us about this place? The things he reckons the acts here get up to on that stage . . .?' His expression dropped as realisation dawned. 'Nay. You've not . . . not thee.'

'Aye, that's right, I'm no better than I ought to be – I wonder who I get that from, eh? I'm my mother's daughter, all right.'

'Don't.'

'What, it's the truth, ain't it? D'you know how old Coral is, George? Twenty-nine. That would make her thirteen when she gave birth to me. Thir-bloody-teen! Can you even fathom it?'

'Our parents don't have to define who we are. They don't, I mean it. Take it from me.'

Recalling Hyacinth's revelation regarding his father and less-than-pleasant childhood, Jenny sighed. 'It's all so wrong, though. And don't even get me started on just who the hell got her into trouble, who my father could be—'

'I'll not,' he butted in gently, 'for right now, none of that matters. We're talking about you and this place. You can't stop on here.'

'Solomon's ain't so bad once you get used to it.' However, her attempts to make light of the facts were

246

usurped by a blush. Her anger sparked again. She began walking away. 'Oh look, just leave, will you? Go on, go. I ain't worth bothering with. Do yourself a favour and just forget about me, and don't come back. That goes for the rest of youse.'

'Even Noah?'

The breath caught in her throat.

'Well, Jenny? You not going to visit him yesterday, was it because he's dead to you, now, as well? Because I'll tell you summat, that's what he believes.' George nodded. 'Noah worries you've abandoned him.'

'Nay, nay! Never. I just couldn't bear seeing everyone, having to dwell on the truth ... Course not Noah. Never him. I love the lad, I do, I ...'

'Lass, lass.' George was at her side again in seconds. He took her in his arms once more and held her whilst she cried. 'Him and Nobby, Martin and your Coral, even Hyacinth: they all miss thee, want thee home.'

'And you?' she whispered, lifting her face to gaze into his eyes.

His head moved closer to her own until his mouth was but an inch away from hers. She felt his heart banging through her own chest. He licked his lips and she thought he might kiss her, but instead he breathed deeply, nodded. 'I've brought the brass with me to pay Sol what's owed – come back with me. Say tha will.'

'I *can't*.'

'Why not?'

'My family, George, they lied to me. Nowt's the

247

same now. I don't know who I am any more. They've hurt me so much; I won't forgive them.'

'Give Coral a chance to explain. She's a shell of herself, Jenny, honest. If you could just see her—'

'I'm sorry.' With great reluctance, she extracted herself from his blessed hold and stepped back towards the door. 'Please tell Noah I'll sort summat out, find some way to see him soon. I'll be in touch. Goodbye, George.'

'You don't get rid of me that easy. I'll be back, Jenny, I will.'

'Goodbye, George,' she echoed on a soft sob before fleeing inside.

'Another drink?'

Staring morosely into her glass, tears running unchecked down her cheeks, Jenny nodded.

'Sod 'em, girl, remember?' Cassandra urged. 'You don't need them.'

I do, and I want them, too, she said in her mind. *I miss them, all of them.*

'You know what you need, don't yer?'

Jenny shook her head.

'A change of scene. A few of us are away to Bolton the morrow. Come with us.'

'What, to that glorified brothel?' She was aghast. 'Not on your bloody life!'

'Don't exaggerate, Jenny. Brothel indeed.' The woman tut-tutted. 'It's a variety hall. Very varied it is too,' she added, grinning. 'Anyroad, you'd not have to do owt you ain't comfortable with.'

'Nay?'

'Course not, you blockhead. Sol leaves that side of his business up to his acts entirely. He gets a cut of our earnings, like, naturally, but we basically make the decisions. Really, I reckon you'd enjoy it up there. We allus have a reet good laugh. Think about it, eh?'

'Aye, I will . . .' And she would, too, she realised.

Never would she engage in anything that Cassandra and the others evidently did there, but the prospect of getting away from here and all the pain, forgetting even for just a short while, was an irresistible one – more so than ever since her meeting with George. Seeing him again, and hearing what all this was doing to her poor sweet bro—Noah, she corrected herself, her chest constricting, had almost killed her. Moreover, the laughter she'd been promised would be welcome. By, it would.

'You made your mind up then? About Bolton town?' the woman asked later as she escorted an inebriated Jenny back to her own room.

Jenny's response was slurred but forceful with defiance. 'I have, aye.'

'And?'

'I'll come.'

'Ay, good on thee!'

'Sod 'em, eh?'

Cassandra winked. 'You'll not regret it.'

'They're all right, ain't they? They're safe?' Jenny asked the following day when they arrived at Victoria

Station. The huge, hissing monster that had just juddered to a stop at the platform spewing steam had turned her spine to jelly. She hadn't even seen a train before, never mind set foot on one – never had she been so afraid.

Cassandra and some of the other performers making up their company found her concerns hilarious. Doll, though smiling, was the one to stem her misgivings.

'You can sit next to me – I'll look after you. You've really nothing at all to worry about, deary. The journey will be over before you know it.'

Though far from convinced, Jenny murmured her thanks.

She'd been surprised to learn that Doll would be accompanying them to Bolton. She'd raised the subject with Cassandra, who had told her he always came and was very popular on the trips. As the woman had pointed out, opening Jenny's eyes ever more to this new world she'd been thrust into, men liked all manner of things in private – and, for some, their sexual proclivity wasn't confined to women. Doll took full advantage of the fact and was rewarded, at least in a monetary sense, handsomely.

To Jenny's sheer relief, the train journey did indeed go without a hitch. Doll, whom she'd got to know better during the ride and who, so far as she could ascertain, was an altogether decent fellow, had worked wonders for her nerves with his assurances and non-stop chit-chat. She arrived at Trinity Street Station, therefore, in good spirits. Next came the walk to

Deansgate, which was a short one, and there the variety hall was; they had reached their destination.

The interior, though not as grandiose as at Solomon's, was nonetheless imposing in its own right. The layout, however, was completely different. For one thing, this establishment didn't possess a stage. Nor was the seating arrangement like that of a typical theatre. Here, there were no stalls or balconies. Instead, round deal tables with average wooden chairs dotted the floor of the generous space, some thirty in all she'd have guessed, glancing around.

How one was meant to perform in such a set-up was beyond her. And perform they would before that *other* aspect of the evening got under way – Cassandra had told her so.

The group piled into a single room on the first floor, and after emptying out the travelling trunk and getting changed into their costumes, they settled down for a brief repose before the show opened. Cassandra had brought along half a dozen bottles of strong spirits, which she passed around, and they drank and chatted at ease. Then someone stuck their head around the door and nodded, and suddenly the pace switched and everything seemed to be happening at once. Her brain foggy from the alcohol, Jenny found herself swept along with the rest, down the stairs to the main area she'd observed earlier.

It was now a hive of activity and teeming with people. Men predominated – the only females to be seen were the would-be performers and those flitting about serving drinks. Jenny held back, feeling suddenly uneasy, but Cassandra wasn't having that. Taking her by the wrist, she pulled her behind her into the body of the room.

'Just follow my lead, you'll be fine.'

The following hours were what Jenny could only describe as a circus show of depravity in all its forms.

With the absence of a stage, acts were expected to simply drift from table to table, and at each conduct intimate performances to these separate groups thus; the concept was to Jenny's mind wholly uncomfortable – and unnervingly personal.

As the minutes had worn on, she'd noticed the audiences becoming unashamedly free with their hands. More alarmingly still, the performers appeared to actively encourage it.

In hardly any time at all, the atmosphere had altered completely. Some girls, laughing and teasing and seemingly enjoying themselves, were soon sitting in the men's laps. Others were openly kissing. Jenny was so shocked and appalled that she almost turned tail and scarpered there and then. However, the contents of the bottle she'd had thrust into her hand, and the next, soon proved helpful in numbing her somewhat to the goings-on.

Neither was she herself immune to the spectators' attentions. The men attempted to inveigle and cajole her at every table, but she'd step back from arms reach and shake her head. Mercifully, her decision not to engage physically was, albeit reluctantly, accepted and, as occurred at Solomon's, they would instead explore every inch of her with their eyes.

Later in the evening, she became aware of small pockets of people leaving through a side door that led to the rooms above. Doll, she saw, was amongst them. It didn't take a genius to figure out what was happening. Now was her time to bow out and leave the others to their business.

Peering about blearily in search of Cassandra, Jenny finally spotted her at a distant table. She was sitting with three men and had her breasts exposed. Averting her gaze quickly, reluctant to approach, Jenny called out to her that she was leaving. The woman raised her hand in acknowledgement and, without a backward glance, Jenny made her thankful way upstairs.

She reached the room they had spent time in upon their arrival in Bolton, got undressed and climbed into bed. Almost immediately she had fallen into a brandy-fuelled stupor.

For how long she'd been asleep when she heard the sound of the door opening, she couldn't say. Struggling to open her eyes, she squinted through the pitch-darkness. 'Hello?'

Nothing.

'Cassandra?' she pressed.

'Aye, it's me.'

Thank God. Jenny lay her head back on the pillow once more and closed her eyes.

'No funny business, d'you hear? She's as green as the hills so you be patient with her, take your time. You'll garner better results that way.'

Half lost again in the coma-like sleep, Jenny

253

frowned to herself. The woman's slurred murmur had reached her clearly enough but what it meant, she hadn't the slightest idea. Nor did she have the energy to try to figure it out. She was tired, so tired . . .

'Don't fret. She's in safe hands.'

Again, a voice, only this time it sounded different. Jenny's brow creased further. She attempted to lift her head but it wouldn't obey, felt like a ten-ton weight. Sighing, she gave up.

The door opened and closed again then all was still. Jenny gave up the last of her fight and allowed unconsciousness to carry her off.

When next she opened her eyes, the room was bathed in muted candlelight. In the golden glow, she saw a figure seated in the chair by the dead fire. Though her head was splitting, now she was a little more aware of her surroundings. The few hours of rest had done her some good. She propped herself up on an elbow.

'Cassandra? You can't be comfy there – did you fall asleep? Get into bed with me if you like.'

'Lass?'

The hairs on Jenny's arms immediately leapt to attention. She swallowed hard. That wasn't the dancer – it was a man.

She watched, transfixed, as the person rose from the seat and began walking towards her.

With his back to the light, his face was in shadow, obscuring his features, but nonetheless her assumption was confirmed: they were stockily built and head and shoulders taller than Cassandra. It was a man, all right!

A scream clawed its way up her throat. She opened her mouth wide, but before she could make a sound, he stepped closer to put a hand over it.

'Quiet. It's all right.'

What the . . .?

'George?' she gurgled.

'Aye. Don't worry. It's me.'

He released his hold on her and she gazed up at him, her mind awhirl. 'What are you *doing* here?'

'I might ask thee the same thing.'

Memories of the evening before came flooding back; Jenny felt colour creep across her face. 'You . . . know?'

He nodded.

'But how?'

'Didn't I tell thee I'd be back? Aye, and it's a good thing for you that I did.'

She patted the bed and he lowered himself on to it. Despite her terrible mortification at her conduct being discovered like this – and by him of all people – she was gratified beyond words to have him here with her.

'How did you find me?' she whispered.

'I called at the music hall again. They said you'd gone to Bolton with some of the other acts. They weren't for telling me the address at first, but I made them see sense.'

Glancing down at the cuts scoring his knuckles, she bit her lip. 'So I see. So what, you hot-footed it all the way up here? Why, George? Like I told thee last time, I'm all right.'

'You ain't gorra clue, have you?'

'What d'you mean?'

'I did trail all the way here to see thee, check on your welfare, and I'm glad I did. That one Cassandra that you call a friend, she were auctioning you off to the highest bidder when I arrived. Aye,' he confirmed when Jenny gasped, 'I heard her loud and clear. "Unspoiled and plump for the picking" was how she described thee. And them men down there, them dirty, filthy owd bastards . . .' He paused to drag a hand across his mouth. 'They were lapping it up.'

Jenny was sick with shock. 'What occurred? How are you here?'

'I offered up the most brass for thee, didn't I.'

'Oh *God.*' The shame was crucifying.

'The state you were in when I reached this room . . . I knew I'd not get no sense from you had I wakened yer, had no choice but to let you kip it off.'

'I had no idea, George. Honest, I didn't, I . . . Cassandra promised me I'd not have to . . .'

'Aye, well, the vicious bitch lied, didn't she? She cares for naught at all, that one, but brass, it's clear to see. As for her plying thee with drink – she has been, aye, I take it?' And at Jenny's miserable nod, 'I guessed as much. It's all been a ruse, don't you see it?'

Now she did. She covered her face with her hands. Cassandra had been inebriated enough when Jenny left her to go to bed. Clearly, she'd consumed a whole lot more afterwards – must have done not to have recognised George from when she'd help scupper his entry that time at Solomon's. And thank the

256

Almighty for it. 'Lord only knows what might've happened had you not been here!'

'Well I am, so no harm done.' He spoke soothingly now, seeing her distress. 'Eeh, I don't know. What am I going to do with thee, eh?'

'Oh, George. Oh, what have I become?'

He held out his arms to her and she pitched into them, throwing her own arms around his neck. In an instant, she felt a warm gush of security and safety cascade through her, sanctifying in its truth. She heaved a long sigh.

'All right?' he murmured into her hair, one hand moving up and down rhythmically as he stroked her back.

Snuggling further into his broad chest, she nodded. 'I am now.'

They remained, holding one another in silence, for several minutes until George said, 'You'll come home now, won't you, Jenny?'

There was no hesitation: 'Aye.'

'We'd best start making tracks soon afore the rest stir—'

'Oh, not yet.' She pressed her body ever closer against his, was loath for them to break apart. 'Please. Just a while longer.'

'I'll not risk them seeing you, persuading you to go back—'

'They'll not,' she murmured. 'Never again. Solomon's is in the past now.'

'Jenny?'

She tilted her face to look at him.

'I love thee.'

'What?'

'I said—'

'I heard thee.' Her heart was banging so hard she reckoned it might stop. 'D'you really mean it?'

George's teeth flashed in the soft light. 'Now what do you think, daft lass?'

'I thought you believed me a silly kid. I thought—'

'You thought wrong. I've wanted you since the moment I set eyes on you, Jenny Brodings. I masked it – least I tried to. You're amazing. I didn't believe forra minute you'd look twice at me.'

'Eeh, George, George . . .'

Their mouths met hungrily. A fire she hadn't known was lying dormant burst forth to ignite every inch of her. She threw back her head, her lips parting, as his own found her neck.

'We must go.' George had pulled back. Cheeks flushed with passion, his breathing coming in short bursts, he shook his head. 'Please, for I'll not have the strength to hold back much longer.'

'Then mebbe . . .?' The yearning inside her was every bit as powerful.

'Nay. I'll not take liberties with thee, you're too precious for that.' He kissed the tip of her nose. 'Come on, let's get home.'

To think what those other men had in mind for her, had been willing to pay good money for the privilege, and here was this young fellow before her, choosing to do the correct and sensible thing despite having her full consent . . . he truly was a beautiful soul. She couldn't have loved him more in this moment if she'd tried.

'Let's go home, lad,' she agreed.

Before leaving, Jenny lifted her costume from the ground whence she'd discarded it the night before.

The intricate birds imbedded in the fabric winked back at her in the dawn light and she allowed herself the ghost of a smile. *Goodbye, Songbird.*

With care, she folded the garment neatly and placed it in the centre of the bed.

'Hold on,' George said before they left.

Jenny watched as he took three pound notes from the inside pocket of his coarse jacket. He threw them atop the dress. 'It's finished.'

She nodded. The realisation was like a rebirth.

Taking the hand he held out to her, she led the way from the room.

Chapter 13

THE NEARER THE train chugged and puffed to their destination, the more Jenny's anxiety grew.

Her emotions were conflicted. On the one hand, the thought of seeing Noah filled her with such unspeakable joy that it left her breathless. The urge to be with him, hold him in her arms, was like a living, physical thing. She'd tell him she was sorry, assure him she'd never abandon him, never leave his side again, that he was her sun, moon and every one of the stars. He'd be safe in the truth of her love when she was done, oh would he, she'd make sure of that.

Nor, she wasn't afraid or too proud and stubborn to admit now, could she wait to see Owd Nobby. The help that man had extended to her family, even more so of late, and everything he'd put up with . . . Remembrance of her recent behaviour had her wincing anew. She'd been a spoilt young bitch, that was the top and bottom of it. Ungrateful to boot. Nobby deserved one hell of an apology, and by God would he get it.

And yet, then, there was the other thing. Jenny closed her eyes in despair. The thing that, in complete comparison, had her breaking out in a cold sweat and wishing she could be going anywhere but home: Coral.

Just how could she face her? What would she say?

Why had it had to have happened at all? she asked of the passing frost-coated fields streaking by beyond the window. It had flipped her very existence on its head, changed for ever all she'd ever believed, come to rely on. For what? Was truth really always the best policy? She struggled to believe it now. What good would possibly come from her knowing? *How* could they ever move past this?

George was soon pulling Jenny from her sombre reverie; the journey had taken far less time than she'd have liked. She required longer, needed it desperately, she told herself, must make sense of everything in her mind before the confrontation to come . . . yet would it really have made a difference? Probably not, she admitted. All the time in the world wouldn't help her figure this one out. Surely nothing could?

'Nay, come, you're more than welcome,' she insisted when, upon reaching Nobby's house, George made his excuses to allow them their private reunion. 'Please. I'd like thee to stay.'

He nodded, and Jenny reached for his hand for strength. She took a deep breath and knocked.

No answer.

Frowning, she tried again, harder now.

Still, nothing.

'Could they have nipped out? Happen they've gone forra walk . . .?'

'In this weather?' Jenny shook her head. 'Anyroad, Owd Nobby don't stray far from home; his legs ain't up to it.'

A quick shout up at the bedroom window yielded no response. Nor did she garner results from the neighbours after knocking for answers at several doors. Not a soul, it seemed, had seen either man or boy. Jenny was stumped.

'Happen Coral and Martin might know summat?' George suggested gently.

'I don't know – I've gorra bad feeling about this.'

'You'll have to face her sometime.'

'Nay, I don't mean about seeing Coral.' Gazing back to the house, Jenny wrapped her arms around herself tightly. 'Summat feels wrong. I can't explain it, but it does. What if, what if summat terrible's happened and—'

'Hush, lass. Don't be fretting yourself silly just yet – we don't know what's what, after all, do we? There might well be a perfectly normal explanation.'

'Aye, like what?' she cut in, worry making her tone sharper than intended.

'I don't know,' he was forced to admit.

'We'll have to seek out Coral.' *God help her.* 'It's the last thing I'm ready for just yet, but Noah must come first. I have to know where he is, if he's all right.'

George took her hand once more. 'I'm with thee, Jenny. You'll be fine, just fine.'

Though far from convinced, she wasted not a

moment longer and set forth for Carruthers Street at a smart pace.

Coral's face when she opened the door to find Jenny standing there was one of disbelief swiftly followed by sheer terror. She gripped the frame for support.

'I . . . I . . .'

'Hello, Coral.' Jenny spoke quietly, calmly even – though she felt anything but. Seeing the woman again had conjured up in her a maelstrom of emotions, none of which she was able to pin down and identify. 'How are you?'

'All the better for seeing thee, I . . . Lass. My lass.' She made to rush at Jenny then seemed to think better of it and checked herself. Pressing her fingers to her lips, she asked, her eyes brilliant with tears, 'Will you come in?'

Too choked to speak, Jenny nodded. With George a half-step behind, she followed Coral through the hall.

'Can I get youse summat . . . a sup of tea?' Coral asked when they were seated at the table. Without waiting for a reply, she turned on the spot looking around, as though searching for something to say next; she was as jittery as a squirrel. 'I've, I've a slab of barley cake baked fresh just last night—'

'Nay. Ta. Coral, I need to ask thee—'

'I know, I know you do. You must have a thousand and one questions. I'll answer them, lass. I'll answer them all, whatever it is you want to know, shan't hold nowt back—'

'It's not that,' Jenny told her, silencing her stuttered, almost manic speech. 'What I mean is, all that . . . all that must wait awhile. Noah's the reason I'm here. You see, I can't find him.'

'Can't find him?' Coral slid into a chair. 'Well, where's he gone?'

'I don't know, that's the problem. There's no sign of Nobby neither. No one's seen hide nor hair of the pair.'

'I went round there late last evening to see if they'd had word from you, were that desperate to know you were all right . . .' Coral's words petered off as Jenny glanced away. She cleared her throat. 'There were no answer then, neither. I thought nowt of it, reckoned they were having an early night.'

At this revelation, Jenny's earlier dread returned tenfold; she chewed her nail. 'Summat's happened, Coral. I know it.'

'But how? Why, what could have occurred?'

'I don't know but this is queer and no mistake. It's like they've vanished into thin air. There's no one in there. I banged loud enough to waken the dead; they'd have definitely heard me had they been home.'

'Unless . . .' George looked to the women in turn then sighed. 'Well, mebbe summat's stopping them from answering?'

'You mean an accident of some sort?' Jenny began to tremble. 'They might be hurt, aye?'

'It's a possibility—Wait,' he said in the next breath when she leapt to her feet. 'Where are you going?'

264

'Where do you think? I'm off back there to boot the door in! Come on!'

Having sprinted the whole way, the trio reached Nobby's house within minutes. Just to be absolutely certain, Jenny tried knocking one last time, praying all the while that their prediction was wrong. However, like before, an answer never came.

She stepped back into the road to give herself a run-up.

'Let me, lass—'

'It's all right, George, I've got it,' she insisted.

With her mouth set and her stomach doing flips at the prospect of what they might find, Jenny charged forward and smashed her foot against the door.

Further attempts were unnecessary – it flew wide at the first kick. With a relieved cry, she hurled herself inside, the others close on her heels.

Upon reaching the front room, Jenny came to a shuddering halt. 'Nobby?'

'Nobby?' repeated Coral, louder now, taking in the scene over Jenny's shoulder.

Still, there remained no response from the old man who, to all intents and purposes, sat sleeping in his fireside chair.

Tentatively, they inched their way nearer.

Coral put a hand to his shoulder and shook him gently. He didn't stir.

'George . . .?' Jenny whispered, searching his face for answers.

'He's gone, lass.'

'Nay. Nay, he can't, he—'

'He's *gone*, lass,' George murmured again. 'I'm sorry.'

A low moan leaked from her mouth as she crumpled to the floor at Nobby's stockinged feet. It grew in pitch until she was screaming at the top of her lungs: 'Nay! Not thee, Nobby! Not thee!'

'Jenny, oh Jenny!' Coral pulled her to her breast in a firm embrace.

Their private problems seemed preposterous now, utterly ridiculous in the face of this. Jenny clung to Coral as if she were drowning, which she was. She was drowning in grief and devastation and unmendable heartbreak for this man she'd loved as a grandfather throughout the entirety of her life. She'd never recover from this, never.

'Seems he went in his sleep,' George was saying now, though his words sounded distorted, as though he was the one underwater; Jenny barely processed them. 'He'd not have suffered none, lass, and there's some comfort to take from that.'

She nodded, then: *Noah.*

The name crashed through her brain.

'Noah!' she cried out loud.

George went off to conduct a search of the property. He returned and shook his head. 'I scoured the place from top to bottom – there's no sign of him.'

Where could he be? Jenny was beside herself with worry.

Neighbours, alerted by the hubbub, had begun to

congregate around the front door. Rushing to them, she interrogated them again. However, each insisted in the same vein as before that they hadn't the answers: nobody could tell her where Noah was.

Had he discovered Nobby's body first and, overcome with fear and upset, fled somewhere? No. Jenny discarded this explanation for his absence right away. Noah would have gone straight to Coral to alert her of the fact, she was sure of it.

So what?

Was it plausible that a madman had broken into the house then, perhaps, with robbery in mind, scared the old man to death then stolen the lad away? But who would possibly follow up a common crime by committing such a heinous deed as kidnap – and why?

Her guts turned over and her heart jerked painfully against her breastbone.

There was only one person who would that she knew of. One person who not only had an axe to grind against their family but who saw Noah as a valuable commodity.

'Totty.'

Coral turned to her and frowned. 'What?'

'Vincent Tottington – he's behind this,' Jenny hissed.

'Nay, he wouldn't, he—'

'He *is*, Coral. I just know it.'

Sometime later, having alerted the doctor to Nobby's demise, Jenny, Coral and George had shut up the house and returned to Carruthers Street. Along with Martin, they sat now going over the terrible events of the day.

The medical man who had been round to conduct a preliminary inspection of the body and issue the death certificate had confirmed what George suspected: Nobby had suffered an attack of the heart in his sleep. There appeared to be no suspicious circumstances, which ruled out Jenny's assumption of there having been a house break-in or confrontation of some sort. Nevertheless, there was someone behind Noah's disappearance, had to be. Him being nowhere to be found made no sense. Someone had him under their control. Still, she could think of but one man who might be responsible.

How was this possible? After everything that had happened, they had wound up coming full circle – back right where they started, at the mercy of that devil's son. All that had gone on in between seemed like a dream and a hundred years ago now.

Coral was still insisting that Totty wasn't the culprit: 'He promised me, wouldn't go back on his word. Nay, there's gorra be another reason. Happen Noah was out somewhere and got hisself lost or injured . . .?'

'Well, I think Totty is to blame.' Jenny was adamant. 'We need to find out where he lives. We *must* go round there, check for ourselves. I'll never rest else.'

Martin had been informed by his wife of her recent exchange with the chimney sweep. It had had to be done, for Noah's sake. He'd been far from pleased that she'd kept the secret from him, it showed clearly in his countenance, but he and Coral both agreed that now wasn't the time for their personal feelings to take precedence. The lad and his welfare must come first. Now, listening to Jenny, he was the first to express agreement, much to her surprise: 'I think you're right. But how do we go about getting his address?'

'Happen we might start by trawling his usual watering holes?' she suggested. 'I found him once afore that way, when he owed our Noah his wages. It's a start, eh?'

Martin and Coral nodded assent, the former saying, 'We stick together, mind. If this fella's as vicious as you claim, then I'll not take the risk of either of you women getting hurt.'

Jenny couldn't help but feel touched by the statement. The change in Martin's attitude towards her since his explosive statement was nothing short of miraculous. Guilt was what it was, what drove him, she knew this – blurting such a monumental truth as he had done had been a spur of the moment decision which he deeply regretted. Nonetheless, despite his softness now, his clear desire to make amends, she wasn't dropping her guard. He'd hurt her more than he could know, and not only with his revelation of her parentage. His escalated coldness and all-round mean-spiritedness towards her this past year had ingrained itself in her; he'd made an already hard existence so much more difficult. It would be a long time yet for her to trust him fully, if ever.

'Mary will keep an eye to the younger ones whilst we're away,' Coral stated, referring to her and

Martin's eldest daughter. Now plans were put in place, she looked to have come around to the idea, though Jenny suspected it was more to placate her than from any solid belief still that Totty was at blame. 'When will we begin, then?'

'Later, when it grows dark. The inns and taverns will be packed out in an hour or two, and Totty's bound to be somewhere amongst their number. Best we wait till then.'

Coral rose to make tea, and Martin crossed to the mantel for his clay pipe. Filling the bowl with tobacco, he had his eye on George all the while. When finally he'd lit it and resumed his seat, he said, 'You're quiet.'

'Am I?' George replied.

'Aye, not said a word, you ain't. There wouldn't be summat you're keeping back, would there?'

Jenny opened her mouth in readiness to leap to George's defence. However, the expression on the younger man's face, when she turned to glance at him, stopped her. He looked as guilty as sin. Martin was correct – George was hiding something.

'Lad?' she demanded.

'Jenny . . .'

Oh Lord, what now? 'Whatever it is . . . tell me.'

'I know where Vincent Tottington dwells.'

'You do?'

'I know because . . .' Releasing a shuddering sigh, George put his head in his hands. 'Oh lass, I've been meaning to tell thee, wanted to so much, but as more time went on . . .'

'George, you're scaring me,' she whispered. 'What is it? What don't I know?'

'Totty . . .'

'Aye? What about him?'

'He's my father.'

The room reverberated with their collective gasps. Jenny reared back in her chair: 'Your *what*?'

'I love you, lass, couldn't risk you finding out.'

'But . . . nay. You're George *Sixsmith*—'

'That's my mam's maiden name. I took it on when I finally rid myself of that man. I don't have no contact with him, honest. I ain't spoken a word to him in years.'

'All this time . . . All this *bloody* time?'

'I know how much you despise the bloke and with good reason; I reckoned you'd not want nowt to do with me if you heard the truth—'

'You're damn right there.' Breathing heavily through flared nostrils, Jenny flicked her head to the door. 'Get out.'

'Lass, please.'

'I said get out!' The pain was like a death – she could barely comprehend this, not from him. 'You deceived me, George.'

'I felt I had to, I—'

'I'll not stand for this – can't. Yet another liar keeping secrets from me,' she added, throwing Coral a denigratory grunt when the woman flinched, couldn't help herself. 'I don't ever want to see thee again, George.'

His devastation was absolute, it was evident to see.

He gritted his teeth to stem his quivering bottom lip. 'You're right. I'll go. I'm so sorry, Jenny.'

Tears were building; she blinked them back desperately. 'Before you do . . . the address.'

'Address?'

'Your father's.' She spat out the words as though ridding her mouth of something unsavoury. Indeed, they left behind an acrid taste on her tongue.

He complied, and when he'd gone, she sank to her knees on the hard floor. Coral moved towards her to place a tentative hand on her shoulder, and Jenny didn't stop her. She felt suddenly and utterly exhausted, hollowed out. She hadn't the strength for anything.

'You poor young love.'

'What's wrong with this family at all, Coral?' she croaked. 'We seem to just tumble from one calamity to another. Why? I'm bone-weary of it. We're cursed. Aye, that's what.'

'Eeh, Jenny. I know George's hurt thee, but I don't believe it were done out of malice. Sometimes, folk act out in ways they wouldn't normally, but it don't make them bad people. They just feel they have to, to protect them that they love . . . Please, can we talk?' she continued, taking Jenny's face in her hands. 'I need to explain myself to thee, make thee understand.'

Jenny's emotions were dangerously too close to the surface to bear more now. She shook her head. 'Not now, but we will. Later. All right?'

'All right, lass.' Coral sniffed once, twice. Then she

nodded firmly. 'Let's see what that Totty has to say for hisself, shall we?'

'Aye. Let's fetch the lad home.'

The abode they arrived at, situated in the heart of the worst slums and at no great distance away, was dismal to say the least. Jenny wouldn't have housed a pig here.

The brickwork of the homes, if not too optimistic a description, was crumbling with age and neglect and blackened with over a century's worth of soot from the chimneys of the surrounding factories and works, whilst more than one window had been put through and boasted balls of rolled-up newspaper stuffed into the holes to keep out the worst of the elements. Meanwhile, just to add to the misery, a thin river of Lord alone knew what – raw sewage by the look of it – flowed freely down the centre of the unsewered and unpaved road. God only knew how the residents fared during the hotter months – the stench now, in spite of the weather, was unbearable.

Poorly built and definitely wanting their own streets might well be, but even they were not on a par with this level of depravity.

Wrinkling her nose, Jenny turned to an equally grim-looking Coral and Martin. It was clear they had the same thought in mind as herself: imagining their Noah holed up here was heart-rending. She felt a white-hot rage spark then gush through her veins. Without further ado, she picked her way through the general debris to the front door and knocked hard.

The vision who appeared half a minute later was a shock to the system – Jenny hardly recognised him. She gazed open-mouthed in undisguised horror. It was difficult to know who was more shocked in that moment – herself or Totty.

'You?' His speech was laboured, his breathing likewise. Then he spotted Coral standing behind her and his eyes widened even further. 'What the divil's going on?' he wheezed.

Her lip curling, Jenny looked him up and down. His clothing was ill-fitting and falling from his frame in folds; he'd lost a considerable amount of weight in the short time since last she'd seen him. Month-old stubble carpeted cheeks that were sunken almost to the point of concavity, and deep plum-hued stains lay beneath bloodshot eyes. He was ill and deathly so. What's more, she didn't care a fig.

Letting out a beast-like cry, she gripped him by his shirt front and ran with him, forcing him backwards in a tottering trot, before ramming him against the hallway wall. He sagged, his face contorting in pain, but she wrenched him back upright with unnatural ease; he was as light as a toddler.

'What's going on, you have the gall to ask?' she growled, her face in his. 'You know what well enough. Now, where is he?'

'Who?'

Jenny drew back her arm to strike him but it was held from behind, halting her attack. She turned angrily. However, the murderous expression on

Coral's face stopped her. She stepped aside to let the woman take over.

For what seemed an age, Coral did nothing. Then she moved with such speed it took everyone by surprise. Lashing out with expert precision, she caught Totty with an uppercut that sent him reeling through the open living room door. He landed with a dull thud on the bare flags of the floor where he remained, groaning and coughing for breath.

Martin was frozen with shocked stupor. Jenny meanwhile was filled with such admiration that she found it a struggle not to run to the woman and throw her arms around her.

Her emotions were strange ones. Staring at Coral, she knew a feeling of pride. And she experienced recognition – an altogether new sensation. She saw herself now in this woman, mirrored completely, as she'd never done with the mother who raised her. It lent Jenny a sense of belonging, the like of which she'd thought never to have again. She was a product of the woman's flesh. She was. Perhaps they would be all right, her and Coral. Perhaps they would.

'I know you, Vincent Tottington, and I see when you're lying.' Coral had moved to stand over him. 'To think I believed you incapable of being behind this, believed you respected me enough to keep your word – huh. More fool me, eh? You tell me where my little brother is, right now. Or I swear on all that's holy, I'll kill you.'

'Noah ain't here.'

'Where then?'

'I don't know—Ow!' Totty cried out in the next breath as Coral delivered a harsh kick to his ribs. 'All right, all-bleedin'-right! He's most likely with a fella named Skipton.'

'Skipton?' Jenny asked. 'And who the bugger is he?'

'An owd acquaintance of mine.'

'What d'you mean "most likely"?' Coral wanted to know. 'Are you saying you're not even certain?'

'Well, nay . . .'

'Just what's going on here? It makes no sense. Tell me, Totty!' she demanded.

He struggled into a sitting position and sucked in several shaky breaths. 'Skipton, he were on t' lookout forra lad. He asked me if I knew of any who were small and agile enough for what he had in mind. I recommended Noah to him.'

Coral frowned. 'A lad? For what? Is this Skipton bloke a sweep too?'

Jenny held her breath. If he'd sent the lad back up the chimneys . . . she'd murder him herself. Noah would never bear them again, never!

'Nay, not him. Skipton's a raider.'

Jenny didn't know whether to be relieved at this news or not. She closed her eyes in despair.

'You mean to say he's gorra grip of my brother and is making him raid houses with him?' Coral ground out.

'Not just houses. Businesses, too – anywhere in fact that has owt worth stealing. Raiders rely on lads for their help in gaining access to the properties. A grown

276

man can't fit through narrow gaps – windows, that sort of thing – and so they gets someone smaller to squeeze through and let them in through the door—'

'I think I get the picture. Christ's sake! My brother's been turned into a common thief. And you were the one to make it happen?' Coral's lips were pale with rage. 'I ought to finish you right here and now, you bastard!'

Jenny had tears of fury dripping down her face. 'Noah wouldn't have gone by choice. He wouldn't. He's a good boy.'

'I told Skipton where he lived. He planned to ambush him when he saw him out and about.'

'Spirit him away, you mean?'

Totty nodded. 'As you say, the lad wouldn't have agreed, so Skipton would have to take him by force. That's what he said he'd do, anyroad. Whether he managed it or not, I don't know.'

'Course he bloody well managed it – Noah's nowhere to be found!'

'I can't tell thee more than that.' The sweep spread his hands wide and, much to their dread, they could see that he meant it. 'I ain't gorra clue where Skipton is. He don't stop in t' same place for more than a few days at a time, has to keep on t' move to evade capture.'

'D'you know summat, Totty? I meant to kill thee.' Jenny's tone was empty now; her heartbreak was unparalleled. 'I ought to have seen through what I had in mind for thee, should have burned this stinking hovel to the ground and you along with it. Vermin like you don't deserve to walk this earth amongst decent folk. You don't deserve the precious gift that is life.'

Her revelation regarding what she'd had planned for him had brought his mouth open when she was speaking. Now, hearing her last statement and opinion of his worthlessness, he did something that surprised her: he nodded.

'Fret not, you'll have your wish and sooner than you think. Look at me: I'm not for making old bones. I'll be lucky to see Christmastide. It's soot wart,' he finished.

Jenny had never heard of the affliction. She glanced to Coral for explanation.

'Scrotal cancer,' the woman murmured. Her eyes flashed for a split second with pity, despite everything. 'It's common amongst sweeps, has summat to do with the chimney dust, or so the learned folk reckon.'

'Comeuppance you might call it, eh?' Totty said.

Jenny said nothing. Though she wouldn't have wished such a cruel disease on anyone, she couldn't fail to wonder that God did indeed work in mysterious ways. After all Totty had put countless boys through with those chimneys, it was he himself who would ultimately succumb to their dangers. It really was a queer old world at times.

'So there you have it. I'm destined for the earthworms shortly. You won.'

'There's no winners in this. Noah's still missing. We ain't walking from here victorious.'

278

'Aye well, that's life,' was Totty's only response.

'I see it now, you know, see it all so clear,' Jenny told him. She rested on her haunches before him and stared him dead in the eye. 'It's little wonder George were too scared and ashamed of me knowing you were his father. I'd have lied through my teeth an' all – by, I would.'

'George? My George?' His eyes had grown as wide as saucers. 'You know my son?'

'Oh, I more than know him, Totty,' she heard herself say; the words came on instinct alone and never had anything sounded so right. 'I'm to be his wife.'

'His . . .? You?'

'That's right,' she said, and heard Coral sigh softly in relief.

'Lass. Talk to him for me, ask him to come and see me. Will you? I'm dying and I've norra soul. I've got no one—'

'Come on, let's go.' Jenny rose and, with Coral and Martin close behind, headed for the door.

Totty's pleading followed them out: 'You'll do it, won't thee? You'll speak to my lad? Say tha will. Say it, dammit!'

Jenny didn't look back. Without another word, she lifted her chin and walked away.

'Where the hell could he be?'

It was late evening and Coral and Martin's children had been put to bed shortly before. The three adults were sitting at the table with a cup of tea, which they sipped at slowly, and though a plate of bread smeared with pork dripping sat in the centre, none had touched the food. In light of recent events, their appetites had unsurprisingly flown.

'I don't know,' Coral conceded, 'but we'll find him.'

'And if we don't – what then?' Jenny left her seat again to pace the floor. 'What if this Skipton swine is mistreating the lad? His poor burns ain't even healed fully yet. He must be so confused, so frickened . . . This is my doing, this. It's all my fault. I should have been here to protect him. It were my job, blast it. But nay, for where was I?' she spat with self-loathing. 'Oh aye, that's right: putting my daft pride first as ever, and fast falling into a life of debauchery . . . If owt should happen to him, I'll never forgive myself. Oh, I can't bear this!'

Coral rose to usher her back into her chair. 'Hush now, sit down, else you'll be for making yourself ill, and that'll do no one any good. Noah needs you to be strong for when he gets home.'

'Coral's right,' said Martin. Not a drop of alcohol had passed his lips, his wife had shared out of his ear-shot, since his revelation to Jenny, and it showed. It was like sitting before a new man. 'You did all you could for that boy and allus have. We see it, you know. He's a smasher, aye. A well-mannered, well-turned out young man. That, in no small part, is down to thee. You ought to be proud, Jenny.'

'We will get him back, lass,' Coral added. 'Keep the faith.'

Jenny wished she had her optimism. Truth was, she had a terrible feeling in the pit of her soul that Noah was lost to them for good. The thought made her want to curl up and die. She'd never survive without him. The prospect was inconceivable.

'You look done in,' Coral told her gently. 'You really ought to try and snatch a bit of kip.'

The idea of returning home alone to her cellar – no Noah, no Nobby nearby, no nothing but her brutal mind for company – was a horrifying one. She swallowed hard. Then Martin was speaking, and she turned to him with raised eyebrows. Had she heard him right? 'What?'

'I said you'll stay here in our home with us for as long as needs be. I insist.'

'Eeh, love.' Coral's eyes shone. 'Thank you.'

'Aye, thanks, Martin,' said Jenny earnestly. The relief was immeasurable. 'I'd like that very much. I'll be no bother.'

Though his response was gruff, his gaze was soft. 'I know, lass. Truth be told, tha never were any trouble. I've been a fool, and I'm big enough to admit it now. I'm sorry, for everything.'

When he left them to retire for the night shortly afterwards, Jenny crossed to the hearthside chairs with Coral, and they sat in the dim firelight finishing their drinks in silence. The minutes ticked on, and with them the ever-pressing issue that was yet to be discussed swelled and spread through the air between them like a living, breathing presence; Jenny thought if she put out a hand, she'd have been able to touch the atmosphere.

'Coral?' she murmured finally.

'Aye, lass?'

'I'm ready to listen now.'

The woman took a shaky breath then licked her lips. 'All right.'

Not knowing what on earth was to come but aware she had to hear it – she must if she was to ever try to understand, attempt to get past this – she drew her legs up and wrapped her arms around her knees.

'As tales go, mine's but a short one by all accounts,' Coral began, folding her hands in her lap, spine taut, eyes lowered. 'You know already I were careering around the city getting up to all kinds of mischief – well, I went a step further one night, and you were the result.'

'Who was he, my father?'

'Johnny was his name. He were in our gang of friends, and a year or thereabouts older than I was. And well, one night . . .' She spread her hands wide and sighed. 'We were just kiddies, Jenny. Daft kiddies, aye, with bellyfuls of ale and "you can't tell us what to do" attitudes – stupid, eh? I see it now, course I do, but when you're younger, well, you think you know it all, don't you? You're so desperate to grow up, little knowing what you're letting yourself in for, the hardship what comes with it . . .

'Anyroad, the night you were begot, I'd had a blazing argument with Mam. I'd come in rolling drunk yet again in the early hours of the morn, and understandably she were livid. She called me sinful, reckoned I were on the path to ruin, so I thought I'd show her what I were really capable of! Remind you

282

of anyone?' Coral added quietly, her lips peaking in a sad smile.

Jenny knew she was referring to Solomon's and her disastrous decision to continue working there in spite of the advice of those around her. She screwed up her face, abashed.

'I didn't know what were happening to me, not at first. My monthly curse had only begun several months afore so when I missed a few, I thought nowt of it, reckoned it must be normal. There were no escaping the bump, though, nay.' Coral snaked an arm around her midriff as though revisiting the past. A wistful look entered her eyes. 'I felt you inside me, Jenny, and I knew you were my very own and allus would be . . . Then Mam and Father noticed, and hell itself broke wide. God above, the rows – terrible, it were. Just terrible.'

A lump the size of an egg had lodged in Jenny's throat. 'That's when they decided to raise me as their own?'

'Right from the off, aye. They swore me to silence, made me vow never to utter the truth to another living soul. It were the thought of everyone finding out and what it would do to us. The shame, you know? The name Brodings would have been mud, tarnished for evermore, and you'd have carried the stigma of illegitimacy like a bad smell the rest of your life. I understood even back then, young as I was. Surely you do too, lass?'

She did. Recalling suddenly something Coral had blurted during their recent ruckus – what was it? – Jenny searched her mind and nodded to herself slowly. '*After all I've endured, the sacrifices I've made . . .*' Of course, it all made sense to her now. She'd suspected even before that, though, hadn't she, when listening to Coral's talk of her past and association with Totty, that the woman was keeping something back from her, but never dreamed for a single second it could be anything like what she now knew – and why would she? To her credit, Coral had honoured her parents, hid her secret well. Eeh, but it was all such a tragic mess.

'It must have been hard on you. Pretending you were my sister, I mean.'

'More than you could even begin to imagine. I've been to hell's depths and back, over and over and over again . . . You were mine. *My* daughter, not theirs. I didn't blame them for how things turned out. I never could; they wanted only the best for us, and I was the one in the wrong. But I were resentful, Jenny. Bitter too, aye. Hearing you calling another Mam when I were sat there, aching to have you say it to me . . . I'll never know from where I found the strength to stand it.'

'I'm sorry.'

'Nay, nay, lass! Don't you ever, *ever* apologise, not for anything, do you hear me?' Coral leaned forward in her seat to grip Jenny's hands. 'You was and are still as pure and free of blame as the heavenly saints themselves. I did wrong. I'm the bad 'un. Not you. Never you.'

'Martin . . .?'

'I kept it from him,' the woman mouthed.

284

'You wed him without telling him the truth of things?'

Coral nodded and put her face in her hand. 'I were that frickened he'd run for the hills if he learned the way of things. I trapped him, really. Married him under false pretences, aye. It were cruel, wicked. I were a coward.'

'When did he find out?'

'I unburdened myself of it last year when our parents passed on—'

'*Your* parents,' Jenny corrected her quietly.

Coral winced. 'My parents, aye. Sorry, lass, it's been habit referring to them as so for such a long time. My parents,' she repeated, nodding. 'I reckoned that if Martin knew, he'd see that I had to step up and be a mam to you at last when you needed me most, that he'd understand.'

'But he never, did he? He'd not allow you to take us in, didn't want me nowhere near the house.'

'He was angry. I'd hurt him reet badly, Jenny. He reckoned if he kept me and thee at arm's length then the secret would stay buried and no one need ever know. Embarrassed, he were. Embarrassed of me, of having a whore for a wife.'

'But not no more?'

Coral smiled. 'Let's just say he's getting there. He is trying, lass.'

He was – hadn't she borne witness to it with her own two eyes? 'All this . . . it'll take time for me, an' all, Coral. You understand that?'

'I'd be shocked if it never,' was her ready reply.

'There's no rush, none at all. We'll get there when we're good and ready, aye. I'm just glad it's all out in t' open. I've got thee back. And, by God, I'm never for letting you go ever again.'

Nor did Jenny want her to.

Chapter 14

THE NEXT MORNING, Jenny was up with the factory hooters and, running on grim determination alone, was raring to go. She'd resolved last night whilst lying next to her half-sister Mary in bed – by, but it still felt queer to even think on that – to do all in her power to fetch Noah home, where he belonged. She'd tramp those rotten streets and roads and lanes out there until her toes dropped off if she must. She *would* find him. Whatever it took.

Whilst Coral and Martin had the unenviable task of visiting the undertaker to arrange Nobby's funeral – Jenny wouldn't have borne it, would have found it far too distressing – she herself prepared to sally forth into the most densely populated slum districts to enquire at every drinking establishment she came across over the mystery man Skipton. Someone had to have heard of him, would tell her where to locate him. No man was an island. He must surely have associates? A bit of persuasion and they would talk . . . wouldn't they? Pray God they did and that the age-old proverb proved to the contrary: that there wasn't honour amongst thieves.

Her first port of call, however, before she even thought about beginning her search, was the Balloon.

Coral had asked Jenny before they parted company for bed last night whether, given what she'd proclaimed to Totty, she was indeed prepared to give George another chance. Her answer had come immediately: she was, most definitely, providing he himself would have her back.

She'd hurt him deeply with her reaction, this she knew. What if he'd decided that in fact she was more trouble than she was worth, that he'd had enough of her? Would she cope with such a loss? Time would soon tell.

The landlady was all smiles when she spotted Jenny's entrance. Gesticulating with much zest, she beckoned her across. 'Lass! By, it's gradely to see thee.'

'Eeh, and you, Hyacinth,' Jenny responded with equal fervour. 'I ain't half missed thee. Hyacinth, listen, about all that brass you put towards freeing me from the music hall . . .' Her shame was absolute – the woman was surely aware by now how matters stood, the dubious goings-on at that place – but Jenny knew she must confront it. 'Thank you just don't seem enough. I mean it all the same, I do. And I'll pay thee back, every copper coin of it. I swear to you.'

Hyacinth responded by opening her arms. The bear hug, when Jenny walked into them, sucked the breath from her lungs; clinging to the woman, she smiled through her tears.

'Now then,' the landlady said when they had drawn apart and she'd wiped dry Jenny's eyes, 'I take it you've not took time out of your day to just come and see my lined owd face – am I right?'

'Well, actually . . . I were hoping to snatch a word with George, aye.'

A knowing smile appeared at her mouth. 'He's away ordering a few barrels of ale to be delivered, lass, from the brewery. He'll not be gone long. Sit thee down whilst tha waits and I'll fetch thee a drink.'

'Nowt stronger than tea, please, Hyacinth,' Jenny was quick to say. Even small ale was, and would now remain, a thing of the past. On this she was steadfast.

Throughout the following minutes, as the women caught up on one another's news, Jenny's eyes barely strayed from the door. When at last it opened, she rose slowly and braced herself for the scene to come. However, her worries were soon proven unfounded. George, his face wreathed in shocked delight, hurried to sweep her off her feet into his arms. He held her tightly.

'Oh, Jenny. I can't believe you're here.'

'George . . . I'm that sorry.'

Hyacinth discreetly took herself upstairs to allow them privacy to talk. Sitting down, they clasped hands over the table.

'I were wrong, George,' Jenny began, 'should have given you a proper chance to explain—'

'Nay, I'm the guilty one here. What a thing to keep back from thee . . . I'm so sorry, I am.'

'You had your reasons. I see it now. I went to see your . . . Totty.'

'And?'

Jenny shook her head. She related what had transpired and, when George threw his hands in the air in fury, continued, 'Wait, lad. Afore you spout owt about him that you might regret, there's summat you must know.'

'Regret? Never! He's nobbut an evil, twisted owd—!'

'Vincent Tottington's dying, lad.'

The wind left his sails in a rapid gust. He ran a hand through his hair. 'How . . .?'

'Soot wart, so Totty said. I'm sorry.'

George nodded, sighed.

'Will you see him? He wants you to, he said so.'

'I don't . . .' He heaved another long breath. 'I should be the bigger person, I know, but the things he's done, what he put me through, I . . . I can't.'

She stroked his arm, understanding wholeheartedly. 'The decision is yours alone to make. Just know I'll support thee in whatever it is you choose to do.'

'Even after all he's done to your family?'

'Aye. He's still your father, George.'

'You're incredible, d'you know that?' he told her with feeling. He lifted her hands to kiss her fingers. 'What would *you* do?'

She'd thought never to make it up with Coral ever again at one point in the not-too-distant past – now look at them. Of course, their set of circumstances were different, but it just went to show: you never could tell what might be around the corner. Things occurred, emotions altered. Only people could make things happen.

'I think, if you believe you can find the strength for it, that you ought to go,' she said after some soul-searching. 'Do it for yourself if nowt else. It might just bring you peace, you never know.'

'Mebbe. Anyroad, I can't think on that now. What are we to do about this Skipton one?'

'We?' she breathed.

'Aye.' He rose to his feet. 'Where do you want us to start?'

'You mean you'll help me?' The relief was empowering. 'But what about your work?'

'Hyacinth will understand.'

'Aye – she were sympathetic enough just now when I were telling her what's occurred. Eeh, George, if you're sure? Thank you.'

Wrapping his arms around her, he pressed his lips to her forehead tenderly. 'As if you even need to ask. Come on.'

They scoured what felt like the entire city, flat out without a break, until they were almost dropping with exhaustion. Finally, as midnight approached, Jenny was forced to admit defeat; she steered them back towards Ancoats. 'Let's go home, George.'

'Hey, none of that,' he murmured, lifting her chin with his finger then brushing away with the back of a hand the tears that had escaped and fallen to her cheeks. 'There's allus the morrow.'

'There's no use. Noah's gone, George. He's gone.'

'Nay, he ain't.' His tone was fierce. 'We're going to search and keep on searching until we've norra breath left in our bodies – we'll never give up. We'll find him, lass. You must believe. Say it.'

'But . . .'

'Do it, Jenny. Say, "I believe".'

'I believe.'

'Louder. Mean it.'

Filling her lungs to capacity, she clawed back her will and narrowed her eyes. Her chin went up. 'I bloody believe! Come hell or high water, the lad's coming home.'

For six days and nights, Jenny kept her word. Despite their incessant searching throughout, they had gained not a single lead, but she refused to waver. A breakthrough *would* come. It must.

On the seventh day, in a quiet ceremony, they laid Owd Nobby to rest beside his long-departed wife.

Throughout the sombre service, Jenny had watched the doors of the church, then again kept her stare peeled on the fringes of the grey cemetery as the small group comprising herself and George, Coral and Martin, and several close neighbours, stood shivering around the freshly dug hole, hoping, praying for a sighting of Noah. An ambitious prospect, she knew, but she did it all the same. If, by some miracle, wherever the child might be, he had somehow caught wind of the old man's passing and that the interment was today, he would come. Nothing, she was certain, would keep Noah away were it at all within his power to do so. *Please, lad, please . . .*

'Jenny?' It was Coral. She wiped the tears from her face and sniffed loudly. 'Do you need a few minutes by yourself, lass?'

Snapped back to the present and glancing about, Jenny saw that the clergyman had departed and that the gravedigger was hovering with his shovel a short distance away. She squeezed shut her eyes. Pictures and snatches of speech assaulted her brain: Nobby's smile, the feel of his hand on her shoulder during his regular kindly expressions of support. His laughter, and the roll of his eyes when gently advising her to learn to keep a hold on her temper. His belief in her. His love. *The sorrow in his voice and the pain reflected in his watery gaze during their last meeting, when she'd blasted him for holding Coral's secret . . .* A sob tore from Jenny.

Her selfishness and plain pig-headedness were unforgivable. She'd treated this fine man here lying cold in his mud tomb appallingly throughout his final weeks and now there could never be an opportunity to put it right. Please God he hadn't departed from this life thinking she no longer cared. Please let Nobby have known she hadn't meant it, that he had a piece of her heart then, now, always. *I'm sorry. I'm sorry. I miss you so much already.*

'Lass?'

Jenny turned her attention back to Coral. She nodded once. 'Go on ahead. I'll be all right.'

'You're sure?'

'Aye. I'll meet youse back at the house soon. Don't

worry about me, I just want to say goodbye in private.'

The woman inclined her shawl-covered head in understanding and went to inform the others. A minute later, Jenny found herself standing quite alone.

She inched closer to the yawning trench holding the cheap wood coffin and blew it a kiss. Then she straightened up, clasped her hands in front of her and opened her mouth in song.

Ave Maria had been a favourite of Nobby's. Jenny let the haunting strains carry wide, stroking the surrounding moss-mottled headstones on their journey to the heavens and the newest member therein as it went.

When the affecting hymn was over, she caught the gravedigger's attention and alerted him silently with her eyes that he may now proceed with his task. A last sweep of the desolate land yielded no Noah. She wrapped her arms around herself, turned about and set off for home.

Upon her insistence, the modest funeral tea was to take place at her cellar. Coral had offered to hold it at Carruthers Street, but Jenny had deemed her dwelling more fitting. This was the lane that had been beloved to Nobby, where he'd lived for half of his life and more. He'd made precious memories here, both for himself and others, and the surrounding residents were his friends. He would have wanted it this way, Jenny felt.

She'd scoured the place from top to bottom in preparation. The weeks of lying empty and shut up had left everything with a dust sheen and the air in the underground space stagnant. Now, as she accepted a cup of tea from Coral and sat sipping it seated beside George, she was comforted by the familiarity. Worried that being here again with all its memories of Noah would be far too painful to bear, she'd been secretly dreading it. But no; she realised now her feelings had been skewed. She felt closer to the lad somehow, not further removed. She'd forgotten just how much this place meant home to her.

The table, covered with a dazzling white cloth which she'd borrowed from Coral along with some crockery, held plates of food for the small party of mourners: Cumberland ham cut thinly and garnished with sliced onions, cold pies and a good-sized loaf, with hard-boiled eggs arranged neatly in a tin dish alongside. A small barrel of ale had been acquired for the males, and the teapot was assured not to run dry for the women. All in all, they had done Nobby proud with what little resources they had at their disposal. He'd have really enjoyed himself were it possible for him to be here.

Throughout the next hour, as they drank and ate, they smiled and chuckled and shed a tear or two whilst reminiscing about the old man. It warmed Jenny's heart to witness how much he'd been loved. Eventually, the group began to break off. Neighbours left to return to their respective dwellings and soon only Jenny, George, Coral and Martin remained.

Emotionally wrung out, Jenny knuckled her tired eyes. 'I'm fagged.'

'You look it, lass.' Brushing back a lock of Jenny's hair, which had escaped the pins to fall around her face, Coral smiled sadly. 'How's about I clear away these dishes and then we'll all get off home, eh? You can take yourself up to bed and have a good long kip – it'll do you good.'

'Well, actually . . .' As she'd done earlier, Jenny glanced around the space. That same wave of comfort coursed through her and she nodded. 'I think I'd rather stop here, at the cellar.'

'Aye?'

'I didn't realise how much I miss it. You letting me lodge at your house, mind – I do appreciate it, really I do. Both of youse,' she added, bringing Martin into her gaze. 'But it's time to come home.'

Though obviously hesitant to leave her, Coral respected her wishes with a soft sigh later on her way with her husband to the door. 'Remember,' she told Jenny earnestly, 'if you need owt . . .'

'I know.'

'You know where we are, lass.'

'Aye.'

'You'll be all right?'

Jenny assured her she would be. 'Goodnight, God bless. And thanks, for everything, today. I couldn't have done it without thee . . .' Her words petered out slowly as she caught sight of Nobby's house up ahead. She blinked, frowned, blinked again. 'What the . . .?'

A man pushing a handcart stacked with bundles and furniture had halted outside the door, whilst a woman and child had their hands cupped over their eyes and were staring through the window. Jenny stepped outside into the road.

'Excuse me!' she called out. 'Just what d'you think youse are doing?'

'What does it look like?' shot back the woman, straightening up and placing her hands on her ample hips.

'The landlord don't waste much time, does he?' muttered Coral. She and Jenny had cleared out Nobby's house a few days before and distributed his meagre possessions amongst themselves and his other nearest friends, as he'd have wanted. 'That's what's afoot here, lass – these lot are moving into his place.'

'But . . . today, of all days?' Jenny was incensed. 'The owd fella's barely got comfy in his grave and already his house is being handed over to the next person, like he never existed?'

Martin shook his head. 'Business is business, Jenny. No houseowner will let a property lie doing nowt for very long, not where brass is involved. Don't take it personally; it is what it is.'

'Come away inside,' George insisted gently, taking her by the arm. 'You'll only upset yourself. When all's said and done, it ain't no fault of these new tenants, is it? Besides, they look neat and clean enough – you could have got a lot worse.'

She knew her beloved was right. Catching the gaze of the young boy who was evidently the son of the new couple to the street, her anger was swift to dissipate further still and she felt tears clog her throat. He reminded her so much of Noah. True, this child had sandy hair and not ginger, and he was a little taller; however, his small, impish face and scrawny frame mirrored Noah's completely. They even possessed the same large, innocent eyes in the exact shade of jade. Jenny was charmed.

'Hello,' she said to him, feeling the need now to lighten the mood and start things off afresh on an even keel. However, if he'd planned to, the lad got no chance to answer. Before he could utter anything, his mother gripped him by the shoulder and dragged him behind her, shielding him with her skirts as if afraid Jenny might spirit him away. Her eyes were steely.

'I'll thank thee not to speak to him,' she barked, putting Jenny in mind of a lioness ready and willing to battle to the death to protect her cub. 'In fact, don't even look at him, d'you hear?'

'What?' Nonplussed at the unexpected venomous response to a simple greeting, Jenny glanced to the others. But they looked as mystified as she. 'For God's sake, missis, I were only being friendly—'

'Aye, well don't,' the woman cut in, her warning slicing through Jenny's exclamation like a hot blade through wax. 'Just you leave my son the hell alone.'

'All right, Liz, that's enough,' her husband said quietly. His eyes were gentle, almost sad. 'All's well, wench. You've nowt to fear now.'

The speech had the desired effect – his wife's face relaxed. Bunching together her lips as though she was on the verge of crying, she nodded. Without another word, she took the boy by the hand and led him inside their new house.

'Sorry,' her husband offered to Jenny when he was alone. With that, and without providing any explanation, he turned and focused his attention back on the handcart.

'Well, that was a queer do and no mistake,' Jenny told George, scratching her chin, when they returned to the cellar after seeing Coral and Martin off. 'I can't fathom it – can you?'

'Happen the woman's a bit light up top.' He tapped his temple.

'You reckon so?'

'She were acting mad enough, all right.'

Jenny flopped on to a stool. 'Oh, it don't matter, anyroad. I've more important things on my mind than her.' She cleared her throat to dislodge the fresh ball of emotion. 'I thought . . . well, I thought . . .'

'What, lass?'

'I thought our Noah might have been at the funeral. I were looking out for him, felt sure . . . Daft or what?'

George came to crouch in front of her. He took her hand in his and squeezed. 'Not daft at all. Hopeful, that's all. And that's a good thing. We *have* to keep hoping, must.'

'Eeh, lad. I don't know what I'd do without you, yer know. I mean it,' she added earnestly, leaning forward to burrow herself in his waiting hold. 'Stay.'

'Stay? Here, you mean?'

'Aye. Stay here with me.'

'But, lass . . . it ain't proper. What would folk say?'

'What folk?'

'Well, your Coral and Martin for one. They assumed just now when they were going, I think, that I'd be following them on, on my way home as well. If they knew we were alone here even now, they would be far from pleased, never mind us spending the night together.'

'They don't need to know.' Jenny was growing desperate; thoughts of him leaving her were unbearable. 'Please. They'll not find out.'

'The neighbours, then.'

'I care naught for what any of them might think! The only neighbour whose opinion I minded was Nobby. He and he alone had a right to a say in my affairs, for he loved me. And, well, he's gone now. He's gone. I . . . I miss him so. I . . . Oh!'

'Ay, my love. Eeh, come here. Sshhh, it's all right. Everything'll be all right. I'm here.'

Jenny wept freely against his chest. 'I needed to be back here, back home, you know? It's a comfort, it's true, but just the thought of being alone . . . I couldn't stand it.'

'You don't have to. If it's what you really want.'

'It is.'

'Then I'm going nowhere.'

'Thank you. Thank you.'

Hours later, the single candle cast its shimmering glow on their faces as they lay, arms around each other, in bed. Eyes heavy, Jenny allowed herself the shadow of a smile.

'All right, lass?' George whispered.

She sighed against his chest. 'I am.'

'We'd best snatch some shut-eye. We've another long day in front of us the morrow.'

Her face lost its smile. She nodded. 'Where should we start the search next time? We've tramped every inch of Manchester already, it seems so.'

'I'm for calling at the police station first, I think. I know we decided it were a pointless task, and aye, it likely will be, but what have we to lose? Maybe, just maybe, the law might be able to do summat, you never can tell.'

Though Jenny didn't voice it, she was convinced he was in for a wasted journey. The law cared very little, if at all, for slum dwellers like themselves. Of course, had it been a nobleman's loved one who was missing – well. Things would have been very different. But it wasn't, was it? Noah was, to those in authority at least, a nobody. Just another worthless pauper, no use to society, a mere scourge on the city. They would get no help from that quarter, all right, this she was certain of.

Sure enough, George arrived back from his visit the following morning wearing a bleak expression. 'Well, I tried.'

Jenny handed him a cup of tea with an angry click of her tongue. 'What did they have to say?'

'Not much. The desk sergeant listened to what I had to tell him and said the police would be in touch should they get any information. I shan't hold my breath.'

'Worried was he, this lawman?' Jenny asked mordaciously, then gave a bitter snort when George shook his head. 'Nay, I thought not. Didn't I tell thee it'd be a waste of good boot leather?'

'It had to be done nonetheless.'

'I know.' She let out a long breath and stroked his hair. 'I'm grateful, I am, and thank thee for at least trying. So, where now?'

Draining his cup, he rose once more. 'Get your shawl on and let's see where our feet take us, eh?'

Their day's efforts proved every bit as unsuccessful as the others before it. They reached the cellar at nightfall thirsty, starving hungry and frozen through to the bone.

'I'll get a meal going,' Jenny said wearily, crossing the icy room to get the fire going. 'Sit thee down, lad, whilst I put the kettle on to heat. The tea will keep us going until the grub's done.'

'Actually, there's summat I need to do.'

'George?' she said, frowning, as he made back for the door. 'What—?'

'I'll not be away long,' he told her, and was gone before she could question him more.

Too tired to dwell on the matter further, she concentrated her efforts on her chore.

An hour later, the simple meal was cooked and warming by the hearth, but of George there was still no sign. Jenny headed for the door once more and looked outside. Bar one or two people hurrying for home and warmth, the street was again empty.

Where was he? Would he even come back tonight,

or had exhaustion got the better of him and he'd decided to go back to his own lodgings? She certainly hoped not, was dreading him not returning.

Another half an hour passed before, finally, the knock came. With a small gasp of relief, she hastened to open the door:

'Eeh, lad. I were starting to get worried . . . George? What is it?' she pressed, taking in his countenance. 'Tha looks terrible! Come in, come on. Sit down.'

He hunched over the table and put his head in his hands. 'I shouldn't have done it. I shouldn't have *gone*,' he rasped.

Jenny rushed to his side. 'Why, what d'you mean? Where did you go?'

'To see my father.'

'Totty?' Her brows rose to meet her hairline.

'I had to make sure he definitely had been telling the truth about having no more clues where Noah might be. I had to look into his eyes myself, for only then would I know for sure, would see it if he was lying.'

Jenny's heart had begun to thump with desperate hope. 'And?' she murmured.

'And nowt. He . . . He . . .'

'What, lad?'

'When I arrived he was dead.'

She sagged and dropped into a seat beside him, her heart plummeting like a pebble for both him and herself.

'Cold and stiff as a board, he was. Finished. Gone.'

'George, I'm sorry.'

'Don't be.' He wiped the back of his hand across

his nose. 'May God forgive me, I shan't be doing any grieving. He never earned that right; he didn't deserve it. I felt nowt, you know,' he went on quietly, levelly. 'Not a thing. No regret at not having seen him afore he passed, nothing. That he might just have been able to shed some light after all on Noah, and now it ain't possible, is the only thing I'm sorry for, and that's the truth.'

'Eeh. Bloody families, eh?'

'Bloody families,' he agreed.

Chapter 15

'MORNING—OH. HELLO.'

Despite being convinced she had nothing to be ashamed about, Jenny couldn't stem the blush that crept to her cheeks to have Coral turn up unexpectedly and catch her and George alone together. She waved the woman inside. 'Sup of tea?'

'Aye, thank you.'

George, sitting in just his shirt sleeves, clearly shared Jenny's discomfiture. Discreetly, he reached to where his jacket hung on the nail in the wall and slipped it on.

'It'll have to be a flying visit, Coral, I'm afraid,' Jenny said, lifting the teapot. 'Me and George want to make a start in our search shortly, make the most of the daylight. It grows dark that quick these days.'

Coral nodded slowly and arched an eyebrow. 'You must have set out at dawn, lad, to be here so early.'

The silence thickened as they glanced to one another and back again, stuck for a suitable response. Finally, Jenny threw her hands in the air.

'Actually, George stayed the night. That's right:

he's stopping on here with me to keep me company.'

'I see.'

'I hope so, Coral,' Jenny said quietly. 'There's been no . . . goings-on, neither.' Nor had there been. She and George might be sharing a bed but all the action it saw from them was sleeping. There had been no funny business between them, nothing untoward. 'You've my word on that.'

Eventually, the woman let her shoulders rise and fall. 'I believe thee if that's what you're telling me. Anyroad, it's a bit late in the day for me to be issuing you with dos and don'ts, eh? Be warned, though, lass, you know how folk are; they'll talk.'

'Let them, they can think what they like,' Jenny replied mildly. 'I feel closer to Noah here, but I do get lonely. George is remedying that, so to hell with propriety.'

George excused himself soon afterwards to visit the privy, and Jenny took the opportunity to inform Coral of Totty's passing. 'So that's that. He's gone. If he was holding owt back about where Noah is, he's taken it from this life with him.'

The woman sighed sadly. 'I don't believe he was, you know. I knew the man of old, would have sensed it were he lying. How's George taking it?'

'Not too bad. He seems relieved almost, like a weight's been shifted from his shoulders. Noah ain't the only kiddie what Vincent Tottington made suffer. He led George a terrible life.'

306

'Aye, well, he's paid the ultimate price now, right enough.'

Minutes later, the three of them were standing on the doorstep saying their goodbyes. Coral touched Jenny's arm.

'Good luck. Here's hoping today's the day and youse find a lead.'

'Aye.'

'Noah will be found, lass, he will. I just know it, can feel it in my bones.'

Jenny's attention was caught by the new neighbours' son, who was playing alone happily. Sitting cross-legged outside his house, he was drawing pictures on the flagstones with a stone. She smiled longingly. 'He does remind me of Noah, you know. It's the eyes, I think. Mild-natured he is, too, just like our lad.'

Coral nodded agreement. 'You had anything more from that mother of his?' she asked.

'Nay. I ain't seen nowt of her since. Oh, speak of the devil,' she added when, as though they had conjured her up, Nobby's old door opened and Liz appeared.

Initially, as her gaze rested on her son, she smiled. Then she noticed the trio standing nearby and her demeanour changed. She turned back to the boy. 'Come inside, lad.'

'Aw! But why, Mam?'

'Because I said so,' she responded, eyeing Jenny, Coral and George with open mistrust. 'Now do as I say.'

With his bottom lip protruding and shoulders

slumped, the youngster abandoned his game and tailed his mother inside the house.

'Just what is wrong with her, at all?' Jenny cried when they disappeared. 'It's as though she don't trust me or summat. Does she believe I'd harm the child, is that it? But why, what on earth have I done?'

Coral and George shared a shrug, as baffled as she.

The matter was still on Jenny's mind later as she and George, well into their now-familiar quest, trudged down yet another sad and dreary street. She must speak with if not Liz herself – she was under no illusions that the woman would give her short shrift should she attempt to confront her personally – then her husband, had to, for this strange behaviour was beginning to get right on her wick. She'd finish up clocking the woman one if this went on much longer. Mind you, it wasn't even anger she felt if truth be told, not really; hurt was the overriding emotion instead. Liz had looked at her with what Jenny could only describe as fear mixed with an almost murderous challenge, as if daring her to even think of going near the boy. Why? Could she indeed have a touch of the madness, as George suspected? For some reason, Jenny didn't think so. So just what did it mean?

It wasn't until two days later that she managed to get the man in question alone.

Having nipped out to make some purchases, Jenny was nearing the cellar when Nobby's door suddenly opened and her new neighbour stepped outside and turned left in the opposite direction. Taking the bull by the horns, Jenny rammed the small loaf she carried more securely under her arm and set off on a run to catch up with his long stride.

'Excuse me, mister?'

'Aye?'

'Can we talk?'

He was quiet for a moment before sighing in understanding. 'This is about my Liz, ain't it?'

'That's right. Look, I don't want no bad feeling betwixt us – we have to live together whether we like it or no – but I need to know: what is her problem with me? Just what have I done?'

He dipped his chin. 'Nowt, lass. 'Tain't thee. My wife, she . . . she's troubled. In t' head, like.'

Brow furrowing, Jenny watched in silence as he closed his eyes and waited for him to go on.

'Coming here, it were meant to be a fresh start,' he muttered. 'But she's still struggling, my Liz is. She tries, she does, but the memories . . . God above, near killed her it did.'

'What?' Jenny urged. 'Please tell me – it'll go no further, you have my word. What happened?'

'*He* happened,' the man spat, and his gaze took on a manic look that screamed pure loathing.

'He . . .?'

'Aye, bloke name of Skipton, that demon from hell!'

The world seemed to cease its spinning. Jenny staggered, barely noticing when her shopping fell from her grasp, the loaf following suit to spin into the gutter. She felt her way to the nearest house and rested her head against the bricks. 'Skipton?' she managed to choke out after some moments. 'Is that who tha said?'

'That's right, aye.'

'You . . . you know . . . where to find him?'

'Well, aye. Lass, are you all right? Lass?'

But Jenny was beyond all rational capabilities, couldn't think; her knees buckled. 'Noah,' she breathed as she fell into a dead faint.

'George?'

'Aye, it's me. How're you feeling.'

'Like shit,' Jenny groaned, struggling up. 'Where . . .?'

'You're at home. Do you remember what happened?'

'Nay, not really, I . . . Oh, God!' she cried out in the next breath as her memory swam back, and she made to lunge from the bed. 'Skipton, he—!'

'I know,' George soothed, pressing her back down, and with her head spinning dizzyingly from her sudden movement, Jenny reluctantly yielded to his will. 'Mrs Armitage has told me everything.'

'Who?'

'Liz, lass.'

'Liz?'

'Aye, that's right,' a different voice chipped in.

Jenny looked past George to scan the space through screwed-up eyes and frowned when a figure rose from a stool at the table. 'It *is* thee. What are you doing here?'

Liz moved closer to the bed. 'My husband came to fetch me when you collapsed outside – scared the living daylights out of him, tha did; he hadn't a clue what to do. He told me what youse two had been speaking about afore you took bad . . . I'm sorry,' she went on with a sob. 'I've been a real bitch to thee and you didn't deserve it.'

George picked up the thread of conversation. 'Mr and Mrs Armitage helped to carry thee down to the cellar. I thought I'd lost thee when I opened the door . . . you were out cold, looked bloody dreadful. Liz insisted on stopping here until tha wakened. She wants to explain about her son. And Skipton.'

Having pulled herself into a sitting position, Jenny nodded. 'Go on,' she begged the woman.

'The lad here,' Liz began, motioning to George, 'he's told me all about your young lad Noah. Ech, I'm that broken-hearted for thee, and that's the truth. You see, I understand the nightmare you're going through, aye. I know, for that bastard snatched my boy as well.'

'Wha . . .?'

'Aye. Plucked him right off the street, he did, in broad daylight – can you fathom it, at all? Brass-necked ain't in it!'

'He meant to put your son to work in breaking houses, too?'

'Aye, least them were his intentions, only he never got that far. I saw what had happened, you see, from my window, and so I gave chase. But that divil were too quick for me. A witness what were passing and saw everything recognised the swine and gave me his name and address. Me and my husband hotfooted it to his rooms and rescued our lad within the hour. Thing is, we hadn't reckoned on his character,' she finished grimly.

Jenny didn't like the sound of this. 'What d'you mean?'

'Eeh, he's worse than Lucifer and all of his hell dwellers combined – evil, evil! Aye, and dangerous to boot, I'll warn thee of that now. He threatened to kill us, slit our throats, and I reckon he meant it, no doubt about it. He said he'd make us pay, all three of us. We only got out of there in one piece because I spun him a lie that the law were on their way. After, we couldn't settle; I didn't feel safe in my own home no more. Well, I mean, he knew where we lived, didn't he? It all got too much in t' end – we had to get out, move away, somewhere he couldn't find us. That's how we came to be here.'

Jenny was nodding; it made sense to her now completely. 'You're overprotective of your lad, and rightly so. That's why you behaved as you did when first we met.'

'I can't help myself, lass. I see peril everywhere these days, you know? I meant not to upset thee – I just struggle now to trust anyone, and strangers more so. You understand, don't you?'

'I do,' Jenny was swift to reassure her. Wouldn't she act exactly the same in her shoes? 'I'm glad you got your boy back, missis – now it's my turn.' Throwing back the blankets, she scrambled to her feet. 'George?'

'Don't fret none, lass, I'm with thee. Mr Armitage has already informed me where we'll find Skipton.'

Eyes bright, he smiled. He held out a hand. 'What say we bring Noah home?'

Clasping his fingers, she laughed through her tears. 'I say aye – aye bleedin' aye!'

Cutting rainfall accompanied them on this vital, and what might mercifully be their final, peregrination. Focused, rock-ribbed, determined, they strode towards the neighbouring town of Salford wordlessly.

They veered off Broad Street as per the Armitages' directions and weaved their way through a square of soot-grimed streets. When they reached the correct row of back-to-back dwellings they were aiming for, they glanced to one another and nodded. Then, mouths set, they continued purposely for one house in particular and Skipton's lodgings.

A teenage girl dressed in little more than rags opened the door a few inches to their knock and peered around the crack, her deep-set eyes narrowed in mistrust. 'Aye?'

'Out of my way, you,' Jenny ordered, shoving the door and sending it and the girl swaying backwards into the minuscule hall.

''Ere, what—!'

'Skipton – where is he?' Jenny bellowed, cutting off the stunned tenant with a hand around her throat. 'Tell me, by God!'

'That one? He ain't here.'

'Liar!'

'I ain't soddin' lying,' the girl yelled back. 'Scarpered yesterday, he did. Aye, and good bloody riddance!'

'Nay . . . Nay!'

'Wait here,' George told Jenny. Pushing past the girl, he charged up the stairs.

Bangs and heavy footsteps filtered down to them as he stormed the upper rooms, kicking open doors as he went. He ran back down to the hall and again skirted past the young occupant, this time to search the downstairs area. When at last he rejoined them, his face was tight with fury. 'The lass here's right, Jenny. He ain't here.'

'He is! He *has* to be!'

'He's gone, I tell thee,' the girl insisted, twisting free from Jenny's grip and stamping her foot. 'He's cleared off, owing my mam a week's board money into the bargain, swine. He'll not be back so you'll just have to try elsewhere, won't you?'

'But . . .' Jenny was dangerously close to tears. 'Do you know where he could be, where at all he might have gone? Please, if so, you must tell us. It's important.'

The girl shook her head. 'I haven't the foggiest, and that's the truth.'

George caught Jenny as she flopped, weeping uncontrollably, against the door. Holding her secure in his strong arms, he threw the girl one last question: 'Tell me, when you saw him last, was he in the company of a young lad?'

'You mean his son?'

'My God . . .'

'Little thin thing, carroty hair?' the girl added. Then at Jenny's tortured whimper: 'Why, what's wrong with that, then? Just what's going on, what's he done?'

314

'Nowt, it's nowt,' said George, guiding a devastated Jenny around and back out into the weak sunlight. 'Thanks for your help.'

The girl, clearly annoyed that she would garner no gossip from them, clicked her tongue. Then shrugging, she slammed the door in their faces.

'You can't lose faith, Jenny.'

Lying on her side in bed beneath the blankets, knees pulled up to her chin, she didn't answer, hadn't the strength to even if she'd tried. She was empty, drained dry, void of spirit and soul. To have her hopes dashed like that so cruelly when she'd dared to believe she'd at last get him back . . . Her devastation was absolute. Yet again, she'd let her lad down. *Just a single day too late.* He could be anywhere, far from here by now, for all they knew.

'Noah can't stay lost to us for ever,' George went on. 'Somehow, someway, we'll find him. When we do, he'll need to find thee fit and strong, the Jenny he knows and adores, so you must keep fighting. We'll settle down together when he's back, the three of us, aye. We'll do this place up reet nice, make it into a proper little home, as you've allus wanted. And we'll get wed, Jenny. Eeh, just think on that. Noah will be over the moon, eh, with that? Just hold on, my love. Please, hold on.'

Her only response was the closing of her eyes.

Chapter 16

As MANCHESTER AND the rest of the country got set to celebrate the festive season, Jenny and George stepped up further their endeavours to wheedle out Skipton.

After a shaky start, and thanks to the support of her loved ones and new friends the Armitages, and of course none more so than her betrothed, Jenny had clawed back her enthusiasm with gusto, more resolved than ever before to find Noah.

It was, however, a futile task. He remained as lost to them as he'd ever been.

Coral held on to the notion that her brother would come back, and on Christmas Eve she included him in her purchases of inexpensive gifts for her family. Jenny watched her place them beneath the small tree in silent despondency. The woman might be certain still that he'd be home to receive them, but Jenny was fast becoming unconvinced once more.

The Christmas dinner of a small roast chicken and vegetables was cooked to perfection and on its way to the table when the enormity of the situation, and plain truth of her failure, finally slammed home, snatching away what little hope Jenny had been clinging to for dear life. She snapped. Much to the consternation of the people sitting around her, she put her head in her arms and burst into immeasurable sobbing.

Coral hastened to be by her side but there was nothing she could do or say to comfort her. *Nothing could make this better.*

'I need Noah! I need my lad!'

Though sometime later her tears dried up, her mood was far from improved. She'd slipped into deep and impenetrable depression. She was aware of it, saw it in herself, but for the life of her she'd neither the energy nor desire to drag herself from the darkness. Why bother? It was pointless, all of it. What's more, it for ever would be.

By the time George arrived to see her after enjoying his customary Yuletide lunch with Hyacinth Harewood, Coral was at her wits' end with worry. She beckoned him inside and pointed to a slumped and dead-gazed Jenny, and begged, 'Do summat, lad, will thee? Please?'

He crouched down to her eye level. 'Lass?'

'I need Noah,' were the only self-same words that her brain and mouth would form.

'Right, enough's enough. Get your shawl on.'

It took her several moments to focus fully on his face. 'What? But I don't want to.'

'It weren't a request, Jenny,' he shot back. 'You're coming with me.'

317

'Look, George, I know you're being cruel to be kind here, but trust me on this, I ain't in no mood—'

'Get your shawl on,' he repeated. His countenance was unmoving. 'Put me to the test, lass, if tha likes, but I'll carry thee there if I must. I mean it.'

Despite everything, she couldn't contain a crooked smile. 'George Sixsmith, are you trying to be masterful?'

'If you'll let me,' he quipped, then, seeing her smile grow, he added softly, 'come on. Hyacinth's opened up the Balloon – half an hour will do thee the power of good. I promise.'

'Aye. All right.'

It was a hive of merriment when they entered. At first, Jenny felt rather self-conscious – she hadn't exactly left this place on good terms, had she? – and wondered if some of the customers might be unwelcoming given the behaviour they had witnessed from her towards George and Hyacinth on the night she wished she could erase from memory. However, she needn't have harboured concerns. They appeared genuinely pleased to see her if the grins, cheers and shoulder squeezes were anything to go by. She was more than a little grateful. They were the salt of the earth in here and a greater bunch of people you couldn't wish to meet.

A cup of tea later and Jenny was slowly beginning to relax. It was difficult not to feel wrapped up safe and snug as she let the atmospheric warmth of the place seep into her bones.

'Why not sing us summat, lass? Go on, a little Christmas jingle will liven everyone up even more,'

Hyacinth wheedled, having sidled up to where Jenny and George stood at the counter.

'Oh nay, I don't think—'

'Go on,' George urged. 'The tavern ain't been the same without your pulchritudinous tones dancing about the rafters, and that's the truth.'

Oh but she did love that word, now. What's more, his voice had contained not a hint of resentment – not that she'd have blamed him an iota if there had. By, but she really had struck solid gold with this man of hers. She flashed him a watery smile. 'I have missed it, you know.'

'Then step right up, lass. The stage is yours.'

She sang a stirring rendition of Hark! The Herald Angels sing. As the opening notes left her mouth and the familiar sensations of wonderment closed around her, she knew that her claim of missing this had been woefully understated: she'd been starving for it – her heart, in spite of its lesions, lifted as though it might take flight from her chest. Once it was over, she stood for a moment, lost in its rapture. It was only when she felt the tugging on her sleeve that she realised someone was trying to get her attention. She turned, puzzled.

'Did tha hear me, lass?' an elderly punter called into her ear over the roof-splitting applause. 'I said there's someone waiting by the door wanting to speak with thee.'

'Speak with me . . .?' *Noah! Oh, dear God.* 'Thank you!' she gasped out in the next breath, careering past the messenger to get to the newcomer.

'Best wishes of the season, deary.'

Disappointment like no other tore through her. She shook her head, sending angry tears spilling, and demanded, her emotions making her sound harsher than she intended, 'What the hell do you want?'

'I come in peace,' Doll said. He smiled his kindly smile. 'You're looking well, Jenny.'

'I'm feeling it, an' all, now I'm free from that hell pit Solomon's.'

He inclined his head in understanding. 'You sounded magnificent just now, and quite at home, I must say. You'll have a job for life, here, I'm sure.'

She gave a small curtsey. This was where she belonged and had been all along. She saw it clear as crystal now.

'I recalled you mentioning once where you lived. Alas, a neighbour explained you were absent, but gave directions to where she informed me you were spending Christmas Day – with Coral. You managed to rectify things with your . . . sister?' he finished, evidently unsure how to refer to their relationship. 'I'm pleased for you, truly.'

'Ta, thanks. So what was it you want—?'

'I've seen his face afore – what's he doing here?' said a voice behind her before she could finish.

Turning, Jenny touched George's hand in reassurance. 'It's all right, honest. Doll's one of the good 'uns.'

George nodded and moved off, although he didn't return to the counter. Arms folded, he watched on like a guardsman from a short distance.

'Your young fellow?'

'Aye.'

Doll smiled approvingly.

'Surely you can't blame him?'

'Not at all. You'll do all right in life with him. He clearly loves you very much.'

She returned his smile. Never had a truer word been spoken. How she'd have managed without her man these past weeks, both emotionally and financially, she didn't know. Then, picking up the thread of conversation, she asked, 'So what *are* you doing here, Doll?'

'I wanted to check on your welfare. It's true to say I did become really rather fond of you.'

Her face softened. 'That were nice of thee and likewise.'

'I'm happy you left, you know. I could see right from the outset that you weren't cut out for Solomon's.' He shrugged. 'I always can.'

'Won't you ever consider leaving yourself one day?' she asked him. He deserved so much better than that place.

A wry grin appeared. 'I don't really think the dull and dreary real world is quite ready for me yet. No. The fantasticality of the music hall – warts and all – is my preferred habitat.'

Drinking in his appearance and smiling, Jenny reckoned he probably had a point.

'Oh yes, I almost forgot: there's a present awaiting you at Carruthers Street,' he told her matter-of-factly. However, there was no mistaking the definite excitement shining in his eyes.

321

Intrigued, she cocked her head. 'Doll? What are you up to?'

'Up to? Me?' He wiggled a finely groomed eyebrow. 'Why, nothing at all, deary!'

Jenny opened her mouth to ask more but he put a slender finger to her lips. 'Hurry home and see for yourself. I think you'll be most pleased with it.'

'Aye, all right. A Merry Christmas to you, Doll.'

'And to you, Jenny. A Happy New Year also. Eighteen seventy – a brand new decade into the bargain.'

'Fresh beginnings.'

'Fresh beginnings,' he agreed. A last smile and he was gone.

After informing George that all was well and that she'd be back soon, Jenny slipped from the inn and, going over in her mind the possibilities of what her gift could be, headed the short distance to Carruthers Street.

She was barely midway up the road when she spotted Coral, snowy apron flapping in the winter wind, running towards her.

'What the . . .?'

Oh Lord, something was wrong, had to be.

Picking up her skirts, Jenny set off on a sprint to catch her up.

'Coral? Speak to me!'

'Did tha see him? Did he tell thee?' the woman gushed, and Jenny saw now that it wasn't fear nor horror driving Coral but sheer joy. She shook her head in confusion.

'The fella from the music hall! Did tha see him?'

'Aye, but—'

'I all but collapsed to the ground when I opened the door to him and . . . Eeh, lass! Noah managed to give Skipton the slip this morn and make his escape, but the poor love hadn't a clue where he was – hopelessly lost, he were. He was wandering about when he came upon Solomon's. Recognised it, he did, from summat you'd told him about the frontage having orange and white tiles . . .? Anyroad, he banged on t' door, thinking to find thee there. That Doll bloke came to his aid and fetched him back.'

It was as though Jenny had been cast in stone: she could neither move nor speak, couldn't hardly blink. Her mind, on the other hand, was a whirlwind of activity, her whizzing thoughts tumbling over themselves.

Her gift was Noah? Noah was home?

Brushing past Coral, she picked her unsteady way to the house.

After everything, the non-stop searching, the disappointment of Totty dying without bringing to light any further clue, the elation at the Armitages' information then crushing hopelessness when nothing came of it . . . After all of that, Noah had been the one to do it, succeed, make things right again? By! It was barely fathomable. And how had the lad managed it? Thanks to the music hall, that's what. The one single most regretful point in her life had proved in the end their saviour. Happen everything did occur for a reason; it seemed so. Life truly was a mystery at times.

'Lass.' The woman stopped her as she made to enter. 'The lad, he don't know nowt about Owd Nobby . . . Give him some time afore breaking the sad tidings, eh?'

Jenny gave a hazy nod and stepped inside.

The scene that met her was ethereal. He *was* here. There, look, sitting on Martin's lap by the fire. She had him back. She had him back!

The fog cleared from her brain in a puff. Releasing a cry, she tore across the floor. 'Lad, lad!'

'Our Jen!'

She fell to her knees and took his precious face in her two hands. He looked powfagged, wrung out, but didn't appear harmed in any way so far as she could tell, blessed be. Yet what of his mental state? God alone only knew what he'd been through with that monster . . . Would they ever know the real Noah again? She was soon to get her answer:

'Jen?'

'Aye, lad?' she answered tentatively, in dread of what he might reveal.

Putting his nose up, the boy sniffed the air. 'I'm fair clemmed – is there any chicken left?'

'Eeh, little three bellies!'

ABOUT THE AUTHOR

Emma Hornby lives on a tight-knit working-class estate in Bolton and has read sagas all her life. Before pursuing a career as a novelist, she had a variety of jobs, from care assistant for the elderly, to working in a Blackpool rock factory. She was inspired to write after researching her family history; like the characters in her books, many generations of her family eked out life amidst the squalor and poverty of Lancashire's slums.

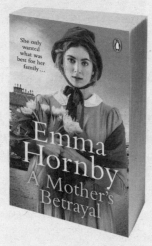

With all the odds stacked against her, can Phoebe find the strength to overcome her past . . . ?

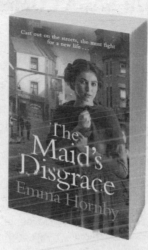

*Phoebe Parsons is a liar . . . a shameless harlot
with unscrupulous morals . . .*

Phoebe Parsons is destitute, disgraced, and alone. After her
mistress tragically dies, Phoebe is forced back on to the poverty-
ridden streets of Manchester by her unforgiving new master.
Desperately searching for work as a domestic maid,
Phoebe soon discovers her reputation is in ruins.

Fearing for her future and haunted by the harshness of her
abandonment, Phoebe finds herself living with thieves and drunks
in the smog and squalor – until she meets Victor Hayes. An officer
removed from his duty and shamed by a cruel lie, Mr Hayes
is a kind face among the uncertain threats of living in the
alleyways. But Phoebe soon realises the sacrifices she
must make to rebuild from the ground up . . .

**As their two worlds collide, can they make a new life
from the wreckage? Or will the judgement of
their peers make a pauper of Phoebe?**

AVAILABLE NOW

JOIN OUR SAGA COMMUNITY

Penny Street is a newsletter and online community bringing you the latest book deals, competitions and new saga series releases.

You can also find extra content, talk to your favourite authors and share your discoveries with other saga fans on Facebook.

Join today by visiting:
www.penguin.co.uk/pennystreet
and follow our Facebook page:
https://www.facebook.com/welcometopennystreet/